XMAN

OTHER WORKS BY MICHAEL BRODSKY

Circuits
Detour
Project and Other Short Pieces
Wedding Feast

XMAN

by
Michael Brodsky

Four Walls Eight Windows, New York

First edition published by:
Four Walls Eight Windows
Post Office Box 548
Village Station
New York, New York 10014

First printing, October 1987
Second printing, March 1988

Library of Congress Cataloging-in-Publication Data

Brodsky, Michael, 1948–
  Xman.
  I. Title.
PS3552.R6232X6   1987   813',54   87-7389

ISBN: 0-941423-01-8 (clothbound)
ISBN 0-941423-02-6 (paperback)

Printed in U.S.A.
Composition by Commercial Typographers of Connecticut
Design: Hannah Lerner

"... a long act of dissimulation."

Henry James, *The Beast in the Jungle*

ABLE TO BEAR it no longer he, Xman, at last decided to depart for good, this time with no turning back. With some money saved, some bequeathed, he and his torn green duffel bag made their way, via taxi, to the airport. Driver, true to type, proved loquacious.

He said, "Where are you going." Xman replied; forestalling the inevitable next question he added, "To make myself unique."

"Do you eat."

"Yes."

"Sleep."

"Yes."

"Shit."

"Yes." The driver's genial shrug left it up to Xman to decide whether he hadn't in fact won his case. He certainly, Xman was forced to admit, had his point: those universal parameters set formidable limits to any pretense to uniqueness.

"I had a chance once to go New York-ward," said the driver after a long lull. Xman could not bring himself—had he ever been able?—to draw him out. Just when it seemed he had no

1

borating, the driver said, "Somebody told me
ʒs of a great one. 'In yourself you are a great
)dy said. 'But I can foresee horror for you in
,. ɪou'll end up alone, spending your nights alone,
ρσckmarked fast-food addict taking dictation from the
stars in behalf of a universal language.' " Taking a deep
breath the driver accelerated for no visible reason. "Then she
said something else: I've yet to understand it." Xman never
importuned but as if he had, the driver sliding his hand
toward the glove compartment and removing a little note-
book grumbled, "Oh all right. Since you insist I'll read it."
" 'You think you are beyond everybody's comprehension:
beyond formulation, beyond bracketing. But I can foresee
your intelligibility as a remnant, a failure, a nobody ranting
and raving against the failed dawn. When your undeniable
uniqueness is projected, the die being cast, upon the screen
of universal resistance something monstrous will ungra-
ciously take place. In yourself you are great but thrown into
the world you cast another shadow.' That's why I never left.
But it's sure to be different for you." Tipping him overgene-
rously was the closest Xman came to asking, "How do you
know." Before quizzical gratitude had a chance to overflow
the driver said: "But: no regrets." He turned suddenly belli-
cose as if Xman's silence was now the sharpest of challenges.
"No regrets because I have tasted fate in her essence. Quite a
gal. That she never came to my aid, made herself known in
the service of a destiny that should have been mine—the
only conceivable destiny given the incomparable richness of
my raw materials—that I have been forced as fruit of her
abstention from all signs to drag on unnoticed—has yielded
a dividend: privity of fate in the perversity of her nakedness
or nakedness of her perversity. Privy to the stench emanating from the fissure between Moira's painted unbreeched
buttocks going about their daily business of doing what she

does best I bear the trace of having caught her at her most unguardedly preposterous when she might have hoisted me up to my true—my assigned—height and out of inexplicable envying spleen did not, went her not so merry way standing still as it were for all eternity."

Some passengers-to-be positioned themselves away from the setting sun. On the roof of the building opposite (a few desk clerks were hard at work on one of the lower floors) the wind sweeping across a wide puddle left little plaques brilliant with sun. Fading totally the plaques interfusing achieved their peak of corrugated dazzle. Besides his duffel bag and the plaques Xman had nothing to hold on to and with so little he felt this was going to be yet another failed voyage out. In a little room next to the lounge where he went to escape the family hordes, an old woman sat down next to him, bit into her ham-and-cheese-omelette sandwich and swallowing with conspicuous difficulty said, "Young man you have the look of somebody who voyages in search of a perfect voyage. But life, young man, is not a perfect voyage. Not by any means. You look round: you notice the defective candy dispenser, the broken glass in the window, the young woman snoring in her lover's too bronzed arms. But isn't it absurd, I ask you, to take every potentially malevolent contingency seriously. As if anything could intervene to make things worse than things as they are. All is doomed. And not doomed. As if the sum of turmoil hasn't been fixed for all time, as if any new addition to the sum won't keep the sum equal to itself whether it grows or cancels. In fact every pitiful little contingency only and merely safeguards the sum and keeps it equal to itself. Nothing can lacerate you any deeper. Always already comprising all possible additions to the fatal sum the lookout for contingencies that can spoil the voyage necessarily spoils the voyage. But just because you—as lookout man—have already spoiled the voyage does not mean the voyage can't still be gotten through and in the best way possible. Once you recognize that you have already spoiled the voyage, once for all and over and over again, there is hope—not for reduction of tension but for—for—" She belched. "Sorry, they just announced my flight." Xman had heard nothing.

On the plane he sat beside a middle-aged man all over whose face was scrawled, I just have to talk or I'll go stark raving. Let me talk, whoever you are. And I'll reward you by thinking of you forever after as one of the ones who let me. "Know New York. I've lived there now going on *n* years. Nobody can make a dent in that babe's armor. She's a tough cookie." Then as if adopting a more serious tone, "It's a tough town." Xman hated people saying "town" when they meant "big city." Just as he hated when "see you later" or worse, "catch you later," was made to mean "until we meet again."

Every so often the beardless stranger came out of his densely worded trance to almost perceive that since Xman was a total stranger with a life of his own he would do well to camouflage his fear of him. And then—but casually to his own amusement and horror—MINGLED amusement and horror as it tended to be phrased in somebody else's true home, the nineteenth century—Xman noted that as he was managing to abstain totally—in perverse self-aggrandize-ment—from self-presentation, the talker was beginning to hate him, with hate taking the form of contempt—Xman could read it in the stranger's bloody sclerae—utterable as the question: What self-respecting being stands still refrain-ing from a dive into the fray of telling what he does and how he does it, in other words, what he is. No longer able to contain himself and at the same time irradiated with the uneasiness that comes of having to confront another in that other's unmitigated totality of tastes and peculiarities that are nothing less than insidious challenges to one's own tastes and peculiarities, the talker finally said, "What do you do," so that Xman could say, "I'm an x." Or, failing that, "I'm in x," or even worse, "I'm into x." As Xman said nothing the talker said, "Look down. It's all grassland from up here. But when you walk those filthy streets you forget about grasslands. It was walking the streets of New York"—as his voice descended to a whisper Xman noted that he had good reason to whisper since everybody was turned toward them in expectation—"that I realized for the first time—a monster—an absolute monster from whose tooth we are all pendant." Xman looked out the window. He could not decide whether he was not in fact MAKING A PRETENSE of looking out the window, merely impersonating somebody with a need to look out the window or rather somebody who looks out the window without any need to look out the window. "Once I was strolling through the sleaziest quarter during lunch hour—when the whole workaday zoo puts on the feedbag, so to speak—and in the middle of all the three-piece suitors beguiling their exotically coiffured secretaries with daring exploits perpetrated in the land of copy machines and water coolers—I saw a dwarf on crutches literally thrashing across Broadway—not far from that island where tourists—but not only tourists, no not only tourists—queue up for half-priced tickets—every step an excruciating tortuosity through the impeding thick summer air. It was then I said to myself, 'You,' I said, 'New York tells you God is the quintessential mad doctor, Mengele given proprietary right over every cranny in the universe, and every man his experiment. God puts man on earth to see how he will fare saddled with every conceivable blemish and deformity, delights in watching him perform according to slender skills and blatant liabilities. Oh course our man God can foresee the end result of all this jabbering juxtaposition of types—in his mind, in his mind—but he can only *undergo* such a juxtaposition when it is played out in sun and shade for his lonely delectation. Our man God needs the world the way every movie "buff"—another detestable word—needs a populated pullulating screen.' At any rate, as I watched the cripple advance—and he did advance—miracle of miracles he did advance—I wondered how I fitted. For I stood back from the fray, even if I was simply one more permutation of given strengths and frailties I stood back from what I and they were doomed to be. Avatars of Spinozistic perfection—yes, perfection, no matter how offending to individual nostrils. I determined that I was as Olympianly curious as the God monster about how all this would turn out, least of all of course how I would turn out. Perhaps the most telling sign of my godliness is my consistently greater interest in how all others will turn out. I wondered whether a scandalous detachment from phenomena—especially from the phenomenon that was I—was already tabulated in the total conception that was I or had the mad doctor—too smitten with Amazonian avifauna—obsessed but occasionally shortsighted—simply overlooked, amid the trappings of an ostensibly infallible banausic scrupulosity, this possibility of monstrous detachment, which consequently had slipped in unperceived and undeleted. Or had he, that mad master of contingencies, allowed for my detachment as a kind of spice in a human soup far too heavily dolloped with self-interest."

As the passenger continued to speak and the other passengers to gape, Xman pushed back deeper and deeper into shadow though the plane was, strictly speaking, insufferably well-lit. The passengers' terror became Xman's terrifyingness. In the bus from airport to Grand Central Station after discovering he had left his umbrella on board he fell asleep momentarily but not before listening intently to a couple, no two, shallow in conversation. Not enthusiastic about what they said so much as recurringly relieved about all they managed to omit, performing their quartet each could trust to the others' never wandering very far from the unspecified key signature of caricatural blandness. No danger here of chitchat over excruciated cripples. As a comet was soon scheduled to make its appearance across the New York sky-line and as one of the four happened to be an astronomer or just happened to know somebody who once knew an astron-omer's maiden aunt the conversation turned naturally to questions of the best rooftop on which—from which—to—to— But to Xman's virgin ears they did not seem to believe in a word they were saying. They had simply seized unerringly and en masse on what might best be said to get them through a bus trip. Or maybe it was simply he, Xman, un-able to imagine conversation propelled by other than ur-gency or by an urgency other than that simultaneously wooing and staving off the unspeakable. Is there any other plane, Xman asked himself, priggishly, pompously. To exist in perfect neutrality was the aim and here that aim was triumphing. The conversation was not about this or that, this or that comet, this or that tennis champion's grand slam—any more than the uninterrupted wielding of a white flag is about anything. It was only when the conversation was in danger of dying down that he (1) became afraid that any one, two, three or four of the four would leap out of the circle of voracious blandness to say, What do you do—What he did, Xman wanted to say, was subsist as a paradox. But he was afraid to say as much, he had always been afraid of rushing when already there, as now, to an extreme—an air-port's, for example—and completely severing himself thereby—as he had already done—from forbears and a tradi-tional line of work; and (2) realized somebody was looking at him from the side. He turned to the stare, rendered all the more terrifying by bafflement at its own powerful insistence.

The stare perceiving his reaction to the chatter behind seemed actively to be discounting its importance in behalf of the bigger game he himself embodied.

With duffel bag he forced himself to walk up Second Avenue though the pair of eyes persisted in invalidating every movement of an itinerary not yet born. He had no idea of walking uptown or down, east or west. From the carnival depths of late-night eateries burning defiantly bright groups observed him, after the initial collision of glances, without the least interest in his kind seen many times before, many many times. Several times he was accosted by derelicts, several times he gave a few cents. At the end of a street (Forty-fifth corner of Sixth Avenue) just where friends had said it would be stood the recommended hotel, Microtraumata Royale, its glass doors parting at his mere approach to reveal a magnificent interior multiplied to infinity by busily festooned mirrors strategically placed. Just before they parted definitively he turned one last time to the street where, as if on cue, a woman was shrieking at the hotel's doorman closing the door on a taxi about to pull away. From all directions and distances the stance of strollers and bystanders slumbering hopefully toward a possible scene of crime proclaimed not shock but relieved delight—shock of delight—that at last rage and disgust were being given a voice. Somebody somewhere harangued in their behalf. Xman wanted to bottle the harangue toward some more appropriate time when a siren suddenly drowned it out.

After squaring things with the clerk—if one may ever be said to have squared things with the clerks of the world— who also looked as if he had seen or smelled his, Xman's, kind many times before—although from what Xman could gather looking up occasionally from the house form he was filling out this clerk had seen everybody's kind many many times before, even Gandhi's, even Garbo's—Xman ascended in one of the hotel's elevator capsules to a room that smelled wearily, like the empty overlit corridor, of carpet. Before putting anything away he turned on the television set next to the window giving on an embrowned brick wall.

Remembering the look of people in the eatery—the look that said it had seen his kind before—in his rage he trembled, moving back and forth, getting from one end of the room, past the television set, to the other without remembering how he had been able to move so far. Rage had paid for and propelled his passage. He was compelled to add but to what, to the shaggy little ghost of an ottoman, "Don't get used to this. If you do, get used, I mean, you are in danger of sponsoring its perpetuity. If you don't, get used, I mean, you'll have to get used later when with absolutely no hope of exit, of transfer, you are in no condition whatsoever to get used."

The television showed a young couple fully clothed kissing passionately with the flawless abandon of billboard figures in a perfume or underwear advertisement high above—he hurriedly opened the door, ran to the end of the corridor, looked out on the town—Times Square. Theirs, a total indifference to life's larger miseries—aspirations—was the kingdom of heaven for those, that is, who cared to be kept abreast of timelessness. As for the couple talking in the next room it was the man, Xman decided quickly, who was completely without hope or at least without the equipment for synthesizing its grosser manifestations. What talent, sneered the woman. You never had any. Since I've known you you've done nothing but wait. He put his ear to the wall, he had a hatred of noise. I thought, the man said finally, after a certain point it wouldn't matter what I did, that I would still have a destiny independent of exertions on its behalf. Unable to bear either voice he lay down: adhesion to surface of counterpane, coarse and sticky, almost glutinous, reminded him

9

his own was unwashed. No good. He was wide awake to the story of his own future, he who loathed stories on principle. You were always hopeless, said the woman. Instantly he was not only wide awake but the last man on earth with hope. As far as he could make out the man was now trying to convince her what she deemed hopelessness was a mere curtain let down to foil his enemies' scrutiny, a camouflage as it were, apotropaically allowing for a going about the real business unseen. He was trying, Xman saw, to make her understand that in calling himself hopeless, so naming himself, what was he doing but erecting a deflected deflecting localizedness for the benefit of those consecrated to stamping him out for everybody's good but his own and, come to think of it, maybe his own too. You name it, you kill it, the man intoned. But once you catch them by letting them think they've caught you—in the net of their naming—you can go on—don't you see—uncaptured and unannihilated. The woman made a mouth sound that must have been shrug-accompanied. So what you're telling me, she ventured, trying to sound skeptical, far away from affiliation with what she was in fact on the spot inventing and therefore infinitely close to, is that playing hopeless is like playing dead—a prop. But you don't trap them—you don't trap anybody but yourself. People don't bother, the man insisted, with somebody who appears to feel hopeless. They let him alone. The woman must have shrugged again for the man said, It's true, as if insisting against all odds embodied in that shrug, then the voice sagged, suddenly disbelieving its forcefulness. Xman too was about to sag, before, that is, suddenly becoming shot through and through with unaccountable vitality. Thanks to this man—this voice—hopelessness, bad luck, failure, were no longer shapelessly and ubiquitously impending as they had been, Xman immediately saw, ever since he set foot in the taxi to the airport. They were instantaneously shrunk to the dimensions of the highly contoured figure across the partition so that in contrast Xman might feel infinitely strong. As long as he sustained the high—the very high—contrast between them he would be able to avoid all pitfalls—all labels. Exertion—mighty and infinite—was suddenly no longer impossible, even here in New York where, judging from the complexion of the merciless night sky, exertion must indeed count for very little. Exertion was no longer futile now that he had managed to extricate himself from the shadow of the other's failure to exert which failure in fact absorbed all failure to exert. Whatever he, Xman, ended up doing would perforce shine in contrast to this man's doings which added up to nothing from all indications but third-rate forage for a bovine shrew's reproachful rumination. There was no longer anybody else in New York against whom Xman would be required to compete. This man absorbed—was—everybody, all of being, and in contrast consequently to everybody—this everybody—else Xman was on the verge of doing very well, now even almost liking the coarseness of the counterpane.

Adjacent to the television screen he continued to listen to their dispute. What baffled was the man's refusal to learn to learn how not to provoke her. After this brief interval Xman already knew what to avoid laceration must not be said. The man—the only other man in the world—on the contrary welcomed feints that brought him to a threshold of incomparable invigoration. You say you are glad to be named—hopeless, she said. Then why don't you call anything else by its name. I call you by your name: Fa— I don't mean just me, she retorted, but in a voice strangely artificial. You don't call the hotel by its name. I can't call it by its name when its name is a pretentious absurdity. Calling it by its name I yield to that absurdity as something different from the barest most blatant pretension as if I buy the illusion it is trying itself unknowing to foist off. Better of course if it does not know: this makes the illusional absurdity somehow richer . . . for unsuspecting bystanders, that is. At any rate, I don't want to have to read pretension off a slate of coercion. For this implies I buy not only the particular illusion but my own being in a world of such illusions. I am not in the world, not for one minute. The conversation sounded more and more rehearsed. I don't want to be sucked in. That is why I always make it a habit to affix precautionary pincerlike "thises" and "thats" to any name I am forced to intone. Every proper name, full of absurd resonances the entity impaled cannot begin to appropriate, is a pretentious bid for significance. During a long silence the sole figure on the screen addressed its adversaries somewhere in offscreen space, which assumed greater and greater menace. But sometimes, continued the man, whom Xman dubbed (-)Xman, I give beings the wrong names purposely to watch them thrash, fail to emit the tics characteristic of the essence assigned them via the name and buried in its folds. I watch them fail to fulgurate essence the name says they involve. And I begin to be deeply touched by the fatuity of these creatures going about their business trying ever so hard but failing flailing all the time to emit—transmit—what the name proclaims, going about their business in—as—the shadow of a consummate failure to authenticate—give life to—the caption so magnanimously assigned them. They move me. Similarly, I have captioned myself. I have entitled my striving, or rather my failure to rise to the occasion of any other caption, *A life*. This is the caption assigned to those who have proven inadequate in their doings to the doings of any other possible caption. And muttering my caption as I go about rising to the occasion of the slender doings forever failing to rise to the occasion of an authentic caption, I am invested with a pathos and wish to weep, weep, do you hear, weep. The truth of the matter, Fa, is that I am sometimes terribly ashamed of my ability to miss nothing and see all. And this phrase—caption—*A life*, I mean—somehow soothes my shame over a hypertrophied vigilance. If on one hand the caption indicts and renders pathetic my inadequacy in the realm of hairy-chested exploit, on the other it detoxifies my voracious apperception and cuts its godlike enormity down to size The phrase—as if furnished by another—soothes and satisfies one who always rises too high yet never high enough in the direction of occasion. In a word, Fattie Lu, or is it Fattie Mae, the word tells me I am doomed through being unable in princely dedication to all that is too absolute to contend with this world. I am doomed, my flight has not flown. Once again, hearing (-)Xman Xman was instantaneously catapulted to invigoration, flights he had not even known were flying all at once and in all directions. Once again in well-timed opposition to this monolith once again conveniently embodying all men Xman was catapulted to a uniqueness forever beyond the monolith's reach. The caption, (-)Xman went on, I like it. No matter how much I see there is still a seer—the seer embodied in the caption, *A life*, the shadow thrown by the caption *A life*—outside myself, far outside and yet alarmingly—appallingly—close who, from above and all sides, computes every contingency self-aggrandizing collision with which has come to nought. In this case—and in this case alone—being named, being captioned, is restorative, soothes me against my hopeless craving to "make a name" for myself, by affirming my right to a certain . . . powerlessness. For what precisely does the phrase *A life* celebrate but that certain powerlessness in the face of exertion thereby paradoxically fortifying me for renewed exertion. From a certain perspective—that of the caption, *A life*—I am not responsible for the failure of my exertions—for all exertions are, by definition, failures once situated in that wider

13

perspective. If I am placed in this dingy hotel room in company of a shrew—this after all the years of storm and stress—then I am not to blame. Life foiling my greatness has put me here. I should stop feeling tormented owing to all world will be missing if my projects are not achieved, owing to world's decree for that decree also brackets, comprises, subsumes, supposes the subsequent privation. If life does not wish to exploit my talent to the limit, then three cheers for its own privation, I say. In other words, in addition to excruciation at my own failure and all the hardships to which it exposes me—each and every very much associated with the proud man's contumely—I must also suffer shame for the inconvenience of losing out on some of my not so inane projects nipped en route to fructification. No, no, no. I refuse to suffer excruciation as a monumental inconvenience to some other. Even if that other is the world. At any rate, you see, Fa, it is not quite true that I never call things by their proper names. When you impose a resonating name on some unsuspecting entity—which may include yourself—then the naming necessarily secretes a pathos as irrefutable as the Eisensteinian variety—farrago of cripples and sun-saturated parasols come to greet the battleship's scandalous triumph. This pathos oozes out of the interstice between name qua carapace and entity's core striving in vain to overwhelm, appropriate and discharge as autochthonous whatever name evokes. Yes, yes, Fa darling. At first I too felt my targets would strive for nothing but flights from my labels until I discovered that the majority dreaded nothing more than emergence from the floodlighted radius of experience subtended by these labels. Anything not "covered" by the labels immediately becomes unassimilable threat to being. So—I have no objection to inventing names but I will under no circumstances parrot the disgusting concoctions devised by those in love with their own densely populated vacuity. Such names are the treacle of incarnated delusion. Here the woman snorted. So everybody's name is necessarily a pretension they cannot hope to live up to—or live down, as the case may be. Only you have the right to lull yourself to sleep in the shadow of a caption like *A life*. A caption is not a name, he reminded her, vehemently, a little too vehemently, Xman tended to think, but not, he was obliged to add, if all this was being staged for the edification of some third party, some young man from the provinces embarked on— He, Xman, shut his ears and began shouting louder than his mind could think. That caption, my dear Fa, said (-)Xman at the same time that what sounded like a fist crashed against the wall behind the television—had he shouted that loudly?—is a much needed sabbath from the penal servitude of having always to be striving.

In the succeeding silence Xman tried to cover his life—his own life's striving—with the phrase, *A life*. But there was no resonance. "Perhaps," he thought, "it is because I am young compared to the man behind the screen, and there is not yet enough pathos-laden disproportion between strivings and outcome. And so it is not yet the moment for resolving that disproportion into the crystal dewdrop of a phrase such as, *A life*." You don't call things by their name, the woman suddenly shrieked, because by naming you—I mean one—necessarily yields to the world, to being in the world. And you—*un guerrier così codardo*—are mortally afraid of that leap into being. Somberly, almost stolidly, the man replied, Why should I leap into being. It's a play of masks, of pretenses, of the same phrases endlessly repeated. I want to destroy all that. Fa clicked her tongue as at some irksome peculiarity too etiolated even to qualify as peculiarity. That's why it's best, the man went on, we give this hotel the provisional designation of Shitkicker Arms or Tub of Farts Bed and Breakfast. For an instant Xman was no longer frozen in opposition to (-)Xman but living in and strengthened by the long shadow cast by his voice. This man's courage of refusal to name glimpsed the possibility of a similar courage. The hotel room was suddenly a dead space, the mere sign of everything outside itself impinging mercilessly in an effort to provoke a name. Not naming, said the man, as if before the blackboard in a packed amphitheater, is a first step toward refusal of things as they are, of the stench of things as they are. Then the voice became as if strangled by a sob.

In the past my being was undergone as a monumental and calculated challenge to the being of the clan, those sickening imbeciles among whom it was my misfortune to pass my youth as we speak of passing gas. And so I had to exaggerate into a hideousness susceptible of labels pejorative enough to put a lid both on their malevolence and my own violence smoldering just beneath the surface of its fatuity this unsuspecting capacity to incite and inflame. And when I was sure of the label I breathed a sigh of relief and spit out my disgust all in the same heave. Such was my exultant shame at being doomed to emanate what the label said I emanated. Crouched just beneath the label's lid for as long as the "shameful ignominy" lasted, I was spared the far greater excruciation of crawling out in conscientious quest of whatever had been causing such discomfort to the dear folks with whom I was doomed to share a Procrustean bed and breakfast. Don't you see, Fa, overweening fear of turning into myself was transmogrified into not-so-overweening fear of the denigrating label hovering in the shadow of every act, every gesture, every syllable consecrated to such a turning into myself. Yet would fearful hunger to turn into myself have been so great, you may ask, if the Procrusteans had not been so single-minded in attempting to suppress that hunger. I don't know. I do know that all striving—the slightest deviation from complete immobility in prostration before their every whim—was severely "frowned upon." At this point unmitigated hilarity at so genteel a caption for so grotesque a company. But I was so tormented by the inviolable play of essence in my depths that surely I cannot be blamed for striving to synthesize from innumerable shreds and patches of derision and disapproval a replacing accessibility. I know what you're thinking, Fa. That I'm being too harsh. In fact, you're thinking, such derision and disapproval masked an almost childlike enthusiasm over the ingenuity of that patchwork of foolproof cure for inviolability to which, therefore, they hoped deriding to yoke their own. It's just that I can't help looking back and regretting all those years spent synthesizing a sum of symptoms grotesque enough to ensure subsequent fall into the trap of this or that label: familiar, uncomprehending, lavishly lacerating.

Surprisingly all the woman—Fa—had to say was, Call it by its right name. Tsimmytsummy Arms Supreme, supreme one, that is, among those exquisite wreckages celebrated by the quondam bard of Valvins. Say it. He must have made a gesture of refusal for she clicked her tongue loudly. To Xman, the gesture meant: Saying *that* name necessitates an irreversible contortion of my backbone. The woman began to scream hysterically but he was beginning to have trouble hearing owing to what sounded like the arrival of a large family party in the room on his other side. Loudly susceptible to novelty they were a noisy lot, the kind of plain folks Hector's steeds were doubtless forced to drag around Central Park at high noon. Then he again heard Fa say, Say it. You can say the name. Say it. You're just pretending not to be able to say it in order to have a symptom at your disposal. But this is a mere degenerate case of symptom. It's far too calculated to be a symptom. It, this symptom, is supposed to make me recoil, draw back revolted—but of course not revolted enough to be unable to diagnose. You need my diagnosis, diagnosis puts me where you need me to be, diagnosis PLACES me. Yes yes yes, you pretend you are revolted by naming, labeling, but all this pretense—and it is all pretense—serves one purpose and one purpose alone: to force me to label your refusal to do your naming duty as something far more grandiose than the paltry little contrivance it turns out to be so that once labelled you can stretch out at length and at leisure on the rack of the warmingly familiar revulsion you consider yourself free to deduce from what you deem my diagnosis. Not only am I fixed—stationed—where you most need me—in parental revulsion triggering diagnosing outrage—but you yourself are conveniently put out to pasture in the very denigration you were heartfully repudiating a short time ago. But I don't want to be responsible for placing you, as the Procrusteans apparently placed you, since placing you places me or at least distracts from more essential tasks. I don't want to be forced to decipher the sand you throw in my eyes to keep me from colliding with your essence. In fact you no longer interest me. At least not as you did when you were a raw recruit. At the words "raw recruit" there was suddenly an alarming casualness in her tone. I'm leaving you, she said. This evidently meant walking to the window and opening it wide on the night starry or starless depending, so Xman had discovered from his brief walk, on the sidestreet.

Xman was surprised. The fact that (-)Xman embodied a symptom, a tic, however calculated, did not leave him— Speaking more to the brick wall than to (-)Xman Fatima added, I too loathe captions, darling. I wouldn't be caught dead in the toils of this one—oh, so you hear it too—declaring, for the tepid delectation of frumps and slobs, AFTER A TOUGH DIAGNOSING SESSION LIFELONG PALS RELAX IN A SWANK HOTEL CRANNY. The fact that (-)Xman embodied a symptom, a tic, however calculated did not leave him, (+)Xman, free to soar symptomless in opposition to the all of being now symptomed. On the contrary, he felt a sudden sodden infirmity in his very vitals, a certain quivering predisposition to what some fat old German would call Symptom-Synthesis. This time (-)Xman's ploys did not leave him free to be all he, (-)Xman, was not. This time he was ranged with his quasi double on the same side of the clinic fence as victim—and perpetrator—of symptoms wielded as truncheons but against whom and against what. Give me a symptom and I will move the world, so what if ultimately against myself, was (-)Xman's message, and it was fast becoming, alarmingly, Xman's own. (-)Xman began to weep. But again, to Xman's ears, even half-battered by the family's house sounds, the weeping had too much the quality of demonstration, was too much the work of a seasoned performer running the gamut of emotion purely as an exercise. I thought we wouldn't have to talk about all this, said the man. Fa replied:—she too sounded as if demonstrating a universal truth for the benefit of some third but somehow losing her hitherto firm and subtle grip on didacticism began to bellow, snort and sneer—It brought itself up, it erupted. Shrug? There are still too many unanswered questions connected with what you call—the symptom. I have a suspicion that even before the symptom—the tic—the ploy—call it whatever you like—was barely formulated you found yourself—it found itself—tabulating all those activities for which it might incapacitate you legitimately—you the supreme loather of everyday life. For isn't this the function of the symptom—legitimate, seemingly legitimate, incapacitation. NO NO NO. The aim of the symptom—a true symptom, fool—is to divest itself of the overt content responsible for its upsurge in order to establish a broad network of relations impossible outside the bounds of its good auspices. But you have never been able to think in these terms. For you symptom means disability checks, for me something entirely different: window on the world—or on world's destruction. Barely a conceptus your symptom was undoubtedly already big if not with itself then with computation of just how many areas of expertise it could be depended upon to obliterate AS FAR AS YOU WERE CONCERNED. And at the same time, given how mindlessly conscientious you can be once you put everything but your mind to it, you must dread incapacitation for routine as perhaps more strenuous ultimately—more strenuous, intricate and humiliating—than simple participation in the daily grind. At any rate, there is no place for a symptom in my network—I mean a symptom on those terms. I have always had other plans for the symptoms in my domain.

I have an infinitely more pragmatic attitude toward symptoms. Side by side with your cringing opportunism is a feeble and garrulous delusion of grandeur, equally if differently opportunistic. You dream of a symptom—a shame—so enormous it will create a fissure in being. (Remember, any such fissure is as momentary as a ripple in capsized azure.) Through some beneficient symptom you see yourself as so enormously flagrant as to be at last without all labels, inconceivable to the delicate and malevolent—delicate therefore infinitely malevolent—sensibilities of being. But it is when you are apparently most catapulted to the very outskirts of being's ozone, when you feel—through your symptomal shame—most relegated to the hideous margin of the goodly pageant—that the great world to which you so erroneously ascribe such delicate sensibilities has no trouble labelling you away forever. There is always a name—a label—allowing for the simplification of phenomena. It is only the likes of someone like you who fidgets in the face of ostensible phenomenal intricacy . . . The great world can never be accused of such fidgeting: it goes straight for the straitjacket. Despairingly drawn toward the lodestone of your very own den of iniquity—yes, like Gunhildo, just like little Gunhildino—an embodied fissure in being so you think you are in actual fact oh so colossally at its very heart accessible to any old sentinel specializing in rudimentary detraction. Here you are wielding your symptom like a cudgel and convinced you are thereby like Samson not only pulling down the temple canopy but blinding everyone in sight when—once again in actual fact—you are blinding nobody but a swarm of supremely expendable extras while the true judges sit quietly appraising the production values of this not completely unamusing posture. Take it from me, the world comes to terms all too easily with your "vast blinding shamefulness." What you dream of as too vast and hideous for conceivability is in fact a mere bonbon in the maws of the powers that be. So either you take, like me—though no one can be expected to attain my heights—a more pragmatic approach—one more consonant with . . . our aims—(she whispered something that resembled "destruction of the universe")—to symptom-making or it's bye-bye. Xman heard the man weeping. The tears moved Xman more deeply than he had ever dreamed it was possible to be moved. Up to now whenever he thought of his own fate he only felt rage. Shedding tears for this other he was suddenly able obliquely to shed a few tears over his destiny, failure of same. His own confusions were now lost to him therefore purified in the confusions of this other, this (-)Xman. The latter murmured, My symptoms are not just a vengeance on reality. I know it is not a vengeance, she went on, very sweetly, as if all was at last and for all time forgiven. It seemed to Xman that both he and (-)Xman must have their heads poised at the same angle in anticipation of Fa's formulation. I just wonder how much calculation was already prefigured in the symptom, how much energy of calculation contributed to the possibility—in other words, the inexora-

bility—of the symptom. How much was calculation responsible for propelling it into existence. How much calculation,
or rather let us call it speculation, was intrinsic to its forma-
tion. In other words, to underwrite passage of the symptom
from nothingness through the eddying narrows of development there had to be a kind of advance purchase on acts sure
to be sabotaged. I foresaw nothing, the man whispered. It's
only now the symptom is fully formed that all these inter-
connections have sprung from its forehead. You mean, she
murmured, it's only now that you've started to sabotage
acts—our acts—through the good auspices of the symptom.
Now that it's fully formed—but not before—the symptom
thinks itself into obstructive connection with other states of
affairs. But I'm convinced—and here her voice became quite
dreamy—the symptom was always thinking itself into sabotage. Because only by thinking could it come into being and
the only kind of thinking a symptom undergoes is sabotage-
thinking. It seemed (-)Xman was about to gasp forth a counterthrust. He did not have time. Birth—and when I say birth
I mean birth of the birth—of the symptom catapulted you to
a plane of unforeseen possibilities. Although you might not
have been able to say so, from the moment it was a something the symptom was already thinking sabotage. But it was
always the wrong kind of sabotage—sabotage in the name of
your incapacitation, exemption. Your symptom was incapable of thinking big simply because it was always already
weighed down with your sickly solicitations in your own
behalf. Your symptom was never permitted to think: What
bereft of this purulent ballast of overt content can I do for
the cosmos. If only we could harness your symptom for
there is more—far more—than a circumstantial connection
between true work and true symptom. Maybe, the man stut-
tered, it's merely a defect—One of your many, she suggested.—that I see the symptom simply as an obstruction.

Whenever we have a meeting and we have had many meetings with delegates assembled from—Xman had the impression she had quickly covered his mouth with her hand.—I begin to be afraid of the symptom. I'm afraid that if I speak I won't be able to "say names." I live in fear of dysfunction consequences. The symptom doesn't seem to have much of a content, said Fa, but not hopefully as Xman might have expected. And it must have abundant content if you are to prove your mightiness by abundantly eviscerating that content. Yet (-)Xman, judging from her tone, no longer seemed to be an enemy: they were both united in the face of a common problem. And yet their union had, once again, a heuristic quality, a preplanned pedagogic intensity as if even discord had been deployed in the service of some benighted third. The more in the form of a frantic pacing from television set to window and back again he considered it, the more did (-)Xman's comment beginning with "I begin to be afraid of the symptom," or did it begin rather with "Whenever we have a meeting," stink of too rapid abject capitulation. Unmotivated, merely demonstrational. How had (-)Xman managed to reach this point. What I mean, resumed Fatima as if in kind response to some classroomwide blank stare, is that so much of this symptom—this terror of naming names—becomes mere terrified anticipation of the consequences of the symptom . . . giving free rein to itself, I mean. Definition of the symptom pretty much becomes: dutiful credulity in the face of its possible upsurge. The symptom is a potential space, a pleural cavity dependent for upsurge on the expansion and contraction of a horrified—always ready to be horrified—credulity. You mean, said the man, always a little too eager to be enlightened, judged at least by the tediously exacting standards of a conventional dramaturgy, there is no symptom apart from terror of the symptom. And once again it seemed as if all real conflict between the two had broken down and what was left was starkly instructional give-and-take devoid of plausibility though not of its own peculiar brand of pathos. We're going to try to use your symptom, to make it part of the work from here on in. You mean, he replied, to devote its every other waking moment to the project. Imbecile, she retorted. Everything is a joke to you. And for a moment they seemed comfortably adrift in the old contrariety. But as you see with your tic—your symptom—you cannot fix me as some benevolent reprobating clinician. I've bypassed you, bypassed IT, choosing instead to go after the network of relations in which once given free rein it owes it to itself to be caught up. Suddenly their television—it had to be theirs for the loudmouthed family had uttered no sounds for quite some time—was turned up very loud. As from a very great distance he heard them laughing, thinly and in a thin unison that enraged and fascinated.

Hearing loud pounding on the other side of the wall opposite Xman realized the family assumed the noise was coming from his television set. Before he could decide whether or not to pound back a protest at being accused unjustly he heard a far less contentious—an almost friendly—knocking at the door, which he was able somehow to detect above both television and continuous pounding. Opening wide he quickly directed with a stab of erect forefinger presumable head of temporary household standing forthright on threshold to real source of a disturbance unspeakable at any hour. All at once, however, all noises stopped together and head of household at last able to get a few words in edgewise said, "I'm from Joliet," with a slight belch. "In Joliet we have a real family network, friends, spiritual orientation, co-workers we insist on being fond of as if they were our very own—and this sentiment persists outside the workplace—loving neighbors, and community rites, to say nothing of true blue regular backyard world culture in a nutshell, as it were." Before

Xman could say the words he suddenly believed might change his life and thereby spare him recourse to the dubious resources of a Fa, say, or a (-)Xman, head of household added, "We have shared beliefs regarding how life ought to be lived. Life isn't just a carriage ride around Central Park in the dark." Xman felt that if only he could say "How's the weather in Joliet," he could become another, the other among others destined as a unique product of nowhere to succeed in New York. For a split second the phrase, "How's the weather in Joliet," had seemed a mere dizzyingly ironical consummation of counterfeit existence, implement of choice in keeping a household hound at bay. But now with hound on the verge of leaving his life forever Xman craved this phrase that already departed was impossible of retrieval. "Sorry to have disturbed you," said head of household with exquisite politeness. "Good night," he added, walking backward toward where a large family awaited him. At first the lost phrase had seemed the vehicle of massive impersonation. Swept away it now stank of the only conceivable existence worth craving in this slagheap of unhooded carriage rides.

No matter how full it appeared the bus always managed to admit a few more fancifully attired matrons on their way west or was it east. Stepping out of the hotel and feeling immediately as if he had been lured from a fixed point into vast chaos he had been tempted to run back and rip the TV antenna out of the box in order to be possessed—accompanied everywhere—by a substitute. Above the chatter of children just disgorged from various private schools, to judge from their too studied disarray, one of the bus's many "struggling young actors moonlighting as waiters" spoke proudly—just as Xman caught sight of a regiment of icicles depending from the black walls of the brief east-west tunnel—of how he had gone with his agent, Laura Forza del Destiny, to see the new play by . . . Xman could not catch the name of the play because with the bus swerving from some tiny hummock directly beneath the icicles his attention was netted first by a derrick in the far distance, grazing, then by his own recurring terror of what was likely to befall him in this jungle of derricks. Now he would never know what play it was the young actor and his Pallas Athene had gone to see and loved with all their heart. The young actor should have gone on speaking so Xman, no lover of life, could decipher this honeyed openness to all experience. Not just honeyed, Xman had to admit, but overwhelmingly intimidating.

When he got off the bus, reluctantly turning his chilled backside on the Metropolitan Museum of Art and on a demure little path at the corner of Seventy-ninth and Fifth leading with a minimum of hubbub into the depths of the park, he passed the glass-enclosed outpouching of a restaurant whose habitués evidently had just been confronted with the unsightly pavement spectacle of two derelicts cleaning their toes. They looked at, or rather down, Xman, as if to say: You, you there; do something, something at once; why, this is unheard of; when such vermin do not take care of their even more vermined own; in this day and age; here we are minding not only our own business but that of our freshly sculpted endive pasta when who—what—should come along but; oh no, oh no; waiter. Frenzied bejewelled gesticulation toward the eatery's innards. Once the maître d' arrived: Kindly put those masses of purulence and their ineffectual steward out of our misery forever. Forever, do you hear. He passed other derelicts, some did not clean their toes or their crotches, some wheeling carts from which "an impressive array" of bags in all shapes, sizes and colors dangled ponderously, ponderingly even, merely spoke to themselves in the accents of alternating outrage and commiseration. Passing them he did not feel as he had in the hotel eavesdropping on (-)Xman and *his* Athene,—that these creatures were kindly absorbing all his quirks thereby leaving him free to soar high above frenzied and bejewelled verdict. These did not absorb all he was on the verge of synthesizing. He could easily become polluted by their way of life. It was tempting even if he hadn't come to New York to derelictate, could have stayed on in C— —and become one of their ilk though being a *derelict* there wouldn't have resonated with the same skyscraperly prestige. Saying the word he both killed the event it staked out in the world and framing perpetuated it. Just before entering the building whose number corresponded to that scrawled on his gangly palm he stopped at a sidewalk kiosk adjacent to a souvlaki vendor's sclerae-searing fumes in order, purchasing the *Wall Street Trencher and Gavottenik,* to impersonate a successful young executive-in-training with boundless ambition and, to use Fa's phrase—but was it hers?—a network of connections, equally boundless. Scraping together the necessary nickles and dimes his eye was caught by the cover of *Persona* magazine just below one flaunting a pinkish female rump (one buttock only, if you please) and to the right of another's ocherish male testicles in the throes of ecstasy appropriate to such contraptions. Far more disorienting however, than hairy testicles colliding with broad daylight was the title of the *Persona* cover story: LIFE AND DEATH OF THE ALL-AMERICAN BOY scrawled in red across the face of its subject impishly beaming into the very anus of eternity. The kioskite hastened to agree with Xman's straining eyes: "You said it. A crying shame. A clean-cut kid like that and in a plane crash." Looking him dead in the palm awaiting its wash of small change Xman said, "If I have to die I vow here and now—nine o'clock in the morning on"—he looked up and away—"Park Avenue neither in death nor life will I ever prove susceptible to such a story—worse, to such a caption—in short, some easy print-greasy encapsulation of street meaning targeted at the gum-chewing delectation of fops and frumps."

Jed Perlmutter turned out to be middle-aged. Tics did
nothing to humanize him. Xman could not quite locate a
center of gravity. Perlmutter himself seemed in quest of
same and sensed, to judge from his eye movements, it might
be found high above his desk or toward a side window smothered in ferns and giving on a water tower pasted to a billboard. Perlmutter said, "What brings you here," in an
unfriendly, an almost brutal, tone that nevertheless suggested any brutality was all for the sake of its target. "It's a
long story," Xman replied, and by so replying felt witty or at
least reinvigorated by the distance such a reply established
between self and self, between self and story as slagheap of
incidents refusing to assume the sagittal figure of a destiny.
Yet reinvigoration did not prevent Xman from feeling this
comment obstructed irrevocably what must be reported if he
was to arrive. As if they had just concluded a long discussion
as a result of which he had no choice but to be very favorably
disposed, Perlmutter said, "I'd like you to meet Jensen Mac-
Duffers." He rose, and with the arched-over pittypatting am-
ble of somebody just hitting the open air after an enormous
repast, quite possibly Szechwan, moved toward the door. Just
before disappearing he said, "You must be devastated, not
having a job, I mean." Xman had never thought of himself as
somebody not having a job, I mean. He was merely—exaltedly—somebody looking for a job. Perlmutter had named, in
other words gunned him down just when he was looking
most avuncular, implying he had been insufficiently—(appalling state of affairs)—conscientious in terms not of actually looking for a job, for here he was bright and early on the
very first day of the workweek, but of being devastated at
having to look at all. Perlmutter's almost-out-the-door naming subtended a secret propaedeutic practical devastatedness
of whose existence he, Xman, a novice, could only be igno-
rant. He wanted to run after Perlmutter and point out that

he was, after all, frequently devastated. Only only catching him off guard Perlmutter had consigned him to permanent undevastatedness. Rebuked for not being devastated at that moment Xman dreading suspected he would never get back to devastatedness—now exalted to his sole protection against joblessness—especially in the eternally lingering shadow of Perlmutter's enervating jubilation—enervating, that is, to its target, him, Xman—at having pinpointed—that is to say invented—so prodigal a lapse.

Perlmutter was now sole proprietor of the devastation-phenomenon and had already done all he could to make reappropriation impossible. Perlmutter had left the door open. Looking into the corridor Xman wanted to explain to the yellow wall leaking in from that corridor and smeared with its multigenerational filth (the building was a landmark) that in fact he had been devastated on more than one occasion. But how know when devastatedness undergone was at last more than equivalent to the most conscientiousness-affirming success-guaranteeing dose of devastatedness peddled out in the world. And now—he was almost ready to sob—even if all the previous despair did summate to the requisite level of devastatedness—slyly but surely apotropaic against all imputations of shortfall—naming—Perlmutter's naming—had just killed all possibility of summation. To qualify as novice destined for a success beyond temporary joblessness he must reaccumulating a sufficient heap of devastatedness scratch from scratch. Hadn't he, Xman, in search of gainful employment, wept and crawled and climbed all over himself bleeding from all orifices. Yet the filthy wall told him there was no appeal. His symptoms did not constitute authentic devastatedness as named by the likes of Perlmutter.

A fat shadow advanced across the filth but did not obliterate, did not come even close to obliterating, the mash of cigarette stains, fingernail- and footprints, wisps of dried and faded excrement. "Jed tells me you're a raw recruit," said the fat man before he was even close—before his shadow was even close—to the desk, nicked and gnawed, Xman now saw, in many places. "I'd like you to meet Tom McTom Tom. Or is it McTomTom. I can never get the name straight and yet we go back thirty-six years, can you beat that. He could give you a better idea of the layout. How much are you looking for before we touch bases. I mean, What are we talking about, what ballpark." Always exhilarated by any implied characterization—"raw recruit" would, in this case, do very nicely—that served to annex the utterer as an instant guardian busy classifying, bottling and shelving him away in behalf of a soon-to-be-divulged larger truer destiny, Xman nevertheless resented being in the hands of this vintner, however masterful. He longed to put himself in a more undefinable if precarious position with regard to MacDuffers who after screaming, "Polly where the hell is Tom McTomTom," into its mouthpiece dropped the phone and proceeded to wait hands folded feet on desk. Rather than smile reassuringly at the raw recruit, as had to be customary under such circumstances, MacDuffers chose to stare at the ceiling or let the ceiling stare at him, as if bored with Xman, the ceiling, the phone call, the whole bloody business of contending with raw recruits of this type especially when in his day a raw recruit— Xman was tempted to sulk at this absence of reassurance when MacDuffers, breathing through his pudgy fingers as if after a manicure added, "You have this hangdog look, young fella. It may be attractive to women—then again, it may not, not knowing the circles in which you travel, got a woman? At any rate what if I had reassured you, I mean, while I was on the phone, said, 'Don't worry, this McTomTom is a real ace. He'll get you fixed up. You would have bristled and bridled, take an old fart's word for it. It would have stunk to high hell of inadequacy, my reassurance, committing the colossal sin of making sayable what should go beyond saying. Beyond thinking even, am I right, sir? I should be so concerned about your fate as not to be able even to conceive of having to reassure you. And in any case if I had tried you would have picked my reassurances apart like a second-rate turkey roast. Make that fourth-rate—at any rate the saying would simply have invoked a superabundance of more comprehensive reassurances stintingly—appallingly—left unsaid. You would have said to yourself, 'Why does he say, Don't worry. Does he think of me as one so fragile that the minute he's on the phone I require a tranquilizer.' You see what I'm getting at, young fella." As if to Xman's strategic demurral MacDuffers went on to say, "I know you're jobless and you're running out of time. You may have a family to support. There might be some gal who won't let you inside her pants if you don't—at any rate, you're jobless and you expect me to downplay this stigma of being more trouble than you are worth by emphasizing its badge-like secondarily sexual scintillation as the proverbial step backward before the great leap. You know, the Rastignac Syndrome. But I can't play that game." As Xman said nothing, MacDuffers asked what kind of work he was interested in—not necessarily the kind of work he was interested in doing just the kind of work he was interested in. Xman could have kissed him for making such a fine distinction but only for a second. The urge passed. Noticing, however, that a label with his name (typed) slid under a piece of plastic was gaudily pinned to an unnaturally large pinkish left lapel Xman wanted less than ever to reply, yet couldn't decide whether label, lapel, lighting (one of the scrolls of fluorescence was flutteringly shot), sirens below, smudged yellow taxicab reflections in ninth, tenth and eleventh floor windows across the street, or the way MacDuffers's pudgy little fingers oozed

over the back of his curule chair thereby permitting especially flagrant beringed pinky (with its tiny chaos of golden
hairs between the first two joints) grazing contact with the
stem of the tensor lamp behind, or some memory of long
ago, or some indecipherable physiological impasse of here-
and-now's anus, bowels, penis, penis sheath—stymied reply.
Straining to see out the window behind MacDuffers for a
moment Xman could almost believe silence was in direct
response—contrast—to the thrust of the plane trees adjacent
to—hadn't someone told him, the kioskite, that was it—the
Museum of National Historiography slantingly striving to
haul earth's intolerable obstructiveness to expansion either
downward or over their mottled shoulder. Only then it became evident that he could not name his line of work precisely because that line was simply too too good for the
world as known up to now, what with its sumps and sties
and worse, its stridently good-humored apologists for the
existence—nay the proliferation—of both—too good for this
ubiquitously foul-smelling puddle reflecting only shattered
flight (birds, helicopters), turbulence (twigs, purplish rack),
and outrageous complacency in the face of stark want (See
the essay: "Social Utility of the Flutter of Tennis-Ball-Green
Penthouse Canopies high above Puke- and Piss-Mediated
Derelict Powwows," *Journal of Contemporaneous Contempt*, August, 198–). Yet without having spoken, without
having even attempted to speak, he was already exhausted,
laid out, ensepulchered—yet here was MacDuffers having
the audacity to exhume him with a probing belch—by all he
could be saying to ridicule and refute himself. What the hell
do you mean, you little squirt, by too good for this fucking
fuck of a world. Hadn't the directrix of the orphanage on the
outskirts of Cincinnati always sneered at the first sign of
what she all too eagerly took to be pretension: Who the hell
do you think you are, charity boy. We've worked ourselves to

the bone and you've been nothing but trouble. Before utter-ing, muttering, the shard of a syllable Xman dislodged a plethora of counterstatements from the non-site of non-say-ing in which miasmic puddle of plenary refutation he felt obliged to drown.

The remark even unspoken, because unserenely un-spoken, quickly became a mere placeholder for all that might have been and still could be said to triturate it. Again out of the blue, MacDuffers said, this time examining the beringed pinky. "Speak up, speak up. You wanted to say something like, 'My line of work is too good to talk about. I won't name it before the likes of you.' Oh I'm not laughing. I believe all my raw recruits when they say, or don't say, as much. The remark, by the way, is most vulnerable precisely when it possesses—as it certainly must in your special case—the highest degree of truth. Knocking it down as so much bombast is not very interesting. You'll find, young fella, that the closer your true work—sorry, your personal project—oops, your true work—comes to being 'too good for this world' the more you should expect yourself to renounce the pleasure of saying, 'This here work, this here project, is too damn good for this here world, or that there world, or this here world.' For if your work is too good then the remark becomes irrefutable. And that's exactly my point: You don't want, especially in your condition, to be irrefutable. You can't afford, especially in your situation, and not this early in the game, to be irrefutable, to be condemned to the stasis of irrefutability. You need contacts capable of irrigating the des-ert of the true work. You want to touch bases—sure you do—with a lot of nice guys. How nice? As nice as the phrase 'A hell of a nice guy' permits." As if summing up and having clearly completely forgotten about McTomTom MacDuffers said, "I'm going to hand over your resume to somebody I'd like you to meet. And soon. They should meet you." Xman was beginning to know without knowing he knew this kind of talk was an attempt to give him, Xman, a sense of Mac-Duffers's sense of his, Xman's, uniqueness in order to camouflage his, MacDuffers's, not-so-unique hunger to be rid of him at last.

"I know what you think. I'm trying to get rid of you. It isn't true. Or rather it is true precisely because your very being alerts me to my profound inadequacy with regard to the vending of such beings. It isn't true. It's simply that the Finaglie brothers, Amos and Alphonse, are extremely busy and I want you to get to know them before they're off again to Crete, or Tripoli, or Taxco, on another business trip determining the fate of billions. They should meet you," he repeated again. As he walked out the door, Xman hated MacDuffers's panicked craving for some sort of consensus on the Xman Affair to be obtained at no small cost, no doubt, to his already badly callused feet. And what kind of consensus was he, MacDuffers, seeking. Thinking of Xman as a shit was he so scandalized by the extremeness of his reaction that he needed some backup or truly impressed was he simply eager for the corroboration known tangily as feedback sure to put him on the right track at last regarding where to situate the little devil, organizationally speaking. Or did he have absolutely no opinion whatsoever on Xman as man or beast with him, Xman, representing no more than what he must always represent and embody to all these associate creative directors, executive managers and vice-presidents in charge of operations, namely, a grain of doubt, some less than scintillating shard caught in the hierarchical gears that must under no circumstances (see addendum to memo 69Bib) be left unturned. The MacDufferses of the world did not consider or care that these encounters were nothing less than a mammoth grueling undertaking for the Xmans of the world and must, to remain sufferable, necessarily correspond—always from the point of view of said grains, shards, Xmans—to a mammoth interest, or at least curiosity on the part of the powers that be.

No answer to these questions from the elevator buttons, much less from its denizens intent on high feed or a trip to the bank or a quick rendezvous with Bob, computer programmer on the way up and boyfriend of the week. And why shouldn't Bob hold up his head proudly as computer programmer on the way up. Intent on finding out to what degree he was marketable Xman took the subway far downtown: it turned out the Finaglie brothers, or The Twins, ran an employment agency on a very high floor of the World Trade Center. The view behind the leaden receptionist proving truly magnificent Xman thought of jumping to freedom but stopped short upon realizing he was debating whether or not to take his jacket with him. Seventy floors below he was convinced he discerned a puddle whose presence between two hydrants momentarily cushioned the prospect of jumping—made it real, possible, painless. As it turned out he discovered he had taken the wrong elevator and was obliged to return to the lobby. This time he was alone with a pair who evidently worked in the same office. The male, smiling significantly at his fellow passenger as just in time he eluded the closing doors and noting the soggy paper bag held discreetly away from the big white bow consummating little white blouse's zigzag of frills—discreetness carried to the point of flagrancy—said: "Why so late when you're supposed to be an example to all the rest of us." Xman began to feel loathing neither for one nor for the other but rather for the soggy space between thick with the aftertaste of faint flat amenity. Oh yes, the big white bow was sufficiently repulsive but it could not be taken to task for inspiring loathing as he loathed. So accosted the woman assumed a bilious tinge. Late, she was caught by a co-worker. Her culpability named,

she began to speak, Xman watched her try to displace rage
from her captor to the exasperatingly long line of construction workers who if truth be told had just a few minutes
before spitefully chosen to obstruct her passage to the probable matutinal corn muffin/sugarless milky tepid tea/green-
ish orange. In that confined space with the yellow light
hopping from number to number—they were at this very
moment within the two—no the three—no the four—no the
two-digit range—Xman continued to watch her try to slide
exasperation in raging shame at co-worker within to work-
men without. And he watched both her and the hopping
light with far more than the mere interest of a MacDuffers
or a McTomTom for it was up to her to dispel the nothing
less than universal loathing and disgust engendered by this
littlest of little scenes but the more she attempted to displace her rage the more bloodless, slithering, and abject she
became. Yet it was not her specifically he loathed. It was
only later, seated at last in the right office, that of the Twins
Finaglie, exalted issue of Gall the Unmitigated, filling out
his application that it came to him. Now Xman understood
why he had felt he was going to choke, felt the slightest
breath would burst the bounds of his chest cage. That scene
in the elevator had been big with a caption. And the caption
was . . . THE GANG AT THE OFFICE. A caption for rancid
humanity in its rancid nudity. He never wanted to be captioned: Wasn't this what uniqueness meant: to be beyond
caption. The co-worker in frills had bristled at being named,
at having her lapse named, unaware that she and the other
were flailing beneath an even larger lid. But this would never
happen to Xman. And at the same time he still did not
understand why he had felt choked. It had little or nothing to
do with the propinquity of a caption, it had nothing to do
with a caption, it had to do with . . . something to do with
disjunction between what she, the frilly one, had pretended

to be feeling toward the regiment of construction workers and what she was really feeling toward . . . toward . . .

Disjunction. When he heard a voice say, "Hi there, Xman. I'm Rose Baldachino, Xman. Come this way, Xman," he made a point without knowing he was making it to raise his head very slowly from the application attached to the brown clipboard. She skimmed the form as she led him to her office beyond the labyrinth of cubicles. Her high heels exaggerated—as is so often the case with this breed—the toss of her rump, irrefutable sign of convivial efficiency. He was glad—sky-blue glad—by sheer chance his head hung on one side, ample protection against the blast of pain induced by the sight of that rump. "So Xman," she said, sitting down. "What have you been doing, Xman, and how can we help you, Xman." He strained to see outside the window, open to gusts of cold city air. If only he could see a tree, any tree, an elm, a shingle oak, a samara from said oak's agon of boughs, even the sagging shadow of a leafless nodeless petiole—seeing in the sense of affixing that shadow to his being as a signature is affixed to a death warrant—he would find himself somehow beyond her capacity to bracket and crush him between spiked heels with this unendurable false familiarity. Yet was he strong enough to venture beyond her capacity to crush, spiked heels or no—toward the peculiar comfort proffered by a total lack of spontaneity. And why should she proffer spontaneity. Was there any room for spontaneity in a world demanding confrontation with its MacDufferses and McTomToms. This wiggling rump had wisely learned simpering improvisation had to be abandoned double quick and at all costs. As if in answer to his musings, she murmured, "I'm here to help—Xman." She had clearly forgotten his name and made a quick leap to the top line of the information sheet. Hearing her voice he knew he would not have the strength to venture beyond her brittle surface. Only as Xman

+ samara, or as Xman + shingle oak, no longer the Xman of
"How are you, Xman" would he be her prey no longer. But
she persisted in blocking his view, her kind always would,
was she adept at this interviewing strategy, of course she
must be. He was sure that once able to look down down
down he would find all—more—than he was looking for.
With only a glimpse of the wall outside her window decid-
edly unsmothered in ferns—what did this mean—quick—
quick—MacDuffers's had been smothered in ferns, hers was
not—he knew lower down said wall must at this very moment be making everything as comfortable as possible for
the encroachment, vast, scrawled, forever two-dimensional,
of the blue-gray shadow of some burled and mottled London
plane whose very impatience of posing would be responsible
for the authoritative flourish of the sketch's haste. On the
lower reaches of this wall would soon be enacted the definitive conversion of a chaos of peeling, gleaming, damp tinsel
into the sacred calm of flawless midday shadow. But here
was Ms. Baldachino sucking him through the fissure of her
rump deep into chaos. And just when the emergence of
shadow was informing him that the true work—the long
awaited true work—this true work—some true work—had
not a little to do with—with—with—conversion of—
into— When he was halfway through the sentence he heard
himself saying, "The first summer after podiatry school I
worked on a construction gang out in the Berkeley hills. The
foreman was almost castrated." Before she could ask Xman
added, "He gave too many orders to his men. For the most
part drug addicts in the uneasy throes of rehabilitation they
had a hard time accepting orders." He wanted to add: "An
order is a window on death." "Did you get along with these
. . . other workers." Rose B. handled them with pincers. Secretly he thanked her for letting him feel superior to her
squeamishness. Xman could not bear to answer. Did it mat-

ter. Her question embodied not only its answer but also his failure to know the truth at the heart of the correct answer as well as the particular mode of presentation his failure to know would inevitably take. Xman quickly coined an adage to be savored, squirrellike, in privacy: In the presence of the Rose B.s of the world all failure stinks of inevitability. It didn't matter what he answered, what he said, what he—presented, of a lie's glaring failure to know its smothered kernel of truth as the most glaring—nay incandescent—nay glaring—presentation of that truth in spite of itself—himself—itself. The struggle toward and attainment of enlightenment was already packed tight into Rose's rump and leading question. Her question already comprised what it pretended to seek and was out only to measure how far answer could diverge from core of impugning truth hidden at its heart. She was out, the slut, to scan the angle of divergence subtended by a core of truth blithely bypassing its own emergence. The angle of divergence, here was the key to his entrapment. All Xman said was, "For some of them an order was a window on death." Sensing, oh horror of horrors, that she was growing fond of him, he was terrified even more than if she had threatened to evict him on the spot. As if rebounding in time from such rashness, patting the jet-blue-black under a sparkling snood she said, "So Jensen sent you. Let me tell you about him. What holds for him holds for Jed too. Sometimes I think they're the same person—you never see them together. Both are married, both love their wives—Bertha, and their kids—Freddy and Fredda. He's pleasant enough when you first get to know him. Or think you are . . . getting to know him. Until the inevitable moment when pouncing he goes straight for the jugular. Begins to insinuate—in a jugular vein, of course. His so-called generosity, which between ourselves is nothing more than a cramped desire to toy with human frailty, has once again washed

somebody up on our shores. Not that we mind. That's what
we're here for. That's what we're paid our pittance for. And
every lackey loves a pittance." A pretty young woman entered without, as far as Xman could tell, having knocked,
and handed Rose B. a cherry-colored folder. Without opening
it, without even acknowledging another's presence, although
the shift to a new tone of more formal authority all too
keenly suggested acknowledgment, Rose said, "I may be getting something in soon. Of course, as you might have
guessed, I have nothing, absolutely nothing, now. "But,"—as
if recalled to what was demanded professionally, "I don't just
want you to take it. Simply because you're in an . . . interim
with regard to what really matters." This comment made,
Xman thought, as an all-or-nothing bid for recognition of her
merciless acuity, restored Rose, Xman also thought, to eternal favor in Rose's eyes. No longer could she be accused of
succumbing to sudden fondness for a stranger, especially
when he was not a particularly tall, dark or handsome stranger. Looking at the young woman Xman tried to understand
"interim." "I know your kind," Rose bellowed, as if to strike
dead his gaze and his gaping. Turning to the young woman:
"The kind with delusions of some newfangled personal project's ultimate triumph on these our fair shores. They spend
half their office time on the phone making personal calls of
no substance purely to affirm differentness from all the others." Still looking hard at the young woman: "You are selling
all this eagerness now because for the time being and perhaps for all time—haha—you are depleted, washed out, at a
loss, stymied, eclipsed. You're between engagements, so to
speak, and so you come here manifesting an enthusiasm
without bounds that you can't possibly sustain. Or maybe
being sick to death of struggle here in the big city you've
made a resolution—a New Year's resolution several months
before it falls due." "I've just arrived," said Xman, also look-

ing at the young woman, either from the most outrageous defiance or the most abject mimicry. She went on: "You've cut yourself off definitively from the project. Without it you're free at last to see what you can make of yourself. At this very moment you're looking back on it, an obstruction, an accretion from which you have at last been able to prove yourself detachable. You'll swear at any rate it is detachable. So here you are, telling me not to worry: Xman's come home to mamma York free at last to function creatively, rid once and for all of a mere accretion that is at the same time indistinguishable from his very being or rather from his hallucination of that being, but no matter,—do you hear, Rosalie, his very being, indistinguishable from his very being of hallucinated being—and when active merely repels and discounts all other tasks." "You make it sound like Vesuvius," said a voice, his. Although it might be better to pretend to have absolutely no idea of—no familiarity with—the subject at hand, Xman was afraid by seeming not in the least to understand of losing a vital connection heralding the beginning of the end of centuries of vagrant pilgrimage. "At this very moment you may be feeling free of yourself at last—a delightful feeling at times, I know from bittersweet experience—free of all that insists on making you you. Free to participate in projects totally alien to needs always too deep for articulation but never deep enough for total obliteration. But I don't want to catch you at an off moment, your least representative, in fact. Is this the real X-man—sorry, Xman— or a stand-in pending bluer skies. Or stormier." He hung his head. This mute avowal drove her to what she clearly took to be greater—transcendent—mercilessness of lucidity. "Take it from me, Xman, you're never free of the accretion. Its detachability is an illusion of the pitiable kind. At times you may very well think you are functioning independently—of the accretion, of your fealty to its lawgiving musculature.

41

But it's then you are most entangled in its coils—propelled by it and it alone. Yes, yes, I know. How many times have you found yourself bemoaning this behemoth's setting strict limits to activity in other spheres. Did it ever occur to you that the behemoth fuels all such activity. What do I mean—what am I driving at. Simply this: If the project, the true work, the shenanigan, is a trap it is also a mainstay. Always behind the scenes of this other activity it forbids you to be intimidated by inevitable failure to keep pace with all associated pettiness. Not that I would ever dream of laying a charge of pettiness at the doorstep of this 'other activity.' It pays our rent, eh Rosalie. At any rate—so so so—you come here at a moment when you happen to feel free of all that makes you you—the way Jensen MacDuffers occasionally feeling free enough of all he is becomes infected with this germ of a need to help. Yes, for two minutes—I'm sure he didn't speak to you longer than that—he was able to stand far enough apart from himself to applaud an imposture. Never forget—he wasn't talking to you he was listening to himself impersonate and you, dear boy, were simply the echo chamber of Sarastro's impersonation. You come to me as if you have already turned over a new leaf but I smell the impatience—the hatred—that generally overruns everything you yourself have not set in motion. So why, Rosalie darling," and here she turned to Xman at last, "am I wasting everybody's time sending him to this interview. I must be mad, simply mad." "Too bloody kind for your own good," murmured Xman with what he hoped was an audible twinkle of irony. The woman addressed as Rosalie said nothing, nor, apparently, was she expected to.

"Young man, you would be far less dangerous admitting outright your commitment to a line of work patently hostile to anything I for one can dig up for you." This was the first time anyone had honored Xman's velleities with the name of personal project, with the name of work. Before he could much relish this discovery—and at any rate hadn't MacDuffers blusteringly deferred along the same lines to—: "Now don't get me wrong: I don't think you're purposely trying to deceive me. A woman of my vast experience knows better. What is far more dangerous I think you're actually trying to work yourself up into a trance of . . . otherness, all you are not and cannot hope to be. And this for my benefit and that of my little friend who will, I hope, become your little friend before very long. Seriously though, first find out what you are before you come here or anywhere, panting to get on with it, hawking this unsubduable eagerness to tow the mark. An attitude, I might add, completely inappropriate to the type of assignments I have in mind." Here she looked at Rosalie, not a cue, an empty look, expecting nothing, not even the slight smile of discomfort that played around Rosalie's ample rosebud lips. "What is the appropriate attitude," he found himself asking, intrigued by the Xman who would ask such a question. To his knowledge, he had never before made his acquaintance, that of one humbly inquisitive. "I know it when I see it," Rose snapped. "And I also know an irresponsible spate of eagerness sure to come to an end. And what will I be left with when it is over—I who must hold up my head at all costs among employers of all coats and colors. What will I be left with. I'll tell you what. Reports either that you have fled or driven by the dreglike virulence of a rage without end ended up sabotaging the whole works, stealing—merely to discard them in some wastebasket—the most vital of vital documents."

Xman did not know how much to tell her, how much he had to tell her. He did not want to betray himself yet as a rule felt strong and sure only within the toils of a candor that documented and decomposed his fluctuations of uncertainty. Should he mention that up to now everything born of the personal project had necessarily been born into a status of exile he had no idea how to modify. As if prompted by this moment of silence Rosalie went to the three-drawered file cabinet near a side door and opening the middle one with an effort so harried he wanted to jump up and help, more than help, fold her in his arms against the excruciation of having to take orders from the likes of Rose B., but was she in fact obliged to take orders from Rose B., and if so did she mind; never mind, only in her fate could he weep at his own so what if by misrepresenting them both—drew forth a salmon-colored folder, dogeared and streaked with soot, which she placed discreetly a little left of center on Rose's tennis-ball-green desk blotter. Waddling about in her chair to suggest she was far too big for it though she was in fact a tiny woman with an enormous coiffure, Rose grasped the folder as if it were being spitefully withheld and said, ever so sweetly, "Well, maybe I was a bit hasty, Xman. I think we'll be able to place you with no difficulty, Xman."

It was now he began to tremble. Why was she suddenly taking to him, was she taking to him, yes she was, here and now, and if she was it must mean merely that she was suddenly finding him to be nothing less than a locus of market-abilities of which up to now he had had absolutely no inkling, he who had always berated that is secretly lauded their dearth. He shivered, felt he was coming down with something, a cold, more than a cold, the Bangkok flu good surely for a few decades incapacitation until all this zeal blew over. For he sensed she had suddenly sensed that if he, Xman, was here at all, if "at his age and after all he had gone through or relinquished" he was still presenting himself and halfway presentable then he was one—one fungible entity—to be gotten cheap, very cheap, very very cheap indeed. And she must be always in need of cheap labor.

Now that she had the folder she was turning its pages

rather perfunctorily all the time striving to make the per-
functoriness, fast turning out to be the very backbone of her
enterprise, pass for unfazed conscientiousness in the face of
some very fungible entity's flagrant inadequacy for even the
meanest in an appalling scarcity of specimen slots. Looking
up after having, Xman was sure, read nothing Rose B. said,
"I'm so afraid." "Afraid of what," Rosalie said, with irritation, but discreetly, as if its target was somewhere out there,
equidistant from all three. Rose chose not to take note of the
irritation: "I'm afraid he won't profit from any spot I may get
him. As soon as a situation becomes unbearable, that is to
say, the least bit challenging, he'll shift." "What do you
mean *shift*," Rosalie murmured, putting back the file. Rose
bristled but mightn't this interplay have all been arranged
beforehand. "There'll be an intricate play of the mechanism,
child. The situation will be bracketed, bracketed away, fixed,
as raw material for . . . the other project." And here, momentarily forgetting herself, or at this moment perhaps most
self-possessed in, by, impersonation, she jumped up and putting her arms around the younger, larger woman embraced
her passionately. "So before he learns to adapt the situation
to which he might have adapted is identified, whisked away
and reformulated beyond, far beyond, its capacity to teach or,
in his terms—the terms of an Xman—torment. Before he can
learn from his difficulties the personal project has snatched
them away to be pithed and gelded according to departmen-
tal specifications. His enterprise is a phantom: Doesn't he
know there is nothing more fascinating than the work I can
put his way. Now all I have left," sitting down, "is a bad
reputation." "I'm prepared to give myself to—the situation,"
Xman suddenly said, not that he pitied Rose B.'s plight—he
knew without knowing that her kind was never plighted—
but he did want to get as far as possible from where she
seemed on the verge of depositing them both. "Yes, yes, yes,"

Rose began, having very quickly abandoned her tone of lamentation, "but before you can respond already it has been domesticated as a datum, drained of all color local or otherwise to become the livid archetype of itself, an allegorical shard whose sole content is utter irrelevance to all needs but one and that one not a living need. My dear friend, a true-blue situation in the workplace is not like a symptom. It is not to be drained of all content." Xman began to weep. "The symptom, as I understand it, whatever that symptom may be, must be drained of its content in order to function—in order to skid into a network of relations. The true-blue situation—the kind you eschew—depends completely on its content for purposes of overwhelming edification. But I do not pretend to be an authority on symptoms, like some people. At any rate, the symptom is in here"—she jabbed her sternum with a surprisingly stubby thumb—"the situation is out there." "It's true—" he looked at Rosalie as if she had made some move to protect but in fact she was far from intervention. "I tolerate history—my personal history—with difficulty. I've always preferred categories to real live-wire events. Contaminated by the archetypicality of my objects I too am projected into a dream time."

After this Xman heard about Rose B. only from Rosalie, who tried to spare him the details of humiliations endured daily. Yet on those occasions when she did speak he found himself heartily resenting the intrusion of her torment into the limpid space of vacancy set aside, by unspoken mutual agreement, for the only woe that mattered, his, a grisly myriad though when it came time to disgorge he proved incapable. Rosalie was not alarmed, however, for in the *Lady's Home Buttfucker*, published biweekly, (*Your Man* subsection), regarding her or anybody's man for that matter, she had read that ". . . Embodying the effects of his futile trek through the discontinuum he inevitably suppresses their causes, and by withholding specific details thereby converts his own humiliation into the bomblike instrument of another's. But don't worry: Just show love and affection. Try a new sexual position, airier lingerie. Withheld humiliation becomes a sagittal figure pointing you . . . wards. He watches you suffer and he cannot stop making you suffer. But don't despair: Try pot roast served meringue-style the way our grandmothers did. For he knows he can stop, recant, at any moment. It is only when he is a little distance away that he smells the irreversibility of what he has said or rather what he has refused to say. In your presence he is very much the child refusing to utter because uttering reminds him mother was not there to witness and ratify. So serve him animal crackers in bed—reinvent your connubial bliss—lick the bacon and eggs off his toenails (as long of course as he agrees to give you the same licking). He's just a big bear: He wants to feel superior to your knowledge of the event that has wounded him. And it's simple—you weren't there. And yet your ignorance, your benevolent eagerness to know, enrages him because it leaves him alone with the event that is ostensible basis of his superiority. He and his tormentors share a common heritage—the event and its aftertaste. He is one with his tormentors inside the event in opposition to you outside. But when he remembers with whom he is inside, namely his tormentors, he can only rage against your abstention. He wants you to make little of—to annul—the humiliation without his having to name it. Or if he has to name then he wants it to be done quickly, at breakneck speed, faster than he can be reminded of the inexhaustibility of what he is naming. He wants to dazzle you with his familiarity with the event and your quiet and respectful dazzlement only reminds him you cannot save him from its virulence. Never despair: Rent a pornographic film and watch it together. Study camera angles as in their emergence they cast a shadow on previous camera angles, note how their very being retrospectively modifies the meaning of their predecessors. Until he has named his humiliation he isn't quite sure he has been humiliated, in and out of employment agencies for example. But naming the humiliation he knows he has been humiliated and that humiliation, named, will reverberate into eternity. Only he mistakes the bitter taste of utterance on his tongue for a certain skeptical demeaning look in your eye. You are not to blame. You love him. Then cook for him, sew, show him just how independent you are. Only don't, for Christ's sake, smile and say he is heroic. This simply means he is infirm and therefore that every effort no matter how ordinary is, under the circumstances, heroic. This simply means his heroism as you conceive it does not translate, no not in the least, out of the domain of infirmity. Don't take him seriously. It may make him uncomfortable to be taken seriously. He may be much more comfortable, your man, striving to be taken seriously."

Rosalie put down the article. In her studio apartment high above the Hudson River they made it a point even before the dishes were washed (which disturbed him tremendously) of going up on the roof to regard the sunset. It was on the roof he was most given to withholding causes of raging melancholy. In the darkness just before they went down he tried to make amends for bad manners—for "bringing his work or rather lack of it home with him"—by analyzing himself as a type. She tried to make his type correspond to the *Buttfucker* type. Over and over she was harshly evicted from the collision of types. He read her a passage from the *Man's Outdoor Buttfucker* and hoped it would more than speak for him—would sound as if he had written it with more than his own blood, Type AOK, no X. "Be proud, he-man, last of the wild eastern cowpokes, for your type, oh man of men, is governed by what your type proudly refers to as a fear of the banality of finitude. Before your type, he-man mouth, opens that orifice to speak, before your type has barely formulated what it has to say, refusing to foresee the modifying influence not only of an interlocutor but of the saying itself, with or without interlocutor leaning provocatively against the lamppost, it has undergone the trajectory of the unformed and unsaid as a being taken nowhere—precisely nowhere. And as it is with your saying so it is with your tastes, predilections, fancies, yessirree he-man old chum old fart. No matter how exotic these tastes on the verge of sharing them you have always already unfurled the grammar of their finitude's subterranean betrayal of your most scandalous secret linked to ultimate limitations as somebody who likes X. Somebody who likes X. Tastes, he-man, betray you as a somebody. Sharing—admitting—your tastes delivers you up to a caption's pouncing." He paused. Just before the trapdoor closed on a given night's ration of water towers he felt obliged to read on a bit: "It's not as if you loathe the little lady. It's not even as if you loathe your love for the little lady. It's the caption you dread: SHARING PET PEEVES WITH FRIENDS. Or, AMBITIOUS YOUNG CITY DWELLERS GET TOGETHER AFTER A ROMP THROUGH THE PUBLIC TOILETS ON FORTY-SECOND AND NINTH—seriously, it's the captions you dread and dreading loathe to the point where you cannot move, act, be. And unfortunately, buddy, old buddy, this war with captions and captionable acts is never terminated, exploding you to total transformation as somebody in the world at last. For I know you only too well, good buddy, old buttfucking good buddy. Every torment, tormenting because captionable, and tormenting, I might add,—and even more tormenting, I might add—when subject to more than momentary caption-deprivation, every torment, good old buddy o' mine, is simply brashly ultimately superseded by some other's relegation to the same sootily fatuous and abject posture—of captionability. So brace yourself, old buddy, and love the little lady for all your prick and balls are worth for the little lady's the only thing you've got, that is outside of a horde of scowling ancestors not a little bit responsible for the forthrightness of your dark dank and dirty predicament."

One night, just before they came down, Rosalie said, "You remember the way Rose B. spoke to you. She often speaks that way but with you it was as if for once she was hitting the mark. Not that you are what she claimed but there was something in your eye, there still is, indicating you wished more than anything to be as she said and that you would do all you could to become so." And for a short while after he was able to laugh at the gruesomeness of going at his age from agency to agency in quest of what all his peers no longer had bypassed contemptuously decades before. For wasn't he, according to Rose B. or to his expurgated version of same, through sheer force of will set apart for a loftier fate IN THE DREAM TIME. This vagrancy was merely an interim stint: gratuitous impersonation of failure, misery, self-loathing, utter lack of distinction. The disjunction . . . disjunction . . . disjunction against the fur between what he was and what he was obliged to be was occasion for the starkest merrymaking. "Thank Rose B. for me," he told Rosalie. "Don't worry, I see beyond this miserable shuttle to the program she has sketched for me no doubt in spite of herself." He did not elaborate except to point out that though searingly distinct at the boundaries as of this moment his personal project—the personal project—was somewhat appallingly hazy with respect to internal configuration. More frankly Xman did not know what to do with all the energy triggered by astonishment over the disjunction between what he was to become and what he was obliged to be here and now if he wished to sire that becoming. Suddenly without knowing it New York was opening its doors. He found himself moved by the sublime and the beautiful as it manifested itself—as they manifested themselves allowing for those cases where they were not on speaking terms—in the various art forms. More than moved: Suddenly he couldn't get enough. On Rosalie's meager earnings they took subways and buses to ballet, theater, movies, concerts. Walking to work—employment agency after employment agency—he could barely stave off disembodiment before scenes of the sublime and beautiful to come and gone. Of course there were always jarring moments when mamma York asserting the right of her slime made the juxtaposed sublime and beautiful appear ridiculous, as if it had missed a beat and that the most vital. Yet when there was no slime to contest the hegemony of the sublime and the beautiful he grew even more tormented. Though he found himself requiring Rosalie by his side every time he decided they must at all costs treat themselves to ever more massive dosages of the compound, he could not bring himself to forswear the fiction that shepherding her into the darkness of the movie theater or the semitranslucence adjacent to the ballet stage was nothing more than a mentorly duty peripheral to profounder and more delicious excruciations best savored singly. Rosalie still had no sense of what bearing all this could possibly have on a personal project, a true work. He felt no need to explain to her, much less explore for himself and wanted only to strangle her when she failed to press his hand in response, for example, to a particular shot sequence or intricacy of corps movement. Rosalie read, this time in the autumn foliage issue of *Woman Beware Daily*, that her "man will always try to make you feel as if you have just committed an unpardonable faux pas with respect to the sublime and the beautiful when in point of fact he is afraid to be confronted on his own with that sublime and that beautiful and will therefore go on—as long at least as you let him, you pretty little thing—perpetuating the fiction of your unseemliness. But let him, let him. He needs you to reflect back to him as from a stump of gleaming pewter this puny desolate version of the life-lie. In other words, your presence is a necessary impediment to annihilation at the hands of Messieurs Sublime and Beautiful. Your presence as putative pupil circumscribes rapture and the only bearable—conceivable—rapture is a circumscribed rapture."

One night, as they were walking home from one of these disconcerted assaults on the sublime and the beautiful, ostensibly in order to avoid ending up with his one pair of decent trousers stinking of derelict piss, Xman tried in vain to sidestep a derelict crouched in shadow. Catching his eye at the very height of his ridiculousness skirting an imaginary zone of intersection the derelict mused, "Don't you know, Xman—you are Xman, aren't you?—I'm one of a horde—a horde of hierodules—working—a swarm of artisans—working—day and night to stitch together in the form of a fabric hitherto manifest only in the latent creases induced by—his"—here he turned to Rosalie—"refusal to collaborate in its production—nothing less than your destiny's rightful due. Lady, we're stitching together a fabric from the tatters—our only blueprint—of his abstention from all forthright participation in what should, if he were half a man, most concern him. Proceeding by spurts and therefore completely at odds with our bliss-inducing notion of natural growth he has consistently abjured any sustained effort on his own behalf. Leaving it all in our hands he then goes on to sidestep us as too too foul-smelling for even the barest sign of recognition." Just as they moving off to melismatic moans of "Hierodules!" "The hairy horde!" "Fabric destiny!" the man cried but in a register far more peremptory and matter-of-fact, "By the way, those creases I spoke of, creases of abstention, can be noticed sometimes in the late afternoon sky. When by old zephyr head brother cumulus is hammered out to a very fine consistency—beyond cirrus and evil, as it were."

As they walked on Xman shivering said: "I'm coming down with something." Before they even reached Columbus Circle he collapsed on the pavement. Looking around imploringly for help she tried to lift his less than perfectly shaped head from the cold filthy surface as the few pedestrians in sight passed blithely by. Only the contraction of their buttocks suggested hurry to get away from what, knowing old mamma York, might very well get out of hand. Remembering the man in the hotel room, further remembering his voice and realizing the derelict's was very similar he was able not only to rise without assistance but to note: "One day still a child I noticed not far from the orphanage an insect moving in a circle on the pavement. In those days asphalt was an amalgam of shit, piss, phlegm, rhythm and blues. At any rate, clearly there was nothing to be afraid of from an insect moving so absorbedly. Yet I was afraid. For it was not implausible that the insect might leap up from encircling absorption to direct attack on the first bystander who, mistaking circular movement for obsession, chose to believe himself completely disregarded. I knew the circular movement all the time summating to crisis point was the search—the hunger—for obsession. Crouched in the periodicity was a mounting intensity, a brute accumulation of force starkly unrelated to evolution or natural growth. Suddenly the insect dashed out of the circle and stung me, the bystander. Had I become the obsession, target of obsession, or somehow triggered ultimate rage at obsession's eternal absence. That's all he was, an insect. What he said has nothing to do with me. He can't caption me!" And grasping and squeezing her delicate forearms (he could feel the bones through the skimpy cloth coat) he shook her endlessly to prove his point, right under the statue of Christopher Columbus.

At the next day's employment agency—there was one for every day of the week and then some—he was, after successfully, nay triumphantly, passing the typing test ("Xman, where ever did you learn to type so beautifully?"), subjected to a slide show deep within its labyrinth of windowless cubicles surrounded by well-lit offices for company folk. The first slide said: "Naked you are, friend, when you refuse to collaborate in your own destiny." The second: "You are at war with life when you refuse the first move, the first step. Here at Schlumpbuddy Slumptime, founded by no less than his Right Honorship the Right Honorable Schmendrick McKendrick—" His sole companion, a ghetto black, turned to him above the patter and said, "It's up to life to make a fool of itself first. Whatever effort I make is only all too quickly entangled in my actor's helplessness. Keeping myself as free as possible of vulgar upthrust, serf's momentum, waiting sedately intrigued beyond my own despair I give no sign so as to be able to detect the sign—the definitive sign—from life itself. But of course as we both known the sign withheld is the ultimate sign. My loyola friend Barthes made that clear to me once. Look, I've seen this show before. The only life worth having—take it from me, you won't get it on the silver screen—is the life that makes itself known in the face of anybody's refusal to collaborate in the confection of that life, or to subsist on anything more than marginal forays into the heartland of survival. This is the only game I am willing to play with life even if my own must be sacrificed to that game." Turning back to the tiny screen Xman realized they—or rather he, since the other had by his own admission seen this star vehicle (the undisputed star being the very Reverend Schmendrick McKendrick) many times before—had missed several slides. Number six proclaimed: "Avoid like the plague what we call praxis of passivity. In short, get

moving." At that moment the receptionist entered to announce: "Can you be ready for work tomorrow at nine? It's
only for a day or two but it could, Mr. Xaman, very well
blossom into something permanent."

As he walked toward his temporary cubicle that was in
fact less, far less, than a cubicle, with no windows or doors
or cabinets, just a chair and a heap of metal oblongs standing
in for a desk, he wavered between complete despair over the
derelict's verdict—diagnosis—and startled joy that after all
he was still free to . . . be on the margin of being where his
core was intact, unnamed, unsuspected even by himself.
Once again his passivity was back where it belonged, somewhere north of tact and south of dare. Just before reaching
the non-cubicle he was informed by one of the receptionists,
who clearly belonged to that confraternity of miserables ever
eager to side in a pinch with their oppressors against any
upstart daring to pose a threat to the cubicle nature of
things, that Fish wished to see him. "Double-quick?" Xman
inquired, although she did not wince fleshily at his quick
wit. Marching toward Fish's office he tried to hold himself
with the dignity both appropriate and crucial to prisoners en
route to the scaffold. Leaning on water cooler adjacent to
john an employee in upper-echelon shirt sleeves was edifying
a secretary whose upper-echelon eyelashes were clearly entranced by the muscular rump of a delivery boy deliriously
puffing on a butt above his salver of styrofoam cups: "The
gods," he intoned, "the *dei otiosi* have withdrawn into the
nether sky and left me but their flunkey." Shirt-sleeves
turned significantly to rump and eyed him with contempt,
turned back to eyelashes. "The supreme gods never had any
need to justify themselves and consequently never enjoined
the construction of fanes and statues in their honor. The
sight of a priest made them sick. But their flunkey—my
demiurge—is of a different breed. He is forever justifying his

existence, proving he has enough work to do so that he is not recalled to that netherland strangling on the hoary roots of cumuli. So what does my demiurge do. What do you think, Doris." "I'm not Doris," she replied. "At any rate, Hannah, my flunkey-demiurge justifies his lifetime annuity to the higher-ups by torturing me with scraps of ostensible good fortune. I'm forever on the verge of getting out of here forever. According to my tormentor, that is. The flunkey/demiurge that is. My tormentor and I have a strange relation." Xman thought he was waxing almost wistful over this recurring blight. "Just when I am about to abandon everything, hand in my resignation to that stinking insidious Fish, and when the torment of being in turn abandoned itself fades so great is my disgust with life, my loathing of its rules, regulations, routine, I hear him—following in my footsteps, panting to run up to me. "Here Shitman, here look—for Shitman is my name. Look, the Society for Derelicts Anonymous. They want you. You and nobody else. It's your big chance: international civil servant, benefit package to make any flunkey turd's mouth water, security from cradle to grave. So, dear boy, everything is taking a turn for the better: Why look up: the very rack is caught in the tinselled treetops and the horizon is turning an unforgettable eternal shade of hymeneal pink.' Don't you see he—the demiurge—the flunkey depending from the tit of this or that *deus otiosus* retired into eternity out of disgust for the whole human race—he—he—is afraid I will do something drastic and thereby deprive him of what hitherto has been an ideal site. Seeing me sulk and grit my teeth he hurries up to his equivalent of Mount Olympus to demand of his version of the reigning father of godlets some viable stratagem to keep me going at any price even if that price must be the price of a little good fortune. And so a windfall is arranged, like the letter at the end of Ashton's *Enigma Variations* when all the characters are conveniently on stage. But I refuse to go on serving as occupational therapy for this varlet. Oh I see, I see. You, Harriet, are like all the rest: You expect me to take pity on his fear of the power of my hopelessness when finally undiverted and unsapped by measly makeshifts, courtesy of the sleepers on high. I see, I see, I'm supposed to succumb piously to his humble need for this reusable site of infinite misfortune—this reusable site that is I. But I refuse. Can't you see, I refuse!" A shriek then the sound of spring water being poured into a paper cup.

Seeing Xman's retreating back the rump announced, "I told myself if they could hold themselves with dignity when no longer able to shield themselves against the empty stares of their traitorous co-workers—and don't let anybody kid you, babe, that's the true horror, the emptiness of the stares, their failure to formulate any recognizable human emotion and the brash bovine flaunting of that failure—if they could suffer all those who came out of idle curiosity—and there is an excruciatingly thin line between the idle and the morbid—then so could I. And so here I am with the styrofoam cups always ready to be called into the Fish's inner sanctum without flinching." The delivery boy cleared his throat with pride. He must be tossing his butt in my direction, Xman thought. Approaching the inner sanctum of the Fish, going past the desks—real desks—of the clerks, secretaries, administrative assistants, assistant administrators, assistant administrative assistants, all of whom must know who he was and where he was going—he tried to parasitize the hypothetical valor of those who, condemned to death, were necessarily far more naked than he not because the world knew the details of their crime, its every nook and cranny, that reason was uninteresting precisely because interesting on a tabloid—a captionable—level but because they were absolutely visible, they reflected back to the gaping toothless multitude—the delivery boy's "brash bovine flaunting" mass of "the idle and the morbid"—a humanity without subterfuge—or rather, a mortality without subterfuge because no longer subject to modification or delay.

In a tempest of panic Xman thought of altering his route to this Fish. He agreed with himself: The condemned man is most naked in his inability to vary his route to the scaffold. Since the sign above the water cooler declared: "Following the assigned route, workers,—but assigned by whom—is equivalent to allowing the mulish multitude of employers to peer up your anus from a dulled disavowed curiosity sensorially unlocalizable and incapable, amid the dark hole's—your dark hole's—smelly intricacies—of which, worker, you have every reason in the world to be proud—incapable of the construction, I too am so constructed," Xman tried even harder to vary his route but without success. He heard drumbeats. Looking across the hall to a little anteroom he saw what looked like a flunkey saying, "Goodbye." A shrivelled old woman squinting and wrinkling up her nose came out of the toilet and, to distract attention from where she had been and what she had been doing, announced to the receptionist just outside the Fish's office, "I'm going down now," in a grating cowlike voice, a voice that had clearly passed the menopause and was acceding just as blithely to a postclimacteric of folk piety. Once within but well before he could advance on the one vacant seat within (Fish was nowhere in sight which was just as well since he had a magnificent view of the Hudson's bile salts) the receptionist cried out, "Hey, where are you going," in a particularly malicious tone that indicated she was only pretending not to know who he was and taking a particularly insidious pleasure in treating him like a common thief (which in fact he was having already during his brief tenure stolen reams of paper, paper clips, pens, and for no reason since he had no clearly defined project to develop on his own time, as the saying goes. Turning around fiercely his glare silenced her, or so he told himself: She went back to filing her nails ("file clerk," he murmured as if it were an imprecation), extremely long and red, the kind that tend to leave tracks of vehemence on a lover's back and backside. Yet she looked too bovinely self-absorbed for such merciless abandon. When he turned around Fish was at his desk, playing with his pens under his very own portrait in oils, patches of shadow in just the right places. Staring, and not just at the broad desk and its accoutrements, he felt rage toward the project-to-be, the accretion, the vocation, the true work for it was immediately clear he might have been a Schopenhauer, a Dostoyevsky, a Voinitsky, more— a Fish, if only he hadn't been stymied by its phantom importunity. Fish, with his stubby fingers, manicured nails, bifocals, shoulder-looped turquoise sport shirt, was what he might have been if he hadn't had the gross misfortune to be himself. And what was he, he wondered—quickly—quickly—he sought to discover the answer before the Fish who, he saw, was looking over what looked like his resume.

Without looking up Fish remarked, "This pink slip affixed to your status sheet indicates that you consider yourself weighted down with some odd form of prowess." He knew it was a form of prowess, he knew it—but then again, it might not qualify ultimately as prowess. Eating away slowly, inexorably, with termitelike rapacity at the conventional—the indisputable—prowess he might have boasted or rather at a not-so-distant and yet all-too-distant capacity for conventional prowess—(Wasn't he rubbing noses with the possibility of such prowess at this very moment?)—it—it—it—this odd form of prowess rendered him, when all was unsaid and undone, indistinguishable from a chambermaid in her decline and therefore incapable of confronting the likes of Fish on his own sacred ground or rather within his own sacred

waters. "What is this prowess and how will it finally manifest itself," Fish muttered, at the same time making a slashing notation on the pink. How and when. Xman felt chilled,
feverish, on the verge of collapse—no, no, he musn't, not
here, not now, Fish was not Rosalie. Thoroughly sympa-
thetic to the vicissitudes of this latent prowess Fish opened
wide his chaps to say with a conspiratorially ironic drawl,
"How are you finding the workload?" Before Xman could
explain that as of this moment he hadn't yet begun his smiling nostrils added, We both know you were destined for bigger and better things. Smiling, Fish looked as if already he
had the answer, as if the question all too magnanimously
embodied the affirmation of Xman's latent sinews—as if
they were both allied against all absurd drudging demands
that he deviate from ceaseless cultivation of the powerful
secret life of those sinews. How absurd that he, Xman,
should be forced, said the smile, or rather the creases of the
smile, or rather the spaces between the creases. Then the
smile no longer accompanied the question, it lay in wait
behind. Fish's tone changed all of a sudden. Looking at this
watch he said, "There are two subjects we must discuss. For I
have been observing you carefully, so very carefully. I desperately wanted you, from the moment you set foot within
these hallowed halls, to continue on a permanent basis but
unfortunately what with the wage crisis that is no longer
possible. Surely you've heard about the wage crisis: In a nutshell availability of derelicts for paraprofessional chores like
those you have been so assiduously engaged in here is drasti-
cally lowering the wage ceiling. I'm well provided for what
with the cottage out in the Hamptons and my property just
off Lake Geneva and the Tanganyika settlement—at any rate
it's your kind I'm worried about. Given certain aspects of
your personality—or should I say personalities—it may become difficult finding comparable employment. And it

pains me more than it will pain you—of that I am sure—to speak of them, those painful traits, I mean. One overriding delusion seems to inform your every movement. At the same time I have absolutely no fears where you are concerned: You've sidestepped every trap we've set for you. No, you'll go far, very far." Although Fish clearly expected him to squirm, strangely Xman found himself sitting absolutely still throughout the pause. "I was referring a moment ago to the delusion of the sheer gratuitousness of your acts—your corporate comings and goings, as it were. Whenever we assign you a task—whenever we give you an order—set you down in other words beside a window on death—we feel you are about to leap up and run away, as if all this did not really matter in the least, as if it were a kind of absurd punishing whim on our part—and on yours. I don't know what your finances are, young man, but it is as if you are working for no reason at all and, reawakened incessantly to the absurdity of such a course, on the verge of smashing everything in sight." To Xman's imminent demurral the Fish very abruptly—more abruptly than he had ever heard him speak, Xman heard himself think, as if catching the other's fever of fabrication of their long partnership at the job site—said: "Point number two. Yes, Brunhildine." One of the receptionists had taken the liberty—or rather her exaggeratedly high-heeled shoes had taken the liberty—of tiptoeing with a message clipped to her claws into the Fish's adytum beneath the sea. "The applicant is here." She seemed unsure whether this should have been said in Xman's hearing. "All right, all right, Brunhildine." Fish smiled to Brunhildine's receding backside. "As I was saying, Brunhildine. I mean Xman. Point number two. Perhaps more vital than number one is this outmoded hunger to be unique. You wish to flee every task or smash it to bits as if it were a piece of imitation crystal. You don't want to become one with a job well done. You want to be recognized for standing outside your task, for having created through sabotage, through—terrorism—an entity far superior to any completed task. I must warn you that given the present state of the market—with the wage ceiling falling ever falling—it won't be difficult to find thousands eager to be stereotyped in the very manner you loathe. Why such specimens dread nothing more than the conspicuity of uniqueness, however—rudimentary. They want to be one with, lose themselves in, the task at hand. Why they positively rhapsodize at the barest mention of stereotyping. Now, now, now, Xman," he suddenly added, changing his tone to one he obviously believed more considerate of the other's—the underling's—feelings, one that emphasized how it was making a point to treat him, Xman, underling, as if he was a human being. "With regard to their stereotypical drive toward success—different, far different, from your 'hunger for uniqueness'—have you ever taken a walk up, say, Third Avenue in the early spring. You should, you really should. Papa Fish heartily recommends it for ailments of all kinds. Look at the people around you, striving with all their heart and soul to be . . . what they are condemned to be, in terms, for a start, of race, religion, ethnic ethos, etc. . . . To the likes of you it will I'm sure seem nothing more than an unbelievably tiresome noisomely predictable descent into hell but these folk—and some from very good families, some from very costly condominiums a little way away—the Luxe Eterna, the Versailles-Chambordeaux, the Coq au Vin Armes—these folk are not fatigued by their unending saga of self-affirmation at all costs. They are not suffocated by what you alone perceive to be a self-imposed straitjacket. They don't want to obliterate past and present. But you, Xman, you seem to be constantly wanting to start from scratch—to be recognized, enshrined, as starting from scratch, zero point, nowhere. And nobody starts from nowhere, dear boy."

Out of the blue lowering his voice and his eyelids all in the same spasm the Fish moved toward him across the impressively battered old desk and said, "What is the meaning of all this shit of drudgery, after all. You know and I know it's horseshit, the kind that lines the gutter along Central Park South. But if you have a personal project, Xman, and if I read you right I think you do—then the drudgery, such as we tend to offer here, can help distract you from waiting for the project to take form and having taken form bear fruits, garner plaudits, a place in the sun of eternity." Removing a scrap of tobacco from his tongue he whispered, "Excuse an old man's blubbering." His eyes began to water, he looked much older than his years, much fatter, he blew his nose, yet his embarrassment seemed an imposture designed to suggest something dire and crucial had been divulged on the spur of the moment. Xman turned away from his thought by turning his back on Fish.

"You know, Xman, you have been caught several times making phone calls that have nothing to do with your work here. I, personally, don't give a good Goddamn. But you know, Xman, no matter how much you may wish to sustain a pitch of anonymity, of mystery, of . . . unbracketedness, of not really being here with Brunhildine and all your other co-workers, there is a certain indubitable sense in which you *are* here. Like all the others you are being robbed of time, precious time. The same time, life as time, time as life, is being subtracted from you as from all the others, Brunhildine and company. And you will continue to be robbed no matter how many outside phone calls you end up making to prove that your gaze is forever outside the cubicle, outside the sum of cubicles. In short, your efforts to make the phone call a sagittal figure of repudiation always backfires and you find yourself more deeply enmeshed, more deeply . . . labeled. In shorter, Xman, no matter how many phone calls you make to the world outside to prove that you are not really of this world—to affirm yourself yourself to these walls and to the world within these walls as incontestably beyond these walls—" "Windowless," Xman felt compelled to mention. The Fish nodded at this testimony to the power of observation, a small point in his favor. "No matter how far you try to displace yourself, Xman, the fact remains that you are in, of, this world, and are being depredated as baldly as all the others. And remember, do not be fooled by the Brunhildines of this our world. Just because she has no outside calls to make does not mean she accepts the bracketing or is unaware of it. Perhaps she too felt the same unspeakable urges when she first arrived. But with time she may—I don't say she did but she may—have realized its futility and thereby transcended the outside-call phase and so perhaps is now more than ever *of the cubicles* but in a lofty relation of ironic resignation. So that when I call Brunhildine as I did a short while ago I am calling perhaps only to her surface.

"Imagine a young girl, a beautiful young girl such as Brunhildine must certainly have been, arriving in New York City several years before you. She takes a job in an office. She has come here from a suburb backwater in flight from the possibility—the heinous possibility—of becoming one of those superannuated virgins who, living out their days with bleating egotistical parents of the Smallweed variety, never quite overcome infatuation with a pink and jowled boss-infatuation founded foundering on a deliriously masochistic immersion in the work overload contrived by said boss with squealing salivating delight. She arrives in the city and is on the lookout for traps, pitfalls. She vows never to be categorized, filed away. Constantly baffled, thwarted, in her efforts to remain aloof from all straitjackets she persists in her refusal to be pigeonholed. She wants, as the saying goes, to be seen for herself.

"One evening—the sky a flawless crystal, the sun setting, moon rising over the gingkoes' yellow more luminous than any orb—walking past Columbus Circle as was her wont after work—she loved to walk and at any rate must save on subway fare if that lovely little item draped every lunchtime around an unnecessarily haughty-looking mannequin was to be hers at last—she could not help, with her step more and more electric, wondering how to avoid becoming indistinguishable from all these other pedestrian wage earners ending up in all directions subsumed and carried forward by the message, as they indubitably were, of the underclothed melancholy guitarist paper-bagged in protest of the Iranian regime who had managed to set up shop directly across from the winged statue. In spite of herself she found her footsteps were struggling to outface the rhythm of these haunting strains. And in this way she also found she could not escape becoming the subject matter of these strains, the undulation of the strings a skewed commentary on the futility of a workerly life. And she, Brunhildine, felt particularly bitter for she had been wrestling with this very problem over the last several days and nights, namely how to assert her uniqueness at five o'clock or at lunchtime when she emerged from the workplace FASTER than it could be subsumed and smothered by the ubiquitous caption from nowhere: 'The fact remains that she is a wage-slave,' one of the multitudinous. And she had resolved the problem somewhat to her satisfaction by making a detour both in time and in space, exiting always a little after the lunch hour had officially begun and through rarely frequented side doors stinking of piss, feces, fly-infested garbage, collapsed plastic boxes of salad bar leavings—slimy salad bar leavings are all the rage now, Xman, my dear.

"Yet for all her stratagems here she was once again challenged to the quick. She continued walking a little more

quickly to demonstrate her indifference to the guitar's melancholy strains, its irrelevance to the mismatched strains of
her own life. But even more quickly she noticed that those
who like her, walked most quickly away, were always the
most subsumed by the strains of the melancholy guitar, by
the commentary buried in its strains, interrogation of this
their lives, such lives, such routinized lives, scandalously
contemporaneous with the slaughter of innocents—men,
women, children, sheep—elsewhere. The fast movers were
the most—at least in her eyes and she felt sure in the eye of
all of being—subsumed by these strains taking their time,
noting, bracketing without apparent condemnation (the lack of
overt condemnation made condemnation far more peremptory, far more virulent) all this futility of hustle and bustle to
which she, little Brunhildine Jones, contributed no more and
no less than her share. Against the strains of the sad guitar
the machinelike status of her co-workers was enhanced beyond recall. But how could she, Brunhildine, escape the tableau, escape the straitjacketing. The soundtrack became
equivalent suddenly to a long shot, the strains were looking
back on the target of their commentary from a great distance. For a moment she became that universal spectator
looking back at a race of scurrying ants from the vast height,
the infinite distance, not of condemnation, not of judgement, but of something far more virulent. And at the same
time she underwent all the opprobrium of, antlike, being
looked back at. How could she, Brunhildine von Cool, née
Van Der Kool, twenty-eight, single and employed, hope to
escape framing as target of something vaster than judgement. It was then—then—then—she remembered the statue
itself, hardly, it is true, to be compared with Símon Bolívar
astride his steed of freedom further down on Sixth or even
with Governor Seward, patrician and cross-legged, cross-
town off Twenty-third, to say nothing of Cuyahoga's Pinoc-

chio Jenkins toying in broad daylight with his nickle-plated
tickler close to a secluded arbor in fashionable and pretentious Soho where the upwardly mobile accountants and lawyers look like panhandling artists. It was then she—a mere
twit of a thing—a girl—hit upon the idea of looking very
fixedly, very intently, ELSEWHERE, outside the frame, and
in this way, with her eyes glued as she walked to the statue
and nothing but the statue—*Chris über alles*—for the very
first time she felt outside the tableau, at odds with it, totally
indifferent to it, nuances and all, and thereby successful in
eluding the gaze of the universal spectator the music had
become. She was no longer, intent on Chris, delivered up to
the message of the music as the message of her futile being's
scandalous preoccupation with its own doings and undoings
when elsewhere—elsewhere—elsewhere—she was no longer
delivered up to the music as message of her being indistinguishable from all these other beings trying desperately to
obliterate the encroachment of that message. Looking at
something outside the frame—looking at something ELSE-
WHERE even if it was not the ELSEWHERE IMPLIED BY
THE MUSIC'S VERDICT TREMULOUSLY WITHHELD—
looking at something outside the frame, not quite clear to
the frame, she was proving stronger than all the forces that
had striven to keep her in the frame, of the frame. She proved
stronger than the soundtrack. The soundtrack no longer
spoke for, to, of, her, no longer spoke her unspeakable. It had
nothing to do with her. For whatever else it did this music
did not subsume a pointed and obsessional absorption (an
absorption such as she was now trying to peddle) in some
mysterious spectacle outside what it framed of 'mechanized
modern life indifferent to suffering.' The soundtrack had no
comment to make, no caption to devolve, on her gaze. She
felt the certainty throbbing through her. By fixing her attention on the impresario of Pinta, Nina and Santa Maria she

was proving—she proved—she was proving that she and her footwork were no longer absorbed in their own petty problems all the time that the Iranian regime was continuing to perpetrate atrocities. For here she was absorbed in some mysterious something outside herself and those minutiae. She was obsessed with Christopher—or perhaps with the wind whistling through his right armpit—no, with Christopher—who had come to these filthy shores well nigh over . . . She was obsessed with the illumination at the spectacle's base. She was obsessed with the absence of living wings on the several tiers of the pedestal. She felt she had escaped fixation at last now she had proved—now she was proving—that in certain cases the potency of offscreen space may very well vanquish a soundtrack consecrated to smothering and transforming everything into one more fulguration of a street-corner ideology.

"In fact Brunhildine felt so emboldened she entered the park itself, something she rarely did, especially at nightfall, when so many transactions of an ambiguous nature never stop unfolding in its dankish depths. Triumph or a misguided sense of triumph disorienting her she was quickly stabbed several times, incapacitated for several months, almost left to die in the world, no health insurance, blood oozing into gingko trash, I found her, put her on the payroll, moans beneath a lone star sky, made sure she was entitled to all I knew was coming to her before letting her type a single memorandum. Now she is eternally in my debt. There are things far worse than to be bracketed, Xman."

That night on the roof he recounted what had passed. Unlike herself she was a little brutal naming what he refused to name. "You were dismissed." Then she smiled kindly, through her tears he began to have a new vision of himself, he did not like the vision derived from this half-successful attempt to smile through her tears, it drove him to the exasperation of shouting so that even the slumbering belly of the Hudson might hear—"It's all only temporary, Rosalie, my dear. For a lifetime, maybe, that's all." And oddly enough the Hudson did wrinkle its ursine belly shooting forth a ray of salmon-colored sun so lurid Xman was obliged to shield his eyes. "It's all a way station," he murmured, more to himself than to Rosalie's tears. What he really wanted to say was, Your cancelled check is your receipt, as a second choice, One size fits all. He looked around; nothing justified such uttering.

In the quiet dark of their apartment Rosalie asked what he would do now. When he did not reply, preferring to go on washing the dishes, she ventured, "Rose Baldachino spoke to me today about your project. No—not another Fish out of muddy water. She has the name of a project analyst. It seems you can go to him, talk about your plans, however vague, and he will tell you what he thinks, try to put you in contact with the relevant figures in the field." He wanted to lash out savagely at *relevant figures in the field*, but managed to contain himself and in the morning dutifully took down the telephone number scrawled across a scrap of paper left on the hall table, a wreck they had picked together up off the street.

This turned out to be a character very different from the Fish and from Rose B., or so Xman had to believe. This was someone who promised fulfillment in the plane of the personal, on a massive scale in other words, for Mitch Rollins had an almost frighteningly just intuition of what his, Xman's, true work must be. "Has to be to justify so much frustration, rage and impatience and such an unswerving sense that all this struggle (let's see you've worked for Fish and Company, you've been to the Finaglie twins, MacDuffers Frères) is merely 'for the time being.' "

First off, Rollins made some disparaging remarks about

money and those clients who insisted on discussing that matter first and foremost. He could only say how pleased he was Xman was not one of the ones who proposed to stymie all true progress by focusing on the inessential. This was nothing less than a delicious invitation to confederacy against all those saddled with accretions, excrescences, not true vocations sustained by an armature—the only conceivable armature—of frustration, rage and impotence, unswayed triumvirate.

Rollins did, Xman had to admit, have the unfortunate habit of once very excited finishing almost all of his pronouncements with an indecipherable mumble but at the moment this seemed, like everything else, part and parcel of a grandiose charm. And in any case Rollins's office windows gave on the city's very heart, a neighborhood at once in decay and on the rise, a sweltering swarm of vacant lots, brand-new hi-rise lofts, cheap China Chili cafes and exquisitely overpriced glass enclosures opening onto the derelict pavement. So much delightful detail to agglutinate while Rollins was in the john: Across the street (records, scores, busts of old masters) an employee carried gingerly a glass pot minus trailing plant up winding stairs at the very moment pretzel vendor was dragging his car uptown, the wares in question heapingly impaled at all four corners. In a word, in tracking down Rollins Xman felt he had at the same time tracked city to its soft palpitating core, replete with pigeons festooning the wrist of a streetlamp.

"I saw a pretzel vendor," said Xman, gleefully, when Rollins returned. "You've come to the right place," Rollins riposted with matching glee. Xman gathered that each day marked (with tall austere Rollins in the midst of all the bloom and boom) the coming to life of a new gourmet shop, yet another boutique fantasque, and ventured to say as much. "Did you bring any samples," asked Rollins ever the intense professional on the lookout for aptitude in the raw but when Xman replied in the negative Rollins waved away his previous question as if it was totally absurd, supererogatory, an insult even, smiled apologetically as if to say, How could I have so dared to tarnish a global commitment renowned for its conspicuous freedom from any demand for vulgar instances. Too too weakly did Xman sense Rollins was simply presuming too quickly on their alliance, worse, their unanimity and with regard to what precisely.

"You seem to have an eye for detail," Rollins suggested, lighting a cigarillo and as if sensing Xman's uneasiness. "You walk a lot—from employment agency to employment agency. Try to make use of your walks, and not just to mewl." On his way home—he was too excited to take the subway—he saw: A workman shirtless on a rooftop opening a can as he looked down. Moving onward a small distance and turning back he wondered if in fact the workman wasn't looking down from a rooftop, shirtless, as he opened a can; or rather, looking down from a rooftop as he opened a can, shirtless. For the very last time, at an intersection devoid of collisioning traffic he, Xman, looking back wondered whether in point of actual fact the workman wasn't looking down shirtless as he opened a can on a rooftop.

Coming out of the men's room of a new hotel planted between Fifty-sixth and Fifty-seventh, Sixth and Seventh Avenues, he saw: a delivery man arms resting on a dolly loaded with beer cartons watching an adolescent scrape dogshit off the red carpet running into the doorway of a restaurant. He tried not to look back because he knew that if he looked back—

Under the statue of Bolívar he wondered if what he heard himself seeing so differently moment to moment might not have something to do with this true work, this phantom personal project, less his own than Rose B.'s and the Fish's, flown off as it had on their wings of reprimand. He didn't know if he liked the idea of the true work's affiliation with the contingency of such observations. If he hadn't had a full bladder necessitating a visit to the john at telephone level in the Hotel Honeydew he might not have emerged at the very moment an adolescent scraping dogshit off a carton of beer— He was about to run back into the hotel for it was there in some unoccupied stall still smelling of the last occupant's businessman's lunch that the answer must be crouching. He did not want a personal project dependent so much on words and not so much on the words per se as on their anastomosing into configurations that evoked what turned out, as now, as a few minutes before, to be a reality impossible of appropriation from any coign however prostrate.

In his despairing fear of depletion, of ultimate charlatantry, he decided to wait for a bus on the corner of Fifty-eighth and Ninth, telling himself as he stamped to keep off the chill (there was no chill) that he was once and for all done with a quest for the true work. But then, the pavement of headlights advancing up the avenue insisted on contrasting so starkly with the orderliness of the double row of street lamps evidently await-ing instructions from a bloated new moon inserted biscuitlike into a little tissue of cloudfog that he, Xman . . . Only was the double row of street lamps in fact as orderly as all that or was he hungry simply for a contrast capable of converting the chaos before him into a bona fide phenomenon worthy of acquisition. He had only succeeded in smothering any possibility of "phe-nomenon" however remote by inventing its armature. Looking back and far down the avenue he did not know what he saw, was supposed to see, as true worker or civilian, what the biscuit overhead insisted he be seeing. For when at last he began to see, what he saw challenged everything the thought embedding "a sharp contrast" said he or anybody with even the most jaundiced eye necessarily must see.

All the way up Riverside Drive under the elms noting no possibility of phenomena, he murmured, underlining incontestable relief, No more phenomena. But then he heard the lady behind him say: "But the absence of events, Bertha-Jayne, is even more loathesome to Harry and me than events themselves for what is absence, Bertha-Suey, but a mere jumping-off point for a veritable pullulation"—she pronounced it "pooloolayshun"—"of contaminants." Presumably Bertha-Suey-Jayne turned to her pal and sniggered, "Do you really believe what you have just succeeded in thinking or have you simply been cajoled, Rhodonda-Luke, by the nervure of syntax."

At the corner of Ninety-sixth into whose translucent samara heaps pigeons skidded shamelessly he was about to note an artifact of sun reflected in the windshield of a parked car (he did not know one brand name from another, Porsche, for example, from Linzer Torte; Borscht, for example, from Woyl's Woist; nor did he care: he was simply not a red-blooded American boyboy). But before he could even begin to apply himself to noting, hopefully in preparation at last for some not-too-distant upsurge of the true work's incunabula, he was overcome to unconsciousness by a thought that he would have given anything to be able to pawn off on Rhodonda-Luke or even Mahilda-Sue, namely: Orb is superabundantly reflected in the depths of car windows but never directly visible above. He waited for the observation to justify itself metaphorically by telling him something about his own life. But he had only one half of the metaphor and who could be sure that its sole purpose was not insidious overthrow of all possibility of starting from scratch with details out there: sun, the setting sun, reflected dying in the slightly dusty windshield of a parked—

Finally the bus stopped not far from their rooftop's base. Descending Xman looked around and before he could fix on any likely building block he heard himself think: It is the moment when all apartments are still dark but storefronts glaring. He immediately asked himself if there was indeed such a moment or had his thought simply created it and if the latter how now contend with a world deficient in that moment. Advancing toward Broadway he heard a voice—where had he heard that voice before—say, Words can be found for any horror therefore any horror is possible, in and off the planet. Then after a voluminous belch redolent of coriander and curried lamb chops, Every thought must, to qualify, be wrested from a monolith, a vast embodied resistance otherwise it simply does not qualify. An immediately preceding thought can, of course, function as resisting monolith. Footsteps gradually drowned out the voice, the face to which these footsteps presumably belonged—it was not the derelict's!—examined itself in all the shop windows or rather examined the contents of all the shop windows until that unmistakable moment of solemn stiffening when the gazer catches his own reflection. Xman was struck, thoroughly undone, by the humorlessness of that moment. Or was he simply imposing "humorlessness" on an event completely innocent of same in order to smother it utterly *in utero*. Or was there after all an event to smother. Although these encounters seemed to have some connection with the possibility of a true work he did not know if he could want to sustain the pitch of their ominousness even in behalf of so exalted a non-event as his salvation procurable, presumably, through that work. Get a job, settle down, he heard somebody's voice say. Xman shook his head against the nonexistent chill. He knew he didn't know what to do with these events, these collisions with chaos that could then be deemed events. Put them in a story, he heard somebody say, and guffawed long and loud, longer and louder, all the way up to the eyrie.

Just as, full of the global commitment, he was preparing to describe Rollins and the view from his office the Single Room Occupancy Hotel across the street forever on the verge of demolition began to howl. Although he bypassed it as if it was Twenty-third on the Number 2 IRT Rosalie, he saw, was listening intently.

Sounding strangely familiar an old woman stood at her window and cried: "Oh you rich people across the lot. You're full of disease. You're contracting the disease at every moment. You talk about us, about me, but you're the ones covered with symptoms. We inhabit the age of the symptom—if we can be said to inhabit what evicts us propulsively and perpetually to boot like shit into a stinking void where rents get higher and higher. We live in the age of the symptom but we cannot even fuse with our symptoms and claim them proudly, whatever they may be, as our own. We stand away distractedly from the symptoms we have lured into twilit life or that have been foisted upon us by the rich folk convinced they have better things to expropriate. They take our goods, our very possibility of survival, and give us their symptoms. And so we, the poor, stand condemned, not so much for the brute content of our—your—symptoms, as for a failure to recognize them as our very own whatever their provenance.

"Yet why should we assume them as our own. They are yours. You are the ones in despair not we. Yes, you are in despair even if suddenly you feel beyond all predicament because beyond MY especial predicament. Swathed in furs, chains, pigeon feathers you are infinitely beyond the despair you think you have, for good, foisted off on us. On ME. It's my fault. I've made the mistake of confiding in you, you bastards, that is to say, I've spurred you to a euphoria contingent on contradistinction. But suddenly, as with despair, it is as if, euphoric now, you have always been euphoric. My troubles buoy you to differentness, goad you to flaunt—I see you flaunting behind your lumpish curtains—an instantaneously immemorial differentness from me and my symptoms that are of course you and your symptoms—and I include even, especially, pissing in the snow under the double-jointed catalpas. I've seen you, squatting on your hind legs. Don't think that my misery in contradistinction to which you—but never mind. Don't think my misery abolishes an ever-aching perception of such stratagems. I am aware. I know what's going on.

"For too long I've been ashamed of this ability to perceive what's going on. I always thought of perceiving as stooping to perceive, a concerted wallowing of the gaze in world's sty. I was ashamed of my ability to fix and focus on certain details thereby showing I was of the world, more of the world than I cared at any given moment to admit. But I see now I can perceive, miss no trick of the pavement, yet be completely elsewhere. Seeing everything I am still far less of the world than any of you, sure to be counting your dividends this very minute.

"But if I am in despair you too are in despair, dividends or no dividends, and both of us can't bear to hear what wonderful comfort is in store for us, me because my being is an embodied objection to all of existence. Through my torment I combat all of existence. I am that slip of the pen in the demiurge's scrawl that refuses to be corrected.

"But you refuse comfort on other grounds. You rich folk are despairing always over something, which is just the beginning of despair. Here, cigar-smoking Louie has fifty thousand more shares of AT & Tit than you do, and there, Schmucky has evicted more tenants from his rattrap in five minutes than you can ever hope to do in a year. Don't you realize the apparent target of the despair—the searing pain—is in fact a mitigation of something deeper—a despair so deep it cannot express itself. So all manifestation is ultimately mitigation and here you are complaining—that the faucet leaks and that the maid was late and that the mink hasn't yet come back from the deep freeze along with its wearer, hahaha and will therefore not be wearable in time for the teratology ball "as per your instructions"—I know the elegant terminology of mindless hausfraus. But be assured your despair is deeper than mine for you don't even know where to begin looking for its cause. You've thought of the deep freeze—even you, obtuse as you are—and of the stock page of the *New York Times*. But then again I wonder: In fact are you in despair. Perhaps you are the blessed of the earth, having completely bypassed the need for some kind of, pardon the phrase, spiritual nourishment.

"But who cares, who cares, for the spiritual nourishment of the rich. It is of the poor I come to speak, but not to praise them. The poor, the poor, who are they. The poor hunger it is true, and desperately, also true, but not, as is commonly believed, after bread. The poor hunger to finish—to be finished—with *the task at hand* and as soon as possible. The poor cannot stop not working to pay for the brown bread and alcohol but struggling to see present as final task after which there are no others and consequently last remaining obstruction on the void. For their lives are too cluttered with each new rag simply enhancing localizedness therefore vulnerability. What is the function of each new rag but to serve as victim-finding service for their tormentors, landlords, etc.

"The poor are those who, like me, have never been able to achieve a position in the world, a no-nonsense stance founded on pride in the pride the world takes in one's brand of hard labor. Which is not to say I have not labored with the best—and worst—of them, and oh so desperately, in my chosen field. And not merely to be unique, as some do who shall forever remain nameless. But all the labor all the striving,

never summated to a sense of being set apart through expertise within the jungle of perches whence all other fat cats
look out with that assurance slightly tinged by skepticism
marking the true, the authentic, professional—fat cats who
are well-paid and furthermore know they are well-paid but
are never delivered up to paroxysms of startled unworthiness
every time they are well-paid. All my toil has simply never
summated to this capacity to look out from my eyrie in
unjudging appraisal of all the rest, of all that incessantly
forces itself, barteringly, upon the unwary soul. After all
these years I am living in a tenement on the verge of eviction
and still capable of being undone by the slightest sign of
appreciation—as if it has come too easy. Too easy. Without
enough meriting struggle! Enough meriting struggle! And
not only am I recurrently undone by the slightest sign of
what retrospect quickly identifies as anything but guerdon
however belated—but also—and in my vitals mercilessly by
the feeblest sally whether launched by the most insignificant little hoodlum emissary of the landlord above-mentioned or some cute-assed half-breed little figure skater
wiggling her contempt at the outlandish purity of my raiment. In short I am forever being undone by the slightest
humiliation as well as by the slightest hint of success, which
of course never expands beyond the merest hint, merest
whiff as of some prohibitively expensive perfume.

"So, you rich bastards across the way this is what it means
to be poor. Poor at last, as when the weary jet setter remarks
to the pink Persian moquette adjacent to the crapper's Car-
rara marble: Home at last. This is what it means to be poor:
to have no context. But that's wrong: I have a context but it
must be recreated from scratch on every occasion without
any circumambient clues to guide the masonry. For the ambience I am always nothing, more inconspicuous than a Fili-
pino busboy worked to the bone in some fashionable East

Side ristorante. And recreating it from scratch I must wear that context as one wears the most unwieldy suit of mail—as Dickinson's anguish wears mirth—not because I am particularly fond for I am not particularly fond of it but simply in order to have something to oppose to the agglomeration of ideologies with which not only landlords' hoodlum-flunkeys but the world at large—what is world but a criminal at large—is trying to suffocate, to obliterate me. So I end up a tireless proselytizer for myself. Like everybody else.

"And all this because my life's work never took off. All this because my chosen project—vocation—never found its place in the sun. For once one's vocation finds its place then one's place falls into place specifically through proliferation of those specialized grievances that situate one incontestably in ebbing, I mean being, and as an entity of the most unimpugnable high seriousness. This is what the poor hunger for most—not bread, not circuses, but specialized grievances bred by specialized tasks that command their own price—grievances that unify the sensibility and reduce world events to a common denominator of greater or lesser helpfulness with respect to one's vocational goal.

"Don't play dumb with me—you've all listened to doctors, lawyers, accountants certified public or otherwise, massage parlor managers, chatting at lunchtime all the way down to the lobby of the Empire, the Flatiron, the Grace, the Chrysler, the Seagram, the—you get my adrift. You've seen them—heard them—luxuriating in their—in their grievances and almost believing (before they hit ground floor) in the authenticity, the intensity, of those grievances. Only before they can give themselves to the grief, the grieving, they are simply too much overcome by the delight in a specialized vocabulary—an artisanal argot—able to exclude all other occupants (we are in the elevator, remember) from comprehension—participation—in the rigorous riotous delights of a status (quo) apart. Focusing on grievance—how this patient insisted on subsidizing an anal canker that even the awesome tribulation of virginal lively and beautiful everyday was powerless to jeer into nullity, how that federal courtroom adversary had the audacity to fart at the height of a particularly piquant peroration in favor of death to all tyrants (and paupers, derelicts, chambermaids, night watchmen), how yet another poor taxpayer contracted the absurd fancy that his government-cheating machinations were literally invisible compared to those of corporate-bloc heads and of the government itself—they authenticate themselves, opposing themselves to the world they thereby situate them selves within that world but within a special purlieu reserved for . . . those to whom such a purlieu is reserved.

"But I, dear friends, rotten friends, stinking friends, friends filthy rich and just plain filthy, I, for one, never found a specialized vocabulary of grievance to set me apart. Specialized grievance is, after all, the banausic's prime tool. For my vocation comprised—comprises—I am Duchess of Malfi still!—an unending monologue indecipherable even to colleagues on high. But don't get me wrong. Even as a pauper on the verge of eviction with nothing to show for my painstaking I don't envy such fools: On those few occasions few and far between when I found myself fattening comparably on drivel peculiar to *my* line of work I was immediately terrorized, nauseated, by a presentiment of IMPERSONATION. This is of course a mammoth theme that can be developed only at greater length. Assume for convenience sake, my trade is . . . beef, every conceivable ramification of beef and beefiness. Every time I heard myself spontaneously berating A, B, or C for failing to furnish my custom with grade-A sirloin or even grade-B ground round I immediately saw myself—I simultaneously saw myself—captioned as: BEEFER DISCUSSING THE HAZARDS OF THE TRADE, or,

BEEFER RECOVERING FROM STRAINS OF THE MAR-
KET'S HEYDAY. And I wanted to puke the beefiness of this
caption, the unutterably stringy fiber of its fabulation. In a
sense then I have chosen to remain poor, poor, poor—this is
not a consolation, awareness of my responsibility excruciates sometimes beyond endurability—poor of grievance, caption, vantage, status, to say nothing of cash, cash, cash, cash.
If only I had continued to ply my trade or better yet—and
more to the point—the talk of my trade—I would not be
consigned and at such a late date to this SRO on the verge of
demolition. If only I had gotten used—and damned be captioning!—to a tone of grievance—if only through the tone of
grievance peculiar to a young tradesman I had procured my
very own inexpugnable and eternal leverage in being—in the
shit of being—my own site as it were—I would not—obviously, you say—be where I am now. But at the same time I
would have been obliged to forfeit the dubious delights of
excoriation, denunciation, revulsion, perhaps after all my
true—truest—vocation—excoriation of those artistes, yes I
give all you lowlives the benefit of the doubt—those artistes
for whom the road obviously has not been so long nor so
hard. I loathe compassion but I am obliged to point out that
in my case, the case of a poor sinner, exalted beyond exalta-
tion by degradation beyond degradation, the road was sometimes so long and so hard it completely disappeared over the
nape of yonder copse and at the same time roadless, roadless
and roadless I found myself very much at the very heart of
the busiest intersection of all thoroughfares but with none
of the expertise one quite as a matter of course ascribes to
those who profess to find themselves at such a juncture. At
any rate, good night sweet princes, I loathe you all."

Xman and Rosalie looked at each other in the dark feeling
sure the ranter must notice the look. Xman was about to
shut the window when surprisingly Rosalie said, "Leave it

open. Why are you closing the window." At first he had no answer, then the answer came, he did not want to give it, stated the opposite. "Her ranting and raving can't have any bearing on anything I try to do." "The true work, the personal project," said Rosalie. He shrugged again. He saw that she was authentically offended by his shrug. Couldn't she decipher beneath a mere mask, mask of a moment's monolithic deprecatory incredulity the hope that feared its own enormity. Couldn't she decipher the shoulder sneer. She could not, took it for no more than a shoulder sneer.

Unexpectedly she turned to him again and said, all the time Fa—it had to be Fa or (-)Fa—went on ranting to the four winds of hell, "You speak of earning your bread and make light of it. Now you make light of what might appertain to the true work—the personal project. I wonder if anything interests you." "The personal project?" he sneered. "Why mightn't what she is ranting be a . . . building block." He said: "What she says is idiotic." "That's because you're afraid it might undo you completely," Rosalie said, turning away as if in disgust but in fact out of diffident concern at having been too harsh. As there was no response she added, "Maybe you should wake up to the fact that in your kind of personal project what end up as basic building blocks may first be experienced as abominations, shapeless threats to that project, colossal invalidations of one's claims to workership. Maybe you should wake up to the fact that if your project is all it claims to be then it has no choice but to welcome interlopers—nothing is alien, it's open season. The question becomes only whether you are up to such a challenge." She was almost inaudible now with anguish on his behalf. He went to the window, leaned out to feel supremely visible to the rantress. On she went, in silhouette. Her tone became sweeter but there was something even more alarming in the sweetness. She said: "I am now speaking to those of you who are new to its streets, squares and circles, new to its injustices. Not that I hold you less accountable.

"I am just delighted that you have chosen New York for New York is a city of delicious and unsurpassed heterogeneity. I speak from the vantage of the rich for it is their well-being that interests me. Yes, yes, yes, I can hear you all protesting my inconsistency even if that inconsistency is working suddenly in your favor. Of course I am all for the poor, needs of the poor. In fact I am a member of a cell, a true-blue communist cell. What is this SRO but a vast communist cell. That is why the capitalist-pig landlords have enlisted the aid of their flunkey-hoodlums to smoke out its occupants and destroy it. But we cell members—committed till death do us part—we cell members have needs, after all. We're human. And to be human being the need above all to make distinctions, set oneself apart, the only way one cell member can set himself apart from all others is in the superior thoroughness of a reverence for the swells and shits with which specimens *your* cells evidently abound. Not that I don't loathe cell members who, unconsciously and self-contradictorily, prostrate themselves before such swells and shits: doctors, lawyers, real-estate brokers, related sharpies of all shapes and colors. But I am forced to recognize that the claustrophobia induced by cell life—by life itself some of you cynics will declare—ends up producing a cell member of a certain type, namely, the type under discussion. He/she cannot endure the shabbiest sign of initiative-laden brilliance issuing from the vocable-forming hindquarters of any of his congeners. And that is because antedating claustrophobia-induced irascibility—you cynics are right, up to a point—is a deep-rooted and impermeable sense of inferiority that associates initiative-laden brilliance only with the swell and shit class. And though a cell member of this type may profess to loathe swells and shits more than anybody on the lesion-mottled face of the earth in fact he/she loathes his fellow cellmates even more. For when you get right down to it what do these cellmates embody for a fellow cellmate of a certain type—not shared dreams for a future more felicitous and more just but the bad smell inseparable from being compelled to fight in one's deprivation and despair for that future while the fat cats and their plushly obese kittens ride by—but never mind. Signs of initiative-laden brilliance only threaten his/her deeprooted conception of cellmates as utterly devoid of said brilliance-laden initiative. At the same time crushed by a sense of inferiority this cellmate is inundated with an arrogance that demands prostration before himself though not before himself specifically—prostration rather before his own prostration—incontestable sign of superiority—before the swells and shits to whose obliteration he claims to be consecrated. And this is how a cellmate of this type wields power within the cell, basing his unspoken superiority on the ability—on more than the ability—on the craving—to lick the dirty butts of you shits and swells all the time you are made targets of official denunciation. For this cellmate type, equality is in, of, the future, the dim future, but in the meantime he/she needs to act out some little fantasy of strict hierarchization in which he, of course, is assigned the supreme position ALL OF COURSE IN THE NAME OF THE FUTURE GROWING DIMMER EVERY MINUTE. Ostensibly amused but in fact outraged incredulity at their inability to recognize, accept, reverence, the untraversable gulf separating mates from swells and shits ultimately browbeats these mates into a stance of devoutly-wished prostration organized, of course, around the still point of his own most superior because most arrant prostration. In other words, the more he licks the dirty ass of your ostensible superiority the more he is entitled to hegemonize over his congeners obliged to somehow follow suit. But, I repeat, we here at the Proletariana Arms are not cellmates of a certain type. Not as long as we watch our step.

"But getting back to you—the sooty, shitting, swelling shits and swells—I want to do all in my power, a mere charwoman I, a mere wardrobe mistress, to make your—their—stay here at the capital of the Universe, copious and resplendent. I want your—their—each and every sunrise to trumpet forth a diapason of unutterable only ostensibly incompatible delights. I am living proof life can be irrevocably lost when on the basis of a mistaken notion of incompatabilities far more is rejected than assimilated to its, in fact, mercilessly prehensile and eclectic tissue. I wish to athetize all notions framing New York as dull-wittedly maiming all its inhabitants to a same sameness. Look around you, denizens of this deep. Look at that tug coming up the Hudson and that barge going down. Look uptown, look down. Look at the cars on Riverside Drive. Look at all the demolition sites. (Don't worry, the threadbare inhabitants have all been relocated thanks to the unstintingly strenuous efforts of their dear-hearted oppressors-extraordinaires. Why, there goes one. He's come all the way from Cigarsdale just to be able to attend in person to all these ponderous instaurational doings.) Look at that porter in the hi-rise to your left and my right. He can go to the lobby's big bay window and look to the trash festooning the sidewalks any time he likes. Any time he likes! He is under no duress, any time he wants he can temporarily sever his connection to the task at hand. Now seeing the ladies and gentlemen festooned in their furry rags bypass him without a word either of greeting or adieu what comes to mind exactly. Hopefully not some banal overcooked reflection on the maleficences of the chrematistic temper in our or any time. Really, I expected more of you than that. So, if you are at all like me and I know you are, irreverent, effusive and as openhearted as the city itself with inexhaustible supply of booby prizes, then you are sorely tempted—no compelled—to think and do more than think: utter out loud: How wonderful, life. How variegated. Each man, woman, object, entity, child, in its specificity. Its luminous specificity. No job—that of tug, porter, shitkicker, urinal-licker—to be contemned, no station fleered, no pretension to dignity flayed—at least outright—for every entity, every task, blends unstigmatized—at least outright—into the vast benign (benign because vast) heterogeneity. One stench, in short, cancels another. All work according to their capacity and let no laborer (the deeper his boots descend into the shit the better) be labelled less than exalted. Now, mind you, each laborer is not exalted, worthy of respect in himself. Let's not go overboard. Let us not overvalue the merely banausic. But from the point of view of the heterogeneity necessary for nourishment of the idle rich—who are never idle, this is a defamation most unworthy of their impious underlings— each component is to be *labelled* as worthy. I hear some of you out there already grumbling that to accept each man in his station is tantamount to abandoning him eternally to that station. But if you grumblers will only step back a little distance you will see that what matters is the bright heterogeneity—the motley—a riot of color and only apparent disharmony for the delectation of New York's finest.

"So, boys and girls, tomorrow morning when descending from your spacious hatboxes aloft the gloam of New York's gauzy soot into the maelstrom of matrons fashionably attired for the day's feeding and hurrying off beneath the stunned gaze of derelict street sweepers invisibly entranced—descending say NOT as might have been your wont before we talked at such salubriously great length: Look at that hideous bitch with her toothless smile for whom the longanimity of her fellows is little more than an occasion for subaesthetic rapture, NOT: Look at that bitch thinking herself a beneficent detached observer of the scene failing to unfold when in fact she is observing nothing but her own smug high tolerance for squalor's matutinal harlequinade, NOT: Let's blow this fucking bitch out of her coign of mobile vantage (for you know bloody well the coign will be quickly usurped by some other bloodless darling in a Bergdorf-Gucci hat and in actual fact requires no occupant whatsoever being aggressively enough its own rheum-infested roving eye, present everywhere, visible nowhere, missing nothing, misinterpreting everything,—eye of the paradigmatically anonymous well-heeled spectator accepting without taunt and without compassion every form and grade in being's greatly overrated chain and whose cowlike ruminativeness phagocytizes event as nothing but outpouring of myriad pinpoints of color, less than local and more, far more, than global), NOT: To accept each man in his station as this bitch does is to eternally condemn and abandon him to the soulless rigors of that station (for such cavilling is, I repeat, tiresome), NOT: I want to catapult him outside the lattice of things as they are (for that is tiresome, darlings, too)—descending say NOT this that or the other but, How delightful this heterogeneity comprising and embracing ('Give dada, kiss') each man in his station if not quite in his humor. How beautiful, each man, woman and beast in its specificity so what if, here, the racked rotten specificity of anguished routine, disquiet, desperation, rage, envy so deep it no longer knows its target, there, somewhat less racked, that of frivolous irascible surfeit incarnated this very minute and for all time as the mammiferous matron in the Bergdorf-Gucci hat-o'-nine-tails . . ." Here the voice, for it was no more than a voice, became completely inaudible, as in the hotel room long before. Televisions seemed to go on in all the apartments around her, tuning her out and not in a friendly way. One home screen seemed bigger than the pane that framed it.

Officially in search of work, any kind of work, Xman went on walking the streets, Fa's monologue his unflagging soundtrack. Afraid only of soiling his only decent pair of pants, afraid in fact of far more, he discovered all the places where he could urinate in peace before embarking on one more foray. There were, for example, the hotel on Fifty-third and Seventh, and that between Sixth and Seventh smack in the middle of Fifty-sixth. One advantage, the only one, of being dressed for an interview was that he could enter these havens without awakening suspicion. Sometimes there was an attendant with a little plate full or not so full of coins. He felt obliged, upon emerging from a stall, of inducing a substantial tinkle. Moving from agency to agency he was tempted to call Rollins but abstained. For one thing, public booths stank of urine and he could not afford to so impregnate his clothing. "I'll end up your biographer," Rollins had said on that first occasion before disappearing down the hole of another mumble. Toward four after too many typing tests and filing tests and good-with-figures tests he decided to dial, just as he began leaving his name, a voice broke in, that of Rollins, good sign.

"Sorry to bother you," Xman said, trying to sound brusque therefore offhand. "It's just that there are moments on the streets of New York when—" "To all my clients. Much love. With regard to your projects, also much love. Learn wherever you are—and even if your clothes stink of urine dialling from the hallowed halls of the Donnell or the Epiphany or the Mid-Manhattan or the Bloomingdale—learn to use everyday shame as a building block FASTER than you allow it to incapacitate—talk you into incapacitation—for the project." Just as Xman was about to hang up definitively Rollins did break in—also definitively—with: "Hello Xman. I could try to con you—distract you from the case at hand. I could tell you that as your biographer I intended from the very beginning of our long friendship to prove—and deftly—how susceptible all this misery is to articulation right down to the urine stains around your cuffs and the dogshit clinging to your holely soles. You do stink of piss, don't you. All supplicants do. Though we both know time is hideously running out I could tell you what now feels like stigma will someday take its place as one more secondary sexual character in the inevitable bracketing of incontestable success, one more low point—perhaps we might even angle it, with respect to the tabloids I mean, as *the* low point that triggered the inevitable thrust forward and all within a framework where the lowliest fart is dramatic, scintillates allegorically, so that the little man on the street on his way home from work, after having read his Xman so to speak, may be able before the sagging hellos of wife and kids—but never mind. I could dazzle you, but why bother, with all that is to be. That is not my function. And I know you are much too smart to be unambivalently licking your chaps at such a prospect—I mean of your life and hard times reduced to a mere STORY. Required rush hour reading, as it were. For you know as well as I that stories tell one thing and one thing only: How X—not Xman—became reconciled to his mediocrity and how recovery of that mediocrity, long lost amid the baleful blossoms of a veritable Rappaccini's garden of protracted adolescence, became, amid the differently scented blossoms of sudden middle age, an occasion for rejoicing—if not on the part of the hero then at least among all other stooges essential to the drama. You know as well as I that in our time, a time of voracious blandness, the possibility of true originality—genius—has been mastered, overcome, filed away, as laughably obsolete. All lessons have, blessedly, been learned and the only genius worth revering is a genius for mediocrity, blending into the common shrubbery. Since, therefore, we both know what we both know I am not going to distract and bedazzle your plight with promises precisely because I intend to keep those promises and then some. Knowing those promises will come true can only get in the way of your plight's upsurge and resolution. For all intents and purposes, plight is your most precious possession, bud. Now go to it. Scrape that dogshit off your heel. Oh yes, and call when you have to." Then, out of the blue, "How is the job hunting going," Rollins said sunnily in a tone Xman needed to believe minimized that hunting's relevance to a true true worker's destiny.

"It's difficult sometimes," said Xman, suddenly reminded of the creature screaming from its window on death. Now he was one of the heterogeneity providing cackling nourishment for some dowager wavering between a mad dash through Boomingdoyle's and a more leisurely stroll through Lloyd and Tyler's. "It's just that sometimes it hits me, in the middle of the afternoon usually. I'm running out of time, as you so rightly point out. And I feel worthless and pointless, like one of millions." "As you speak, Xman, as you name your pain, I think you are beginning to be aware of how easy and how tempting for some biographer—some Rollins— some storyteller—to summarizingly recuperate all the pain as a story's mere moment, all this urine-scented shapelessness bound neatly together and made to tip toward . . . ineluctability." Rollins sounded as if he had inadvertently stumbled on this *mot juste* so what made Xman so adamant in thinking all this stumbling was an imposture, the most exquisite of impersonations. How easy for some Rollins to encapsulate and acquire what poor Xman, out on the hot pavement or rather in, momentarily, from the hot pavement, can never, at least from his present vantage, hope to acquire,—what, in actual fact, completely unfixes for acquisition—even—especially—of oneself. As Xman was trying to decide whether or not he wanted his plight to conform, storylike, to the contour of some lean and hungry biographer's greed, Rollins very nicely and kindly said, "I'm working on your project. It's of an intricacy, I think—but I also think there are many people you could and should meet. You should meet—" and here Rollins rattled off a list, presumably of New York's finest or at the very least semi-finest. "Remember what you are going through may seem to give off a terrible stench—like your cuffs and shoes—but from the other side of the abyss—I am there but you, of course, are not—but be patient, patient, patient, patient, patient, patient, patient, patient, patient—at the very worst as far as I can see—" Here the voice was ousted by that of the tape: "To all my clients. Much love. With—"

Feeling better inexplicably he walked through the streets repeating Rollins's title: Project Coordinator, the syllables were nothing short of hypnagogic, several times (on Fifth, Madison leaning against a shoe store window, Third) he was on the verge of swooning. That evening, after their visit to the roof, Rose Baldachino called. Rosalie showed complete, and as far as Xman could see, genuine surprise. "I though she was done with you," she said, passing him the phone. "Or you with her." "There is a man named Xaviero," Rose B. said. "He seems very interested. I wouldn't steer you wrong." He had only one vent for the spleen induced by her, by anybody's, high seriousness when it came to work other than true. But there was, appallingly, scandalously, more here than mere high seriousness, namely, self-interested coercion trailing its commission payable once the dunce in question was made to steer himself right. So what, then, if Rose B. was a noxious mixture of the forthright and the manipulative. Why shouldn't she be and why shouldn't he, Xman, be able to contend with the mix without shrinking to nothingness and beyond. Though he categorically discredited a ridicule impeaching the unimpeachability, the racial purity as it were, of just such things as her vocational high seriousness, it now became excruciatingly difficult to ascribe the term *high seriousness* to her coercion. To emerge at all cost from a complex situation Xman quickly invented the gratuitousness of the ridicule he was, in this special case, too terrified to flaunt, finding it easiest to treat coercion as yet another chimera of that ridicule's frivolous unjustifiability. Through excess of ridicule hadn't he always put himself—comfortably—in the position of a child needing rehabilitative reprimand yet here he was perceiving as more than a child and with a ridicule alarmingly cogent the childish insistence and insistent childishness not so latent in a conscientiousness with every moment more and more widely diverging from the straight and narrow of disinterested parental concern.

Rosalie woke him early as she did every morning for he had a tendency to oversleep dreading as he did, as he must, the new day. He loathed not only the rising but the getting dressed, the eating, the shitting, the washing of the buttocks after the shit, the getting dressed again, the closing of the door, the running back from the elevator to confirm the actual airtight closing, the running to the subway station against the stench of the streets and the people. He had a habit, once the toast was too thickly buttered then smeared shamelessly with apricot jam (not always lumpily redolent of high quality), of opening wide his mouth to slurp the too hot coffee. These little things disturbed her. Watching her lay out his one pair of good pants, newly pressed, starched shirt, tie, he said, "You turn away, Rosalie, my love. You didn't reckon with a guy who at breakfast plummets ass-first into a jar of imported preserves—imported, however, from one of the less fashionable pseudorepublics abutting on the smelly perineum of the tundra-laden monster to the east, land of Chichikov, Tatiana's letter scene, Modest's brutish promenade (before it was sweetened up by Maurice)—a guy who chews with his mug wide open on the brand-new day. But I do so, Rosalie, only because I am suffocating here— suffocation is a leitmotif running, so it would seem, through the desert of my life. I eat with my maw wide open to maintain always open a window on—death. I mean the world. I mean death. I mean the world. I mean death." Rosalie nodded in a way that chilly retrospect, synthesized slapdash on her way to the bus, construed as hopeless.

As Xaviero, the party in question, had his office near Twenty-third on the East Side Xman had a little time to sit in Eliad Square beforehand and watch the leaves fall from the white poplars. At the beginning of descent they fell with slow almost leisurely somersaults, only further down did these somersaults accelerate into figures of illegibility once the pretense of reascent at any moment could no longer be sustained. Xman thought of running back into the subway's stenchy dark, but with these leaves skidding toward the pavement's fiat he knew there was no turning back, against the fur, against the fur, toward some dream time of inexhaustible reversibility of acts great and small, small, even, as the fall of a pygmy poplar leaf. The leaves not in themselves but as he heard himself seeing them fall had everything to do with the true work, its possibility and incessantly painful birth as exclusive proof of continuing progress. But he was not ready for a true work, not here, not now, comprising such confrontations as he was having with—the leaves, the dead leaves refusing to rise. The condition of the leaves as he heard himself seeing that condition reflected the "bitter truth" of his own but who said he was ready for that truth brought in such things as the leaves to the brink of clarity. By moving forward involuntarily Xman saw that one of the evicted/seceded was whirling upright, completely upright in midair, carolling on tremblingly supportive petiole as if entreating reassignment to the heights of the trunk, all the time pretending the carolling was solely for the sake of carolling. There had to be a way out of the irreversibility circus, the plight of whose performers was so poignantly—elementally—depicted by a single pygmy poplar leaf in Eliad Square. The minute he saw he hated him. He tried to smile, knew he was failing, saw that Xaviero did not seem to care. For Xaviero he was one of the many miserable crawling toward the teeming center of his, a prodigious universe with their goods barely marketable precariously perched on hairy foul-smelling snouts.

"The job calls for impersonation," the fat man said. "Can you handle it." Xman was at this point unsure of how eager he ought to appear: Too much eagerness was easily despised, he knew from past experience or had he simply read it somewhere. "Are you sure you can handle impersonations?" Xaviero repeated. "Yes," he replied. He tried to sound as indifferent as possible. But would Xaviero see through apparent indifference to the last, authentically daring, ploy of one who, terrified by the prospect of verdict, strives to appear to stand outside all concern with categorizability. But perhaps this was the stance with which Xaviero was most familiar. And he clearly wasn't interested in the particular distance Xman had had to traverse to practice this stance. All Xman allowed himself to say was, "I feel completely outside of being so I easily impersonate those who think they belong on the inside."

"Are you a Jew. I mean, officially outside of being. And if so, doesn't this therefore somehow call into question your credibility as one spontaneously outside of being. I mean, once officially named and labelled as one outside of being are you still outside of being in the only manner that lends shape to such shapelessness. I mean, doesn't your official unreality—your published exile—somehow neutralize that unreality and render it merely nominal. Decorative even. I mean, if you have been identified as outside of being then you are not so unlocalizably amorphously outside of being as you might wish. In short, I don't know if I can use you." Yet somehow Xman felt he would be recruited.

That night the telephone rang as Xman knew it would. This had less to do with self-assurance, he told himself, than with a slumbering passive fatality. Before it rang Xman said to Rosalie: "I wanted to speak to the big fat bastard about having long been haunted by a talent for dissimulation, always less or more than dissimulation. Always generating personae (goaded to produce them—the more unspeakable the better—but I will contend with that subject elsewhere), always in advance of those personae so that by the time my tormentors (whose numbers were always swelling daily— minutely) got around to a label—a caption—sufficiently denigrating I was far far far beyond its pertinence. Rosalie, I'm hard to figure out. I am and I am not tormented by the labels—the captions—to which I incite my tormentors. On the one hand I dread the deflation—the annihilation—I must believe with all my heart and soul to be inherent in a label such as shitkicker, fuckloader, pansy-nansy, tit, *tzigane*. On the other I dread emerging from the sheltering radius subsumed by the label. Outside that radius is a vacuum waiting to suck me into madness, far far away from any possibility of 'health and happiness.' And that's why I'm right for this type of job."

"Maybe," whispered Rosalie, as if she could sense the phone was about to ring, "that was a way—that bubbling up of typeable phenomena—to keep them far far far from your essence. You threw in their eyes the sand of impersonation. You had to believe enough in each impersonation to induce a label believable—defensible—to your tormentors. For they had to spew their labels back at you with the overriding conviction that they were at the very least annihilating your essence. But deeper down you knew those impersonations were only agony's changes of garment. Agony, YOUR WARDROBE MISTRESS."

The phrase *wardrobe mistress* resonated strangely for Xman and even more strangely made him think of the woman in the hotel room his first night in New York. He let Rosalie answer though she was in general terrified of picking up the phone as well as of making calls. He went into the bedroom, keeping the door open and began to play with a portable radio as if he were "tinkering" with its innards, he knew he was not really "tinkering," he was simply refusing to respond to Xaviero's call. Never had he had any talent for "tinkering" or allied activities. But under the circumstances—under the circumstances and within the straitjacket of the context—the impersonation—of one tinkering, of one who enjoyed tinkering—was as real as—far more real than—truth.

He clung less to the tinkering—he did not cling at all to the tinkering, he had not the slightest idea how to go about tinkering—than to the "idea" of himself as one who tinkered, as one who took to tinkering like a fish to water. He found himself clinging (all the while letting Rosalie flounder on the phone) to this entity as he rarely clung to the doings of his true self, intrigued by its caption: Someone with a radio who is so absorbed tinkering he doesn't hear the phone ring. This pleased him, this absorption in activity beyond vigilance, alertness, attention to personal advantage, beyond capacity to perceive as the rantress had self-condemningly perceived, all this pleased, made a man of him at last.

This was all a lie—this was an . . . impersonation but it didn't matter for the temptation to be another was too great and he had succumbed and consequently transcended himself. The temptation to impersonate one whose range of perception was much restricted, given the purity of his absorption in a task—an authentic project, unlike his, always playing possum—this temptation was too great.

Rosalie called, over and over. He knew he was refusing to answer but for seconds at a time he was unsure about what he was doing. Was he refusing to answer or was he in fact out of earshot so great his absorption in his work. This latter possibility became true the moment he thought it or rather he thought in a way that made the question of its truth irrelevant. He knew he was only pretending to be one so absorbed that he could not hear but the pretense produced an exhilaration that cancelled out all sense of pretense. This was after all what he wanted to be above all else: somebody so absorbed in his work he heard no voices, somebody absorbed in his work to the exclusion of all other stimuli. He had no work, no true work, no personal project, that was a fraud. But he had acquired this entity, this pretense, this impersonation. The shame of impersonation was cancelled by the joy of acquisition. He had become real at last—but as another and for minutes at a time.

"It's him," Rosalie called. "Xaviero," he corrected. She hated when he kept people waiting. Instinctively she felt it was her responsibility to make him acceptable to the outside world. He was her project. But he was not keeping people waiting, he was simply trying to be the type he was impersonating to the best of his ability. "Does he say what he wants," he asked, stolidly, remaining where he was. In her eyes he wanted to appear indifferent to worldly advancement, which was absurd, since she knew he must be waiting for Xaviero's call. They both knew he needed a job. But this did not detract from the urgency, the urgent requirements, of the moment, the moment's impersonation, impersonation's moment. Each moment then existed on its own terms and nothing was more important in this moment out of time than to appear—thereby be—indifferent. Miming indifference he became indifferent, a veritable species, of which indifference was the merest secondary sexual character. Rosalie's eyes said: "And this is why you will never succeed. Because you sacrifice the long term to gratification of the moment even if gratification is in your case abstention from self-gratification. You carve the moment out of time and abstain from it totally."

"Hello," he said finally. "Hello," Xaviero replied, quizzically, suggesting restrained and condescending ministration to a neophyte's understandable but nonetheless laborious anxiety, or adroit rectification of the same neophyte's mere and simple overeffusion that would not do and would have, oh yes indeed and before too long, to be tempered even further, redirected, overhauled. Out of the blue Xman heard himself think: *He* can only impersonate when not being paid. "We need you," Xaviero conceded finally. Xman heard what sounded like another voice in the background. An operator cut into the proceedings, all at once they were definitively cut off. He waited a short time, thinking of nothing, not even of how he might be needed, how could anyone need him, Xman, then slammed down the receiver. He dissipated his fear of so rash an action mustering a brusque bravado toward Rosalie's inevitable motherly alarm in the face of this one more proof of his churlish ineptitude. He turned around, sure enough she was poised in tormented anticipation. He wanted to strangle her: Why should she be considering this not even burgeoning relation to Xaviero of such crucial importance. Did his whole being hinge on it. With terror he now wondered, did his whole being hinge on it.

The visceral throb of a massive bassline was unmistakable. Before he could focus on the constricting horror the vibration induced he was forced to focus on an imperceptible transition within Rosalie's alarm. It reminded him of something. It was not so much as if this something had anything to do with the true work. Rather it was as if setting up a connection between the imperceptible transition within Rosalie's alarm and this . . . thing to be remembered had in spite of itself something to do with the true work, the personal project. Could it be the true work was the slagheap for such connections, could it be the true work stimulated such connections in order to acquire them as so much slag. Making the connection would somehow put him on the road to the true work, or would it. And then he would no longer need Xaviero, maybe not even Rosalie—but this last was a thought too grim to be borne, at least here, at least now, at least now when needing her was all he knew. The bassline continued incessant, incessantly on the verge of . . . poplars. Yes, on their way home from NYCB one sultry Saturday the poplars had been bent back by wind as each shaft expanded its sheaf of upright branches fanwise. Bending backward against the sultry windfall had triggered an expansion fanwise. Just as Rosalie was now . . . just as Rosalie's disgust at his, Xman's, irresponsibility vast and disgruntled, was imperceptibly transformed into alarm at his inevitable reaction to noise. The bassline was crawling more and more insistently toward grim audibility. "Forget about the music," Rosalie cried. "Call him back." Neither his neighbors nor the builder hoodlums responsible for such paper-thin partitions between one hovelette and another cared for his true work, his personal project, and the solemn peace and quiet its everpresent imminent possibility solemnly required. Suddenly invaded by an insidious throbbing this tiny space was too large, vast as an echo chamber on the edge of the Mojave Desert. Suddenly, as suddenly as it had begun, the throbbing stopped, as suddenly as Xaviero had stopped their interview hours, centuries,before. Did this throbbing have something to do with Xaviero, was it a coded missive of conditional acceptance. He knew he should try to reach Xaviero but was afraid to initiate any movement lest it provoke a resumption of the throbbing bassline *en forme de* Brobdingnagian vengeance on a lapse in the usually paralyzing vigilance that was his only protection against the upsurge of phenomena, in other words, world.

He knew Rosalie was exasperated but he had to say: "If I make a move it will only induce the noise. Remember the film we saw: When the camera moved it induced the movement of one of the characters—one of the other characters I should say." Rosalie began to pace back and forth: "Should you risk anything knowing you may be cut off by death. Noise is the angel of death." She began to weep. Because her weeping said: "I don't know if I can live with someone so tormented: What will happen to my *joie de vivre*?" he felt impelled to attack her. As long as I am vigilant, he wanted to tell her, no phenomenon can upsurge for why should it upsurge at one carefully guarded moment rather than at another. No—that is not what I mean. "What I mean is—there where I am or rather where my vigilance is there no phenomenon's upsurge can hope to be. For my nonbeing is contaminating. Or maybe I, Xman, am so replete that the space subtended by the wakefulness of that repletion can support no other tenant. Too much and no being at all, that is my problem." He shook her back and forth in rage and fear, she wept more loudly. Her despair was nothing more than a mammoth provocation, an insidious attempt to cut him off from the mammoth quiet indispensable if the personal project—the true work—was to give a sign at last. He went back to the bedroom, to his tinkering. He felt an irresistible, or rather well-nigh irresistible, impulse to smash the gadget. Just before he succumbed the telephone rang again. "I'll take it," he cried, surprised at the loudness of his own voice. This was an Xman he clearly did not know, hadn't planned to encounter, an entity he had no desire to acquire. Through the corner of his eye he saw her lower her head, saddened somehow, at this point clearly nothing he did could reassure. She was too decent to admit he was a great disappointment on all counts and fronts.

Unnecessarily the voice said, "Xaviero here," then clearing its throat, "Can you make it tomorrow in a building at the corner of Lexington and Forty-fourth." Once again unnecessarily, at least from Xman's absence of vantage, he added, "It's a beautiful building. The kind they don't make any more, a landmark sandwiched between two greedily compact horrors compliments of the not-so-recent real estate craze. There's not much filigree but what there is is prime: The nooks and crannies positively ooze an exiguity of scrollwork that puts us—at least some of us—into a rapturous trance." "What is it," Xman asked. He himself did not know what he meant. "Patients are coming," Xaviero went on but not in response to the question he seemed not to have heard. "One is coming with his doctor, a von der Schmücke. Rose Baldachino mentioned that you attended podiatry school for a few weeks, or was it days"—"Minutes," Xman audibly retorted—"and so you should have no trouble imitating—impersonating—our version of the good doctor who beneficently dispenses the treatment on hand. You should have no trouble impersonating, shouldn't have any qualms about impersonating. We're a race of impersonators. Is that blasted utterly leafless elm down in Madison Square Park, five feet from Seward's crotch and fenced round lest it rant and rave itself into yet another lunch hour epileptic fit, ashamed of impersonating an elephant and with such elan that even grown and half-grown secretaries, accountants, clerks, and lawyers are mesmerized into throwing peanut husks and anything vaguely resembling said husks into the burnt-out annulus between barricade and bole scrappily allotted to its horary captivity in and out of season? The true dispenser of the treatment is a . . . partner. But he is unpresentable except to patients. They accept him whereas any self-respecting colleague never would. More's the pity. We need someone clean-cut and a trifle . . . tormented. I'll explain our point of view. Very briefly," and here Xaviero became almost as incoherent as Rollins when he chose to wax eloquent. Xman tried hard to concentrate—paying attention, after all, could lead to being able to contribute to the rent and, better still, think unmolested and unvexed about the true work's possibility. "We treat folks with a special kind of sickness with special signs and symptoms (the sign, of course, stands in for the symptom's purposeful failure to make itself known to the instruments presently at our disposal). Of our patients we cannot say that at some specified date in the past they contracted the disease. Before our very eyes they are continuously contracting it. We pity them for they never have the look of those who have at last superseded that moment when the disease might or might not have been possible. Someday we may decide to distill, bottle and market our pity for fifty dollars an ounce at Bloomer Doil's. At any rate, this state of affairs, where the disease is being contracted at every moment, implies this was always the case—the disease was always being contracted at every moment. But we never give up on them, my partner and I— he is at present overseeing the production of a pornographic film in Yugoslavia for eventual dissemination among the sexually dyslexic. In other words, he traffics in goodwill gestures, teaching aids. He is what is known as an old-fashioned good German even if he isn't necessarily German. And I, dear boy, am what isn't known as an old-fashioned good Argentinian. Xaviero am I. In any case what we try to do is make these fools jump through the hoop of their own glutinous particularity into what aborigines crouching amid the luxuriantly thorny foliage of my country's copious river valleys refer to as the dream time. And when we introduce the cure we also acquaint or rather reacquaint the incurable party with the origin of that cure, or rather with the story of its origin: How, for example, Poseidon Pete, the great farting whale, was, when suffering from excruciating toothache miraculously cured JUST AS THEY WILL BE by the reticulate worm Sammy sticking his fuzzy forked tongue up the mewling mammal's prodigiously dentate asshole. We encourage them to stop thinking in worn ways. Teeth, especially when they excruciate, penetrate to being's very vitals, and are not always—in fact are rarely—located in the mouth. Fixed location in the mouth is a mythy camouflage. Teeth, like liver, heart and muscle curd, are everywhere. 'Teeth in the mouth alone' is a pretense of stability, such entrenchedness is a magical if massive masquerade against the brute fact of mad mobility. The fact is: we primates can't locate our organs nor should we try to. Fact is, their very being illustrates nothing except Heisenberger's (sic) Uncertainty Principle. At any rate once our patients are able to conceive of the alligator worm sticking its tongue up their ass to remove the stinging tooth, once they can allow themselves to yield to the gravity of the tale—then they stand a chance, swathed as now they are amid the paraphernalia of the dream time when toothache and the cure of toothache first burrowed up the ass of being, of being sublimely cured. But old notions die hard and resistant rigid and reluctant patients die even harder as you can imagine. In short, our cure rate is not statistically significant. And this is where you come in. Are you still there? At any rate, we are not, my comrade and I, the slaves of statistics. Forever in the vanguard we are willing to endure the inevitable martyrdom of those in the vanguard. Yes, our patients die—unbearably painful deaths, sometimes—but it is we who endure the biggest excruciation of all, namely, the ignominy of our colleague's tactful skepticim. We are creative. No, we create. And besides, we have property: he in Auschwitz and I in the Bolivian hintertropics—but never mind. Forget I said that. It's a lie: We have no property. What do you take us for: trust-fund hippies? Our faith is our task and our task our faith and not a penny more do we have to show to the deposit window every Friday afternoon. In any case, why don't we let bygones be bygones and meet as I suggested on east or is it west Twenty-sixth Street in that landmark of landmarks with all the musty charm of an old carriage house. From afar it gives off the whiff of the old world and an old world charm that is in such short supply these days. Oh I could weep. In any case, once we get our patients to participate in the dream time's archetypal moment of cure they are cured. Only they don't know it. Now comes the hardest stage—convincing them they are cured. Convincing the little pygmies there is nothing wrong with their . . . physiology. Of course I don't blame them. At the height of crisis every natural act—shitting, pissing, breathing—is called into question as they all wonder: Can I manage it—pissing, shitting, breathing in this new neural landscape. And at the same time physiology—the autonomous working of physiology—for that working has a way of persisting beyond doubt—belies the virulence of the crisis. In the midst of profoundest torment they find themselves rejoicing one and all at the imminence of a good shit, piss, breather. Obstructing disease with the normal working of physiology it is no wonder they obstruct the working of cure. They get in the way of health just as they persist in getting in the way of disease. Frankly, Xman, patients are a nuisance. Disease and its treatment should be able to proceed without them. Disease and its treatment would be quite tolerable if only these panicking bastards could be made to refrain from rearing their ugly heads, kidneys, testicles, mother vulvas, ureters, the works. So that one of the prime components of our highly successful and innovatively efficacious approach to arthritis of the soul so to speak hahaha is to create that void in which true illness makes itself known at last. We view not only the patient but ourselves as obstructions, nuisances, hindrances, on the way to the disease's unimpeded manifestation. Do you follow. Look, there is a disease, a miserable loathsome disease that any halfway rational creature wouldn't be willing to touch with a ten-foot pole, much less with scalpel, much much less with a few therapeutizing words. We see we are confronted with a disease. So what do we do. We get rid of the patient with his tedious chronology masquerading as meaningful biography—a sum of symptoms that have nothing in fact to do with the disease. We must get rid of the patient who brazenly eclipses the disease with all the suavity of moon eclipsing sun. We worship disease quite frankly. It is patients we loathe. We don't set up a Faustian opposition between life and disease, pure law-abiding health-giving life and evil old disease. No, it is the patient who is without doubt the devil, an unwitting stupid country bumpkin of a pumpkin-headed devil, the fat churlish straggler at the country fair whose rugous rump persists in stenosing our dazzled perception of the bearded lady's antics. Yes, yes, yes, I admit it, disease is our bearded lady yet the patient insists on deploying his own comparatively anemic anomalousness across her horizon. And we too, we helpers, are also an obstruction. So what do we do—we try to maximize the contrast between ourselves and our patients so that out of that sacred space purified of the influence of both the disease may ooze at last, incarnated in symptoms that are its own and not the patient's. But then of course, my partner and I, we grow tired of such an approach—we grow tired of flagellating the shadow we profess to cast over the disease in its purity, we grow tired of casting aspersions on patients casting their frivolous shadow over the possibility of a disease. Why, we have become as humorless as those fat-assed Germans who clunk their sausages during Tristan's [sic] Rhine Journey at Baby Ruth (sic again). So we hurry up and accede to a new stage marked by the discovery that it was our sick dedication to the purity of the disease essence that caused our patients to be sick in the first place. But first we have to indict the clinic—our clinic—for breeding obfuscating complications in the primordial entity. As it too quickly turns out, the disease we saw, Gottfried and I, was never the real disease for it had been covered over with the excrescences created by too free intermingling of patients with patients and patients with patients, to say nothing of patients with clinic air, clinic air with patients, air with air, air with walls, walls with air, toilets with walls of air, and air with toilet walls, these last so cockroach-laden, so mossy and so disfigured by inept graffiti. How can we treat disease in its pure state if we—Gottfried and I with the foul effluvia in our clinical gaze—and the clinical ambience itself abounding in pollutants and mutants to say nothing of the urban tumor in whose heart our practice must be fixed—from humanitarian motives of course—we wanted to be accessible to the thickest ladleful of the human soup's stooges and lackeys from all walks of life and death, as it were—if all this renders that pure state well-nigh illegible. In any case, finally we—he and I—attain to the last stage. We cease to view the disease being contracted at every moment as a purity, as an entity—the entity—soon to emerge unscathed from the violaceous void. No, we are through as I say with visions of abyssal purity, we are through with this invocation of purity's demon goddess, the alligator worm. We discover that the disease *does not exist*. It has a configuration—like lightning in summer's midnight sky—but no being. The disease does not exist but this nonexistence does not prevent its tracing a course not so much within the body of the patient,

which it barely traverses and then with the profoundest contempt for the bumpkin's entrail circus, as within *our* soul,
pandering to our base hunger to name and acquire especially
what does not exist and thereby festoon the vacuity of our
professional annals with yet one more account of still one
more discovery of one of being's farthest outposts. The disease does not exist, I tell you, even if you, Xman, wanted, for
example, to murder mom and dad at age eleven. The disease
does not exist. It never existed: neither in the clinic under
our rumbustious touch's parody of palpation nor in the patient's tender flab. The disease does not exist. And once we
cure ourselves (it is a laborious process that must, to be
effective, be repeated over and over but like Johnson's Milton
Gottfried and I, lovers to the last but of what, I ask you, of
what, were born for what is arduous)—once we cure ourselves of a belief in the disease then we can begin to begin to
begin to attempt to situate ourselves in such a way that the
possibility of patient-cure may one day present its possibility on the salmon-streaked horizon of progress. But we make
no promises regarding even the possibility of such patient-
cure. It's every man for himself and this truism is never so
true as in the realm of patients. We make no promises and
that is why we have sought you out, Xman. Because every
line in your youthful preeminently inexpressive face makes
no promise. We know you will be able to peddle the disease's
nonexistence with a straight face, with the dissimulated arrogance of if need be martyred commitment to the lost cause
we never had the courage to espouse much less invent. What
am I saying, drop that, drop that from the record at once,
dearest boy. In any case, the disease has a configuration but
no finite existence: The disease—any—consists of the same
worn elements rearranged and juxtaposed along diverse sani-
ous pathways. There are never new facts merely new combi-
nations of the old facts, each and every sclerotic as an old

hag's buttock or an old fart's erythematous right testicle. With what antediluvian ingenuity these well-worn pieces of subclinical shit rearrange themselves for the delectation of a diagnosing nisus. And so we come up with a—verdict, a diagnosis and an adage to soothe the most savage beast. And just when the fool is about to run out and get squashed by, say, a truck or invest his last nickel in the latest fatal panacea we stop him short and announce that though incurable and a combination of infinite and infinitely intricate elements the disease does not in his case exist. And then he is more tormented than ever. For his very existence depends on the pertinacity of the disease entity. What can he be expected to do in old age without a disease to his credit and all his friends, worse his enemies, possessed of an ailment, a glorified grievance as it were, of their very own. What is he—or she—to have, what can he or she hold up as counterpoise to all that boasting. For every man needs authentic grievance to make him an everyman wholeheartedly convinced (without of course giving it a moment's thought) that he too is situated in being. And this is where our true cure comes in. Our true cure for the disease that doesn't and cannot exist. We provide them with signs and symptoms. We fabricate signs, allowing them a minimum of two or three: one linked to fever, another to testicular throbs (right side, if you please), a third to suppuration from unlocalizable but mammoth cerebral sore. And of course they toddle off thrilled. For they have come through, they have left the disease far behind, conquered its nonbeing, annihilated its nullity, and from its spacious and accommodating void extracted those few and precious signs bespeaking disease but even more the desperate cunning of the "medical intelligence" hungering after some—any—target. We let them get off scot-free as it were with signs that are not so much symptoms as substitutes for eternal absence of symptoms (like some eternal Frenchman's eternal absence of a bed). And when they come back moaning and groaning that friends and relatives have rejected their paltry little panoply as bereft of underlying substratum, consistently pulsating hypostasis, then we tell them to tell every last lying bastard to shut his butt and to intimidate their dull-wittedness by asking, point-blank, whether they in fact know what any jackass knows, namely, that there is no such thing as disease, hypostasis, entity,— which is not to say the disease is a nullity, species of nonbeing, ghost of a ghost of some anal canker, the very formulation we—Gottfried and I—were forced to reject centuries ago when we were fortunate enough to come upon the unpublished work of one Heinie O'Mengele: What's wrong with you, don't you read the medical journals, even the vulgates make a point of making frequent reference to the pressing need for abandonment (heart-rending to some) of a point of view that was for oh so long oh so near and dear to our hearts. Alas now we see the disease exists but as a constant sliding away from the bracketing straitjacketing lattice of localizability. Disease for us—as for any man with half a brain—can only be such a sliding away from specificity, an incessant deviation from typicalness, from type, from any form of German-heavy conceivability. The individual's essential aberrancy—yes even the heartiest conformist's—triggers a veritable chain reaction whereby the disease in its Mephistophelean playfulness mimics at every stage the patient's essential deviation from norm and itself becomes an embodied deviation—the displacement of itself. And with such notions lovingly affixed to his butt our jackass of the moment usually goes away soothed if not convinced.

"So that now, hopefully, Xman, you can see where we are coming from, to coin a phrase, and why we, my partner and I, stand in such great need of your services. We need you to stand guard—yes, nothing less than stand guard—over the essential deviancy of the disease entity, which does not not exist, let no half-baked perfect Wagnerite notion lead you astray—the disease exists, in all its hideous splendor. The disease exists and you are to be sentinel on the frontier of its intrinsic and incessant deviation from norm that also exists if only in the dream time—against the fur, against the fur, here pussy, there pussy, everywhere a puss pussy—you know, you know, when the alligator worm Nabucco licked the ass of the nanny goat Kundry and the dandelion lay down with the lamb or was it the scapegoat, I forget which. Do you see, do you see, I mean the role you are going to play. When we first called upon dear Rose B.—who is herself an incessant deviation from the norm, as I, as your dear wife, as your dear children, grandchildren, greatgrands, as their aunts and uncles, as we all are incessant—humph—when we first called upon her the job description was a far paltrier version of what it has since become—just in the last five minutes talking to you. Now we've discovered we need more than a pimp, more than a public urinal-licker and kicker, more than a buttock-spreader—what we now need is a man for all seasons, a Renaissance man with an Enlightenment sense of humor, a spiritual centaur with three bagpipes sticking out of his backside whence periodically emerge strains worthy of the great Felix at his most elfin, worthy of the great César at his most plangent, of Buffalo Bill at his most mythically oafish, you get my drift buffalo man. But best of all you will be standing guard, making sure—better, certain—no half-assed patient's personal physician dares to impugn the essential deviancy—think you can remember that phrase?—of the disease entity as it is known and loved across the land, from Madison Square Garden to Grand Canyon Gardens, a desert condominium representing the *ne plus ultra* of luxury living." There was a deep sigh. Somebody seemed to be in the room with Xaviero. "And once our patients leave us forever we are not the type to try to draw them back, to create a factitious dependency. We are not the kind to exhibit them every Sunday at Bicêtre or Bethlehem for a nominal fee. Once they are cured, once they are cured of disbelief in their glorious deviancy incapacitating them for all susceptibility to cure, then we become like the mightiest archers of old commissioned by the city of Paris to drive each and every indigent from the august gates. We drive them out into the sunshine of the great big beautiful world. Yes, yes, yes yes, my dear. We have made mistakes. Gottfried's investment in Bolivian tin mines—I mean, what am I saying, I meant—I mean—in our treatment of our dearly beloved patient family. With so many patients how could we not have made mistakes. Many resent being one of many, one of an infinite series, so to speak, growing daily more infinite. But so what if throwing themselves fatally in front of some truck in the middle of that great big beautiful world aforementioned those many make it a point to shower us with curses. Errors made in one patient are rectified in the next or in the next after that. It all cancels out and he and I, all down the ploys— I mean the joys—of rec tification—tribute to our conscientiousness—dream of nothing so much as one day being able to retire to some sunny little concentration camp in the Bolivian rain forest—a kind of Dachau-sur-Amazon, if you will, and of course you will—you're a Baldachino boy above all."

"So," Xaviero concluded with a sigh that was far more courtly than could have been suspected from his previous breakneck volubility, "we will see you tomorrow." Then he slammed down the telephone abruptly as if he, Xman, had been guilty of trespassing on a fellow mortal's precious time.

Xman looked at Rosalie suddenly hating her for her poorly masked eagerness. But she was, after all, a mother-to-be and was only looking out for the being inside her. Xman only hoped labor and delivery would not end up conflicting with a very important mission—a visit to NYCB for Balanchine's Divertimento from *Le Baiser de la Fée*. "You have another assignment," Rosalie said, trying to manifest in visage and voice uneasiness lest deflected by the vagaries and vulgarities of making ends meet he abandon the true work. But eagerness and relief evolved faster than uneasiness. All he said was, "Have to go for a walk." "Where are you going," she asked. "On the roof?" They were both alarmed at the separation. She drew toward him, with a shudder he pushed away her approach. Though it was drizzling slightly up and down Broadway he took no raincoat. He walked up the two small flights of steps separating their apartment from the noisy smelly corridor, dirty also in spots, only to regret, in the darkness before the elevator, that he was compelled to go out now at the very moment when there seemed to be no noise from neighboring apartments save the intermittency of what sounded like something light being dropped onto a wooden floor—when it seemed a good time and a good idea to reconsider all the raw materials of the true work for who knew when he would have the chance again. When he could see the river through the trees of Riverside Park he began to breathe more easily, why he did not know, after all the river stank, never washed its belly. Entering at Seventy-second he made his way to the marina, dangerous this time of night, but what did it matter, how could anything happen to him now the worst had already happened.

He needed to clear his brain of Xaviero. Lights in condominium apartments across the river on the New Jersey cliffs indicated evening was about to begin for so many even if for him evening was over for good. Leaves blew under the great mottled planes, he surprised himself charging through the high grass and weeds that separated tennis courts from road at the very edge of the water, he was too tired to look for balls, he wasn't too tired to look for balls, he simply did not want to acquire anything for he did not feel he could at this juncture defend what he collected, he had no contoured being capable of defense, acquisition could not, as usually, induce a contour, would only exacerbate his already expanding amorphousness, so he steered clear of theft, he would only have to leave them behind, the tennis balls, green and gray, when he was arrested, for impersonating a physician, and what a pitiable commentary they would constitute once the stealth and preparation recruited to their confiscation were no longer living beings able to distract from the act in its nudity, its superfluity. Watching the willows within grazing distance and whatever boats, large or small, passed by he sat down finally, invisible to himself, on a ledge overlooking the bloated stream. From one of the boats in the marina a voice cried out hysterically, "What are you doing here." Another voice, meditative, and unruffled, replied, "It is pleasant to walk out of an evening, convinced you are done for and that an urban forest walk is the best remedy for ungovernable ills. You smile, having triumphed at last, waltzed by failure into a stupor of contentment that knows there is nothing left to preserve and defend, no scrap of the ostensible latent (which has never been anything but a burden, an atrocious mythic burden) to hoard against slights." Xman waited. The voice was dead.

"No longer any pretext for hurrying through the day's regimen in order to not so much recommence as be once again in readiness for the impossible upsurge of some completely unforeseeable vantage on the possible upsurge (the last having supervened in that year of our bawd . . .) of the—" Xman couldn't make out the last words. They sounded alarmingly like "true work." After an acrobatic plummet into silence: "Delightful to smell the air sanitized by a supersonic whirr of tennis balls, shiver of loverly trysts fixed beneath the willow's gibbet—it is delightful, I mean, knowing of one's prior craving to be like one's neighbor at last, to say nothing of one's neighbor's neighbor. Yet—" and here the voice became husky, genderless, suffused with excruciating despair at the same time it most seemed to be simulating ecstasy of grief, "—all too soon, long before the last lighted tug has pushed the last barge into the abdomen of urban dust"—Xman looked, there was no tug, no barge, just the Hudson's oily paunch as ever refractory to reflection of those condominium lights)—"one becomes disenchanted with this far-off and once novel intention of saddling oneself with the carcass of IMPERSONATION of any number of a billion fellow drudges. Lying down one then considers what is left, nothing, nothing, but a lewd leap into the estuary's maw of livid shoals barely eroded by the babble of Wall Street ichthyosaurs. So on one walks, realizing even this, this extreme occident of desire, is doomed, doomed, most doomed in its very extremeness to . . . intelligibility, is by no means unassimilable to the tongue-clicking compassion of neighboring drudges within a certain fixed radius without bound who will have no trouble subsuming its inconceivable calamity with a goodwill marred only by the vaguest vexation at eternal half-sleep intercepted." The other voice sobbed: "Once I thought the leap into cold shoals would obliterate my name—obliterate its *conceivability*—when it was, in actual fact, at the very moment of that leap I was most nameable." The other other voice fell like an understanding nod of the head: "Afraid no doubt through leap—and what is the symptom: Leap or fear of leap—of destroying world—rending irreparably the tissue of being—when all along, world—more than capable of accommodating itself to your daring—your iniquity—had been pushing you toward the tortured daring of that symptomatic leap, that leap into symptom, so that you would at last be cataloguable, known, put away, straitjacketed forever as the one who leaped and failed and forever held his peace." The other moaned assent, adding, "And I cannot even call my suffering—a grief festooned with the failure of symptomatic leaps—my own, very own. An annoyance to world—universe—being—it is something for which I am forever making excuses." "And miracle of miracles annoyance to the universe—eminently characterizable as 'fragile' and 'with enough problems of its own'—becomes more lacerating an occasion for shamed guilt than the initial grief. And you continue to undergo the excruciation sponsored by the universe as a colossal impropriety gratuitously perpetrated against its hard-won and otherwise perfect and exquisite calm." A long silence broken only by a hunger for it to be broken. They—other and other other—broke it finally with the unison of: "So on one walks bent on refusal to comply with tragical specifications so easily processed and discarded, under cowl of night forced to swallow still another humiliation until, having dived so deep, there is over and over amid the seaweed and the stench (but not of seaweed) this hunger to dive out drinking in some detail however innocuous yet vestigially redolent of heroic failure to have wrested from the monolith of world's consummate indifference to anything more pondered than a casual stroll down the sidelines of preoccupation with things as they pretend to have to be a consummated nuptials with the hyacinthine bronzed brawn of everyday eternal truth. Quick. A drumbeat sounds and, much as one loathes noise, even in the key of fate, much as one loathes any attempt at forceful penetration of the evening's maidenhead, is greeted with relief forever grateful for the emergence at last of some perturbation made to the measure of a sourly vigilant susceptibility so taut with contradiction it borders on insensibility. So what if each new throb heralds a new intransigence of woe, proof once again that the world has no intention but to withhold all confirmation of one's prowess as a gatherer of exiled sparks." Xman felt all this should have been—should be—

reminding him of his own vast experience—on the bayous, in sunny Seville, on a junk off the Hong Kong coast. He thirsted to hear more. One of the two moaned. It seemed unbearably close, through closed eyes he could smell fetid breath, he blinked at the figure beside him in the icy grass. "Ah Xman," it murmured, "I simply had to catch your eye before the proverbial 'first day in the office,' what I told you about disease was all wrong, I'm afraid our conversation was tapped by a certain terrorist mamma named Fatima Buck— never mind, I'm afraid now you'll hold all this against me forever, I didn't mean a word of it, do you think my partner and I could ever be so unfeeling toward our flock of pigeons, could we allow you to come away with so many misconceptions, induced I might add"—here he tapped Xman's knee-cap—"by your own all too forgivable haste—after all you are young, my dear boy, too young in a sense to be part of the team, it's all right, Gottfried has told me to tell you we both forgive you wholeheartedly for missing nothing, misinter-preting everything, all we said about the cure and the pa-tients and the doctors in general is simply not true. Not a bit. You ought, with your experience, to have been able to read between the lines and know we sensed we were being bugged and understandably resorted to a code enabling us to give life to our deepest convictions by campaigning for their opposite. You should have tried to decipher the code as you will one day soon have to try to decipher symptoms. Do you see Gottfried on our little yacht. Wave, wave. Never mind, he's going to sleep in the hold. With his girlfriend—he pre-fers women, the fiend. I have to listen to their gasps all night long. We live on the yacht—with Tanya, his woman: good for a fast getaway. Not really—we adore New York, the shops, the spectacle, the violence—in short, the heterogeneity. Never mind, never mind, no heterogeneity, forget that line, in any case it isn't ours. It's Tanya's. Look up at the sky. The evening light as Tanya never tires of repeating—we found her in front of some SRO threatening the fat slob of a landlord with illegal eviction—has a charm of no common gravity. I wish gainfully to employ its silence. The charm speaks for, or better yet against, our laudable efforts thereby usurping the prerogative of our most malevolent because most indifferent enemies and rendering innocuous their halfhearted and all the more insidious thrusts. In any case, I won't bore you with the exemplary temerity of a struggle to make our comprehensive cure for diabetes, arthritis, heart failure, terminal cancer, muscular dystrophy and obsessional neurosis the toast of the century. In short, we orient our patients toward success, or rather, as our detractors point out, toward the success syndrome. No, no, that's not it. Gottfried, Gottfried, stop porking Tanya and help me, help me. No, he's asleep, fast asleep, in preparation for tomorrow's confection. He's terribly thrilled about meeting you. The office is positively aflutter with anticipation of your advent. But before you go I do hope it's clear at long last that all disease is pretty much nothing more than madness. Yes, madness. Any ailment, any congeries of rotting viscera, is the product of a defective outlook, a perversion of logic, of language. So we enter into the game, Gottfried and I. We play the madness game. If the patient thinks, for example, he is suffering from a limp prick then we do not deny the limpness. We follow limpness to its bitter conclusion high above the acacias and a little to the left of the maidenhair ferns. We bring the patient paroxysmally to a point of crisis by pointing out ever so tactfully that if the wrist is limp—is as limp as he says—then he himself and everyone and everything around him is sinking slowly into the other, nether, world. We make it a practice to abide by the laws of the country in which the madman seeks to find himself. Only we manage to foment a revolution in that country of course never availing ourselves of foreign agents, oh never, never, never, never, never, never. No, we confine ourselves to native stock that will force the madman to abdicate once sitting on his throne suddenly becomes too dangerous, too threatening to well-being crowned or uncrowned. Though we make of one of the elements of madness a foreign element we never exit from the raw materials with which it furnishes us. Only we are clever enough to transform one of those raw materials into a contesting element. An autoimmune phenomenon rears its ugly head at our prompting and the madman heretofore propped up on the inexpugnable stilts of his defective syllogisms suddenly finds himself allergic to what has until now so obligingly buoyed him up above the crowd of merely routinized workaday drudges he professes to loathe.For disease is nothing more and nothing less than arrogance—the arrogance of idleness camouflaging fear of inadequacy by an arrogant refusal to submit to what conveniently it deems servitude and in point of fact reduces only and overwhelmingly to the tasks that make men men. Disease is arrogance. This is the essence of disease, arrogance generated by a deep deep deep-rooted fear of work, of taking orders, which goes back to that long sleep before childhood. In any case, we play the madman's game. We cater to his presumption in fixing on some totally useless image when billions are being slaughtered daily—over religious disagreements, for example—in hijacked airplanes and pleasure boats: Innocent women and children—men are never innocent—bombed out of existence to feed the fatuity of a few feeble despots-in-training. We try, then, to shame the madman out of preoccupation with an image—one image—any image—no, in actual fact, the most shamefully insignificant of all images. For, in actual fact, the sick man's shame is not this or that tedious detail out of a tedious personal history far far far from the dream time—against the fur, against the fur—some safe

cracked or buttock pierced—but rather his farcical preoccupation with any shameful detail whatsoever whose only
shame is its mammoth insignificance. Get the picture. Now,
now, boy, I don't mean to frighten you by showing how selflessly we strive to shame the madman out of preoccupation
with this or that image's fungible parody of shamefulness.
Street-corner shamefulness. Remember, it is a solitary image
no matter how many components its insignificance recruits
and lays claim to. It is one image, remember. But we show
that protruding from the image—sticking right out of its ass,
so to speak—is a counterimage—a (-)Xman so to speak—
contesting and virtually annihilating the primary image that
owes, in the sick bastard's eyes, no small part of its indelible
prestige to the illusion of indestructibility. The limp prick,
the limp prick, for example. It seems to be limp for all eternity. Its limpness now is indistinguishable from limpness for
all eternity. But then we show that it is sinking or rather that
the image of such limpness has already given birth to a sinking earthward, ever-earthward, under-earthward, for all eternity. This monstrous scion of mere limpness—a limp penis
pulled toward the earth's molten core—ultimately destroys
for good and all the pure indestructible beauty of limpness
with a mere flick of the wrist by stretching it, the limpness
not the beauty of the limpness, so far earthward that it totally relinquishes its feathery identity. So that don't you see,
don't you see, what is your name, ah yes, Xman, Xman don't
you see that disease is nothing more than a deformed relation between two images or rather the construction and subsequent misperception of that relation. And we must correct
the misperception by emphasizing the retrospective illumination cast by the second image on the ashes of the first. We
show that the second at once creates and resolves the ambiguity, the genius for spectator disorientation, resident in the
first. And by so showing we ourselves are permitted to par-

ticipate in that ambiguity, to undergo its oscillation among several possibilities just before that joy-ride oscillation is foreclosed on a 'coming to rest at last.' And so you can surely understand why we always remain grateful to madmen for such enrichment (making it a point to send them New Year's greetings whatever the annual state of our finances)—an enrichment that literally catapults us out of a marshland of mere passive spectation into the far more verdant realm of hard labor. So, we show that the second image instead of affirming the indestructible purity of the first effectuates its derogation through extreme formulation of grosser implications. So that what do we discover. Simply that disease is more, far more, than preoccupation with an image. In fact it has nothing to do with such preoccupation, nothing whatsoever, and be you damned to hell if you dare to suggest such an infamous possibility. Disease is that special case of the everyday *démangeaison ontologique* where unbeknownst to the sufferer an image's grossest implications are played out *in extremis*—and always within the everyday ostensibly neutral confines of the victim's routine. He does not know he is suffering, much less in thrall to an image. So this is disease. This, finally, is disease: not to know, to know nothing, to seek nothingness, to achieve nothingness at the prohibitive price of whatever meager prospects remain for enjoyment of health as defined by six-figure-income experts. In short, to be diseased is to be all the time announcing symptoms' surcease ultimately and all too quickly indistinguishable from flaming onset. Gottfried and I have devoted more than our lives to making the world a better place for such onset, no site—Beirut, Treblinka, Kent State, Cambodia—bereft of our (some say too fussily decor-obsessed) ministrations. We were there. Prompt courteous service, that's our motto or should be once we get around to incorporation. Know a good criminal lawyer, by any chance?" Xaviero breathed deep of the night air. Now that they had advanced hand-in-hand, arm-in-arm, into the wee hours it was time, he announced, to get some shut-eye in preparation for the next day's gambols. "For there is much to learn, much to learn. And," (guffawing), "if we can bring this off it's sure to make our name in the company—internationally even, for the world is petit by the light of the lamp of animal cunning. Just remember that line and you'll go far, little Xman, little Ostrogoth with eyes of icy blue. Hahaha." Xaviero seemed to be laughing less at Xman's inability to laugh than at his naive sublimely fresh and disarming discomfiture at such inability.

Armed or saddled with this counsel Xman wended his way home believing above all in his heart of hearts that Xaviero/Gottfried resembled nothing more than Johnson's dynamic Pope/Swift duo: curers where there was no disease. At best they escorted their unwilling victims along a steep thoroughly supererogatory detour to dolefully inevitable death. Gingerly Rosalie asked how was his walk. He was about to reply when something in her tone—a certain Franckian plangency of hesitation between tones—alerted him to what was really expected from his harsh knotted reproachful physiognomy. A long silence was broken less by the indefatigable chant of the SRO lady (Tanya?) than by Rose Baldachino's even more forceful emergence from the cramped bathroom to say: "And so, onto his constitutional incapability of responding to a normal question like, How was your walk, posed of course, as such questions always are when the questioner is Rosalie, with the very best of intentions—launched as it were with solicitude born of the profoundest love—to his constitutional incapability is now grafted an obligation to IMPERSONATE the being anticipatorily traced by the heart-rending tremor in that question, Rosalie, my sweet. In short he is obliged to play the role specified by your not-so-latent terror of how he will respond to such a question. Setting foot through the door—I admit, I did not see him enter—he might very well have been intending to speak or at least let himself be cozened out of a vindictive (never mind toward whom) silence. But now you are making it clear you defer above all to his probably rage-laden incapacity, his iron-clad reluctance, to ... BE, it is as if he must fulfill this dreading expectation at all costs. He cannot, no not at this late hour, but does the hour have anything to do with it, see his way clear to wresting himself free of the effect your tone's sludge of perceived suggestion has on him. He needs to do your bidding—to impersonate the one you are waiting for, ostensibly in dread, perhaps in the rapture of dread. And at the very moment when he is as close as he will ever be to a willingness to be straightforward!" Xman said, "Leave me alone," to all this but he knew he was speaking more to Rosalie than to Rose. "He is giving you what you want, he is raging against the day's drudgery, a lifetime's drudgery, only now his rage is differently targeted—at his susceptibility to your susceptibility to his perceived power of suggestion, rage at his own fear of disappointing your dread, the maidenly dread you turn on at will. As he entered—again I didn't see him actually *entering*, I was flushing the toilet—something wrong with the chain by the way, you should call the plumber, Jake by name—without naming him directly—without labelling him outright—as your tormentor—something in your tone named and labelled him all the same according to specifications of expected, that is to say, dreaded, functioning. Now, listening to himself as that dread must be listening to him, whatever he says, whatever he doesn't say, sounds like gross, the grossest, exaggeration, that is to say, dissimulation, vastly incommensurate with whatever he may or may not have endured on his solitary trek past the tennis courts of courtly Riverside Park. Hearing himself point to his pain ('Leave me alone')"—here Rose B.

pointed at his groin—"he quickly checks whatever the pointing points to his having endured in order to determine whether it is indeed pain and not some abject simulacrum. In short, is he overstating the case. But in a split second it seems like grossest understatement—the pain was far far greater than what is adumbrated by a mere less than dear, Leave me alone. And now once again—synthesized as a perverse and gratuitous attack on the scope of your solicitude—like overstatement. Whatever he is enduring, my pet, it is clear he does not want to coincide with it through naming. At least, not in your presence, Rosalie, my pussy. Coinciding in your presence with that pain he simultaneously concides with his reluctant love for you. And that is simply unendurable."

Kissing Rosalie passionately on the cheek Rose B. sat down by the door thereby affirming that she belonged neither to the apartment nor to the world at large. She did not look at Xman so much as beyond to what she was preparing to say. Standing at the window with her back to her Rosalie murmured, "Maybe now isn't the moment—" "—And though I loathe I understand him perfectly—that's the marvelous and terrible long and short of the matter. He comes home. You, Rosalie, need him to evince something you can seize upon and misinterpret to your heart's content as giving forcible expression to your ostensibly deepest fears and suspicions. So what if his being veers elsewhere. You need a field for free exercise of your symptom and you'll be damned if—I pity you both heartily for I know that somebody—some organization—is going to come along and make use of two such shipshape symptom-machines. There's gold in them there ills. At any rate sensing your smothered demand he is eager to comply for in spite of himself as all these upsurges of rage and disgust he is very much the complaisant compliant little snotnose who wouldn't, no not for anything in the world, dream of disobliging mamma. At the same time he has no real difficulty doing the rage and disgust you or rather your symptom requires for rage-and-disgust laden denunciation of being always manages to catapult him outside damned coincidence with himself. But are rage and disgust performed at your bidding authentic rage and disgust. At any rate what has self-coincidence ever yielded but a caption. And there is nothing he fears and loathes more than a caption. Why is he in New York, after all, if not to elude all captions en route to an ineffable uniqueness. But what will that uniqueness procure, you might ask, I might ask. What is to be gained from being declared definitively supremely unique? Ask him, ask your little man. At the same time he wants to be deciphered in his futile craving. For what is his true work but a work of incessant interpretational decipherment to which he is unable to give himself from the laziness of fear. And so he seeks some kind of crazy vengeance and vantage (both) on his own sloth by making you the true worker he ought to be. His fearful sloth is your project. Listen to me, Rosalie: Let others fall into the trap of defining that true work. I do not pretend to number myself among the better minds required for a task so exacting and exiguous, never mind the billions recently slaughtered in Cambodieland. And at the same time his true work achieves its only meaning only in contrast to such atrocity. In short: He wants to be deciphered himself before condescending to become the reluctant slave of intepretation."

"What do you mean, 'deciphered,' " he finally mumbled. "I'm miserable, loathe my life, and I have a wife to support." "She is not your wife," Rose Baldachino cried." "She has been supporting you, you no-good, you low-life. At any rate, why can't you simply be 'coming home from work or the search for work or the flight from search.' Why can't you simply be 'man coming home to woman.' " "You mean," he spewed with a virulence that frightened him, "why can't I be the dapper family man. And it is true the family man is so fascinating as an object OUT THERE right down to his squarely cut nails and yet so excruciating as an object IN HERE." He jabbed at his navel with an unwashed thumb: It smelled of Riverside Park's grassy slopes of mud, dogshit, cellophane. Rose Baldachino sneered as if all her worst fears were suddenly bearing fruit. "All roles are ridiculous and inaccessible, is that it. All roles are impersonation. But the rage they induce: Is it for the roles themselves or for your simple inability to live them as anything but a cripple." Turning to Rosalie whose body was half out the window Xman cried: "Hi honey. I'm home." He noted a shiver as she leaned out even further downward on the smoggy night. "Hi honey I'm—" "Enough," Rose B. decreed, rising and advancing on the minuscule alcove that served as kitchen. "It's all ironic depiction. You're so steeped in irony there's simply no getting back to the intrinsic lesion that makes the irony necessary, is there. I knew you were hopeless the first time I met you. You tell yourself the person with whom you are failing to communicate could never speak to your essential being anyway but wouldn't it be too excruciating having that being addressed at last. Though Rosalie tries all the time to speak to it your irony defends against penetration. In any case, what you think is your essential being—a mere knot of ravenous and tantrumly pretensions to a uniqueness that will supposedly absolve you of all need to strive, contend, make do, compromise, transact, laugh, cry, as one among millions—simply does not exist except as a delusionally intermittent throb in the bowels of self-loathing. You think your irony eludes all brackets. But it does bracket you—as one with a hungry pretense to being outside being. And sometimes the nostalgia—to be in the world, to live your body as others do theirs—breaks through, doesn't it, that is, when you allow Rosalie to allow it to break through. But I simply cannot have her exhausting herself playing your game, actively interrogating your fleshly soul and soully flesh with an eye to their true cravings. I cannot have her forever deconstructing your poetic transformation of those cravings into their lordly opposite—lordly rejection of all finitude. No, no, no. My Rosalie was put on earth for better things. I'm not necessarily talking bigger. But certainly better. I cannot have her eternally deciphering your confusion. You come home enraged—disgusted with your own nullity. She smiles—you ridicule the smile. But deep down you are grateful. You are simply postponing gratitude. Why can't she decipher the sneering as the schema of delighted celebration of your good fortune in having stumbled on such a masterpiece of nature to come home to. For Rosa is a masterpiece. Why can't she then decipher your sneering without your having to descend into the abyss of direct communication, that canaille-ridden outpost where *I love you* has the audacity to mean *I love you* and nothing more or less than same. Since you find it so easy to transform celebration into sneering denigration surely she can transform the sneering back into its original form. But there is no original form. The sneering sneers and is nothing but sneering. There is nothing lying in wait especially if she cannot detect anything lying in wait. You see, Xman, if you were a truly ethical soul then perhaps I could apply to your paroxysms the notational poultices of my late friend Sir Soren O'Grady-Kierk. But you are not of the ethical stamp. Your quest for uniqueness has nothing of ethical fervor about it. How I wish I could say: In order not to be distracted by finitude and relativities you have placed irony between yourself and the world. At any rate Rosalie can no longer be expected to penetrate to the delight beneath the shroud soaked in sneers and forever likely to remain so." Slowly Rosalie brought her body back among them. Kneading her brow with both palms—she was terrified of wrinkles and the abandonment she was told they provoke—Rosalie murmured, "I was a little discontented tonight. That's all. A little afraid. Can't it be that when he senses that discontentment—which has nothing to do with him—Xman gets afraid—afraid and enraged at the accusation crouched in the shrubbery of that discontentment. And so—and so—" She began to cough. Xman resented wanting to come to her aid under Rose Baldachino's watchful eye—this would seem too much like doing her bidding striving to turn over a new leaf within seconds flat. He could not bear to give Rose B. this satisfaction but how did he know he would be giving her satisfaction. Wouldn't she in actual fact prefer that abstaining from all recognizable human feeling he drive Rosalie to flight and into the welcoming arms of some profitable businessman, doctor, lawyer. "Rosalie darling. Always giving villains the benefit of the doubt. Clearly my own life hasn't been enough of a lesson, enough of a guide to the perplexed. At any rate, according to you terrified of your discontentment he makes it his business to rush toward discontentment even faster so that now afraid of *his* slipping away you end up forgetting your own all too imminent flight. I don't know, I simply don't know. I mean I simply don't know when it comes to the Xmans of this world—so self-righteous, so ready to lash out in rage at the slightest provocation—least captionable of all when most, at least in their own eyes, delivered up to the dime-store grandiosity of one more tirade indicting this that or the other injustice perpetrated upon them or their seedy semblables. He reminds me more and more of my old school chum Fatima Buckley and her sidekick Siegfried/Mahatma. Never mind I'm sure he'll end up with somebodies just like those two misfits." In a hushed almost reverentially envying voice or rather—for suddenly Xman had witnessed this scene unfolded unfolding and about to unfold many many times before and forever

playing itself out as less itself than its abject failure to conform to the arcane specifications of the archetype of which it
was never any more than the puniest instantiation—in
short, another failed stab at the dream time—"in a hushed
almost reverentially envying voice"—for apart from questions of archetype Rose B. now was (and perhaps all along
had been) both playing the scene for all it was worth and
standing outside pointing to the playing—*in a hushed almost reverentially envying voice*—Rose B. insisted, "Look,
come home with me tonight. I'm afraid for you. I'm terrified
for you. Aren't you afraid to be around him. I mean, now.
Aren't you afraid he will simply jump right up and rip your
womb—our womb—to pieces or blow both you and the
teeming fetus to kingdom come. I'm afraid for you. I'm very
concerned. Oh, how so very concerned am I. A widow myself
and so much concern. For Rosalie, you are the incarnation of
the future, that full belly of yours points to what cannot be
inventoried, bracketed, mastered, in the here and now. And
more than anything he—or rather, the likes of him—wants
nothing so much as to eat up and spew out the here and now,
to come to the end of all here and nows, so as to be at last
free to move in on the true work above and beyond all works
because fattened up for the kill by his epical abstention from
all kill. Yet here you are tenacious, heroic, shamelessly proving there is no inventorying in the here and now, the frame-
able here and now. For you are in process, my darling,
maturing slowly, ripening ever so delicately. And he too is in
process for the here and now he wants to frame, straitjacket,
bracket away to slagheap irrelevance, is in process (and therefore refractory to all framing tactics, diagnosing strategies of
the prematurely handheld camera). Rosalie, at long last we
are talking evolution—development—maturation. And if
there is anything he hates it is evolution. So full of torment—his own nonbeing so much an anti-evolution, so

much a saccadic propulsedness (over gulfs starker than hell itself) from moment to moment—he can only recoil from the development going on around him and recoiling floridly revile its rugged essence as nothing more than—indistinguishable from—bombardment by the contingencies inimical to development. Rosalie, he wants you in his frame, framed beyond appeal. And you *are*, so to speak, in the frame, in his frame. Yet your belly points without pointing beyond the frame. He covets (without knowing he covets) its vectorly vantage on a world outside the frame, time beyond the frame. He does not want to know he covets that time beyond the frame because to know is to invoke and thereby insure the sabotage of malevolent contingency, in other words, life itself. Never forget, dearest little Rosalie, you are big with a future—the *disorder* of a future—outside and beyond the frame. So you are not quite *of the frame*. Just as he will never be quite *of the cubicles*. Yet he needs you to be completely inside the frame so that after cataloguing, inventorying, classifying, he can throw frame and contents out the window—throw even the window out the window—and proceed to get on with the not so busy business of contemplating that absence of all conceivables frames and contents whence the true work (with a little luck it might deign to obliterate them both) is supposed, in certain vicious circles, to arise. He wants to throw you out the window. He'll kill you, Rosalie. I know he will. He'll never forgive your gestation of a content beyond the frame. Get out while you can, come home with me, back to your old bed. Come home with me, he'll never forgive your belly as a vectorly vision of the future, in other words, of hope. He loathes people who wear their hope on their sleeve. You know that. I don't have to draw pictures. Go quickly before it is too late." Xman was not moved to terror by the sneezes, coughs, and rapid blinks bringing Rose B.'s speech to an end.

129

Rosalie was now standing directly over Rose B. in a glaring
light that gave a lachrymal quality to the eyelash shadows
spilling over flushedly exquisite cheekbones. "I think you'd
better go, Rose." Rising Rose Baldachino said, "Will you be
in tomorrow. We have that semiannual sales meeting with
Jed and Jensen." Xman could not make out Rosalie's reply. In
the hall they whispered for a long time together. Noting the
intimidatingly interrogatory twinge of his features as he lay
pretending to doze on the uncomfortable red couch Rosalie
sat down next to Xman and said: "She said many women do
as I do." "Don't forget," he sneered but with an overlay of
simulated torpor to soften the blow, "I'm also and above all
incompatible with myself." He was suddenly terrified she
was about to announce her desire to end their relation. "So
that," Rosalie continued, "they can play out more visibly an
unresolved incompatibility with themselves. I have choreo-
graphed that incompatibility 'on' you. As Rose got into the
elevator—oh yes I must call Jake—she asked if I was playing
out this incompatibility in order to resolve it once and for all
or perpetuate it forever in a kind of maddening repetitional
fandango of the same gestures, questions, ploys. For example, when you came home and I looked at you with fear as
the schema of reproach or reproach as the schema of fear—"
As if in his sleep Xman replied, "I don't want to discuss
that." Though his eyes were closed Xman knew Rosalie had
just nodded apologetically. "She said in the beginning it
must have been so easy to jettison myself, I must have had
absolutely no sense of self-betrayal yielding myself up to the
oceanic rapture of being in you. She told me she was sure at
that point there was no self to betray for my self was the
other's—I mean your—self. She also said she thought I was
slowly beginning to precipitate out of the solution of that
rapture to discover"—here Rosalie became almost inaudible—"grudgingly"—normal tone again—"what had been re-

linquished, or blithely cast aside by you or me, I forgot whom. I went down with her in the elevator and in the lobby—don't worry there was nobody about—she assured me in the beginning—at everybody's beginning, that is—there is a tabula rasa of infinite depth in which to drown. She had tears in her eyes—somebody was ringing—she must have been thinking of Soren Kierk, her first and only love killed in action at the Battle of Copenhagen. Then looking me straight in the eye, piercingly yet with infinite compassion— oh Xman, she is more, so much more, than an employer— she told me all the time I was drowning I had certainly been tabulating grievances, violations of the protocol respecting those lost at sea. But I love you."

In spite of himself—he wanted to fall asleep once and for all—he jumped up and dashed into the kitchen. Though impossible to ignore the multitude of cockroaches plying their featureless trade over sink and stove he tried to put them out of his mind long enough to bite into a soggy peach without puking. "I need to refresh my mind," he announced over his shoulder to Rosalie hesitating in the brief narrow hallway. "You won't leave me," she cried. "It's you who want to leave." It would be so easy to take her in his arms and reassure her with a kiss, yet because it was so easy it was indefinitely postponable. Walking past without the barest acknowledgment and lying down on the sofa, still red, still vindictive toward buttocks and spine, he applied himself with all that was left of heart and soul to falling fast asleep. Later that night with Rosalie asleep from despair, he presumed, he went back into the tiny kitchen more windowless than ever and plastered his ear to the wall. It was as if he was back in his first-night hotel room and instead of provocation from boorish next-door neighbors was awaiting further dispatches from Fa/(-)Xman. No distinct sound, only a cosmic visceral humming, greater, far greater than the ploy of mere neighbors, as if the world were bees and nothing but. Here in the great urban slagheap the universe was spinning toward opposition to the true work.

Overhead there was a brief, almost apologetic, scraping of what sounded like chair against tiled floor. He shrugged this away as beneath the contempt of his vigilance. Beyond this scraping there was no message, as from a beyond, on how to go about proving the yet-to-be fabled potency of his vocation was more than a hyposecretion of sebaceous glands. Of course the scraping of chair could mean: You have to think of more than yourself, there's Rosalie and the child in her belly. But the scraping could also mean: Don't bother demeaning yourself through exertion. Your future splendor comprises this long fallowness seasoned with imposture when nothing much seems to be happening. Emptiness is a test—a necessary part of progress. All at once through a tattoo of discrete taps the message was clear: indistinguishable from its decipherment: The true work exists to make you feel its exigencies are betrayed at every moment. Understanding at last Xman breathed a sigh of relief. Rosalie was suddenly beside him in the kitchen. "I had a nightmare," she whispered. "I was a saleswoman in a shop run by Rose B. She owned a mongrel. It was trying to bite me and so as not to offend her I had to pretend I was not being slowly bled to death. I was in fact profusely bleeding. Yet just as I was on the verge of death I begin to understand what made her sick. I realized I was so used to the expediency of flattering in the name of my tormentors' well-being that I was only just beginning to distinguish between truth and falsehood." She went on to explain how Rose B.'s truth was her sickness, which she, the shopgirl, suddenly began making every effort to judge absolutely and no longer in terms of relative progress meaningful only within the sphere of the sickness's abjection. The beast biting her thigh was, she came to see, speaking for that sickness as a permissible viciousness and for its need—its right—to be at all costs attended to. Yet the minute Rose B. sensed she was being attended to—in the manner to which her viciousness had become accustomed—if only by respectful silence—that viciousness demanded, so that she, its perpetrator and slave, need not be thrown back on too invigorating a whiff of her own dire inadequacy, some sign of reciprocal helplessness to which she in turn might minister. But the shopgirl refused to manufacture this plausible symptom of helplessness flattering the witch's sickness through synthesis of a sibling. "I stood my ground though gnawed. But you won't leave me, Xman, right. You won't throw me over." She clutched him passionately. Her body, warm from the sheets, had an irresistibly delicious odor. Able to classify it to himself as irresistible he threw it over, with panic he watched her go back to bed soothed by her recounting for he needed her to protect him against noise's onrush or rather become the receptacle of all his unfocusable rage toward noise and all that was not noise. For the noise was beginning again. Yet he was tired, tired less of the noise than of his compulsion, like clockwork, to react against the noise according to what were now institutional specifications. Tired of not so much noise as belief in the malignant and labyrinthine intention at its heart, alone at last in the kitchen he found himself thinking back—with nostalgia—to the interval of alarmed shiftlessness, despairing unwantedness—in short, unemployability—just before Xaviero arrived on the scene. Looked back at the trek from agency to agency became shorn of all that had made it unlivable. Seen as a picture—from without, no longer lived—from within, it no longer evolved expanding from a knot of suspicion, fear, rage, humiliation. He turned on the radio. Over one of the Chopin nouvelles études—the one that expires with a groggy but authoritative little trill in the bass—an ingratiating voice announced: "Let's look friends at retrospect, particularly the instant retrospect shorn of contingencies among which figure most prominently your overriding reactions to everything foul and unpleasant impinging THEN—at some time in the past. If you give yourself to instant retrospect—we also carry a decaffeinated version—your THEN will be recovered refunded, but as a picture remarkable for its four-cornered equanimity and such as one might stop to admire in a museum. All the unpleasantness," (Xman filled in long trek through agency slime, especially foul breath of interviewers always worthy of renown for bad breath, nose-picking, ball-scratching, sly contumely of potential employers, dearth of unshitspattered toilets), "will prove eliminated to make way for details you were unable to acquire consciously in the throes of anguished absorption in the THEN as unadulterated pain-event and nothing more or less than pain-event. Protectively enveloped in your preoccupation with what had been the pain-event's here and now of brute survival this miscellany of privileged sights and smells comes back fresher than in its sidestepped half-life." Xman shut off the tiny soundbox a trifle brusquely. Someday nostalgia might similarly coat this little interval of fractured calm grazed by Chopin's wing, this little scene of Rosalie tossing and turning against the cockroach-infested kitchen wall, completely delivered up to the nightmare that was the underbelly of her mongrel life with him and he to the terror ostensibly induced by a nearby shoe or faraway chair scraping against an uncarpeted stretch of flooring, neither near nor far. In fact, hastily fabricated retrospect was already shearing this event of its pain-content, its fleece of panic and futility, and leaving him a beguiling shag. He lay down beside her on the thirdhand mattress they called home. The odor of her naturally perfumed flesh was again irresistible and again he resisted or rather postponed a satisfaction that was so easily procured, so imminent, available at any moment—indefinitely. Waiting fully dressed for dawn's fragrant drizzle to his surprise he was already looking far back on this interval barely over, barely begun, depopulated of its core of anguish at the very moment when that anguish promised to be greatest. He was already looking back on the decor: bed, kitchen wall, scraping chair, smell of sleepy flesh flayed once over lightly by the harrow of nightmare, as mere props of the scene, as shammingly homespun filigree trying to create a scene. With dawn an even newer interval was arising, he felt it in his bones, veins, pores. This was the Interval of Budding Opportunity heralded by Xaviero and yoked as opportunity oh so often was to yet another yelping stranger's blurred and whimsical vision of the public weal. But yet another instant retrospect would surely flush away its own peculiar crop of propulsive anguish.

The next day he rose early, took another walk past the equestrian statues of Central Park South. In the middle distance he very quickly spotted, chewed up and spewed forth a figure from the now distant past—the Fish, Fish sans Brunhildine, jogging fashionably, a bandanna tight round his bald pate. He almost expected to see her beside him, taking notes, amanuensis on wheels, so to speak. Crossing the street just as Fish was about to enter West Drive he heard him call, weakly, querulously, but imperiously, "Xman, Xman." Maybe it sounded imperious because as of this moment Xman had no faith in his own substance. But faith or no faith he kept walking. Thanks to this failed encounter he was no longer Xman. And he felt, walking on and on toward Fifty-seventh not far from where Rosalie's obstetrician held court, absurdly triumphant as if this willful repudiation of an undeniable bond constituted the beginning of true success as impersonator, as . . . being. Not having responded to the querulous petulantly idle curiosity, owl-like inquisitiveness, of this male fishwife augured well, supremely well, but for what, oh, for the future. He, Xman, or rather his impersonation of all that Xman was flagrantly not, had triumphed over the Xman that was too real and therefore had to be suppressed in the name not so much of the true work as of a true work's possibly someday making its way among sharks and scoundrels—the Xman that had always been too volubly eager to empty itself totally—deliriously—under the first comer's scalpel. Standing at a point midway between the former Huntington Hartford Museum and a men's clothing store (corner of Broadway and Central Park West) forever on the verge of permanent close-out a derelict in dark glasses and shredded trench coat intoned, "You'll have to kill me. I know too much. But how are you going to do it. You'll have to kill me or . . . I'll kill you. They'll kill you." Xman stood perfectly still pretending to stare into a gourmet delicatessen. An expensively wrapped Granny Smith apple seemed to agree with him that the core of the utterance was: I'll kill you, even if the utterer was doing everything possible to attenuate and mislay his lucid rage amid the trappings of a halfhearted delirium. Then the utterer added, "What ever comes of openness but the world's dry diagnosis fastening gleefully on this or that symptom and bypassing the incomparable uniqueness that sponsors such symptoms and more far more than symptoms. But how can uniqueness—true uniqueness—survive without shrouding itself in symptoms as I shroud myself in dark glasses and a trench coat. First comers always miss the irony in self-depiction. Don't they see the depictor is all along saying: 'Look at this happening to me, all this degradation, all this humiliation, me, the man set aside for the most dazzling of destinies. See how far from true destiny my life has deviated.' " Xman remembered (-)Xman, now promoted to the status of old old friend, who

had begged for diagnosis in order to bind and thereby incapacitate his diagnosers for other—all other—functions.

He breathed deep passing the Carnegie Hall Cinema.
Hearing heavier breathing beside him he turned, it was the
Fish, slowed down to a trot. "Didn't you hear me calling
you," he cried. Xman did not know what to answer. "So you
did hear and you didn't want to stop." "Look, I'm in a hurry."
"As you turned away I caught that look on your face." "What
look." "The look of somebody who more than anything
wants to spill his problems in your face—who needs to exte-
riorize a 'struggle with deep roots'—and yet who rebels
against the slightest insinuation of defect, the slightest suggestion concerning how to change a painful state of affairs,
rebels against what is voraciously perceived to be crude
cruel insinuation and that, frequently, turns out to be only a
restatement of what he with lesser lucidity himself presented. So maybe it's better you didn't start talking to me
about how things have changed for the worst. This way you
are spared the excruciation—the excruciated relief—of a displacement of anguish from the real problem at hand—inability to hold down a job, failure to face reponsibility as
husband and father—to my—the other's—searing failure to
grasp the far more esoteric essence of your predicament. For
what I'm supposed to grasp I guess is that your predicament
has nothing to do with your essence. All that has happened
or failed to happen is a colossal fatuity, a veritable blueprint
of martyrdom in our time designed to demonstrate how far
the life of greatness can be made to deviate from its true
destiny. But I don't buy all that." Fish, Xman saw, was keeping up an almost imperceptible jogging pace. They were now
nearing Fifty-third where out-of-towners dressed with bland
boldness were stepping out of taxis onto the gilded steps of
the Hotel Americanacopabana. Xman said he had to go—he

needed to use the men's room. "Just remember," the Fish cried, "if you dump your problems into somebody's lap full of infinite qualification that somebody—if he has half a brain, that is—is going to pay attention not to the infinite qualification but to the bottom line: Where is this guy Xman situated on the social scale. Buddy boy, don't make your war with yourself into a war against the misunderstanding of others. In your war with yourself you stand half a chance of winning." As the Fish receded Xman noted the graying hair on his inner thighs was pasted glistening to their flesh . . . also graying, no, to their robust flesh, simply.

After the men's room, an old friend though not so old as (-)Xman—there was no attendant so he didn't have to leave a tinkling tip—Xman took a bus downtown. Normally he loathed buses but there was plenty of time. He watched the people getting on. You never know what expression might turn out to be useful, he told himself. Some felt ebullient after the double triumph of having caught the bloated vehicle before it pulled away from the curb and put just the right amount of small change, without collapsing, into the slot but were quickly squelched against the crude limits set by those already seated and intolerantly judging. In homage doubtless to Xman, father-to-be and all around regular-guy, one passenger, tie hanging loose, was speaking to what looked and sounded like co-workers about how Petey or was it Howie woke him up every morning just before the alarm rang out. The co-workers nodded in a unison of bovine understanding. Grumbling through his reasonable well-cut beard he immediately put his co-workers at their ease. This was something he, Xman, would never be able to do. Did he want to. Here was a specimen to emulate—copy—impersonate, he wanted to take notes on every gesture, every inflection. Here was a man who did not threaten his fellows and gals, gals and fellows, who was at home in being. And here was a man who set everybody else at ease in being, should they wish to be, by incessantly—Xman was sure this was no isolated case—bracketing himself to easy intelligiblity. They loved him, these co-workers, they were lapping him up, young father true to form, publishing a familiar and light-hearted complaining approach to paternity, deviating not a millimeter from the rigorous specifications of the fathering genre. He was in thrall, he seemed to—he did—say but without rancor, and this reassured their own thralldom. Once father-to-be exhausted all specifications of the genre co-workers began to chat among themselves. Sitting on the bus Xman felt as if he were waiting for the elevator in the World Trade, or the Grace, or the Flatiron, or Woolworth, or the Chrysler, or the Olivetti. How he marvelled at their ability— he knew all their names now: Denny Stone, Monica Boobka, or was it Boobka, Jezebel Jencks, Jezebel Crawford, Tushina McKendrick, Schmendrick McKendrick, Schmendrick Harcourt-Brace, and Hefty O'Wixzc—to express amazement, conviviality, curiosity, about the flattest matters all in a single bus ride: the sneakers of this one (Tushina Harcourt-Brace McWorld), the piebald parasol of that (Schmendrick MacPhendrick). And each seemed so delighted to be part of the group travelling east or was it south and to be paying his way keeping up somebody's end of the conversation. Ungainlier than most, Xman heard himself think though he knew this was simply not true. Their chatter held up a caption affirming: We are part of the team. We constitute the work force, we are man/woman power. And this positively fascinated Xman, more than the turretless turrets of the Avenue of the Americas, more than any number of ochrous flashes of the Palisades—he couldn't get enough. Yet he thought he knew he himself would never be able to tolerate such encapsulation. As he watched listening and listened watching he said their names over and over again, especially the names

Denny Stone and Monica Boobka, and was amazed, over and over and over again, that when he captioned Denny Stone as DENNY STONE CHITCHATTING AND CHATCHIT-TING VERY COMFORTABLY WITH HIS CO-WORKER MONICA BOOBKA said Denny did not dissolve away but on the contrary and in high contrast persisted more heartily than ever inside the shell of the caption. What fascinated Xman was Denny's obvious complacency, his FEELING GOOD, damned good, ABOUT HIMSELF, a phrase Xman loathed with all his heart and should yet why on earth should he loathe it. What fascinated Xman was Denny's prideful complacency in being able not only to chat but to continue chatting come hell or high water—to sustain a chat even when content and inflection had been used a thousand times before. It was Denny's delighted self-satisfaction at being able to dig his snout so deep within the asshole of amenity—of . . . being that more than fascinated Xman, that almost paralyzed him. Looking at Denny and Monica B (indisputably Couple Number One on the Dance Floor of Being's All-Night Marathon) he kept seeing the caption, DENNY STONE CHATTING WITH MONICA B AT THE ELEVATOR. He wanted to blow them to smithereens for dragging him into the precincts of their caption. He wanted to annihilate them so that he would never again have to be outfaced—tempted—by such captions. He wanted them dead. But they were not dead, not yet. Posing the appropriately coquettish questions about her sneakers and bustline and of course her plans for the holidays (a big three-day weekend coming up for drones) and noting how those holidays matched her skirt yet clashed with her undies, Denny was obviously very much alive, more than alive, delighted at being able to affirm his ease in humdrum relations. So what if Monica B was not only not particularly attractive but governed also by a slightly bovine shyness bordering ever so

subliminally on the sullen though for all her sullenness
Monica B. Boobka clearly considered herself a valued member of the group and valued that valuedness. Maybe Denny,
Xman thought, confused that sullenness with the most aro-
matic rarefaction of feminine wiles and was spurred thereby
to ever more jaundiced feats of rancid reparteeing. And
Monica reluctantly responded. Over and over and over, faster
and faster, faster than the bus, faster than the fast-food-joint-
sponsored blimp above their heads, Xman said her name.
Because he was baldly intrigued that these creatures had
names—Monique von Boobku, for example—and stuck by
their names, clung doggedly to the particularity embodied in
their names, and even managed to blossom forth just as doggedly from that particularity, not necessarily as flowers but
as beings nonetheless, and aggressively intact. He was baldly
intrigued that these creatures held on to their names, held
on against obliteration of those names in this or that caption
captioning what was for Xman a positively lethal banality,
mediocrity, blandness and lethally contaminated thereby.
On they went, unobliterated by their captions. Monica endured the repartee. Although her slightly bovine sullen endurance said, I'm Monica Boobka and when I get home to my
TWO-STORY residence in Queens, New York, I will become
the true Monica. I am holding her in reserve for my big
strong husband (he's almost paid off the whole mortgage)
and my little son and my little daughter and bossy all-knowing ma whom I simply must call about THAT sale THEY are
having next weekend across from Howie's barber—although
her slightly bovine endurance said all this that slightly bovine endurance was still very much of the repartee, very
much of the caption bracketing the repartee. How he loathed
the repartee, them, everything about this filthy stinking bus.
It deserved to be bombed out of sight. Angrier and angrier he
grew more and more fascinated—he underwent raging fasci-

nation as a suffocation deep within his chest cage—by the caption he intoned over and over and over: Monica Boobka, Monica Boobka chatting with Denny Stone, or rather not so much by the caption as by Monica's blithe refusal to be done in by the caption, to disintegrate gratefully in the soggy beam it projected over her comings and goings and those of her goodly companions, to long for some kind of counterfeit unstraitjacketability outside the fancifully festooned frame of the caption. He grew more and more fascinated, less and less eager to leave the Schmendricks and McKendricks of this world. More and more fascinated was he becoming by the caption he loaned them and that had quickly become their purulent and delicious stench—a homegrown peasant stench, fibery and robust, stench of uninteresting shyness and even more uninteresting warmed-over wit founded on ability to function in a group abiding by the rules of the group. He loathed all groups, more than ever. Why bother trying to succeed. Hopeless, hopeless, hopeless, he was not made for this world. Too good for this world. TOO GOOD FOR THIS WORLD; *that* caption turned him into one grandiose guffaw. Denny obviously found himself interesting. Or perhaps interestingness or noninterestingness was beside the point even for the likes of Lenny. The point was at all costs to affirm his being to—through sustained conversation with—one Monica Boobka, alias Boobku, a.k.a. Monique von Boobie, vocation: co-worker, fellow member of the team with whom one Denny Stone, vocation: also co-worker, instinctively felt a kinship transcending trivial questions of personal affinity and transcendently rejoined the camaraderie that moves mountains, hills, hummocks. How he loathed those hummocks! There had to be a way to blow them up, those hummocks. There had to be a way to wage war on those hummocks. Their being together in the bus comprised the stance of definitive commentary on working in and out of unison all day long day in day out, definitive allusion to the secrets of nonexistent but very real fellow feeling born of little cubicle jokes and shared collisons with cubicle nice guys and cubicle bastards. Xman continued to repeat: DENNY STONE CHATTING WITH MONICA BOOBKA. A firm sense of personal identity was exuded from every pore of Denny's repartee in spite of the caption with which Xman, a mere flea, laboriously assailed his indifference. Denny did not fear caption. Monica was dreaming of a sale on parkas—in Queens, New York, Queens, New York—that went far far beyond the only fantasmatic virulence of captions. Xman looked at them—for the last time, he told himself, for the very last time—and thought: And do not accuse me of feeling superior. And do not exalt yourselves for rejecting me. At any rate, I am too engulfed by fascination to feel superior to you and you and you entrenched in being's treacle, hard at work proclaiming yourselves and your names immune to capture by captions, and taking pride—inane and necessary pride—in yourselves, whatever you are, whatever you call yourselves. Monica Boobka, he whispered. Denny Stone, he whispered. But neither was the least bit obliterated by all his—Xman's—fiery captions exuded of contempt for this sorry little butt-ended enactment of repartee-streaked camaraderie indistinguishable from the five o'clock sharps or rather flats enacted on every landing of every building in Manhattan. Monica Bubu, he muttered. Denny Stone and Monica Boo, he murmured. And their conjoint being blithely stood its ground against the captions once more. Gloriously self-sufficient they seemed to welcome caption, revelled as if frozen on the broadest billboard in "The Times Square area." Caption clearly put the finishing touch on a species of selfhood to which poor Xman would never accede even if he ultimately chose to stop conniving to hold himself aloof from caption's superbenevolent infringement.

He wanted to arrive neither too early nor too late. The door was already open in the office on the twelfth floor. Xaviero was smiling, a new artificial smile. He took Xman by the crook of the elbow into an antechamber facing the haze punctured here and there by the flues of Queens over the East River. Pearly-rimmed black-bellied cloudlets were as if let down on strings, but, Enough of this, he wanted to say to Xaviero, why should the very landscape be obliged to participate in the gross impersonation about to unfold. Putting on the immaculate overstarched white jacket Xaviero held out to him, all he could manage, as Xaviero complimented the subduedness of his blue tie, no green, was, "It was strange seeing you last night. I didn't know you and your associate own a boat." Making a mock bow he said, "I didn't see you last night. And we don't own a boat," the last without the slightest conviction. Xman was put behind a desk, Xaviero leaving him to greet arriving patients and their doctors. Sitting with hands folded Xman heard himself say, "I'm being carried away by the role." After several moments Xaviero popped in to announce, "It's normal to be nervous." Xman was incapable of replying, "I'm not nervous," even if this was in fact the case. To speak in any sense of nervousness—to deny nervousness, for example—was to render nervousness conceivable therefore likely. Xaviero stared for a long time then said, "Fine, fine. You're doing superlatively: You conduct yourself as if you have been at it all your life. But remember, don't become offended if I correct you—yes, right in front of the doctor—saying, Do this, do that—yes, right in front of the doctor. So what if all that meddling—for that's how neophytes invariably see it—undermines ostensibly unfissured flawlessness by pointing to impertinent little pockets of fluctuating flaw. You'll come through this, Xman. You're probably afraid you'll be so good your services will be too much in demand. And that will take you further and further from the true work. But you will pull through." Xman wasn't sure what this meant except that it held an edge of menace. "And if you do pull through, dear boy, it might be—that is the risk—as another, alien, completely uncongenial to yourself." "But he's learning," said a nauseatingly ingratiating background voice that had to be Gottfried's.

But in fact the figure popping its too-ruddy face into the doorway frame was subsequently introduced as the redoubtable Dr. Q., long time attending on one of the pair's most troublesome cases. "I'll leave you two to your jargon," said Xaviero whose tone of ostensible disapproval poorly masked rapturous admiration. "As you probably know," announced Dr. Q., putting his cards on the table, "my patient is afflicted with a rather troublesome symptom. Or rather in the midst of feverish activity my patient longs for nothing more than a symptom she can name. Feverish activity: Do you understand what I mean by feverish activity? At the same time she dreads the annihilation sure to follow upon naming. You know how it is." For a moment Dr. Q. seemed about to forsake his impeccable and doubtless hard-won veneer and succumb to the oohs and ahs of degenerate confederacy against all these hypochondriacs making it more and more difficult for men of integrity to pocket a few dishonest greenbacks. Then he recovered himself and laying some impressive pieces of parchment on the table said, "Look here. Regard this map of the emotions, so to speak. Look at how close to each other body and soul seem to be in this patient. No need to transmit qualities to each other for such qualities are already proper to both. Body is always the immediate expression of soul and vice versa. And so my patient anywhere she turned unable to escape herself had no recourse but to—a certain activity. At any rate my patient was brought to the attention of Xaviero and Gottfried because of what was in fact a symptom. Call it X. I need not go into details. For I ask you, one medico to another, how but through cancelling its contents can the the symptom become a placeholder authorizing that multiplicity of relations unthinkable if I—if she—had confined ourselves to the literal horror of its initial meaning. In any case, X reared its all too ugly head about the time she, the patient, entered into relation with a subsection of a major international terrorist group working out of one of the city's major department stores. At first she was afraid to be unable to calmly face the challenge. Would she manage to throw that first bomb, permit herself to sacrifice innocents to the great cause—establishment of a homeland for magnates unjustly uprooted owing to mere treachery and greed. Don't be fooled: These terrorists are working for the powers that be. Their cause is the legitimation of the haves and the further debasement of the have nots. But terrorism per se does not interest me. There always were and there always will be such animals. Inevitable injustice on every level inevitably breeds them. What interests me is—but you've already guessed it, Dr. . . . Xman, is it. You have guessed it, haven't you. She gloriously overcame all trepidation. And yet—and yet—X did not cease with her triumph. In fact, she gave herself to X with redoubled passion, if one may speak, that is, of giving oneself to a symptom. What's that? What's that you say?" the doctor suddenly cried out a little truculently, not, Xman needed to believe, from any particular animus but rather from some kind of unlocalizable physiological turbulence. "Ah yes, of course, you New York mavericks will explain that the symptom—in this case X—not quite a symptom, not quite an activity, not quite in . . . being, if you understand me properly—that the symptom was simply in lag of the good news that all was well with Brunhildine who was getting on quite swimmingly in that international milieu. But such an explanation does not interest me, the redoubtable Dr. Q., in the least. And that is why I am here—to protest—precisely because such an explanation does not interest me in the least. Not even if it is true—not even if it is the true explanation. Hahaha. For such an explanation requires no active collaboration from me, the physician. I must accept it passively, no way of obliterating the normal hunger for verification through a strenuous undergoing. And I am no fond friend of passivity, my dear friend. Perhaps you are. I need to collaborate in the explanation. I need to work hard at the ultimate explanation so that what is purveyed in that ultimate may be verified through my visceral undergoing of its moments each and every of course resistant to my undergoing. I must swallow it bones and all and spew it forth undergone, certified grade A exegetical beef. But none of this happens with your fashionable 'New York explanation,' namely, that the symptom was in lag of the good news. Such an explanation simply parasitizes the quirks of physiology—and a constructed physiology at that—for who knows how long it takes for news, good or bad, to burrow deep into the spaces among rotting viscera? Second, such an explanation neither embodies nor drives toward the kind of ambiguity that should be our stock-in-trade. Surely you must know ambiguity is the self-respecting physician's stock-in trade. Surely as a physician consecrated body and soul to your vocation you must know it is off ambiguity that the symptom—I mean the vocation—must feed if it is to be a vocation at all. But where is the ambiguity when you tell me over the phone—as you did three weeks ago—and thanks again for

147

returning my call so promptly, it was so very kind—that the symptom simply is in lag of the good news and so investment in the symptom is redoubled.

"In short a symptom must embody a contradiction in terms. So what do we get, my dear Xman, may I call you dear colleague, for I must tell you, I like you tremendously though steadfast in my loathing of your politics. Rather what do we have. We have a hunger on the part of Brunhildine X to indulge in self-flagellatory activity X well after the provocatory fear and anguish have ceased. So that X suddenly is truly an unknown quantity, it exists beyond any formula, any category. Some would say Brunhildine von X persisted in X beyond an authentic need for X in order for once in her life to create and acquire some entity insusceptible to brackets and bracketing. For what was her life after all but a series of minute destructions always according to institutional specifications. So she fabricates a symptom—the venerable X. But when excruciating torment is no longer the case what happens? Simply this: The symptom, the X factor, becomes—no no no not an expression of torment, there is no torment, remember—but a skewed celebration of removal of the vigilance—the proprietary right—long exercised by the torment, up to then ostensibly the symptom's sole inducement to exist. Skewed and celebratory said symptom sets out on its own toward deliriously unhinged free expression, torment or no torment. X is then both avenue of escape *from* the torment induced by confrontation with the life-or-death challenge of international terrorism and reward for meeting the challenge with flying colors." Not knowing where the words came from, Xman asked, "Did Brunhildine von X ever exist in the absence of torment. Overwhelmed by provisional abatement in conspicuous torment she simply redoubled all efforts in behalf of the symptom's persistence, always presenting those efforts as a celebration of the removal of all tormenting snaffles to putatively craved well-being. But well-being was not craved nor was it ever craved. All that craving of well-being, all that courting of well-being, was a farce, a bloody farce, do you hear me?"

"But that is wonderful, wonderful, colleague." The redoubtable Dr. Q. apposing his sweaty palms positively foamed at the mouth with approbation and amazement. Xman began to be afraid: He did not want to be adept—if adept was indeed what he was beginning to be—at this new rent-paying chore. He needed to be found out and soon. He got up, walked to the window: Morning's clotted cumuli compliments of cosmic central casting were gone. "From what you tell me of Fraulein X—" "Yes, yes," Dr. Q. panted eagerly. "—It would appear she must go on being allowed to allow symptom von X to bubble up unmolested. You might as well know, Dr. Q., that anybody accepted for treatment is necessarily exceptional. And how is exceptionalness best manifested? In a proliferation of baffling symptoms, of course! Symptoms like the dread of impersonation proper to any vocation! The terror of impersonation proper to any vocation! The loathing, do you hear, the loathing of impersonation proper to any vocation! My life, I mean the life of our patients is a continuous discharge—of symptoms—and to a far greater degree than for others. Perhaps President Xaviero von Kulp has already intimated that we are thinking of changing our name to Symptom Society US of A. Symptoms make for uniqueness. In many ways, our patients are nothing without their symptoms. Don't get me wrong: Symptoms are painful and try to rid themselves of an inherent lack of reality through what we refer to in these not so hallowed precincts as—accelerated manifestation. Many physicians— I know you are not one of *their* number—confuse such accelerated manifestation with the smugness of dazzling vibrancy. But I know you do not look upon the symptom's

saraband as a floor show. A symptom wants to die to its
stench, its lack of being, as quickly as possible. Yet why is
the symptom saddled with a lack of being. Precisely because
the symptom's being is an embodied contradiction in terms.
As we saw in the classic example of Fraulein von der X. From
my point of view—the point of view of a philanthropic specialist—this contradiction in terms is thoroughly delightful,
there is nothing more remarkable, more truly real, take it
from me—this is thirty-odd years of experience talking and
not through its hat or its ass—than such contradiction in
terms. For it invites collaborative decipherment, the infernal
bugaboo of audience participation on an intimate scale. For
mass audiences always try to resolve a contradiction, to
bring manic oscillation to rest. Unfortunately, patients arriving here are unable to see themselves in the new light of
the symptom and persist in condemning themselves according to what they take to be the world's terms. You might say
that compliments of the symptom they have a vocation at
their very fingertips. Yet they try to disembarrass themselves
of the symptom as soon as possible. Ever so quickly, before
you can say Vasana Cittavritti. And how do they try to disembarrass themselves of this best part of themselves, this
dazzling core of potentiality. Some go the pathway of renunciation and restraint. Not that there is not much to be said
for renunciation and restraint in themselves, out of context.
For if our patients succeed in refraining from a particular X,
Y or Z they not only purify themselves but appropriate a
true and powerful force vastly surpassing the meager context
of temptation that teased it into life. But the trouble with
such force is that it threatens the whole economy of being. It
may very well cause the Empire State Building to topple or
all the female customers at Bloomingdale's to undergo men-
strual cramps at the same moment. Being simply cannot

endure such a masterly renunciation of its dubious plea-
sures. Therefore being retaliates via a tantrum. Being turns
symptomatic when confronted with the upsurge of a force
more powerful than its most powerful temptations. At any
rate, such renunciation does not lead to vocation. And we
must never forget that is why our patients are here—to
achieve a vocation. Vice-President Gottfried von Schmendrick may have hinted that we are thinking of changing the
clinic's name to Vocation Center of All the Americas. But
more of that later. Either our patients refrain from the symptom or drive manifestation to the breaking point, the very
peak of delirious contradiction. And in this way the bidding—the will—of the symptom (driven more than anything
by a desire to manifest itself, to see the light, to actualize
itself outside a putrefying latency) is done. But this will is
subsumed in turn by one even larger. Manifested to the
breaking point the symptom perishes and through extinction escorts the patient—an infinite sum of such symptoms—closer to repose. But what is this repose but refusal of
self as a sum of pullulating latencies striving toward the
sooty light of 60-watt bulblets. So damned be repose. Patients are not here to sleep. We offer no advanced degree in
napping at our institution of higher learning and higher
earning, hahaha. For symptoms can be profitable. But more
of that later . . . when we meet for dinner. Do you have any
preference—Creole, Pakistani, Ugandan?" Xman cleared his
throat and with startling rawness added, "All kidding aside, I
hope you are aware dear Doctor, herr Doctor,"—here Herr
dear Doktor eminent though he might be in and out of his
putative field of expertise positively bristled at the allusion
to obtuseness latent in Xman's masterfully adversarial
tone—"that our patients come seeking not reconciliation
with self through pallid eroticization of the doctor/patient

dyad but—but—but—total emancipation from self's outworn tonality. But emancipation is not repose. New York is
emancipated but it is hardly in a state of repose, hahaha. Our
patients are taught to seek to shed the self by actualizing a
maximal number of symptoms. For it is only by shedding
the self—its noisome particularities—its noisome allegiance
come hell or high water to those particularities—that one
can enter at last into the majority of a vocation however
humble however exalted. Vocation above all, that is our
motto. As God is our co-pilot. But you must be wondering:
Don't we consider symptoms part and parcel of the self's
noisome particularity? No no no, not at all, on the contrary.
When we speak of particularity we speak of a straitjacketed
quasi-maniacal predilection for what one is in any case condemned to be—hereditarily, ethnically, physiognomically,
ectoplasmically. And the symptom sides (and with what,
you may ask) against that craving for a well-ordered particularity. Our patients learn to actualize their symptoms but
through a special technique taught only within these purlieus actualization no longer implies extinction and death-
like repose. Just for the record—the broken record—no
symptom is ever overcome and shed. Simply superseded by
some other it is relegated to a stance on which the usurper
soon to suffer a similar fate can cast an instantaneously
retrospective beam of sooty fatuity. And so on and so forth.
So through this special technique—available in colloidal
suspension only through our mailing house in Secaucus—
actualization of the symptom no longer comes to mean extinction. In short, we have effected a revolution whereby the
life-giving symptoms of our vocation-seekers can see the
light without disintegrating. For it is in the foul rag-and-bone
shop of the symptoms, or rather, in the spaces between
symptoms as sharply demarcated gobbets of purulence, that

incunabula of the vocation are to be exhumed and worked over." Xman very quickly shielded his eyes as if their weep ing was due to the intense haze even if there was no haze, only the minuscule blight of tepid overcast against which backdrop a few black-bellies, nacre-rimmed, perdured. "So now, Dr. Q.E.D. you hopefully understand that our patients are all driven by a hunger for emancipation from particulari- ties of the straitjacketed self—every self maimed to the same sameness of predictable differences. Only the uninitiated will believe that symptoms—bedwetting, for example, pref- erably at an advanced age—stand in the way of said emanci- pation. But nobody—nobody do you hear—will ever have the audacity to number our patients among the uninitiated, the brute benighted. And once these patients come to realize— and if they have half-a-brain up their butts they come to realize pretty damn quick—that their symptoms are also striving toward emancipation, wish to bask in the half-light for which our planet is justly famous, that blinding light favorable to the deployment of an equally blinding self-con- tradiction justly characterized by some of our more mallea- ble sages as the bedrock of being on or off this planet's rotten husk—once they come to realize symptoms are also crawl- ing toward the light favorable to dehiscence, death and resur- rection then they easily accept the apparent obstacles put by those symptoms in the way of emancipation. For in a very short time they will have learned that when we talk voca- tion we are talking haphazard obstructions forever in the way of its arborescence. When we talk vocation we are talk- ing parasitization of the symptom's vision of the world even if that vision seems to go against the grain of the vocation. Our patients come to see things our way—the company- way—that is to say, they quickly find themselves feeding off the apparent obstacles embodied in their symptoms. They come to accept what in fact turns out to be not obstacle but mere delay, mere and ultimately fruitful prorogation of emancipation. They find themselves living emancipation not as endpoint but as inexhaustible process. They find that delay—detour—is essential if vocation is to bloom. And vocation does bloom. You have only to examine our active roster of doctors, lawyers, accountants, dentists, college professors, doctors, lawyers, doctors, lawyers, doctors, lawyers, diplomats, typists, overqualified administrative assistants, overqualified office managers, programmers, typists, typists, typists, dentists, dentists, typists, dentists, typists, orthodontists—to convince yourself of the gamut of the bloom. What is our secret. For, I'm sure you'll agree, this is no time to be modest. What is our bloody secret. Simple: We allow the birth, bloom, subsidence, resurrection of symptoms to stand in the way of swift emancipation so that emancipation can ultimately give birth to the warts and wattles of authentic vocation. We allow symptoms to play themselves out as necessary detour for patients in quest of a vocation. In short, we permit ourselves to derive maximum benefit from the discovery that emancipation and vocation are nothing less than mutually exclusive."

So as not to seem daunted by this young whippersnapper who at any rate hardly practiced what he preached, Dr. Q. said, "I must take my patient to lunch. In addition to everything else, I am striving to cure her of the anorexia your cronies have succeeded in inducing." He rose brusquely without sign of farewell and left the room. A minute after he was gone Xaviero hurried in and said, "I heard it all, I heard it all, you were passable. I must admit, however, that you did apply to perfection all the lessons I taught you, especially those of last night on the horse's-assy slopes above the river Hudson. There might be a permanent full-time position for you from all this. Something truly secure in the works, something to make your—our—name in the company. for we are judged by the company we keep." Xman was tempted to respond but felt it was not the moment to say he tended to dread the kind of cradle-to-grave security Xaviero seemed to have in mind. Then remembering Rosalie's swollen belly he gasped at the recurring nightmare of his own "irresponsibility." "Why don't you break for lunch too. There will be some more stooges coming in later but after your encounter with Dr. Q. they needn't prove too difficult. Not to someone with your . . . credentials." Poker-faced Xman observed, "Credentials are the work of a moment." Xaviero gigged conspiratorially then vanished as quickly as he had appeared. But had he appeared quickly. "Just one minor point," he simpered with wormlike affability. Looking him hard and straight in the eye, Xman braced himself for the most pernicious of all bugbears—constructive criticism. For wasn't such criticism all too often contingent on some organic exiguity not worth a fishwife's fart—a flea up the ass, a dull throb between the balls. "Xman, Xman, Xman, I see you looking a bit constricted. I couldn't improve on your eloquence. But your comprehensiveness—your capacity to cover all essential points—left something, no everything, to be desired, not that our favorite gasbag necessarily noticed anything omitted. It suddenly occurs to me you seem to have forgotten the most important point of all—laid out in great detail on the grassy gassy slopes above the Hudson—I am referring to the components of therapy—our therapy. We utilize, remember, the principal of the label, the caption. After a few preliminary sessions, each client—I loathe, I positively loathe, the word *patient*—is given a label in and out of which he or she is obliged to thrash indignation and outrage. We choose the labels at random—you know that. What interests us are the

patient's frantic efforts to outwit the malevolence of a massive inaccuracy parading as incontrovertible truth. Through
the thrashing protest we are able at last to discern the true
state of the patient's soul and prescribe a course of treatment
(of course in which labels are no longer permitted to figure)
conducive to the flowering of an old-fashioned vocation. And
you forgot all about this, Xman—I mean, how we invent a
label at random to determine the patient's mettle, so to
speak, as he thrashes against the label. You also forgot to
mention how some of our candidates—those subsequently
dropped and none too tactfully, I might add, hahaha: Spare
the rod and pass the ammunition—willingly succumb to
their label, positively salivate in proximity to its hindquarters simply because they cannot conceive of life outside the
label as anything but a vacuum eddying toward madness." At
this point Xaviero went quite mad himself as twitching and
giggling he scratched balls, nape, and belly simultaneously
until recalled to order by the tocsin of his partner's nonsensi-
cal shriek that at the same time made clear it would brook
no further frivolity.

Xman was not hungry but descended to street level anyway. He had to see Rollins, talk about this newfound newfangled success and what it might bode for success of the true
work, the personal project. As Project Coordinator for half
and that the better half of New York—yes, he had heard as
much—Rollins would surely be able to determine whether
or not he was at a crossroads.

Xman walked down to Soho where Rollins had his newest
office. He was always changing, his secretary said with a
bright smile, New York's brightest. Rollins did not refuse to
see him but seemed to be trying to seem busier than usual, it
was as if he was irritated by the presumption on Xman's part
of a continuity in their relation. But was theirs a relation:

Once again words might, under his very nose, be anastomosing to invent an impossible reality faster than he could challenge the invention. As if to win Rollins's solicitude he painted the impersonation session in colors direr and grimier than those with which he had in fact come through. In a single bolt Rollins rose from his desk, muttered, "imbecile," and closed the door, all the time preserving a tiptoeing mysteriousness that had become, for Xman at least, his trademark. Long after Rollins was reseated Xman continued to be astonished. But he forced himself to say, brutally, "Well, as one imbecile to another have you dug up any projects on which I might exercise the talents you seemed so sure about not so long ago." Mumbling ever more quickly and incomprehensibly Rollins clearly seethed at this question daring to stain the enormity of his commitment by stooping to solicitation of positive instances. "If I—Rollins—one of the busiest men in New York—have never stooped to demanding positive instances of a putative genius for some specific vocation why should I—the above-mentioned Rollins—be harassed by the willfulness—the positive scandalousness—of a subneophyte impatience for proofs, proofs, proofs of strenuous exertions on behalf of that genius. Hildine!" In came the little secretary, no longer all smiles, her nose wrinkled in anticipation. In a voice politely flaunting enormous restraint Rollins said, "Hildie, do we have any proofs, proofs, proofs." Hildine shrugged and exited. Xman looked at Rollins, he did not know what the spectacle meant. "I am making definite provisions for you, youngish man, but they take time. You come here out of the blue with your dozen canvases. At least half of that dozen portray naked women in the throes of catamenial cramp with blood or feces or both emerging from the anus and you expect me, on the basis of such a potpourri, to make you a deal." Once he

had corrected Rollins—his canvases were still increate—
Xman made a feeble effort to depict himself as still, but had
he ever been, a good investment. Never had he nor would he
ever stoop to truck with anuses, female or otherwise. Rollins
sighed impatiently as if what in point of fact he now most
needed to hear was nothing less than a staunch avowal of
even stauncher commitment to anuses, preferably female.

The silence becoming unbearable, Xman reverted to the
subject of impersonation. He loathed himself trying to win
Rollins over through analysis of what had not yet even become a predicament. But couldn't this be a predicament too:
predicament's failure to emerge into the maturity of authentic predicament.

Finally Rollins said: "Imbecile," but this time gently, and
most to himself, like a mandarin (Dung, no Dung-Ho, Dy-
nasty) on the commode. "You weep over your fate. Don't you
know that the humiliation and the excruciation serve a vital
function. They not only distract you from the excruciating
slowness of recognition for what you are one day sure to
produce but are also a source of raw material."

"But the point is to get to enrichment faster than it can
undo me." Rollins looked up. "Did you say something. Your
problem," he went on, "is that you metabolize every painful
situation—long before it is even the least bit painful—as
RAW MATERIAL—you bracket it away as a datum long before it has evolved into the excipient in which you have the
luxury of immersing yourself." Xman was disappointed.
This was reminding him of something somebody had said
long ago. He could not remember who, only he instinctively
knew that the sharpest contrast ought to have been maintained between Rollins and that phantom. And it was not
being maintained, which only proved—

"I thought you said I should look for raw material," Xman
sulked.

"But you're going about it the wrong way." After a long pause in a simpering glassy-eyed tone that was new to Xman's experience of him Rollins said, "Did I ever tell you about my friend, the great creator Z. He always made it a point to throw himself heartily into what he called 'the disaster of the everyday.' There was that time— But then again, you are not Z." This was Rollins's first adversion to a paradigm. Loathing him for the invidious pusillanimity of such a ploy Xman at the same time shuddered for the ploy's true measure of Rollins's obviously qualified championship prodigally tinctured as it was with exasperation and reluctance, in other words, spite.

"And what is Z doing now," Xman said, in as casual a tone as he could muster. "Oh," Rollins replied, monumentally condescending, and waved his hand as if to obliterate Xman's blundering intrusion into a reminiscence too beautiful for words or at least for the kind of words he was obliged to use with somebody like Xman, "he dedicates himself totally to *his* project. Last time he was in town he begged me to drive him to the public beach. He wanted to listen to the sound of receding wavelets over multicolored pebbles. He specifically instructed me: The pebbles had to be multicolored. He had a way of listening—" Rollins was clearly enthralled by such a fulguration of the workerly consciousness in play; Xman's skewed exclusion added to, perhaps created, his enthrallment.

Xman wanted to weep for the hopelessness of it all. The only way to alert Rollins to his being was to analyze its inadequacy and he was sick of analyzing his own instead of the world's truer, more dastardly, inadequacy. "According to you before I can throw myself into an event a shift—an intricate play of the mechanism—files it away as usable only at some later date. Yet mightn't it be true, Rollins—I mean Mike—that the true work files away the event, files away and breaks it down into assimilable form before, that is, it can incapacitate me for labor in its—the true work's—behalf."

"Well, first of all, Xman, we, I mean you, are not quite at the stage of laboring in behalf of the true work. At this point you are lucky if you are merely waiting for upsurges of a possible vantage on the true work. You are not Z, clearly you are not Z, why at your age Z— Second, the true work would never stand in the way of authentic enlightenment-laden suffering. Now and again the true work may choose to appropriate a sick fragment, the way a concerned parent chooses to remove a splinter from the tender flesh of its firstborn, the way a begoggled motorist chooses to remove a fallen log from a particularly sharp curve in the roadway. But in the large it only seems the true work eliminates vital elements of what is sure to become inseparable from its own being. In actual fact it is you, always you, who, once fodder for the true work attains a certain inevitability, delimits, contours, brackets, consigns to the slagheap. You bottle away your only real conduit to true discovery. For example—instead of remaining uptown with your boss and living impersonation to the very limit you run away as fast as your legs will carry you, you come here bleating, painting the blackest picture you know how, you arrive with the barest shards of an experience expecting me to help you denature and bottle them away. That invaluable experience—yes, invaluable—I'm all for experience—can't get enough myself—is now rendered for all practical purposes useless to the true work. That is, if you and I are speaking of the same entity when we speak of the true work. Are we?" he asked, slyly, provokingly, as if all further connection between them depended on the answer, as if Rollins could hardly be expected to go on "handling" him if the answer did not turn out to be the only conceivable answer. Then, in a resonant bass worthy of the Old Testament or Verdi's Amonasro Rollins raising a forefinger (nicotine-stained) intoned, "Woe unto him who dries up the springs of torment before they have gushed their fill," trailing off, or so it seemed to Xman, in voluptuous contemplation of, say, the inerranable exploits of Z, so different, so vastly different, from Xman's . . . virtual absence of same. In a whisper Rollins added, "Before your copious inadequacy has been beneficently flayed on its rack the vital phenomenon has become: the archetype of itself, its intensity (what you refer to as its excruciation) as shrilly futilitarian as the screeching tail of a peacock. Or might I say the screeching asshole of a peacock."

Xman knew there was no point changing the subject. "I know you: Having transmogrified the blessed event into its own archetype you hope it will smuggle you, unnoticed, into the dream time. Don't you think Z also hungered for a little junket in the dream time. But he went about it another way. He went about it like a man. If he hungered for a little whiff of the dream time—time out of time where acts are no longer irreversible and the stench of a personal history is obliterated via participation in the gestures of being's all—he never confused that hunger with a hunger to produce the project. When the day's work was done and only then he would settle back, against the fur, against the fur. That was his key phrase, his watchword, his shibboleth. And slowly but surely he would row himself back to that moment just before time—history—irreversibility—unleashed itself on his head, on his world. He made it his business to focus on an unpleasant task of daily life and consecrate himself to both its conscientious execution and the excruciated memoration of that execution every day day in day out . . . for he knew—how foolish of me, he knows—he knows instinctively what is given to very very few of us to know, namely, that the tedium of flawless execution of the lowliest tasks cannot continue indefinitely without foundering on the glacier of mammoth reparation in the form of explosive change." Xman wanted to suggest that it was precisely the nature of tedium, of routine, to continue indefinitely. But how could a patrician, a parlor anarchist, like Rollins be expected to understand this nth law of tepidynamics. "Don't you see, he exhausted all his former lives, exhausted brute duration itself. But I don't think you are ready to relinquish all *your* former lives—you are too attached to them, for all your anathematizing of those lives." Then feeling he had been too harsh or in order merely to bring the interview to a close he said, "I've talked about you to some friends." Xman tried to make his silence mean what he could not bear to bring himself to utter. Rollins shrugged as if in fact the fatal question, What did the bastards say, had been asked anyway. In desperation Xman cried out: "The destiny of the true work: It puffs along with excruciating slowness." "That is because one's products, once complete, deliver themselves up though quite of their own free will to the less than solicitous rhythm of the powers-that-be and that rhythm is a rhythm infinitely slower than any mortal rhythm after birth. But we're hardly at that stage, are we. Where are your products, I mean, it would have been understandable for Z to have complained like you, years ago, before he was enshrined as the prodigy he indisputably is and will always remain. But you, now really." Xman wanted to run back Xaviero-ward as if there was his true home at last. Xman wanted to run. Clearly Rollins could not be depended upon to make everything better by rescuing him from a lifetime of Xavieros. Xaviero did, in fact, call that night to tell him not to try so passionately to engage visiting physicians (Why hadn't he, by the way, returned that afternoon. Just as well, thin flow of stooges.) in a tourney of eristic passion, but rather to point to his own passion, but passionlessly, as it were, as to some

tried-and-true therapeutic device, no gadget, in the engagement and disengagement of whose gears disorderly disorder-
ing passion was never permitted to play, lubricatively
speaking, even a bit part.

After what he hurriedly tried to establish as the failure of
his interview with Rollins, Xman was more docile that he
might otherwise have been. When he arrived at Xaviero's the
next day a man was already seated in the waiting room,
beside an excitable-looking lady of the exiled-countess variety—exiled, however, most probably by way of Flatbush and
the Duchess of Duckworth Beauty Salon, corner of Fifth and
Fluke. "This is Doctor Quixot," Xaviero simpered, as the
person or rather the personage in question rose to full
height. The woman too began to rise but subsided to pos-
tural incoherence before she was anywhere close to complete erectness. "A miscarriage of justice, a miscarriage," the
doctor exclaimed through pearly gritted teeth, more gritted
however than pearly. "At any rate," seeing he was not getting
the hoped for rise out of Xman, "I received a copy of your
brochure 'To the Physician'—is that the name of it." Was the
question a trap or prelude to a round of completely inoffen-
sive chitchat between colleagues. "In fact—or should I say, in
farct—I've brought it with me." Xman watched inexplicably
spellbound as the fattish tallish robustish fellow removed a
tattered blue pamphlet from an expensive-looking through
unmonogrammed leather portfolio. Xman hoped that this
look, now fixed beyond modification, was one not of apprehension but calm pleasure, as at the imminent prospect of
fruitful confabulation with a colleague peaked at the same
level of substantial expertise. He hoped he was looking like
somebody familiar with people pulling out brochures in a
hurry.

"There are certain questions I have," said Dr. Quixot. "You
speak here, page xi, of encouraging the patient not to think

of himself as sick." Xman looked Xaviero-ward, said, "I think we can discuss all this in my office," to which Xaviero replied with authoritatively subliminal nod accompanied by brief eclipse of eyeballs under heavy lids. As they were going into the office—Xman had no idea where this office might be—the doctor whispered, "Doesn't it somehow stink of platitude to make saints of the warped." Xman shrugged just before he reached "his" desk. The gesture was new to him, intrigued him, became the very paraph of his impersonation, did it belong to him, to whom then did it belong.

Once they were both seated with lady patient lost to mauvish shadows in the corner the doctor said, "Oh, oh, oh, so easy to impugn things as they are. And leave the madmen alone. Sick of all these sickening bourgeois folk who live madness, vicariously of course, as some kind of verdict on the comfy little life they cannot begin to have the courage to confront and overthrow." Adjusting the Venetian blinds behind—they reminded him grievously of light-and-shade effects of the orphanage days—he needed to be doing something in order to dissimulate self-preparation—Xman said, "It may be easy to impugn things as they are en masse but it is quite another matter to pinpoint specific targets of revulsion. Oh, oh, oh forgive me, I don't know what I am saying." He applied the underside of his forearm to the abundant sweat of his brow. "Oh, I'm going to faint. Someone should be telling me this. I should be listening passively, taking it—drinking it all in. I should be imbibing these thoughts at the foot of some massive master instead of spilling the little I don't understand in front of sparrows like you—I don't mean, esteemed Doctor, you are a birdbrain. It's just that—" He was on the verge of a symptom, an impossible symptom, a symptom that transcended what he perceived as its immediate and vulgar formulation—a dead faint. "It's just that I can foresee, more than foresee, taste, somebody telling me exactly what I am telling you. But I am not ready to tell what I am almost ready to hear from alien though guiding lips." He cleared his throat. The mauvish lady seemed to stir in shadow. "I don't know about your patients, Doctor, but mine are masters of this art of pinpointing—the given. And not just the technological, real estate, and corporate givens. At any rate, what we call sickness with such a self-satisfied air of flourishing is simply the 'uncanny' ability to shift attention from the gangrenous root of things as they are toward those moments when the things solidified and stabilized one way rather than an infinity of others. My patients are aware of so many simultaneous alternatives. With respect to the patients themselves, one not so careful look from top to toe and you are never allowed to forget they themselves never forget they embody merely one among infinitely many possibilities. And at every minute they fight against and try to uproot that one possibility. Through the transparency of their impersonation of what they are, what they are condemned to happen to be, I am able to take note with spectacular clarity of all these other possibilities. At the very moment I am solicited to observe their embodiment of apparently only one possibility among too many it is as if they are about to shed its skin in favor of—of—nonbeing. Being is too restrictive. Sickness—mental, physical, pastoral-tragical, tragical-comical—is nothing but the struggle to get past the single possibility of the sickness toward that infinity of which it furnishes the nastiest teasing glimpses. Sickness—madness—is nothing but the excruciation of a vantage on all that might have been— should have been as long of course as it is not." Xman lay in wait for the expression on Dr. Quixot's face. He looked as if he was about to sneeze, the lady in shadow was writhing a dumbshow of approbation. "Don't you see, don't you see," Xman cried, emboldened by the lady's writhing as if it was "in his favor," "what we call their sickness is simply a sick-ened awareness of how appallingly feeble is this one variant of being with which they are saddled." He felt once again on the verge of fainting; the craving to faint must have some-thing to do with a vague sense of a wider, far wider, applica-tion for his present assertion. "Their sickness, then, is merely the clogged gateway to elegiacal vantage on a horde of missed possibilities. Is it any wonder then that their embodi-ment of what they are—that is to say, the appalling and feeble possibility with which they have, through no fault of their own, been saddled—becomes nothing more than an impersonation thick with ironical sideshows, slashed by the milkiest and sometimes the lustiest accents of disavowal? As if I, for example—I received my degree from—in the year—as if I were to impersonate the glorious healer I indubi-tably am." The Doctor squirmed. "We are all impersonators, Herr Doktor!" Xman cried, suddenly beside himself, sud-denly convinced he would at least, at last, find in the lady in shadow a fierce partisan of paroxysmal disgust. "Herr Dok-tor, Herr Doktor, your New Year's Eve impersonation of Joan Crawford or is it Garbo, is only a degenerate case of what I'm—we're—talking about." The lady was suddenly—as sud-denly as he had waxed paroxysmal—very quiet, still, seemed to be clicking her tongue in disapproval. At that moment the door of the consulting room opened. Xaviero marched in. Xman hadn't noted his absence. "What is going on here. Slob! Incompetent! We could hear you at the other end of the clinic. The side that faces the East River: The police just called. You're interfering with river traffic. That tug out there painted pale blue, for example—do you want us to be evicted." Xaviero stared hard—exophthalmically—at the raw recruit. Xman could not prevent himself from smiling slyly. This, he saw, heightened Xaviero's disgust for his very being. "Now, now," he surprised himself saying, "I was merely explaining office politics and, incidentally, my 'theory of sickness,' to use the highfalutin phrase you had the goodness to teach me, to this bedraggled colleague of yours, especially since he and the missus seem to be on their last legs spiritually speaking. At any rate, he is no colleague of mine. You can be sure of that. I was merely pointing out all authentic being is impersonation for if truly authentic it is necessarily sick with the bracketedness—the suffocating demarcatedness—of itself, as one more alternative among too many, as one turd too many amid the too myriad heap of dogshit or is it horseshit extending, on a clear day, from Bolívar equestrian to Christopher C astride little more than his self-importance." Xman waited. Surprisingly, Xaviero took a ringside seat next to the lady in shadow.

"I am sorry to say, Xaviero, that I will very shortly be leaving your employ for good. I find both you and my—your—colleagues too shortsighted, far too limited. I need something more than the medical profession—something better than any profession. I need something consecrated to the destruction—on a grand scale—of all professions. For what are professionals but misdiagnosers: you, Xaviero, and they daily commit egregious errors of diagnosis and treatment convinced, nevertheless, that all will always be well since errors committed with one may be rectified in the next patient or the next after that. No, I cannot function that way. I need guarantees or a sphere where incertitude does not have repercussions for those I loathe. For I loathe my patients, as do you. Hasn't my esteemed colleague here been telling me, for example, that in his view the sick are those who because they wrestle unendlingly within an obsession are incapable of seeing: sunsets, bicycle wheels crushing 'helpless' old ladies, masses of bluish concrete falling from the heights of skyscrapers onto the pickled rumps of—etc., etc. In contradistinction I believe only the obsessed see truly.

167

For they see things as things must be seen—as embodied conflict. They are, the truly obsessed, obliged to wrest the target of their seeing from a monolithic sludge that does all it can to prevent seeing's emergence. But in vain, in vain. Or rather, every seen becomes an obstruction to contemplation of the one thing that, obsessionally, matters. So that the exasperated effort to remove thing seen from the obsessional pathway is the form seeing necessarily takes with form thereby all too accurately—all too sublimely—miming intrinsic and inevitable content of thing seen as site, locus, of unbearable tension—configuration of widening struggle. A sunset is after all but the triumph of bloated orb over massed array of slumberous vesicular rack.

"In any case what disturbs me most is esteemed colleague's insidious—yes, insidious—technique of keeping his patients at the end of torturous tether. He ostentatously abstains from labelling them as sick"—here Xman looked Xaviero daringly dead in the eye—"all the time all too clearly convinced—and letting them know he is convinced—of their sickness. So the subject of scrawnily eroticized encounter becomes my colleague's 'admirable restraint' with regard to a situation that cries out for label. I, for one, make no bones about labelling my patients—correctly, no aleatory caprices, I leave the avant-garde to the avant-garde—nor about telling them point blank how sick they are and of what their sickness consists whereas this little worm hems and haws a glorious abstention from label for all to see, or rather smell, all the time sourly holding feeble abstention over their wearied heads. And of course he demands something in return, doesn't he, my dear." This was Xman's first direct appeal to the lady in shadow. She extended her arm as if reaching toward him across a vast distance. And all down its duration she tried to give, or better yet, locate the impression that this gesture of mingled supplication and command had begun long before any invoking horseplay on Xman's part. "Of course he demands something in return. He demands that one never give way to outburst, curative outburst, beneath whose foaming searing brine even the most Poseidonian physician may be drowned forever. No, and the little lady over yonder will surely bear me out, won't you, little lady, in return for his supposed broadmindedness patient is expected to remain forever civilized, drinking in words of wisdom that cannot possibly serve any curative function because they are simply that—words subsisting at the level of words and tracing no blaze along and among the spaces of subterfuge-laden viscera. He never allows you, does he, madame,"—here she rose, collapsed, and began crawling toward him over the tiled floor—"to enact the despair that is forever gnawing, gnawing, gnawing." As she went on crawling he realized her crawling resembled Tanya's shrieking. In its "grim inexorability." Xman rose from "his" desk with a smothered cry of triumphant anguish and standing over the prostrate creature tried to lift her up into the muted mauvish light of late afternoon. He found her far more resilient, far less classically prostrate, than he had imagined. In this case images rather than words had anastomosed inventing a reality he had not been quick enough to challenge. As usual, too passive. "Get away from her!" Quixot cried out. "You poisoner," he added without conviction. Xaviero was clearly at a loss. "These are strong words to use to a valued member of my staff," he ventured, tittering. "Not that I don't agree in this particular case, of course, but still—but still—the proprieties . . ." The veiled lady made what sounded like a growl. Jrgrgwgwbugrll, she intoned. Turning away Xaviero as if to the four winds muttered, I have always felt strongly that it debases somebody to label his greatness in this way. Ggjjgzzjj, the patient pursued. And less effervescently, Vzvzvz. As an already timeworn if

169

not time-honored denizen in the realm of disjunctions Xman, and this from the very bottom of his wild tyro heart, hungered to call attention to, to intercede in behalf of, this yet another among so many already encountered on the sidewalks of Gotham. In this case the disjunction was between what was heard/perceived by Xaviero and what was meant by the veiled lady. And who was to say that he, Xman, mightn't make his name if not as company flunkey extraordinaire then at least as true worker tabulating just such radical disjunctions between, for example, what is simultaneously seen and heard in a subway toilet, smelled and seen in an East Village soup kitchen, heard and tasted amid the hills and dales of Central Park, or failing these between what is lived and subsequently rehearsed in a therapy dive just like Xaviero's, or failing this between what is seen and the time allotted to the seeing when said seeing is especially difficult to gulp down even amid the austere trappings of a Soho art cinema. What she, the veiled lady—creature eminently worthy of Ashton/Elgar—was proclaiming here of latent, precocious, belated or posthumous genius unattended and unsung, was clearly not characteristic of what she allowed herself to proclaim—and did she ever in fact muster enough bravado to proclaim—elsewhere. She was proclaiming hereabouts what, Xman was sure, she permitted herself under no circumstances to even whisper elsewhere lest she fall prey to the debasement Xaviero had just evoked so cavalierly. Extrapolating mercilessly, Xaviero was going about his business making it his business to postulate a seamless continuity between what his madmen brought him here and what consequently they must bring elsewhere when to Xman's virgin sensorium at least it was clear what they brought or rather bought here was self-reparation in the shadow of Xaviero's good intentions—reparation in the name of interminable pretermission elsewhere. In short, for dazzlingly accoutred derelicts like the veiled lady Xaviero's was a warm bath in a cold cosmos. Too lazy to undergo their life outside the bath through ceaseless deduction from particulars (how they rubbed one buttock with a washcloth, how they applied the pink heart-shaped bar of perfumed soap to their privates) Xaviero preferred to create a blatant blanket one-to-one correspondence between bath and all that was not bath, thereby calling eternally into question, at least for one as acute as Xman hoped someday to become, the very status of the bath as warm, as bath. Xman wanted to cry out that what the veiled lady proclaimed in his, Xaviero's, presence, had never been, would never be proclaimed in all that was not warm bath. To others the veiled lady would never have proclaimed her genius but coming to Xaviero she was completely outside herself. And so she could allow herself this little fit of self-definition driven by accumulated exasperation. What she was with Xaviero and what she was outside Xaviero's precincts were both irreducible to that ever-elusive being that was the real veiled lady now prostrate before Xman's wonderment. Coming to Xaviero was a vacation from essence AND everyday existence away from Xaviero was a postponement of essence. So of the vacation and the postponement was born the veiled lady's truth, a truth that issued steaming and smelly from the buttocks of the genius-proclaiming phrase, Vhshdg dbsbd tutu. Seeing the lady in question was not likely to emerge from—relinquish—her prostration—seemed to love it, seemed, in a word, content to arrest emancipation at this intermediate stage of enthralled and enthralling defiance, Xman fled. Before leaving the building—"forever" he told himself—he could not however prevent himself from returning to the consulting room for one last peek. A disconcerting spectacle met his eyes: The lady hadn't budged. Xaviero and Dr. Quixot were whispering in a corner but not that which had formerly been her province. Periodically they referred in uni-son their spidery gazes to the case still in question. "Don't worry," Xman began, in response to Xaviero's throwing out his arms at once accusatorily and apotropaically. "I have only one more thing to say and I'll say it all the same—quickly—so you two lovebirds can get back to deciding on how to dispose of the corpse. She's not long for the world, poor thing. I think it is disgusting—truly disgusting—that this colleague of mine, no longer esteemed, is encouraged to ostentatiously abstain from label and hold such abstention over the heads of his flock when it would be so simple to label—label the right way—thereby allowing the sick one—the tormented one—the right to protest and struggle against the inadequacy of that label. For the right label is always inadequate precisely because it induces a sense of helpless-ness—or rather even greater helplessness—in a being already too much overwhelmed by the world's too massive rightness on all counts. For what is cure, gentlemen, but self-affirma-tion through struggle—as struggle—against the blatant in-adequacy of more than adequate correct label toward a flickering but ultimately localizable core of truth. And what is that truth but the truth of the original label but arrived at via the patient's own slender means. Look at her collapsing there under the weight of symptoms. Knowing how difficult it is for symptoms to impose themselves on the body impoli-tic at the very least you should have the decency to obstruct and thereby stimulate their evolution with labels—right la-bels, always the right labels. Don't just stand there—give names to her symptomatic crawling and slobbering. Good-bye." Just before the door closed Xman heard Xaviero slimily affirm: "Our therapeutic approach has nothing to do with labels, imbecile! We are enlightened. We are the vanguard."

Stepping inside their hole—he had now come to think of it as a hole—it was the winter of '76, just before the rents started their obscene climb toward inaccessibility for all but international drug moguls and their molls—he decided on the spur of the moment not to denounce Xaviero and Co. That was tiresome—and even worse, captionable: Pretentious failure denounces his rejectors. No, he could not bear to be cocooned in such a cartoon, at least not tonight: his first night off the job after such glorious careering. Instead he found himself whinnying, "Hi honey. I'm home." Immediately fascinated by the creature he found himself adumbrating in the syllables, he could almost smell—touch—its slightly acrid breath on his own face, the breath unmistakable of the family man. And at the same time he felt sorrow that he would never evolve into this family man, this mythical figure both ridiculous and awesomely inaccessible on whom he must vent impotent rage rather than investigate a flouting inability to join its ranks in other than italicized regalia. "How was your day," he said sneeringly when he saw Rosalie approach from the bathroom where the light was on. The intensity of the raw bulb when it was not quite night depressed him infinitely and somehow vindicated a sneering ironic depiction of what he would never be.

"I've lost my job," he told her. "I quit," he added, seeing for a split second disappointment and anger, daring her to give way to disappointment and anger on her own behalf and that of the unborn. His sneering allusion to the usual lack of butter, eggs, and bread dared her not to move away from her own discontentment to exclusive consideration of his own, the most mammoth on God's unwilling earth. He dared her torment not to accept interment/internment in the night courts of his own until further notice. "I'm doomed," he said, through gritted teeth. "No butter, no eggs, this hole, I'm doomed. I should never have been born."

She was about to make some comment but refrained. And to muffle any possible expression of discontent, disapproval, disagreement, realistic fear, he had to run to her, as so often before, or was this the very first time, with the most extreme formulation of what he perceived her wanting though not daring to say. Armed to the teeth with this most extreme formulation he was thereby . . . thereby . . . arranging to be spared any further provocation. "I'm doomed," he added, once more. Regarding the brilliant electric blue over the Hudson's left thigh he had spoken, decisively, out of the blue.

But Rosalie had still not (as far as he could observe from her reflection in the depths of the pane competing for his full attention with the sunset beyond) completely abandoned her preoccupation with his newborn joblessness. He refused to believe in her concern for his welfare. So he added once again, "I'm doomed." He saw her move slightly and as if to stave off a movement too decisive for their relation he said, "I curse this life. I loathe life, the laws of life. I should never have allowed you to get involved with me, made you pregnant."

Despite all his efforts both to intimidate and appeal with pronouncements on the order of, Life is a shit, Rosalie could still not be shaken from asking, "What will you do now." He waited a moment at the window, went into the kitchen, bypassing her without a look, opened the cabinet, took one of their few plates and threw it against the refrigerator door handle. After a long silence, which he underwent terrified of her reaction, Xman said, "There's your answer." Over and over he played back her question to reinduce the feeling that had somehow permitted him to give way to such an outrush. Spent, he was now totally dissociated from his plight, free, untouched, unlesioned. So why had he smashed a perfectly decent plate. In retrospect, the hastily concocted retrospect that was the only retrospect his kind ever knows, the question seemed less a provocation than a pretext.

174

"What was so horrible about my question," Rosalie asked herself out loud. Now she stood at the window, the sunset less fierce. "Unless it was less the question than the distance you have come from that core to which the question, in all innocence, spoke and of which it painfully reminded you. And so you had to get away from the question as quickly as possible."

As nothing further was to be gained—true, or invention of anastomosing words?—from remaining together in the same room—their apartment was nothing more than a big room, Xman noticed that now—they decided to take a walk. On too-too-too fashionable Columbus Avenue, bending over to scoop up a dime or quarter, he couldn't make it out in the thick-thronged dusk, he felt a discreet tap on his back, not far from the sacroiliac. He turned around, the face flowered familiar. "You remember? The cab? The way to the airport?" At first Xman was exhilarated by the emergence of this "figure from his past"; it meant the fates were gently smiling, scattered threads of his being were at last converging on a common fabric—a fabric of destiny—or at least on an old-fashioned loom compatible with that destiny. But as the cabdriver rambled on and on about his newfound success in this city of his wildest dreams, about his spacious apartment on Manhattan's spacious Central Park West, it became clear for the moment no further work was being done on Xman's fabric. This aggressively former taxi driver did not ask a single question about his, Xman's, work, true or otherwise. For one who had been just recently transformed into a *coqueluche* of the Columbus Avenue street scene, Xman's true work, clearly a chimera, was better off consigned as quickly as possible to the distant past. Hungry for friends, Rosalie willfully misunderstood, or so it seemed to Xman, her man's relation to the taximan and with her usual generosity suggested they three proceed to rest their weary bones amid the chatty chiaroscuro of some less than fashionable café. Seated with his cappuccino in the Seven Plagues Bar just off Seventy-seventh, the ex-taximan thanked Xman for suggesting New York though Xman had no recollection of having made such a suggestion. He waited. "At first I was a little afraid of coming back. But then, watching your fat—no your skinny—rump wending its way toward the international departures terminal I said to myself, 'Hell, if that slobotomized carcass can do it so can I.' " He looked around, wishing he could say, The sky is getting overcast, or, The clouds are charged, electric, vesicularly purulent. But no such luck. And he could not speak in the absence of context. Yet neither could he have spoken in its presence—that of sparked cumuli—which would have rendered speech—naming—labelling—superfluous. The ex-taximan was looking at him as if he was supposed to answer, answer to something. There was no way out of this moment of excruciating pain, excruciating because its emissary, the ex-taximan, was busy reminding him he was a nonprince without a fate. Before Rosalie, motivated by politeness, aching curiosity, and a pressing need to, as usual, compensate for Xman's blatant because constructed lack of conversational elan, could ask any further questions, such as, How big is your bathroom window, or, Does your landlord give heat in midseason, and thereby satisfy a curiosity that, given their own straitened straits, was nothing less than morbid, the ex-taximan, still sniffing too complacently at his own hindquarters, probably unwashed since the now legendary drive to the airport at C——, rose and announced, "I've got to run. I have to see this woman—Rose Balda—Rose Baldo—Rose Baldi—she's absolutely marvelous—been getting me all these jobs one after another—" Left alone they began to argue not so much with as beyond each other, deep and far back within their respective dockets they struggled in self-defense against an imminent verdict of perpetual abjection since it was appallingly clear he, the ex-taxi man, had shamelessly expropriated all available, all conceivable, riches as well as all available space for their flaunted deployment. He, presently the only man on earth and their only competitor on the international scene, had done a good—an impeccable—job of doing them in. Rosalie diagnosed this young man—Xman corrected her: This was by no means a young man but Rosalie waved all his objections away as being of no importance and they were, Xman had to admit, of no importance—to be typically self-important, inebriated by his first whiff of success, of easy money. Xman shook his head uncertain if he was denying the young man's self-importance or somebody's misguided belief that such a worm had something to feel semi-important about. Rosalie had apparently long before made peace with the inhuman monstrousness of the non-young man's condescension whereas he, Xman, was still grappling with the conceivability of condescension not merely as a force in the world but as a force directed his way.

Rosalie looked away. Rarely moody in this way—always at the service of others' moods—she suddenly frightened him. The true target of her resentment remained unclear: Was it this young man refulgent in his new marketability or the ignominy of Xman's bypassing just such marketability when it had all along been staring him in the face and being now forced to contend, minute by minute, with the consequences. How dare there be such an alternative when he, Xman, the unwitting father of her child, was consecrated to peddling something so fatuous as the true work to come.

Retracing their steps down Columbus Avenue—they, or at least he—underwent this retracing as a punishing admission of defeat—all he could remember was the young man's conspicuous omission of questions regarding his particular progress. Hadn't that topic been uppermost during the ride to the airport. Focusing in spite of himself on this omission it began fast to stink of the scandalous, the heinous, the— calculated. Because he had more energy of rage than he knew what to do with—and of all places on Columbus Avenue where everyone looked so unenraged, so delighted with things as they incessantly turned out to be—Xman applied himself with gusto to the work of wresting maximal malevolence from the monolith of the other's breezy self-absorption. Forcing himself to undergo indifference as calculation was, however, as unrewarding as ascribing insidious intention to his neighbors' visceral basslines. But just upon reaching a pitch of unbearable anguish they glimpsed a child being lifted high into the air and sustaining all through the experiment a look of the purest seriousness, unencumbered forthrightness of ozone-tinged deference to its own wonder. The look contrasted all too baldly with that, purposefully vacant, of diners staring out at the bag people—the cart people. These LESS FORTUNATE severed from their audience by a sheet of the slenderest glass were forced to pasture on nothing more delectable than dogshit-seasoned asphalt. In front of a movie theater a very long unmoving line attested to the unexpected popularity of a film rereleased after decades of smug neglect. When they arrived back in their apartment—the hole, as he called it again—Xman put some objects in order, threw some others away, felt much better. Knowing it would frighten her, especially now, when she needed to be reassured about their common fate, "I could impersonate a derelict," he told Rosalie, lying down with eyes closed and hands on her belly. He hated her for needing reassurance, especially now. He hated himself for refusing to be able to furnish the few simple words "any pregnant woman needs to hear."

He felt wicked, beyond resipiscence, looked around. The room, the single shoddy solitary room was in perfect order.

Unbearably happy, so great was his delight, at every object in its place and the wide deathly-still space between objects, he could not for the life of him understand why he was therefore incapable of exiting from this cruel abstention from reassurance. He could not speak the necessary words, not even now, when it would be so easy, ostensibly so easy, here amid the flotsam of his little kingdom swept clean and its every denizen accounted for.

When he was almost sure she was sleeping, at least dozing, he said, softly as if afraid to provoke the cockroaches, "Rosalie, Rosalie my love, in the midst of these most excruciating torments I still tend to look upon them as mere preparations for those to come. Nothing I undergo, no matter how humiliating, is real except as a preliminary sketch, blighted preview of what the others—ever so more real—undergo when they decide to 'do' suffering. I haven't yet come to accept my history yet only by accepting that history can I go beyond it, beyond its sickening irreversibility, into the far brighter reversibility of the dream time, where blind Orion with a monkey named Cedalion on his back is forever searching for the rising sun. And unfortunately, Rosalie my darling, I cannot set you apart from all the others. You don't help me to escape my history."

By the way she opened her eyes—as if challenging a challenging sunburst—Rosalie showed she had been awake all along, listening intently. "So you want to reduce everybody and everything to the same common denominator. You want to reduce life to a unique and overpowering homogeneity. Like our lady friend across the way"—she pointed to the window—"you denounce any kind of motley. You can't stand being duped and exploited by the Xavieros of this world and then coming home to me, who does not dupe, maul, gudgeon, trepan, bait. For if I do not dupe you—if I care for you—why don't I do something, why am I not powerful enough to

179

annihilate the Xavieros of the world. I am not powerful enough." She rose with difficulty, her face became flushed, there were tears in her eyes. "And it isn't even as simple as that. You don't want me to annihilate Xaviero. You want me to annihilate your hunger for humiliation at the hands of the Xavieros of this world. Just as you need Xaviero you need me to reactivate your self-loathing. And with me your injustice—your cruelty—becomes a pretext for self-loathing. But I won't tolerate it. Do you hear? I've endured enough with Rose Baldachino all through the years. No more vampires." "A hearty true work stew requires generous dollops of self-loathing," Xman said for what seemed no reason. "Yes," he added, conceding, "reducing the revoltingness of life to a unique overpowering and apparently masterable homogeniety is easier to bear. I can't shift gears."

"You'll have to," she said, sinking back. "Maybe if you can make me loathe you then the loathing of others can be twisted into concealing as does mine—but only up to a point—passionate parenting love." A pause. "No wait," she added, seeing him turn away gritted to the window. There was something infinitely moving, infinitely voluptuous, in that, "No wait," put forth by protecting fear of his inability to contend with darkly suggestive truth. The voluptuous gentleness of "No wait" put him at a crossroads, at the point of giving way. But he knew he would not give way, that he would choose to resist. Because he was so very much on the verge giving way could be held indefinitely in reserve. Her entreaty had an odor that choked his chest. Because the voluptuous gentleness was localizable—and only for a matter of seconds—in her tiny wrist or imploring forearm, he jumped out to squelch—to punish—it. Holding both arms, one at the wrist, the other at the level of forearm, he shook her back and forth, over and over, with no release from suffocation. Even before he finished shaking he began to have stirrings of guilt. Uttering his rage through the shaking did away with it forever after but being a fast learner he saw from her recoiling features that nothing was resolved in the long haul. Out the window through the gauze of leafless branches monoliths melted in the setting sun. "I'll reform," he told the leafless branches. Rosalie turned over on the bed. "We need a bed," she said. "Furniture." "I'll reform," he repeated, expecting to be absolved. But she did not refute him, she took him at face value. But uttering, "I'll reform," immediately killed all desire to reform, divulged the absurd irrelevance of trying. Emboldened by the absurdity of what he was saying he elaborated on it. The sketch as sketch intrigued him. "If only, my dear—the "my dear" he knew from experience inaugurated another epoch of irony—"I can make up my mind to reform and become a good citizen like the ex-taximan you were so insistent about taking to tea. But I can't reform, Rosalie, my dear. Because the deepest outcry comes not from me but from the innards of the true work and the true work has a nasty habit of demanding its due in all weathers. Whenever the true work finds me weakening— more thoughtful of you, that is, and of our little life and of Xman, Jr.—then like those stone lions thrown on the mercy of montage it rises up to reproach me for what might end up looking like abandonment. Who, if not I, must speak for it. Not that they are—these true works, yes, works, for they are multiplying, don't you hear them deep down in *my* womb— yes, my womb, my womb, my womb—particularly enamored of my defending orations—for they are only too well aware that my course is of a staggering brevity, utterly incommensurate with the noisomely monumental—utterly inconceivable—span of those powers-that-be whose duty is to someday confer a value on their—the true works', that is—abundantly noded meandering. So is it any wonder they turn from me, my true works, since through me there is little likelihood they can insinuate themselves within the public domain. And as they turn blithely away from my decrepit incapacity to induce within that monumental span a swing from scant to gradual but thereafter unswerving and sure-footed notice—the long road from pretermission to apotheosis, as it were—so I turn vexation from myself onto innocent bystanders such as you." He waited, he heard her breathing deeply, she was asleep. He went on: "And this absurd fealty that I insist on harboring only saps me for jubilation within the precincts of any other enterprise—not that the true work is exalted enough to qualify for the label of enterprise. Oh no, no, no. Oh no, no, no. Doggedly obstructing and ultimately obliterating any other version of prowess—haven't I said as much to Fish?—not that whatever I do in the domain of the true work qualifies as prowess—not that I hunger after any other form of prowess—lucrative or otherwise—it's only that the persistent derision of others almost makes me wish, on occasion, around holiday time especially, since holiday time is 'family time' and I loathe family time with all my heart and soul—makes me wish I could end up slobbering after some gilt-edged version of prowess acceptable to the slobbering powers-that-be—obstructing prowess, then, the true work makes me sometimes wish I could hunger after prowess." "You could look for another kind of job," she whispered. "Xaviero isn't the last man on earth."

He tried to calm himself. But he was only calm enough to rage against the daring intromission of anxiety into a situation where at least from the vantage of another hastily improvised retrospect had reigned only serenity. "I'll kill her after all," he heard himself murmuring to the gauzy branches. For one of his absence of dimensions the only viable antidote against any new anxiety—anxiety with or without plausible instantiation, with or without target—

was its immediate transmogrification into "only remaining obstruction" to the stainless steel of well-being. And at the same time—when it rains it pours—he was burdened by an anxiety flowing freely from two situational tits, coexisting though mutually exclusive in Boschian simultaneity. Visited with all the anguish attendant on what smelled like chronic unemployment he was at the same time saddled with, hemmed in by, inexhaustible responsibilities inseparable from gainful employment by the likes of Xaviero and his kind. All of a sudden he did not want to be severed from the Xaviero family and just as suddenly thanks to Rosalie's last remark knew reintegration into that family was in fact but a phone call away. He was in short burdened with the simultaneous summated horror of two mutually exclusive states of affairs. Yet he had to suffer this affliction if, standing at the window, always standing at the window in the shadow of the trees and Rosalie's half sleep, he wished to repudiate the miseries of one in the refuge afforded by the other. For this was the only refuge he now knew, that afforded by misery. Or were the words simply anastomosing once more. Suddenly it all came back to him what his old pal—not the cabdriver but Baruch—used to say: Xman, my schmuck, if you are stupid enough to end up afflicted, make sure affliction can be associated with as many causes as possible. For you will be less afflicted through the very fact that keeping track of so many causes necessarily eats up no small portion of the energy pockmarked for what I call The Affliction Indulgence. And this he was doing now, far from his first home, a home, in fact, away from home, standing at the window of their blessed hole awaiting the firstborn's knock.

He turned: Rosalie was asleep. The sight of her sleeping, pregnant, so terrified—and enraged—him that he couldn't bear to stay in the apartment another minute. How dare she just . . . lie there and sleep when they were on the verge of eviction. He heard the first faint murmurs of a visceral bass. Time to flee, he would return to Xaviero, apologize, promise to be more discreet. He walked through the park in the darkness, just as he emerged a bus passed, reflecting yellow flashes of taxicab like so many lesions along its obese flank. Another bus passed, still not his, and swerving slightly from a Houyhnhnm whose bucket of grain was more the feast of a mock-retinue of filthy and quick-witted or rather quick-in-stincted pigeons than its own humble repast preparatory to dragging yet another lard-load of hideous-looking tourists around the fringe of the park—swerving slightly reflected not only puny taxicab flanks—not only the puny facade of the Plaza Hotel—not only the faces of the urban leper patrol out to squander its breadmoney—not only the skyline of night's rigorously enlightened cells (like a page of sheet music with too many, far too many, notes to the bar) but all of the city's past, present and future trumpeting forth of the same voluntary on sottish themes of icy privilege squelching the mass. And he, Xman, was interwoven, with or without a destiny, into the tapestry of that mass. In short, the scroll spread out on the bus's—so what if it was another bus, a third or fourth or fifth—flank recapitulated his whole history, the history of a noble tragic race, a race of one. He followed the bus to Columbus Circle and Chris on his unwieldy stilt. Tonight the southwestern horizon was swathed in white cumuli and with a cape ominously convoluted as if cut from the same cloth, he seemed twisted in entreaty, emulating unawares the fountains frothing for dear life through a scrim of dirty-limbed locusts. And then he swerved and twisted no more, looked as if all he wished was to lie down in the sepulchral concavity fashioned out of the slightly perforated Huntington Hartford Museum facade. It was that moment, big with windy dust and the afterstench of noon's souvlaki vendors smothering the spittly musk of horseshit, when the city squats to piss before stepping out in top hat and tatters. Xman heard himself say: But how can I say this of the greatest city on earth, etc., etc. He told the voice to shut its sacrilegious trap and as he hurried downtown it complied.

Checking the time in the big confectioner's clock lording it over the Twenty-third Street bogland he suddenly had a "terrible craving" for Center Drive, not so much for the drivers, nor even for the horses, but rather for the horseshit strategically heaped to intercept the ravening headlight beams. Hungry however to acquire a force surpassing all temptations Xman tried instead to look as if he were leisurely advancing on Second Avenue and walking about prepared what he would say to Xaviero. In a cheap restaurant's glass enclosure giving, without too much preamble, on the dirty windy street a Live Lobster sign was plastered right above the bald pate of a fat customer picking at rusty salad leavings. Exalted by his rootlessness, Xaviero's former star pupil entered the mock-crystal palace, tapped the fat man on his well-padded shoulder and murmured, "Granted, you're a lobster. But are you alive. That's the question we must solve before the night is through." And for a split second but no more it did seem as if Xman's whole future depended on the solution. Then guffawing with factitious irrepressible effusiveness that made him suspect he was going mad, quite mad, Xman made his way to the Xaviero building.

He wondered if he shouldn't say, Xaviero, here I stand before you. Take me back. Once seated in the antechamber usually reserved for local doctors come to pick a bone or two with their patients' new found big-city savior, he began to feel better, then worse, then best, then worse again, then worst. Colliding with him, Xaviero wasted no preambles. "Oh dear, I have many harsh criticisms to append to your performances, Xman. I'm not just speaking of your unspeakable insolence. That we can ascribe to the follies of arrogant youth, too sure of itself, too short on the acuity born of experience and the all-too-rare high style that eschews the supreme vulgarity of wanting to prove a point. In any case, the craft, Xman, the craft. You are deplorably short on craft when it comes to impersonation. And without craft you are no better than a dead man. And not a dead man's dead man either." He tried to snicker to himself, to remain buoyed up in the shadow of the true work, to mimic—to impersonate— the lady patient in the mauvish shadow of her sublime resistance to cure. "So again, you are once again in the unenviable position of finding all vocations, all jobs, all stints, all petty little excursions into the banausic and chrematistic and back again sterile and hideous and fatuous, without however being able to hoist a frenzied repudiation of said vocations and jobs and stints with palpable proof of bigger and better things. The trying and true work refuses to collaborate, so it would appear, in your reprobation of The Common Pursuit. Here you are big with contempt for all our huffing and puffing—all this stage business as it were—but incapable of disclosing what gives you the right to reprobate without appeal.

"But I knew I would have trouble with you. Rose Baldachino, do you know her, recommended you with very definite reservations. But I won't say: I should have known. I won't do that to you, Xman. You merit a dressing-down, no doubt about that, but I won't go so far as to say, I should have known. I watched you circle around Dr. Q. and Dr. Quixot. You made them feel terribly uncomfortable because *you* felt terribly uncomfortable. It was as if you didn't have enough room. Do you have any idea how graceful a true . . shaman is. I mean, the authentic ecstasy specialist. Wearing costumes weighed down with more than forty pounds of iron, steel, and copper, a professional hysteric can perform his dance in the constricted space of a yurt crowded with gaping potbellies, all this without getting in the way of anybody's sacred spectation. So what is your excuse, little man."

Xman tried to look downcast though use of the phrase "professional hysteric" made him feel triumphantly light-hearted. "But as I said, I knew I would have trouble with you—the minute, that is, Rose B. spoke of your conflict. Oh, she thought that would make you interesting. She knows I'm a sucker for torment—the mystery of torment, specifically in youngish males. You have just to mention that somebody is in conflict and I become their humble and obedient servant, Yaws, etc., so to speak. I want to help, I want to suck them clean of the juices of that conflict, I— But as I was saying I knew I would have trouble the minute she spoke of—how did she put it—dedication to a high ideal working more or less only for the disjection of forces that might, in another lifetime, in another cosmos, have worked toward good. Oh no. Oh no. I don't ask for details, always gruesome. Asparagus the gruesome details, that's my motto, vegetarian since Haight-Ashbury. All I now want is that you manage to make yourself oblivious to the true work. Kick it aside for as long at least as you are here. Let it enrich your travails in an obliquely constructive way." Xman replied, "And if I manage such obliviousness." "Well, well," Xaviero huffed, "you will have managed such obliviousness, that's all." Xman turned to the big bay and looked down. "But couldn't mine turn out to be the preliminary sketch of a global oblivion. If I myself can forget what right do I have to expect this fucking world not to. Isn't the trick to keep myself wide awake at every turn and alert at every moment lest my own obliviousness give ideas to the world at large. For the world at large is forever on the lookout for models to plagiarize: It does not share my overweening hunger to be original at any price. If I go on, as you request—" for a split second Rosalie and her—their—

unborn passed before a consciousness of working toward his own ruin, "—if I function and for the likes of me functioning is self-oblivion, then I merely demonstrate that with respect to the monumentality—do you hear, monumentality—of the true work, indifference and oblivion are indeed possible—possible!—and for all eternity. Like everything that partakes of my essence, whatever that is, this will to obliviousness is strong enough to will its own echo on a cosmic and eternal, in others words irrevocable, scale." He waited. "Then get the hell out of here and never come back, goddamned fucking turkey," Xaviero said. But he sounded as if he were impersonating what he hoped the words were inventing. Not giving himself time to think, Xman picked up a paperweight in the form of a shaman with massive buttocks dancing over his own corpse and threw it at his "erstwhile mentor." It was unclear whether he ducked in time. A typewriter platen, at any rate, blue with pinkish streaks, looked as if it would remain dented forever. Softly closing the Fire Emergency door that gave on a staircase smelling stiffly of piss Xman heard a low moan. On his way uptown Xman realized he should have established whether or not Xaviero would be willing to supply him with a reference. In his present state of mind the gnawing importunity of such a question did not appear incompatible with the event of a few minutes before—an event, as he told himself, he had merely witnessed from afar.

He wanted to be able to say to Rosalie he had walked the streets in a frenzy, yet when he arrived home she was gone. Feeling as if they slept in shifts, he lay down on their mattress to deploy in that way the corpse of his culpability. Whatever he might say to defend himself or show a colossal contempt for self-defense, his corpse could be depended upon to say it more truthfully. Entering, seeing him lying there she said, "I was walking on the roof." "I threw a paper-

weight at Xaviero," he noted. He underwent a giddy euphoria sitting up in bed and at the same time underwent the
giddy euphoria as an impersonation, an impersonation asserting its sovereign right independent of any solicitation by
context. "You did well," she replied. Quickly he tried to
smell out any inauthenticity, there was none, she was forthright. The insistence exasperated him. "I didn't do well," he
spewed. "You were justified," she went on. He went to the
window, not a single star, only the window-studded cliffs of
New Jersey, again, like a page of sheet music with too many
notes to the bar. "To speak of being justified: It robs me of my
wrong, don't you understand. To speak of my act in such a
manner does it a grave and terrible disservice, you're trying
to rob me of—smother—its sheer gratuitousness." "You
should be relieved. I never saw you working for Xaviero anyway. We'll manage." "I should be relieved, I should be relieved, yes, but ONLY in the context of a full acceptance
of—delectation over—having done wrong, irreparable
wrong. A wrong for which I must take the consequences."
He had no clear idea of the consequences, he only knew at
this juncture he was supposed to hear Xaviero's "horrible
moan: horrible not because of its loud excruciation but for
its very undemanding softness, its almost sugary good humor, etc., etc." He turned around, now she looked frightened, the confidence of a moment before was whisked away,
he almost wished it back. "I may have killed him," he added,
to punish her first for trusting him, standing by, and second
or third for this unforgivable lapse from the equally essential
comforting good humor of trust.

"You did well: Xaviero was monstrous." He wanted to
laugh at her characterization. Xaviero might be many things
but he had never been monstrous. He intrigued himself attempting to imagine not Xaviero's monstrousness but rather
Rosalie's imagination of that monstrousness. He tried to put

himself inside the shoes of her puzzling generation of that monstrousness. Did she believe or was she typically shunting aside all questions of belief. In the face of a pressing need to nurture, appease, was she proclaiming truth, her version of the truth, or merely peddling the most expedient restorative. "Rosalie," he said quietly, "when you say Xaviero is monstrous do you really believe it."

"You did well. That is all I can say." This insistence on the probable monstrousness of Xaviero as immediate cause of his unspeakable act was becoming a foothold for him too. He tried now to create some kind of connection between Xaviero and his outburst. Had rage motivated the outburst. Hadn't it been rather an IMPERSONATION of rage, an attempt to prove at last that he was worthy of Xaviero's confident respect and as more than an impersonator. He tried to create a connection—a Rosalie-type connection—but the connection broke down like a woven footbridge under stress. The effort to create and cement such a connection lost interest in its raw material and instead craned past Xaviero toward something preformal, virtual, monolithic. And from the vantage of that antediluvian slush bashing in Xaviero's roost no longer had anything to do with Xaviero

"But he was monstrous! he was monstrous!" Xman turned back to the window, his way of stopping his ears against browbeating his misdeed into the ever-so-righteous issue of Xaviero's bad manners. Contemplating the righteousness of his crime he felt especially doomed. Or was it rather a case of: Contemplating the righteousness of his crime he felt "especially doomed." Thinking of the dented platen and the room—his former office, office for a day—in total disorder, he said, "I wish I could go back." When she smiled in what she thought was a consoling manner he knew she had misread him. "I tampered with order, I tampered with my love of order. If only I could have forced myself to remain . . . ensconced in the heart of order. Because if I am not ensconced in the heart of routine how can I be located by *them. Them.* The horde of hierodules striving day and night to weave the tapestry of one man's fate along the tatters of his abstention from the monumental vulgarity of self-propulsion—in other words, self-promotion. Yes, yes, yes, I know. I want to have it both ways—destruction to soothe the savage breast of a monolithic rage with neither provenance nor issue AND flawless order once the craving to destroy has been quelled and all aftereffects take on the stench of pure gratuitousness."

"You need to rest," she said. "You really need to rest."

Reducing his bloated global anguish, his monolithic rage, to a mere need for rest enraged him even more. Clearly Rosalie was constitutionally incapable of undergoing his rage's globality as somehow far removed from—infinitely beyond—the middling contingencies too much in their midst though capable of serving, until that rage's overpowering sourcelessness could be proudly worn, as its supreme source. She was constitutionally incapable, but who wasn't, of sharing a resuscitating descent into the propagation of disorder with its luxuriant aftermath of regret for supremely gratuitous violation of what, in the dusky shadow of penitent exhaustion cast by satiety, seemed suddenly so easy to have respected and upheld. As the river flowed below, Rosalie was proving capable of one calisthenic only: mildly frantic inventory of the sins and solecisms vindicating Xman's murderous plunge egregious, perhaps, for all eternity. Then she began to weep. "I feel that I am responsible. Your act had a single message: I'm in despair. And wherever despair is, there Rosalie is responsible. I've learned that living and working with Rose. So I have to placate—I should have placated—your despair. Placate, placate and placate. And on a certain level it's comforting to believe whatever transpired between you and Xaviero is my fault since as my fault it is a malleable excruciation, fertile in not so much relations as self-referential praxes by which to prove at last my worth to you, blemished by my fall."

"I'm sorry for Xaviero," he said, finally. He was trying to become contrite reciting the words of contrition but an aftertaste of impersonation dragged him down, inauthenticity enraged him, made him want to strangle Rosalie. "Throwing that paperweight I'm back where I started—no, further back because I begin to have a reputation that will keep me out of respectable circles. Why oh why did I do it. Just when everything seemed to be going along so beautifully—just when I was just about to face the future with the security of an intact apprenticeship behind me. Just when working at a normal job—the nine to five route, you know—was becoming a kind of cushioned sleepwalking. Why did I destroy it all. Why did I destroy our future and future of our unborn child?" But he saw reflected in Rosalie's face growing alarm, or at least perplexity, at what he knew to be his growing exhilaration, his growing delight. "But don't you see. Don't you see. I had to—I had to—I destroyed our security, I destroyed our future, but I acquire . . . tension. Of course I see the value of this tension only for moments at a time. But if I sustain my perception of that value for more than moments at a time I will be on the road to . . . acqusition of the tension. And tension acquired is tension valueless. Tension's value stems from standing in the way of its own acquisition, any acquisition whatsoever, of objects, for example, in relation to whose sharply defined contours one defines one's own. One might say tension, compliments of my misdeed, has acquired *me*. And in a flash—here—high above the flowing Hudson River—how privileged we are to be allowed glimpses from our monad, Rosalie, my love—my deepest darkest love—I see that it is tension and tension alone that feeds the true work." At the same time he felt somebody should be telling him this and he would not assimilate and believe until told. "The true work is a desert irrigated by tension. I know, Rosalie, you have been trying to mitigate the tension but there is no going forward or rather inward if you have as I do a loathing of declamation—without prostration before the absoluteness of that tension. Don't think I'm not afraid to admit its absoluteness. I'm afraid I won't be able to see beyond the admission assuming there is something to see. But maybe I am simply failing to see that admission may trigger a total transmogrification by which a fertile abyss, a whole new swamp of possibilities, is opened up to the marketplace."

Rosalie was still weeping. "I still say: If only he had treated you with more respect." He put his arms around her neck but not to strangle. "Rosalie, Rosalie, dearly beloved, we are not gathered here to seek out causes commensurate with what is after all too global—too lofty—to take comfort in causes, now are we." He could feel his hands tightening. "If only the chambermaid had farted in my ear instead of on my right testicle that stormy night in Karlsbad de Janeiro—if only—if only . . ." He wrenched his hands free of her person. The temptation to destroy was becoming too great. Now that she was out of reach he could allow himself a greater, stentorian, abusiveness. "I'm sorry but I simply can't bear it—this hunger to plausibilize, that is to say, straitjacket away—my sins, my enormous sins, my wretched sins, me a father-to-be—this feeble attempt at attenuation that only damps the bracing therefore immensely therapeutic certainty of TERRIBLE WRONG DONE—perpetrated—against the powers that pretend to be—this bid for mitigation via appallingly conscientious inventory of all crimes committed against my state by said powers or their flunkeys too innumerable for the active roster. Don't you realize you're robbing me of the one act (albeit the infinite sum of minutely anastomosing recoils) by which I participate in the intricacies of El Dream Time—time out of time—when all differences were—are— volatilized away into the aroma of the primal soup, when no thing was the *cause* of anything else, when the lion and the lamp chop lay down their arms in the mauvish shadow of the—when—when—" Rosalie was still weeping. "Can't you smell that I don't want to be legitimated; to be even a mixture of the legitimate and illegitimate is already an excruciation past mortal bearing. Don't you sense that I might be strong enough—whatever may be my weaknesses elsewhere, my infinity of weaknesses elsewhere—to suffer the legitimacy of the boss's revulsion—of his mandate and my wanton destruction of that mandate."

Standing before the kitchen (there was no door nor would there ever be one) she was as if standing in the way of his participation in that dream time of tigers running roughshod over the common run of flamingo-fringed gibbons without so much as a ripple of scruple staining the superbly stained hide. She for one would not relinquish his personal history, a loathesome chronology whose slime subsumed an alcoholic mother, a crippled father, a tyrannical maiden aunt with far too many animal lovers, a prolonged orphanage stint, a . . . He whispered to the depths of the kitchen, to the refrigerator's ghostly hum: "Only by knowing I have done wrong can I come through, can I come through and *come* through the act." She stood her ground, holding her belly. She was sweating profusely for the cloth of her dress clung to her abdomen. Her clenched palms said she would scale down his egregiousness to one big mitigation, a deformed fetus of mitigated outrage, neither fish nor fowl, a not quite teratomal challenge for the potbellied obstetricians.

"If only the boss hadn't treated me like a dog . . . So you think it is conceivable that he—that anyone—could treat me like a dog." He stamped his foot. "It is not conceivable." "Get me some . . . aspirin." He did her bidding, relieved at this opportunity to show some hopefully recognizable human decency. Yet when he reached the street he no longer wanted to buy aspirin—to do a good turn for any human being. He himself was not human, he was shit and as shit he had no obligations. This was the privilege of shit, especially when dried, colorless, and spurned even by the hungriest flies. All around him denizens of night proclaimed his revolt against the powers that be in the person of Xaviero to be nothing more than a temper tantrum, a sulk in assassin's borrowed finery, a flunkey's parody of protest deep within being's mire for all the finery's insistence that his true domain, anybody who was anybody knew this, was the far purlieus of that being, there where nonbeing's barbed wire ("No trespassing") slashed all other sentinels to bits. Couldn't they see what they took for a tantrum was in fact a meditated verdict on being from outside far outside and from someone with absolutely nothing any longer to gain from being. Couldn't they smell that what might initially have been triggered by a desire to be received in the parlors of being on equal footing with derelict dowagers, dowagettes, potentates, and other slobs—in other words properly and according to one's worth (weight in gold dust multiplied by a factor equal to the sum of one's piss and one's puke divided by somebody—anybody—else's blood and guts or was it by the length of that else's perineum)—had exploded into total disgust with anything and everything capable of arranging such a reception. Couldn't the lights of dear old upper Broadway see that his sabotage had shifted gears in midstream.

He was going blind: All was haze beyond the haze of street lights and headlights. Only Rollins could restore him to being, salvage his sense of worth. He was worth nothing. Calling, hearing Rollins's voice, with horror he recognized Rollins was impersonating a project coordinator. With each utterance he tried without success to become an authentic, at least a convincing, impersonator. Xman spilled his beans into the receiver. A tough banged on the booth door. Xman thought to himself: At least there is a door to mutilate. "I just called to find out how things are going." The tough continues to bang, bang, bang, warning that West Seventy-second is about to throw itself into the Hudson. Rollins sighed deeply. The sigh expanding to deeper and deeper silence Xman looked around desperately. Outflowing presumably from between the scrawny legs of a derelict sprawled in front of a bank, the Bank for Shavings, Inc., a stream of piss reluctantly reached the gutter. He tried to describe it to Rollins, all of a sudden he wanted to describe something beautiful, to overwhelm him with the irrefutable cast iron of his project's awesome vision, but quickly, quickly, long before Rollins could recoil and crawl away, deftly as always, down his smart crawl all the while labelling him as one among oh-so-tiresome many, hard at work purveying . . . purveying . . . purveying. He needed to speak so that Rollins would be overwhelmed to rapturous awe—that is to say, annihilated—faster than he, Xman, as one among so many equally perfervid purveyors of beauty parts, could be forever embedded in their sequence never to be heard from again except through the auspices of this or that caption. "The piss, the piss, Mike, you should see it. There is—I have a derelict here—Mike, I think he's hot—New York's hottest young derelict—and his topcoat is—New York's hottest young topcoat—" Xman felt that Rollins's silence was busy tabulating, filing him away and not even, least of all, for future reference, but dead-lettered. Long before he began Xman knew he had been refuted, refuted in both the target of his rapture and in the not-so-latent aim of that rapture—to command Rollins's absolute irrefutable self-annihilating fealty and not just for all time.

Before he could overwhelm Rollins Rollins had succeeded in overwhelming and shredding him with a simple roll of the eyes of silence. Smirking, smirkingly unscathed Rollins had done him in faster than Xman had been able to transform him skin and bones into awe's avatar.

"And his legs are spread out over the asphalt where only this morning housewives, fishwives, ninety cents a pound, three fifty a quarter-pound . . ." But he sensed that putting forth more of the meat and potatoes of rapture would only make it easier to bracket and do away with him finally. "Not that I don't want to be done away with," he murmured. Now for the first time Rollins said, "What?" with a sensual whine of almost morbid curiosity. Quickly he added, "You know, I have shown some of your samples to friends, close friends. In the know, as they say."

So they hadn't been enchanted with his samples, but what samples was Rollins talking about with such conviction. "So you were once enchanted with me, Rollins, but with no one to buttress that enchantment you draw back, afraid. You begin to hate your minion now he has been responsible for marooning you far from those you deem, with ever so much—unreciprocated, I might add—high seriousness and low fervor, your dear dear friends. I on the other hand have no dear friends, no talent, you must know, for dear friend-ship. I've estranged you from a hallucinated connectedness to others, to this pisser here, for example. The spontaneity of your awe—an awe that, in its first gasp, had been so sure of ratification or perhaps been so drunk on itself that ratifica-tion didn't matter in the least—is now coagulating. Better this way—you didn't improve—you wouldn't improve—on further acquaintance, and here I am, with aspirin to buy, murder on my hands, felled by the merest prefatory whiff of the rancidity to come. You stink worse than my chimera here, my specimen of beauty, my pissing topcoat—the hottest pisser in a city of very very hot pissers." He let the receiver drop, opened the booth door, threw a nickel at the derelict, eluded the thug with exemplary *quant à moi* and to his pleasant surprise discoverd that Seventy-second west hadn't the least intention of throwing itself overboard. He was preparing himself, making ready, but for what. All he knew was surprise at the reserves of energy he was mustering for a floundering ever westward, or was it east. On Amsterdam Avenue to the bottom of a poster proclaiming the muted marvels of the NYCB—a long-lost Balanchine (divertimento to music by none other than red Hector whom the master had reputedly disliked along with mad Modest and loutish Ludwig) had just been exhumed from the fast-fading memory bank of some self-styled *prima ballerina assoluta* residing in Monte—another, diminutive though far more colorful, was affixed. Xman read: "Everybody needs a job. Respect your job. Respect yourself." Some scholiast, however, with an affinity for extreme oxblood had decided to take issue with such stolid urging and poured forth peripherally another perspective on the marketplace: "Everybody has a real job. The real job, schmucks, has nothing whatever to do with taking orders. An order is a window on death. The fake—the money-making—job is a window on death. Yet the real job is always less frightening when performed in the shadow of the fake's shrill exigencies. Against the resistance of factory/office/emporium/schoolroom materials we shape our real tools, our real products. For we, the real jobbers, evolve only through obstruction. Trust not, therefore, the sweat-of-his browbrow who though pretending to be obstreperously outside the pale of factory smokestacks belching forth artisanal blood at a rate of so many carcinomas per millisecond in fact never misses an opportunity to dance a ceremonious and shameless prostration before the pale powers-that-be. Rather trust the man who admits outright

that even if it seems to go against the factory/office/empo-
rium/schoolroom grain and everything they stand for, or
rather in, in actual fact the real job feeds from that grain's
bucket.

Although middle of the night it smelled of dawn. The
distant skyscrapers were more than steeped in fog, they were
slowly emerging from a primordial stew. For the first time he
was here before them and each finial, each ledge, each set-
back, had to be wrested from the shapelessness of that instant just before being is once again unleashed on the world.
He was making ready to go to Xaviero, his only friend. Yet
just as he felt himself crawling toward that hardy specimen—toward a new day of impersonation—he was suddenly
overcome by an importunate plethora of tasks, all true work
adjuncts demanding immediate attention and, to judge from
their tone, not to be fast-talked. Moving toward Xaviero, impersonation, bread-earning drudgery, reality as others knew
it—as the young father in the bus knew it—was not then a
moving TOWARD but the dislodging OF a whole subsection
of potential true work exigencies and of whose existence up
to this point he had been completely unaware. Crawling
toward the slimy little cubicle in which his schedule of vi-
gnettes was fixed, he, Xman—Xaviero was not dead, couldn't
be dead, absurd idea—was being awarded a privileged
glimpse of the dislimned continent of his life's work such as
he had never before dreamed much less lived it. The only
vantage on the true work, then, was authorized by movement toward Xaviero's slimy marshland—he was not dead,
he was not dead. On Amsterdam Avenue looking into the
lobby of a hi-rise next to the bus stop he observed a little boy
seated in his father's lap, the porter who swept passing and
repassing with his broom. As if aware of the child's eyes he
went to the window and looked out, past Xman, from his, a
porter's, point of view just another morsel of superannuated

199

city dust, thereby proving he was under no duress to finish or begin, could sever his connection to drudgery any time he wished. Xman thought, looking past him toward the imitation parquet floor he refused to slash clean, The temptation is to think: How wonderful, life. Each man, each woman, each being, in its laudatory specificity, no task to be contemned, all merging unstigmatized into the vast benign heterogeneity, the great beyond of the subhuman soup *she* had ranted against. Let no labor be labelled as less than noble. Though he, Xman, loathed it, especially with a memory of the lady (Fa-, Tanya, Brunhildine) screaming out her window still dagger-sharp, he was astonishingly big with this point of view (he shook his head with so fatuous a grin the porter turned away with even greater disgust than that with which he began, Xman was sure of it, his rounds)—but not as Xman. He was big with this point of view as some bejewelled bejowled matron, simpering hausfrau, farcical female poised to contemplate the city's slime panorama as if it were the painted backdrop for an operetta, might be characterized clinically as *big with bauble-lust*. He was big with impersonation of one whose point of view he loathed but Xaviero was not here to applaud and correct. The broom as it grazed the dull surface under the obscure eye of father and son looked as if it had just finished muttering, Better never to have been born or once ejected . . .

No bus in sight. He stamped his foot. Raged. Raged against having to work for a living with no real sign of the true work in sight, but what about the dislodging of those importuning—so what if only in the shadow of the fake work—adjuncts a short time before, raged against ending his rage, raged against a rage that would never end, raged that this was by no means the very last upsurge of rage pinnacling to annihilating reparation, raged that this was indubitably the very last—the final—upsurge . . . to be repeated endlessly, however, and without appeal. Betting on the progress of two race-horses, two old gray mares masquerading as stud farm prodigies, he hardly knew which of the two he wanted to declare the winner, which to lie down and die with. Did he want alleviation to intervene faster than total and unmiti-gated final rage could guarantee . . . guarantee . . . an eternity of the total and unmitigable.

Not knowing what he wanted he walked and toward dawn found himself in the middle of an island on Park Avenue. He caught the saplings at the moment when their imprint ef-fects the first almost imperceptible shift in the day's distri-bution of dewless (he loathed dew) light along the blades. The message of the blades was: Xaviero is dead. Just before a huge truck bore down on his even huger inattentiveness to signals he thought: It would be not in the least implausible or untimely or unjust or unkind to be knocked down and straight into hell by one of these monsters, the kind, he had nevertheless to concede, whose ghostly flank is, on hazy autumn days, not infrequently stippled with the blue of plane boles signposting its itinerary. It would be a fitting conclusion to what otherwise would not conclude. No dan-ger of my feeling, if I happened to step back just in time, Whew, now that was a close call, hell yes, now that put all my . . . "petty grievances into perspective," boy am I glad to be alive, boy do I want to be alive. If I happen to be booted into oblivion by one fell swoop of the fender's kneecap there will be no antepenultimate *frisson* celebrating the soaring grace of all the . . . littler things. For wasn't it obsession with all the littler things (shadow of plane boughs, porter sweep-ing nondescript lobby at dawn beneath jaundiced eye of pop and junior, or was it mom and sis, steep cliff stuffed with too many eighth notes) that kept me all along from making a big fat killing. The littler things dragged me down to their level. The definitive expression of an inarticulate seething will

201

find its perfect incarnation in the fender's unprefaceable slash. In the truck's dirty work the seething will have at last come to birth. Bye, Xaviero. There was nothing to leave behind, no sudden therefore nauseating illumination, easily refuted, no fleeting therefore heightened therefore indelible appreciation of commonplaces ignored for so long compliments of the daily treadmill. For too long he had been wading in the commonplace book, attentive to its smothered luminosity, while others, cruder and more calculating, more . . . enterprising, had advanced toward . . . toward . . . while he . . . he . . . rowing against the fur . . . against the fur . . . dutifully pursuing the signposts that promised only two more miles to Illo Tempore Tavern, half a mile to Auberge d'Arcadie

Just before the metal slashed his thigh he did see a life unfolding before him only it was not his yet not totally unfamiliar, rather a gloss on the sum of excrescences that had been his life. And as he waited for the truck to come again, to remarry with him, he remembered a thought of someone, who was it: You may come through but not as yourself. Yourself is no more.

There were suddenly two Xmans running toward fusion with the truck's flank: the one who spread the thighs of his receptivity to impregnation by the truck's dappled flank and the second, the new, Xman who, now that rapture was past, must find habitation for these fruits of collisional impregnation, some simulacrum of vocational haven.

Just before allowing himself to be felled he twinged at infidelity to the program he had mapped out coming to New York. For what was submission to the truck but recourse to a remedy. And hadn't he promised himself to abstain from remedy barring apotheosis well-earned. Allowing for amelioration wasn't he laying the groundwork for infinite prolongation of his plight. Nevertheless he forced himself to walk the truck's flank, a firmament of hazy cirrus, a field peppered with dandelion shadows.

But just before felling the truck he wanted to leap forward, not to meet his opponent/savior head-on but to protest that even before this confrontation could swell beyond localizability it was bracketed, familiar, invoking an infinity of facsimiles.

Just before he was felled by the truck he was felled by the torment of being annihilated less by the truck than by the insidious and unlocalizable virulence—a veritable idea—at the heart of the monster's trajectory. Yet wasn't this his true work—here it was coming to him on Park Avenue herself— to make the brutal and monolithic mindless mindlessness of being correspond to some secret intention spinning out its contradictions within that monolith.

But just before annihilation he was made to wince from nave to chaps by far more than truck descending on unwary flank, lightly dotted with the hairs of adolescence. He was giving himself up to be rid of the voracity of a perception that missed nothing and therefore disqualified him at every turn for promotion to the ranks of the unseeing. Not pure enough not to stoop to the perception of detail he could count on the truck to excise this shamefully uncanny ability to focus, fix, that proved he was more, far more, of the world than he cared at any given moment, and even at those ungiven or given grudgingly, to admit. He was looking to the truck as to a model in but not of the world. He wanted to be like the truck which with unconscious mastery all up Park and all down Lexington had managed to set limits to its own perception-voracity by expropriating more and more of the world's prowess and bulk. The truck had trained itself to mime and thereby absorb more and more of the world's force and was therefore unconsumed by a slobberingly voracious need to annotate that world as a substitute for vanquishing it. That was why he wished to fuse with

They—Rose Baldachino, MacDuffers, Perlmutter—all felt obliged to bury the hatchet so what if in each other's flesh and pay a visit to one Raw Recruit Who Had Gone Astray in the Biggest Little Apple of Them All, Partner. Easily enough they discovered he was recuperating at B——B——B——Hospital, all the way up Fifth and right across from the reservoir, briskly cerulean beyond the paste of catkins and the magnolia tabernacles upthrusting their wine-dark knots. Once they were inside his room a heavy silence fell. As Rose B. was leaving all the time telling him she would call he shook his head distractedly like a child trying to absorb and profit from a consolation he cannot comprehend so overwhelmed is he by a pained sense of abandonment that is already a *fait accompli*. Rose felt duty bound to share her observation of the sky, just turned black and blue at the behest of a drumroll of thunder, and to complete the clinical picture a tiny patch of sky above the water towers (Xman's room gave on a somber courtyard's trash) had turned what could only be deemed an electric salmon suggesting the twitched and tortured flesh of a reptile at some too skilled thaumaturge's breathlessly galvanic mercy. "You shouldn't be here," Rose announced. Since imperious brusqueness came easy to her she could assimilate it to a feigned solicitude thereby giving it, so she thought, just the right touch of authenticity.

She looked at her confederates and after a long pause, still maintaining her look, went on, as if now her saying was less a saying than a commentary on their unforgivable blank incomprehension. "You should be back home in the bosom of the family. They're looking at you here but how can they see what's wrong. Your condition can't be deciphered. It was long ago obliterated by the stenchy effluvia coming from the corpses all around you. You are not a corpse, Xman. I knew that the minute I saw you."

"What made you do it, boy," MacDuffers cawed. The nurse entered and urged caution. "Caution it is," replied Perlmutter, ever the ogling harlequin. And before the nurse could close the door on her shapely calves and rump, he cackled, "And plenty of it."

"Xaviero," Xman murmured.

Rose stamped her foot. "Don't blame him, Xman. That's unmanly. Furthermore he's crippled for life. Had to leave the States in a hurry. To recuperate somewhere in Bolivia."

"He never wanted to know *me*," Xman said. "Not even through my impersonations: least of all in those. I was desperate, I needed money, so he had merely to hint at what he wanted done. And what he really wanted done was precisely what he made a point of prohibiting as out of the question, out of the question, my boy—hideous, horrible poses too gross for mention much less enactment. Pretending to guide me he was always hinting at what was most worthy of detestation and so wasn't it only natural that I try out those impersonations he appeared most to detest. I became the map on which he could pinpoint the Unspeakable According to Saint Xaviero. From the minute I started working, Rose— and he and his partner can verify it—I was never content to stand still and be merely myself. From the minute I entered his shabby little storefront, I showed myself alert to new possibilities, ready to tear them apart inside me, and he spurred me on as if to say, 'Go ahead, boy, try on the unspeakable, the raiment I never dared—dare—try on myself.' And then—every time—it never failed—whether I was Doctor Impecunious P. Bottomworth or Father Mustapha G. J. Mustafa O'Brady—once I was fully attired from the security of his vantage outside impersonation he would turn away in disgust. He had only to hint at what was in his terms and in what subsequently became my own hideous—too too hideous for words—to be sure I would be sure to tamper with what was never—do you understand—not under any circumstances—to be tampered with. And then of course joining the medicos he was ostensibly in business to outface and outwit he turned away in stately disgust and outraged exemplariness—his trademarks, as it were—from this . . . spectacle. In other words, once I—I—Xman—had gone to the trouble of decking myself out in all the colors of the unspeakable, the prohibited, the heinous, he was able to duck his head, swerve away in manly outrage from this unforgivable assault on his good will and that of his clients all the while lapping up its extraordinary reverberations."

"He never forced you," Rose bleated.

"No he never forced me. He's a good soul, a decent soul, a noble soul, or you would never have recommended him to me or me to him. Intentions forever in the right place and with a self-proclaimed authentic love of life—and even worse—respect for life—the forms of life—also self-proclaimed. But this same Xaviero—this self-styled pillar of the community—was always harping on those aspects he most detested of the doctors who came to defy and expose him— and so it was only natural I try them out, those hideous aspects, set them before his famished roving eye in a test tube, as it were, susceptible to mastery. What I most hold against Xaviero—or the whole world for that matter—was the relentless insinuation that being myself and myself alone—concentrating on a single point, as it were—was harsh and selfish, a shameless refusal to furnish some little something extra, more than earned befriending me as he had out of the blue. Seeing me be myself and myself alone made him sick and at the same time the slightest deviation toward impersonation necessarily stank of the gratuitously hideous.

He wanted me to incorporate all of being into my impersonation, to cram as much as I could of the unspeakable into my
shabby garments. You see, his wardrobe mistress was very
severe. His wardrobe mistress . . . his wardrobe mistress . . .
but that is another story or at least fuel for another story. I
was to be the heterogeneity right outside his door. And
then—when I was fully decked out, lost beneath the rancid
night of my skin—when at last I embodied the chaos of a
sick heterogeneity for one impeded even in beginning to impersonate himself—then from the phantom security of his
phantom vantage on that chaos he would turn away foment-
ing a riot of disapprobation and displeasure among the pill-
pushers he was supposedly out to gudgeon. Why did he hire
me, Rose—you never told me the real reason, you cunt. Turning away from my unspeakability, without a word, with a
parody of gentlemanly restraint suppressing manly reprobation, gave him an enormous sense of power—the power that
came from impersonating what he would never be—a man. I
was needed to catapult him into his own poor parody. All he
ever cared about was the delicious sense of mastery that
comes from a mere turn of the head—away, far away—from
an assigned site of unspeakability. I was set up to embody the
unspeakableness, the hideousness, the dark purulence, of
being's all. Turning away from me—a mere gesture, mind
you—he had a maddeningly heady sense of repudiating everything loathed within himself, the world within himself
that he plastered onto me, helped me to patch together with
no small help from the pusillanimity of innuendo. He didn't
care whether I—he—won or lost at impersonation. More
important was to play against my impersonation—to impersonate outrage at that impersonation and thereby generate
belief in his own imposture. Don't you see—he turned
away—and the gesture created his meaning. In its course he
caught on to what might be reaped from the gesture—in the

midst of the gesture he caught himself looking at himself from outside the gesture and what did he see but a magnificently restrained palladium of all the all but extinct manly virtues."

"I never knew," Rose said, playing at tightlippedness, Xman thought, as if it were an avant-garde exploit. Oddly enough to Xman's ears, still partially bandaged, she sounded sincere. Mumbling, hoping his usual incoherence would bale him out, MacDuffers said, "All this just doesn't square with what I know of Xaviero. He wasn't just a good man. He's a good man's good man." Perlmutter muttered something that to Xman sounded like, "Shit all shit," but precipitated out of instant retrospect proved to be, "Nothing like old Xavo."

"I never knew," Rose repeated, oblivious to these weaksister protests. She glanced at Xman sideways but something in the skewedness proclaimed that ultimately they would have to confront the matter at hand, namely, the creature stretched out half-naked before her on a hospital cot, sick with fatigue indistinguishable from disgust or whatever else such creatures managed to make it a point to be sick with.

Xman took pity on her and said "How could you have known. I myself never knew: My life with Xaviero was in unstable equilibrium until this very moment. Only by speaking—breaking the sound barrier, as it were—did I begin to understand. Or rather I created a framework—a structure of perception—in which Xaviero was suddenly . . . possible . . . conceivable. Up until now this was not the case. As in certain films praised by that American, Burch, the dimensions of the Xaviero affair remained impossible to gauge until my construction made the scale obvious—a scale of mutual revulsion one might, in this case, say. But of course the beauty stems from the retroactive ambiguity of those dimensions, doesn't it, Rose. Now we see that the Xaviero affair was not what we had all thought: It was never a question of impersonation in behalf of an Xaviero intimidated by the medical establishment. No, my impersonations were, we discover, in behalf of an Xaviero impatient of impersonating, through me and at my expense, whatever he was not and never would be. The doctors he recruited were all so many shreds of thrift shop decor. And at the same time none of this is as neat as Burch, for one, makes it. For the deferred or retroactive match he talks about does and does not occur in this case. Your—our—previous knowledge of the Xaviero affair does and does not defer in this case. Your—our—previous knowledge of the Xaviero affair does and does not succumb to this 'new light' thrown on its vicissitudes."

Rose, for one, seemed reassured and altogether buoyantly said, "Come and see me when you get out." Her hair, jet blacker than ever, was snooded into a big bun, her lips were overpainted, her robustness had much of the manufactured and the moribund. He saw they were eager to go. "Excuse me, oh excuse me, all three of you, how silly of me not to have realized immediately my suffering can be nothing more than a terrible inconvenience for such busy folks. I myself have a positive horror of inconvenience so I know what you must be going through. I know your preternatural quiet, good cheer, humbugging moderation mask depths of—of—nurse—nurse—" He collapsed on the pillows into a fit of hilarity. "One doesn't even have a right to one's own suffering, any more, isn't that the truth, brothers and sisters. One is always inconveniently shaming someone or other. One is aways nothing but trouble to some sickening ancestor, to say nothing of the unspeakable mother and father waiting in the wings and applauding their right to deplore one's latest fall. How, then, can one go about acquiring one's suffering, stamp it with one's very own colophon or imprimatur, when that suffering is all too quickly transmogrified into a terrible shame FOR THEM, THE PERPETUAL BYSTANDERS, WHO THANKS TO ONE'S ALL TOO TYPICAL IGNOMINY WILL NEVER AGAIN BE ABLE TO HOLD UP THEIR HEADS. These bystanders—these Roses, Jeds, and Jensens—always lead one to feel one is the best candidate, yet look at the less than luminous plague one has concocted out of such superlative raw materials. One is always the best candidate after the fact. I see it written on your faces: I am my own worst enemy. So what. I still have a right to assume my shame as if it were my very own. I'd rather be condemned for my shame than for the failure not to have assumed it in time."

"No one is ashamed of you," said Rose B. "We're just a little surprised." She looked around for support. "I let myself get hit by a truck," Xman said, "to be rid of my history—a history of murder, he's dead, isn't he—or rather not so much my history as what is doled out as history through collision with fools like Xaviero, he's dead, isn't he. What trace can I hope to leave—besides the imprint of my tossing and twisting in their Procrustean bed. I came to New York to be unique. But I don't know anymore. Ah—the pain that just hit. To hell with it, in this town uniqueness consists only of the drudgery of serving the likes of Xaviero, footnoting his atrocities. New York certainly won't miss me. New York— uniqueness factory—bringing forth every minute some new fetus of sheer wondrousness having absolutely nothing in common with all other specimens already stretched to bursting on the incubatory rack. In fact, the more willfully different each new clump of fodder targeted at the media threshing machines the more rapidly that clump resolves between the furrowed bladelets into the all too familiar shreds from which at all costs it wished to distinguish itself. I want something different—" "What! What!" cried Perlmutter, with a thirsting impatience he tried without success to make contemptuously ironic. "He's simply afraid of free-dom. The minute he begins to feel its stirrings he delivers himself up to the garbage truck, which proceeds to shred and dump him you know where." Rose walked to the window, looked out, added, "I call this man a coward." "The only reason I tolerated my own history for so long was the thought it would end with a catastrophe of renewal. I tried to create that catastrophe. But you cannot, I discovered, create catastrophe. It must, redounding to your credit, be visited upon you." She shrugged. "Living the events was intolerable. Remembering them even worse. I began to remember even before I was halfway done living them. Not that they were necessarily horrendous in themselves. For, when you come right down to it, 'you guys,' what was the worst I ever did: Yes, I farted in the face of Xaviero's most formidable oppo-nent, the perilous Doctor Pipi. No, these events are abso-lutely horrible simply because they belong to me alone and are irreversible. I had to confess—disgorge—these personal events—these sins—to someone. So I confessed to the only one able to listen, really listen, I mean the truck. Leaping toward the truck served—was made to serve—when all else failed. Leaping I yielded in one vast spasm all I had accumu-lated of a personal toxicity. I had tried other channels of repudiation: blood, stool, urine, semen, pus, snot, more pus from hastily concoted pustules worthy of Jenner, but these failed, failed me markedly." "How can we help," Jed said at once humbly and truculently, but with an overriding sulking bovineness that made Xman want to bash him right in the puss. "We can tell him a story." "No more stories, no more stories," he cried. "Sick to shit of stories." "But this will be a good story," Rose insisted, with a pouting sweetness utterly alien to her being, particularly to her snood. "What the hell kind of story," Jed said, as if standing up on the invalid's behalf against any untoward insinuations. "A good story, a good story, the kind of story that will place him right smack in the crotch of the dream time, where he seems to think he belongs. The kind of story that will cure you of your truck-fearing lust." "I was not frightened by the truck," he cried. He tried but could not rise. "I'll tell you a story that will catapult you right out of your sickeness into a time before sickness came into the world. After all, you're so fragile in your very being, you take every murmur as a sign that to survive you must relinquish yourself and become other. And what is the horrible catastrophe you shrink from—what is it but to be yourself at last. The horrible catastrophe is your kernel of dark selfhood fleeced of all festooning prostrated mimicry. If you do not change, so you think, into something other than yourself you will be destroyed by the inner momentum of that self. But you destroy yourself every minute you refuse to be yourself." Jed Perlmutter entered the conversation—had he ever left it?—with clearing of the throat, supreme sign of supreme tact about to irradiate all that comes after no matter how much what comes after stinks of a flagrantly tactless overstepping of bounds. "I know what you are going through, Xman. Every second is too miserable a specimen of the virginal, beautiful, lively today to be worth making an effort on its behalf. You postpone yourself, alas, thinking you can always backtrack." "Will you shut up and stop coughing," Rose said. He did not stop though up to that moment Xman hadn't noticed him coughing. "I'm going to tell him a story—the story of his illness and cure, and, more important, the story of the origin of his cure." They all looked at Rose as if she was now the repository of great secrets. "But is he sick, that is the question. So why, if he isn't sick, if he is only pretending to be sick, must I squander—on him of all people—the story of the archetypal sickness and the archetypal cure. Let's leave him to his peace and quiet." The two men hung their heads as if outwitted. "All he has to learn is not to allow himself to be disturbed by external stimuli to the point where out of a kind of exasperated perversity he refuses to function in the domain of the true work." He couldn't believe his ears: Why was Rose espousing the true work. "He must stop refusing to be in being simply because the ambience is less than perfect. He must learn to welcome everything that opposes the true work. The true sign of the true work is frustration. He must come to realize the true work is indissolubly bound to the utterly haphazard obstructions that manage to seem to get in the way of its expansion. So, young man, always be grateful for obstruction." Xman murmured as if on the verge of sleep: "In other words, the kind of obstruction represented by Xaviero." "Xaviero is, for all practical purposes, dead," Rose said. Jed Perlmuter stepped in. "So according to you, Rose, the true work is feasible only within the domain of the kind of excruciation you traffic in. But I think Xman here is pretty much his own man. I think he can bloody well count on his own skills without feeding off some sideline." "I never said he wasn't his own man," Rose interjected not because she believed in Xman, Xman thought, but because she did not want to appear to be peddling an easily bracketable point of view. "I, for one, know Xman is able to look his true work in the face without flinching and decree its evolution without a preliminary shot in the arm compliments of the Xaviero-Baldachino paramedic squad. His true work doesn't have to feed off Xaviero-work and work like Xaviero-work." Rose sneered: "It's ridiculous to talk about what he can and can't do—what the true work does and doesn't have to do—since he is nowhere near being one with his vision. He has visions but not a vision." "All I'm saying, Rosie, is that there has got to be a way out of this shabby predicament where the true work begins to throb only in contrast to and as a parasitic offshoot of some hateful little chore. Why do you think this

poor bastard threw himself on the mercy of a fucking truck."
Xman wanted to jump up and kiss Jed on his jowls. "That
hateful little chore, as you put it, Jed darling, paid for Rosalie's visits to the obstetrician, the redoubtable Doctor A——"
said Rose. Bypassing obstetrician Jed pursued: "You want
him to think the true work only conceivable in symbiosis
with a daily grind's slime and immeasurably enriched by the
obstacles that daily grind puts, gratis, in its path. Perhaps in
the beginning when the tyro, waxing alternately tepid and
torrid, is busy contouring the work. But once the contours
are fixed—" "The daily grind is good for him," said Rose.
Never had she looked so pious-cowlike. Jensen's throat-clearing seemed to say he felt obliged to break in. "We can't offer
you the kind of cosmic cures Rose B. here claims she has in
stock but we can liberate you from the diseased thinking she
peddles. After a certain point submission to the daily grind
is not strength but slavishness, bankruptcy not ingenuity.
What my colleague here—and he was never more my colleague than at this moment—is trying to say is that all isn't
lost, all enrichment isn't necessarily cancelled, if you aren't
finding yourself incessantly beating your head against the
wall of the daily grind's absolute refusal to share in the ecsta-
sies of your vision." "No wonder his employment record is
so shabby—nobody has encouraged him to go forward, face
the music. Why do you think he tried, unsuccessfully I
might add as in every other domain, to do himself in—
shame, shame over the shabby employment record. I don't
say he should revel in the daily grind given his pretensions to
a true work but he should find a way of interweaving the
fibers of both tapestries." Her face was suffused with an
imbecile grin. At no moment had Xman hated her as much
as he did at this moment for she was one with the phrase,
"interweaving the fibers of both tapestries," and he hated
that phrase more than anything on mother dearth. "But," he

said, "can I get to use the grind's obstacles faster than they incapacitate me for the true—for any—work. Can I assimilate them faster than they incapacitate me for the true—for any—work. Can I assimilate them faster than they overthrow me." Rose's shrug made him both ashamed and angry that his suffering could be so easily labelled, bracketed and triturated. Or rather it was once again as if the excruciation he was undergoing, bandages and all, was less important than the excessive space the excruciation insisted on occupying in Rose Baldachino's exitless gallery of ordeals borne with exemplary longanimity—as if all could have at last been lovely in her lovely world if not for his untimely anguish. He rebelled against this reaction to his torment, gargantuan as a foregrounded big toe in Mantegna, as simply *de trop*. How dare he vex her with such unthinkable little freefalls into predicament. "Well," she sighed, "we want you to get well, don't we, boys, up and out of here very soon, back on the job. I didn't want to mention it but since you insist I have an assignment for you. Nothing temporary this time: full-blooded permanent and not a thing to do with Xaviero." An imp within prompted him to say: "And what's so very wrong with Xaviero. I liked the work: Even when I was deep within impersonation I always felt I was outside looking in and from a distance infinitely greater than that of Xaviero's maladroit scrutiny, and from that infinite distance pointing to the message embodied by my chosen stance, free to come and go, as it were, however grimly I might have been disdained by this or that visiting quack."

When they were gone he looked out the window to an offshoot of the park. Observing blue spruce coats he told himself: They will outlive me. Though this seemed to calm him the full moon rising in his mind's eye immediately destroyed the moment's timelessness, insinuating its and by extension his tired self-importance among proceedings that with the right visual instruments were very quickly resolvable into a total absence of proceedings. And so the moon, jaundiced, smelly as Gorgonzola left to the skunks, instigated a rebirth of the old agitation to proceed unique and uniquely, dared to insert a timed note into the cadencelessness of the dream time's unfettered music. And it didn't help that within seconds that old devil moon was caught in the teeth of a derrick grazing beyond the union-fixed workday limit.

Coming for him a few days later Rosalie asked if he was well enough to travel by subway since she had no money for a taxi. But why not walk across the park, past the little lake, the fringe of gauzy willows, past— She explained they had moved to a slightly larger apartment, a subsidy, she mysteriously called it. All the way home amid the slime and stench of the New York City subway (commuters were due for a fare hike within the hour) he cursed his—their—fate: You had to be fat as a pig to succeed on this earth, etc., etc. And as if to prove his point at every stop—especially Jude Street East and Fawley Square West—more and more of Gotham's ghostly damp and wretched—more and more of New York's positively charming heterogeneous known at a drop in a hat to throw themselves gratis and unsolicited into the Central Park gladiatorial pit for the delectation from on high of New York's best-dressed—managed to cram themselves ingeniously into the ever punier space.

A tall fat man leaned against the door combing the boil on his neck. After a while the strumming—especially noteworthy in this colorless riot of damp and sweat—began to seem so restful, indrawn, so much hypnotized by its own absence of momentum. But then Xman remembered how insects moving in a circle will often leap forward at the very moment they seem most hypnotized to anodyne eternal circularity.

Out on a little island in the East River the first thing Xman noted were the noises from neighboring apartments. It made them both despair, especially her, despairing over his more vocal despair. At the same time they laughed over the ubiquity of their despair and their unanimity in the face of it. When he lashed out at all the fat hideous cows and pigs sucking the city dry, accumulating a pretty little nest egg while he—while he—was obliged—obliged—all she could manage was a shy expostulating sorrow. He lashed out at her, told her what he knew she longed least to hear, that he should never have married, he couldn't manage responsibility, someone with a true work had to take vows of eternal— etc. And as he lashed out absurdly he saw once again that his suffering was immediately expropriated, this time as her unending shame. He lashed out even more venomously.

As the throbbing bassline grew lashingly louder and louder he said, "They'll get their comeuppance." He shrieked, hating the absurd wishful banality the minute it was uttered, hating himself for having instantaneously exhausted what should have been shored against an occasion even more dire. But could it get direr? When more than now would he need this invocation of comeuppance. "They will," Rosalie said, trying to inject conviction into her hopelessness.

"No," he suddenly shrieked. "The imbeciles, the bastards, the fools, the bastards won't have their comeuppance. But I will go on enduring comeuppances since I am a verifiedly usable site of—of— Why do you expect comeuppances for neighbors upstairs and neighbors down. In a story—the kind Rose B. threatened to tell me—these monsters have their rise and fall but only because the story must have its rise and fall. Morality is the story's shortcut to, excuse for, equilibrium. The ethical curve is sketched to fulfill an aesthetic—that is the story's corporeal—need." And now he hated her for not replying. He took her silence to mean he should return to Rose B.'s and inquire about employment opportunities. Before he could even open his mouth Rose said though she had no jobs she did have a story.

"The office, grim and dismal, gave on a small courtyard. Out of sight the Hudson continued to flow, the young man presumed, into sodden tributaries. He kept reminding himself this was permanent—the real thing. So very quickly he fell into a relation of utter passivity with the others, the endless countless others. Ashamed, however, of his desire to lie down and die he made his way quickly to the urinal, this before his status as a permanent employee entitled to all, or almost all, company benefits could be publicly, celebratorily confirmed. He was reassured by the long line of urinals, the superabundance of stalls beyond. Clearly this was a real, a full-fledged company. Although he did not have to shit he entered one of the stalls, without removing his clothes sat down on the toilet lid, and turned to the wall. A scrawl in a hue somewhat lighter than Lincoln Center's incarnadine ('Trust not the man who. . . ') read: 'Don't be afraid of your passivity, schmuck. On the one hand passivity freezes, yes true enough, reinforces a sense of despair, truer still. In back of all this failed fermentation, however, is an indefatigable optimism, curiosity about how opportunity to emerge at last from the shit will make itself known, and from this curious optimism even you, schmuckface, are not immune. And you are of course correct, putz, when time after time you find it inconceivable that you yourself through your own puny efforts can possibly make a difference—locate survival—for whatever you touch is immediately contaminated with your helplessness, your valuelessness. It is only what comes to you that matters. Continue, continue then, to be passive, on or off the john, so that life's intentions toward you can be made known at last. For the only life worth having is the kind that makes its intentions known at last and without your having to yourself enter in its grubby arena of half-light transactions and soggy compromises.'

"Among his co-workers thinking of himself always as of course completely dead he made it a point never to say, 'Have a nice day,' or, 'You look nice today, Tushina,' much less, 'Billie Sue, you seem somewhat under the weather.' He assumed they must bristle terribly at being bracketed, defined, however amiably, and trounced thereby in the universal game of warring self-assertions. Abstaining though from amiability he (naturally?) begrudged them theirs, underwent each specimen— 'How are you today, Pman?'—for that was the young man's name—'Nice weather we've having Qman.'—for that was his alias—as a leeringly purposeful attempt to torment and humiliate his speechlessness, make him envious of a vastly contrasting fortune-filled felicity.

"He strove, did Pman, harder and harder to be dead, his desk had the orderliness of a tomb. There was no way at this point to see the true work—for he fancied himself a true worker, whatever that is—to see the labor to begin laboring in behalf of the true work's not quite imminent possibility of possibility—as pointed toward anything but posthumousness, more than likely posterity-free. Some of us are born posthumously, his friend Freddy O'Nitch had once said, outside the Ecce Homo Turkish Baths down in—in— He had to live his life here in the labyrinth of cubicles according to this dire knowledge or absence of same. But the key, he told himself—wandering form desk to john and back again, forever dreading encounters with his co-workers, especially those who liked to chitchat and chatchit while relieving themselves—the key is to live this knowledge or bloody absence of same as more than an incantatory cancellation of its ultimate realization. He was bloody well going to die true workless, projectless, and he must not expect indemnification for the undergoing of such a truth. The key was to let the dire knowledge or absence of same penetrate his bloody being awfully. But no matter how he tried to globally appropriate this resignation there was always some fringe of young man peeping in in expectation of prodigal recompense for so much resignation, tastefully deployed. This capitulation to a posthumousness was in fact an intermittent capitulation, prisoner, if truth be told, of its own systole and diastole. No matter how hard he tried after Friday's paycheck despair he always awoke to Satyrday morning's skewed baptism of quasi-riotous expectation. But of what? Of what? Always waiting for bad news, more bad news, he felt his proleptic despair to be genuine. Yet no matter how intense his anticipation, how lucid his resignation, by the time the inevitable did roll around, anticipation and resignation had contracted and volatilized away, had become the sign, the category, the archetype of themselves for which—according to the felicific calculus relevant to such forms without content—reparation was due.

"Though he found it hard to remain a sagittal figure of posthumousness, only posthumousness had the power to furnish captions of a teleological surety for what bubbled up incessantly from his site of putrefaction. Only posthumousness could transform chaos's homogeneity into the dazzling heterogeneity that sprouts from one fixed point's intersection of all avenues of awe. There was no awe for his likes now. But wait, but wait, he told the labyrinths, and the typewriters and the windows of which he caught a glimpse only barely in the course of a day.

"To his co-workers Pman was a miserable being but much to his regret miserableness was never accepted—in other words, did not startle to speechlessness—once and for all. And on a bright sunny day when least expecting it he would be told, 'You seem kind of sad.' But hadn't this been established long before and for all time. He, who prided himself most on a grim gapless consistency, was being informed there were lapses in his armor. For, 'You seem kind of sad,' meant: We are noting your impersonation today—at this moment—of one always sad in order to cast retrospective Burchian opprobrium on those many times in your past when, unbeknownst to you, your impersonation failed miserably. Or, 'You seem kind of sad,' could also have meant: You are always glacially—impeccably—sad but we choose just today and for some special reason to call attention to what is ostensibly, tacitly understood to be, beyond sayability, beyond conceivability. They seemed to snicker not so much beyond his back as at an angle—the acute angle whence amusement is most lancinating.

"Botching an assignment he was always sure he heard them snickering. Yet when these co-workers were similarly humiliated and then bounced right back with a smile he was even more enraged. For bouncing back, contrasted with his brooding miserableness—proleptic coloration against inevitable dressing-down for inevitable ineptitude founded on inherent indifference to anything diverging from the possibility of the true work—must mean their bad fortune was not bad as his was, invariably, bad. They were clearly in possession of some parergon making setbacks insignificant in this sphere. Or they sustained a secret and invisible bond with their tormentor, who was also the young man's—Pman's—tormentor, the less than redoubtable Mr. O'Kay—a bond perhaps fortified by vicissitude. In short, his jealous rage over this intrinsic ability to adapt to circumstance, to rebound from mishap without hoarding incriminatory instances, grew from day to day until transformed ultimately

221

into a murderous obsession with their less than licit secret fund of strength not bravely constructed from scratch of self in the face of circumstance but wheedled out of O'Kay on the sly and guaranteed consequently to keep them smiling under every conceivable lash of exploitation.

"But he was most enraged when, after observing him praised for a bland piece of botchwork, they—the ubiquitous co-workers—still found the smiling strength to say, 'Good work. Have a nice day. Damned good show.' Did this secret fund—this hypostatization of his own exorbitant despair but with the sign rousingly reversed—secure them against all puny successes of others (mere ripples on the belly of well-being) or were they merely heroically dissimulating, sealing off their anguished envy from his observation with a phrase or two. And so never did he bristle so bitterly as when he heard from the depths of this or that cubicle, 'Good work, Pman. Have a hell of a holistic day.' For this 'Good work, Pman,' and 'Have a hell of a holisic day, Pman,' did little more and little less than consign him sempiternally to the slagheap of susceptibility to simple-minded praise for simple-minded bedpan-Charlie-type chores simple-mindedly well-done, Charlie. 'Good work, Pman' told him point blank and without sugarcoating that his good luck was a crutch they were very well able to do without, thank you. They were after bigger game but this did not prevent them from observing the amenities where small fry were concerned. They were all sublimely superior to the contingencies that accounted for his institutional euphoria. From their exalted vantage the boss's secretary's assistant's kind words on his dexterous shredding of paper clips marked him the way a mongrel is marked by uncontrollable baying at a half-moon slab of raw rotting tripe. Their 'Good work, Pman' sketched the bark he ought to have emitted as at fleeced cerulean curdling the glass at the end of the optic nerve. He envied their refusal to be envious, to be anything less than goodness gracious and if they did not show the symptoms of envy either they were not envious, thanks to the gargantuan guerdon wheedled as a lifetime annuity out of fat O'Kay, or simply putting up a good show, better than he could have managed, he knew, under similar circumstances.

"Once when as a reward for having attended to his little tasks with such numbskull alacrity he was allowed to depart early they again wished him a lovely evening again with no sign of resentment which good wishes meant only they were delectating over some bacchanal about to unfold in the loathed office, now a domain of delight, and to whose unfolding his sickly presence had been the sole impediment. In short, he was not to be envied, his early escape was no windfall, he had simply been jettisoned in preparation for some bureaucracy regatta to whose jolts and surprises he was not, under any circumstances, to be privy.

"It was simple, they all loathed him, were conspiring against him. From the depths of his monstrousness he concocted a unanimity they never dreamed—take it from me—they shared. Telling him to 'Have a good evening' even before he was fully dressed to leave depicted, defined and designated him as the prey of contingency, the plaything of circumstance. By so depicting, defining and designating they proved themselves to be beyond—outside—depiction, definition, and designation—outside, then, the most chloroforming categories of medieval thought, outside the contingency he chewed up so gratefully—gratefully, that is, according to the interpretation he imposed on their fluttery lighthearted farewell. Spewing forth their send-off they became superior to all contingency—for all contingency was suddenly embodied in his departure—they became mysterious and inconceivable. Mysterious and inconceivably immune to contingency they were only too happy—always according to

223

Pman's interpretation of this or that tiny little phrase of greeting or farewell—to relinquish momentarily their vantage out of nowhere in order to escort him to the all too localizable threshold of immersion in that out-of-office babbling and gamboling to his wild heart's boobied content that knowing him as they did would have to be his first priority once he hit the streets. They used—he felt it in his bones as he stood by the elevator and grew sick with mad protest that he, Pman, Qman, Rman, progenitor of a true work as true as any man's, should be so discarded, he, he, Pman—they used the euphoria with which they saddled him via their felicitating 'Have a good evening,' or 'Don't take any wooden nickels,' to plausibilize—always according to his interpretation, remember—to plausibly camouflage their eagerness to get rid of him as quickly as possible. 'Have a good evening'—as if in response to his euphoria—was in actual fact his order to go, to make himself scarce, euphoria or no euphoria. But why, why, what were they planning behind his back in the depths of the labyrinth. Were they . . . terrorists. He hated them, hated them all, the nameless faceless pastes. He could barely restrain himself from running back to formulate what had suddenly already formulated itself in his bowels, inexhaustible source of shit: Only by manufacturing his euphoria—once again, how many times, Xman, do I have to remind you, only according to Pman's interpretation—could this eviction at breakneck speed seem a plausible, nay, a gracious, response to circumstances rather than a crude hurried molding of same. He wanted to shout: YOUR EAGERNESS TO GET RID OF ME IS AS IF IN RESPONSE TO MY UNCONTROLLABLE EAGERNESS TO BE GONE. You're impersonators. All life is impersonation. All this—my dear Xman—through sorcery of the phrase, 'Have a hell of a holistic evening.' All this—the monstrous idea at the heart of

their monstrosity—through the sublime witchery of a simple, 'Good work old shit.'

"But he did not go back. He formulated nothing before
their very eyes. He went down in the elevator saddled with
this crude cruel luck at being able to leave early. He gritted
his teeth at every floor as the elevator picked up more and
more drones. What could he do with these few hours? Saddling him with this crude cruel destiny they had expropriated the only destiny from his absence of vantage worth
having—a destiny unuttered and unsketched and foiling all
conjecture and thereby derogating blandly all others. They
had constructed him as the enviable one— the enviable one
they did not however envy—in order to carry out some
deeper darker terroristic purpose in his absence.

"The following day he forced himself to take the initiative.
He said—as a monumental mammoth and yet ultimately
impostural—transvestitial—vengeance on being—'Have a
real nice day,' when one of the foremost drones was about to
leave the labyrinth. He felt as if he had mercilessly incised
her, or his—he, Pman, was not sure of the co-worker's sex; all
he knew was that he/she was taking a course in Gender
Management at the New School—privacy, the secret intention with which he/she had hoped to escape unscathed. Yes,
by his intonation the young man wanted, 'Have a real nice
day,' to mean nothing less than 'Fuck you. I've done it—fixed
you in being. Tit for tat. Tat for tit. Just when you think your
departure is unnoticed and therefore unlocalizable, unsay-
able, I, Pman, alias Qman, alias Rman, a.k.a. Pman, impale
it. With your labels ("Have fun in the whorehouse, Pman")
many a time you called me into the frame from outside the
frame in order to call attention to your own unsituatability,
unlocalizability, your perch outside being. By saying "Have a
real nice day," for once I'm letting you bastards know your

so-called good fortune is not my bad fortune. My good spirits are a coded message to the effect that I am, for once and at last, repository of a global security outfacing—O'Kay or No-kay—all species of adversity.' Yet watching the co-worker depart stigmatized by his 'Have a real nice day,' the young man grew sad for what was he doing but impersonating his co-workers in order to undergo the delectation he supposed they had experienced ushering him out so blithely. Yet he felt none. He was trying through impersonation to discover whether the blitheness irradiating their features had been dissimulated envy or despair, or authentic blitheness stemming from global security. Through impersonation he was trying to resolve an ambiguity that continued to torment him.

"He stood there, long after the co-worker had left, trying to make the nonexistent ambiguity decide in favor of one alternative. It was like straining to relieve himself without success. Either he, like they, had a secret 'out' and enjoyed flaunting its propinquity by showing himself undaunted by another's good fortune, or he had no 'out' and was desperately keeping up a brave front in the face of that good fortune snatched from his clutches. He had been shortchanged: He did not experience the euphoria attributed to his co-workers, nor did he detect signs of envy among them. He/she had simply thanked him and gone a long way down the shaft. Only they, his opponents, were able to milk this game for all it was worth, straitjacketing misery in a protocol of bliss. When they had said, 'Have a nice day, Pman,' and 'Fart one for us, Pman, old tit,' the 'Have a nice day, Pman,' and 'Have a nice lay, Pman,' were simple placeholders vastly vastly repelling all that might have revealed a true state of affairs, with soundtrack ultimately triumphing over image. They had made his early departure mean (for him, for them, for all of being) what their words said it had to mean. But he, in contrast, was left in the lurch by utterance, it fell flat, on his lips sounded stale. Uttering their utterances, impersonating them, impersonating them as if his life depended on it and in this case for no pay, wielding their little phrases of farewell, of come and go, had not procured him, no, not by a long shot, the delight, triumph, aggressive release he knew had to have been theirs, having deftly extrapolated to such rapture from his own despairing sense of having been so thoroughly vanquished. Their utterance, their borrowed finery, had not served him as it must have, oh there could be no doubt, served them. The wardrobe mistress had dressed him in the lowliest tatters, mere flakes of raiment, or rather the costliest garments became mere flakes when draped on his cadaverly shoulders.

"Clearly their utterance did not exist eternally. It allowed for one-time use only, like surgical gloves, and they had expropriated it before he could get to it, before he could desire, know he desired, to get to it. 'Have a nice day,' emerging from their multiple mouth had been at once an empty pleasantry and a savage and delirious transcendence of all that pleasantry suggested of envy held in check. The little phrase had managed to straitjacket his whole being, convert him into a termite easily assuaged by crutchlike favors from on high, while inertia, bondage, nonmovement, had become, also through the phrase's wielding, a kind of infinite clandestine mobility. Bondage was now simply the broadest vantage on the fatuous doings of scullions such as he. Through their wielding of the little phrase, 'Have a good shit, Pman,' bondage had been transmogrified into the exorbitant fringe benefit of those lucky enough to be left behind at the last minute—those lucky or willful enough to have engineered purely through utterance a being left behind. Wielding their little phrase bondage had been bludgeoned into a foothold, a pivot, whence others less adroit—especially one other—

could be lured, puppeteered into manifesting an essential and irrevocable futility, big with blundering locomotion and its heady susceptibility to garish farewells. So it's no wonder, he told himself standing there like a dunce in the labyrinth of cubicles, it's no wonder I tried to wield that tool in order to procure myself the same fringe benefits. The more they pelleted me with the little phrase, the little phrase I am trying now with so little success to make my very own, the more all that exertionless exertion proclaimed their ability to elude fixation simply by uttering such a phrase. Over and over they transformed me into the known by uttering their little phrases. Whereas I, using the same phrases, simply watch them fly back at me like raw egg from a squash racket.

"Then he encountered their slip-ups when fractures in monolithic unlocalizability showed through. When A, B, or C slipped up they would invariably proclaim the slipping up to have been going on purposefully for the longest time, as part of a grandiose program of defiance—terrorism, in other words. And it became clear to him, Pman, that these workers, normally so conscientious, would stop at nothing to lure him from the straight and narrow in order to have companions in misery. In his presence A, usually so conscientious, would profess a flagrant indifference to lapse, taking his silence for credulity. And how our young man—Pman—envied this impersonation, this cancellation of true feeling and true self with a proclamation. How he envied this swift and streamlined overriding of the disjunction between ideal feelings and real feelings through a displacement of focus onto his almost farcically deluded failure to join in the sabotage. And this was when he began—I don't know if I should mention it—to contemplate sabotage as a way of life, a sabotage that would also annihilate these pseudopractitioners. Of course from their perspective he was such a stick-in-the-mud. Although A tried to be casual about his refusal to subscribe to the newly inaugurated program of lapses Pman's refusal to contribute personal instances of ineptitude was a clear-cut irritant. Pman only wondered why Aman, Bman, and Cman couldn't live heroically, candidly. Why had the datum of a single lapse—it could happen to anybody—to be transformed into the focal point of a new policy. But if Xman's—I mean Pman's—silence enraged it also soothed: Subterfuge had passed muster with one who struck the perfect balance between possesion and deprivation of the facts of the case. Pman hated A as he was later to hate B, C, D, D_1, and E for making him caretaker of this desperate ploy—to remove the stench of lapse by contriving to make it partake, this lapse, of the larger stink of a concerted program of lapses, lapse now metamorphosed into definitive verdict on the absurdity of conscientiousness and competence. But all the time denouncing, these others, Pman knew, were planning to resume their competence as soon as possible. Perfectionists all, as only petty functionaries can be, so overwhelmed by the stench of a single lapse they had devised ploys to inter that stench. Reinstalled once more within their shells of competence, they would be the first, Pman knew, to deride his own future lapses. For now he hated their forcing him to acquire these observations encapsulating the disjunction between what they proclaimed and what they truly felt. He wanted to steer clear of acquiring such observations. He hated such observations. For a moment he would have given everything to destroy a world capable of delivering its denizens up to such observations. They destroyed his sanity.

"Collision with the world had produced an inviolable acquisition. His co-workers had marooned him to acquisition of a specimen of bad faith. He suspected such specimens might constitute no small part of his plan. For like you, Xman, Pman had, or thought he had, a plan. And he also suspected that true components of the plan—the true work, if you will—would ultimately be definable only in terms of a mode of acquisition as excruciating as this resulting in a specimen of bad faith. And the mode of acquisition would invariably, he suspected, be collision, collision of a specially painful kind. And the mode of acquisition would also be indissolubly bound to venturing everything as he had ventured everything in acquiring however reluctantly—however excruciatedly—his observation of a disjunction between the stated and the felt among the co-workers. Venturing everything, he suddenly knew, was possible only in the realm of total uncertainty fostered by collision and vice versa. So here he was, Pman, with his first authentic acquisition. He knew it was authentic because he was still trembling and he was uncertain as to what he knew and did not know regarding its very nature.

" 'I hate them I hate them,' he told his . . . companion, when he arrived home. She asked him why he couldn't bear to be alone with his observation (she did not call it an acquisition, or maybe the companion was a man, Pman may have preferred men) without hating it, without feeling betrayed to labor in abandonment.

" 'Why can't you keep your observation and still maintain a vibrant connection with the beings who brought you the observation,' asked the companion. Pman could not answer, he could only hate them. It was too much to be the receptacle of insidious human foible and at the same time know the plan would advance only in symbiosis with such slime, oozed into the vaults of his apperception for transformative safekeeping in perpetuity. Then he burst out to his lover, 'How much longer do I have to endure the ooze of their—humanity's—sores into the bedpan of my accursed omniscience?' But even before he finished the sentence Pman knew the answer: until he was finished with the plan, until he washed his hands of it once and for all, assuming, of course, it was not coterminous with his life. The lover said kindly, 'How much longer will you have to go on witnessing and metabolizing the disjunction between what THEY say and THEY really feel.' In tears Pman added, 'How much longer go on witnessing without being able to wound to irreparable enlightenment, without being in some way rewarded for seeing to the very heart of the beast.' And for your information, Xman, the heart of things comprises a single bedrock—disjunction—between what they feel and what they say they feel.

" 'They ridicule my conscientiousness,' Pman went on. He was now entwined in his lover's arms. 'And I don't mind so much what they say as the disjunction between what they are able to say and what I am able to say. I loathe them for calling attention to my conscientiousness since I have always abstained under similar circumstances from deriding their efforts to be good little boys and girls, beloveds of the O'Kay. I have always pretended not to notice their strenuous efforts in this department. They make me aware of the impossible distance I would have to traverse within—' (he impaled his sternum on right thumb several times) '—before having the courage—offhandedness unmarred by trembling anticipation of rageful vindictiveness—to speak as now they speak, to deride as ever so playfully they now deride.' When his companion asked if that in fact was what he wanted—to deride as THEY derided—shrugging he replied, 'I suddenly desire to do what they do simply because they do it.' 'You are too tactful for that kind of thing.' 'Yes, I am good at tact—simulation of nonseeing, simulation of a being always elsewhere than at the scene of the crime. And what is my celebrated tact but a ploy, growing with each passing day in direct proportion to a sense of encroaching doom. Tact is a foothold, keeps me geared to earth in preparation for some

new failure, some new slash from a fellow worker. Tact is
both a form of readiness for every new disaster—I believe if
only I keep my eyes open at all times I can prevent every
horror's emergence form its dowdy little hole: Pain is a punishment for suspension of vigilance—AND a strategic—a
calculated—bid for reciprocated preferential treatment in
the face of imminent failure. For even if all my failures took
place long ago they exist now when now named, uttered,
implied by derision. If unnamed, they will not occur, will
not be. I'm tactful so they won't name me in my failure. So—
I am proleptically tactful to ward off being named in my
failure—that is to say, my essence.'

"His companion shrugged as if to say, What does this have
to do with us, entwined in each other's arms. But she or he
or she or he shrugged, Pman felt, precisely in order not to
have to say, 'You are not a failure.' The shrug allowed him/
her to imply he was not a failure or to furnish him with
some kind of token assurance that he was not a failure all
the time keeping his/her own counsel.

" 'Yes,' Pman sneered, but it was unclear whether the sneer
embodied awareness of the ambiguity of the shrug—the
shrug going just so far in the name of his well-being. 'Why
should I care what they call me. If I am afraid they may call
me a failure it simply means I already believe I am one—in
relation to the plan, I mean. What would such labelling be
but the skim-off of my own excruciated internal monologue,
echo of a lesion's wail.' He sighed. His companion had gone
to the very edge of their rooftop and was looking over. He/she
turned. 'Did you hear me?' Pman insisted, trying to mask
the plea at the very core of insistence. 'Echo of a lesion's
wail,' he/she responded dutifully, then returned to his/her
station. 'But my own self-indictment is endurable. Each repetition of the indictment annuls its possibility, cancels it
out. Self-utterance kills its target. Other-utterance brings

target into being—forever and ever. Words kill phenomena. Words bring phenomena back to life. I kill my failure calling it by its right name for I can conveniently take being's ensuing silence for incredulity or forthright contradiction.' 'You aren't a failure yet. You're still young.' 'Others bring my failure to life calling it by its right name—calling it by its right name they extrude it into the brute world, out of the warm womb of abeyance. So I am careful not to bait this extrusion, I pretend to be unaware of *their* absurdities, the pitiful disjunction between what they pretend to be and what they truly are, between intention and performance. And I'm such a good impersonator, my darling'—here Pman reached out for his lover's genitals—I cannot say whether male or female for at that moment Pman himself wasn't sure what he would find— 'that these buffoons end up taking my tact for a certain mindlessness, a certain naiveté, whereas all along it is a calculating stratagem. My vigilance—my perception of things—eats up circumambient phenomena so quickly—so voraciously—without the turn of an eyelash, the blink of an eye, that after engulfing the landscape in one fell gulp there is always lots of time left over to play at obtuseness, at laboriously slow assimilation of what was in fact digested long before and is probably at that very moment emerging from between my buttocks as so much ferritin-encrusted slag. What allows me to impersonate'—here he again leaped for the genitals in question—'the man who sees no evil—no lapse, no sign of failure, falling short—is my uncanny intuitive ability to smoke it out immediately at the drop of a hat. It is my quickness of assimilation that allows for a successful subsequent impersonation of varying degrees of obtuseness, Aman's, Bman's, Cman's, I mean A, B, and C's. I would make a good terrorist, a good spy, but never mind. I chew up the bric-a-brac of being so quickly on any single occasion there is no further distraction once I put my mind to imper-

sonation of *he who chews at nothing*, not even his own cud.'
'But you waste so much energy impersonating for the benefit
of your co-workers.' 'Yes, when I could be channeling that
energy into getting ahead sucking up to Mr. O'Kay. But I am
never able to apply my talents or carry out orders (windows
on death) in the domain to which I have been officially assigned. It is always after the fact, posthumously, when I am
no longer feeling coerced, that I flower according to specifications deliciously defunct.'

"After this discussion Pman felt he had annihilated all he
had striven to create through tact and would have to start
from scratch. Talking about his ploy endangered it, made it
unreal, once it existed in the realm of language it no longer
belonged to itself. It would never prove the equal of the name
to which it had given rise, in this case, tact. Pman felt he was
now living not so much in the shadow of his co-workers' ill
will as beneath the contempt of the name, the label. He was
a poor peasant living in the shadow of a mock-Etna. But
more than ever he tried, amid the stray sunshafts that penetrated darkly the labyrinth of cubicles, to be present always
with the right word of unseeing consolation and support, the
apt phrase of obtuse camaraderie. And aside from the effect
it had on others there was a pleasure positively voluptuous
in standing aside and hearing himself utter these words of
obtuseness, thereby acquiring the impersonation adumbrated by their tatters. And none of these co-workers—neither Aman, Bman, or Cman—seemed to suspect that the
foundation was a special pleading on behalf of what he did
not want to hear mentioned—his own status as one very far
down the totem pole, one who had never been able to make a
go of it and must therefore accept the consequences, the
slaving away for brutish O'Kay. None of them suspected a
kind of unspoken coercion, as willful and despotic as the
said O'Kay's fiat of so many reams of completed correspon-

dence per hour, to be treated as he was forcing himself to treat them. He was accumulating a capital of comforting gestures—a sum of abstentions—to which he might refer ultimately if his own crying need for gestures equivalently comforting was not met. In short, abstention cried out for exemption. All this game playing, Xman, was a cry for reciprocity. Just as he successfully suppressed all spasms of *Schadenfreude* when they received their daily dressings-down so he expected them to unite with him in rage against his oppressors also their oppressors. Even then we might say he showed the embryonic stirring of the terrorist spirit. But enough on that subject. Many—not only Aman, Bman, and Cman, but also Dman, Eman and Semen—were incapable of meeting his challenge of reciprocity although these were always of course the first to come crying when one of O'Kay's sublieutenants in charge of budgetary submatters took them to task for failing to mail off a basket of fruit to the proper bigwig or overcharging some other bigwig, equally fungible, on a wholesale order of pinkish green brochures outlining the O'Kay approach to eternal success. For O'Kay was in the success business.

"One morning, Nman, who as co-workers went was more than tolerable, called his name. 'Pman,' was all she said as she skirted his cubicle, smaller than others. He cringed, he could not bear it. This was a terrible infringement on his privacy, an allusion to the fatuity of his pursuits, and a prophecy of even greater disappointments to come. Yes, he could tell form the tone, he wanted to walk away from Nman, but there was nowhere to walk. Her calling, 'Pman,' functioning as pure prophecy intoned with the purest malevolence he naturally hated her, hated her for he knew she was *their* envoy. And then when he realized hers was a prophecy with respect to what was already—supremely—true, that is to say, his abominable failure or rather his failure to experience that indubitable failure given the plan's refusal to give some indubitable sign—when he made this discovery he could only guffaw. But he smothered his guffaw—guffaw at his farcical distress at a prophecy regarding what was already blatantly realized—because he knew someone from Aman to Zman, perhaps Semen, would undergo the guffaw as an invitation to ridicule, and that ridicule, beginning as ridicule of a guffaw's unseemliness, might leak into ridicule of the plan rendering its failure irrevocable and eternal. For as it now stood, his failure—his failure even as a clearly demarcated failure—was a temporary truth, a provisional mechanism with just enough of the lubrific stuff of the apotropaic to do away with that failure before it became ultimate and eternal. They, including Nman, did not know his failure was a kind of playing at failure, a vigilance lest real failure rear its ugly head. If he was able to go on impersonating failure it would never land amid the branches of his being. Impersonating failure Pman warded it off through what he referred to (a secret between him and his pillow) as inverse omnipotence. Impotent as he was, so withdrawn form real being, whatever that was, whatever he enacted—whatever he impersonated—would always remain at the level of impersonation—outside real being—and would never be reflected IN being. Whatever he embodied—strictly outside the pale—of being—would never find its correlate in being, given that he was such a beingless worm. Being—reality—so he reasoned to that bolster—would never allow itself to be sodomized to the point of reproducing whatever he chose apotropaically to embody. Whatever he shaped would never take shape in being precisely because he, an impotent, a passive thing totally withdrawn from the ways and means of being, had shaped it. There could never be any correlation between his inside and the outside to which he prodigally lent his dread of plagiarism. But if impersonation of failure with regard to the plan dispelled the incubus of authentic failure it also kept him from any kind of substantial effort in behalf of the plan.

"On one of the many 'next days' of his working life the co-workers Aman thru Zman enraged him so much he could not refrain form calling—me. I was not in so he called Mac-Duffers who for once turned out to be available. 'I don't mean to be ungrateful, Mr. M, or is it Mr. D, or is it Mr. McD,' Pman began, in a loud voice that carried through the labyrinth, 'but I think I'm reaching the end of my rope with regard to odd jobs, temporary or permanent. When I was a little greener I made myself believe that all these jobs were slumbering toward culmination—toward a real destiny. But none appertain in the least to my destiny. These jobs, sadly enough, have made up my life but that life is completely inimical to my destiny—an antidestiny. Believe me, Jem, can I call you Jem, I mean Jen, I've tried to throw myself whole-heatedly into these obstacles. I convinced myself—maybe for minutes at a time—that they were summating, paving the way toward the vindication of inexpugnable teleology. But now I see obstacles exist merely to plausibilize other obstacles, to alert them to a usable site. Jen, there is simply no limit, no least upper bound descending to put a lid on my excruciations. I've tried here, Jen. When I am knee-deep in the shit of meaningless toil I tell myself, Pman, don't despair, nothing is wasted, nothing is obstruction for one whose life is a destiny. Counting invoices for O'Kay you are in fact exerting yourself—being exerted—on behalf of the plan. As you stretch and strain your muscles scuttling foam from the smelly hold, you are in fact riding the breakers of an exaltedly tempestuous teleology. But I was a fool. There is no destiny utilizing all this waste for a higher purpose. That is why'—whispering—'I thought of terrorism. Life as I live it is thoroughly and utterly incompatible with destiny—thoroughly corrosive, in fact, of destiny—the destiny I might have undergone and of which, from time to time, I catch glimpses the way the weary traveller catches glimpses of distant castle masked by soot of nascent poplar, smoke of still dormant sallow. My essence is elsewhere. I am convinced that essence is to be found in a concerted program of worldwide destruction. Destruction is the only way out of the horrible prospect of "those who come after" being able to feed off the fruit of my present labyrinthine chaos. They'll use my excruciation here as a primer whence to pilfer and go scot-free. They'll have no trouble, these afterfolk, of recuperating my anguish as a mere moment, how susceptible it will all seem, this struggle, to distillation into purest dogma. I am overcome and incapacitated by the enormity of a chaos but they will—the afterfolk—the afterfolk—don't you understand—have no trouble chipping off its minutiae and agglomerating them into a uniquely lucrative program'

" 'And who precisely are they,' MacDuffers said. Although this sounded like an authentic quest for elucidation, Pman took it as an attack. He changed the subject: 'I used to think there was a horde of artisans on my side working day and night on the fabric of my true destiny. But in fact they are on hand only to procure me a wispy intuition of the true destiny forever out of sight so I can be tormented, so I can go on being tormented to the crack of doom by the breadth of deviation from what might have been. They are the anti-artisans.' Pman realized to his horror that he was screaming. There was now silence in the labyrinth of cubicles. Everyone was clearly listening. But he could not control himself. 'You are the anti-artisans. I'm sure of it'. 'I'm convinced that you do have a destiny but your big mistake is to repudiate it. For that is what you do when you take its essential building blocks for excrescences superimposed on an exquisite perfection. You must force yourself to go out and greet each and every, no matter how excruciating, and as quickly as possible, so that you do not find yourself drawing back to dwell on its fortuitous obstructiveness. Remember: The excruciation does not issue from these events but from your insistence that they are detachable through the foresight of rapidly supervigilant reaction. Remember too: The moments of calm between events do not constitute the real destiny. A true destiny is never in tune with itself, is never Titian's Venus in postorgasmic repose. It feeds feeds feeds on obstruction.'

"Pman looked up. All his co-workers were hovering in the doorway. Only when he said, 'I can't remember anything now, Jen,' though he was not speaking into the receiver, did he realize why they were standing about. He was weeping profusely—weeping—more than weeping, shrieking and moaning. He fled their curiosity, dropped receiver in his flight.

"Full of murderous rage he directed himself to me. He had no choice, he told himself. I was the one he had to see. I was in some way responsible that it had come to this. He did not know if he would kill me or merely speak his mind. All the way here he could feel my jugular yielded up to the pressure of his fingers.

"Seeing him I did not allow myself to show fright or panic. Or perhaps he was in no way menacing, only pathetic. 'Well what will you do now?' I asked, holding my ground.' "

"I don't know." After a pause: "What," Xman added weakly.

"I said what are you going to do now. You need something to hold you up, something to cling to."

"Rosalie."

"No a symptom."

Rose sneered. "You know from the start I never took this business of 'the true work' very seriously. But I sensed im

239

mediately that you were somone who could be put to good use chained to a symptom. Oh, it's very difficult to produce a symptom, more difficult than producing this absurd true work. Oh, so you don't think it's difficult to yoke the body to participation in the symptom's genesis, expansion. But then again if you do succeed in producing a symptom expressive of all your agitation—despair—hopeless failure—you can return to it over and over and over. It becomes a usable site, usable for expression of a wide variety of torments and crises. A symptom comes into the world encountering so much resistance, so much incredulity, far more than you pretend to have encountered and continue to encounter with respect to your picayune little parody of a work. Oh I'm sure you have never looked at things that way—you are always the supreme underdog. But any true symptom is a bigger underdog—until, that is, it becomes a full-fledged symptom. Do you think your—or anybody's—puny superconservative organs wish to lend themselves to the expression of this or that anguish, this or that fit of despair. If only a symptom could get along without old man body. If only we could get along without our bodies. No, the body does not want to get all entangled with what thrives on contradiction—that is to say, the network of ideas determining the symptom. For only ideas that are mutually contradictory give rise to the symptom, to the need for a symptom. Xman—forget the true work. Get yourself a symptom. For example, you want and you don't want to kill somebody. But as I just said, once you are lucky enough to get yourself a symptom, to find yourself symptomed, then you need never worry about a form of expression for all your worrying contradictions. You will find you have made a truce with yourself, in spite of yourself—compliments of your dumpy organs—to the effect that whenever particularly tormented future ideas are in need of manifestation they will have no trouble letting off steam through the flue of the already-created symptom. Isn't that wonderful. So Xman, get yourself a symptom, get yourself— with symptom. You simply can't continue this way—running, like Pman, from job to job. What are you going to do now?"

He no longer saw her, barely heard, dropped into a chair by her window.

What. What are you going to do now.

Looking out the window, he vaguely discerned the window frame.

"Life is a prison. I know better than anyone. But only when you accept it as one do you begin to make progress, only then do you discover those marvelous escape hatches peculiar to prisons, only then do you begin to breathe freely in the midst of global asphyxiation. For once you have established that your residence is indeed a prison you are supremely qualified to pick out, amid the slime of neighborly small talk and other ungainly resonances, this or that wretched gillyflower shaking in the sooty breeze, this or that lizardly fissure of cool silence amid institutional stampedes. But what are you going to do now. You see what happened to Pman. You're not made for the labyrinth of cubicles, you're not made—nobody is made—for 'the true work.' Only for a symptom are you made. And the supply is running out."

What are you going to do now

that lilacs are not in bloom to pay the bills, appropriate the necessary frills.

What are you going to do now to make the frog community wake up and take note at last of your croak as unique among croaks, far beyond croakdom yet necessarily identifiable as some form of croak—prolapsed into identifiability— if for no other purpose than to be singled out, decked out for

apotheosis, as croak beyond croaks. For yours must be identifiable as a croak if it is to end up as Tussaudian croak to end
all croaks. Croak, croak.

But what are you going to do now about this absurd craving for transcendence when Arts and Leisure, or is it Home,
section of *New York Times* has proven definitively that such
a craving is passé, *outré*, or simply *de trop* amid the harsher
than harsh disagreeabilities encountered by town-house denizens, East Side and West, straightforwardly in search of a
halfway decent venison salad to feed their fellow revellers
after a hard day at Berghuff Tucci.

What are you going to do, orthodontically speaking, about
this absurd predilection for gritted teeth all down your spine.

What are you going to do, oncologically speaking, about
this never benign lack of easy money.

What are you going to do, deontologically speaking, about
the mother-to-be and the baby-to-be given your manifest
loathing of distraction from possible upsurges of the true
work particularly during those star-studded moments when
there is absolutely no sign of its imminence, absolutely no
word from the artisan horde—yes, that irrepressible horde
again—putatively hard at work weaving the final strands—
into—into—

What about total despair and yet, given the slightest—the
barest—the flimsiest—hint of a kind word from the bowels
of the good earth, this twinge of amnesiac's deprecatory unworthiness in the face of triumph come too easily and far
too soon.

What about hemorrhoids—spoor of the shit serpent.

What about life offscreen, outside being.

What about preoccupation with equity as a mere refuge
from personal disappointment, conveniently displaced and
expanded to world-shattering dimensions of dimensionlessness.

What about crooks, hustlers, landlords, and "the world's most ruthless magnates" unconscionably using bullhorns, hoodlums, fire trucks and kind words to evict aged tenants from crumbling brownstones and laughing ever laughing at the boundless naiveté of these poor slobs incapable of taking life seriously enough to think of ways of beating it at its own game. Maybe they—the "most ruthless magnates" are the most naive of all.

What about the possible naiveté of the above construction with its mawkish punchline.

What about the naiveté—the straitjacketable naiveté—of all constructions.

What about the pathologic implications of the need to flagellate the need to erect such constructions over the corpse of one's failure to thrive in a world bereft of the efficacy of such constructions.

What about this need—this need to have the last word on one's folly—as a solipsistic parody of vengeance wreaked on an opponent completely oblivious and yet to be satisfactorily identified.

What about abstention as yet another fatuous because solipsistic vengeance on an opponent completely oblivious—his royal fartness, 'All of Being."

What about the god from the blood of whose dismemberment blooms the heterogeneity of sacred space. What about the *dei otiosi* yawning deep within the cumuli of sunset, authorizing their dimiurge flunkeys to wreak the havoc that was their trademark once.

What about the "gathering shadows" of popular fiction and international terrorism.

What about the hopelessness of attempts at self-betrayal.

Night was falling. Rose had her coat on. "I have an appointment," she said. He could see her more clearly now. He held his stomach. The sight of her sickened him, he turned purple with the asphyxiated and impatient craving to spit his tripes.

She held a portfolio under her arm. He advanced on her, she advanced her arm to ward him off. More effective was her saying, "The suicide attempt has preceded you everywhere. Nobody is going to hire *that*." She was suddenly speaking with the exaggerated twitching affirmativeness of somebody who is unnerved by the imminence of a confrontation dreaded for the longest time. It did not sound as if this had been rehearsed but rather as if having to no avail promised herself time and again to sit right down in the breakfast nook over the decaf and muffins and prepare for the inevitable return of the world's biggest schmuck she was now stumbling all over herself to give the impression of a spontaneity expert beyond the need for union-fixed rehearsal time.

"By the way," she said, sitting down at her desk, "how is Rosalie coming along. She never talks to me about her personal life."

For a moment he looked closely at Rose B. Rather than face the cold he was "sorely tempted" to "open his heart" to Rose, to tell her Rosalie was in fact doing just fine but that he only hoped she did not decide to give birth on that special day reserved for Balanchine's ballet about a village boy and girl and the fairy that threatens to carry him off forever, on the same program with the one, sublime he was told, about a young poet at a ball who gets entangled in the malevolent intrigues of an irresistible coquette and after inciting the host to ungovernable jealousy himself becomes enthralled by a phantom sleepwalker dressed in white and carrying a candlestick. Eluding in their pas de deux every trap he clumsily sets for her, in the end she literally carries him off to another world. Or so Xman wanted to think. And all of this to the music of Bellini: The blackamoor duet danced to the *Norma* Adalgisa/Norma duet; the ball's set piece purloined from the *I Puritani* polacca; an air from the first act of *I Capuleti e i Montecchi* finding itself the dark angel in the serpentine poet/coquette pas de deux; and *La Sonnambula*'s "Ah! non credea" used epilogically as the sleepwalker stands over the poet's corpse. Xman wanted to tell of all this. The anticipatory rapture with which he could infuse at such a time hunger to see this ballet—time of his wife's pregnancy when every normal man is sickened with uxorious delight at the prospect of participating in a facsimile's advent—at such a time this sort of rapture must signal indestructible uniqueness. Surely Rose could not help collapsing before his prostration before the prospect of dazzling configuration after dazzling configuration of diaphanous dryads. He was tempted—oh never more than now—to foist off his prepackaged uniqueness on one who viewed him as the lowliest of failed clerks. But he forced himself NOT to speak. He forced himself not to attempt to sell a uniqueness that would only be straightjacketed—bracketed—in other words, shrugged off. For Rose had an infinite capacity to assimilate—equalize—all tremors and upthrusts. Restraining himself he sensed immediately—oh to be in better shape to appreciate and applaud—a new epoch being ushered in. Was he mad to think it might be the epoch of the true work. He had restrained himself knowing this fast-talking cow, this seamy profit machine would never be dazzled to reverence, awe— even sullen curiosity—faster than her engines could find words to bracket and thereby volatilize him away as one more specimen of the tiresomely bizarre. He had kept—oh miracle of miracles—his own counsel, no matter how much he had wished to speak of and thereby fuse with the sleepwalker—too good for this earth—to become as beautiful as he imagined her to be and to remain as beautiful in the eyes of the cows he despised more than himself—especially in their eyes, the cows he despised. He had dimly perceived that she would have pigpenned him to fatuity faster than he could ever have disarmed her, inducing prostration before something unearthly, far far more beautiful than whatever was put forth as desirable by employment agencies and typing pools and cubicle labyrinths festooned with greeting cards heralding the wearisome joys of this season or that.

"Waiting anxiously," he said, poker-faced. He continued to say, to express, nothing. "If there are going to be hard feelings—" He felt himself beginning, after this sulking rejoinder—but to what—to get enraged again, to want to strangle her. Calmly he said, smiling, "As if our relationship has ever partaken of anything that might by any stretch of the imagination be considered an alternative, a contrast—to hard feelings."

"You're fragile, Xman. Your self-esteem—"

He begin to breathe hard. But the room did not spin. "Self-esteem, self-esteem," he tried to sample its taste. "Self-esteem, self-esteem," she prompted. "In the service of the true work I relinquished my concern with self-esteem quite some time ago. Maybe I've misplaced it, in the heart of an aerolith or under a sofa." "Or under a truck." "I hardly intend to go to pieces over your puny little reference to my . . . collision with the truck." "Temper, temper," pacing. "As for this truck business, Rosie—don't mind if I call you Rosie, do you—I feel it's my duty to inform you that you've hooked onto a completely irrelevant aspect of my being. It's a completely unrepresentative outcropping, so much sand thrown in the eyes of amateur exegetes struggling to undo me with the proper proper name. You thought you were annihilating me with an allusion to my trucklike essence. But in fact with all this babbling you have done me the service of distracting attention from its real site." "Good luck," she murmured. "Love to Rosalie and—to the little stranger." He had his hand on the knob. "You'll need luck. Because after your suicide attempt . . ." Outside it was night, he thrashed past passers-by as if struggling toward the gates of the city. Where were the gates, what were they, and to what did they lead. He tried desperately to put Rose within a framework enabling him to look back at her with pity immune to the slightest surge of bile by thinking of what was plaintive and beautiful, say, the toccata from Widor's Fifth Organ Symphony, but to no avail. Her viciousness triumphed over every effort to mitigate. He was still looking for the gates, involuntarily he fished in his pockets, torn, for loose change as if these gates might in fact levy a toll. "Rosalie." He murmured her name. The only other word that soothed, caulked the wound that was he walking, was, "No." No, no, no, no, no. Although he spoke without moving his lips, without a single twitch, still people looked, and as if he was not merely moving his lips but also scratching his balls, etc. Though he had no balls, not at this particular street-corner, in this particular glare, though at the next, who knew what he might claim as his very corporeal own. He was in the very heart of the urban slime, Fifty-ninth and Third. Up toward Sixty-third and First three old folks watched him pass. He was moving fast, he knew, clearly absurd. But clearly they did not know each other well enough to unite in mockery of his absurdity, the absurd flare of his trousers, the absurd contortion of his immobile lips. Then what united them. He had to know before he left them far behind forever, for it was clear he would never see them again, on First or elsewhere. Then he saw—collided with the context at the very moment when turning a street-corner he was about to lose it forever. They were standing—of course, why hadn't he thought of it sooner—in front of their just-about-to-be demolished tenement house, sandwiched between Versailles-Fontainebleau Condominium Towers—"an experience in urban sensuality"—and a string of gourmand boutiques where the illegal immigrant underclass wrapped

247

and beribboned the venison pâté consumed with such bland voracity by its betters. Obviously they had made the foul mistake of not keeping up with the times. Members of the demolition crew and what looked like emissary executives from the corporation very much responsible for this derrick-created prestidigitation passed by with evident distaste as if the dialyzed piss with which the trio (never a triumvirate) had ostentatiously befouled its paper-thin bedclothes was still warm. A lady carrying three shopping bags all the time wheeling a huge shopping cart to which a far greater number were attached made a point of looking back with the hugely italicized distaste of infinitely preferable mobility. Yes, the face of the city was changing.

"Yes the face of the city is changing." In the midst of his rage—his profound and stalwart communion with these three elderly vagrants—he heard himself impersonate a bland organization man or bejewelled dowager remarking on the plight of his or her congeners (several times removed) with the mildest amusement in delight that the city still managed to furnish for the sake of the jaded eye-catching examples of change-movement-transformation. He found himself impersonating. He was no longer himself, he was impersonating, yet he wasn't being paid. He remembered Rose. He needed a symptom: A symptom would get him through, steady as no malacca cane could.

He refused to turn the corner. He would stand his ground until he was Xman again—not Organization Man X or Dowager Y—straightforwardly compassionating with these misfits. He looked hard at the emissaries in their three-pieces and for a second—on this particular street corner, perhaps on no other—he was sure that when it finally came to birth the true work would do them definitely in, reigning forever and ever in their stead. But then they made a movement— the landscape shivered—a spark fell from the topmost story of the wretched little hovel about to drink at the same chimera as the derrick's maw—and Xman—he was Xman now, deploring the cruelty of change—he was Xman—excoriating the brutality of the city's doings to its aged and poor and mad, never forget the quite luminously mad—he was no longer the chortling dowager McD in need of a little local color to perfuse the pale paste of her flabby buttocks—and Xman—Xman now—only Xman—watched helpless as they managed to claw themselves free of the storybook frame in which they had been placed in order that he, Xman, might undergo in peace the suturing prospect of a redemptory true work. For it is only within the frame—carefully walled off from offscreen space in which such vermin tend to circulate at highest speed thereby coming to conclusions that bury us all—that comeuppance is feasible. For the frame stipulates the framed product must undergo a rise and fall, a trajectory. Now they were outside the frame, these three-piece suiters running loose, instructing their henchmen to keep the skulduggery coming hot and heavy. The three vagrants-in-training watched the derrick's maw as if hypnotized. Xman faced instead the music of the derrick's jib, metronome of those virtuosi who wished to transform mamma York into a temptress of glass and steel. He decided to walk, which meant putting one foot in front of the other. Then he thought: Why bother, like an actor—he was now impersonating an actor, any actor, an actor about to be evicted from his brownstone—who realizes he is performing long after the last spectator has straggled out into the chilly midtown night. Decision to walk may have begun as a craving but was now dying as an incentive to said craving—a spur to said craving—now that said craving had suddenly lost all potency of pulsion to instantiate authentic being in being.

He walked on uptown toward Seventy-second. A woman ran across the street. For a split second he felt Rose was wrong. He no longer needed a symptom. Watching the woman run he no longer needed anything for clearly she needed nothing beyond her own unfathomable momentum. He knew there was a bus waiting on the other side of the street. He was glad she was running to the bus especially since this bus in no way diminished the intrepidity and bravado of the run's mad dash but there was a desolation he could do nothing to conceal when it opened to admit her. This was a big letdown, more his, of course, then hers. Though the tonic of exhilaration for having arrived in time—*her* and at the same time his having arrived in time—was mounting exponentially it activated a simultaneous ascending curve of pain alerted to its one and only golden opportunity—his lapse, in disinterested exhilaration at a street scene, from vigilant expectation of more pain. Rose was right: He needed a symptom. Something to allow him to contend with these letdowns. Every street sold its letdown, that was the glory of New York.

He crossed. It began to rain. The traffic, including the bus in question, at least for him, advanced madly toward the park. He wanted the rain to stop. It was the sole impediment to well-being: not having lost yet another job, not having conspired to lose it, not the true work's refusal to rear its head, not Rosalie's imminent delivery, but the rain. Obstructed by the rain well-being was suddenly luminous, dimensionless, unending. He looked around: The traffic was gone. For a split second—at this particular street corner—the disappearance of the traffic meant rain's surcease. Awareness of his mistake made him feel heavy, too heavy, as if his arms were weighed down with the sale items with which their few cupboards over sink and stove were cluttered. He was convinced he was carrying packages in the rain and as the woman who had entered the bus was gone, gone across Central Park into the Hudson River, there was no hope of succor from that end. He sighed: The sigh imagined how agreeable it would be to be free of packages. Forever. And suddenly he had the thought: He had the look of one who, though now unencumbered but used to being weighed down, was in fact looking around hungrily for some thing to haul. But he had the thought as that troublesome dowager D again, or was it as organization man P in his impeccable three-piece suit of mail. He didn't know where he was: in the dowager or in himself. Suddenly there was a passer-by. At first he thought it was the running woman come back to offer him food, drink, warm clothes. All along the street she looked into shop windows but there came a moment—a moment privileged as that when the traffic's disappearance becomes the pattering rain's surcease—there came a moment—a moment—the moment—when the solemn stiffening, the almost imperceptible pout going from rosebud lips to the very tips of the toes, announced that after so much intermingling with foreign particles she had at last caught her reflection. During this moment, now that, all these moments in the cold and rain, he was suddenly feeling so close—close—close to the true work's upsurge. It was as if behind the solemn stiffening and instantaneous disappearance of bull-headed traffic undergone as end of the rain the true work—behind—behind—filial from first to last—was emerging from no belly but his. Not Rosalie's but his own. The solemn stiffening evoking an infinite realm of mixed feelings at reflection caught at last and the sudden disappearance of traffic misinterpreted as the end of rain were the true work rearing its ugly head at last. In the distance a flue nourished with its noxious spasms a whole firmament of overcast. Grotesquely foregrounded were his lips. He could see them ever so clearly. He had to change their expression. Quick, before everyone found out. For to every spectator they had to be registering an expression of—of—instead of a

251

merely mindless physiologic reaction to a swarm of phenomena too lowly to disentangle and enumerate for the benefit of the census takers. He had to change the expression of his lips, for the expression of those lips—those lips—those lips—were those of somebody who went beyond destruction (through a symptom) of his self to destruction of everything. Dangerous lips.

He tried to think of the true work. He tried to think of going out and acquiring a symptom, something to express his contradictious attitudes toward the true work. Instead he could think only of a truck. Any truck. He needed a truck, its white mass bordered with yellow lights, redolent of skin's rancid night. Only collision with a truck could strengthen him for the collisions to come.

He found himself walking again toward Park. "Nothing like Park in the Eighties," he heard himself say. He was not saying it as Xman but as some normal everyday Joe proud of the wife and kids, proud of his ability to keep up the mortgage payments, proud of mom and dad's pride in their kid's ability to "hold down a job," stay gainfully employed through thick and thin.

Park Avenue meant trucks going at full speed. Park Avenue meant escape from the true work, the symptom question. He stood on an island, similar to the island of that other time, but this was not at all like that other time, this was a completely different time, absolutely no similarity between this time and that time. It seemed to him if he was careful and made sure no one was looking he could leave his lips here, on this tight little island fringed with nodding scraps of begonia-simulating cardboard. A couple overtook and passed him. They were already in the middle of the street so eager did they seem to get to the other side, to Lexington, Third, Second, First, East End, Schurz Park, the River, the river beyond. Absorbing all impersonation into

the massiveness of their welded self they left him momentarily free to be Xman. But their mere presence, well-fed and
well-furred, evoked unemployment, the responsibility he
was refusing to face, what he might miss if Rosalie chose to
deliver on the night set aside months before for what was in
fact too too crucial to miss. The true work would never
upsurge if he was not contaminated first by the sleepwalker
lifting her poet in arms deceptively frail to carry him off and
away forever. He needed to be buttressed first by the sleepwalker's indestructibility.

The traffic showed no signs of stopping, the couple would
be here forever, they obstructed the view of the true work,
they reminded him of his unemployability. With his right
foot he stopped the flutters of a washed-out tabloid, lifted it.
He tried looking at the fine print, not as if the tabloid belonged to him but as if totally unfamiliar with its format he
had stumbled on a copy for the very first time and was therefore assessing it with the innocence of casual skepticism—
with no preconceptions. Which was in fact the case. Only,
impersonating what was in fact the case transformed him
into all he was not—one in, of, the world, no longer impatient of its pace but perfectly adapted to that pace, perhaps
even a little behindhand—at any rate, peaceable consumer of
worldly produce. The impersonation of what at this very
moment he in fact was transformed him into all he was not.
From this sprig of impersonation he wished at all costs to
hang indefinitely or at least as long as it took for the true
work to sprout from its nodes. For absence of preconception—he was sure of it—here and now—in the middle of
Park Avenue—was the only fertile field—the only true manure—whence a body of true work could spring fully
formed. He wanted them to turn around and catch him in
this moment of impersonation. Rapture, awe, before one so
innocent, so free of preconception, so free of attaint by such

a planet would surely defang them. And once defanged they could help, they could help procure him his place in the world. They had the look of . . . powers that be. And in fact he had just procured the scrap of newsprint—it did not belong to him—it never would—he had never before seen such a layout—not in all his years of news ingestion—so it was not an impersonation, this eager innocent curiosity. He was truly eager and innocent. But no—no—no—it would only succeed as impersonation. Only impersonation insisted on dying. Holding the rag he had absolutely no desire to read on and was completely disgusted by the way the black print seeped into his fingertips already contused.

They began to speak, waiting for the light to change. Talk, yes, like normal people, normal married people. The female mentioned someone who was making fifty thousand a year. Xman felt more unemployed—unemployable—than ever. He was demolished. Then the male—the husband—the lover—said: "I'm hungry." And now—now—just as in the hotel room—yes he recognized the voices—this had to be a Fa and (-)Xman—now he was no longer intimidated. For in saying, "I'm hungry," the male—the husband—the ruthless and powerful magnate—constructed and embodied the world's—all of being's—triviality, futile preoccupation and left Xman free, scot-free, to impersonate—no no no, more than impersonate—embody—the only high seriousness left in the world as the only conduit to true success—true success as mammoth reparation for all that abstention (always in high seriousness) from unappeasable hunger and thirst, supremely frivolous in their pertinacity. Having deduced, in other words constructed, the couple's amends-laden triviality—correcting their unpardonably high-spirited allusion to big salaries, civic responsibility, employability—Xman felt better, much better, almost strong enough to cross the street rather than wait for the truck. When he turned back though in fact his eyes had never left them they were lost to sight, even on the other, the Lexington side. His only foothold, his only pivot, was gone. They were gone before he had time to ask them what relation an impersonation such as that performed for their delectation could have for the true work. Could such impersonation be recuperated in behalf of the true work. Could the instant retrospect for which he was surely famous on both the East and West Sides recuperate such impersonation as a commodity, a component, a building block of said true work. Was, then, the true work the sum of such impersonations—their retrospection concurrent with—maybe even in advance of—maybe even IN ADVANCE OF—their enactment. Was it the duty of the true work to somehow yoke these impersonations into semi-plausible connectedness and consanguinity. Was then the true work a being concocted from an infinite sum of nonbeings. In short, Xman was put on earth to enact his impersonations for the benefit of folk like this vanished Park Avenue couple in order that later the same minute such impersonations could be molded and contoured to conform to the contoured Procrustean bed of the true work. It didn't matter what, who, when, how he impersonated. What mattered was the simultaneous transformation of such impersonation by instantaneous retrospect with an eye on, to, the true work. A cyclist passed, proud and indefatigable in the rain. He didn't want to follow the cyclist with his eyes. Especially now that he was buoyed up by a mammoth high seriousness doomed to conquer all. But the high seriousness had dissolved away having resisted volatilization for so long compliments only—in the vivifying beam—of that fat man's chitchat about hunger, thirst, genital cravings. Now he was nothing, Xman only, equivalent to nothing. As Xman he cancelled himself out. Nothing remained but the cyclist's retreating buttocks. It was the turn to the cyclist, then, that dissolved away a vitality at its peak. Why hadn't he been content to live within the boundlessness of that vitality. Why could he only exist afflicted by some solicited soliciting marginal irritant capsizing ultimately a vitality afraid of its own conatus. Why must he live on the margin of himself. Why was his being obliged to advert to another's—on the margin of his own and which marginality became the inevitable shrine at which he felt obliged to prostrate his self-loathing. It was too late. No true work. Only a symptom—fleeting—this hunger for the cyclist—surely this hunger was a symptom—it had to be admitted—a symptom, made to the order of Rose B.'s domineering insinuatingness. Only a symptom but not one to buoy him up in the interim before the true work upsurged. To be buoyed up by the symptom—surely that was outside Rose B.'s field of bracketing conceivability, surely that stratagem would do the old cow in. Too late: only silence, only the truck, only the bier of the street impaled on a rainstorm's cracked axis. No true work, no employment, no proud self-sufficiency. Filial—it—it—could have been born once. Only a symptom as fleeting and meaningless as a rainstorm. But wait—wait—here was instant retrospect, what had he been thinking? Something about why he could only exist afflicted by some solicited soliciting marginal irritant capsizing ultimately a vitality afraid of its own conatus. Yes, wasn't this the story of his life, life of Xman, he who loathed stories above all else. Hadn't he just taken the momentary excruciation wrought by a symptom and transformed it into an observation. Couldn't he somehow use this observation. Couldn't this predicament, this lamentation over predicament, be recruited to the work soon to be at hand. Couldn't this predicament no longer predicamental now it was recruited to thought—to observation—be recruited even more heroically, even more thoroughly, to the true work at hand. Couldn't he trying very very hard begin to smell the configuration of the true work from these pinpoints of utterance derived from observed unworthiness for any earthly activity whatsoever, least of all a true work. Too late, too late. It was simply too excruciating to preserve these shards of instantaneous retrospect toward some final purpose—some destiny. Best to be rid of these observational uttered shards as quickly as possible. They stank.

He walked and walked, toward Forty-second, impediments on the way to the true work everywhere: ashcans, tree limbs, shopping carts, puddles reflecting the confectioners' clocks abrading a skyline of soot. Too many impedimenta leaving no alternative but to walk faster faster faster ever faster tearing at his own flesh and chitinous exoskeleton in order to make way at last for the true—the true—for he did not want the true to be born of collision with objects. Collision with objects—take the cyclist, for example—only produced symptoms that recalled him to his unworthiness, his ignominy. Collision with cyclists, for example, at best produced symptoms that brought him to the threshold of articulation and beyond. And he did not wish to be saddled with the articulations that commemorated a sodden humiliating collision with objects—with cyclists—with these cyclists and trash cans and frondlet-fanned treetops. Get yourself a symptom, she had said. And he had got himself a symptom—had got himself *with* symptom. But symptom bred utterance or at least a hunger for utterance: "Why could he only exist afflicted with some solicited soliciting marginal irritant capsizing ultimately . . ." Or rather symptom, as he lived symptom, was indistinguishable from utterance. Symptom bred utterance, was utterance. And utterance bred a hunger

to acquire the utterance, to insert the acquisition in a sequence a—story. No, no, no, no. No symptoms, no utter
ances, no acquisitions, no insertions, no sequences, no stories, no . . . true work. For there was no way around uttered
and acquired symptoms to the true work. On Broadway he
looked down a side street. In the shadow of many many
hours past midnight a man and his deformed aged son,
propped half-a-buttock each on the same hydrant, were sharing a hard-boiled egg. Why these objects instead of any others. Why not a ladder or a condom. This pair—this father and
son—were immediately already known, too well known, too
well inventoried in their every nook and cranny. He was
saddled with the excruciation of arraigning—conceiving
something like arraignment for—a father and son. Why this
father and son. Which was not to say he was a partisan of
that father and son over there. Nor was he peddling partisan-
ship of mother and son, mother and daughter, pimp and slut.
Why—anything. Why anything when he did not need anything, did not want to need anything, did not know how to
learn to want to need anything, want to learn to need anything. He abolished the side street, an already plotted—an
exhausted—itinerary. Still he wanted to walk down that side
street. But this want—this hunger—was also an already exhausted itinerary. The man, his son, the egg, the reflection of
the lights of Broadway on sooty finials—these were all so
many hungers—pretexts for hunger—cast aside as impediments on the way to—to—for he knew how they ended. Anything was an impediment whose ending was known. All of
this was a known schedule, an already plotted itinerary. All
of Broadway, all the self-important marquees, all the
wretched plotting transactions in trash-eddying doorways,
was the already known. None of this could lead Xman where
he needed to go if—if—if— Of course: "Why could he only

exist afflicted by some solicited soliciting marginal irritant
. . ."—shards of this type could begin to lead him where he
needed to go. But he simply refused the excruciation attendant on such being on the right track at last. He—Xman—
failure by trade—wanted objects to yield him a true work
without his having to endure the utterance-breeding collisions crucial to the prenatal evolution of that work.

To a stranger he said, "If only the true work would unfurl
its plumage like a deck of cards." He smiled, knowing he had
somehow to dispose of his lips. His lips gave him away. And
not only to the cyclist. The stranger did not answer. So he
screamed to Forty-second Street itself: "Why doesn't the true
work unfurl." The street, normally brazen, rasping, rheumy,
did not answer. It looked as Rosalie might have looked at
such a juncture. It did not answer yet in its delicate fili-
graned hands this refusal did not in the least publish skepticism or ridicule, became profoundest solicitude. He looked
askance at the street as if the street were in the wrong. Yet
was the street after all doing any more than trying for all it
was worth to remain tactfully tangent to the curve of his
telling, of his refusal to tell. And it was he who was infuri-
ated by such respectfulness taking seriously his pronouncements. More than the world's unconcern (New Year's Eve, he
realized, and in Times Square) it was the high seriousness of
the little street enduring oh so patient and ever so resplen-
dently (as if it did not have enough to contend with in the
form of exhaust fumes, postadolescent riffraff, fulsome overflow of trash melting in the absence of starlight) the agglomeration of potbellied clouds at its tip while striving oh so
diffidently oh so stalwartly to master his refusal of mastery—it was this exemplary striving that drove him to total
despair. How could he complain in the face of so noble a
little fellow as the street. And at the same time he hated the

street for making him bear full responsibility for his uttered anguish at the same time that avowal was supposed to do— and almost did—away with it completely.

Rose B. was right: He needed a symptom to oppose to the street, any old symptom, my kingdom for another cyclist, lean and in the bloom of youth. He did not have the courage to face the street unsymptomed. That bitch Rose had seen to it that he emerged from her cubicle sapped of all strength. No use blaming Rose. But there was no symptom willing to vomit itself forth from the bowels of his being. Or rather he harbored no credulity for a possible symptom's upsurge. Only sodden tears, crust of paroxysms passed. "I need a symptom," he murmured. Especially at the corner of Forty-second and Eighth where the bright lights were too bright, almost searing the very covers of pornographilia imbricating newsstand walls. He turned—"on his heels," he murmured and felt better for one, no, two and a half steps—toward Park. Just before turning away high above Times Square he read the following illuminated ticker-tape message: "In the face of life one can only continue buoyed up by credulity of alarm for surprise upsurges of the symptom as—as—" turning away for an instant he noted that Rose's face imposed itself upon the tip of the Chrysler Building in the not-so-distant future of vagrancy "—as—as—incarnation—only conceivable incarnation—of life itself. The powerlessness that informs as a matter of course one's relation to life—to being—as a New Yorker, a New York animal, of course—can only be attenuated in the restricted field of exercise of the symptom and its outpouchings that replace, as controlled though hardly masterable microenvironment, life—life itself . . ."

With the ferule used by schoolmarms a man on a soapbox was pointing to a chart fixed on a portable easel. He was saying to a thumb-sucking crowd of ungainly thrill seekers:

"We live, my dear friends, we live in the age of the symptom. THE AGE OF THE SYMPTOM"—he pointed to every letter of the phrase each in a different faded color—"but we are out of joint. The Lord has granted us this largesse, each and every one, but we are out of joint, I say, we reject what has been granted oh so prodigally. We are permitted to drink at the same chimera as the good Lord or at least his underlings and out of that collaborative pang the symptom is born. But what do we do. After we have lured the symptom into twilit life we stand back and are condemned. We stand condemned but not as you may think for giving way to the symptom—to excess—to abandonment. Rather we stand condemned for failing to appropriate the symptom as our own, our very own. We are out of joint and all the merrymaking in the world won't get us out of joint—I mean, out of disjointedness. We are behind our symptoms, in gross lag of them. And so what do we do—we walk the city streets estranged from the very best part of ourselves, hoping in vain that some object will rekindle—refund—that best part or rather our belief in that best part. For the symptom is our only horizon over and beyond a miserable wandering down city streets in the wretched labyrinth of cubicles. And sometimes we are ready to throw ourselves in front of a truck—yea, in front of a truck—yea—rather than resolve our uncertainty over the symptom—over having and yet not having the symptom."

He could not bear to listen any more, even if/as the voice reminded him of (-)Xman. At the same time he could not tear himself away, it began to pour down, the speaker did not stop, saying: "And why are we afraid to become one with our symptoms? I'll tell you why. I'll tell you why indeed. Because we are afraid to be labelled not so much as symptomed but as symptomed particularly. And so we abstain, we abstain miserably. Not realizing that giving way to satisfaction of the symptom might procure us, become indistinguishable from, the life or death leap to a new plane of being. Compulsive pissers—for once piss in your pants and damned be the upturned noses. Shitters—shit your fill and damned be the menacing nightstick. But we stand still for fear of the symptom. Which reminds me of the Man on the Bench."

Most were moving off, except one or two, Xman edged away from these stragglers. Didn't he have an appointment with Park. He did not want to be identified with the stragglers. He was not strong enough to embrace the plight of his homologues, to see them as serving a function beyond exacerbation of his own visibility. He did discern, however—but only fleetingly—that such visibility held up before him on—from—all sides might be used—or rather the excruciated protesting utterances to which it gave rise might be used—in the true work, a true work, some true work. "He was not strong enough to embrace the plight . . ." might be used, might be assimilated to the context of its congeners. But he was too frightened to provide the context, the congeners. "He was not strong enough . . ." flew away.

"Let me tell you the story of the Man on the Bench." The speaker looked around, clearly undaunted by the sudden dearth of auditors. The fewer the better was his ferule's philosophy. His easel was collapsed, the ink on the chart had flowed away into the asphalt, mingling with the chipped and reflected neon.

STORY OF THE MAN AND OF THE BENCH

"He was a man like any other and yet totally unlike all others. He was a man hard to define, fragile of temperament yet with nerves of steel. Loathing the world he fancied himself completely outside all predictable human response to, in, that world. There is no beginning to describe how much he loathed the world and the infinite predictability of the world. Each time he heard a conversation he writhed at its flawless reproduction of everything heard before, on airplanes going to Belfast, on steamers traveling up and down the Mississippi, in the parent-infested playgrounds of Central Park, in public toilets, female, in hospital recovery rooms, in airplane no-smoking sections.

"His loathing, his refusal to believe that people could willingly, even euphorically, reproduce the already known, the already seen, got him into enormous difficulties, mainly with himself. When he saw, for example, a fat hausfrau with the dimensions of an opera singer but with diapason no greater than a single half-step and that emanating from an orifice not usually associated, unless serendipitarily, with exertions worthy of the great Gioacchino and the even greater Giuseppe to say nothing of the also but less great Vincenzo and Gaetano, manic-depressive to the bone—when he came across such a creature he always said, 'She cannot be what one might, at first glance, think she is.' But within seconds she proved herself to be that and much more of same yet totally brazenly indifferent to the straitjacketing verdict of self-caricature. Until he, the Man on the Bench, began to realize that almost everybody is enclosed in his caricatural function—as we speak of an algebraic function—better yet, a geometric—and likely to remain so, blissfully closed off from the ruinous difficulty of hungering after uniqueness. Which hungering—AS EVERYBODY KNOWS—is ultimately the most susceptible to straitjacketing caricature.

"One evening returning to his hovel from the work site he overheard, struggling to unearth key from hip pocket, the following exchange between an adolescent and the mother of that adolescent's adolescent friend:

" 'Hello Mrs. Shitt, it's Jasper Merdy.' 'Hi Jas, what's up,' returned the frump, the whining casualness of the abominably ubiquitous 'What's up' not quite disguising intense unease. Perhaps Jasper had called her away from the john at the very moment when— After delivering his reason for this surprise visit Jasper said: 'Catch you later,' (meaning, *So long*), 'you're looking good.' And this—all this—to the hideous slutlike frump, hair dyed bright orange, feet shod in impossibly shiny little white fur-lined bootlets.

"Needless to say this little interchange drove our man wild with rage. Yet why did the use of this or that populism enrage him so. Why, why, why. He told himself, our man did, that he was not revolted by populisms per se, some new expression in itself become common currency, precisely because some new expression, some new shred of failed argot, was never *in itself, of itself, for itself,* was always already a repetition of what somebody somewhere—some somebody preeminently somebody—would have said under the circumstances or better yet having once jerked circumstances into plausible connectedness with shred of choice. According to our man each new shred was the vehicle of an impersonation and so our man must loathe such impersonation, stark symptom of the hunger to stink a little of one's *constructed* betters, to wit, those using shred in question with greatest ease. What kind of uniqueness was this. He visibly spat, our man did, on the notion of such distinction, the hunger for such distinction, distinction as no more than a very bracketed being very much at the straitjacketed heart of being. He visibly spat right there in the corridor smelling of hair spray, chuck steak, and festering newsprint. There was no way, lubricating spit or no spit, into or out of the unfissured blandness inhabiting such a peculiarly universal craving for instant distinction. There was no way into (or out of) such unfissured blandness.

And concurrently there was, spit or no spit, no way into intercourse—into connectedness—with these universals craving instant distinction—these impersonators—these phantoms—phantoms because forever volatilizing away through *utterance of a certain sort*—or so they hoped—into their constructed betters. So how was our man to reach them, touch them, stroke them, be reached and stroked, even caressed, by them. For even if he told himself he was revolted by this particularly voracious hunger for unique- ness—a degenerate case of uniqueness, as it were—a unique- ness violating all his tenets regarding what constituted true uniqueness—distinction—inconceivable, unutterable undi- agnosable distinction in uniqueness—what really tormented was the sobbing intuition that these impersonators were lo- calizable nowhere for touching, stroking, kissing, licking, comforting AND touching, stroking, squeezing, tasting, em- bracing, nuzzling HIM. What really tormented was that they were inaccessible because always elsewhere, always other, that is to say, always incarnated in this or that uttered shred of contemporaneity certain to invoke and capture the beings they hungered to be—the only conceivable beings—the be- ings scandalously at ease—in and out of ease via the mighti- est legerdemain—with this or that latest butt-end of small talk, table talk. Help was nowhere to be found. Healing touch was nowhere to be found. Healing touch—longed for and loathed—would never be found even if it was ultimately longed for at last without loathing. These beings were out- side themselves searching for their billboard betters, there- fore incapable of ministering to our man's deepest needs, still unavowed. They had no hands for stroking, seizing, quenching, lips for exhaling, kissing, firing, for such chattels were on permanent loan to the beings they intended to be- come—through utterance, mind you, of a certain sort. No- where to be found. So he hurled himself into the wilds of the city. The memory of the interchange, its defiant use of popu- lisms, made confinement within four walls impossible, es- pecially—though he would never have admitted it, would never with the equipment then at his disposal have become conscious of it—four walls graced by no ornament or sign of life. He met another man—on a park bench. He immediately decided that this man was ALL HE WAS NOT. And he immediately began to loathe and love him for his achievement, right down to the very balls—of his feet.

"He looked around and, after a long rainy winter, suddenly saw himself enjoying the first signs of spring in spite of himself. Yet he did not want to have the tastes of others like this other man beside him on the bench. It was unendurable enough to see those other *at* their tastes and preferences the way he saw pigs at feed in the Children's Zoo.

"So you can understand that he did not know what to make of his rapture over the first buds, the first catkins, the rainbow of cirrus lording it over Belvedere Lake. Did the rapture have anything to do with the Other Man on the Bench, somehow in his infinite vitality—the vitality of a lean and long-limbed cyclist—granting him, the Man on the Bench, the right to have his rapture in its—the long-limbed vitality's—shadow. He could not quite decide what to do with the Great Lawn before him, obelisk to the left of him, Belvedere Castle and Winterdale Arch somewhere to the right. At first he tossed and turned on the bench, telling himself that it didn't matter, this fleetingly heretical rapture, because he was universally known to hold particularly aberrant views of springtime. For example, he had always made it a point to insist that the first buds, stitched taut to the branches, followed a route completely different from their stays. And there was the whole question of spring itself: He wasn't fooled by this particular day—moment—of calm. For spring as he knew it in this city sandwiched between two mighty rivers hated definition, definably gradual evolution, as much as he and would begin soon enough masking itself in the terrible rains sure to flood not only Belvedere Lake but the reservoir too and the pond at Central

Park South and the Pool on Central Park West and the Bowbridge Lake. Spring as he knew it would, to avoid destruction through self-definition, the excruciation of a name: spring—take refuge in the illegibility of torrents. Anything, anything, to avoid an orderly development, maturation, growth. Anything to avoid the inexorable gradual convergence on an utterable essence. And then, when it chose at last to stop the rains masking essence, spring would present itself in the unrepentant seething of that essence. By then, of course, the city would be well into winter.

"But breathing in the thin fragrant air, knowing that his pupils were abnormally dilated, his penis abnormally distended, he could not escape the implication of these telltale signs of his own relish. No different no doubt from anybody else's relish. If truth be told, he was at once pleased and alarmed. Like *the others* he was suddenly a man who appreciated springtime. But then he was overcome as if with a terrible spasm. Suddenly he saw himself caught and captioned thus: It's good to be alive. Anything but that caption, of an indescribable billboard banality.

"Out of the blue this other man, a kind of yokel who, it seemed, aspired to become the conscience of all the troubled souls dispersed like him beneath the great oaks and magnolias—out of the blue this figure, without turning but ostentatiously ingenuous, content, continuing to look out at the lake with its light infantry of rushes and its not-so-distant prospect of more peace-loving sallows, said: 'This obsession of your: It's standing in the way.' When our man asked, 'What is standing in the way of what?' the other, with what our man took to be a venomous little chuckle, said: 'You're just trying to muddle the issue. Instead of plastering me with all kinds of ill intentions as foreign to me as—if Miss Dickinson is to be trusted and she is—always—firmament to fin—instead of insulting me down your hairy snout—I never let myself be insulted—by anybody—why don't you run over to that little pergola there—yes, that one, in the shadow of the obelisk where the fat man and his son are sitting, sharing a hard-boiled egg and try like all hell to disentangle the skein of events responsible for the present state of affairs in which a grown man—a grown man—maybe coming home from the wars your dad didn't want to come home to your leering fishwife of a diseased mom—'

"Our man grew irate, leaped up, and facing his opponent said, 'For you I'm just one in an infinite sequence. And your tedium—inspired by the dismal repetitiveness of its members—spares you the excruciation of confronting me in my nudity.' The other man continued to sit very contentedly on his bench—it was now his—among the mounting number of sunbathers and picnickers—hairy and lithe in equal proportions—looking on with a kind of fatherly pleasure at the season's doings. But he scowled whenever he chanced to look in the direction of our man on the bench making off to a patch of brindled shade. Our man—our man needing no introduction—ultimately settled on a patch covered with dog-shit and unruly tufts of burned-out grass, right next to a twin-boled beech. The way the two, diverging from a common trunk about a foot off the ground, managed to maintain their entwined equilibrium despite impatiently striving centrifugal gyrations of boughs, branches, and twiglets, filled him with a wonderment that momentarily blotted out all memory of his mortal foe.

"Yet waxing truly rapturous over the beech's itinerary he purposely reminded himself of the other man, his stance, his inflection, the hairy litheness of his long limbs, though without looking in his direction, either to determine whether such rapture could survive the return of the tor-

ment incarnated in that other man that had been so conspicuously absent during its—the rapture's—genesis or perhaps
to wrestle afresh with that incarnated torment now he was
so much strengthened and comforted compliments of
beechy rapture. At any rate he quickly lost all capacity to
connect himself to the fate of the beech and found his atro-
phy coupled anew to the man on the bench. What had the
worm said, something about being his worst enemy, no
doubt, diagnosis being the last refuge of quacks. And yet to
his horror he discovered he was outraged less by diagnosis
than by the possibility of its failure to survive subsequent
life-events stretching and possibly—ultimately—impugning
its venomous accuracy. Would it survive, this hoary beechy
diagnosis, onslaughts of experience intent only on rendering
it obsolete, yes, even in his case, where everything remained
the same and life-events had a way of being sent up the river
for twenty-five times life. And then it came to him, what he
must do, spring or no spring, lawn or no lawn, obelisk or no
obelisk. He had to run right over and demand a refutation.
He was ready to relinguish
      his kingdom for a refutation.

"It was as if all future functioning—in the workplace, in
the unornamented hovel, on the subway between workplace
and hovel, in the subway urinals, would be impossible in the
shadow of this egregious slur. On his manhood, he added
guffawing wildly. He did not know what functioning, exactly, he had in mind since most of his life—as we have
seen—was spent in flustered flight from the specter of captions for the very functioning he was now afraid would be
stymied. Suddenly captions no longer mattered. So what if
once—long long ago—he never cultivated friendships lest
seen chitting and chatting with Tom, Dick and Harry Janos
he thereby invited the annihilating caption: Friends having a

good time, or the slightly less denigrating: Friends having a good time at all costs. Captions were no longer to be shunned even if they set all activity ablaze.

"But he did not go. Days passed into decades and the sage on the bench was always out, gathering around him more and more recruits ripe for discipleship. And this gladdened our man in some obscure way. One day the rawest among this ever-increasing number—though perhaps he, the man on the bench, I mean, the Man on the Bench, designated him so out of spite or worse, a need for foothold in inchoate differentiation amid all that chaotic coming and going of apprenticeship, nay, cult worship—came over to where our man was sitting, at the very edge of the rush-fringed lake, at the very edge of the fringe of being. The castle seemed remoter than usual. In the other direction, the baseball players looked especially vigorous under the full-blown willows. Though here again, 'remoter than usual' and 'especially vigorous' might be, unbeknownst to their eerie progenitor, mere techniques for establishing nodal points, footholds, slapdash differentiating criteria, amid all the chaos, the heinous homogeneity.

"It became obvious the would-be disciple wished to speak his mind. Finally after much placatory hemming and hawing he said: 'You know, you really should come over. That man over there—he'll teach you something it might take you years to unravel on your own. He'll teach you to become completely aware of what other people are feeling. And what they are thinking when thinking becomes a way of camouflaging what they are feeling. No, don't move off. He'll teach you how to master the thoughts and feelings inside yourself—the thoughts that play with you. And then when you've mastered every feeling/thought you'll be able to foresee every situation such feeling/thoughts can possibly produce, every destiny such feeling/thoughts can possibly etch in acid. So armed you'll be able to disappear from the sight of other men. Do you understand. Nobody will be able to impose the sickness of his destiny as your destiny because you will already have mastered all the feeling/thoughts such a destiny strives to emit. And you will be able to help others, help them out of straitjacketed misery inseparable from a particular destiny emitting so many feeling/thoughts per minute, virtually indistinguishable one from the other yet stinging with all the daring of authentic uniqueness. You'll be able not only to extrapolate from a mere shred of feeling, shred of thought, to a whole destiny, a vast network of excruciating situations, but also to cry out, "Stop. Don't do that. You're operating at the behest of a sick mixture of feeling and thought," to every dupe so stymied.'

"All our man could say, looking at the rushes surrounding the great gaping hole of the lake, was, 'Go away.'

"The other went away without a word. More than ever he hungered for a refutation from the other man, *this* other man inundated by a following that not only passively imbibed but actively sought to convert. He hungered for a refutation the more the man on the bench thrived. Or perhaps the other man, for all his apostles, thrived neither more nor less. Perhaps our man, in his misery, had framed and within that frame had decreed a kind of trajectory for his mortal foe—a trajectory that would highlight his own mounting abjection.

"Their paths crossed. Their paths crossed several times in all weathers. The other did not seem to recognize our man, our man thirsting for a refutation. Our man felt he had been absorbed back into the landscape of rushes and willows, had become a beech sprig or rusty twig of dogshit. The other man clearly had too much to do breathing in the vapors of sunlight to bother himself about our man. But wasn't there the very slightest false note in all that active rapture: Wasn't

271

there just the slightest hint of oppressively elfin daring, of aggressive insistence, of—of—impersonation, in all that actively deeply inhaling rapture. Passing the other a phrase came to our man soothing him like a symptom: One man killed the other man. Finding this phrase very soothing he intoned it more and more. But then he heard another sentence that did not soothe, oh no, not in the least: One man brought old pains to the other man as if the other man were the provenance of those pains.

"Sometimes the man—our man—in search of a refutation—in search of a refutation SO HE COULD PROCEED AT LAST—GET ON WITH THE BUSINESS OF BEING ... ON THE FRINGE OF BEING—witnessed the other man swallowed up by the typically great distance separating them or rather, our man, after yet another brutal spin in the centrifuge of that dizzying distance (consigning him in self-contempt to the very bottom of the barrel of being for though he never would have admitted it in his case being now was inversely proportional to distance from the other man) found or rather lost himself envying this other man's exalted ease amid his own insignificance brought boisterously to life by perspectival ploys that rendered him, always the other man, little more than a mere pinprick beyond turrets, tunnels, trees. And the other man looked so blithe our man began telling himself it was only his—the man in search of a refutation's—obsession—that made him believe he—the other man—was willfully withholding what might so easily be dispensed. As easily as he was throwing crumbs to the sparrows and pigeons he would soon throw him a crumb of refutation.

"One day the light—with the derricks suspended over the churned-up meadows—had a beauty stranger than usual. There was no plausible cause for its shimmering. It fleeced him of anxiety and in the absence of that anxiety he was able to sequester and scrutinize the light without anxiety going out at the same time ostensibly to meet but in actual fact to obliterate the lovely little specimen, artifact of midafternoon urban dawn. As if suspended from the derrick's highest point the light found itself pincered in an absence of all hovering cause for anxiety within and without. But there was no remaining indefinitely in the shadow of that light not because the light was itself fading into the straightforwardly vaporous smear of five—six—seven o'clock but because our man—the man in search of a refutation and needing no introduction—and whose future projects refused to ripen without the go-ahead of momentous and global refutation—our man could feel the other man, proud progenitor of labels and friend to New York's myriad friendless, about to descend on him with all the precipitancy of a derrick's bob. It was a strange new feeling. The other after centuries of apparent indifference was about to attack. So he had no choice but to break off a particularly sharpshooting bough from the double-trunked beech and approach in self-defense. Spectators gathered quickly round the falling form with a tentative grudging absorption, as if this little scene might turn out to be but one more unsuccessful bid for media coverage—the only arbiter of any phenomenon's authentic being equipped to roam the unpatrolled streets of Jungle City. Under that sublime light they knew they were now obliged to do battle whether they wanted it or not. For there was the crowd to contend with. So our man and his other man proceeded to do their utmost to wax warlike, that is to say, engage in confused affectless feinting. Occasionally the arm of one touched the shin of the other or the elbow of one grazed the sternum of the other or the shoulder of one tickled the hip of the other and from that fleeting connectedness was kindled less mutual rage than unfeigned delight at the prospect at last of collaborative zeal dirigible against the slobbering expectations of the strabismal lunchtime crowd, their true enemy. Yes, the crowd was their true, their only, enemy, the hungry crowd that did not even know it was hungry but was nonetheless not above giving slumbering heed to some vague intimation from somewhere a little to the left of Belvedere Castle's Horseshit Valley that it might indeed be craving some little blood, some little pus, some little pussy bloody sputum shed, some tiny terminal pang dehiscing from between a pair of tactfully collapsing thighs. Yet at the very moment when the promise of more than mere rancor—nay, of eternal friendship without peer—seemed about to ooze from their interplay our man needing no introduction broke his sibling's neck beyond appeal. The whack of the connubially blissful double-trunked beech bough against the tangle of less blissfully intermingling tendons, muscles and nervelets made the light turn sour, worse, forever lose that palpitating freshness redolent of dusky dawn and dawny dusk. Once his opponent was definitively down our man turned to the crowd as if to say killing had not turned out so satisfying as he had hoped since his victim, this ragged heap that had fallen before his very eyes, was not quite—had not quite the panache of—the label's perpetrator. His grimaces of stately convulsion had cheatingly transformed him into something just a wee bit to the right or left of that primordial malefactor whose crimes against humanity couldn't go unpunished indefinitely. All for nothing.

"As he was about to be escorted away, the disciple who had tried to talk to him at the edge of the lake came up and said, 'I won't say I told you so. But if only you had returned with me that day. In any case—' and turning to the police officers in charge of the case, the dead man's chief disciple (although perhaps this title 'chief disciple' was just another effort on our man's part to differentiate the mass from itself) said: 'Can I just tell him a quick story before you cart him off.'

The officers shook their heads wearily but soulfully. The disciple shook his head also as if signalling that now he would begin and make it quick. 'I just feel the whole bloody business could have been avoided if only this man here, whose name I still don't know, had trusted his rapture. But he didn't know what to do with that rapture. So used as he has been to envy, misery, confusion, regret—all the diseases born of cruel labelling and typecasting—he's a good example of a man who can't understand the most rudimentary up-surges of life-affirmation. It undid him. He reminds me of—' Clearing of throat. 'Many years ago Bob O'Bannion left his office one night. Around five-thirty-five it was a particularly foggy dusk in midsummer when he left that place of hardly gainful employment to brave the subway platform crowds at Twenty-third and Lexington. It was a particularly difficult period for Bob O'Bannion for he was subjected to protracted telephone conversations with his parents, both dying, though at different rates. The mother, Mother O'Bannion, was making sure to stretch out the dying process to the very crack of doom so that a maximal number of beings might suffer her exasperation at life's difficulty to the hilt. For her aim, Mother O'Bannion's, had always been to disseminate enough bile among as many as could reasonably be expected to puke at the very sight of it. Through her unending com-plaints and outraged intolerance for all circumambient signs of life, however feeble, she was clearly husbanding a massive strength against those "final moments" that were in point of fact very far off. And when Bob O'Bannion was not thinking about these aged parents he was thinking about the person who employed him to run errands well into the wee hours. One day he had gone into her office just before his perfor-mance could start falling off perceptibly. He knew he was simply incapable, given his father's disrepair, of typing quite so many thank-you notes and cutting and pasting even the

minimal number of brochures for the variously handi-
capped. As elliptically as he could he explained why. And
she simply lapped it all up: In the delight of the moment—
delight at being called upon to melt his legendary glacial
reserve—it was making his name in the company—"making
his name in the company," truly a loathesome phrase—delighted she simply forgot to go swimming in her customary
slimy depths of trivial obsession. Nor did she require as was
also customary that he venture out beyond the shoals alone
in quest of this paper clip, that invoice number. Only gradually, when he refused in the days that followed to come forward with details equally gruesome highlighting parental
disintegration and connubial crises—when she realized he
could not be depended on to be consistently producing more
snaillike extrusions of confidence—gradually she came to
herself and donned the gilded rags of an erratic irascible
viciousness that made her the slimy terror of the labyrinth
of cubicles where O'Bannion was not so slowly being buried
alive. For he had generated a fissure in her being and refused
to keep refilling it. And it would take so much time to dry
up. So she went on humiliating him with redoubled force.
That very day they had had a big battle where, only partially
successful in humiliating him before the whole staff, she
had nevertheless managed to empty out the whole labyrinth
of cubicles so it could witness his comeuppance. Bob O'Bannion of course fought back like all the O'Bannions before
him. Hadn't he always loathed this little runt of a glorified
file clerk struggling to lord it over—of all people—him—Bob
O'Bannion, last of the fighting O'Bannions. He fought
against humiliation and he fought in the name of regret at
having divulged all to this runt. Even if he hadn't divulged all
he felt sick with having divulged all. He hated her because
she made him feel as if he must remain faithful to the predicament he had injudiciously set before her. Now that he

was struggling to surpass that predicament her expectation that he would go on feeding their connectedness intervened. For Bob O'Bannion knew her—only too well—oh so much like his mother she was—what with her airs and foul perfume and last but not least her demand that lest she be thrown back on too invigorating a whiff of her own inadequacy he continue to supply her with signs of a helplessness whereby the relation, through her indispensable succor of oohs and aahs and how bloody terribles, could perpetuate itself to infinity but never against the fur. In any case, as he hit Forty-fifth between Fifth and Sixth he was hard put to explain why it was he was suddenly feeling so rapturous. There was no reason, simply no reason on earth for this untidy smile to be slackening what he took especially at this moment to be his prize possession, uncompromising vigilance. In point of fact he considered vigilance to be one of his features, on a par with mouth, nostril, nostril stamens, eyebrows, in point of fact the most striking of his features. And this peerless feature owed not a little of its peerlessness to being localizable nowhere. He became terrified. He looked quickly around. Though like his good pal Soren Kay, lover of freshly baked boysenberry Danish pastries, he loathed consensus—he was after all convinced that business transactions on the basis of probabilities had nothing to do with true being—at this very moment he needed the support of others. But no support did they lend. No one had his look of rapture. He was all alone with it. So he began to denounce the rapture and asked himself why, why, why, in the midst of his torments and burdens he had been called upon to feel unhinged to the point of effervescence. And then—in the middle of the roadway of his life—he farted. He allowed himself to release seminoxious gases without a care as to incriminating sounds and smells. He simply—farted. And it was only then with the odor mounting to the skies and the sound reverberating from the Forty-fifth Street piers to the opalescent barricades of Beekman Place that he could say he sensed he was beginning to learn to accept the concreteness of his rapture without soliciting causes, having divined such rapture would disappear soon enough not because of external circumstances but because of its own rapid trajectory aiming toward total extinction. His rapture was like a gas—a fart—expanding. The gas fills space not from desire but from submission to its own laws indistinguishable in this case from the law of others. And something warned him against trying to prolong the feeling not from delectation but from a need to warp it into a specimen at last compatible with circumstances. But he did not heed the warning sufficiently. And so at the corner of Forty-fifth and Park allowed himself to be truck-shredded. It was never ascertained whether he was trying to kill his rapture or by his collision with the truck deform that rapture into compatibility with circumstances. It was never ascertained, not even at the inquest, after scores of witnesses had descended upon the dungheap of consensual truth. It was never ascertained.' The disciple wept. Our man was led away."

After hearing the speaker (Xman was the only auditor left though the torrent had diminished to what newscasters might do well to call a seasonable trickle) he felt more than ever that he had to get to Park. Something about the story haunted, yes, the man in search of a refutation had felt that the other man—the man withholding refutation—despised him for being one in a sequence of madmen. And what if throwing himself in front of a truck once again was looked upon as a mere dullwitted repetition of the first throw . . . of the dice of his nonbeing. But this was different. This would be a totally different collision, he was sure of it.

By the time he reached Park, however, all calvaries converging on Park, he was hoping the collision would be absolutely the same since variation only masks a brute duration's
tedium thereby insuring the plausible infinitude of that tedium. Whereas insane repetition, as he had lived it ever
since arriving in New York, yet this was a deliberate falsification designed to render his experience here meaningful: In
fact he had always lived insane repetition—always seemed—
at least from his vantage—his instantaneous retrospective
vantage on previous vantages bypassed or forsaken—on the
verge of exploding into the definitive impossibility of further
duration. So he wanted the . . . attempt to be the same, if he
kept everything the same then he might be exploded out of
time, into the dream landscape of archetypes where the tiger
rides roughshod at last over the lamb's fuming corpse—

He awoke just as the white coat closing the door disappeared.

He rose, stumbled toward the door, opened it slightly. This
first time he laid eyes on her she was at the very end of a long
corridor, seeming to instruct the doctor on duty.

She had a hideously deformed upper lip, her hair was cut
short except for a long tail that descended almost to the level
of the collarbone. He found himself less astonished by her
hideousness than by the quiet pride she seemed to take in
that hideousness.

It gave him hope, he, Xman. For he too was hideous, or on
the verge of hideousness or forever prey to the possible upsurge of hideousness. Yet, if someone like this, truly hideous, could walk tall, walk proud, then surely he, who was
by no means hideous and at worst trembling on the verge of
hideousness—but perhaps he was all wrong to reason so.
Perhaps an infinite distance separated him, a mere postulant
in the hallowed halls of hideousness, from the being who

279

had chosen or been chosen to take the quantum leap into hideousness. Through the quantum leap into authentic hideousness some qualitative transformation occurred that made it impossible to extrapolate back to and toy with one's own potential hideousness. Perhaps the leap into authentic hideousness was incursion into the very heart of being insuring all verdicts emanating from that heart were immediately and forever annihilated. And since he had not taken that phantom—no, that very real—leap then he must not expect to parasitize its profit.

She advanced from the bottom of the corridor, passing door after door. Just when her features seemed to be getting clearer she vanished. From his cell (at least when the nurses did not interpose themselves) the surrounding slopes, verdure hugging the steeps for dear life, changed vertiginously from red to gold to blue and back again. At the moment when he felt himself beginning to begin to get absorbed in the rare vehicle cutting a path through that cropped mutability he heard her—it had to be her—speaking just outside the door about his condition. She seemed to be omitting no detail, no symptom, past, present or to come. Over and over the word "symptom" fell like an overripe fruit. Though her conversation was one long digressing further and further from any stable site yet over and over he—or his name that went unspoken—was the only fish stupid enough to be caught in its skein. There had to be some way of turning a corner to put him forever outside the track of a pathology plotted by such a voice. From fragments overheard it would seem she knew completely what he was bound henceforth to confront. And at the same time within the folds of her bland catalogue of his infirmities and their infinite ramifications reposed for moments at a time at least the key to escape. The cataloguing was indispensable preliminary to escape. She had to lay him out flat before putting him back together again as another. When she alluded to matters that obsessed him at all times (rent, price of food, high cost of education, government cutbacks for the "arts") these matters became real for the first time in a new unpleasant way. "So what you're saying," the doctor mumbled, referring to his chart less to retrieve relevant details than to hide his discomfiture, "is that once you begin speaking of matters that commonly obsess him, gnawing lacerating worry, which was his typical approach, is not only no longer gratuitous but flagrantly deficient. Long, long ago—according to the notes taken by Nurse Brains while he was in a postsurgical coma—a particularly voluble coma, I might add—whatever worry he chose to expend on such matters very quickly became excessive—heroically supererogatory confection or discharge—meriting total banishment of—or rather an indefinite 'freeze' on—said matters. As long as he kept to his worrying he thwarted—or so it seemed—the incessantly threatening emergence of the target of worrying, always at any rate already emerged. The minute he began to worry—or so it seemed—the target lost—transferred—its actuality to the worry—do you hear— THE TARGET TRANSFERRED ITS ACTUALITY TO THE WORRY INITIALLY FOCUSED ON THE TARGET—and obligingly became no more than a slenderest possibility of regeneration. His life—and that of his companion and the unborn—became that slenderest possibility and nothing more. Worrying in his peculiar manner disembarrassed him of excruciated belief in a target of worry. All worrying became—is this your 'theory'—gloriously proleptic, in other words, gloriously gratuitous. Target always managed—how nice—to make itself scarce—must note this on the fever chart—as mere hecatomb flung in the groin of some thaumaturge, some troublemaking, easily suborned, lackey-demiurge." "We'll speak later of his demiurge. Or rather," she guffawed, "we'll speak later of my theory of his demiurge."

This hideous creature was changing everything, suddenly confirming a reason to worry. He thought he could see the doctor through a crack in the door. Was he trying to escape her. Or did he simply have to see the doctor trying to get away if he was to see them at all, see at all.

Once the doctor began speaking his inflection had said he was not in the least intimidated. Taking a deep breath Xman tried to determine how this new development would affect his status. For his status did not establish itself once and for all, oh no. Every datum modified that status. The doctor's intrepidity of tone was one such datum.

At that moment the woman broke in with: "For one thing he is totally passive. He does nothing to advance. His already shaky status unconsentingly is contingent on modifications within and between the lives of others. Take the young woman and the unborn, for example. At this very moment he must be shuddering at how your refusal to be intimidated (by whom? by me of course) might affect his status. And then he begins to hunger after some change in status. Strange lad. That is why we are hoping to interest him—but never mind. At this point I think he is hungering after . . . results. For his so-called true work—surely it's in his history—has yielded absolutely nothing in that line. And what is work without results for someone like him. Basically, a derelict, a professional orphan. I'll tell you what work without results turns out to be: a sham, that's what."

There was a silence. Then Xman heard the doctor speak: "But doesn't the true worker know the external result—the acquisition—that seems to be within his power is a bald contradiction in terms. In fact it is not in his power and so he chooses to remain in ignorance of accomplishment. For to become aware of what he has accomplished *so far* would only kill what he has accomplished so far and revert him back to zero. Results—acquisitions—reduce tension. And the true worker knows that only infinite dialectic tension is his soul helpmate."

The doctor was trying to help him and the woman was trying to undo him but their contrary doings had the same effect. As they spoke of "work" it was as if all he had achieved in that domain were immediately cancelled. With the concept mediated by these two, differently expert, there was no way back to work, true or otherwise. They had appropriated, these two, not the means of production but, far more dire, the means of conceiving of production.

They had appropriated the means of conceiving of production, as if their sole purpose was to crowd him out.

"And of course you have heard," said Fatima—for this was how the doctor addressed her, "how whenever event produces a certain level of excruciation in his self-styled sphere of true work he immediately calls in his emergency unit to confiscate what he must perceive as mere artifact to be fed to the true work *only at some future time*. But I won't go into that. It's too well-known. And in any case we—I mean I— take a different view of this ploy. From our—my—point of view this is a symptom and any symptom is useful—transformable. There is no growth apart from symptom growth. So I am by no means disheartened knowing he refuses 'wholeheartedly to live his events.' Such living is vastly overrated. If this refusing to live is symptomatic then what counts is to live the symptom with passionate intensity and wholehearted commitment even if that commitment is 'in spite of oneself.' "

The doctor cleared his throat, or so Xman thought. "Why does such a mewling ploy make him symptomed. Why aggrandize the procedure with so fanciful a label. Let it rot nameless. If his work is the true work—some kind of true work—then for his own protection he must be able to defang and warehouse rather than let himself be totally undone by the malevolence of contingency—contingency malevolent by definition when it is a question of a true work wishing to engulf, imbibe, become all of being. I know *I* had to learn similar tricks during my medical school and internship days. Old Professor Zang Froid (rhymes with 'void') used perfervidly to enjoin us to remember that for the living organism protection against stimuli is far more important than their reception."

"He shrinks them down, these stimuli, to such a degree they no longer have any contour. But then again, I DO NOT LOOK ASKANCE ON SUCH A PROCEDURE. I am unique in this regard and wish him to know I am unique. So what if this symptom incapacitates him for the true work. For the true work—a true work—definitely exists. We—I—deign to consider his likes precisely because he is a failed true worker who, hopefully, will carry that sense of failure around with him forever without, again hopefully, doing anything to correct it. We seek out and recruit failure. We need failures tormented by their sense of failure. And these two failed . . . attempts brand him supremely as a failure. Otherwise do you think I would be wasting our—my—time. We prefer him just as he is—symptom and all—especially symptom. But I think we have just scraped the surface of that symptomatology. We are delighted that he cannot manage to be omnivorous, that he finds it impossible to dwell in the midst of an ostensibly fructive heterogeneity WHERE ALL IS FODDER FOR THE TRUE WORK'S MILL. We are delighted he sees only obstructions and malevolences where others— healthier hulks—might see choice grist for their mill. We are delighted that he views all phenomena as obstructions to the true work as if its actual making—the actual true working—is every step of the wobbly way an aesthetic entity—as if every stage is a final product in its own right that can only fail if every condition is not test-tube perfect. A FINAL PRODUCT IN ITS OWN RIGHT, do you hear. We are positively thrilled he has the soul of a rank amateur, an inarticulate seeker after the sublime and beautiful. Please let me know, doctor, when the little rat is ready to leave."

All the time they were talking about him he was completely bypassed. Before he could formulate this thought—a shard of the great heterogeneity, or rather, shard of collision with same—he heard the doctor say, point-blank, with no rancor and perhaps with a certain collusive relish: "You want to rob him not only of the true work but of himself. You want to transform him."

He felt very dizzy, drained, clearly Fatima was one of those beings—often owllike or bovine—who make one come away—no matter how tight-lipped one has made it one's business to be—with the sensation of having spilled all, more than all, more than it is ever possible to contain. And there was the further sense—which was not the result of intercourse with most owls—that based on this unlocalizable garrulity one was incapacitated, degraded, for all future experience. One had provided Fatima—his abstention had provided her—with enough raw material whence to construct an already toppled future.

He jumped back into bed just as the doctor entered. "How's the patient," though without the rosy jowls that normally go with such an outburst. "How's my big big boy." Xman murmured, "Fatima." The doctor admitted a woman by that name had stopped by but said nothing about Xman. In fact she had come to see one of his most challenging patients, fellow by the name of Xaviero McShayne, who had just expired in an adjacent ward. "Really," the doctor persisted, "she had nothing but kind words for you and your

doings. She said she had heard about you from a Distin-
guished Project Coordinator by the name of Mike Egg Rollins. You must have heard of him, she said he's the positive
toast of Soho. No, I'm wrong. She said he's positively the
toast of Soho. No, no, no. Positively he's the toast of Noho."
"So, Doc," Xman intoned, positively astonished by his sudden ability to cut this babbling short, "is there any way I can
jump out of the skin of my apparently solipsistic commentary on SOMEBODY—Fatima by name—and paint at last a
true portrait of the despicable little bitch FASTER than the
commentary flings me back into my most humble hole
through its disobliging sketch of my own symptomed sickness. Doc!" Xman cried—and though he listened intently to
the timbre of the cry and tried to stand completely outside
its reverberation he could not determine whether his throwing all caution—all urbanity—to the four winds of hell was
impersonation or not—"just tell me if I can get to an objective commentary about old Miss Fatima faster than incarcer-
ating self-depiction overtakes and does away with me IN
YOUR EYES. For this is for your eyes only. In short, Doc, can
I sketch her portrait in distemperly fashion faster than
sketching hers I sketch my own. Because I think, in all due
immodesty, that I'm the man for the job. Why shouldn't I be
the singing Sargent of my day. Tell me, Doc. Tell me if I am
diagnosing myself correctly. Isn't your job to assess my diagnosis and if it stinks of heavenly competence expropriate it
as your very own?" The doctor for a minute looked away as if
he saw fit not to protest against the diagnosis of himself not
so deeply buried in the folds of Xman's impersonation of one
throwing caution to the winds. Didn't he know from bitter—
not for himself but for them—experience with billions of
lunatics that protest as pathologic refusal to conform to the
contour of diagnosis as given—given as the sun, rain, and
stars are given—only strengthened its (incipiently feeble)

impersonation of unswerving curve of truth sketched in the three-walled laboratory of the patient's soul.

Before Xman could take the absence of an answer from this new version of "on high" to heart the doctor barked, "But do you really want an answer, my dear Xman. Wouldn't an answer, yoking itself to, digging its ungainly lineaments deep within, the connective tissue of the question, only be a kind of . . . subtraction. What I mean is, what is your question but the real site of all the activity making you—at least in your own mind—Xman the Unvanquishable. It's a swarming net of contradictions—like a symptom—and how does one begin to answer a swarming net of contradictions. Xaviero tried in his way and look what happened to him. Unlike him, however, I refuse to erect a credo over such a swarming net of contradictions. I don't think you want that swarm marred by anything as vulgar as an answer. Am I right, man, am I right."

Before Xman could answer, the doctor said, "What I mean is, there is no answer that would satisfy not because of the inevitable inadequacies of answers A, B, C but because built into the nature of questioning—your questioning—is answer's intrinsic repugnancy. But in answer though not necessarily to your question I *can* say that if you want to get to depiction faster than self-indictment gets to you then you have no choice but to compare Miss Fatima to—an insect!" As if patient's eyes were popping out of bandaged skull, the doctor said defiantly: "Yes, precisely. To be sure. This insect is among the most putrid and venomous. And yet possessed when it is so inclined of a mesmerizing torpor that drives it round and round. But I for one am always prepared for the insect's totally unexpected leap toward direct attack on the proverbial innocent bystander, his sole crime the misguided belief that he is completely outside the circle of remarkability—in the clinical sense—and therefore forever disregarded by the bright beast in the throws of obsession. And of course someone—something—someTHING like Fatima is always convinced that she is performing the most difficult leap of all—not the one designated by Balanchine for the 'Darting Finger' Fairy in his sublime yet still sleeping version of 'The Sleeping Beauty at Bunker Hills'—in the *Entr'acte Symphonique: Le Sommeil*, to be exact—but that where a man shoots down from stratosphere back to starting point just as the most difficult decision in the realm of the spirit is that unassisted by any kind of therapeutic distance and with no decor to rouse to awareness. But Fatima avoids that most difficult decision to become what one already is by leaping claws outstretched out at another." The doctor's voice grew very low, almost inaudible, as if reminiscing about something particularly painful which had not yet lost its sting. Xman was first to turn away from the exhumed mound called Fatima toward a distant skein of branches crawling parallel to the ground and through whose virtually denuded intermingling could be glimpsed little tulip islets nodding in a total absence of wind. ". . . nodding in a total absence of wind . . . ": The phrase itself seemed an islet cut off from a mainland true work that had sunk into the sea. When he turned back the doctor was gone. Rosalie was in the room, rocking an infant in her arms.

She laughed sadly. "The night he was born I thought you didn't come home because you went to see that ballet. Then I found the tickets in the little envelope on the kitchen table with the date. So I knew you hadn't gone. Would you have still gone if you had at that very moment—at that very moment—known—known—"

Seeing her and the child he turned over, to hell with the excruciation of awakening raw sinews, and murmured, but loud enough for her to hear, "This stinking business of staying alive."

Though she brought the infant close to the bed and pulled back a piece of knitted cloth ever so slightly he was terrified of looking. Something prompted him to say—hadn't the slightest idea whence it came—"A piece of true work if ever there was one." But the minute he was done he clung desperately to the possibility that, after all, his delivery might still be considered a glaring impersonation of paternal pride. "The face is a sketch," he stated offhandedly, to get a grip on himself. "And either the sketcher was impatient of the raw material's paltriness or was, on the contrary, so overcome and reduced to helplessness by the immensity packed into such a small domain and overcome as well by the limited time at his disposal that he worked far too quickly—put in the mere signs of eyes, nose, mouth—in a word, features—expecting to return later." Rosalie he knew listened to nothing but his grotesqueness. Infinitely jealous of the little thing and the infinite affection lavished on it before his very eyes what maddened most was the sense of her sense that she was acting as much for him as for herself and that he would, must ultimately, be infinitely grateful. And then he began to feel pity for the little thing as unconscious victim of such enmity. But he felt pity only insofar as he could sustain the pedal point of the little thing's imagined unconsciousness of the enmity hovering over the cradle she made of her hands, for when he finally managed to look into the little sketch's eyes, construing its look as a direct confrontation in unflinching interrogation, he no longer felt pity.

He thought of weeping to catch her attention. "He's so much like you," she said, strumming its underlip, thick, almost bloody, with a forefinger.

"Another little practitioner of the sublime and beautiful: Did they tell you I'd be let out soon." She took her time turning to him after presumably digesting the question. "The doctor said it depends on your morale." "No morale worth a shit." She winced slightly. 'It's so quiet here," she said, going to the window but not looking beyond the smears and fissures in the glass, so he needed desperately to believe. "Do you want to hold him," she said. He did not answer at once, then striving not to make it sound like an answer, said, "You feel hundreds of miles away from the urban smile. From the plethora of problems and disappointments hatched and trapped in that slime."

Very abruptly Rosalie turned to him and said, "I'll come tomorrow again, I'm not working for her any more, she seems to have disappeared off the face of the earth. We can go for a walk by the lake." He did not answer, just before she shut the door he cried, "A lake is just a wall of water." At its edge the next day a father was teaching his little daughter how to fish. He saw a woman resembling Fatima disappear into the shrubbery shrouding the hospital in hot haze, he said nothing to Rosalie who was in any case absorbed by the father, a real father.

From the depths of the shrubbery, or perhaps form its heights, it was hard to say, a man's voice cried, "I'm getting out. I'm tired of the racket." The voice reminded him of somebody's. "You can't get out," said Fatima. Her voice also reminded. "You're in too deep. You—or rather your symptoms—have made too great a contribution to the cause and at the same time not enough of a contribution."

There was a sound as of spitting. Xman found himself moving further and further away from Rosalie and the child, fortunately she was transfixed, or so he needed to believe, by the little girl and her real father. "It's never too late to get out." "It's always too late." After a long silence Fatima went on, partly smelling her advantage and partly, Xman felt, to suture her own discomfort at having been so successful demolishing this essentially feeble specimen. "Dear boy," she exhaled. "Our work is an activity intrinsically defined, more than defined—driven—by the unwavering belief that at any stage it is clearly too late to withdraw and at the same time is no stranger to the very logical deduction that given the fluidity of our workaday and 'fast-changing world' it is *always still possible* to get out. Out of this tension hangs a tale—and a lifelong commitment. Contradiction is the key here—the strengthener—as it is with the individual symptoms that have made our name." No answer, Xman looked back, Rosalie was still entranced by father and daughter at the very edge of the lake, momentarily duckless. "In short our work expresses several meanings simultaneously. As one of our founders almost said: In all the world there never was found two sleeping partners better suited to each other than passion and contradiction. But why am I speaking of contradiction when you have never been able to endure the contradiction crucial to our line. No—the contradiction has nothing to do with the fact that set down in the midst of existence you found yourself so different from all the others. No—the contradiction you are unable to endure is that saddled with so much ostensible inner commitment to the true work your appearance is—must be—just like other men's. You were never able to refrain from calling attention to your long act of dissimulation. You were never able, as Soren K and Henry J both in younger days urged, to work yourself up an incognito—the best incognito of all—that having the appearance of all others, that lined with the manifold composite rag of the finite, that interwoven with the various predicates of what we call a human existence." "So I'm a coward." The sky was suddenly overrun with clouds—big, expressionless, and black. The infant began to cry, Xman wanted to strangle it on the spot especially as Rosalie began to wrap it ever more tightly. The black clouds hovered above the rooftop of the hospital with foam rubber ineluctability. Yet not far distant from and sometimes even conjoined to these carcasses were filaments of an unspeakably buoyant freshly laundered azure. From the way the occluded sun failed to fall Xman realized it was that glorious moment of protracted peace he used once to spend, far from the public eye, with schoolchildren and other residues on city street-corners haunted by propagandizers for a quieter, less chrematistically inclined, time. He looked up to no light from the sky, only soot, only gore. The most authentic radiance came not from that defective dome rarefied away to the tones of a tiered abysmal smudge, but from heaps of fallen leaves, linden and gingko. Only through gaps in those that still, precariously, hung did the sky miraculously recover its inflection of precipitous pollenous blue.

"If you are a coward then it is indisputable your cowardice is far more difficult than heroism. Heroism, in fact, comes more easily to you than cowardice. Stunned passivity can easily pass for heroism—at least stoicism—whereas coward-ice, at least as we have on so many occasions seen for the likes of you, involves a realignment of the whole mecha-nism. Physiologically, friend, you were made for heroism or rather for a certain impersonation of what is easily taken to be heroism requiring least output and thereby threatening least your governing credo to the effect that once set in motion—having at some minuscule gap foiled a hypertro-phied, normally gapless and incessant vigilance—there is no way to alter anything, now existing retroactively from all eternity against the fur, against the fur."

The man said nothing. "Through your specious brand of heroism you were successful with both Xaviero and that monster Baldachino. Points markedly in your favor."

"Rose Baldachino," the man corrected. "In any case, Fatima, there's no point your trying to get on my good side. I have no good side. From whatever perspective I'm mutila-tedly unphotogenic. I'm getting out, don't cotton to your version of protest. The program pretends to loathe life as it is—the sickening heterogeneity that merely serves as spectacular food for the cows roaming through our fair city's courtrooms, boutiques, boardrooms, museums, clinics, opera houses. But this is not the correct approach to a world inducing profound disgust. No, no, no, not this puny seditiousness. Such an approach, Fatima, is alas very much of the world. Can't you hear the caption setting ablaze all we do. Can't you perceive the framing every time we throw our grenades: AFTER LOVELESS CHILDHOODS THEY NATURALLY HATED LIFE SO THEY REBELLED THE ONLY WAY THEY KNEW HOW. This is one of many captions floodlighting our acts, our very being, each time we get ready to—to—lend our targets an enhanced solidity by mapping out a way of blowing them to bits. We are hungering for a comeuppance, everything we do serves merely to enhance the conspicuity of a disaffection that craves only to be taken to task, preferably across smelly pimpled buttocks. Ours is an embodied, an aggrandized, symptom craving rehabilitation and demonstrating our profound belief that the fault is not in the world but in ourselves that we and our underlings are underlings."

"We elaborate symptoms—the need to throw grenades, for example—in the hope of inviting cure, is that it." Xman thought he heard a sage nod through the flicker of branches. "True rage and disgust, dearest Fattie, perform their daily grind with unimpeachable scrupulosity. It all goes back to what you were telling me a moment ago—to live the contradiction between one's innermost passion and outermost impersonation of one far far far from passion. Scrupulosity defies all commentary, all caption." "We don't care if we are captioned. It does not invalidate the program, as you call it." Xman wanted desperately to hang on to her statement though not to the shriek on whose rooftop it hitchhiked. Yet no matter how deeply Fatima might burrow into disputation with this recreant she could, he felt, at any moment leap out of her vicious circle, discover and obliterate him. "You loathe life," the man repeated. "I love life. I fight for life—for the preciousness of life." "You are hatred and nothing but hatred. And embodying it completely and utterly—stinking of it—there is no element of your being refractory to hatred— you cannot make your way to it gradually, sagittally, vectorially. You incessantly gobble it up before it becomes an entity to be pointed to and examined." "Go then, go," Fatima said. "Become a derelict, sit under sky-blue skyscrapers with your back to life. Do you know what a skyscraper looks like reflected in its congener across the street. Its contours are melted down to the clarity of a crumpled shit-brown paper bag's. Go and sit among the others who talk only to their own stench." It seemed Fatima was speaking not so much for the benefit of the man before her as sagittally for some third's. Xman felt a tap on his shoulder, turned, it was Rosalie. "Too cold for the baby out here. I'm going back to your room." Afraid to miss a word of the conversation all he said as if telegraphing a long message: "Can't now. Sky—too beautiful." Rosalie nodded sadly, with his back immediately turned to her no more of him than that back presumed she was wending her way back. Oddly enough there was no conversation during this interval as if Fatima had very kindly been making a special effort to have him catch up. "So you intend to return to your own program—the personal program—the true work. You were always declaiming your plans for some old true work, deploying its always too inchoate anatomic deformity not, I suspect, in the hope of hooking onto my lavish sponsion but rather of inducing—through a farfetched and far-flung oratory already doing most of the hard work of deriders and parodists—some kind of diagnosis, caption, verdict, capable of putting whatever remained of its lingering blood supply to permanent sleep. You never wanted support for the true work—which seemed at least as far as I am concerned always bounded on all sides by an infinity of virtually indistinguishable facsimiles—but rather signs of a contemptuously parental—in other words, authentic—concern infinitely deeper, infinitely more sincere, at least in your eyes, than mere support. And only the hopelessness, absurdity, delusiveness of the true work could hope to elicit that personal interest—that parental concern. In other words you lived for contemptuous solicitude not for the true work." No longer a voice, he was face to face with Fatima in all her burnished glory. Xman turned away as if blinded by a burning bush. Father and daughter were gone, under the watchful eye of a fashionably dressed woman and her son attired for prep school though it was Saturday, or Sunday, or both, an emaciated figure whose face looked ruddy and ravaged was now sweeping the leaves, linden, gingko, at the lake's rim. The bleached blond hair, skin bronzed to cracking point of infinite anastomosis around eyes and mouth, bejewelled arms, were typical of a certain class and more particularly of its aspiration. Propelled suddenly by something stronger than the strokes of his rake the sweeper walked away from the little heap of gingko and linden, away from the bleached blonde and her brat, just as he did once before, Xman thought, but where, when. Xman turned to Fatima as if she might know, she stared straight ahead. Facing the sunset the sweeper leaned on his rake as if to say, I can walk away from all this any time I want, I can exit any time I want from the . . . wisp of heterogeneity devised for the delectation of frumps like you.

"I know what it means to feel like him," Fatima whispered. "To want to walk away from the prop one has become in order if only for a moment not to be identified with its putrefactive content. I wasn't always Fatima Buckley. Once, long ago, I was—I was . . . I was. . . " He waited. "But I don't want to tell the story." The man with the rake jumped at her shriek then rested his arms contemplatively once more. "Every time I feel myself on the verge of telling I want to flee. I am suddenly assaulted by a plethora of immediacies immiscible in the muddy solution of the story yet which cry out with a passion of ruthless importunity the story will never know. And what is a story but a vastly expanded and extended caption enshrined in an amber forever on the look-out for yet another fly-by-night. And anybody who knows me knows I repudiate all captions. I'm already so busy repudiating the caption-to-come I can't even focus on the landscape. Did you ever have that feeling, young man. It happens every time. Just as I am about to tell the story that justifies me utterly and completely the movement toward it induces an avalanche of compossibles demanding my immediate attention where before—just before—there was only a vast dim dearth. But I'll tell you the story because you need to hear it. (You're not cold out here, are you?) So fasten your seat belt and don't be intimidated by the imperturbable if slightly acrid warmed-over charm of our svelte stewardess in charge of anti-suffocation operations. For like the hero—or rather the heroine—of my story she is appalled at the straitjacketing, the captioning, that qua stewardess she must endure at each takeoff smearing the receding earth with the spoor of this beastly having to serve willingly. But look—the hoarded horizontal thrust is about to become repudiating upthrust and that loudmouthed frump entering the international *arrivistes'*—I mean arrivals—terminal is suddenly no bigger than the tumor on her devoted—too devoted—husband's spleen.

"Soon we'll be looking back on life as we know it as on some dead thing. In any case, once upon a time there was a

poor little wardrobe mistress. And she was warned by the
staff and on several occasions by the master choreographer
himself that her tardiness—her chronic flagrant reprehensi-
ble lackadaisical disrespect and disregard for the rules—
would simply not do, would no longer be permitted.
Wardrobe mistresses, she was told, were a dime a dozen. The
stars and their retinue had to be clad and on time every time.
If she was to earn her keep then she had to relinquish this
unwholesome brooding over the past as muddy firmament of
malefic cluster points, points of origin, points big with bifur-
cation, trifurcation, quadrifurcation, whence things might
have turned out quite differently with her ending up forever
free à la Violetta in her famous *cabaletta* of the straitjacket
conferred by the much-coveted position of Wardrobe Mistress to a Vast and Innovative Ballet Company, in fact the
world's vastest. She had to relinquish all this in order to
clothe her charges appropriately with a dignity worthy of the
master's antiminimalist aesthetic. And she had to relinquish
this unwholesome preoccupation with the absence of a tolerable past for other reasons. For there is no story without
characters and characters will simply refuse to character-act
if not suitably clothed, preferably like the figures on their
hand-mirrors fringed with acanthi. In short I depend on her
to get me through my story. I simply will not tolerate fai-
néantise.

"In short I was not always a revolutionary but I was always
out of joint with things as they are, crucial to the making of
a revolutionary. But let me tell you how I managed to thrash
my way out of the slime and take upon myself the responsibility of awakening all the other straitjacketed wardrobe mistresses trapped in their windowless little shops far far far to
the right or left of the applause applauding its own incomparable luminosity of discernment. I managed to uproot my

self from unwholesome meditation on those points—those moments—of origin, of choice, that hadn't seemed like moments of choice for I had been far too excruciated at the time to look in other directions—those glimpsing an impinging superabundance of alternative choices. Instead I chose the direction of my tormentors—the fleering jeering multitude whose dank taciturnity insisted I comply with my one choice and one choice only. But they are not to blame. Or rather they are to blame as long as blaming them—cursing them eternally—does not get in the way of my friendly smile just before I launch another grenade. Yes, they are to blame. Yes, that is the truth. However, not truth but its wily suppression makes for any form of advancement worth a damn on this damned planet. So in the Myth of Eternal Wardrobe Mistress there are no villainous shamans. In the Personal History of the Wardrobe Mistress there are villains numberless. However at this stage of the game I prefer myth to personal history, in other words, personal tragedy. In short: What's the point of blaming, I mean, what's the point to my—to our—progress—our suprapersonal progress.

"You know there is a charming story about a people that revised the story of its hero to meet certain archetypal specifications. Marko Kraljevic was his name. You see a priori I am by no means against transformation of everyday slag into the almost-gold—in other words, the lead—of archetype. I'm not one to berate somebody for such a ploy. So, Xman, you've come to the right place: Feel free to go on using your mechanism to consign event to the slagheap of archetypal gesture.

"But returning to the subject at hand. Yes, I was a wardrobe mistress and whenever I close my eyes I have the breath of the master's lackeys full in the face. There they are, huffing and puffing, dragging me toward the stage to watch the assorted, the ill-assorted, performers. But I was unable to focus on those I had clothed, preoccupied as I was with this life having nothing whatsoever to do with its destiny, unfortunate product of having hurried slapdash through the moment of choice, imagining I could rectify and recuperate later. But how recuperate what the recruited nearest to hand astink with a coercion so vast there is no locating its center has crowded out. Though at the moment of choice it did not feel like coercion, only the simplest way out of an impasse, a temporary stopgap. Choosing for me had always been choosing wrong so as to have some kind of foothold in the plethora of choice directed toward that time out of time when I would be able to choose truly at last, weigh alternatives as calmly as a diamond merchant. But life has not cared for this point of view, at least not as passionately as I might have wished. I had from life's point of view no point of view whatever. But what is amazing is that after one or two suggestions I was completely transformed. For they simply reminded me—as lackeys are wont to do—that my work as wardrobe mistress was by no means gratuitous and that I had to discipline myself accordingly in order to go on paying rent, food and dental bills, subway fare. In any case, much as I loathed the lackeys, to say nothing of the higher-ups of whom they were the merest pale simulacra I was nevertheless grudgingly grateful for their relieving me of this painful labor of fidelity to an outworn misconception. They reminded me, by telling glances more than by words, that it was not a matter of sheer perversity but of brute survival driving me back to the dimly lit worktable day after day. It was not merely a question of thwarting nobler aims just for the sake of thwarting them.

"Though I hated the humiliation of reprimand by these lackeys—so what if my comportment or lack of same had been one long provocation—I found myself grateful for their timely intervention for it immunized me at last against the toxin of uncertainty: Should I stay or should I leave. It was no longer as if I hadn't chosen and was therefore saddled with the dire consequences of all unmade choices.

"Yet a second later I couldn't bear to go on. I was finished: But I owed something to my creatures. They wanted their moment in the sun. Of course they didn't know how well off they were in their latency, shielded from the thankless rigors of realization. They knew nothing, poor dears, of the bliss of failed extrusion into the world where all are indistinguishable, especially in the spotlight whose inexorable glare maims to the same sameness of refutable dungheap brummagem. The only moment worth cherishing is that—and if one is lucky it lasts forever—just before one is obliged to go on. The only moment worth fighting for. And little did they know that if and when I permitted them to open their toes at last (having costumed them according to company postminimalist specifications) they would hardly emerge as full-bodied beings contoured by the welts and warts of an irrefutable flesh. They would be there to embody—in the form of thoughts defending against—the menace of contingency. And the sum of thoughts becomes more often than not the overarching buttress in whose cool shadow the story mossily peters out.

"Of course they hated me, these creations, as they hate me this very moment of my striving to deck them out in the flesh and blood of discourse. But in fact they should have blamed the wardrobe mistress from whose dank womb I finally emerged just as now they should blame not me but the storyteller from whose womb I may never emerge. I never promised them anything. It was she, stuffing their costumes full of pins and their heads full of shopgirl fantasies. From the very first—in the recruiting office bordering the docks—I told them to expect nothing, only the hardships of an ephemeral eloquence with none but an imposed—a forced—relation to what came before and was to come after. From the very first I told them to forget about evolution, maturity, character development. In my world there was, is, no place for evolution, maturity, character development. Anyone found evolving is shot on sight. Through me, a mere wardrobe mistress, they learned that the purpose of dance steps is to cut off contingency at the root before the infection of evolution—character development—sets in. Through me they learned—many refused—they were a succession of steps and nothing but a succession of steps. Through me they learned every step is a warding off of danger. What was vital for them as dancers—what is vital for them as fixtures in my story—is not that they evolve but that every step— every thought as a step of the mind—cutting off the possibility of loathesome gradual evolution at the root—be uttered—I mean danced—in time. One of the conscripts had the nerve to suggest that my hunger to have all steps spoken—I mean danced—as quickly as possible and at breakneck speed stemmed from a fear not of external contingencies bombarding them into illegibility but rather that allowed to incubate lingeringly—as over Sunday brunch—these steps might prove connected to their fellows through more than mere force of the master's will. The little marplot had the insolence to suggest that left in peace—in other words removed far from the vicinity of my throbbing impatience—such steps might very well throw out roots toward one another in a soil surprisingly loamy and accommodating. And of course you know what all this latent consanguinity points to—a story, yes, a story. Why the little shit had the audacity to imply that my steps were by no means insusceptible to inclusion in a story—one of the so-called story ballets—with a certain cohesiveness. In other words, the apparent heterogeneity masked a kinship and a story was very much adumbrated by that kinship. But take it

301

from me—my story—my story—what you are—were—about to hear contains none of the steps constituting it. None of these step-points, though they constitute the story curve, are on that curve.

"They all protested against being mere beasts of burden—speeding vehicles on whose bristly backs or rather on whose sun-dazzled hoods the steps sought to hitchhike into the darker sunlight of articulated frenzy. Clothing them in minimal finery I intended to bring them to the threshold of an eloquence free of character, free of story. But you cannot clothe such creatures in finery however minimal without expecting them to immediately make the quantum leap into the grosser expectation of sporting 'a character all their own.' I found subsequently, much to my dismay, they would not wear anything—not even a mere rag, a strip of dung-spattered pelisse—without inferring entitlement to an authentic role in a story. Certain ideas will take root, all our insistence notwithstanding. Don't you see, even at that early point, I knew that stories are a drug and if we are to arise like lions after slumber in unvanquishable number then we must throw off the chains of stories—stories—stories.

"I've developed quite a reputation, been called unfair to my puppets, unfair to their expectations. But it was never I who excited those expectations. If I had granted them free rein they would have turned sluggish, and sluggishness is one thing I cannot tolerate given the hot haste in delivery my thoughts—my steps—demand. Their haste is their pathos and their pathos their grace. Their haste is their Petipatic purity of line. One minute more and they disintegrate. Ah, what to do with such performers. They all wanted to dance their pasts—you know the unique and irreversible time before identical to everybody else's time before, how grandma abused them, what mamma did to their privates that turbulent night in the toilet, what pop almost did, half-dressed on the landing with the full glare of the new gibbous upon his too avid haunches. Always the same past so there is not even a remote possibility of dialectical enrichment—all this dredging up merely to realize the shopgirl's dream of a lifetime: to be in character, to make the spectator undergo. But didn't they realize—don't they know even now as they clamor for me to turn them into rich and robust 'characters'—that the spectator never undergoes anything except the duration of certain steps' utterance. For thought-steps fight their way free of the story the way the spectator must ultimately fight his way free of oppression, a wretched life throated to the tune of landlords and corrupt politicos. The thought-steps are an example—an incarnate placard, as it were—advertising nothing less than the possibility of total liberation from the opium stew of stories fabricated for the sleep-delectation of bedraggled mass-media off- or rather iff-shoots. The thought-steps incarnate nothing less than successful repudiation of everybody's beginning, middle, and end. But they wanted—they want—their character. They want—wanted—the spectator to undergo their pain as character X and Y. Only in the gaps, my friend, only in the gaps between steps does the spectator undergo and then at cross-purposes with himself and what he thinks he is seeing.

"Fools! They had to see their steps as take-off points to mawkish self-discovery in which the audience would certainly share. They forgot that they existed to make the steps live and not vice versa, they existed to allow the steps their brief life during which passion struggling to create the dialectic surface tension between step content and passion beyond and inside the step could become the content in depth of the spectator's experience. For the step incarnates beauty and passion precisely because SOMETHING is desperately trying for its brief duration to reach the surface of the utterance—I mean, enactment—before utterance—I mean, enactment—is over. And the struggle of the spectator to undergo the struggle of that SOMETHING to reach the surface becomes the embodiment, the content, of true passion. Thus the spectator does not undergo used-up worn forms of passion, passion linked to the already exhausted ploys of this or that character-type, this or that plot-twist. The spectator is called upon to undergo, almost assist, speaking maieutically, the failed emancipation of passion from the step's depth. The spectator is called upon to undergo the torment between passion and step, passion—whose threatening upsurge is 'remedied' by the step—attempting after having been its immediate progenitor to break through the crust of the step as pure form.

"This then is the job of lackeys—to speak—I mean, dance—steps so that the trajectory of imprisoned passion can be sketched. There is not much difference then between a terrorist and a dancer. Only the terrorist has the whole world for spectator. I always urged the importance of dancing quickly and cleanly—throwing the bomb of one's body, as it were, as efficiently as possible along the tottering line of light connecting dress circle with farthest pit of the gallery. I always urged the importance of dancing quickly—before the steps were sucked into the fog of malevolent contingency— all contingency is by definition malevolent to steps until, that is, these steps absorb the malevolence in a flash and are immeasurably enriched by it. Truly creative dancers are able to not only elude but use the contingencies invoked by the urgency of their steps—unconsciously solicited by those steps in the innocence of their urgency—make them pretext for the generation of other steps. But my aspiring characters never had time for such extracurricular work. They hungered only to be recognized as Lord or Lady de la Tour de Balls or Fast-fingered Eddie Boy Blue. Or as the irrepressible Granny-Shit Willickers, hag sister to Madge the Witch or

Tchaikovsky's Carabosse. Some of them, turning their back on what was less decree than enlightenment of the purest kind, had the effrontery to suggest thoughts were not done in by external factors but rather by the malevolence with which I myself saddled them. For in their view all these thoughts were essentially the same thought—step, I mean— the thought—I mean, the step—of destroying the world. Or perhaps, said other would-be dancers, I saddled these skewed aggressors with my not so latent rage toward the thoughts themselves, in which I had evidently to be always wallowing in order to feel piggishly alive. For you see by this time I was a choreographer in my own right, my talent had succeeded in chloroforming the master who now treated me with infinite respect.

"To this day I myself don't understand the haste of my thoughts: my haste over the thoughts. But it was not their place to question. Maybe each thought—each step—secedes from itself, finding itself too unworthy to linger over the furry contour of its own eloquence since it is clearly not THE thought—the thought that will wounding it to irreparable enlightenment transform the world. And so in despair the thought altruistically making way for the thought—THE thought—hurries to spew forth, denature and destroy itself.

"Every step—every thought—thirsts for extinction. I extinguish them in the story I refuse to tell. The story is an orphanage that confirms our most unspeakable fears concerning public service institutions.

"In any case, after reprimand by my charges—for no matter how exalted my function I always listened to the grumbling in the ranks in order to learn from my inferiors—since before the world can become a world of equals there must be inferiors to carry out the arduous duties of transformation— after reprimand I trained myself to trot out my creations more amiably. But at the same time I encouraged them not to think of themselves as characters, to realize they were still nothing more than mouthpieces—or rather, body-pieces—of a moment, as long as it took for one configuration to melt unlocalizably into another. And then as I began to see the fruits of my labors I also saw that these mouthpieces were in fact transformed into what they had always been: a horde of hierodules working day and night on behalf of my rightful destiny. Yes—as soon as they began to become the embodiment of a succession of steps it was clear they were more, far more—they were the handmaidens of my destiny and I their leader. These were no longer failed characters packed into leotards but artisans, true artisans riding the mottled steed of assiduity on behalf of a mammoth repara-tion for services rendered over too many lifetimes by one poor little wardrobe mistress about to come into her own at last. In return for my having stitched together so many ex-pressive garments for these long-limbed monsters and taught them how to move around in them to maximum effect they had chosen working day and night—and unsolic-ited—to stitch together the definitive fabric of destiny from the tatters of a lifelong abstention. And suddenly I saw why I had abstained for so long. I hadn't wanted any gesture of my own, any brutish exploit, to interfere with their perception of where the fabric most needed reinforcement or an effect as of gossamer—their perception of my purest need defin-able only in the absence of all I might—but didn't—do to satisfy—in other words disrupt, trivialize and obliterate it. So, between performances, they worked stitching and pleat-ing, taking their cue as to form and texture from those creases obligingly made in the potentiality of the garment by an intrinsic lifelong refusal to work at slave wages for its jowled manufacturers—taking their cue as to true commit-ment from my sublime example. (Hadn't they seen me sacri-ficing whole weekends to the completion of this or that set of costumes for a Monday opening night?) Suddenly it became clear that though reduced to the most incredible misery my life was—thanks to these puppets turned artisans—germinating in secret. All of a sudden I realized that those clients who ostensibly had paid me no heed in their gallop toward the footlights—no truck for them with the boss's lowliest drudge—were in fact my supreme slaves exclusively obsessed by my inevitable accession to the throne of destiny among destinies. I and no one else was queen of the hive, sure to see the piecework I so passionately loathed, every blessed stitch of it, go up at last in flaming homage to my belated but nevertheless still somewhat welcome apotheosis. But I never allowed myself to get carried away. Success is, after all, one stance among many, one more way station toward what is always bigger and better. But more of that later.

"So that thanks to the haughty clients who turned out after all to be most obliging servants of her lordship, I was able to reach some form of limit point. For I was so tired of being under the sway of—forthright souls all—those jailers in being's maximum security prison whose vigorous talent for inhumanity stems by the way from the mistaken but all too common belief that with their own straitjacketed hops, skips, and jumps actualized by puny surrogates they have nothing more to do than gloat over transcendence cheaply bought in the form of servitude even more cheaply eluded.

"And who were the jailers after all—not the choreographers brutally thrusting blueprints under my nose—as I indicated I superseded them—nor the even more noxious assistants—not my fussy clients who were always complaining—they felt obliged to if they were to qualify as more than rank amateurs—about the texture of this tutu, the length of that tunic—no, the most pernicious jailers were the steps themselves to which I had for so long subordinated the dance. For so long the dance seemed inconceivable if it did not conform to the contour sketched subliminally by the progression of steps. Freed of my enslavement to the steps— the step packets—I realized all at once I was put on earth to confound and refute all stances perpetuating heterogeneity—the stewpot of rank injustices—to destroy the world as we know it. And only my obsession with the individual steps doing their duty of resisting the progression of a story line kept me back. But once I observed the dancers busily if subterraneanly at work stitching together the garment of my evolution I forgot about the steps. I forgot about keeping track of the steps with which I always managed to saddle my conception of the dance, never tolerating a single loss in the course of its unfolding.

"But tut tut tut I see I have offended you. Is there any point, you must think, dwelling on the doings of our leaders, since it is their doings that have produced the world I am consecrated to destroying—those bright beasts we turn to in a moment of crisis simply because they are there—there— everywhere—caparisoned in the eye-catching dowdiness of their own secretions, buoyed up by rumor's pertussal homage, spleens robustly hypertrophied thanks to substantial donations from the rabble and the rabble-rousers given to hanging from the rafters in corporate boardrooms. Look, look, bright boy, you needn't protest. How dare I begrudge your striving for promotion when clearly all my rhetoric has to offer is a dagger thrust right up the bowels of your complacency and emerging from the rosy-lipped mouth, engine of lies. Go forward, bright boy, after your convalescence, that is, toward a plowed progress. Forward, forward. The cattle cars stand at attention and the mothers and children weep against the grain of the goose steps. But I won't comment, don't worry. I abstain from social comment as of this moment for what is it but a way to explode one's infirmities to the proportions of universal ague. The universe is charming. The little cubicle on the margin of the hacks is the only conceivable habitation fit, in fact, for a kingpin. Any defects I can pinpoint simply indict my own personal maladaptation to a perfectly acceptable if somewhat malodorous cosmos. So go forward, take orders, parasitize the sooty ozone that gives such a gratingly familiar twang to the voice of your betters. Try, try, try, at all costs, to make your meandering aspirations—for what is a man without aspirations—conform to the clear-cut directives issuing from the orifices of these simpletons. Don't let their project, as perfect arena for deployment of a wanton expertise, get away. Don't hesitate, even, to loan the dears a pair of scissors with which to fix the area under study and formulate the 'parameters of the project,' multinational, of course."

The voice was more than ever that of the woman in the hotel room. "Don't let me stand in your way," she said. "But I might as well tell you: Both Rose and Xaviero are not . . . as they have been. Don't plan on going back to their halfhearted support. Xaviero is dead and you may very well find yourself a wanted man. He just couldn't convalesce fast enough in those Bolivian hinterlands. Rose B. may be recuperating, last I heard, from a severe blow to more than her pride. But what are Xaviero and Rose B.: A certain taxi driver made sure that you encountered them once you departed from your city of origin. A certain taxi driver whom you later met on fashionable Columbus Avenue and who drove you wild with envy. In any case, they are all so many obtuse angles on the universe as it is meant someday to be. Though essentially dull-witted, though essentially limited—especially in their commitment to profit, profit, profit, and devil take the cripples and the misfits—whereas we blow them up altruistically intent on a better world for their congeners—there were momentary chinks—as you know better than anyone—

in that monumental hebetude whence peeked here and there a kind of slumbering acuity in which you participated, whence you learned. I do not deny that both Rose B. and Xaviero were teachers—master teachers—perhaps the very best our fair city has to offer but it was always as if—or almost as if—merely to examine the effect on you, a patent neophyte and therefore good for a laugh—the intelligence was peeking through the hebetude or the hebetude through the intelligence so that either one or the other or both were an impersonation of the rankest sort. So retrospectively hebetude becomes a calculated insidious hebetude—a constructed dull-wittedness. Just like the noise in your apartment—" "What about the noise?" "I think your start is the answer to that question." "So it was you—the throbbing bassline—the visceral insistence across the paper-thin partitions—" Fatima lowered her head proudly, suffused with a delight that accepts full responsibility for its consequences.

"We—I—had hoped that in your struggle to isolate the intention behind, within, the brute force, you might have awakened to the connection between noise and the noise made by the likes of Xaviero and Rose B.—capitalist pigs of dissimilar but ultimately identical species. Xaviero pandered to the medical moguls and Rose slobbered before the hindquarters of what our foulmouthed euphemists refer to between slices of toast lightly buttered as 'the business community.' They too had a secret intention, an acuity throbbing at the heart of their apparent hebetude, an intelligence of which they were in large measure unaware. The message was: Abandon us, we're the dead, we're the past, join Fatima, Fatima and her boys." As Fatima began at this to laugh uproariously the very clouds seemed to join in her riotous ode to humanity's imminent springtime.

Seeing him turned toward the hospital she said, "There once was a young man who aspired after the true work. So he took a cross-country bus ride and when it thundered over the Great Plains he watched the raindrops fall on the panes. Some slashed the glass like meteors, so inflamed by a sense of purpose they were willing to accept quick extinction if that was the price—and it was, oh it was—of achievement. But the inflamedness of purpose immunized them against all sense of penalty. Other drops slid a very small cautious distance and then simply swelled, swelled, swelled, so many burls on the trunk of being, refusing to burst and die. At that moment the aspiring true worker realized he was at best—at very best—a true worker *manqué* and more akin, infinitely more akin, to the bulbous mourners than the splendid astral bodies he so passionately worshipped from his coign. So where do you go, Xman. Do you join the true worker *manqué* on his cross-country voyage of painful discovery. What becomes of you once you leave these hospital precincts, these shabby purlieus. Where are you to go with your absence of a history, your hungering after a vanished true destiny, your greater affinity for possible upsurges of the true work than for the work itself, your greater skill at staking out possible vantages on the next possible upsurge of the true work than diving head first into the very heart of the heart of that work.

"Where are you to go with your hatred of stories and your equally passionate hatred of the absence of stories—this proliferation of thoughts refusing hospice in the story's sludge." She waited until a ripple covered the scummy lake then said: "You can always skid toward evening. But Xman—to leap in front of a truck once, twice, may be regarded as misfortune: To leap thrice will look like carelessness."

Xman surprised himself. He did not respond to her remark as to a wound. He heard it the way he might have heard or just failed to hear a bird in flight squawking through a samara-peppered thicket—the sound of an ax far off in a cherry orchard and so, looking up and away from the hospital, from Rosalie, from the child, he skidded toward evening, one blue-black element among too many.

"So," she finally said. "How was the glide into evening. Look, Xman, you're a man of many facets, many . . . symptoms. I can give you an opportunity to put your rage to good use. How many times have you come home to that little creature, what's her name, yes, Rosalie, with your disgust, your obliterated sense of worth immediately instantly transformed—at the mere sight of her—into discontentment with your . . . relation. Ugh! Loathesome word. Never touch the stuff. Quick, a chocolate. Before she can reach you your self-loathing puts you out of reach. You've tried to weep at the painful truths she or rather her unbearable devotion has dredged up, unbearable, by the way, because uncontingent—dredged up for your instruction." "I've tried to weep," he admitted. He was weeping now. "Yes, you wept—to make contact with some facet of your being beyond ubiquitous rage, rage jealously filling every crevice that might have been rented out to other emotions. But these emotions can only 'give mortifying pleasure' to others whereas rage— Surrender to these emotions would constitute a lapse from vigilance. So in your terms, Xman my dear, rage is vigilance. Rage is a mammoth vigilance. Rage is your lookout. Therefore you can understand why we want to work with you. We need somebody who is most under control when most delivered up to rage. Our business after all is rage of a certain genre. Rosalie, in her own quiet way, has of course guessed your secret hasn't she. Hasn't she." "What," he replied as dully as a gingko leaf. "She has guessed the rage is a ploy—an impersonation of rage—though no less real for all that—masking its true heart of . . . hopeless contentment. You speak of your hopelessness, your sense of doom—this, how did you put it, 'stinking business of staying alive'—merely to throw her and everybody else—her AS everybody else, what a fatal mistake that, no greater disservice can be done to a great love such as hers—off the track. You are never more comfortable than when decked out dependably in rage, flitting from impossible situation to impossible situation—Fish to Xaviero to O'Kay. Oh, that's right, O'Kay was Baldachino's phantom. Yet ashamed of so clinging you have devised imprecations implying a nonexistent schism from that to which you are only too welded. You are not hopeless, simply camouflaging hopeless contentment at being shiftless and living off Rosalie's trust. In spite of herself she has detected the hopeless contentment at the heart of anathematizing hopelessness. And all along you thought you were inconspicuous: that your tantrums were so much sand thrown in the eyes of the little one's perspicuity. Too many times you've tried to damn yourself before she could locate you. But she has succeeded in locating you." "It's just that she tries to mitigate my excesses—" "And I am proud of you, Xman, proud that you refuse to mitigate those excesses. But making them out to be worse than they are is sometimes—not always—a form of inverse mitigation, if you like. I was proud, however, to hear how you destroyed Xaviero's office and almost strangled Rose B. in her boudoir."

The moment Fatima murmured this last it became true. Xman's undergoing of its elusive intriguingness constituted its truth. "And Rosalie means well when she tells me I am not being singled out when I return from a hard day's nothingness. I am not being singled out: She thinks she is helping me, reassuring me. Doesn't she see—" "That your only consolation is the sense that you are indeed singled out for the most excruciating of all torments? No, she does not see. Or perhaps she does see and stemming from the leafy roots of her tender soul is rage at your delusions of uniqueness. But we can use that uniqueness—that delusion of uniqueness—

for the delusion of uniqueness constitutes authentic—the only authentic—uniqueness and remains—that is the glory of this delusion—delusion still. We can use it—you. Xman, look at me." As he had been staring intently he could not understand this exhortation. Was its purpose to cast a retrospective Burchian glow of transformative enlightenment on the staring as suddenly a nonstaring. Was she asking him—wardrobe mistress still—to undergo his staring as the negation of itself in order truly to live it. Something in her look terrified him: a kind of bovine accusativeness that was itself not aware whence it accused.

So he glided on, on he glided, as she had commanded, into the domain of evening. No longer blue, darker than black. For the first time in centuries he was amazed by something other than the landscape's retrocession. He was taken by its fecundity best exemplified by a stretch of discarded tires, wastebaskets, cigarettes, old-age homes at whose curtainless windows the residents were about to become visible. He took his bearings: on one side death, invisible and discreet, on the other a horizon just short of ineffable owing to the fragile clarity of sailboats about to collide but always at last in different planes. And everywhere bodies turning as on a spit. He sidestepped the flab on his way to the shadowy filth beneath the boardwalk, zone neither of death nor life, but of an after-dinner paroxysm redolent of undigested tripe. Right across from the theater of the eastern seaboard (undulations right on cue, breakers collapsing neither a second too early nor too late) were tiny castles in the air, moats choked by exploding foamlets. He fled. Anathematizing the tires and the flab nevertheless he quickly underwent an ungovernable nostalgia for their shapes, their smells, especially when a red wound of setting sun abandoned untended throngs of titmice. Yet here he was back among the patients, who insisted on picking ears, noses, assholes, or whatever other orifices were being promoted all down the main corridor by super-conscientious nurses. He had glided out of evening back into his room, no more evening, evening threw up its hands at the ungovernableness of man, relinquished the reins to tougher gum-chewing night. He walked faster and faster, tried to escape evening's harsh verdict. Then he began to walk neither to escape nor draw closer but in order to, as it were—like some indentured land surveyor—appraise the extent of his own incarceration grown hoary with age. Fatima's words haunted him until he realized (lowering the blinds) she had not spoken them. In any case Fatima ought to have said: "You have chosen the true work so expect nothing: no results, no certainty. And don't take the easy way as a town crier of your own failed inwardness as you did just a minute ago parading down the shingle's titmice-and-tire-laden main street (sound effects compliments of that 'hot' new rock band, Surf, Inc.). Remember this is the true intrinsicalness of the true work: It rebuffs all recompense, all result. The true work exists to make you feel you betray its requirements every moment." The door was opened slightly. Shadows of doctors and nurses, ministering nurses all, expanded heavenward and were vaguely touching—would have been touching but for the all-too-typical stridency of their efforts to hide a sense of doom, no longer impending. These efforts, he wanted to announce, were simply too much out of keeping with the state of martial law sketched by the first stars and irradiating impartially the face traced in the spaces between. He closed the door, on the table was a note, he lifted it heavily as if it was Rosalie's body. The note told him she had decided to leave, had reached her limit of tolerance. She had thought with the baby at least— She was out of the nightmare, which was all life with him had been, could continue to be, for too long she had refused to make the distinction between nightmare and non-nightmare, for nightmare

315

is to be at the very heart of nightmare noting alternatives as forever out of reach. And suddenly he hungered to be Rosalie: to impersonate her, or rather to impersonate her decision—to be her decision—not to endure any longer. He envied with all his heart and soul her ability to have reached this point of refusal to continue in the same mode. And with all his heart and soul he wished to become that heroism, to earn it, to direct its beam on the flotsam of his own life. If he had been cruel he had also been driven by too many factors to which he would have liked to say more than ever as Rosalie now was saying: I will not endure more in the same mode. He envied her exit. He grovelled at the feet of her exit as he had never grovelled at her own, or perhaps only in the early days when they left the dishes unwashed to struggle on their rooftop amid the ocherous beams of Hudson River sunset, unbracketed. He sought desperately for situations, continuing to pace, in which he might say as she was saying: I will not continue in the same mode, I am exiting from the nightmare. He thought of Fatima, and for a moment, impersonating Rosalie, impregnated with the courage embodied in the words that now haunted his every movement, felt able to overcome, consign her to oblivion. Then the ability to impersonate faded and he was left with mere hunger.

But miracle of miracles, instead of throwing himself out of the window he found himself safely disembarked in a little pool of lampless landing communicating through its rickety flight of tattered steps with the outcries pullulating on the landing below. Here, within the shabby precincts of the hospital, he, Xman, was surrounded by friends or at least acquaintances—far more than he could have ever imagined given his loathing of his fellow mortals and their gaseous ways—their blithe repetition of everything he had ever heard long before he heard it even for the first time, their blithe refusal to escape the straitjacketing invasion of a privacy disowned at every available opportunity. They, these home-grown outcries of the congenital and chronic, whisked him back without ceremony to the shabby precincts of battle with things as they are.

He was once again confronted with whispered impreca-tions behind rickety partitions pretending to be sturdy walls, vacant lots over which from time to time a derrick's con-science-stricken presided but only on days of flawless blue when its corrective services were least needed by residents happy for a stippled moment in and out of want. For want, didn't he know, is not without its mindless disfigurements, its bashful filigree, at least until the homicidal pigeons waken us to the ultimate intransigence.

He was slapped back to reality just as Fatima was having the audacity to say, Stick with me. Loathing Fatima was easy but what was the alternative. He breathed deep. She took this for his coming obediently to attention. "The doctor let me in again. I couldn't leave on such terms, I want us to be friends. Especially now you've nothing and no one. Remem-ber, Xman—three suicide attempts would look like careless-ness. You simply weren't made for the simple life with Rosalie and the child, with the likes of Baldachino and Mac-Duffers. But you should be proud—you made an honorable attempt even if its failure was known in advance and already foreseen retrospectively as an interesting bit of biographic footnote, as it were. Stop blaming yourself. You are not, after all, the young man by the lake. Or rather, you are too much like him to be capable like him of living in the world. Only in a story—ugh!—can such a specimen survive for as we both know a storybook character is guaranteed a bracketed rise and fall, to say nothing of the fringe benefits of all that comes between. But without its framing mechanism induc-ing—" Xman was tempted to glide back to the evening's blue-black.

"Before you go, Xman, for your massage in ward ABC, let me tell you the story of the young man by the lake. He sat down at the edge of the lake. Just as you might have done if I had not accosted you. He looked around, thought he was enjoying the contrast between his lacerated uncertainty and the calm of nature's walks and willows. Or rather he was enacting the contrast for the benefit of . . . storyteller. And being so busy working for that storyteller's benefit he was completely obstructed from seeing the archetypal element in his life. At last he was an archetypal figure. Seated at the edge of the lake. What made him archetypal at last? We'll soon find out. What obstructed him from enjoying his own archetypality? What made him want to wish it away with all his heart and soul? But in those rare intervals when he was free of torment he easily envied those embedded in just such an archetypality. He envied the ease with which they delivered themselves up to the story in which he, at least, knew them to be embedded and in which he was unable to fit. But that was because it was their story. Not his story. He could only begin to marvel at that story from a distance, as a potential acquisition, a potential result. When inside the story he was undone for acquisition of himself, of the story, for self-differentiation, for being. He needed to acquire what he lived, and living and acquiring are incompatible—as you know better than anyone. Except of course when one is a terrorist or rather when one is living that vocation to the hilt or correctly or both. The need for a trace was doing our man in. He, the young man at the edge of the lake, was terrified of coinciding with himself in the story, for once he coincided with himself there was no acquiring the story—no acquiring himself—from the outside. For one who is one with his story there is no fetishizing the story.

"So he rejected the story for in his case a simple truth must be stated: The story was not compatible with its elements. Yes, this is the simple and horrible truth but I think, Xman my boy, you're strong enough to take it. You've got enough hair on your balls to take it. But in fact this truth—not about your balls—is a misrepresentation of the truth—as are all truths except those that issue from the treadmills of Fatima Buckley. No, no, just kidding. In his case the story was incompatible not with its elements—and we will be coming to such elements shortly—for his elements like anybody else's were authentic building blocks of story—archetypality—destiny—teleology—incompatible not with its elements but with the machinations of his dread, his refusal to shoulder and live inside the building blocks. The story was, in his case—the case of the young man at the edge of the lake—for he was a case—incompatible with the symptoms—the symptoms—

the symptoms

elaborated to prevent himself from participating in the building blocks and thereby living the story. So, do you understand, in the case of the young man at the edge of the lake in early summer the story was incompatible not with its elements—and we will be getting to those elements very shortly—with its legitimated building blocks—and we will be getting to those building blocks shortly—elements of tension intercalated into the edifice of being like chunks of finely hewn ashlar—elements of uncertainty, tension, and conflict—incompatible not with its elements but with the symptoms he elaborated to erode the building blocks expanding in the leisurely sunlight of the story's unfolding.

"Over the story that might have been—that of a young man about to ask for a raise from Mr. Fish or Mr. O'Kay—there, you know the theme of the story at last, you big old naughty lusty boy—arched a symptom's willful and malefic collision with each moment of his plight as traced by the story. And thanks to the symptom's ruse he managed, poor fellow, to confuse—fuse—the aims of the symptom with those of the story and to make his story nothing ultimately but the absence of itself—in short, a promenade of collisions of the symptom with what might have been legitimate triumphs over moments of plight. But what can you expect— only a terrorist knows how to put his symptoms to good use AND enjoy these legitimate triumphs over moments of plight.

"When he first sat down at the edge of the lake he rejoiced when he realized what he was: Any young man seeking a raise at the workplace. He rejoiced for a moment when he heard himself speaking, so what if for the time being only to himself, for all young men in search of a raise. But his tragedy was to believe that his plight could not become quintessential until all eye-choking tension had been precipitated out of the distillate. He tried to blink away his predicament, or rather the tension of that predicament, incompatible with the unfolding of an archetype—the predicament as the archetype of itself—as if the archetype could be separated from the predicament in all its bloodiness, all its messiness. Bloody, chaotic as it might be it could never begin to approach the bloodiness—the chaos—the homogeneity—imposed upon it—and this is the whole point—by the symptoms working overtime to sabotage its deployment. In short, he tried to blink himself away but he would not go away and make way for the archetype in its purity for the archetype couldn't go on without him, without his messiness, without his chaos. He closed his eyes to the toy sailboat that swam into his clotted ken.

"But when he opened them, the same flesh, alas, as before, pale and too too hairy and blemished compared to neighboring flesh assaulting on all sides—flesh compatible with archetypality, destiny, teleology, story, being, flesh of pretty young men who spent their days on park benches with sunglasses suspended fashionably, he presumed, from a button on their shirtfront or pushed back tiaralike into bleached subliminally ruffled hair. Opening his eyes he saw, alas, he had not blinked himself into beatific nonbeing. He was no closer than before to embarkation for the Cythera of archetypality on his own terms. He wanted to cry out. With all his heart and soul he wanted, then and there, to cry out. But to whom could he cry out. He was not as lucky as you, Xman. He did not have his Fatima Buckley at his service. It came to him, sitting at the edge of the lake but no longer, alas, the young man seated at the edge of the lake, that the story did not exist, could not exist. His story—the story—his story could not exist—and this was the verdict from on high, at the level of his sternum, that is—because according to the sternum's presiding authorities, authorities feeding off an ever more invasive symptomatology, that story was incompatible with its elements—the only true—the only possible elements.

"And in case, Xman, you've just turned on the radio—WFAT, to be precise—we're talking about the story—the impossibility of the only possible story—that of the young man with a hunger to ask for a raise at the edge of the lake. The story that could not exist simply because it could not tolerate its own elements—their messiness, their unpredictability—superimposing on their failed deployment collision of the symptoms with those elements. The story could not tolerate its elements, or so his symptom decreed. His symptom (authoritarian, cowlike) simply confiscated the story's prerogative. He told himself, the young man at the edge of the lake but not the young man with a need to ask for a raise at the edge of the lake in early summer, that he simply could not persist as a young man with employment problems because the story of that young man would only attack as foreign bodies its primordial elements, calcining him in the process. Primordial elements such as the need to decide how to approach the boss, he of the furry forehead carbuncles, what time of day to choose, how to contend with the jealousy or, in the case of inevitable failure, with the churlish *Schadenfreude*, of his co-workers, those compelled to feed at the same trough, namely, Prissy, Kissy, Mack and Michelange. The sailboat under the azure looked, from its zigzagged veering beneath the cirrus streaks, as if it believed he was saying goodbye forever with his gaze. But in fact he was waving goodbye to the story that might have been if it had not been destroyed by the very incidents—the intrinsic incidents—crucial to its unfolding yet that ate away at it *like a foreign body*. To get his story going he needed some element of tension, some foreign body at its heart. But once that element made itself known—once the hunger to get a raise made itself known—and without a raise how could he pay the rent on his hole on the Upper West Side, how keep pace with the rising cost of cat food, his only source of nourishment and only when it was a sale item in local supermarkets—it proved in its tension-laden propulsion too paroxysmal for the leisurely progression of the story as decreed by a symptom waiting only to pounce from not so afar. He, the young man at the edge of the lake but no longer— had he ever been—embedded in the story of the young man at the edge of the lake with employment, housing and nutrition problems—he, he, he, could not, would not, set foot in being as propounded by what he had always detected and longed for in the stories of others, namely, authentic predicament. But he did not have a Fatima, Xman, to harness his symptom to a mammoth project that would not—not ever— be done in by the machinations of the dread embodied in the symptom. So he took refuge in dens of iniquity—but more of that later—at the clubhouse—more of the alleys and byways of nonbeing, later I say. You'll meet him and hopefully he'll unfold his hideous tale for you. But he could not bring himself to set foot into the possible authentic being of his story until all the authenticity of being—but in terms of his conception of a story mere dross, waste, detritus, discharge, rheumy obstruction—was obliterated. This he called resolution of preliminary difficulties! He did not realize you cannot be saturated in the life-affirming tension of the story and at the same time indulge in rapt contemplation of yourself as a character in a story—acquisition of oneself as a story character. Ultimatum was in the cirrus-scented air: He would set foot in the being of the story once everything redolent of the tense uncertain electric richness of being had been drawn off and conducted away.

"But Xman, what I want you to take away is not the odor of the lake, nor the meandering of the toy sailboats, nor loverly trysts beneath the willows' gibbet—what I most want you to take away, though you are clearly going nowhere, pacing back and forth here in the hospital cubicle before the note left you by the beloved, what I most want you to acquire is a sense that the young man at the edge of the lake was damned not because he was sabotaged by a symptom but because he made such ineffective use of said symptom, creating a thoroughly artificial and gratuitous—even perverse—opposition between symptom and story. Ultimately the symptom in its ostensible hunger to destroy and attack became a provocation to attack. It led to an endless chain of ineptitudes that provoked scorn and contempt. In short he forswore attack by provoking—straitjacketing—others to attack him for an incorrigible ineptitude, a colossal failure to coincide with his story written clear as grimy day across his features."

Fatima breathed deep. They had penetrated far far into the night. Xman wanted to ask if the young man railroading others to raids upon his symptom's sequelae was not her companion in the hotel room, his, Xman's, first night in the throbbing crouched calculating urban rete. His gaze must have asked the question with more thoroughness of eloquence than his voice ever could have mustered, for shaking her head with glazed ambuscading sclerae she replied, "I never spend my time in hotels with men I loathe and detest."

He was about to run from her, from what he thought she promised, but just before trying he saw himself as in a vision totally transformed. He was both the Xman who had serious employment problems and he whose flights flew toward an authentic empyrean of true workery. He more than viewed this integration—this cohabitation of incompatibles; see: So much of his life had been founded on and stymied by a rigorous and thoroughly false vision of incompatibles—he underwent it in every viscus. He now felt as if he had come to a sudden halt after breathless flight down hill and up dale, he began to wipe his brow with his fist in a certain way—perhaps the way people did after they had stopped running— although this did not describe it. Only he knew this gesture sealed—was like the finishing touch on (though in fact it single-handedly invented)—an impersonation: A sublime impersonation of . . . a . . . self . . . that was . . . he looked at Fatima but could not go on. She terrified him and at the same time his terror spurred him to his new flight of formulational ingenuity: The gesture sketched a being undone by neither employment—employability—problems—nor the excruciating pleasure of the true work—a being that rose sure-footed above these incompatibilities, these antinomies in the plane of being as a thinking being, and whose levitation was fuelled by the sense precisely that there was no such thing as incompatibilities, a being that accepted the ways of the world without rancor and made it its business to parasitize those ways however incompatible to enrich the ways of the world. A manly being therefore, a being too lofty to be offended by imaginary slights and rancors. In fact, a blond beast in all his Viking glory if ever there was one.

Then the blond beast vanished, a failed acquisition, flash of true being as imminence of its acquisition, as other—all he was not. In the little hospital room that had voyaged far far beyond its capacities into the sea of black night he was once again shipwrecked amid the hoary shoals of his old self's inability to coalesce with its particles. But wasn't this non-sum of immiscibles better than the baroque fiction of healthful self-compatibility inlaid into an inaccessible, a phantom, plane like a shrivelled oak leaf under ice.

"What will you do when you get out?" Fatima asked. He did not answer, standing still he was running, running, running, from Fatima, though he hardly knew where. "When you get to New York," she persisted, paying no attention to his refusal to communicate, "there is a hotel near Times Square. We own it, your room is paid for in full as long as you need it. And there will be a check waiting for you—to take care of your immediate needs."

In Times Square he said to himself, Times Square is a sewer but a lively one that happily makes no claim to advanced plumbing. He walked along, he, Xman, newly released from the State Hospital in Bronxville, renowned for its refined anti-semitism and authentically quaint main drag. Two young girls in T-shirts with under their faded leather jackets various insignias he refused to read were eating two-toned ices out of furrowed paper cups, the kind they used for urine samples out there. These two turned to cackle brutally at an old woman whose electrified hair was dyed the rhubarb of one of the ice tones. Further on he glimpsed a billboard completely taken up with an advertisement for perfume in which a bared torso raised itself above a woman swooningly swept into a mock-epic of staggered calisthenic coitus. There was no possibility of winning Rosalie back with his body, his soul. The body and soul of maleness were expropriated—and for all time—by the billboard image. He ran down Forty-second between Seventh and Eighth and then between Eighth and Ninth, past the Port Authority's tiered ramps dotted with bulbs, toward dusk coming from the opposite direction to cover the dying blue with light gray. The hordes by and large kept pace with the clouds except for one derelict who refused to walk any faster than was compatible with cautious disentanglement from less the tatters of his topcoat than the gilded threads of meditation. Xman side-stepped the stench. But not before noting the giveaway accoutrements of all derelicts eager to remain in fashion, or "hot": the pair of laceless sneakers worn by middle-aged hairy-backed handball players on the courts of the Bronx forty years ago. There was of course the obligatory musician, open instrument case bespeckled with small change. He had taken up temporary residence on Theater Row where, among the now demi-fashionable Off Off Off Off Broadway theaters with their parasitizing café-boutiques, an old lady, well-dressed, did an about-face—back toward the derelict—and did her best to italicize its double take—a mixture for Xman of disapproval, disbelief, outraged compassion. But how far did compassion stretch. To what degree could he, Xman, depend on her likes should he end up in similarly sneakered straits. Did her gaze impugn the wretched specimen of urban slime or the society that had molded or rather failed to mold him or the ostensibly different society that blithely condoned such a state of affairs—stasis running rampant, so to shriek. A chic young couple of pretty things—he looked like a dentist, she perhaps was a newly created vice-president and executive creative director overseeing outgoing mail expedition at an advertising firm firmly entrenched in the Flatiron or the Grace or the Chry-

sler or the Kissmyarse—laughed as at a novice street vaude-
villian when said derelict, sneakers and all, began dodging
cars, trucks, taxis, buses, bicyclists in a truculent though
essentially halfhearted effort to get himself killed. A dishev-
elled young man on a bicycle purposely added the derelict's
unwashed toes to his bumbling itinerary. At Tenth Avenue
he found himself moving downtown, faster and faster and
faster. The streets dutifully receded, their recession extending—this had to be its meaning—the promise of permanent
escape from Fatima. But then, after swallowing a few more
in the direction of Herald Square, he was obliged to note that
the receding perspectives assailing, buoying him up, had
themselves given up, like the spray at Columbus Circle diminishing to a trickle. These sidestreets as well as Tenth
Avenue herself had carried out very brief experiments in
depth—penetration to a perspectival depth. All he had left,
advancing, always advancing, was a brief and abortive suggestion of infinite distance. Though he went on the city no
longer seemed to want to go on. It reared in response to his
footsteps but only for a few inches simultaneously drawing
back on its hindlegs. Now it seemed as if every pilaster,
every girder, every shred of superannuated filigree had chosen to congregate here, at arm's length, baiting in simulation
of ambush. Were these shreds of landscape the celebrated
hierodules come at last to claim their cacique. He held his
breath. Fatima had her artisans, had he come at last upon his
own working day and night, grimly and without surcease, to
stitch together a simulacrum of variegated destiny from the
tatters of abstention he preferred, in moments of conniving
lucidity, to call timely withdrawal. Were these the hierodules—these fire escapes, girders, street lamps, metal-muz-
zled storefronts. Or were they Fatima's armored lieutenants
off from work and out prowling to lead him back to the
Times Square hovel where a new life was sure to begin. But

327

they had to be his hierodules—by the mere process of elimination, he needed a destiny more than ever, something to
oppose to the one Fatima seemed to be holding in reserve,
made-to-order like a shroud. He wanted this countervailing
destiny to shine as brightly as Second Avenue during rush
hour, streets paved with headlights, asphalts transmogrified
into a substanceless foggy glare that all things considered
was strangely not without substance.

Xman ran, further and further from Fatima and her min-
ions, her minute men. Then out of the blue he hurried—just
when he was about to debouch on the pigeon-infested won-
ders of Herald Square, the shoppers gone—back uptown to
Fiftieth Street and Eighth and vaguely remembered a vast
patch of ground exposed to the four winds and unseeing gaze
of Sixth Avenue skyscrapers, a mere scotoma in their mind's
eye. There, and there only, corner of Eighth Avenue and Fiftieth—sporting a cinema specializing in all-male pornographic films—he could feel he had at last tracked the city to
its very heart of surprisingly soft entrails. There too, the
city, feeling netted and exposed, lay down and played dead to
conceal thereby its real core and essence. Tonight he could
not stand the city's impersonation—soft belly playing at total capitulation—nor these perspectives that hideously tormented with their incessant ablation of an at best
supposititious depth. The smell of gingko escorted him even
further into the sludge of festive putrefaction where there
was no depth and where there would never be any. It was
here, however, in his favorite spot, if one so amorphous could
speak of a favorite spot, he began to feel followed. At first he
was afraid it was Rosalie, he could not bear to think of her,
nor of the child, he did not want her to see him, he was afraid
of how he might react to her expression.

He swerved toward the gutter, someone behind also
swerved toward the gutter. Turning to observe his hounder, a

tall man, not unattractive, of an uncertain age and crowned with a balt spot, he now had no alternative but to board the IRT at Seventh and Fiftieth and head for the Village where he would be truly lost in the crowd. As he began walking faster to reach his goal his hounder also began walking faster, they were yoked along the same frayed rope whose fibers were the fibers of—of—

Suddenly, once on the platform—but stupidly, stupidly, he told himself—he was after all through with all that—Xman felt he might begin the true work at last thereby throwing off Fatima's fetters forever. Stepping into the car—no filthier than it had to be in order to qualify as a bona fide New York City subway car—he immediately observed a fat repulsive-looking woman—who hadn't even the excuse of middle or old age to justify her repulsiveness—placidly insinuate both copious buttocks into a space that could by no stretch of the imagination be deemed viable, not even for the most emaciated commuter, a young man residing, say, in Soho, but in a garret, though there are no garrets in Soho, and hard at work on a canvas so comprehensive it is sure to interest every gallery on his block even if every gallery on his block and even on the next is indistinguishable from a FINE BOUTIQUE catering to young unbattered professional folk. The woman adjacent and now subjacent muttering something disgruntled the fat one turned sideways with the elephantine contempt of placidity from which malevolence threatened to rise like a fart. However, the triumph of the butt spoke directly—instantaneously—to her pasty face and thereby extinguished the not quite latent retaliatory bovineness that might, under circumstances distinctly less epinicial, have belched slowly forth with all the désinvolture of smoke from a flue sandwiched between two water towers, the trio sandwiched in turn between mother dearth and a typically milky purple sky of vernal and electric Gotham.

The women sickened Xman yet the very sickness seemed to bring him to the verge of the true work. Revolted by her malevolence he nevertheless or necessarily understood it, was inside it, watched—no made—it happen. Yet he would not be good at salvaging this woman from the slagheap. The true work clearly had something—everything—to do with this specimen but he could not possibly use her as a building block faster than he allowed himself to be disqualified for use by revulsion. The true work clearly had everything to do with this woman or rather with the insinuation of two buttocks in the space unallotted and the subsequent bovine simper of unachieved contempt. Yet he was allergic to the insinuation of the buttocks as building block. He was quickly developing an autoimmune reaction against this insinuation of HIS buttocks as element of a true work whose upsurge was still *awaited with anticipation*. He was no good at salvaging such an element. He was good only at destroying it.

The conductor's voice blared over an unlocalizable loudspeaker . . . Xman thought: . . .A sensation comparable only to that induced by the diminishing incoherence of the conductor's voice when the door of the car finally closing, it assures all passengers within that the warning of a delay does not in fact apply. What was the "sensation comparable." As the local glided into Forty-second, the express gliding in simultaneously on a not so parallel ascending track Xman thought: . . .A look of rapture so intense it could be compared only to the paroxysmal impatience of someone who, observing the express pull into the station, waits for his local to come also to a halt and open its doors.

Rising to leave all the time observing the push and pull Xman thought: . . . Feelings that can only be compared to the little eddies in the subway at rush hour of those getting out, those struggling to move more deeply in lest they be ejected by egress-seekers, and those attempting to retain their place at all costs no matter who is trying to get in, who out. But what kind of feelings were these. These subway events all had to do with the true work, he was sure. But the true work was slipping away forever. These subway events were vehicles for expressing feelings that could be expressed in no other way but as these events. No. They were, these subway events, the feelings. No. Wasn't the true work—the true work—the true work—fading fast forever—the only arena where such feelings, such events in the form of feelings, could become clear. Closer, closer. But the true work would never be existing, especially not now nor ever again what with a pursuer hot on his trail since Eighth Avenue and Fiftieth. What were the feelings comparable to these subway events, feelings induced by the subway events indistinguishable from the events themselves. Wrong question, wrong question. He was getting closer to the true work but only now with his pursuer also getting closer closer then close.

There were no subways. Yes, there were subways. Rather, there were no feelings to which these subway events as subway feelings could be compared. He thought: irony, first that the workaday world of subway routine's rolling-pin flattened despair and rage and disgust could create quasi-poetical states, states of ecstasy capable of the most exquisite qualification. And clearly these states, so exquisitely calibrated against . . . themselves, had metamorphosed into gold standard against which all other nonsubway states must ultimately be measured. Each subway state effervesced as if summoned forth directly to ease the passage into spectacular clarity of some prior state, some more significant storybook state, such as might, for example, be undergone painlessly by some young man at the very edge of some city lake—when in point of fact the invocation was a fabrication, an ironic commentary on the true state of affairs, namely, that of each subway state's complete autonomy and lawless-

331

ness unto itself. Each subway state, each subway feeling as event, only appeared to be ancillary, handmaiden of true because storybook feeling coming obstreperously to birth. Irony that through such half-assed metaphors (. . .a feeling that could only be compared, an eddy that could only be assimilated to, a pain in the butt that could only be depicted referring . . .)—bodies without heads, heads without bodies, pineals without conaria—such half-assed metaphors ostensibly in search of their better—their storybook—half, he, Xman von Dungen, a failed failure, a handmaiden of Fatima Buckley von Dungen and her gang of merry mischiefmakers, should be proving and worse seeing himself prove that no states, no feelings, no events, were comparable—that each appertained onto itself and could be depicted only in terms of the minute details of its rise, peak, subsidence, into the residual dust of perplexity. He would never—he knew it now, once and for all time—locate the other side of the metaphor. There was no sentiment, no feeling, comparable, for example, to the precise sentiment of paroxysmal relief occasioned a short while back by the arrival of the local at the very moment the conductor of the express hacked to bits across the platform . . . And only in the domain of the true work could this incommensurability of that paroxysm with any other be highlighted, enshrined as more, far more, than a shortfall. But the true work was gone, gone into something a little less exalted than the promised land. But only in the domain of the true work, gone or not, could subway events as feelings and subway feelings as events both and either apparently maieutic to the momentous articulation of feelings more worthwhile because more conventional because more at home in the storybook world of young men weeping into their beers at the edge of some urban lake, what the French call a piece of water—only in that domain could such feelings as events and events as feelings stand out proudly

332

rebuffing all connectedness to feelings never coming—never allowed to come—to birth. There, his true work was all cut out for him. For of what did the true work consist but giving these feelings as events and events as feelings room to breathe apart from the common run of expectation that they ferment a story. Of course, of course, he, as a true worker, would make—would have made—every effort to unite these imcompatibles into some semblance of a character farting or even shitting or some pretense of a story out of its cradle endlessly rocking as long as he could be sure—and he would have—would have had—every reason to be sure—the true story was all along and ultimately nothing but that of their—the subway events as feelings and feelings as events—Herculean efforts to unmake the Procrustean bed piously provided for a snivelling repose. The true work—the true work—was—gone. Gone, gone. Gone.

Xman squinted at the graffiti scribbled around a poster-length puff for the latest Broadway hit: *Son of Soren K*, Part II. The oxblood cadence was all too familiar. "Dear Nobody (How tedious and toadlike to be somebody): I don't know the answers. I know, however, that my questions sketch a domain that is more than a hiding place. That domain is the domain of my very own true work and nobody else's. Workman, be proud of your own brand of work and the pride will create a domain all your own." He almost heard the scribbler pause for breath. He caught sight of his pursuer hiding not very adriotly behind a stanchion. The space between them emitted an odor of piss so strong it could pass for disinfectant—part of His Honor the Mayor's campaign against sciamachy on public thoroughfares now that the Fair City was capital of the Twentieth Century.

As the express entered the station—its predecessor had been a no-passenger specialty of the house—he, Xman von Dungen, thought: Now is your chance. Now is your chance now you've discovered a little of what the true work busies itself with when it is not canvassing on behalf of the latest eunique. You've been beatifically saddled with these butt-ends of sensation, observation—sensation as observation—observation as articulation—articulation as sensation far more excruciated than any sensation in itself—you've just discovered yourself to be one of the few burdened with hearing a language every time you witness a spectacle—well well well: It is only in the domain of the true work you can discover what to do with your articulations, namely, purposefully fail to make them part of a story, the greatest story always told, your story, everybody's story, the story of the young man at the edge of the lake, about to fall but never falling in. Retrieve yourself. Enter the domain of the true work. Say: His feeling was so intense it could only be compared to the rapture experienced by subway commuters when, the doors opening in the middle of the darkest smelliest tunnel known to pangolin, the conductor announces in his rasping twang ... Say THAT and watch it—this subways event as feeling—blandly yet voraciously usurp the ostensibly primary place of HIS—that is to say, the young man's—feeling which is after all nothing more than every young man's feeling— Retrieve yourself, enter the domain of the true work at last and discover that these events as feelings, feelings as events—building blocks and building blocks to which you are not allergic, don't be fooled—must stay just as they are—comparable to nothing and certainly not to some nobody's conventional sniggling at the edge of a piece of water festooned with toy sailboats. Discover that they are incomparable not from sublimity but rather from exiguity, a burrowing exactness with a charm all its own and perhaps, when that all is said and done, not too far from authentic transcendence.

Entering the express and seeing his pursuer enter the next car he thought or rather heard someone whisper—but it was not his pursuer for his pursuer was definitively within the confines of the next car—"Better to destroy a world capable of producing such events rather than attempt to organize the feelings indistinguishable from these events in a manner impervious to the invasion of a story's falsehoods and falsities." Then he, Xman, definitively thought: "It is in the domain of the true work and that domain alone you will discover what can or cannot be done with the morsels and shards acquired on your trek through the continuum, that is to say, from jakes to john and back again. You will discover that nothing and everything can be done and so you will have a story allergic to itself on your hands. The story will be allergic to its building blocks, will be repudiated by its building blocks. But you will not be allergic to the building blocks. All the young men at the edge of a lake whom you recruit to embody the building blocks AS PLAUSIBLY AS POSSIBLE will very quickly become allergic to their building block-dependent function. But you will grow immunized compliments of their susceptibility."

Knowing his pursuer was beside him even if they were separated by several dank bodies he, Xman von Dungen, resigned himself at once to its being too late for the story therefore too late for the flouting of Fatima. Simply he was put on earth to destroy an earth that produced events ultimately indistinguishable from his feelings and encouraged feelings immediately indistinguishable from its events and therefore incapable of authentic assimilation to the cement substance—integrity—identity—of the feeler. The feeler was—in such a world, stinking, loathsome—a mere succession of events, prey to imploding contingency, buttressed only by the shrapnel of incessant susceptibility. He was put on earth to destroy not to exalt as incarnation of his own backbone the refusal of world events (become his very own personal feelings) to succumb to a story's universal syrup.

Thinking only of Fourteenth Street, of Greenwich Avenue's public garden and Hudson Street's faintly beachfront charm, he heard the unmistakable voice of his pursuer. This meant the Fatima influence was becoming too strong—even if he loathed the phrase, "The Fatima influence was becoming too strong," as too much a storybook influence too easily and without the slightest upsurge of backbone yielding its embryonic autonomy to that, even more embryonic, of a story's shabby possibility SOME TIME IN THE NEAR FUTURE—even if he loathed the phrase the fact remained that Fatima's influence was becoming too strong.

His breath was not heavy nor was it redolent of garlic, cheap cigars, processed cheese. He therefore intoned: "What is a true work, Xman. A true work, Xman, is a work of interpretation, a madness of interpretation. Sometimes the fates are for one's interpretation, sometimes against. In your case, Xman, they have always been against. But Fatima is all too willing to salvage your run ins with the fates and transmogrify them into something fragile, rare, usable. The true work, as only the best of your—no another—kind know it, is a thrashing clear of all labels, all brackets—all diagnosis—in the name of interpreation. For the world—our stinking world—needs interpreters. Nobody will deny that. Yet some of us—despite the ostensible message of our wildest dreams of predestination—are simply not made for interpretation— for the life of interpretation. Some of us are not made to interpret, or if you prefer, discern world events as some form of world feeling—instantiated backlash—on the part of this niggardly monster we call being. Some of us are not willing to admit that no matter how strenuously we thrash toward interpretation—differentiation of event from mere eddy—we fear far more than we thrash. Yet what do you fear, my little Xman. We fear that no matter how hard we thrash, no matter how supple and irreparable our strokes of havoc, these strokes may be all too easily resolved into the phrase, AND DESPITE EVERY EFFORT HE DROWNED. This is the danger of strain, of thrashing, for a certain type of failed true worker. Down at headquarters we call them: the Almost Trues. For a certain type—the Almost True—vitality— thrust—thrashing—ends up as nothing more than its own danger signal and, though it seems to steer glidingly clear of everything that strives to hinder its progress, signature of its own extinction. For the Almost True the more it thrashes the more it feels itself thrashing toward the inevitability of a name that obliterates all progress, all result. And there *is* authentic progress, authentic result, in the case of the Almost True, more so perhaps than for the authentic true worker priding himself on having eluded a straitjacket every step of the way to victory. It is precisely because he is so unusual, so unique, so prolific, that the Almost True attracts an annihilating label, an obliterating diagnosis. So my chickadee of an Xman, an axiom seems to be emerging, doesn't it, from a little exercise in applied geometry. And the axiom is this: The more one struggles, the more heartily and hardily one gives oneself to the fight for interpretation of being (all of course in the name of posterity's saner privacy) the more one is in danger of perceiving the hazardous possibility of failure, resolution of all effort in a name that obliterates accumulated fruit of effort. The key word, Xman, is *perceiving*. Perceiving a hazardous possibility in the domain of the true work is indistinguishable from inviting—actualizing— that possibility. You have already actualized—perhaps you are just on the verge of actualizing—it. It. The more one unites all one's forces in the name of a interpretation that will outface the monster—the more contoured the enormity of that commitment—the more that commitment becomes an easy target for a name, any name. For all names are one name—defeat, despair, disappointment. Any striving susceptible—conceivable—to a name is doomed, and rightly so. Of course I am speaking of those who perceive things in this manner. Perceiving things in this manner they are necessarily doomed to doom, to name, to obliteration in the name. And you are one of those who perceive in this manner. On several occasions you yourself have admitted how guilt-ridden and disgusted your omniscience—your inability to miss anything—has made you. You yourself have admitted how you envy innocence—that is, the ability to miss events, the capacity for authentic obtuseness. I am only paraphrasing what you have told others.

"At the same time, Xman, as an Almost True you dread something even more than the definitive annihilating label for all your thrashing. You dread venturing so far out into interpretation there will no longer be a label. On the other hand the label is loathsome, on the other other it consoles. For sometimes the reality one is obliged to interpret and thereby defang is so frightening, degrading and disgusting that through contamination one seems oneself to be beyond even the crudest labels redolent of fright, degradation, and disgust. So, Xman, in the course of your thrusts in behalf of the true work of interpretation you have never known if you are going away from or toward labels, away from or toward a craving for labels. Your particular ambivalence toward labels is very much linked, if I may say so and I may, I truly may, to your status as Almost True. All this does not wish to imply that while pursuing the true work of interpretation you have not had good—exultant—experiences with labels. There were moments—I happen to know for a fact—when reality— being—the monster—spoke to you respectfully, in a hush of rapturous delight as to a bridegroom. Yes, at those moments it seemed as if the monster was forsaking his monstrous pride so great was his respect for your keenness, your adroitness, at unravelling some of his enigmas, articulating the aim of some of his cruel experiments. One of our cabbies spoke to you of those experiments, I believe. But then, Xman, of such solicitousness you become suspicious and rightfully so. Somehow your self-loathing always greater than your bubble-bath vanity and in the long run more trustworthy suspected that this rapturous admiration was nothing more than the merest gratuity that someone or something having transcended all connectedness feels—but only from the heights of well-being—a certain undenatured concern slightly more intense than disinterested curiosity for disadvantaged brethren wallowing below. Instinctively you knew that when the hush of rapturous delight was vaguely audible the sting of the name was never far off. And so you steeled yourself but in steeling yourself you lost all spontaneity and aggressiveness in behalf of interpretation. In short, you lost your touch. We want to help you regain that touch—to undergo a new—our special—brand of interpretation—that explodes in the same flourish both its target and the caption always trailing behind or in front of one's—your—involvement with that target. In our domain, in the house of Fatima, Xman, involvement with a target is not captionable. Our kind of interpretation explodes all labels and all captions."

Too cold to sit outside he chose a small table in the depths of the cafe, the Figaro on Bleecker. Across the street was the more modestly appointed and therefore more intimate Borgia where he had frequently gone with Rosalie in the days when he was forever on the verge of having all New York at his feet. Once seated Xman watched his pursuer walk almost idly past this joint without even giving it, much less him, a scrutinizing look. Just before he disappeared from the win-

dow frame he began to remind Xman of somebody—maybe
Fish, O'Kay or MacDuffers fifteen years younger. He reminded him of somebody about to issue an order thereby
furnishing a window on death and cancelling a possible upsurge of the true work. Within minutes he had presumably
abruptly turning on his heels reentered the frame, thereby
robbing Xman of one of his few true possessions in a long
time, a phantasm of offscreen space. Observing the ex-phan-
tasm sit down at an unoccupied table paces away so that
they were obliged to face each other over ashtrays, paper
flowers, menus, Xman tried to calm himself by saying this
was a completely unexpected encounter.

From the way staring out into the empty street he gave his
order it became alarmingly clear that here was a man working for Fatima or working as he preferred to put it for the
likes of Fatima. Perhaps she had telephoned him immediately after he, Xman, had escaped her clutches. Now he had
left that small town housing sanatorium, main street, town
tavern, depot, movie theater, she was making sure he was
under constant surveillance. Two flutists began to perform
an ingenious transcription of the mighty Mozart K. 448. The
man took this as a signal to move over with his drink, some
indecipherable concoction that gave new because frightening meaning to the dismal expression, all the colors of the
rainbow. Done they came round demanding alms though
Xman for one had heard almost nothing over the trucks flat-
tening the manholes. But even with no more than ten dollars
in his pocket he couldn't very well refuse, especially with
this lackey interpreting every movement and especially
every abstention from movement. His espresso was, after all,
steaming too opulently for pleas of poverty. And there was
even a stick of cinnamon on his saucer evidently placed
there for the sole purpose of putting the finishing touches on
this portrait of affluent man about town. Surely said telltale

cinnamon stick definitively gave the lie to any trickling ru-
mors that he was undernourished and underdressed. "What
are you doing here," he said finally to the man of uncertain
age who, though far better dressed, hadn't for a minute hesi-
tated about not flinging a coin at the pot of these presumptuous amateurs.

"We have been quite interested in you for a long time. We
think you are our man. The one we need. Especially now
that you have renounced the true work forever." There was
the flavor of a foreign accent somewhere in all this gibberish.
It might be very well situated along his right big toe. Xman
refused to ask, "Need for what," for to answer was to, in
some way, accept the conceivability of the situation. For the
time being—a time being that might very well last a lifetime— Xman needed to think of this situation as inconceivable. "We need you for our campaign," the uncertain one
ventured. "And in any case"—another sip of the unmentiona-
ble farrago—"Miss Fatima always trained us according to the
following axiom: Once you have chosen your target stick by
him. The moment of choice is sacred. One must abide the
initial intuition whatever circumstances abound later to render that choice unattainable and absurd." "Campaign
against what," Xman asked, and asking he was suddenly
assaulted by a plethora of viable targets. "You know against
what, my dear," said the foreign accent. The very air seemed
to cry out against the powers that be. "And what is it about
me that makes you think me . . . recruitable." The other
laughed a laugh suggesting that with such a figure every
move must be, alas, calibrated and yet that took in everything: sitters, squatter, servers and strollers. The laugh's omniscience restored Xman to long-lost offscreen space. On-
and offscreen things, the laugh seemed to say, are too too
loathsome for words. And it was certainly true, Xman
couldn't contest that point of view.

341

The official answer was far more sober: "Because of the wonder with which you regard nature. You are constantly marvelling, interpreting, explaining, transforming—though less, much less, of that last for the time being. But with time— In any case you, better than anyone, know that thought is so many furrows made in the field of being. But you are not content with making furrows, incisions, no, someone like you wishes to extract the vital substance from those fields in being—with or without dandelions. But as our Malaysian brothers have taught: You can only extract ore when the mine is not aware of being robbed and exploited. And that is what we teach—but no more of that now. The night is young. We have chosen you, Xman, because you are a witness saturated in wonderment. You are too good for this planet. You have many a time trasformed objective nature into an objective form of your own existence. But you are not—no you were never—satisfied with mere wonderment, the mere passivity of wonderment. You are not passive, Xman. Get that out of your head right now." The other sippers and chatters looked up from their concoctions for the foreign accent was losing control. Though perhaps this was a calculated, a very calculated, loss of control. "No, no, no," calming down, "you were never satisfied, my dear, with wonderment, mere wonderment. From the very first you projected your sense of an intention—however snakelike, however insidious, into the very heart of the great out there. And so it is not quite correct—except perhaps in the biography that will be distributed to schoolboys—that you were excited by nature per se. No, no, no, it was always the secret intention—behind the noise in your apartment, for example—that caused you to transform nature, which you in fact never gave a damn about—into a distinct conception as object of consciousness. Nature began to hold a place in your wild Irish heart only after undergoing some kind of elementary transformation in spirit—transformation into virulent insidious artifact—archetype—archetype for which fools mocked and reproached you—fools on the order of Rose—"

Xman waved his hands. Although at this moment he loathed Rose and her semblables somehow he could not endure hearing them denounced. "You have always needed the stimulus of nature," the foreign accent went on, instinctively steering clear of what he had perceived displeasing, "in order to give objective form to your own existence in the abstraction, the archetype, you created out of what assaulted you or what you provoked to assault. But you are not completely free, Xman. We hope to teach you to find the stimulus within yourself, without having to react to the noise or the hideous workload in the labyrinth of cubicles. We hope to teach you to find in yourself the material and organ of expression. It is not only in contrast to the hatefulness of the factory—of the labyrinth of cubicles—that your vision can shine. All enrichment will not be cancelled once you stop beating your head against the wall of the labyrinth's sooty refusal to share your ecstasy. Your vocation is not inseparable from its obstructions, its symbiosis with their slime. Your vocation, if you stick with us, is to obliterate its obstructions, one two three. You will find that you can carry out the activity you were born for without the spur of despair over its impossibility. It is possible, Xman. Possible at last. Congratulations on finding us, dear dearest Xman. Up to now of course you have been frustrated, unable to exalt the paltriness of phenomena—noise, for example; the disjunction between what they say and what your co-workers do—what they are and what they say they are—to the level of the idea that seethes, positively seethes, within you. But the incommensurability of shape and idea, monolith and mind, is not insuperable. Destruction unites them in one fell swoop. Congratulations once again on finding us before it was too late."

"You found me," Xman said, without a trace of coquettishness. He was so surprised by his lack of coquettishness he was almost convinced he was impersonating one denuded of all coquettish susceptibility to lewd flattery.

"We found you because you showed and continue to show great promise. Your thought is excited by an alien existence—by the alien as obstruction—but the thought is in many ways free because it transforms the stimulus— the obstruction—through its own operation. So many never advance beyond the struggle to produce some kind of contesting transformation. But this is only the beginning. Some day you will be able to transform the stimulus—the obstruction—the shard of doomed damned heterogeneity—before it transforms you. For when you transform it in thought what is it in fact doing but transforming you. Soon you will be able to take the idea—inside—the phenomenon—and there is always only one idea behind any phenomenon—brute heterogeneity for the delectation of THEM—and throttle it. After some preliminary training, of course." Here the man took another sip of his drink but as if to downplay his own enthusiasm, rather enthusiastic peddling of a product. Grasping the handle of his cup Xman raised it to his lips, it began to tremble, his hand was trembling, a symptom, a symptom. The other eyed him obliquely as if perfectly attuned to the perfectly timed unfolding of this new development supporting his contention that no matter how hard he, Xman, tried, he could never be outside their not so simple faith in his abilities. "You see," the other said. "Yes," he replied, without quite knowing why. "Now you know you are a man saddled with a symptom. And the symptom—like so many others—is the fruit of that connection with nature we just finished extolling. Lots of poor souls have been let out of state institutions just like you—one sees them wandering through the streets, East Side, West Side, all around the slime, And though they furnish an unpardonable eyesore to bejewelled bespectacled matrons and their escorts, to say nothing of calculating younger versions of these too heavily buttered artifacts—in short, that sector of the cesspool seeking no more—at least for the moment—than to finish its quiche Lorraine and tortellini alla pana in peace—do you hear—in peace—though unquestionably a blot on the landscape but prey to every hoodlum and landlord this side of Dante's deepest *bolgias*, they are, don't you agree, far more sinned against than sinning. But your symptom, it can be put to use, good use. Through the symptom, through a veritable potpourri of symptoms, you will be able to deform—destroy—nature, smelt it down to a supple simple form we can use. We want to harness your symptom to our machinery. With your symptom as lever we can move the world. For only symptomed can you transform phenomena without, transforming them in thought, being transformed yourself. Only a symptom renders one intrepid enough to transform, destroy—transform—the world. And why should you have to invite phenomena, so to speak, into yourself. They shouldn't be allowed to make a mess on your carpet. No, go out and make them bend to your will on their own ground. Well, so what do you say. We're telling you that although you are one of the indistinguishable myriad let out of the asylums, indistinguishable and undistinguished, we can transform you—if, that is, you are willing to put your symptom at our service." As if to prove his willingness Xman dropped his cup, it shattered, the sippers looked up from their sips, his hand continued to shake.

Sitting there, in the dimly lit café adjacent to the pavement, a pavement of living lesions, he himself its progenitor

did not have such a bright view of the symptom already
assaulting him. If he could only get away from this lieutenant, no this lackey, of Fatima's the nascent symptom would
go away. Yet in spite of himself, of his hatred of being overcome, he found himself tabulating, tabulating, tabulating—
not how the symptom could, as this lackey said, move the
world—what did he, after all, care for the world—but in and
for how many acts it could incapacitate him. He wanted at
this moment not to attack the world but to be put out of his
misery, to have a licit excuse for putting himself out of his
misery.

"Stop it! stop it!" the lackey suddenly cried so that everyone looked up. "Stop this ridiculous shaking. You'll have to
do better than that. You must let the symptom do all your
thinking for you. This is just a sham—stop it." Xman looked
away as if overhead gulls were swooping in leisurely arcs of
vaguest apprehension. "Stop it, stop it, stop it," Siegfried
repeated. "You are so calculating. This has always made me
hesitate with regard to your putative rightness for the post.
So what if it's been vacant for years—we can wait a few more
years. Instead of giving free play to—luxuriating as it were
in—the symptom you are still caught up in questions of
meaning—origin. We've told you and on several occasions
that the symptom embodies an overabundance of meanings,
all contradictory, all cancelled out. This preoccupation with
an ultimate meaning is of course your way of doing everything imaginable and then some to hold yourself responsible
for the symptom, of making yourself feel the symptom is
entirely the product of your very own slimy depths. And this
preoccupation with holding yourself responsible for an entirely personal product is your way of never letting go, of
forcing the symptom to ride pillion on the wings of your
own sluggishness rather than submit to its dazzling potential for untrammelled flight. You give yourself too much

prescience and power with regard to the symptom—allow yourself to feel terribly responsible for its insinuation into every possible life relation—remember how Rosalie winced when, on Columbus Avenue and at the very height of the tourist season, you shook your cup of Java in the same manner—without, alas, losing one whit of its unbearably mawkish inflection of top-heavy literalness. You torment yourself over responsibility for that literalness because preoccupation with responsibility succeeds in camouflaging a much deeper dread—that of your ultimate powerlessness in the face of the symptom's ultimate capacity to overrun every aspect of your life and railroad it to incapacitation beyond your wildest dreams. In short, you are always tabulating the symptom's capacity to incapacitate, vindicate your truancy, in the small. But in the large, Xman, you are a scared rabbit. But don't insult my intelligence with this absurd pretense of a symptom, although I'm sure you've discovered innumerable uses for it—this absurd pretense of a symptom. After all it got you out of a relation with Rosalie, with the child, with Rose B., with MacDuffers, with the Finaglie twins. But this fluctuation of makeshift utilities has nothing to do with the symptom in its essence purged of visibility. And of course these utilities of which you are forever in search are mere degenerate utilities. They have nothing to do with our kind of utility. At any rate you must call a halt to this search for origins. Yes, I know you have been told that at the time of its administration rehearsal of a cure's origin allows it to fulfill its function flawlessly. This does not apply in the case of symptoms. Yes, I know: Once you understand the origin of your symptoms you intend to take that origin for an unshakable foothold in the manipulation of such puny utilities as you have uncovered. Just remember, however, that the origin of your symptom—or symptoms—has nothing to do—absolutely nothing with the utility we envision for that symptom in our system of purposes, or cross-purposes, as our detractors are all too eager to say. Whatever exists in our system, no matter what its puny origin, is immediately or inevitably reinterpreted, transformed, redirected by some superior power." "What is that superior power," Xman could not help asking. His interlocutor went on as if he had not heard. "And once you discover—that is to say, become the vehicle—of your symptom's utility in our system never believe, no not for a moment, that now you understand its origin. The eye was not made for seeing, nor was the penis made for pissing or fucking. Let us be clear about one thing right now: The utility of your symptom—and there will be many—is only a sign that some superior power has imposed upon its adolescent formlessness the character of a function directed elsewhere. In fact, prepare yourself for a continuous succession of utilities emerging in truly random fashion. One utility merely supersedes another, there is never any question of course and effect." Xman wanted to refuse to obey but could not. "Stop it!" the other cried again. "You do a disservice to all the young men who have given life to their symptom and their life for the symptom. Birth of the symptom—any symptom worth its salt—is identical with, inseparable from, a leap to a new plane where prompted by the symptom's torturing tortured relation to the world new thought possibilities sprout unforeseen but not inside your head—not on your carpet—but on the world's own turf."

Xman surprising himself said, as if remembering the not so distant past, "I don't believe in symptoms. They have no content. The symptom is all terrified anticipation of the symptom-to-come. A symptom is simply the potential space, the pleural cavity, of its imminent upsurge." "Yes, yes, yes," said the lackey, his foreign accent at once more pronounced and more elusive than ever. "All that may be. But when it is most threatening or you most credulous we want to catch that symptom in order to direct it missilelike away from your body toward those who should be its target. We want to catch your symptom in our sieve before you begin to forget that it exists simply as a consequence of your terrified anticipation, your credulity. Never forget, dearest Xman, your symptom is a beautiful creature of destruction akin to the sleekest warheads."

Consious of how little he actually owned, Xman said: "But I don't want to be robbed of my symptoms. Mastering the symptom I master life but under controlled conditions. But what are we talking about. I don't have any symptoms." "What about the need to collide with trucks? The need to torment your lady love—what is her name, Rosa, Rosetta, Rosalie . . . " Then, as if brushing away this allusion—more insignificant than failed—the lackey, still sipping and seeming with each sip to grow fonder and fonder of that whence he sipped, rebounded with, "we want to extract and isolate—buy—your symptoms, before your credulity makes you their target. Look, Fatima spoke to me. She said you were having some difficulties since you got out of the hospital." "Isn't this a bit early in our acquaintanceship to be speaking of my difficulties. I don't know if I like your approach to things as they are." "And what, pray, is the proper approach to such things. Working in offices with all the other drones, like Rosa B. and MacDuffers and that crowd. For some of us that is an impossibility, Xman, and more than a temperamental impossibility. To live that is inconceivable."

Though for a moment it appeared as if the lackey was waiting for him to respond he quickly changed his mind and hailing a waiter said, with all the tumultuousness of afterthought, "You think then it is easy to tear down structures—a lintel here, a cornice there. Let me tell you, son, it is very difficult—I might even say, extremely difficult—to pinpoint and articulate what is wrong out there. There, I mean, where thing are as they are. Take it from me, it's hard to emerge from homogeneous slime and looking back locate these specific components that are just a little more homogeneously—archetypally—loathesome. Take it from me, I'm a veteran amphibian.

"First of all, it requires enormous effort to accept the horror for what it is, contoured, fixed, delimited, undisappearing. No point, my dear, in managing to turn one's head away and back in time to witness everything having turned out just as one had all along wished. We—we—never mind who—have managed to prolong our momentary glimpse of the unendurable into a program, a policy. Might I say as a result of having surveyed from very far and up close you too have accumulated a veritable horde of targets out there: targets of loathing or at least anxiety over whether or not definitively to loathe. But you are still unable to fix on any one target for any length of time. You are unable to stop oscillating among so many fungibles in order to single out one, especially virulent, as the primordial cause of tormented loathing. These targets, what are they but interchangeable landing sites for anxiety's bright birdman. If you at this point may be said to be anguished it is less over this or that target than over the possibility that at some future point you may be unable to alight on any target whatsoever. You are still very much—too much—in the space between targets, Xman. We need to have you come out of the space between.

"Oh Xman, my dear, I do not minimize your torment. I better than anyone know it is extremely difficult to create order out of chaos by pinpointing specific targets of torment. It is extremely difficult to root out sources of lacerating disquieting disgust when they have always already stabilized—when they have settled long long before and are therefore possessed of an inexpugnable birthright making them as right, so to speak, as rain. When things have stabilized it is

350

as if they have stabilized in the only way possible. We—the vanguard—through countless misadventures too numerous to list much less authenticate at least to the satisfaction of shivering neophytes—have always been able to discern its cleft in the sludge at the very moment when one choice, one form of stabilization, outshouted all others. And we are sick, heartily sick, to contemplate the ramifications of the choice—the clot of degenerate meanings, so-called significations, that pullulate around the site of choice like so many pubic hairs about a drain—meanings, that is, for the multitude only too eager to believe what these degenerations tell them life inexorably is. And what they want least of all is to wake up one morning and discover all that darting and fighting and consuming—consuming—consuming—was not in the least living." As if responding to Xman's uneasiness he coarsened his inflection and said, "Let's take an example".

It was only now that Xman yawned, felt heavy, stupid, uneasy. "Look out the window. Why I'll be damned if that helicopter's path isn't being reflected in the glass surfaces of that building over there. Yes, that's right, that one." (Xman had given no sign.) "There, there, that chrome and glass monstrosity dedicated to making a few men wealthy at the expense of many. Quick, the helicopter's spoor is being reflected in the very depths of the glass, among whose less mobile captives may be numbered black-eyed cumuli and rind of moon (*zeste de lune*). But just when all that—landscape—is reflected it seems to fold up and melt away. To crumple against the trajectory of our gazes, isn't that right. Now: Why does that have to be. Why do we have to settle for that? Why do we have to stand for that particular cleft in the sludge. For around that cleft, as I have already pointed out, a host of other possibilities, equally undesirable, equally irrefutable, come to congregate like a horde of our typically urban monkeys at the scene of one of our typically urban

351

crimes. Having tracked down and isolated one more target of revulsion how do we go beyond it, transcend. Why this and not another. And why another. Why must we waste our time loathing this and dreaming of other possibilities. Why must we." (This very last uttered almost with a child's rancorless chagrin.) "Why any state of affairs whatsoever. But no, but no, we want to change the world for good, don't worry. We wouldn't do away with everything. Another example: As I was pursuing you past a token booth I noted a brown paper bag stuffed in the groove through which the tokens are dispensed. This sign meant she—the clerk—was not dispensing at this time. Why this phenomenon instead of any other? And for the phenomenon, why this sign instead of any other? Get my point."

The lieutenant looked him dead in the eye but he could not understand what provoked the look's forced intimacy, this lackey was clearly trying to unearth a latent kinship with the crowbar of his bushy-browed too declamatory gaze. "Let me," he said "give you still another example that may be hitting closer to home." Clearing his throat and finally attracting the attention of one of the waiters he ordered another dose of the indecipherable. Xman noted they treated this lackey with far greater respect than him, didn't they see he had contributed his well-nigh last coins to the YMPF (Young Musicians' Pension Fund). They treated him, in other words, "like family," a phrase Xman loathed more than any other in the universe. "One of our group—you'll be hearing more about him as time goes on—went ferreting out sickness and corruption in one of the major corporations and I mean major, not one of your Rose Baldachino/Finaglie Twin contraptions. Go see her one of these days. She's at death's door, the old slut. He pretended to be applying for a job. You know the approach: interview with the rather irritating personnel manager who ends every sentence with comma followed by your first name. After sitting with the bored receptionist sucking on a green lollipop he had to descend a long long corridor past two co-workers talking about what television program they had watched the night before, past two others whispering their discontent over some new maneuver of their boss presumably and what is more believing in their discontent as if it did anything more than establish their belief that they too belonged plausibly in being, past the boss himself (his daughter whimperingly at his side) talking with a lackey outside his office. And as he—our man, that is—walked past, this flash of the boss suffused with self-importance talking to a lackey who was as lackeys are all servile readiness—an embryonic smile poised against any sally that must pass unquestionably for wit—and to his daughter—a hunk of painted repulsiveness giving herself the airs of a raving—a wanton—beauty—this flash suggested, no more than suggested, secreted—a caption, the only possible caption: CHATTING WITH THE BOSS AND THE BOSS'S DAUGHTER. Or, if you insist, Xman—and I see that you do—we will accept one other possibility: TAKING A BREAK FROM THE DRAWING BOARD. But that's all, we won't accept any more proposals. The winner will be announced at a drawing to be held— And of course our man, trained in the Fatima school of universal skepticism, wondered how any one with the slightest trace of self-respect could bear to lend himself to participation in such a situation, repulsive less in itself than in the caption it excreted. He continued down the hall to wait for his inquisitor in a tiny unoccupied office. Presently a weasel's face, replete with well-groomed little mustache, stretched out from what in the rathole adjacent had to be a weasel's body to call him in. Who should it turn out to be but the lackey who a few minutes before had been so eagerly chatting with his boss. Rising he took his time so as not to feel he was doing this idiot's bidding although such lingering he knew was strictly speaking against the rules, our rules, that is. For when we send one of our men on a job, Xman, we expect he will give himself wholeheartedly to impersonation of the panting postulant. Otherwise how can he—and we—hope to penetrate the inner sanctum. For the first weapon of penetration is understanding, my dear boy, thorough invincible understanding of the facts of the case. But moving from room to room he could not bear to submit to what he rightly perceived as the appropriate caption. The caption is—was—do you give up?—all right—the caption was—INTERVIEWING FOR THE POSITION OF FIRST COOK AND ASSLICKER AT FARTMAN BROTHERS TRUCKING COMPANY. Once again, we will accept one and only one other possibility—GOING ON AN INTER-VIEW AT FARTING SISTERS EDITORIAL POOLHOUSE. Note the excruciating banality—so banal it is almost as transparent as the most exquisitely cut crystal—of the ex-pression 'interviewing *for*,' to say nothing of the equally in-sufferable, 'going *on* an interview.' The jargon of the moment never fails to amaze me, Xman. In any case you may be wondering why I call them FartSchlocka Brothers in one caption and Shitkopfer Fathers in another. Don't worry. The building blocks of a story should issue in contradiction. This happens, alas, all too rarely, but when it does it proves conclusively that the story is not a slavish mirror of scul-lion-riddled reality but a self-contained entity doubling back on, at war with—and thereby fortifying—itself.

"At any rate our man ultimately entered the adytum of this lackey all too proud of its accoutrements. But just as he was settling uncomfortably into a wooden chair he caught a glimpse of the little weasel with his little weasel mustache in a photograph on the wall behind them. Now, so fixed did our man become on this particular detail he forgot to re-spond to the inane questions of his host with a suppliant's requisite alacrity—the alacrity of one whose one and only concern is getting the job. Now it is true we always encourage our man to focus on details but not to such a degree that impersonation—the only conceivable conduit to a far greater plethora of same—becomes jeopardized. In any case, the photograph as he later described it showed captain of weasels—sorry, Captain of Weasels—(sitting at the very desk against which our man's chair now abutted) surrounded by a half-moon configuration of sublackeys conspicuously standing—I mean, STANDING—and while so standing making sure to smile only the palest facsimile of that smile being smiled while sitting by said Captain of Weasels, head of flunkification services—sorry, Flunkification Services—at Fart-Town Business Systems—sorry, Fart/Town Business Systems—(FBS). Slogan: We cater your farties. We questioned him for further details. He could tell us nothing further, didn't know what A,B, or C was wearing. Normally a good cadre he had focused on one element only—the cleft in being—the fissure in the preformal shit, primordial slime, virtual snot, steaming soup of latency—fissure wrought by incursion of captionable meaning. Meaning as parody of meaning. Our man thought he would have to flee not so much the photograph as the caption crying out from its depths or its surface or from the unlocalizable shuttle between its surface and depth. Like Foucault's clinicky gaze his too had the paradoxical ability to hear a language—in this case, a caption—as soon as it perceived a spectacle—in this case, circus act. He thought he would have, our man, to run away. Then, after a moment's fortifying vertigo, he explained that his collision with one puny unit of meaning only affirmed the decision to resist and ultimately annihilate all like units of meaning, all the bric-a-brac of loathsome finitude always concocted by somebody and imposed on somebody else. As Fatima later told the cell: He went away a flunkey and came back a man." "But that too is caption," Xman noted. "Despite his fear of being undone by the photograph he remained to carry out his assignment to the bitter end: the collection of data, attainment of familiarity with every object in and out of every corridor. His first assignment was—but more of that later."

Xman found himself on the verge of saying that for all his, the foreigner's, talk of annihilation he saw rising above the implied ashes the same hierarchization, the same labored preconization of rising from the ranks slowly but surely, the same exploitative utilization of others that must have been so conspicuous behind the little weasel's every breath. But he said nothing now.

"I do not claim," said the lackey, "that we alone are disgusted with things as they are. Many experience the same shock of revulsion. For example, walking to pick up a paper this morning I passed the Off-Track Betting Establishment on West Seventy-second Street, right off Broadway, near the old subway kiosk like an island floating in the middle of the Seine. Just as I was about to hand over my coins to the Arab one bettor waiting without said to another: 'Everyone is out for himself.' At first I became very excited: Here was a fellow rebel, rendering a concrete diagnosis on a special situation. But then as he went on talking I saw that he was making, on the contrary, a general statement. And this immediately transformed him into the merest purveyor of platitudes. As the verdict on the workings of a particular subgroup of the population supposed to be but in fact not bound by solidarity his comment has punch—possibilities, as a Broadway investor might say. As a general remark, a limp outcry—I can't say what accounted for the imperceptible shift—it became the lyrical flight of somebody without the slightest capacity— worse, desire—for flight, lyrical or otherwise. And it wasn't as if the comment had come at the wrong time and in the wrong place. For such a comment any time any place is inopportune. For such a comment is superfetatory. Presumably aware of the general truth at all times, the true rebel never considers giving voice to it. It would be too inconceivably fatiguing to attempt to extract from the monolith of one's nisus the precise expression of its core. So general a truth is too obviously ingrained to be susceptible—conceivable—to speech. If this general truth was not inconceivable to the loser's everyday speech clearly it would never become a goad to effort disgusted with the proroguing ploys of that speech. What I'm trying to say, then, Xman, is that there may be people who sound a little like we do. But always remember there is a vast difference between saying and doing. And in this case saying—conceivability for saying—implies the inconceivability of doing. You see why."

Xman hoped one of the waiters would say, We're closing. But they gave no sign. The lackey went on, "Getting back to the weasel with the mustache—he had been staying late that night. He pointed out, our agent, how proud he, the weasel, had been of his dedication. To make a long story short we made short work of that corporation—from the boss down to the most exploitative lackey. We spared the gum-chewers, of course. And all data was procured through our man's interview visit. We would never have managed the project if our man hadn't managed to get his foot in the door, if he hadn't become rightly so enraged by one detail: one contoured unit in all that chaos. And once again—even though we feel he spent too much time excruciating/delectating over the group portrait—don't think it's easy to pinpoint a target. We have to get our targets right. Each is unique and at the same time they are utterly indistinguishable: Yes, that's right. Once again my story debouches on a contradiction. Once again my story debouches on a contradiction. In any case we want you to share in the pinpointing and field work. If we didn't think

357

you had the right stuff why would our girl Fats have been out there crouched near the sanatorium and by staging a combat with a less successful recruit on his way out making way for the likes—and the dislikes—of you. In other words, Xman, this is to confirm our offer of employment made on the grounds of the state hospital in that year of our bawd . . . We want you, Xman. You might even go so far as to say we are 'on' to you but in a friendly way. And one day you'll thank us for being on to you long before you were on to yourself. Even if, strictly speaking, you are always on. So, tell me, once you finish your drink will you come with me back to the hotel to meet Fatima and the boys. You'll find us tough but you'll find us teddy.

"You seem to be hesitating. I can't believe it. You seem to be hesitating. Obviously you are not aware of the fringe benefits of terrorism—the terrorist package, as it were. You are employed. You can advance. Free medical care after the first two-cent deductible. The hierarchy wants you. The organization needs you. Your co-workers love you. Your superiors revere the very crapper you unload in—as long as you get the job done the best way you know how. Oh I see, I see. You're afraid you'll be asked to abjure a former self—a former priggishness, as it were. None of that here. A true member of our tribe never abjures any prior phase—he loves and loathes all phases equally." Xman made a tiny demurring gesture that began and quickly ended at the very tip of his Adam's apple. "Oh, I know, I know, it isn't from pride that you refuse to abjure that former self—that priggish piggish somewhat beefy fainéant of yore. It is simply—oh don't I know it: Hell, I was young once—from principle. Yes, from principle. You simply will not submit to that all too foreseeable convention whereby the shadowy figure entrenched in an art product is obliged to trace a transformation—and as if that isn't bad enough—a transformation OF A PARTICULAR TYPE. So

you see I understood: You contend there is a far greater complacency involved in such a transformation—the tedious
transformation every last spectator is waiting for. You will
not have to abjure your previous selves—only seem to be
doing so all the time maintaining friendliest relations with
their soft cores. Let me tell you a little secret, Xman von
Dummkopf. We recruit only those for whom every new gesture, act, proclivity, necessarily partakes of the grossest rawest betrayal of some previous self. For example, on their first
mission we require that our tireless apprentices—lifting
high the pink grenade above their newly shaved head—remember some gesture, some act, some inflection—in short,
any old snippet redolent of the basest most shameful self-
surrender—that in their own eyes totally incapacitates—dis-
qualifies—them for consummation of the act. Experience
has taught us that cultivation of this sense of lacerating
incompatibility is—GOOD FOR BUSINESS. It gets the job
done. Our stooges—I mean our stout-hearted men—should
never be too comfortable with themselves. What I mean is—
if they do not abjure prior selves neither do they abstain
from trying to abjure. They live an impossibility and it is
most important that impossibility be undergone at the moment just before grenade is released from sweating palm or
vaulting groin. In fact, there is no release without a sense of
impossibility, no release without apparent stymying of release compliments of the fear THAT I AM NOT WORTHY
OF THROWING THIS BOMB INTO THE HEART OF THE
COMMERCIAL DISTRICT—IT IS ALL THE MOST FATU-
OUS—ULTIMATELY THE BLANDEST—IMPERSONA-
TION—IMPERSONATION—IMPERSONATION—
BECAUSE EXACTLY THREE YEARS AGO TO THE DAY I
FOUND MYSELF PLAYING WITH MY PUD IN THE
HEART OF A THOROUGHFARE VERY MUCH LIKE THIS
ONE TARGETED FOR—FOR— And before you can say,

Masturbation leads to blindness, senility, and the production of imperishable masterpieces, the flight has flown and our global statement against things as they are has been made. In short, in short, in short—don't forget the ten-cent deductible—after that, it's smooth sailing—our terrorists— our version of the terrorist animalcule—never forgets for a bloody millisecond that he may only be impersonating a terrorist, that he may be the last thing from a natural. He is always remembering signs and symptoms of a hideous unsuitability for the calling. He is always remembering—long before he has even begun to begin initiating the gestures preparatory to tolerable practice of that calling—what makes him fatuous and abject, egregious and incompetent. So you see, you'll have no trouble fitting in."

The lackey walked quickly and was always a few paces ahead of him all the way uptown via Seventh Avenue. Following through a doorway whence the other made it a point to beckon seductively Xman found himself in the large living room of what must have been once, long before, the quintessential townhouse. Fatima, yes it was she, stood holding forth at a blackboard in a voice many tones higher than that glimpsed through sanatorium shrubbery. Seeing her stop dead in the tracks of her lesson the others turned toward him, grudgingly, appraisingly. Ultimately their gazes all rested on his cicerone as most powerful member of the group. Then, just as Xman was resigning himself to this essentially pitiful figure, here prince among princes, another figure emerged from the shadow cast by a high console. What with his gnarled limbs and his overall refusal to comply he immediately seemed qualified to assume the role of the first's most rabid adversary. Among all the others he seemed and through every movement to belch forth a categorical refusal to be dutifully dazzled by the cicerone's reputed transcendently virtuosic lightness of touch in their common genre even if—after innumerable common failures to say nothing of correspondingly innumerable half-successes perhaps more unspeakable and unsightly than the failures that at least have the satisfaction of being laws unto themselves—his cohorts were convinced that when he whose name Xman still did not know placed this or that grenade in the middle of this or that booming thoroughfare the idea—the idea of Our Lady of Fatima—was at last given flesh fleshed out and saw at last the light.

Xman refused the seat offered by a dwarf, intent as he now was on his café companion whom everyone, except his archrival, referred to as The Lieutenant. Xman looked closely at The Lieutenant but could discover no special sign of election. In fact, The Lieutenant looked least likely to fulfill the ideals of some visionary master. The others were lither, more alert, and had a more traditional gracefulness. As if guessing his confusion the dwarf whispered that there had been a period during which The Lieutenant was away, having quit this for another network. Over that somber stretch Fatima with the perversity born of desperation elevated her residual faithful to positions of marked consideration, especially as all along they had been vociferous in their hope of recuperating the other's prize morsels. But now, once again, every fecund chimera devolved upon the lieutenant for trial and execution. Once again he became the only conceivable conduit from idea to flesh. Only The Lieutenant's—so Xman gathered—thew and sinew of exquisite receptivity was commensurate with Fatima's dazzling rapidity of creation, sleek transmogrification of collisions with brute matter into programmatic configurations of genius demanding only the right votary to make them like the costliest incense hover palpably so to speak. During a conspicuous lull The Lieutenant turned to him and said, "When I came back into the fold, the only conceivable fold, some were happy, others weren't so happy. But when I am working with Fatima, mapping out our strategies, I feel I am in the only conceivable domain for true work—for the deployment of talents that some consider minimal, others not so minimal.

"I don't mean to cast aspersions on rival organizations," he said in a voice loud enough to be heard all around the room, and even in the next, where Fatima was attending to a small collation, so that Xman wondered if flattery hadn't played some part if not in establishing then at least in consolidating a preeminently enviable position, "but the other masters used only a small part of my natural endowment whereas with Fatima Buckley née Balanchinadvze I am always finding myself utilizing every fibrous faculty. Working for Fatima is like preparing a puree into which no leftover goes untriturated. Do you think she'll tire of me eventually." His face crumpled up, his voice quivered. Diligently, Xman thought. He went on pleading and for the duration of his refusal to answer Xman felt, as only a few times before, completely outside the human condition. This bid for solace transformed him, its instrument, into a blatheringly loquacious ninny and he, Xman, totally mute, attained thereby (saddling The Lieutenant with an envying perception of that attainment in actual fact brought the attainment into being) a position outside being, a stance superior to all stances since The Lieutenant's stance, importunate loquacity, was for the duration of Xman's refusal to answer it, the only stance, the only conceivable stance, better yet, the only stance in town. Now Fatima was again in the room he reverted to a more usual quieter tone: "With Fatima no faculty, no fiber, is left unstressed, unstretched. You're going to find working with her a real treat." The word *treat* did not sit well with Xman. It seemed to shift—no overturn completely—their respective centers of gravity. Addressing the company at the buffet table with most of their backs to him The Lieutenant continued: "When I am working for Fatima I am completely outside whatever was predicted for me as infant, child, adolescent, young man on the make. I no longer—fall into place, or rather, fail to do so. I am totally outside whatever the powers that be—parents, schoolmarms, drill sergeants— foresaw as the only plausible outcome for my want of plausible aspiration." He walked to the window and looked out. Dawn was not far, Xman detected a rufous glare made more urgent by the obstruction of honey locust frondlets and the shriek of sirens. He turned around, nodded back to the backs of the company. "The horizon and I, we have both escaped the future laid down by the powers that pretend to be. We have catapulted ourselves outside the domain of a conceivable destiny. When I am working for Fa——, I am outside my case history, outside the life that was never really mine anyway. That is why we approached you, Xman. We felt immediately and instinctively that you too awaited a destiny that belonged to you truly instead of the life with which you were saddled as through some mean trick. Oh yes, I have worked for others—those myriad who putting up their shingle give themselves a name without even the shred of a strategy— those blind obliterating the blind. I could never bear to take orders from them. An order, after all, is a window on death so that if I am going to die it had better be for a cause I respect." "Tell them about those orders, Liu," said Fatima, helping herself to some cold cuts. "Those orders did not simply irritate me. They refunded me to an amorphous virtual preformal not so latent slime of rage, down there in chaos before the world was saddled with a point of origin. And so it has always been: It takes just this sort of little discontent to send out flayed roots, trigger and sustain a cosmic connection with the discontent beyond discontent, the rage and revulsion beyond contingency. (A truly ferocious feline never stoops to lap up the mere cream of contin-

gency.) But how was I to express a rage that uttered might
swallow the world, that was bigger than its target, bigger far
bigger than all targets." "Bigger than all targets except ours,"
Fatima added. "In our line of work the rage is made to the
measure of its targets. Always." "Before I met Fattie—this
rage far beyond anything that could have been provoked by
the arrogance of petty souls—petty monoliths—produced
not ever-expanding strength but fear of strength—fear of the
slightest show of strength—shame in the face of prodigious
strength. Who knows, maybe this reversion to primal rage
was a device—perhaps the rage itself was and is a fiction—to
induce a compensatory refusal to manifest even the tiniest
specimen—of rage—lest that iota overrun the world. At any
rate this is how I took orders from everybody before Fatima.
Isn't that right, Fa——, darling. Every remark was a wound
less wounding than calling my very being into question, trit-
urating to nonbeing. And I always wondered, If I don't fight
back am I still a man, a contour. Am I already living a posthumous life with the villain getting away unscathed. So I
reached a point—always in the other networks, never oh
never in this—where I hated receiving orders less for themselves than for the chain of events—thoughts—they set in
motion. There was no saving face short of the other's total
obliteration. Even when there was a chance I could bury my
rage and disgust in the work at hand—the project sketched
by the order—I chose not to, choosing instead to burrow
deep into its most insidious implications of irrefutable pusillanimity. And this refusal to be displaced I found on several
occasions to be more a source of torment than the act over
which it pretended to suspend judgment yet with never a
suspension of its lacerating inexorability. More a perpetrator
than the act itself. In short I was my own worst enemy until I
found Fa——. Yet by its very excess, exorbitancy, insatiabil-
ity, rage called a halt to itself. Living at the tip of the cosmic

rage, always about to be ejected from its terminus and therefore always on guard against making a fool of myself I made a
point of acting as if the furthest thought from my mind was
rage—the way the great Stephanos did on the Rue de Rome
millennia ago. In short, in short—before I met Fattie—when
I gave myself to the other networks—merely hearing the
simplest order ('Clean the toilet bowl rim after you shoot the
ambassador from P——. Call our secret agent at the Nicara-
gua/Barcelona interface after you wipe the butt of this unwieldy little—not so little—Fourth World despot.') quickly
enough I found myself delivered up to rage primordial—Gall
the Unmitigated—and as this sublimely temperamental diva
simply refused any truck with her considerably less gifted
epigoni—little irritations, mild oaths, premature ejacula-
tion, nail-biting, bed-wetting, pickpocketing during a businessman's lunch on Amtrak—there was never any escape. I
was driven to rage—extreme rage—and that extreme rage
was worse than useless. Before I met Fattie Belle Jones."

At the conclusion of this delivery, which Xman could not
help feeling was nothing more nor less than a thinly veiled
paean to the likes of one Fatima Buckleyville Buckley of the
Louisville Buckleyville-Buckleys, a.k.a. Mustafa MacDougal
Streete, The Lieutenant turned to her with a sickened rather
than sickening lackey's smile that said: So how did I do, tell
me before I—oh, cursed spite—blow your brains out, you
brainless slut. But she, always the dowager, pretended not to
be seeing not so much his stance of appeal as her own panting hunger for just such an appeal on this floodlit stage of
underlife. It was then she tried once again to bring the meeting to order as if all personal considerations (however lofty
the person considered) must fall before the question at hand.
Yet she seemed at the same time to be furious to be saying
farewell to The Lieutenant's adroit prefiguration of hagiogra-
phy. The imperiousness of her inflection now worked an

equally adroit Burchian retrospective modification of The Lieutenant's paean which after a thump of the gavel she did not wield became mere gibberishtic frivolity. But from Xman's vantage on the fringe of vantage she was modifying more than The Lieutenant's now inept paean. Assertion of her bovine being's brindled busyness with a state of affairs that only she, Fatima, was not on the verge of forgetting became a slash through nothing less than the obscenity of normal human contact, obscene whenever it bypassed Fatima, center of the universe. Yet when men finally turned their attention Fatima-ward she was not particularly pleased. Focused on her the spotlight focused necessarily on her constant companion in office, namely self-loathing. All their solicitude very quickly became—Xman could tell from her contortions—insufficient, a vast detour, a placatory ploy. The hopelessness of insatiable desire rendered all homage inauthentic. Her sense of being cheated—no matter how great the offering—with its accompanying dim exasperated sense of the futility of all solicitation—the dim exasperated confusion regarding what exactly she was soliciting at no small cost to her well-being—was automatically camou-flaged as a Spartan repudiation of all offering. With their homage they, her disciples, merely situated her in being and thereby subtracted from a dreamed infinitude that shed mere being like so many of last year's pigeon feathers. So here she was, tearing at her hair, telling them to shut up, unable to bear the slightest sign of prostration—or failure of prostration—she felt unworthy though outraged at the first sign of refusal, obstinacy, surrender to the surface of her protestation, its strategic glaze. The cause, Xman was sure, of her sending one of the lackeys out into the street was not his reluctance to put an end to inquiries after her health and toasts to her invincibility but the too rapid termination of such obeisances. In order to repudiate apotheosis—at once excessive and scandalously skimpy—she had no choice, Xman saw, but to invent the inauthenticity—the frivolity—of the other(s). Invented inauthenticity postponed a confrontation with apotheosis so deeply spurned and craved, dreaded and desired beyond all else yet always pitifully unsatifactory, always destined to fall far short of what was merited, merited beyond mere vulgar instances of merit.

Then all of a sudden, as if to prove how easily she was able to exit from the labyrinth of pathology, turning to him she said, "But we have been shamefully forgetting our honored guest. Dragged in from off the street by our supervigilant lieutenant." These last words were uttered in an undertone of contempt, Xman thought but toward whom specifically. He began to shiver slightly. "Even though you are not the toast of the tabloids this does not mean you aren't well thought of in certain circles. We have, young man, been hearing great things about your relation to the true work. Alas, shouldering such dedication to its dead weights and as long as you are committed to the fate of these dead weights and to the magical moment when they are shat upon at last by their rightful due—their rightful due, did you hear that boys, phantom among phantoms, their rightful due, hahaha—as long as you are so committed then you are necessarily delivered up to the rhythm of bureaucrats, detestable mediocrities, bankers, fools, miracle men. Theoretically—oh yes, I know—they are supremely invested with the power of taking the dead weights off your hands and placing them—seeing they are placed—properly. But will they, will they. After all, they are mediocrities and we all know what propels mediocrity. Love of its own stench, for one thing. In short, your dead weights, growing deader every minute, are obliged to follow the rhythm of this bloated sector. And since there is more of you, presumably, in the true work than in yourself you are obliged in turn to follow the rhythm of this bloated sector.

You must go their way, yoked to whatever sphinxlike force may ultimately deign to propel your dead weights into confirmedness. But among us, Xman, you will find a different rhythm. The rhythm of your own very particular destiny becomes equal to the rhythm of OUR true work, our project. There is no trailing behind. No longer is your day-to-day being and its accomplishments cast to the rhythm of bloated determining entities too vast to blow up, enthralled to a periodicity of centuries, millennia." "I'll think about it," was all he said. "Well, there's no rush," she replied, not that she believed this for one moment, Xman thought, but simply because she thought it was most expedient to stroke the ostensibly reluctant tyro's hackles. "Ah, but you're very clever," she went on, smelling an advantage in inhabitual candor. "You know that, 'There's no rush,' doesn't quite mean, 'There's no rush.' But something along the lines of, 'There is a rush, a terrible rush.' We both know the only way you can go about making up your mind very shortly is by keeping in mind the slightly minatory, 'There's no rush.' " He wanted to cry out, You're too obvious. Yet he knew very well her obviousness was her strength, her power and her glory, and did nothing to attenuate the overall torment she induced. The caption: Too obvious, instead of annihilating, simply walled her off from further attempts at annihilation. The caption said the ostensible worst that could be said thereby affording proleptic protection against all future incursions of the worst. So, looking at Fatima, listening to her explanation's echo, Xman wondered how to determine when the worst was truly the worst and when simply the worst as in, The worst is over.

"Here's one of our brochures, one of our fact sheets," said The Lieutenant, clearly at the behest of Fatima who turned away as if her mind was elsewhere. Xman knew she must feel a situation progressed most smoothly when she governed from afar. He made as if to go. "And of course you'll read that here. Where are you going. We have a bed made up for you upstairs." Fatima turned to The Lieutenant whom she called Ziggy and said, "We can't go on protecting him much longer. He hasn't much choice. He is at an impasse with regard to the true work. He knows it. We know it. He wants to finish it, one, two, three, as if subsequent interventions in behalf of refinement are somehow dishonest and detract from the purity of creation. Exactly right—but only in our domain. When we plant a bomb it is now or never. There is no going back in the name of refinement. So, Xman, you are applying our code in the wrong domain. He resents oh so burningly the meddling of the subsequent creators he has to become—the other equally righteous versions of Xman the Creator, marring through their challenge the purity of an initial upsurge. Of course, of course, we understand dearest Xman, but only in our domain—the domain of the bombs and the sawed-off shotguns—does the initial upsurge count for everything. Whatever is added to or subsequently subtracted from that initial upsurge becomes proof for an Xman of nodal inadequacy. Exactly, exactly, but only in our domain. Join us, imp." "What do I have to do." Fatima looked at (to?) Ziggy before replying. "We need new locations. What the vulgar call 'scenes of the crime.' The police are hot on our trail after so many—too many—office buildings. We need bridges, public transportation networks." Xman surprised himself replying without hesitation: "There is nothing to be gained from such an approach." They all looked up form their paper plate buffet leavings. "Either one already embodies all available—conceivable—sites or one is at the mercy of a scavenging depletion that far and wide trumpets forth a scandalous dependence on bits and pieces—new sites as you call them. Remember: The poor paysagiste always blames his site. All collisions with things out there—in the alien medium, alien to the true—to any work—are mere impedimenta to susceptibility to the real raw material."

"Don't listen to him, men. First of all, Xman, we are no longer in the domain of the true work. And second, in your case, collisions ultimately transmogrified into its basic building blocks are always experienced initially as abominable—inconceivable—threats to the integrity of a true work never alas acceding to self-determination—experienced initially as stalking invalidations of your claims to true workership. The observations you have never been able to use—of remarks by your dear Rosalie, for example, when for example she said to your son in his secondhand crib, 'One day you'll have a nice home, a nice family life,' were always simply too painful to confiscate and acquire. Those words— however pregnant with true workability—relegated you to the slagheap of the already defeated, the already posthumous—the slagheap of those incapable of a comeback's dazzle. For your puny likes those words were unframable, to be hidden as quickly as possible from the vibrissae of the true work's casting agent. So don't listen to him boys, when he speaks of the peril of collisions with things out there, things ostensibly alien to the true work's medium. And what, pray tell, is that medium but the sum of reluctant collisions with the most prominent outpouchings of ostensibly alien media." Fatima looked away as if she could not bear to look at him, a nonpaying guest. Some madness prompted him to persist: "In any medium thirst for novel sites is always a sign of defeat." She did not look at him in order, he thought, to pretend to be appearing to be thinking deeply about all he had said but in scrutinizing the space between her and Ziggy he could have sworn she was in fact thinking about how best to eliminate similar eruptions in the future. So there was to be a future. She looked away shielded by a gaze of bovine neutrality crisscrossed by the veins of a sulking skulking rage. In short, if she was not looking at him—not answering him—it was not because she was at a loss for words and therefore meditating a grandiose vengeance made to the measure of such an insufferable loss—but rather—SO SHE WANTED HIM TO THINK—because looking at him, a mere whelp and what was worse a whelp arraigned—only distracted from the obligatory good hard look at the facts of the case which good hard look proceeded to swim with aquiline hyperpropulsiveness far above his head and out of his ken into an empyrean where petty partisan squabbles had long been outlawed as antediluvian. She was always eagerly modifying and developing. Unlike him, a failed true worker, she made sure no collision failed to bear fruit that could be made to hang until overripe from the tree of her enterprise. Through gritted teeth she finally announced, "Ziggy will have a talk with you." She turned to Ziggy, saying, "Show him to his room."

"So where are you from," said Siegfried, turning down the counterpane. "My real name is Mahatma. Don't pay any attention to this Ziggy business." Xman had to admit there was nothing especially offensive about Sieg—Mahatma except his gushing announcement as he puffed up the pillow in its polka-dotted case that he had enormous respect for Xman. Didn't he know Xman was an unregenerate enemy of the unmotivated. At any rate he was not intimidated by Xman the way so many before him had been, immediately converting intimidatedness into contempt, but rather by the silence, the growing silence, which spurred him to look everywhere AND IN ALL GOOD FAITH for some fortuitous flap, yapping adhesion, against which to react but with all the contentiousness of neutrality, with all the manly robustness of authentic opinionatedness. He wanted, this Siegfried, making the bed, drawing the curtains, in this charming little room that might once, and not so long ago, have belonged in a brothel, to be authentically in being with Xman through authentic agitation over everyday matters. But at this moment Xman felt less than ever like arguing over the price of gasoline or human flesh or how this season the California Ku Kluxes were performing on the soccer field. So there was no hook onto which standing here with Xman as dusk fell or dawn rose Siegfried could fasten. No help from Xman in bandaging the silence. Refusing to extend facet or outcropping Xman saw old Mahatma sink deeper and deeper into his depths, one skyscraper smelted down to contourlessness in the cumulus-clotted depths of another. Xman couldn't stop watching—but only from an infinite distance of polka-dotted idle curiosity—as simpleminded but infinitely touching Mahatma saw—felt—himself growing more and more unreal, sure to melt away to nothingness if he did not fasten on some datum, any old scrap he could rend to pieces with this other dirty dog. And all the time he had no idea what he was craving. Fingering the counterpane, almost quilted, stained perhaps by the semen, piss, shit and puke of recruits past, Mahatma-Ziggy was in fact crying out for some—any—subject of conversation as escape from all this raw contemplation of the rawest of raw recruits—Xman—the other—on the other side of both being and the polka-dotted pillow case. After all, Xman was not, as far as they both knew, a woman. Therefore there was no distracting, mitigating, sexual element, no question of a hard-on to caulk the cunt of silence.

And then Xman suddenly felt himself riding a crest of genius—a genius for charity—suddenly remembering Rosalie and the child living on that little island out in the middle of the East River, right across from the now fashionable Sixtieth Street pier to which site of high-pitched promiscuity the island was joined by a walled causeway, suggestive of

nothing less than Peking in the heyday of the Shlong Dy-
nasty. Bypassing all the mockery in Xman's tone, standing at
attention, letting shreds of pleated counterpane drop from
his hairy paws Mahatma became very serious. He looked
hard at Xman but not in a scrutinizing derogating way,
looked him over as if this whelp—this—this—Xman—was
now an infinitely fertile field of possibility cast in a pollenous light of reason. Xman sighed deeply observing Mahatma becoming—developing into—and this all this before
his very eyes—the avatar of a thoroughly indubitably mascu-
line attempt to engage in contention but thoroughly playful
contention—stichomythia as the Greeks knew and loved
it—even if the whole world—all of being—was suddenly at
stake. He was trying, ever so earnestly, to lure Xman to
healthy debate—of the good clean fun variety—over possible
modes of transport to and from the island—that island, that
mysterious island as pretext for their one and last chance to
lock horns but in a friendly way and thereby sidestep the
trap of a morbid contemplation of being passing into nonbeing and back again. Though he saw Mahatma crawling toward some point soothingly moot Xman could furnish none,
could not even meet him halfway—on some puny little footbridge of utterance joining the widening thighs of silence.
The island—this *île joyeuse*—was crystal clear in its ways
and means. Still Mahatma went hunting for details that
might serve as pretext for debate: number of square feet of
parking space, number of apartments in each of the three
complexes: for rich, not so rich, flamboyantly incontestably
unspeakable. And each time he came up with a detail worthy of interrogation—you don't mean just three hundred
twenty square feet of parking? You don't mean just one main
sewerage line going from one end of the island to the other?
Why, we might consider blowing it up!—Mahatma was
clearly exhilarated for it was just this kind of fodder that

kept him far from the unspeakable. Mahatma was clearly exhilarated by all they were not discussing as long as they were—he was—discussing, let us say, sewerage on that tight little island. And at the same time exhilaration could take the form only of robust skepticism, hard-nosed contentiousness, with regard to the details Mahatma made it appear as if Xman was all too assiduously proferring. Mahatma: The true Mahatma drew forth maieutically the absolutely necessary details from which he made it a point to draw back with matter-of-fact skepticism once these details—that had the scandalous effrontery to impose themselves—were exposed to the light of day. He had to keep the contentiousness going, going at all costs, as bandage against impingement of the unspeakable. Mahatma hungered after such details and yet— and yet—Xman was suddenly reminded of the hotel room his first night in New York—yet he rejected the details in their namedness. He could not bear to repeat their names. He had to become immersed in contentiousness over the content of these details faster than their names could impose a pretentious hegemony always threatening to do away with him once delivered up to utterance. And it was just these details—number of square feet of parking space—that soothed Mahatma. And with alarm Xman noted that as Mahatma was soothed so was Xman soothed. Mahatma was soothed by the details only he could not bear the proper names that obstructed his way to them. He did not know if he wanted to call the site of so many square feet of parking space the Chateau Garage nor did he know if he wanted to call causeway connecting city and island Dream Fruit Conduit. Yet Xman noticed he had no trouble calling the club for the elderly by its correct name of Folksy Fartsy Society for the Wrecked. Nor did he have any difficulty with the food cooperative: Pompadour Grumbles and Grimbles Kupe. Clearly there were some names that offered so immediate a passport to another dimension that name bar was obliterated. In other words, the name Folksy Fartsy Society for the Wrecked got Siegfried von Mahatma to a transfigured conception of himself FASTER than he could be annihilated through surrender to the name's utterance. Faster than his being could be curdled or shrunk to nothingness through utterance of some name as gross betrayal of that being in its rawest integrity, the name—that name—Folksy Fartsy Society for the Wrecked had procured Siegfried's metamorphosis at last into her Exalted Worship, Grand Baroness Siegfried von Charlus, duchy of Guermantes-Fatimawitz.

Mahatma dove deeper and deeper into contentiousness. What was Xman's surprise—he was tired, he wanted to sleep—when after stating that he had on several occasions walked across the causeway—what was his amazement when Mahatma took this thoroughly tedious and neutral time-marking remark for inauguration of a new debate, a virile thoroughly depersonalized new bout of home-cooked contentiousness. For here was Mahatma a.k.a. Siegfried beginning out of the blue to explain how if you did opt for the causeway you were necessarily missing out on the far more dependable ferry that stopped, if he was not mistaken—he knew about it from having once sought far and wide for a plausible site of attack on a visiting emir—at a point not far from a point midway between the three smokestacks of the slum factory and the intersection of tiny village green and subway station across from the kiosk frequented by types similar to the mustachioed target they had been discussing some other time in the not so distant future. And once you achieved the termite-infested intersection there was nothing more but go on to couple with the seemingly innocuous little bus that deposited you, if Mahatma wasn't mistaken and you weren't careful, right smack under the vault of ravaged lindens beside the Chateau Garage now in smithereens thanks to one of the their more ingenious sub-sublieuten-ants. It was clearly an ordeal for Mahatma to get past name to blessed detail itself, source of contest. In the town square, Mahatma continued, obviously moved, thick with the stench of horse manure and gingko and where, around the few implanted shoulder-high stakes, their paint peeling away faster than the greasy spoon of a river flowed, elm and oak samaras were reputed to whirl mad as wasps. Mahatma went on and on, audibly and half-audibly, but always and completely absorbed in his contentiousness. But with whom and over what. Who and what, oh Lord, Xman wondered—though he loathed the Lord—was the target of this robust insistence in the face of SOMEBODY'S skepticism, disbelief, misinformation. Mahatma needed Xman as a source of misinformation regarding causeway alternatives if he was to wax suitably—indignantly—well-informed but Xman's misinformation had, as far as Xman himself was concerned, petered out long long before. This contentiousness, Xman decided, as he lay down on the hard smelly mattress, was the schema for a sense of being in being, immersed in being. This creaky contentiousness secreted the sauce of connectedness—to being. The contentiousness was a contraption synthesized unbeknownst to his own panic to place Mahatma. Connected to contingencies he was able to aggrandize into moot points (so what if far far far very far beyond their capacity to sustain plausibly the pedal point of mootness) AND simultaneously supremely respectful of their delicate need to be defended against misinformation, he, Mahatma, entrenched himself at last once again in being. And if there was a comrade as there was at this moment then by focusing on this or that detail—and bypassing the excruciation of naming as fast as possible—he also bypassed on behalf of entrenchment procured for both—in being—the glaring fright of that comrade's essence, first outpost of the unspeakable. By ranting on and on, ranting ever onward, about the causeway and the intersection of three lindens well-nigh obliterated by the turbulence of elm samaras Mahatma was like the true pal who, mythopoeically hungry for a hot dog, doesn't forget to procure his true pal one of the same. Seeming to bypass him, Xman, to focus on what he, Xman, took to be sheer irrelevances of failed routine—whether or not he belched smoke upon the causeway connecting the shit of urban slime with its piss—Siegfried von Mahatma had without further ado procured the two of them a complimentary entrenchment in what most folks in the know take to be the grandstands of being—a season's pass—a lifetime membership. Talking about the weather, Xman knew, was a degenerate case of all this—talking about the weather contentiously, that is. "All you need is the right detail, Mahatma," he said, in a voice full of tenderness and without the slightest trace of irony. "And like Archimedes, Mahatma, you can move the world. And any detail neutral and insignificant enough is the right detail." And though he wished to laugh at Mahatma's fatuous and moving obsession with certain details as a way into and out of being yet all this manly coercion couldn't help reminding him there was no escaping the medium in which such details were countersunk. At the same time he loathed Mahatma for initiating all this directionless locker-room contention for what did it do but induce a simulatory contentiousness within himself. He was beginning, especially as he sank into the stench of the warm sometimes soft bed, to feel the stirrings of a mimicry intense and futile and completely alien to what was—had to be—his true being as a farrago of impersonations past. Was he going to start impersonating Ziggy-Mat when there was no longer any money in it. At any rate, he told himself, he was beginning to understand how terrorists work themselves into a frenzy over a given, a chosen, site.

Just as Mahatma was about to leave discreetly, Xman heard himself begin to speak of the causeway and of the fact—was it a fact?—that if you traversed its tortuosity at a speed greater than 73.8 miles per half-hour you were bloody well obliged to apply the stick shift and travel over the piers toward the model community situated on the same longitudinal belt as such sister cities as Caracas, Merdouille Falls, and Old Balls (Iowa). He continued to speak in order to go on briefly investigating this new being sprouting through impersonation and tentatively worthy of locking horns with Mahatma's for he was fast finding himself intrigued by its expansion toward want, wanting, that is, what the other wanted simply because that other had appropriated it without even bothering to manifest want. Mahatma took the bait, smelled no inauthenticity, began questioning him about the ferry and the causeway, causeway and the ferry. Could a small-sized bomb be hidden there, for example. Yet there was a new note in Mahatma's tone, a truculence and resentment that was slightly alarming. Xman felt he might at any moment run toward and stab him through the abdomen. "I'm hungry," he murmured, wondering if it was to win Mahatma's pity. All through Mahatma's hymn to the causeway he had felt guilty for a lack of enthusiasm in respectful silence sustained thitherto in the key of irony. Now this truculence and resentment induced Xman's instantaneous retrospect proving Mahatma had preferred it, in no matter what key signature. Here he was joining in and by joining in ruining a perfectly splendid conversation, pivoted, Xman now saw, on his comrade's being able to forget and bypass him completely while making hot haste to examine the contingencies—the nameless details—he, dutifully forgettable and bypassable, threw in his, Mahatma's, path. Suddenly, Mahatma, in his apparently childlike obsession with the causeway and the wasps and the paint flowing down the river past tugs and barges, was not as ill-defended and vulnerable as Xman's guilty contempt had needed, long before but no longer, to suggest. Xman marveled and shuddered at Siegfried's ability to purge the landscape of distracting human figures, however tiny, in the name of the technological bric-a-brac that happened to be of burning interest to him. But this facility in displacement of attention from man to (-)man must make it transcendently easy to blow up any chosen site. As far as Siegfried was concerned all sites of any interest whatsoever were unpeopled sites.

Finally, at long last, having exhausted and as if for all time, the variegated splendors of the causeway and its linkages to the slowly sinking mainland, to say nothing of the slightly less variegated splendors of related and unrelated power breakages, smokestacks, and snowdrifts, Siegfried straightened up for what Xman took to be the main matter. "Fatima tells me you are having trouble getting used to our methods. Locating sites for future action." Now, suddenly, Siegfried or rather Siegfried né Mahatma was addressing the raw recruit. But didn't he remember that downstairs he, Xman, had been rebuked directly by Fatima only a few minutes before for the very same reason. "What does all this mean," Xman said, bleakly, blankly, without the faintest trace of interrogation in his inflection. He wanted to become a stone whence Siegfried/Mahatma would literally be obliged to draw blood before eliciting the desired whit of explication. Mahatma, on the other hand, did not seem fazed or wounded by what he, Xman, took to be coldness, was in fact volubilized by it. "Every time she asks you to go out and survey adjacent territories wincing you recoil as if any command—even the purest and in the service of a plan for global rehabilitation—is a window on death. And at the last minute Fatima has to go out and make other provisions." Xman began to panic. Why, Siegfried/Mahatma was speaking as if he, Xman, had been

379

employed by this firm for going on over twenty years instead of, etc. He was reminded of a similar situation: What was it, what was it. Yes, Rollins obstreperously confusing him with a painter who depicting female anuses whence the clotted blood gushed copiously thereby obliterated in one fell swoop of the maulstick the whole of his canvas-buying public.

Out of the blue Xman found himself not only replying but using, to boot, a phrase normally loathed. "You have to understand *where I'm coming from.*" "Where are you coming from?" Siegfried said amiably enough, with no sign of being revulsed either by the phrase or by its repetition. Perhaps, Xman, wondered, one form of revulsion cancelled out another. Or Siegfried might be using the phrase in a literal sense. "From the true work," he whispered, in spite of himself, yet mockingly, and with the purest fervor of entangling Mahatma in a privity without core. He was the vestal ladle stirring the seismic soup.

As Siegfried/Mahatma cleared his throat Xman's voice drifted off and away. The simultaneity of events appealed to Xman. Clearing his throat, less ferocious than restless, S/M looked as if he would have liked nothing better than to break a sausage in two with his bare hands simply from the desire to travel. "To manage the true work I'm used to staying in one place. Though I too—especially when the reworking of primordial outpourings is what is most required—sometimes hunger after accretions of local color, regional data, anything to camouflage the shabby origins and failed evolution of my very own production." He was making reference to the true work as to a long-established fact. "Our work is also a true work," said S/M. "Anybody's work is their true work. But getting back to our work—we don't pretend that work has an essence, a core, as you strut about doing. No, our true work is a network of connections—connections to monsters we must at any price eliminate—connections to monuments and edifices that long ago outlived their allegory to say nothing of their use—connections to public thoroughfares that run over the bodies of millions while of course the managers pocket all their loose change. That is why, Xman my dear, I was once so long ago eager for your investment in a symptom. Oh Xman, my dear young man, I—the whole organization—was never interested in that symptom's overt content. Oh no, never, never, never. Ideally, what should have happened and what may happen still (after all, you ARE young, it is only your soul that is old/young) is, how can I put it—a putting out of feelers on the part of that symptom. No, no, no, I was hoping you would have caught on—sensed that once you had been good enough to induce a symptom it would have been time to cancel its contents. And in that way the symptom would have become a placeholder, a mobile foothold ushering you thereby in and out of a plethora of relations with a facility unthinkable without the mobility conceded by blankness. This was what I—we— were all hoping. That you would take to the symptom like a fish to water—take to its shame and horror—and very quickly, most adroitly, allow forgetfulness to unyoke you from the ancestral horror of that symptom's original 'meaning.' For symptoms have entrée, Xman, it is undeniable, we live in that kind of world, symptoms talk, you can't get anywhere without a symptom, don't let anybody fool you. And our people have an advantage over everybody else for they are not only symptomed but devoid of symptom content. This means they are able to go where everybody with a symptom goes without however being impeded by the viscosity of symptom fever, heat, inflammation, tenderness, redness, soreness, stiffness."

Greatful for a clearer outlook on the symptom still Xman found himself hating S/M the way, he told himself, a true master must hate the epigone who decides the high-flying doctrine must be modified according to Lilliputian specifications if it is to have resonance out in the world of boutiques, video outlets, supermarkets. At the same time Xman more than ever dreaded leaving S/M. For leaving S/M wouldn't he be once again obliged to tend to the true work and tending to the true work—or rather to the little tasks reputed to nourish preliminarily and irrigate the true work if only through pretermission—hadn't he already begun feeling which feeling now invoked albeit shadowily S/M, Fatima and the whole damn gang—that this biding of time, this sum of drudgeries in the name of the true work—was less an incubatory standing still before a great leap of ebullition than a sliding away from competence, from all conceptions of competence. And here was S/M offering him a . . . possibility. Here in this lowliest of hideaways he was confronting authentic reality and the bland presence of S/M was all of a sudden a gust of the authenticity. All that span spent in the service of possible upsurges of the true work was now a complete repudiation of the real. "In short," he cried out, "S/M, old boy, old chum, old fart, old scum"—for he did not think Siegfried/ Mahatma could read such colloquialisms, certainly not in an avalanche—"why it's uncanny but the future you and she are sketching with your toenails—the toenails of your belief in my talents"—he looked for some sign that *talent* was not too presumptuous a distillation of all anterior drivel—"is already shedding an estrangingly fuliginous light on a past once the eternal present of attendance on the true work's upsurge at last against all malevolent contingencies striving to keep it airtight. I was forever counting on this past—the past of the true work about to make itself known and never doing so—to propel me forward and vastward. But now your drivel has completely transformed that past into the embodied repudiation of all true confrontation, into an elephantine void strutting about in the emperor's new clothes. One more retrospective transformation worthy of my old mentor Burch! Your prompting makes it clear that the doings of the past have furnished absolutely no preparation for the demands of the future as prescribed by your likes." S/M said, "You will experience as if for the first time the joy of making history as history was always meant to be made and of forcing others to live that history instead of remaining a simpering victim whose only prerogative—if you can call it a prerogative though why not: It is a prerogative—is to deride those burying you alive." Humbly, less from conviction than a desire to see how facility might sit with S/M, Xman said: "Honest, I didn't realize the true work was swelling in a void." S/M appeared neither comfortable nor uncomfortable. Simply he considered this so much leader before the tape. "Get some shut-eye," he concluded.

At dawn they drove out into the wastelands of New Jersey, or what Xman took to be the wastelands of New Jersey since he fell asleep en route in a tunnel. He paid no attention to the Manhattan skyline nor to the ferries coming and going as he no longer felt obliged to deform details into true work entities. He no longer felt obliged to collide with things in order to wring thoughts from the stone of collision. Everything was simply marginalia on the way to the new work. S/M's bulk out in the cold of the fields protected him from the hunger for objects, for communion with objects: sky, gulls, water, distant piers, not-so-distant piers, tall buildings. "This is where we ultimately had to dispose of a few who didn't perform satisfactorily. Knowing nothing they already knew too much. Not that we haven't allowed others a decent burial." Laughing hysterically Siegfried looked hard at Xman and though the gaze piercingly expected some subtle sign of intimidatedness Siefgried quickly lost track of its purpose and became content merely to swim in it though never far enough away to be unable to discern that this swine of a mere disciple still categorically refused to give some sign, even the barest, of intimidated squirming entreaty. "Is that clear?" he finally murmured belching, gesturing toward the skyline with no sense, however, of why he gestured except that gesturing he hoped to induce gestures that would alert him to the meaning of his own. "At any rate, this is a typical site of activity. I've just taught you how we locate a site. You'll be back to this or some other like it." Suddenly as the New York skyline fainted in a gust of mist Siegfried's features took on a look of ineffable sweetness. It seemed to Xman he must have known Siegfried in another life—and starting from that point in eternity if only he could travel back against the fur, against the fur, to attain the moment out of time— But if this were so and Siegfried's slight twinge of an accent established that it had to be so then Siegfried ought to be infinitely more apologetic for the hideous doings of his forbears than he was proving to be. Weren't some of them still stalking the planet in out of the way tropical sanctuaries where tigers mate with gibbons on little islands too much impregnated with the applause of piranhas.

It was as if Siegfried must hate whoever intended to remind him of how apologetic he ought to be. Forbears' slaughter of millions was nothing to be ashamed of. At any rate having his own problems Siegfried began to describe these fields in detail though he, Xman, could not respond to such clearsighted description of fields, sky above their heads brilliantly blue after days of sooty rain. Yet here was Siegfried obviously waiting for some form of response, he would not rest until acknowledged. But Xman did not flinch, resisting every upsurge of epigonal assiduity. Was this heroism, he wondered, this tight-lippedness, or was it merely his usual awe before any manifestation of being already set in motion and therefore unalterable and irrefutable. Siegfried under a sky of dark blue was just such a manifestation, in communion with the deepest springs, the very anus, of being whereas he, Xman, was all too much and forever on the fringe, peeping in. "Go home," said Siegfried kindly. Xman suddenly thought he must know something about Rosalie he himself didn't know. She wanted him back! "Go home," he repeated, looking over the fields. "Think over what it means to have located a site. Think over what it means to give yourself totally to a cause. Go to Central Park. Just about this time Central Park is the best apology for our doings. Go—you'll see what I mean." He surprised himself walking ahead of S/M, leaves blowing in the wind, clouds blowing through the leaves, rack of gingko, so many corpses, so many unfinished stories, so many sabotaged teleologies, though then again what seemed like flotsam might cohere elsewhere as nothing less than an exquisitely fashioned cog in the divine escapement. On the margin of the field shreds of plastic fluttered in the completely denuded branches of ailanthus—the denudation peculiar to mangy curs or plucked fowl. Superimposed upon the linden wreckage was a reticulum amid which the delicate tea-blossoms would ultimately be fixed and strung. In the clumsy way of mutants a few rare sunflowers sought the niggard light regularly eclipsed by passing trains from whose unwashed windows stared the same unseeing eyes. Xman would remember this site, especially now that the river's truly bilious tinge procured the foamlets their high relief against the wake of ferries and helicopter shadows.

They drove back, oddly, by way of Brighton Beach. Before the ocean: "Choosing a site is of the utmost importance, Xman. I know you feel it simply shouldn't matter in the least, that one site is indistinguishable from another. And that is of course true—up until the point when we set down our flag—didn't you notice me setting down our little flag among the sunflowers blinding the blear?—for then our space is set off from all surrounding space. It becomes sacred, not only to our cause but to all other causes, which our cause parodies with impertinent ease. The flag becomes the fixed point of our orientation. Everything around us—especially the Manhattan skyline—remains larval, virtual, preformal. But our little space is real, shaped, ordered. How did I decide on that particular spot? Yes, yes, yes, I can see the question written all over your little face of clay. Simple: I waited for a sign. At a certain moment in our wandering you looked as if you wanted—were about—to murder me. Did I remind you of someone at that very moment? *Mein Führer*, perhaps. At any rate, seeing you overcome I stopped dead in my tracks and amid the sunflowers planted the flag. My sign was your symptom. Yes, your symptom. You began to dribble and held on to your crotch for dear life—why, as if all orifices were about to flood the world with your discontent. So to commemorate this upsurge of a raw recruit's first true symptom I set down my flag like the Achilpa of yore. Not that this symptom so-called was anything more than the preliminary sketch. But it is rare to find any raw recruit coming forth so early in the game with the barest bones of even a preliminary sketch. It is perhaps more correct to say that our fixed point is not the flag but your symptom. And just as that drooly prefiguration made even me, a senior vice-president and director of operations, foreign and domestic, stop dead in my tracks, so your symptom when it comes truly to maturity will make the whole world stop dead. A symptom worth its salt separates sacred from profane chaotic space. Of course the symptom requires upsurges of that chaotic space's vengefulness to start its ball rolling but once the symptom is well on its way those upsurges are never in any danger of overrunning the sacred. Thanks to the symptom—the sacred symptom—any upsurge is a controlled upsurge, like the bacchanals that frequently conclude Balanchine's pink ballets or the urban violence subjected to the warily mobile framing of a Lang or a Godard. The symptom needs to think itself and by extension our strategy. And the only viable stimulus to symptom-thinking is an ostensibly threatening circumambient chaos of sunflowers, broken glass, swamps, dilapidated commuter trains. For example, you intend to blow up a bridge. How to put yourself in the frame of mind to blow up that bridge and the scrupleless fat-assed politico en route to the homage of his favorite slum-lord. Answer: There is no putting yourself in the frame of mind. The symptom, responding with beatific credulity to the upsurge of the chaos surrounding, *puts* you in the frame of mind. The train roars too loudly, the sunflowers leer too blackly, and suddenly you are synthesizing a destiny for the fat tub of lard laughing all the long way to the bank. IN SHORT, THE SYMPTOM REFLEXIVELY PERMITS YOU TO UNDERGO YOUR RAGE WITHOUT HAVING TO THINK ABOUT REVIVING IT. THE SYMPTOM AUTO-MATICALLY TRANSMOGRIFIES WHATEVER YOU UN-DERGO WITHIN (AS A RESULT OF COLLISION OR FAILED COLLISION WITH THE LANDSCAPE WITHOUT) INTO RAGE, STOUT-HEARTED RAGE. NOT THAT YOU ARE EVER NOT IN RAGE. IT IS SIMPLY A QUESTION OF RENDERING IT LESS LATENT. THIS IS THE JOB OF THE SYMPTOM. So this is why we need symptoms. At any rate, you'll not only be going back to our site but hearing about how an authentic symptom was truly developed by one of our higher echelon people. Tonight, or perhaps tomorrow night."

Siegfried's voice died on the waves, little activity on the boardwalk this time of year, old denizens sitting on benches facing the sea, new immigrants from Soviet Russia, the latter distinguishable from the former by a readiness to forget grievances, laugh louder than the surf, refusal to sit waiting to die by the light of the sun. It grew dark, the sunset set. To Xman's surprise, Siegfried von Mahatma suggested they warm up in a doughnut joint on the main drag, a pair of mental defectives sat staring and laughing. Toward the rear an elderly woman, derelict in training, sat across the horse-shoe from an elderly man immaculately dressed for the season. But what was the season. He wore a hat and his hands were soft like a child's rather than like a woman's. Every time she came out with something tamely scandalous verbatim he ponderously repeated the anecdote with a question mark meant for Xman and Siegfried, who couldn't have cared less, sniffing his raspberry doughnut and chortling over his too-hot tea. The old man expected Xman, then, to share—better witness—amusement and alarm presented as detachment of condescension. Only at certain moments listening intently to this loneliness—it had to be loneliness, no one at that age dressed so immaculately if he wasn't lonelily trying to keep up a standard no longer applicable—the old man forgot the revulsion he felt obliged to feel at her unkemptness. Despite his lag reserved for decrying the propinquity of her stockinged feet and processing the necessary verdict on somebody who took such liberties after such short acquaintanceship, she managed sitting down right next to him to keep up her end of the conversation even without the support of his echolalia. What interested Xman was his saying his wife had just died and that it was such a beautiful day he had walked all the way to Sheepshead Bay and back. Xman, newly alone, was fascinated by this staunch and pitiful truce with solitude. What fascinated Xman was a walk without content, a life without content, so similar to what the Fatima contingent was trying so hard to sell—a symptom without content. What fascinated Xman was a walk as a waiting for death. After the doughnut joint they took one last stroll along the beach, the only other figure a female cop with walkie-talkie. "You seem to be on the verge of a symptom we can use," Siegfried remarked, cigar between his teeth. He bit on it hard as a jogger passed. No problem leaving his car parked in a ditch he insisted that they take the subway back. "Subway leaves fewer traces," he smiled. "No business trips in our line of work. Someday somebody will write a Ph.D. thesis on The Ontology of the Business Trip. Definitely mythology material—capitalist pig mythology, that is—right up there with The Baby Sitter and The Summer House." On the subway platform—the just-departed local had swept it clean—stood a single family. The alcoholic father, not fat but bloated in cheeks and paunch, flat buttocks, eager to win the friendly regard of strangers, desperately kept up his end of the conversation. The alcoholic wife, seated now, looked as if she had heard it all before. To his son the father said that when he used to get up very early to go to work you could hear the incoming train two or three stations away. Though his wife merely altered slightly the stoical look in which contempt was trying very hard to keep itself under control or perhaps had long ago passed into an unjudging reflex of infinite fatigue and though the son did not really listen, Xman found himself closer to tears than he would ever have thought possible at this late date. He was struck by the quiet beauty of the image or perhaps by the capacity of the words to put themselves entirely in the service of the image. When they arrived on close smelly Fifty-third and Seventh Manhattan never seemed so festive, the delicatessens were full of welcome even if the welcome was not for the likes of him. He felt pleasantly exhausted from the sea air, perhaps simply exhausted form an encounter with various forms of dying upright, possibility of death in life, excruciating solitude at the heart of family life.

"Go home," he remembered, walking through Central Park. They were giving him time to decide what he wished to do. Dazed by rage and fear he wandered into a moon world of subluxated catalpa trunks not far from the procession of figures on the Delacorte clock, each singing—or rather embodying—its song before being gone. He sat down in a little playground to watch the children, one of them might be his. Remarking on how unaffected he was left by this thought he jumped up and paced. The mothers rightfully observed him with alarm until a dwarf carrying briefcase and laundry bag, smiling to himself, passed and distracted them. Xman immediately distrusted, hated, the smiling: It had no target. Purely apotropaic it was. Himself absorbed in an unlocalizable target of derision the dwarf could not, for once, qualify as himself target of derision. Just as he Xman had once, traversing Columbus Circle and assaulted by the implications of an electric guitar's soundtrack . . . so why was he reproaching the dwarf. Suddenly the dwarf's dimensions were infinite for he was wedded to the infinitude of a secret meditation. The dwarf was truly towering. He did not need to ally himself with the likes of S/M and Fatima. Nearby on the paths set aside for carriages, Xman noted that at a blast from somewhere the pigeons assaulting grain set aside for one of the tired drays exploded far from their target themselves like so many overgrown grains. He began to feel sicker and sicker, what with the grains and the dwarfs and the mothers. Looking around he tried to pinpoint a target of disgust and panic though no phenomenon could be called to account. It was not so much this or that phenomenon as the proximity of the . . . of the . . . caption that underlay and underwrote them all. It was not so much this or that phenomenon as the caption that seemed to lick its chops over the heterogeneity—yes, the heterogeneity—that rearing its Hydra-head again was clearly made for such a caption. But work with Fatima and S/M would rid him of the heterogeneity and the sickening captions they induced. What was this heterogeneity of dwarfs, mothers, sliding ponds, grains, tired horses, fat tourists impatient of their promenade past subluxated catalpas and into the very heart of the New York starscape but—from the gluttonous vantage of captions—the fount of all captions—a sickening celebration of being—being at any price—a fulsome and mawkish affirmation of being's great and greatly overrated chain and infinite ramification. Anything and everything was tolerable as part of the infinite spectacle making sure, like any conscientious mother hen with too many teats, that one component's hideousness cancelled out another's and more especially that there were no gaps in the continuum of hideousness. Everything here in Central Park, in this playground of tots and derelicts, was tolerable, even refreshing, as long as it caulked some gap as the perfection of its own purulence. Wasn't this what his friend Baruch O'Grady had tried to teach him when he seemed so intent on running away to the big city. "Xie," he had said, "never dispute the ways of the Lord: Everything is simply the perfection of its own purulence and as such supremely necessary." Many of the mothers and many of the strollers were positively delighted by so much heterogeneity, this royal stew of derelicts, toddlers, abused beasts, horseshit, wintry yellow-green, autumnal snot green, turrets and minarets launched high above the park's highest treetops— what was all this but a delectation for members only, whose leisure was crucial to true appreciation of tribulation as festivity. How could he himself escape as one more dollop of garnish thrown to this human stew. He looked around at these foul-smelling businessmen and their fat dowager com-

panions who—phagocytizing a heterogeneity of which the
cement substance, connective tissue, stroma, was nothing
less than human misery—were quite in their element, quite
festive amid the splash of incessant local—nay, global—
color. They needed IT to be there just off but not obstructing
their path back to affluent well-being. And it was possible, if
S/M and Co. were to be believed, to destroy them. He observed the ladies in their blue jeans and suddenly was glad
for them though he loathed them for they proved blue
jeans—how he loathed the phrase, positively execrated its
every syllable or rather its bland absence of syllables into
which one might quite blatantly and indecorously sink one's
teeth—was a universal language if only of crotch and buttock fat and bone. He was even gladder for those jeans
abruptly halting at the level, let us say, of the ankle bracelet
just above the shrill preciosity of very high heels. He was
glad that decked out in jeans, high heels, and furs—against
the fur, against the fur—they felt free to enter the public
playgrounds of the city, no longer obliged to commingle only
with their own kind imprisoned within fortresses on Second, Third and Fifth Avenues. Right outside their door were
these little pockets of heterogeneity—just like this one making Xman reel—in whose muddy depths they might be-
smirch themselves like sparrows enraptured all through
spring's first baptismal bath. After so much commingling
with the doormen and the porcelain and the endive pasta
they were permitted a starveling's glimpse of the hungry, the
half-naked, the half-mad, the poor, the scurvy, the ill-inten-
tioned, the unintentioned, able thereby to come away and
back to their eyries reupholstered, refortified, somehow
buoyed up, braced and refreshed beyond any hydrotherapy
available at the most fashionable health clubs on Park, First
or York. He was glad for them. He was glad they were able to
lower one or two heels into the slough of urban dearth and

lift them out reinvigorated by this sterling contrast with the cerulean vividness of their own security, past, present and to come. Oh how glad Xman was. He was happy that at last the rich need no longer be confined to ghettos, immured away as if a race apart, unsightly and heinous. And he was most enthralled when the envoys of this race—for those who dared step into the heterogeneity were nothing less than envoys, new pioneers—took it upon themselves to mimic every endearing aspect of the poor—gestures, accents, raiment, thereby converting a necessitously grimy stance of desperate struggle into the novelty of fashion-conscious caprice. On the faces of these urban cows in their furs and high heels he saw the same untouchable arrogance that had suffused Siegfried's features out in the killing fields. They could play at any game, at any style, at any body argot, without a sense of ridiculous self-contradiction. With no selves to betray their impersonation of poverty in no way impugned weddedness to big fat bank accounts. They had no selves to lose on the way to the very core of fashion. In their trend-madness ultimately they too became absorbed into the landscape of heterogeneity, relinquishing (gladly, it seemed to him) their role of spectator.

Toward dusk they ovinely migrated back to well-fortified quarters on all the fashionable sidestreets and high streets of the big blond beast of a city, heart of the world's anus. The dwarf followed in their wake and then a cripple mimicking the dwarf attached himself to the margin of their pageant until some supervigilant doorman raised his scepter in a gesture of menace tinged with the most imperceptible mocking courtliness. Seeing dwarf and cripple and pigeons following the droves of ladies in blue jeans and very very high heels, sniffing after the dark blue—the cobalt-blue rumps—Xman was put in mind, so he thought, of the true definition of pathos. Pathos is, he told himself, the world's sickening heterogeneity, where everything and anything can be juxtaposed, made not so much to blend as stand forth in a garish headache-making motley, skin's rancid night mottling the canvas of the cosmos. More than he had ever wanted anything Xman wanted to eliminate all this, every detail preserving its contour yet belonging indubitably to—the whole—the whole—more than he had ever wanted anything (yet was he impersonating such a wanter? did he really want this more than anything or did the words simply attract him? were they not so simply anastomosing faster then he could disentangle them? was he simply succumbing to his secret passion for stories or rather to the exaggeration cru-cial to stories and sketching that of such a wanter, a wanter he would never be?) he wanted to destroy this kaleidoscope not quite gone berserk. More than ever he understood the need for symptom as fulcrum, as pivot, as foothold, as origin on the lattice of slime and shit but a symptom—if it was to be effective—if it was to ramify—if it was to abut on every cranny and stratum—drained of overt content, depleted by hideousness and left to run rampant, to give way to a dizzy-ing yet dizzingly well-controlled mobility.

And yet while planning his strategy, screwing his courage to a symptom's sticking place he had to look around still and admire the city, its skyline-hungry landscape so artfully marred by the downward-tending groping sorrow of the ex-quisitely ingenious poor: From the bare bones of what was rashly repudiated by others they were able after all to eke pleasure and not only on those days of mild azure at the peak of summer's autumn—autumn with as it were none of au-tumn's precariousness—so mild, so dulcet, so vernal, so shadowy—when ingeniousness automatically operates at al-most peak capacity. And when it came to furnishing specta-cle for the rich not only the poor but the very birds knew their place and almost continually kept it high up in the branches or along the humps and hollows of the catalpas bent over or back in all simultaneously deployed stages of arthritic despair and mirthless hilarity with no time at all, no no time at all, for normal duration, evolution, maturity, thereby proving once again and for the very first time that things are what a ruthlessly penetrating intelligence perceives them all at once to be and not what they will someday become thanks to a dastard patience, overrated vice. Something distracted him from the heterogeneity . . . the plaint of the carrousel organ with its visceral swarming inside a beached monster's last plangent meditation and final commentary on all the heterogeneity became, alas, itself just one more cog, no longer plangent, in the heterogeneity machine.

No escape, suddenly overcome with pain he remembered Siegfried's remark about, what was it, recruits, to the effect more or less that if they didn't shape up, these raw recruits, they were disposed of. AS IF THEY HAD NEVER BEEN. He couldn't quite decide what wounded, less the venom of intimidation coiling than his confusion about what was required to salvage his pride in the face of that coiling. "And having this problem with every sentence heard I understandably loathe human contact, calling my very being into question." If he did not react in a specified way was he still a man, yet a man, simply he did not know how to hear the remark in relation to himself, then the remark died and still in the playground overcome with torment he looked around at nothing to account for the torment, but focusing on the torment he was once again and immediately put in mind of Siegfried's remark. Yet he could not accept Siegfried's remark as cause of his torment even if it was the first contender acknowledging the existence of that torment or willing to induce it as protection against encroachment of a void far more terrifying than this or that specific and contoured instantiation of picaro's torment. Rather than cause

of torment it seemed more the thoroughly irrelevant correlate some shrewdly imbecilic observer could be expected to
suggest in order to do away with Xman's unbracketability.
But no, but no, Siegfried's intimidating remark about raw
recruits had nothing to do with real torment. He was only
pretending to be susceptible to Siegfried's remark. He was
only impersonating one so susceptible.

As he could not bear to go back to the hotel where "his
room was waiting for him," he walked in the direction of
Riverside Park, that is, of sunset. Walking he thought of
Rosalie and hungered to see her. And the child, he added.
Before he was even in the door he asked her if she still had
any feeling for him. She did not answer. "Even if my feelings
about you were clear," she said, gesturing to a chair in the
kitchen, "questioning me on the state of my feelings mud-
dles them, turns them against you. If they were pure before
the question—and I have no idea that they were, clear, I
mean—they are muddled, exacerbated, inflamed, hopelessly,
against you now. My feelings and your questions about those
feelings do not mix at this point. Remember how you used to
berate me for asking over and over if you could still find
pleasure with me and the child even if the true work was
excruciatingly slow in coming. You sneered and said the
question was 'all wrong' because it adverted to the waiting—
the brute duration—as to some entity out there from which
you could detach yourself at will and about which consequently some decision could be made. Now I berate you for
the wrongness of your question." She turned in the direction
of the bedroom, so Xman assumed the child must be there,
he heard no sound of quiet breathing, the living room had
been painted a salmon color, there seemed less furniture,
but not more space, all photographs of him removed except
one. Reaching for her hand but immediately hearing the

caption—the disgusting caption—"Reaching Out"—he withdrew. Folding his hands on the table, sniffing he said, "Sexual relations have meaning only with one with whom one has suffered, fought, eaten, drunk, voyaged. Part of the excitement—if at this late date we may speak of excitement—in other words the vengefulness propelling the act stems from the sense not so much of triumphing over as momentarily casting aside all past suffering, stolid silent grieving. It is only as a mutual commentary, a gesture flagrantly IN SPITE OF on the part of two not quite in synchrony that the sexual act begins to mean by shedding all meaning, all nauseating captions. I don't expect you to agree with me immediately." Rosalie shook her head as if this was more, far more, than she could tolerate. "It's too late," she said. "Why," he asked stupidly. Rosalie sighed deeply, went into the bedroom, theirs once but never really, returned with a form swathed in the bandages of sleep. Just when he was about to catch a glimpse of the child—his—Rosalie began to speak, he tried listening, noted that as he stretched toward the little form the little form stretched toward him but with a certain irony suffusing its contortion—as if—as if—this stretching, this gentle stretching of curiosity on Xman's part, was being deemed completely out of character and rather comical. "Why," he repeated, like a tear-choked child.

"In a very small village on the fringe of the Caucasus Mountains"—she was reading to their child, as with very few women glasses enhanced her beauty—"in Central Asia there once lived a poor woodcutter and his wife and their seventeen strapping sons: Sven, Jan, Fen, Yen, Zen, Buddy, Isidore, etc. Despite the brawn of these rowdy but well-intentioned youths for all seasons their father could barely make ends meet. Whatever was available in the way of poplar, aspen, beech, cherry, walnut, etc., was immediately appropriated by more enterprising rivals, with Sven and the missus, Yekaterina Ivanovnanookna, invariably finding themselves besmirched so to speak with the short end of the sapling.

"Many a weary winter's night (the pot of black broth and stale loaf had been cleared away) would find the aging couple crouched—aging—aging"—Rosalie gnashed her teeth—"before the feeble flames staring into the bloody embers as into sibyl's leaves. Before turning in Sven Sr. always cried, 'Why why me. Why me, why me.' Yekaterina Ivanovnanookna—she insisted on retaining patronymic as her only link with a glorious past irradiated by the numberless exploits of her father, the General della Rovere, particularly notorious for the blazing silver pistols athwart the lintel of his manor house in the south—fearing for her husband's reputation among the villagers who managed to make a hearty meal out of any tribulation affecting their fellows tried to restrain such excesses.

"But no matter how Yekaterina comforted and restrained him toward midnight he inevitably reached a pitch of rage brooking no wifely mitigation. For this was her greatest flaw at least in his unseeing eyes, that she was always going about busily mitigating—out of love! out of profoundest love!—his plight, his wretched plight, instead of respectfully permitting him to affirm and affirming bask in the incomparable hideousness of that plight. From previous experience with the General—despite what others might think Yekaterina was sufficiently acute, no Hedda Gabler she, to perceive all had not been paradisiac in that manor house south of the border—her first reaction was to mitigate, mitigate, mitigate. Out of love! of love!

"To her eyes and ears—remember she was wife of a peasant and daughter of a general and never the twain shall meet—and so what if a *général d'opérette*—the globality of torment could always be ascribed to if not immediately remediable than at least localizable contingencies. And consequently she could not understand that this peasant—this old dog of a Sven—this stale black loaf of a spouse—did not want his torment shrunken to the dimensions of distinct causes, did not want his misery made to the measure of the circumstantial. Out of love, I say, out of pure chaste love.

"Yekaterina wanted no truck with the global—the irremediable. So always she began to indulge—from love—in one of her favorite avocations—frantic inventory of circumstances directly responsible for Sven's downfall, fall after fall. She had no idea, however, why this exasperated him and why he was invariably driven to sending old pots and pans in her general direction. Always, always, alas, her efforts to defend him dropped away like a husk leaving only the core of her own inadequacy, at least in Sven's eyes. From his perspective, if such a being can be said to have one, her ostensibly consolatory inventorying mania was a cry for reassurance. What she was really and only saying was, What will happen to me—to us—to our seventeen fine strapping sons of the Caucasus. At least from Sven's point of view. Yet all she really wanted"—here Rosalie sobbed audibly—"was to be touched, to be held, to have her thighs stroked and to be told they were lovely, to be validated in her being, to be— Alas, the poor dear never realized that by frantically enumerating in front of the dying embers and sporadic tips of flame the very real causes of his despair she was, in his eyes, robbing him of that despair as a heroic stance outside time and space, day and dark night, and his only true acquisition and accoutrement, at least since that epoch long gone when he had been known far and wide as Mr. Timber. She didn't realize, poor woman—and what woman ever does—what woman with a need to be touched and held ever does—that by screaming at the fire night after night he was in fact shredding—always in his own eyes, from his own perspec-

tive—the curtain separating his profane and everyday excruciation from a dream time intricate and archetypal outside
of time.

"But she was hungry, Yekaterina was, ever so hungry, to
legitimate his despair, and put it to rest. So they could begin
to hold each other as in the old days. But had there ever been
'the old days' with the likes of Sven Timberson. Always in
danger though completely innocent of interpreting their bad
luck as a punishment she found herself feeling more and
more like an accomplice, accessory before and after the fact.
Though they were victims more and more she felt their vic-
timization was a punishment for crimes unspecified against
truer victims. And so frantic inventorying was always more
than three-quarters drowned out by the wail of truer victims
unknown and therefore assimilable to her inventorying
strategy. But maybe she would have been much different if
he had ever taken it into his head unsolicited to enfold, coddle and stroke her, over and over, over and over"—unconsciously, swaying the swathed sleeping form Rosalie
demonstrated the motion, or a small part of the motion, in
question here—"cuddle and coddle, stroke and enfold unsolicited.

"Maybe the poor woman, starved for love or for the mere
signs of love from which love is so often reborn, could not
understand that Sven, in his stale peasant loaf manner was
in no hurry to be legitimated—to live outside the electric
tension of his despair, the despair of his tension—and quite
content to go on operating a passengerless shuttle between
legitimacy and illegitimacy. 'It's all my fault,' she ended up
saying. 'If only I hadn't . . . ' Which occasioned another bat-
tery of pots and pans accompanying another storm of incoherent abuse. And all she wanted"—sob—"was to be held, to
be touched. This only inspired Yekaterina to go on damning
herself. 'It's all my fault,' she continued. 'If only I hadn't

spent so much time baking bread, if only the kitchen had a firmer roof. If only all pride would not simply go up in smoke in the evening.' And even he, coarse as he was, had some idea what she was trying to do. She was trying to blind herself—numb herself—to the raging sorrow she felt at being a not so much partner in his bad luck as target of his abusive recoil from that bad luck. But if only she could unearth enough hideous flaws of her own with which Sven, presumably, was putting up then she might begin to think of herself as more exploiting than exploited. So she went on enumerating contingencies—flaws A, B, and C, to say nothing of D and E—in order that the disjunction—the overwhelming lancinating disjunction—growing wider each and every day—between his own unpardonable grossness in the face of largely self-created ill luck and her own undemanding eagerness only to render assistance and to be touched—held—touched—touched—a disjunction that was simply too yawning, too unsuturable, too tempting a target for some malevolent third's derisory scrutiny—sure to debouch not that she cared in the least on the suggestion that disjunction be carried to its ultimate conclusion—in order that disjunction might be camouflaged.

"But if it was Yekaterina's conscious aim to narrow the disjunction her spouse sought at every opportunity to widen it and in some way she cheered him on, sensing that only by widening the rift between martyred goodness (hers) and hideous blindness to that goodness (his) could he ever come through. Wanting to rob him of his estrangement not merely from her and their sons but from all of being, wanting to muffle the diapason of outraged despair she had become his worst enemy, far worse than all the rivals he insisted were stealing his timber.

"She thought she was helping by saying, 'If only these rivals didn't treat you like a dog.' But this enraged him—that

401

she should talk of his being treated like a dog, true or not, as if it was conceivable—it didn't matter if it was true or not, it did matter however if it was made to sound conceivable—far more than anything else up to now. What, in his eyes, did all her talk imply but that his temper tantrums before the fire shamefacedly avowed denial of a fair share in being whereas, again in his eyes, if there was one thing all his talk implied—proved—it was that those tantrums each and every the tantrum to end all tantrums and more than all tantrums—somehow managed always to be brought to her live from a vantage on the other side of hope, outside the purlieus of a being he would never stoop—let any man come forward who could say as much or forever hold his peace—to frequent. Instinctively Rosa—I mean Yeka—rebelled against this unspoken stance, project, ploy. When Sven talked—didn't she see—of being treated like a dog he cancelled its conceivability. When she talked of his being treated like a dog she not only maximized but also perpetuated the maximization of that conceivability. She rebelled—she rebelled—for if he was outside being where was she. How could she rejoin him, she who wanted only to touch and be touched. He looked at her and for a moment she once again became the loveliest creature he had ever seen. The perfume of her flesh even within these close burnt-out quarters gripped him suffocatingly in the thorax, desire choked, convulsed him. But then she said, 'If only they hadn't—' and he found himself throwing more and more pots and pans at her perfectly shaped head, all the time intoning in a sneering falsetto, 'If only the sky weren't snot green at last, if only the asphalt was not particularly bulbous with snowdung, if only our neighbor with a slimy cough did not have to catch his throat-clearing on a phlegmy bolus in order to feel better for milliseconds at a time, if only, if only, if only symptom incarnated in thought did not embody too many contradic-

tory states of horror and despair conflated to a single moment of story-foiling, history-foiling delirium, and if only
that capacity for embodying contradiction did not contami-
nate the world itself—the realm of so-called play where, unfortunately, robust forces do contradicting cancel each other
out to the last syllable of unrecorded chaos without leaving
behind as in the realm of thought this or that—the merest
trace each in the other, this or that commemorating of unsightly cicatrice . . .' But Yeka no longer heard for she was
unconscious before the dead fire and her seventeen sons ca-
rousing in the village were but the song of her stupor.

"Mistreated, misunderstood, and exploited, compelled to
feed on a trickle of pseudofelicity, the pitiful byproduct of
Sven's lumpish insusceptibility—Yekaterina Ivanovnanookna could only shake her head in despair. Though by no
means old she could not help feeling her life was for all
practical purposes over with Sven's mind so tenaciously on
other matters. Although at first she thought he might have
met some charming damsel at the bimonthly village market
watching him stare obliquely at the fire forever refusing to
cough up the revivifying oracles coughed up, he protested,
with such superabundance in the time of his father and of
his father before him, Yekaterina had to reconcile herself to a
far more insidious preoccupation perhaps superintended by
some elusive succubus whose caresses were fraught with
whispers of heavenly quietus. She did not know whether to
hate or pity him, caress him in spite of his growing protests
or through a tactic of recoil try to warm the dead blood. She
couldn't help wondering whether it might not be her eternal
readiness that had succeeded in slackening his complacent
fibers. A man craved a certain inaccessibility . . . Tormented
by uncertainty regarding the proper course of action she decided to consult one of the village elders, a professional hysteric, a certified practitioner of ecstasy, mystagogue and

psychopomp, M.D., Ph.D., NSAID. Ike MacDermoto, the very reverend—yes, he, Rev. Ike MacDermoto by name, or rather by alias since this legendary figure was an almost legendary concoction of aliases, one more awe-inspiring than its predecessor though in this case it was absurd to speak of before and after, all aliases subsisting simultaneously like so many warring thoughts at the heart of a living symptom. All were cherished by a populace unduped yet still entranced.

"So on the sly on one of the most blistery days of the year, Yekaterina Ivanovnanookna made her way to the elder's comparatively palatial residence—it bore an uncanny resemblance to the house of her forefathers. There were no pistols above the door, however. The absence of the pistols gladdened and saddened as a sign of both progress and infinite loss.

"She noted her footprints were immediately obliterated, so merciless and persistent was the day's blizzard. Lying in bed with a bad stomach ache and a cold to boot—he was taking refuge more and more, she saw, in physical symptoms—Sven Sr. did not even notice much less question her departure though a highly unusual occurrence. Though relieved at the lack of suspiciousness Yekaterina could not help at the same time pouncing on one more unspeakable affront to her dignity as wife and helpmate, companion and mother, which induced a perverse pleasure in computing all his misdemeanors on her way to the very reverend. Amorphous clumps of ice hung from the shaggy firs and spruces. With oafish calculation they sometimes fell on her head but onward she trudged, invigorated by not only Sven's but also by all of nature's participation in her humiliation. This made Sven less rancid, less culpable. She even lost track of him periodically amid the rigors of the season. Wending her way deeper and deeper into the heart of the blizzard with its pockets of mockingly evanescent calm with every step she found a new susceptibility to chill. Every fascicle and fiber was organ key on which mad fingers played. Yet the snow awakened her, however unpleasantly, to a sense of her own body as Sven Sr. never had. She covered her ears on the phrase, Never would. He had always taken his brutish pleasure and then, while she lay there panting for more, much more, for the finesse of mad fingers as it were, he . . . he . . .

"Several of her sons had it was true at various times made advances, playfully but with an almost truculent insistence beneath the playfulness. Of course, like her mother and her mother before her she repulsed them, and thanks to a deft organic intelligence operating through every fiber of her mother's body she was able time and time again to bring an untoward state of affairs to a more than stately conclusion and at the same time preserve a fond, ticklish, and flatteringly voluptuous sensation of what might have been. The danger passed, she currycombed these events and relished what they had or now seemed to shed of promise, dwelling for example on this son's slightly raucous inflection, that one's curve of a comely thigh, a third's manipulation of a greenish apple to demonstrate the impending disequilibrium induced not so much by his desires as her refusal to satisfy those desires, mirror of her own. Ah, how delicious these recollections had, at one time, been. But now she had no inclination patiently to remember. Now she was intent on one thing: laying her case before the village elder, shaman of shamans.

"At the height of her rage—rage not so much at Sven as at Ike MacDermoto von der Tartuffe's daring possibly to mitigate and do away with that rage—a pure specimen in a world impure which she longed suddenly to preserve intact forever so endearing out in this blizzard was the apperception of an injustice outfacing all competitors—at the height of her rage she found herself before his house. She was relieved and at the same time resentful to be adjourning a fermentation that in a very short time and over an equally short distance had become master of its own little kingdom as Chopin—her father's favorite songbird—had been, she remembered, over his. Where Ike was relief was not far.

"Although still recovering from this access of rage she had enough self-possession to remember whom she was visiting and why. Clearing her throat though it needed no clearing, she prepared herself for the civilities preliminary to a stating of the facts of a case beyond all cases. For though Ike always trivialized these preliminaries he paid in fact no little attention to such phatic drivel ushering in what the suppliant took to be the crucial presentation yet that inevitably turned out to be an epiphenomenon obstinately muddling the heart of the matter. Deep within her peasant soul Yekaterina herself had dim stirrings suggesting these preliminaries were not so irrelevant after all, were perhaps more vital to an apt resolution than the ostensibly crucial presentations ultimately reducible to the same babble of rancor. She was even beginning out here in the windy snow to think that forthright presentation only got in the way of the facts of the case—WHATEVER THEY TURNED OUT TO BE! She was astonished, never had she imagined she would hear Yekaterina G. Ivanovnanookna espousing the cause of indeterminacy.

"Though Yekaterina Ivanovnanookna was a simple woman who would have never dreamed of consciously and calculatingly rehearsing her presentation, what with the long trek through the snow and much bitter thrashing in the semiprivacy of the outhouse she had achieved a certain skill in the deployment of rage. Such ease, she suddenly feared, could only work against the excruciation, the—abreaction—necessary to a true revolution in her domestic economy.

"She wiped her boots in the snow as if it were a delicately woven placemat—a veritable fabric of destiny—and rapped four times (she had had four miscarriages) on the big brass knocker. From its depths with new and surprising sprightliness a ruddy face framed by auburn braids was reflected back in company of fir bough and obolus of inexplicably blue sky. She heard footsteps, always a welcome sound to the weary traveller. Then she thought she must be mistaken when this gladdening patter surrendered to a long and expert silence punctuated only by the flutter of redbreasts deep within the shag of spruce and fir. As one of these creatures dived boring into the remnants of a nest Yekaterina turned away unable to remember if it had kept up its fluttering as it pricked with beak and claws. And it was suddenly of the first importance to determine this, before setting foot within Rev. Ike's consulting room. Without this information, without having satisfied herself on this point, she was doomed to—to—

"Before she could decide whether or not she had the strength to turn back to the bird's doings she found herself in front of Ike himself. Fixing on the floral pattern of an unwashed dressing gown that lent an unspeakable elegance to his bony frame she began to tremble, and trembling, went on trembling, trembling, trembling ever trembling. She could not speak, so busy was she trembling before him, at last, Ike. Why now, she wondered, why a trembling now, after my long trek through marriage, childbirth, wealth of afflictions major and minor, not a solitary symptom to my credit.

"Her wondering need not necessarily have stopped there. She might, for example, have wondered how much of the symptom was terrified anticipation of the symptom's capacity to incapacitate for receiving warmth, tenderness. But a simple woman she turned back to the floral pattern, looked Ike in the face.

"She knew that today under no circumstances was Ike Moshimoto to be addressed as Ike. But what was the alias corresponding to this sudden shift. She did not get very far in her researches for with a brusque arm movement he ushered her in. Through a corner of her eye she noted he had taken advantage of this moment of disorientation, presumably mutual, to try to pick a morsel from between blackened front teeth. Following her into a little room serving as bedroom, bathroom, office and parlor, he sat himself down. Before they went any further—she had never seen him less eager to go further until she realized (though the realization did nothing to reassure her) she had never come to him for a consultation and that all memory of the consultation room was a patchwork of tales, sometimes tall, of neighbors who had over the years positively raved about his curative powers through noble sensitivity to women's ills—she removed a chicken from her basket and placed it discreetly on the table separating them. Just before she let go of its plump thigh she wondered if he was indeed not a charlatan. She tried to oust this thought but it persisted in perching before her as stalwartly as the plucked chicken. It sat there, this thought, as stolidly as she, waiting for him to begin.

" 'Thanks for the chicken, woman,' he said, less with gratitude than in interrogation, slightly ironic and as devoid of human feeling as once again the chicken, three-quarters frozen, one-eighth unfrozen. She shrugged, undone by the situation. 'I come regarding Sven,' she murmured. But saying this she felt she was invoking the ghost of another alias, not today's, and that to do so, here and now, was a slight to him, the full-bodied, strapping and eager thaumaturge planted before her and with every right to be taken whatever his alias

for what he conceived himself to be according to the conception of his clientela. He stared saying nothing, as monolithic
as the wall of snow behind their hovel a half, no ten miles
away. 'I come for Sven,' she repeated, hating herself for wanting to please this quack more than she wished to be healed.

" 'How can I help you,' he said finally, as if deferring to
harassment out of the merest decency. 'Sven Sr. He's twisting and turning with torment.' She tried to warm to Sven's
difficulties so as not to find Hashimoto so devilishly attractive or rather to make her apparent selflessness attractive to
him. 'He'll get over it,' said Hashidemoto. And he was so
optimistic Yekaterina knew he could not be addressing her,
much less the problem at hand. What had she to do with the
accessible vision of a benign future. He advanced, took her
in his arms, and made no bones about desiring her. And as
he penetrated her, deeper than she had ever been penetrated,
deeper than man ever penetrated woman, at least since
Adam and Eve, she realized that an alias was one of numberless appendages lacked by Sven Sr., who had always believed
himself obliged to play one role and that a sour rotten one in
order never to be guilty of impersonation. He would never
lose himself as Ike Dershimoto was able to lose himself in
countless variations on equally countless stance themes
(but all in the key of imperishable self-assurance) so
swashbucklingly that afterward Yekaterina felt she had
passed decades with not one but a superabundance of charming brutes. In short, Xman, I don't share your grim belief in
desperation as a kind of integrity. *Joie de vivre*, that's the
ticket." Rosalie burst into tears, sobbed uncontrollably.
"Best to leave in peace. I can't stand the sight of you." Yet as
she stood at the mirror combing her hair frantically he could
not bear to tear himself from her sight. "It's too late," she
said, attacking the tresses. "I can't conceive of constructing
anything with you. I can't conceive of constructing." Stand-

409

ing in back of her and a little to one, the shadowier, side as
the light from the quavering bulb above the sink fell harsh
on the tiled space between them, he, Xman, he, Xman,
wanted more than anything to be Rosalie—to be standing in
front of the bathroom mirror forthrightly informing everyone and no one that IT was over, that there was no point in
continuing. He wanted to impersonate her—from envy not
vengefulness—or rather her attainment of this radical stance
whence she was able definitively to say no at last to abuse.
Somewhere, somehow, he too had been and for the longest
time under the thumb of abusers. Infected by the absolute—
forthrightness of her presentation all at once he, Xman, he,
Xman, craved a comparable—more than comparable, identical—rabid craving for emancipation.

He left without a word, wandered back to Riverside Park,
not far from where he had first lived with the mother of his
child, for wasn't this the supreme locus of so many inflec-
tions of hope inevitably gone sour and supreme intersection
at last of so much craving—craving initially unmarred by
anticipation of malevolent contingency. He thought of leaving the city—the country. Thinking of Rome, Iraklion, Bangkok, Abidjan he tried to evoke plazas, turrets, catacombs,
beaded curtains, but coerced evocation evoked nothing but
the unappeased hunger to evoke. No, these sites were best
reconstituted from an evocation of the evocation in that epoch preceding frequentation of any of them when they were
still unpolluted by his foibles and he questing for the inflection of sunlight appropriate to evocation of what—all down
his postponement—his abstention—he had in the name of
most perfect rapture—taken to be their essentiality. Just as
New York, the uniqueness factory, was best evoked not here
and now along its dogshit-infested pavements, its fruit
stands deploying plums, grapefruits and kiwis under shrivelled awnings—but through a skewed solicitation of that

time—that time—in the heart of the heart of the country when, infinitely deprived of what he had never seen, he had audaciously—from as it were his purlieu in privation—put it together from scratch, New York—any site—only precipitated out of solution when that solution was the solution of exile.

Later in the day finding himself once again on Park Avenue and just before succumbing for the third time his attention was caught by a few Arabs—not more than three or four—emerging from a limousine. At war with his languid curiosity was a sudden desire to convert symptom (hunger to throw himself in front of a truck) into a contentless instrument of insinuation into the innumerable highways and byways of things as they are. But the symptom refused to empty itself of all content. But the first time, or was it the second, hadn't the symptom managed to empty itself of a little of that content by proliferating various contents just before the fender bore down: (1) slash of fender as definitive expression of inarticulate seething; (2) just before metal slashed he saw a life unfolding but one totally unfamiliar—a gloss on the excrescences that had constituted his life; (3) two Xmans running toward fusion with truck's flank, one ready for impregnation by a dappled flank, the second obliged to find habitation—a story perhaps—for the fruits of that union; (4) submission to truck was nothing but abject recourse to remedy; (5) just before being felled by the truck he was felled by torment of succumbing less to the flank's mass than to the virulent and unlocalizable idea at its core; and (6) he gave himself to the truck to be rid of a perception-voracity disqualifying him for promotion to the ranks of those definitively not of this abject world. And what had he done so far with that symptom-content proliferation as a form of symptom purification. Nothing. So—S/M and Fattie had been feeding him one more line. Surrounding the island

411

of red begonias across from that—in which—next to which—he was standing one Arab—the fattest (was he the fattest or was he, Xman, simply making any distinction whatsoever in order to have a foothold in their chaos) fired at a policeman, a second—the slimmest—at a bystander wearing no uniform. The two men fell, the Arabs returned to the car and drove off. But just before it pulled away he, Xman, managed to prescind from the depths of its windshield a slice of Park Avenue running perpendicular to its true direction (the direction of his two previous unsuccessful attempts) and suggesting—evoking—a city entirely different, akin to New York of earlier, more limpid dreams. The sunlight saturating the frame had an otherworldly inflection, one untinged, one might say, by a profit motive so prominent everywhere and such an eyesore for the likes of Xman but not, he admitted, for those as committed to wan heterogeneity—caption soup—as the big fish they hoped to land. The slice belonged to a world shorn of all the familiar associations that made this nether variant so unbearable. Or maybe the framing, nothing more than the mere segmentation of chaos, made the slice so attractive. Straining toward every detail in the second before the limousine pulled away in the depths of the glass he caught also less an actual ray than a suggestion of sunlight about to impinge on and grow groping down a girder's virgin length. And in its deepest depths like an eyeball relegated for its scorched omniscience to the very deepest pit of hell lay somewhat hazed, somewhat flayed, the sun itself.

Xman shrugged, the New York implied by such a fantasmal segmentation of its chaos was outside—beyond—beyond—his grasp—but not—but not—it was suddenly clear—but not beyond the grasp of the true work. The true work lay in the segment's deepest depths or rather was one with the segmentation as one of its most representative fulgurations. And only in the domain of the true work, only in the deepest depth of the skyline relegated to the windshield of the fleeing limousine would the proliferation of symptom contents come to birth as a unity, as a meaning. Not in the prop and trap world of Fatima and S/M but in the true work. Yes, yes, yes, there was definitely a point to emptying his truck-diving symptom of its content but a point only in the domain of the true work. But the true work was getting away, it was pulling away, far from the curb, far from the virgin girder left to fend for itself under a less than benign sky. The depthless depth of the true work into which symptoms could be emptied of meaning and where such meanings could crisscrossing proliferate but toward an entity vaster more impregnable than a story was gone. The slate was wiped clean. The begonias nodded the indubitability of this lesson learned too late. Beyond his grasp, better fly out to Iraklion, but what could he use as money, marching toward Lexington he caught a glimpse of Fatima whose costume seemed more than consonant with its sickly-sweet bazaarlike atmosphere suggesting every shop was on the verge of final and irrevocable closure. Turning away abruptly but not so abruptly as to seem to be avoiding her he hurried toward Third, broader and less suffocating. When he looked up he was delighted to discover that the sky was not a typical flawless autumn sky chiselling its scintillations out of crystal for what had always been the message of such infinite distance but repudiating delight in infinite mercilessness. Still feeling left to his own devices he wanted to rush out and locate Fatima. For he did not want to be left to those devices, homeless, penniless, among the rich and the brazen, the arrogant and the impudent. Under such a sky—but then again not laboring beneath such a sky there was no need to lament absence of moon softening the blow of such blowsy indifference to the fate of the common man. Tonight, after

all—and he looked up once again to make sure—the sky was
sooty, hazy, shot through with gaslight and itself prey and
receptacle of all the malignant exhalations of this miserable
unmelting pot. It was no longer sky as in (1) brutally blue
night sky; (2) merciless skyscrapers delicately—even meticulously—etched upon that blue and aggressively overprotec-
tive of their bejewelled and befurred denizens against just
such encroachment as Xman embodied; and (3) earth, earth
of said Xman and his derelict congeners encroaching forever
encroaching and thereby responsible, now that he thought of
it, for so much grief and sorrow, so much abject unkindness
perpetrated on Rosalie and on the little one peacefully asleep
in her arms. In that farcical tripartite demarcation of being
sky had been as soulless and geometrical (the suggestion of
illimitable immensity was a ruse) as the chrome-and-glass
monstrosities set off against its backdrop. But tonight, this
very night—a night of discovery for hadn't he come earth-
shatteringly to realize that only in the depthless depths of
the true work could the symptom as symptomless, contentless content, anastomose and ramify and produce thereby
worlds beyond world—etched in soot and delivered up to
dead leaf and axillary moisture, sky was compelled to unite
against all that encroached on his elbow room. Even the
buildings were no longer so far away. Everything that
breathed, especially these monoliths—these condominiums
née Chambord or Blois or Chateau Frontenac-Versailles or
Chateau Blaise-Descartes—was absorbed into the same constricted radius of warmed-over throbbing urban penury.
Looking into a store window he caught Fatima's reflection
absorbed by the same objects. But what were the objects by
which he was in fact absorbed. He was simply impersonating
one so absorbed. Their reflections said they were clearly
enraptured by a painting (dimensions: $4' \times 10' \times 3.096'$) striving to vanquish the inflection of public park's late spring:

luxuriant sun, foliage in the its first fat, impossibility of determining whether the boles solemnly planted at the very heart of a solemn perspective are factitious—mere props— installed rather than organically entrenched—or the perspective itself a mere makeshift. Xman was put in mind of his first meeting with Ziggy S/M with the sidestreets receding infinitely yet giving up the pretense all too quickly. She moved on, he followed, pointing at various mannequins in fashionable store windows she laughed heartily, as if to say: One day our enemies will be nothing more and nothing less than this: a wheatfield of mannequin shreds too minute to winnow. But something in his expression or the tone of his silence trailing behind cut her short. And in some way she seemed relieved to have no longer to peddle her wares. Moving on he felt he was doing nothing less than sublating himself in her stickiness. The more he needed her—for where was the true work now—the more desperately he wanted to undergo what he took to be his only recourse as the necessary emanation of his own, less sticky, substance. In the middle of Third Avenue she stopped beneath the marquee of, what was the name of that little theater, he and Rosalie had gone there once: the Sixty-eighth Street Playhouse. He had no place to go but to her, he felt in his pocket for the remaining bills, yes, he had enough to follow, spotted her immediately.

On the screen someone was saying, "Before you might have walked by. But now you have to follow the rules and behave dutifully. Before you might have shaken hands easily enough for then you had a hundred—a thousand—other limbs untainted, still afloat high above the medium in which I ply my sodden trade. Now there are no other tentacles flying high, only these meager two . . ." with which a few minutes before he had paid for his seat beside her. All the others were either pulverized or busily at work keeping

415

him pivoted, hindered from going impertinently off the deep end and jeopardizing thereby chances for a stable occupation. Sitting beside Fatima was serious business, no longer a mere sinecure through which to obtain raw scraps to throw to beasts incarnating the true work, restless in their spacious cages. Once—but when? when?—he had been able to listen to the Rose Baldachinos and Fatima Buckleys of the world while doing a fandango of derision about their pompous platitudes. But now he was in no position to call them pomposity-and-platitude mongers. These *p*s were to be nothing less henceforth than mother's milk. "What did you think of the Arabs," he thought he heard her whisper. He thought he replied, "They made me think of the true work," but was not sure he opened his mouth. Sitting beside her he was tempted to jump up and run away or to pummel her face if for no other reason than that by stretching her feet in a certain manner she seemed to imply that he was her flunky, lackey, international civil servant with a capital *I*, he was no longer gathering compost toward the true work's efflorescence via simulated excruciation, he was no longer approaching excruciation asymptotically via controlled experimentation. Excruciation was now he, either he cast in his lot with the likes of Fattie and S/M or nothing at all. Planting his feet firmly, gripping the edge of his seat, one by one he had to rechannel each and every tentacle, limb, member that up to now had been making such beautiful music out in the empyrean. They, now teeth-gritting limbs, had to be grounded. He was depending on their memory of his homelessness, joblessness, shiftlessness, to keep him fixed, stable, grounded in respectful servitude to the likes of F/B and S/M. On screen he heard, "You can no longer function in one limb with all the others flying high above your half-hearted commitment to drudgery. From here on in every tentacle, probe, proboscis is recruited to the shouldering cause of groundedness, a being fulcrummed against the ever-impending upsurge of monolithic virtual preformal rage." Slowly but surely Fatima was sinking into his every crevice. Slowly but surely every one of Fatima's and Siegfried's utterances had to be taken seriously, memorized, stored away for safekeeping. Once again from screenland: "Submission is no longer impersonation of submission—gratuitous playacting in the name of the truer work's enrichment. Each uttered command is nothing less than a stake ground deep in the palm of your being, to be pondered by capillaries squelched and mutilated. Survival depends on getting things right." Fatima whispered, "I gather Siegfried has informed you of what happens to recruits who . . . fail. The Arabs didn't." He did not reply. "You must make yourself ready for training soon. You should now be convinced your Rosalie wants no part of you. She has found 'somebody else.' An Ike MacDermitoso. Ike MacTermitoso!" Fatima began to laugh so loud one of the spectators told her to shut her trap. "Just because our victims make a show of fighting back does not mean we are not ultimately successful. You seem to be the type that refuses to act—refuses to budge—without an unconditional guarantee that the adversary in question is reducible to utter prostration before your heavenly capacity to enlighten." She grunted with disgust, with which, Xman felt, pride was mingled for a personal foible long conquered. "Accept, dear boy, the humanness of that adversary. Make your point but don't expect him to rejoice at your eloquence. Why, your true work has frequently survived beyond the disparaging remarks meant to do nothing less than annihilate." Although neighboring spectators began to bristle Fatima felt obliged to continue. "But I must speak of the true work, Xman, I must. There you were today totally preoccupied with that phantom (I refer to your fixation on sun at the bottom of their windshield) when you should have been paying attention to

417

the technique of our Arabs shooting down targets with a minimum of hubbub. And of course we both know you were preoccupied with that phantom (I refer to your fixation on Park Avenue monoliths reflected in the depths of their windshield) precisely because it was unauthorized by the context. You can only give yourself to the true work—though not so much to the true work as to its slender possibility—in puerile defiance of what you are in fact paid—and handsomely—to do. Yes, paid to do. Next time though I am sure you will follow the gestures of our men—and women—with more high seriousness. You withdrew from our terrorist operation into the world of your true work—to escape the world you grovelled at the true work's clay feet. But terrorism is itself an escape from—or rather a corrective to—being, mere being, in the world. At the same time our men manage never to think of their work as such a corrective for such gratulatory thinking would only incapacitate them for action based solely on self-loathing. They think and they do not think of terrorism as corrective to being in the world. Terrorism is of the world and an assault on anything and everything of the world. Our men never allow themselves to resolve the contradiction. Terrorism is therefore a true symptom—the symptom of some superior power organizing greater and greater units of force." A woman's voice shrieked, "Shut up." To Xman, it sounded like Rose B. But hadn't somebody told him she was on her deathbed, having been almost blown to bits by a bomb placed discreetly in the reception area of her office. Disregarding the shriek Fatima added, "I know it's hard to be a bystander. I know you loathe bystanders therefore you must heartily have loathed yourself down Park Avenue way at the very moment when the policeman was shot down in cold blood. You have always loathed bystanding co-workers who snivel, for example, when you, their truest spokesman, are reprimanded by the boss for their crimes." Xman wondered why she was calling him their truest spokesman, this was clearly the frenzied fabrication of a sycophancy with truly perverse ulterior motive. "At any rate once you are actively engaged in our work you will not only be able to act out your loathing of bystanders, all that rancor toward their *Schadenfreude* accumulated over a lifetime—in fact once you have them in your power you will probably lose all desire for vengeance—seeing just how paltry and pathetic they are—but far more important you will also be able to hold them hostage in some marginal phenomenon largely of your own concoction, since never think you will be merely carrying out our orders like some computer science or restaurant flunkey. Think of the Arabs today. They held you hostage in some marginal phenomenon while the real business went on elsewhere. I won't tell you what and where but rest assured the murder of one or two men was a mere drop-in-the-bucket—deflection from the true carnage. True carnage—true violence—is simply inconceivable. Haven't you always loathed people who could speak their loathing. That proved it was still embryonic, ultimately trifling and undistinguished. As a terrorist your loathing—your acts of loathing—will remain truly inconceivable especially with these Park Avenue marginalia to distract from that inconceivability hard at work behind the scenes, beyond the scenes, inside the scenes. In short, Xman, we furnish the only vocation where after the first twenty-dollar deductible, inconceivability is a viable possibility. And, as Siegfried Mahatma von der Dumkpkopff must have hinted, free medical care after the first twenty-cent deductible. Isn't that grand"— Xman hated the use of the word "grand" as a bid for elegant enthusiasm—"especially when our line of work makes us susceptible, here and there, to a few scratches. So—to recapitulate—free dental care after the first thirty-cent deductible, superabundance of marginalia to distract from the true work going on behind the scenes—all the corpses you can eat, so to speak—oops, sorry, no mention of true works and true workers—opportunity to scrutinize an infinity of details better to rid the world of their obstructiveness on the way to—to—to—opportunity for those, that is, who cannot bring themselves with exhilarated patience to gape and groan before the excruciatingly slow deployment of phenomena—opportunity to speed up these phenomena. So, what do you say. Eh." Xman cried: "Please don't mention the true work here and now." Fatima bowed stiffly from the neck up as if to say, So be it, worm. We won't have to tolerate your caprices for very long. Not at the rate you're going. Or rather, Not at the rate you're not going. "Xman, when will you learn that the true work is a mere fantasm. Perhaps it will take—Gunhildo. But never mind Gunhildo." Xman wondered if this was a true lapse or perhaps this apparent lack of control was one more stratagem in overall campaign. "For too long you've been in love with obstacles encountered. These were the signature as it were on indefatigable progress toward—toward— Now we both see that the repetition of encounter with obstacle after obstacle slumbers toward nothing but repetition of the same encounters. One would think you were one of Whorf's Hopi from the way you behave. In our world, repetition is not accumulated toward a monumental transformation, a life or death leap. There is no teleology, no limit, no least upper bound. That is, if you continue in the path of this 'true work.' But perhaps now that you are away from Rosalie you will see the light at last." So many people were turning toward them with disgust that they were forced to leave the theater at last. She dragged him to a near-by coffee shop, at the counter she hungrily drank the juice from her fruit cup. But, he demurred, did she really drink it hungrily.

Hoping he was catching her off guard so preoccupied did she appear with her syrup and black coffee he said "Why did you say: 'Now that you are away from Rosalie.' " She stopped drinking to look as if he had just invented something absurd yet blindingly self-diagnosing. For a second it seemed she was going to do her utmost to sustain this fiction—that it was he who had invented the fruitfulness of his being separated from Rosalie. "Poor thing. When you spoke to her of the obstacles you were forced to encounter I'm sure she must have winced. And you must have winced at your ability to make her wince on your behalf. Not so deep down you must have known that she was suffering your pain far more than you. It was her wincing at what you sketched of an abomination that first made you wonder whether you were in fact in pain. Maybe you were an impersonator. You are in pain. Oh yes, you are in terrible pain. You think it is because you cannot achieve the true work that you are in pain. You think it is because you cannot become a true worker—in other words, Caesar—he of salad fame—that you are in pain when in fact you are in pain because you cannot abide your self—cannot rid yourself of your self. (And that is where we come in. We are the most dependable self-exterminating firm this side of the Ticonderokeefenokee.) You think you are in pain because you cannot become a true worker—rid yourself of your self as a true worker—with true workership a kind of passive receptacle, sump for all the accumulated detritus constituting the very core of the true self. In fact you are in pain because you cannot get rid of yourself, cannot consume yourself. And you have fastened on the true work's failure at the bottom of the windshield to make itself known in order to legitimate your desire to annihilate yourself. Because you are clever and alert you know that someone like Rosalie would succumb to your pain hook, line and sinker—

up to a certain point, of course. She has of course gone beyond that point. No, don't go. Eat your custard pie. All I'm
saying is that pain over the true work is merely the beginning of pain and we, the whole gang, want to be in at the
beginning, to help you by guiding your pain in more fruitful
directions. Stop waiting for a limit, least upper bound slowly
descending on excruciation after excruciation like a lid, an
apotheosis. You know there is no least upper bound. You're
tired out, Xman. I can see it." He was staring at the waitress
cutting a wedge of pie. He turned to her ever so briefly, ever
so haphazardly, as if to say, You are so terrified of my power-
generating connectedness to the wedge of pie that the only
way to endure—attenuate—it is to insist on the innocuous
fatigue—the 'tiredness'— at its heart.

"At one time you believed no matter what you did or didn't
do simply because you were you you were necessarily riding
the wave of a teleology sure to deposit you Olympus-ward, a
teleology that, though seeming over a long enough interval
to be restraining itself from all manifestation—halting all
manifestation—must ultimately dissolve into a kaleido-
scopic superabundance of foamlets participating in the oceanic undulation of—the true work. You see now that
drudgery"—here she nodded to the waitress cutting the
pie—"rides the wave only of drudgery. Oh Xman—we will
help you to rid yourself of yourself only to discover yourself
regenerated. You will ride the wave of our teleology—and
discover it to be your very own. You walk the streets and
panic. You are so much in despair, Xman, that when a little
earlier we threw a few Arabs in your path you didn't even
flinch. You sank into the windshield of their mighty limousine. You are convinced now that the life you are living is not
the true life, that another has usurped your destiny and
forced you to move about in his top-heavy monkey suit. And
this suit is completely incompatible with and thoroughly

corrosive of your true dimensions, the dimensions of that destiny of which from time to time you are convinced you catch a glimpse."

Xman knew he was weeping. "Yes, from my peripatetic perch on the filthy streets of New York I do catch a glimpse of what might—should—have been. Sometimes both World Trade Centers are in the same frame as a piece of horseshit on the Central Park South curb and at the very moment when every event on the face of the cosmos seems to have been sucked into the same frame I feel myself becoming— impersonating what I might have been. And then I lose what I am—it migrates to the body of some pedestrian across the street or amid the unsuspected depths of Central Park, to a squirrel's tail or the double-jointed hide of a pod-overladen catalpa. And for a second—" he was about to call her by her name but he stopped short just in time, overcome with the same revulsion that must have afflicted the man in the hotel room his first night in New York. Saying her name would have been like selling himself to her completely. "Yes," she murmured, motioning to the waitress who was now staring out the window at a derelict muttering to a meticulously attired tourist couple. "For a second you feel ashamed at not having fulfilled our destiny. And then, standing at the curb, overwhelmed by the simultaneity of circumstances, distant and near, big and small, rich and poor, old and young, horse-shit and spire—by the heterogeneity, uniqueness festering in a nutshell—you are overcome by a delicious passivity. All events sucked into the same frame suddenly there is no off-screen space—all is here, here and now—are the world—and you are not responsible for the state of the world, not respon-sible for anything, not even yourself. You are if not a victim then a cognate of circumstantial dearth. Having to bend you cannot be blamed if you have not ploughed through the dearth's monolith to unmitigated triumph. You stand at the

curb sniffing the shit and telling yourself you are not responsible, you go where you are put. Sometimes it is delightful to
feel powerless. Sometimes it is delightful to determine that
the world cannot condemn you because it is world all the
time restraining your powers." "And then all too quickly—
all it takes is the stamping of one of those beautiful beasts
obliged to drag obese tourists around the Park or the flutter
of infected pigeon wings—all too quickly I begin to panic
and feel there is no way out but death—only after death will
I find myself bracketed at last but this time as what I truly
am, apotheosizing captions bubbling up like carbonic acid
from the site of putrefaction. I have it all figured out. Flaws,
failures, and disappointments will stink of the teleology that
eluded me all my days." "Posthumousness will squeeze you
dry of the irrelevant and spew you forth a figure at last,
archetype of yourself." She eyed the wedge. "You can have
that posthumousness now—with us." "And at the same time
I am tormented by this possibility. It is as if somebody else—
the somebody else who has robbed me of my true destiny—
will get to that posthumousness before me—as if it is
something exterior to my being rather than its most pro-
foundly organic extension and emanation—will forestall descent upon my own posthumousness." "How absurd. And
yet how characteristic of our little Xman." "And I foresee all
those who partake of my posthumousness—who will believe
in it—passionately even—perhaps Rosalie, perhaps Rose B.,
perhaps MacDuffers and Perlmutter, maybe even the Finaglie twins—to name a few—and I immediately loathe them
more than I have ever loathed my worst enemies. I envision
them envisioning me already very much dead—staking out
claims to my wedge of pie. For the likes of these my present
state is a mere obstruction. I—my bulk—my living presence—my parody of living and breathing presence—ob-
structs their view of my—and thus their own—futurity.

They wait for me to be delivered up to a simple need to reconstruct me unimpeded by still flailing contingencies. Now I am all incubation. Off its chaos others will someday live." "For us, Xman, your present state is not a mere obstruction. Or rather we want to show you how by making your present state a true obstruction to our enemies—the powers that be—you will truly surely bloom boom boom."

Once the waitress had Fatima's order for another fruit cup she said, "We are not those others. We want to save you from those others." He did not want to hear Fatima's alternative: He did not want her not to be numbered among his worst enemies. His worst enemies somehow preserved the true work's reality whereas she, ostensibly befriending, smashing through the Arabian windshield . . . "Now and then I catch a glimpse of the true work—and it does exist—it appears and then it vanishes on its ever-receding curve and the periodicity of that curve is simply too vast and too inscrutable for the likes of my circadian. My wretched life refuses to slow down for all those who not only spurn my signature of uniqueness but take their time spurning." "Sometimes, Xman, you must say to yourself, 'Stop posing and get on with the business of—' " At a sign of his recoil—what her subsequent discourse retrospectively created as recoil—she said, "I don't mean to say you are posing or that you should stop what you are doing: simply that you are impressionable and must feel: if only I could become a solid citizen—not that we want you to become one. Far from it. But sometimes—not that we feel this way at all, we believe in you, believe in your uniqueness—only we may sometimes deem that you are squandering that incontestable uniqueness on a phantom work, true or otherwise—sometimes—sometimes not we but YOU may tend to feel—must feel, in fact—that what has happened since you arrived in New York is not given a certain past history all that mysterious." "I have no past history," Xman said. "All I mean is your past may have caught up with you—I mean given your contortions here and now—in the womb of mamma York—this is what the man on the street might naturally be led to think, namely, that your past has caught up with you. In other words, it is possible to think of you FOR ALL YOUR CONTORTIONS OSTENSIBLY THRASHING CLEAR OF ALL BRACKETS as one supremely bracketed in his contortions by the past whence he never escaped. Maybe the man on the street would be emboldened—given the fact that your contortions show no sign of letting up—to imply that your past such as it is, does not warrant the exalted present and future you crave. In other words, Xman, you cannot go on pretending to loathe routine—blessed routine—especially when you have—again according to our measly man on the street—the scantiest resources for contending with its opposite, what you perceive to be its opposite. And this is where terrorism, once again, comes in. We offer routine within a context of unpredictability—implausibility—or rather implausibility within a context of routine, routine—deference, on our part, to routine—mounting toward mammoth reparation, on the world's part, for that deference. At any rate, in other words, once again according to the man in the street—who is incapable, we all know that, though he has a wife and family, of moving on—so intrigued has he become by your contortions—your past has simply caught up with you and you have turned out to be nothing more or less than a jowled outpouching of your pathology. Now I know this diagnosis—more like a verdict—is hard to take and that is why we are here—not only to soften the verdict but to prove—some malicious tongue-waggers would say forestall—its relevance. Only through terrorist activity do you escape your pathology, escape yourself as jowled outpouching of that pathology. When you throw a bomb, Xman—when you shoot down a magnate without conscience—nobody can trace you—neither to a permanent address nor to a past life. You belong to history, the history you yourself make."

Oblivious of everything but Fatima's fruit cup and the loathing its syrup induced Xman cried out—so loud that the waitress looked up and away from her drudgery of musing as if she were being called for one of those ostensibly timorous reorders (by an obese regular of some obscenely festooned pudding-cake) that are the bane of big-city waitresses barely surviving on pre-city wages. "Yes, I'm the first to admit that the past has caught up with me. I am the man without a past and my past has caught up with me nonetheless. Yet it is not my past: It is somebody else's past—that other who has made it his business to foil me all his days—that other who wants to feed off my posthumous glory as he has gone on feeding off my true destiny here, where the horseshit on the Central Park South curb intersects the glacial specters of those magnificently palpitating slabs—the World Trade Centers. It is somebody else's past—do you hear—maybe this poor waitress's. It is somebody else's pusillanimity—maybe this poor wedge of pie's. Yes, this past is supremely intelligible, transparent as a corpse's left buttock, but completely alien nonetheless, never mind what the man on the street tells you. Yes, yes, yes, I know what you are going to suggest." He could not bear to look at her and turned instead toward the waitress still turned toward the window, toward the night beyond. "Yes, I can accept my loathsome past only as an alien grafting." Deftly though her mouth was full of stewed fruit (she wiped her chin, ever so lightly bristling, on a tailor's-gore-shaped remnant of tablecloth) Fatima said, "The man in the street would say loathsome precisely because it is so typical. First it was merely typical. It became loathsome by design once you forced yourself to cover up the unsightly wound of the too typical, its purulence encroaching shamelessly on a potential space of mamma Yorkian uniqueness, dreamlike and virginal uniqueness, riddled only intermittently with the spoor of horseshit." "I have no past. I bleat and complain—this is not the form my suffering was to have taken neither in past, present or future. This is not what suffering in behalf of the true work was to have been like."

Fatima laughed sadly or perhaps only loudly, tried to catch the waitress's eye and suck her into conspiratorial melancholy of understated outrage—like the old man in the Brighton Beach doughnut joint. "As if the very essence of suffering is not its inappropriateness, its untimeliness, its bad fit, irrelevance, failure to conform to specifications. But that's the beauty of terrorism—what suffering there is never seems anomalous, leaden, irrelevant. The suffering terrorist suffers exactly the form of suffering he feels he should at any given moment be suffering. But there is very little suffering *per se*. We are in business to make others suffer. Or rather to make their monuments, their monoliths, suffer." "In any case, the past has caught up. In me it is by no means of me." "And yet, you should be grateful," said Fatima, with a little laugh. She waited, as for him to catch on. When he didn't she added, "The only excrescence that finds you sufficiently unappalling to risk a grafting. Alien or not this particular past has chosen to come to you. And you need a past. So this is the past you will acquire and assume. What if you are captured and tortured—you will have, ultimately, to disgorge something in the way of chronology. This past that has caught up with you—riddled with employment agency shrews, taxi drivers, couples bickering behind paper-thin hotel walls, little old ladies eating omelettes in airport lounges, overgarrulous fellow passengers on less than transatlantic flights, SRO orators, ventriloquists using billboards as their dummy— this past with which our likes has become so inextricably bound—this past that we have single-handedly created FROM OUR LIKES—this is the past you will henceforth wear around your neck and be prepared to disgorge—reluctantly of course, with the impeccable reluctance of any true impersonator—at a little more than a moment's notice. Be grateful for what we have lent you, thrown you, you flea-bitten disease-ridden mutt. Be grateful this multicolored patchwork of our network ingenuity has found you sufficiently appealing and appalling, appalling and appealing, to merit its less than loving leap into your less than dastardly depths." He looked away from all Fatima seemed to be saying: across the street to the corridors of a tenement sure to be razed in a few months to make way for yet another hi-rise: the La Rochefoucauld or the Devonshire Creem. He could smell charred steak through the blackened brick.

"You'll have to get used to our tools," Fatima said suddenly. "But with our tools you will be able to save face at last. You remember when you used to go berserk at the noise inflicted upon you from this or that neighboring apartment. And in so many ways you were less tormented by the noise itself—by life itself—than by the dilemma you made it pose. It wished to annihilate you: How should you react and still continue striving to be. How should you react to a challenge that threatened your whole identity." Xman hated "whole identity," identity would have sufficed. "This is how you react to life—to life's most innocuous upsurges. You were reacting not against them (and we were them) but against your compulsion to react against them. How far must you react to save face, literally save face, this is always the question among one of your absence of ilk. At first you positively leaped toward the familiarity of the irritant. But quickly enough you grew tired not of the noise—the phenomenon itself—but of your reaction to it, or rather of your need to react to it, the obligation to react in a certain way that allows of no alternative. And then you began to hate the phenomenon and your yoked reaction less, far less, than the innocent bystanders who refused to help. The phenomenon—the noise or the shriek became quickly enough an irrevocable and intractable force of nature that was not the case with a bystander—a bystander like Rosalie—capable of helping but refusing to help. All rage became displaced to the bystander. With our tools, Xman my boy, not only will you not feel obliged to react to phenomena in the same old way—every way will be a fresh new way and every way will be the same old way sclerotic beyond appeal—you'll throw the grenade at the assigned target and at the same time that you feel an exquisite rapture of release you will also be undergoing an equally exquisite sense of relief at painful choice bypassed just before it could turn into excruciation—but also but also you will—with our tools—you will no longer have to displace rage from, let us say, the employer as authentic root of all evil to co-worker pusillanimously licking his or her chops on the sidelines. With our tools, oh my Xman, no phenomenon will be elevated beyond all possibility of intercession. There will be no more powerless displacing—no more need to displace—to the most innocent and insignificant of bystanders simply because you feel powerless to overthrow the real adversary. By speaking to you of Pman, Qman, and Rman Rose read your future had you stayed within 'the business community.' In a sense her prophecy spared you—superseded—an enactment of all she prophesied. On the other hand she spared you an experience that certainly would have brought you to a pitch of rage so vast—so vast— But maybe old Rose was right. You might have been insufficiently equipped to contend with that rage—to direct it at monuments and monoliths—at systems and concepts—rather than at poor rattled bystander bones. With our tools, Xman, you will no longer have to go about constructing phenomena as threats to your structural integrity in impotent rage at the inability to destroy uncertainty as to whether they are in actual fact threats. You will not have to leap eagerly and inexpertly toward what you loathe in order to determine whether in the interval between two upsurges you have become immune—to your need to leap. You will be able, with our tools, with our tools, with our tools, to destroy before you need to run tests. You need no longer worry about adapting—leave that to your servants, or rather to theirs. You will destroy the world before having to adapt to it." She cleared her throat, asked for the check. "In short, our brand of destruction is everything you want and need it to be at any given moment of your needing it. And never feel you have to need it 'desperately' and at every moment to do a good job. Of course there will be moments when desperate need vitally enhances your performance—when as a result of extreme desperation the grenades and bullet seem veritably to sing through the sluggish air. But there will be other moments when desperation is only a trammel and you would do best to master and shelve it as quickly as possible, or rather, bottle it toward those junctures when it becomes A FORCE FOR GOOD. Once in possession of our tools you will no longer have to torment yourself over noise—noise as world. You will be able to annihilate the world before having to undergo the excruciation of not so much noise as wonderment over whether what excruciates is in fact noise or your misconstruction of noise as still another phenomenon intent on destroying what little you have accumulated, poor boy, of structural integrity. Not that I feel your construction to be a misconstruction. But there are forces at work—but never mind. At any rate you will no longer have to worry about saving face in the face of phenomena. Our targets— our phenomena—are never misconstrued or misinterpreted. They are there to be obliterated, not a whit of ambiguity.

431

You'll know them the moment you see them or the moment we point them out—comes to the same thing. No need, following our instructions, to worry your pretty little head about ambiguity. We'll take that load off your mind. At any rate, you will no longer have to worry about saving face in the face of phenomena. You will have our tools, to say nothing of your own tool—the symptom. You will be able to choose from a wide range of symptoms which is not to say that you won't at the same time be inventing a symptom completely new, impossible to locate on our map of the accessible. Our tools and your symptom will constitute an unbeatable combination. The symptom—devoid, of course, of overt content—will bring you to that raging threshold whence the only conceivable resolution is getting the bomb thrown as we speak of getting the job done." Xman said, looking at but not beyond the windowpane, "So by manufacturing this myth of a symptom you give the raw recruit a sense of his active participation. Even if the symptom can never exist in its pure state—at least in your bomb-throwing realm—even if the symptom itself, content-laden or content-free, does not enhance that raw recruit's autonomy one whit. But most of your raw recruits do buy this song without a melody, so to speak. You pick us to begin with because you know we are symptomed and that so symptomed we are more inclined than the general run of mill to GIVE WAY to bomb-throwing as a rabid dog gives way to foaming at the mouth. You found out about my predilection for trucks, no doubt, and you knew you could use somebody with the 'volatile temperament' corresponding to such a predilection. But not in your realm will I be able to purge that predilection, that . . . symptom, of content. In my own realm, yes, but not in yours. But functioning in your realm, or dysfunctioning as the case may be, is my vengeance, my only vengeance, on being unable to achieve the depthless depths, the content-free symptomal depths, of my own. But never mind, never mind." "From now on, Xman, you will react immediately. There'll be no more wondering: 'Should I react to save face, to prove I am a man, or should I abstain—and thereby induce one more crease in the fabric of destiny at this very moment still being woven by artisans on high, my artisans—yes, yes, I know all about them—in short, should I abstain from reaction lest the shrillness of tenacity transform me into exactly what I fear to become abstaining.' Yes, yes, Xman darling, I know all the ins and outs of being in the world. But just think of what we are offering you. An out all the time that you are very much in the world. Look, Xman, I wouldn't steer you wrong." Up to now Xman felt himself trusting her—instantaneous retrospect immediately transformed all that had come before—of disgust, despair, rage, rampant distrust—into purest confidence—that is, up until the fatal phrase, 'steer you wrong.' Hadn't somebody else used such a phrase. Who, who. Up to now he had been more than eager to trust her as all the others before her and to believe all temptation to mockery stemmed from a failure to value his life in the world. Up to now he had been hearing her with ridiculing disdain because unable to take seriously his own predicament. So how take seriously her taking it seriously. But now a new element—the phrase, 'steer you wrong'—was introduced. With this element sketching the possibility of coercion in behalf of her own violent ends, was ridicule still strong enough to do away with discomfort produced by the subsequent awareness (hallucinated or otherwise) that she was not of a flawless integrity. Up to this moment, it had only been against the backdrop of her—all of being's—flawless integrity, disinterested concern for his well-being—that he was capable of ridicule, indifference to the personal destiny she had expropriated and was magnanimously managing for him. Contrasted with this flawless—

godlike—concern for his well-being as the well-being of the cosmos, purified of any petty concern for personal advancement—his ridiculing failure to take heed became a mere capricious postponement of what was indisputably, irrefutably, in his best interest and his for the taking. In the small he could play at rebellion knowing all the time in the large he was being looked after. Now, however, after the suspect phrase, "wouldn't steer you wrong," it was no longer clear he was being looked after for his own good and for the good of the cosmos.

"Xman, no more will you hover with bated breath over an interval of noiselessness, wonderingly hoping against hope that it will go on forever, or wondering IF during this interval you have unbeknownst to yourself and to your loved ones who don't at this point amount to very many learned how to contend with and live beyond noise. And how many times have these intervals come to an abrupt end as less promise of eternal silence, noiselessness, beinglessness, than fortuitous little lull, muddy little puddle of temporization before the great slash, once again, of being at her most vindictive. How many times have you burrowed your way out or been burrowed out of these cozy little intervals only to find that the interval has taught you nothing.

"And how often have you found yourself overcome less by the noise than by a fealty to reactions past, almost blinded— or should I say deafened—by the scrupulosity of that fealty. So that you were undone not so much by the assault on your eardrums as by terror of deviating one inch from reactions past to the fixed idea buried in the insidious depths of the assault. Your bondage to reactions past—as your only conceivable foothold in excruciation—is ultimately more excruciating—you must agree—than excruciation itself. But there will be no more of that, Xman, it is all over, my dear Xman. A new life begins, corrective to the old, as on New Year's Eve but without the disgusting party favors. No more turning on innocent bystanders in excruciation over excruciated fealty to past reactions—especially when these past reactions no longer apply. No danger of displacement as consequence of the initial phenomenon's perceived irrevocability. With our tools you'll no longer torment yourself over the insidious idea behind the phenomenon—the idea at the heart of its virulent persistence despite your protests—its uncommiseratingly snakelike defiance of your pain. With our tools and your symptom there will be no reason to displace attention to bystanders. Our target-phenomena are masterable with the tools at hand. And there are no ideas lurking at the heart of these targets. They have no heart. They are all surface—surface advertisement of themselves. What you see straight before you is what you slash and explode. With our tools and your symptomless symptom you'll know all phenomena are insidious and worthy of obliteration. Or, think of it this way, with our tools you'll know that behind each and every phenomenon is a horde of malevolent hierodules oafishly rejoicing that their virulence overrules your disgust—or so they think. So they were taught to think by the Finaglies and MacDufferses and Perlmutters and Baldachinos of this world. And at the same time you'll know all phenomena have no behind, nor inside, no depth. They are all surface. And yet they have no surface.

Soothed at sight of the waitress cutting another wedge of pie, was it blueberry or cherry—cherry!—Xman said, "Perhaps the idea I attribute to such phenomena as noise has nothing to do with the phenomenon per se. Isn't the idea more along the lines of: WHY IS THE NOISE STILL EXISTING. SHOULDN'T A KIND OF NEGATIVE OMNIPOTENCE HAVE KILLED IT COMPLIMENTS OF MY EXCRUCIATED RESPONSE. HAVEN'T I RAVAGED IT WITH THE CLAWS OF MY RUMINATION SINCE ANY-

435

THING THAT BECOMES THE TARGET OF THAT RUMI-
NATION, EXCRUCIATED OR OTHERWISE, IS
IMMEDIATELY CONTAMINATED BY UNREALITY AS
THE MEDIUM IN WHICH SUCH RUMINATION BEST
THRIVES. OR PERHAPS RUMINATING EXCRUCIATION
WITHOUT BEGINNING MIDDLE OR END CREATES A
POTENTIAL TARGET FOR ITSELF: IN THIS CASE,
NOISE. THE NOISE IN FACT DOES NOT EXIST. I DO
NOT EXIST SO WHAT I REACT AGAINST DOES NOT
EXIST." "What you react against with us will exist!" "BUT
THROUGH EXCRUCIATION I SKETCH A POSSIBLE TAR-
GET, A POSSIBLE EVENT, OUT IN THE WORLD. SATU-
RATED HOWEVER WITH MY OWN LOATHING AT
FOLLOWING A LEAD, BEING SODOMIZED BY SUGGES-
TION OR COMMAND, BEING REFUSES WORKING
FROM MY SKETCH TO PRODUCE THIS TARGET."

Fatima was not browbeaten. "With our tools in hand you
will know all targets as real. With our tools you will be a
completely new man, made completely over. We don't worry
about what you were before. In fact—in fact—" Xman
couldn't resist: "The sicker the better. The more symptomed
the better." Before Fatima could express outrage he went on:
"You spoke of tools. You must mean guns, knives, dynamite.
But I have never liked tools. Don't you think I could have
forced the true work to show its hand faster if I had tinkered
with its surroundings. I always refused, always gave it maximum time and elbow room. Tools are simply obstructions.
As orchestrator of 'the noise sequences'—may I call them
that—you may or may not have noticed that when busy
protesting the neighbors' flagrant disregard for my right to
exist in silence I used not sticks, stones or telephone calls,
but my bare fist against hollow walls. I could easily have
used a stick, it would have spared me a great deal of excruciation. That is exactly the point: It would have spared me a

great deal of excruciation. I preferred my fist, right from the start: direct contact until the knuckles were bloody. And this, my dear Fatima, is how I would blow up the world if so inclined: directly, with my bare fists, no need for tools, no need for intermediaries, no need for stinking Arabs in seal-skin limousines. In fact I might go so far as to say I chose not to destroy the world precisely because destruction is possible only with tools. I never trust rage and rapture to intercessors. It's like trusting your well-being to doctors and lawyers: Never touch the stuff." "And you get hurt in the process." "Yes," Xman replied, as if suddenly treated to a new, noble, redeeming, radiant aspect of himself. He felt on the verge of impersonating all that was, to his ears, admiringly sketched by the words or rather by their subrampant anastomosis, but where was he to begin. "Maybe by hurting yourself you are distracted from a terrible fear—a coward's fear—of repercussion." This slant on his affairs was less new, less noble. "The more intense your rage the more quickly it loses connection with the ostensible target of rage. Doubting its legitimacy you make yourself suffer to offset the illegitimacy—the gratuitousness. For as we know what characterizes you most—best—what best characterizes your acts or lack of same—is a sense of their pure—purest—gratuitousness—not unusual feeling for one not quite of the world." "Are you suggesting that from now on all sorts of contraptions can be interposed between me and the EVENT." He wanted to add: the event in its skin. Before Fatima could reply—he did not know what reply he wanted or if he wouldn't be enraged by a reply—any reply—Xman said: "But it's not just the tools which make me feel unsuited for your true work. Not just the tools—the fucking tools on which I have bloodied my fucking hands all down my fucking life." Ever so imperceptibly Fatima shuddered—a shudder of interest in one who might—dare he think it—hold the very secret of her being. Fatima's shudder said: What is it then. The time was not ripe, he did not want to launch into a discussion. Or rather the time was too ripe and the force of what he had to say would only be dissipated in the timeliness of the telling.

He surprised himself saying: "In the world of the true work I have always striven to make others undergo—as you wish others to undergo—WITHOUT REALLY UNDERGOING OR HAVING TO UNDERGO THE PHENOMENON THEY SEEM TO BE UNDERGOING. I refer first to its brute duration. Whereas you— In any case, I have always managed when confronting a crucial event that I want others to confront—" Xman was amazed as he spoke at how fluidly he was treating the true work, how eloquently he recapitulated not merely experiences but vast bodies of experience he had never in fact had. Yet there was a certain tremorful temerity in his eye as if daring Fatima to object, to call attention to the fact that in fact he had no history to speak of with regard to the true work. But they both knew—or rather his jaundiced eye insisted they both knew—this absence of a history was not only irrelevant but a force, a veritable and positive force, feeding the eloquence of the moment. "I have always managed to unearth some scrap of purest artifice whereby the hungry little faces who have paid, as they are wont to say, good money, or through the nose, can be distracted from the crucial event supposed to be taking place and that thanks to my ingenuity their eager credulity allows them to think is taking place—in order to imbibe experience of a different—a completely different—order. I have always found a way"— once again Xman was amazed at this recapitulation of a history that did not exist, would never exist—"to keep them, the credulous billions, both inside and outside the arena of what supposedly is taking place. For only whatever deputizes for the phenomenon in its brute duration yields that phenomenon in its purity. Oh how deeply I have always

striven to keep them both inside and outside the arena of
what is supposedly taking place, what they have paid to
see—what they think they have paid to see—and all in behalf of their being able to believe in amid their viscera a
taking place before their very eyes."

"Oh why am I giving away trade secrets—in any case—" he
saw he had Fatima where he wanted her and revelled momentarily in the fact, revelled to such an extent that he
wanted to cry out to the waitress, Another wedge of pie,
though he hadn't even had one. To hell with that: The moment's meaning could be encapsulated in one and one way
only: Another wedge of pie. "In any case without their quite
knowing I manage to keep them out of the arena of a brute
duration through recruitment of a fascinating marginal phenomenon but never so marginal as to alert them to the fact
they are well beyond the phenomenon's core and its brute
duration's unfolding. But never fear, then I bring them back,
at the right moment of course, and what is the right moment you do well to ask but that moment when the phenomenon—the event—the event less than blessed—which
they have failed to witness in its entirety—that is to say in
any phase of its durational development—has been consummated but consummated without having taken place, that
is, without having taken place continuously, step by step,
though enough time has certainly elapsed to render plausible the taking place. Not enough time measured in units of
verisimiltude, no—in these terms no time has plausibly
elapsed. But enough time to induce hunger to be back
whether or not they have been cheated of an entirety. I always manage to manage things so that not only do they not
feel cheated but are inevitably delighted at somehow getting
more than they bargained for—more far more than the phenomenon in its entirety—without the inconvenience of having had to endure a billionth of its fabled evolution,

439

maturity, peak, subsidence, dissolution, in short, or rather, in long, all of duration gone sour with the interminability of everyday life. Don't you see, Fatima, at the crucial moment—when the event should be unfolding—I escort them out of and away from the arena so that said event can presumably take place, mount stepwise toward glorious maturity. Of course once unspectated the event does not take place, there is no summation of discrete instances except that bred by absence conveniently distracted by other, far more interesting, phenomena. I escort them back on time, unscathed, from somewhere inside, outside and on the margin of the phenomenon in question, whose stepwise progression through uneasy stages they have eluded. Who can ask for anything more. As an artisan I hate to boast—artisans should be anonymous hohoho—but this capacity to fix time and time again on some streamlined substitute for the true and laborious consummation of the phenomenon at hand whose beginning—the idea of whose beginning—has been introduced the better to topple and stagnate the drudgery-laden trajectory of evolution and fulfillment—this ability, Fatima, well, you must agree it approaches to—" Fatima spit out a rag of unchewed stewed fruit just as the head of the orphanage used to do. "Don't use that word. I loathe it." Xman shrugged, for the first time. He tried to go on impersonating a shrugger but with the initial gesture further invention failed him. "The measure of my—brilliance as an artisan, Fattie—I can call you Fattie—is this ability to find SOME OTHER WAY of representing the phenomenon to be fabricated. Which, in the long run, is not simply some other way of representing the phenomenon but the phenomenon in its abysmal purity, shorn of its labor of contingency-laden leap from stasis to stasis in the name of creative evolution. You must agree the phenomenon in its wholeness is the bane not only of my everyday earthly existence but, more important, of any true worker's striving to achieve himself. The fulfillment of the phenomenon in its wholeness is the biggest obstacle to my fulfillment as one fulfilling the dream of a vast public." She seemed to be snoring silently over the stewed shards. "All right, all right, I won't call myself a genius, Fatima, but you must admit—even you—that I am kind. I do not wish to inflict on my spectators what I myself have suffered, of, for example, noise without beginning or end. I do not wish to inflict the possibility or my obsession with the possibility of a malefic idea at the heart of the phenomenon's bruteness. I am kind, I am kind. In place of the phenomenon in its brute duration I offer the supreme alternative to suffocating totality. I replace the malevolent idea at its heart with the phenomenon in its abysmal purity achieved in adroit detour through apparent marginality. So don't applaud my brilliance, applaud my kindness. I am kind to my spectators." Xman was intrigued by his use of the phrase, "vast public," in summary recapitulation of dealings too varied and too numerous as if he had blasphemed. In this his moment of staggering triumph needing to induce remorse he added: "I exist to spare the phenomenon its illfated association with duration—with evolution." He could not get over the feeling of having robbed—of robbing before her very eyes—the waitress, now computing somebody else's extravagances. "I escort them back but I haven't robbed them— I've spared them. And they never demand an accounting for what has—or hasn't—transpired: the maturing to full-fledged ripeness tinged with declination. Surely that is the best test of their satisfaction—their heads are too heady to demand an accounting. Yes—they feel blessed with a plenitude though they have been parties to a deprivation, and as I am sure you are all too eager to say, one of the grossest ever perpetrated on the likes of man. They have been deprived of what never took place except within the mind of absence insofar as it was distracted by the sheerest of marginalia weighing at last more than a ton of bricks. A little secret, Fatima, in case you don't know it: The discontinuity and discreteness of marginalia affirm the wholeness—the consummatedness—of the event—the blessed event more vastly than an actual undergoing (excruciation for all concerned, not just the stage manager half-stewed on martinis and the carrot-topped tyke in the peanut gallery playing hooky from the local military academy). Marginalia—details like these furnish people with a greater sense of undergoing than actual undergoing of the whole—the whole blasted process ultimately and very quickly insusceptible to undergoing. Actual undergoing through brute duration is an inconceivable monolith yielding nothing, less than nothing. Undergoing the whole blasted process is a sum of nonundergoings, a sum of excruciated demi-slumbers, a sum of quasi engulfments— even the engulfments are half-assed—by a characterless, yea characterless, immensity. But don't confuse me with your half-assed Arabs distracting from the true carnage with their Park Avenue horse- or should I say limo-play. For there is no organic connection between that horseplay and the overriding overruling carnage you advertise as unfolding elsewhere. If ever I were to witness the carnage consummated at last there would be no sense of having somehow participated— undergone the whole through a part. Their—your—doings are a degenerate case of my strategy. The whole of carnage, as I conceive of it, cannot be undergone in part."

For a split second, but only for a split second, feeling sorry for Fatima as if he had abolished her, Xman adopted an even brasher tone of extreme formulation to camouflage regret and allow her breathing space. "They don't, your terrorist friends, believe in a substitutive therefore constructive undergoing as I do." Her lashing response immediately made him regret having taken pity on one so supremely capable of fending for herself precisely because she gave fendworthy matters no thought. "And who, pray, spectate this your undergoing amid substitutive marginalia. Who are they but the high-heeled blue-jeaned spectators of Central Park's heterogeneity circus, illegitimate offspring of Ophuls's Mammoth, for whose overfed delectation its stock company of ragged saltimbanques are prepared at less—far less—than a moment's notice to cavort." At this time and in this place the answer seeming far too irrefutable, he ran out of the coffee shop—without paying, he heard himself think. Through a corner of his eye he glimpsed Fatima and the waitress behind her calculating the check. Fatima had time enough to say: "Tomorrow—a meeting—organizational—same place," smiling broadly as if she were the devil incarnate. He had just enough time to note the waitress looking as if trying at all costs to escape the frame in which she was embedded with Fatima. Caught by the corner of his eye, in her movements like a squirrel on the margin of a playground repudiating all connection with what might be brewing in Fatima's depths the waitress became the most indispensable and compelling figure in the landscape. Standing still yet all the time in flight as for dear life from the unsettlingly settled frame and its contents, framed she proved there was no abjuring the frame in which one happened to find oneself, abjuration becoming merely an indispensable element of the framing. He, like the waitress, like the wedge of pie she had just cut, was now in the frame with Fatima. There was no way out.

A little distance away he realized he would have to pass this night alone, homeless. He had no money. Should he run back and ask Fatima about lodging for the night. When calmer he walked again past the coffee shop, the waitress was there, alone, he was terrified not so much by as for her now she was no longer bound to Fatima in a common frame. Moving to the back to write the next day's specials on a blank slate she crossed her legs as if on a stool. A waiter emerged from the cellar carrying a small wooden basket of unskinned pink potatoes. Xman turned: The jacketless door-man from a neighboring hi-rise walked to the telephone booth at the corner, leaving the broken door ajar he deposited the obligatory quarter and his eyes remaining fixed on the street began dialing. The thought that the likes of Fatima and Siegfried were training him to destroy a world constituted of such events was somehow a momentary relief. Weren't these details the heart—He stoppered his ears as if it were a question of shutting out an endless flow.

But wasn't the true work equally potent, consigning just such details to the slagheap of quasi archetypes, a depthless depth where rinds of sun and moon ran, alternately, rampant. Standing behind one of the shop's three horseshoe counters the waitress was cutting yet another wedge of pie and putting it on a plate. A woman in a blue business suit—the shop had been empty a minute before!—with irrepressible smotheringly big bow consummating the fidgety tracery of her blouse sat nearby, coffee stains on the office matter spread out impressively before her. Perhaps the dossier of another (-)Xman. Further away shabbily dressed sat a man with no pretensions to business acumen of the higher, or at least more declamatory, sort. He might, Xman thought, very well be the one waiting for the wedge of pie. He thought, though he did not want to think—no, for no money in the world did he want to think: WHO GETS THE PIE. Coming up with this caption he felt as if he had walked straight past the coffee shop window into the greater morass of Lexington Avenue mercilessness. He turned around to realize he was still in front of the window. WHO GETS THE PIE. He had done the event before him a grave disservice—the grave disservice of this caption—yet at the same time seen through the eyes of the caption it was if not exalted then definitively severed from his mainland of churning torment. He still felt he was well past the scene of the crime and must go back though already back. The reverberating caption went on consigning its event to a recent past's slagheap. Still he had to go back to find out who was to get the pie. Everything—true work or terrorism—hinged on going back though he was already back to look more closely though it was strictly speaking impossible to look any more closely at this enigma of who was at last to get the pie or merely to reconstitute behind the enigma an original—primordial—state of affairs crudely obliterated or rendered inaccessible or both by encapsulation in a caption postulating an enigma—a caption—a headline—that until the moment it was uttered had seemed the perfect depiction of respectful distance from. He was standing still on the spot, forever on the verge of going back to solve the mystery. But what if there was no mystery to solve. What if there was only a waitress cutting a piece of pie with nothing whatsoever in mind, as a few straggling customers happening to be still sitting in their places watched or did not according to the mood of the moment. There had to be a mystery otherwise life was not worth loathing. He didn't care who got the pie but he, Xman, bloody well did care if there was a pie, a wedge of pie to be exact, to be gotten. Here, then, was terrorism's attraction: It would do away with both ambiguity and its maddening absence, it would do away with world's refusal of ambiguity-as-sustaining-pedal-point-of-a-life-without-hope-in-the-large. Standing there—here—all he knew was that terrorism would do away with such lacerating puzzles faster than he could solve them.

He fell asleep on the pavement. When he awoke, his underpants soggier and stiffer than usual, the waitress was gone, the shop dark. The waitress was gone, the wedge was out of sight, but the caption remained, full-blown and inexhaustible. And he was inside the caption, he, Xman, was inside the caption, WHO GETS THE PIE. It was warm inside the caption, sometimes too warm, sometimes suffocatingly close. He repeated it over and over in homage to his irresistible nauseated fascination with the image it almost evoked. Such an image—an image captionable by WHO GETS THE PIE—was not one in which an Xman would normally find himself entrenched. Here rather was an image to aspire to. At moments he was sitting at the counter waiting for his pie or resigned to the fact that the pie was not for him, as any solid citizen, with or without frilly bow, might be waiting or resigned. At other moments he was the waitress dispensing pie: He could feel himself rising blithely to the occasion of impersonating a disgruntlement with which he already felt enormous might he say even overwhelming affinity. At the same time on the verge as the caption sounded—as the caption tocsin sounded the knell of parting life—of entering the image shrouded by the caption he felt very much on the verge of annihilation. But it was unnecessary for him to enter the image for he was already there. And he was finding himself revolted not so much by the caption as by the complacency and complaisance of the figure—himself inside the caption's *enceinte*—buoyed up and buttressed by the caption, living off the caption, as it were. It was the blithe self-affirmation of the Xman inside the caption that fascinated and revolted him. For didn't he have a long history of outraged contempt for obliterating captions. Wasn't his true work after all an incessant flight from the captioning of its creator apparent. Yet here full of self-affirmation thanks to the caption, a self-affirmation that was absurd, daring, excessive, scandalous, pompous, brutal, fatuous, inane—here was Xman inside the image, dishing out the wedge of pie (apricot? blueberry? rhubarb? quince?) or waiting patiently for his golden ration along the counter's golden horseshoe. The self-affirmation of this other Xman made him stamp his foot in rage for he wanted and did not want this self-affirmation, he wanted and did not want to be liberated from his grovelling in the face of induced ambiguity, this crawl from doubtful episode to doubtful episode. He wanted and did not want this high seriousness of THE GROWN-UP at peace with his superfetation of captions for what was any life but a sum of captions, no point escaping, better to be grateful for one's captionability as proof of prosperous installation in being. Here he was on the pavement obliterated by a caption yet this other Xman inside the caption was not obliterated, was thriving bulbous beyond obliteration. He felt he could go on forever being revolted and fascinated by this other Xman as he hadn't been able to go on being similarly revolted and fascinated by that other Xman long before who had spread his thighs against the truck's fecundating incursion into depthless depths . . . He wanted to escape this other Xman inside the caption, or perhaps he wanted to escape this disjunction—this not-quite-acquired disjunction between Xman inside and Xman without the caption. And yet—and yet—wasn't this what the true work was all about, wasn't it precisely this kind of disjunction, dislocation, estrangement, that it scavenged tirelessly. But what could he do with such a disjunction between the Xman within and the Xman without the caption. What could the true work do with it. No time, no time. Nothing to be done with such a marred fruit of the perception-voracity, even if the perception in this case bore immaculate witness to a closed-eye seeing from behind stiff and soggy underpants. Half-asleep, ejected definitively from the womb of the true work's hovering in his behalf, he made his way toward the hotel near Forty-second, a light rain was falling, he entered just as Fatima was concluding reminiscences of what sounded like a highly checkered artistic career, something about having preferred,

447

during a tour through the Hebrides, Amelia's first to her second aria in "Ballo." Seeing Xman she directed him toward the kitchen. "Like a dog," he thought. "Like a dog she directs and like a dog I go. I have no choice. Choice excruciates as no dog biscuit can." He ate his fill of fried eggs, Italian bread, cold ham, hot strong coffee with real cream with a trace of cinnamon. Returning to the chamber he remarked that his absence had not been remarked, he was now a fixture, his coming and going had all the portentousness for these flunkeys of steam rising from a bedroom radiator. Looking straight at him but unseeing one of the cell members spoke out. "Louder, Grigorevitch," S/M cried. Xman did not understand why until he noted S/M's pointed stare. That cry had been an admonition not so much to said Grigorevitch as to him, Xman, to pay careful attention. "The symptom, the symptom," the others cried out, as if the symptom in question—was there a specific symptom in question?—were Grigorevitch Ecdysiast Extraordinaire's last shred. Fatima was trying hard not to beam as at the long-awaited prancing of a star baboon. "Years ago it was different," Grigorevitch droned as if reciting a poem recited many times before and to an undiminishing universal acclaim that was only just beginning imperceptibly to pall. "Years ago there was no incompatibility between my shameful acts—between my symptoms—and the true work I engaged in. I was able to wallow in my symptoms as a kind of superfetation of what flourished here. You allowed me the dependable refuge of my shameful acts in times of despair. And what destroyer of bridges and cathedrals does not have moments of despair, eh? I ask you. But yesterday or the day before or the day before that when I was coming out of the den—the place I go to when I want to revel in my slime and in the homologous slime of others—THE OTHERS, the special others—I was suddenly overcome. It was as if in a moment I had crossed the frontier from zero to infinity. Having given in for the thousandth time to my shameful impulse—loathsome, disgusting, imagine foreign clammy hairy hands advancing—" "Grigo," Fatima whispered strictly but tenderly. "—I was suddenly disqualified and from all eternity for continued participation in, reunion with, the true work—our true work. I was polluted beyond participation! Why, oh why, was I suddenly overrun by this incompatibility when incompatibility had never reared its ugly head before. Yes, yes, I know. There's always a first time. But as anyone with half a brain will tell you—ask Fattie, ask S/M, ask Kirillovich, ask Smerdyakovskaya—in terrorism there is never a first time nor is there a last. There is only the eternity of the privileged moment whole." He began to moan and whimper. Fatima said, "Grigorevitch," without inflection. Yet to Xman's eyes and ears this was all too much a constructed confession and upbraiding. S/M noted, "All of a sudden what has been and always will be completely incompatible with the true work—that is its glory! that is its unique contribution to the continued success of the true work—causeway or no causeway"—here he looked with glaring reproach at a spot not three centimeters from Xman's right elbow, red from grating contact with the chest of drawers behind him—"incompatible with the true work, our true work, not some flunkey's version of true work, is found to be—incompatible at last with said true work." S/M looked around with impish provocation, daring them all to prove their ingenuity and refute the absurdity. Or rather uproot and unleash the flame at the heart of the absurdity. They laughed. Spontaneously or from a mere sense of drudgery-laden duty? "My terror," said Grigorevitch with reproach in his voice—how dare they deride his authentic torment, "is that after my shameful—my unutterable—lapse I will be unable to continue with my work here." Fatima said, "You have made it so. Not we. We are

449

good people. We would be only too happy to have you stay on here and harness your shame—your symptomatic shame at loathsomeness—to the true work AT LAST. Up to now your contribution has—I must be frank—been valueless. For the first time you stand a chance of authentic assimilation to the task forever at hand. For too long you have lived a completely uninteresting harmony between the true work and your secret life, neither interfering with the other." Xman was instantly haunted by the ominous ring of "neither interfering with the other." "And that is why, Grigorevitch, *mein Herr*, you have been so ineffective, so uninteresting, a saboteur. Your slime, your loathsomeness, always had their little . . . outlet. The hairy hands and all that. But you must become one with your ills—proudly—before you can profit from them and profiting allow others—your brethren—to profit. You must be willing to solder yourself to your ills come hell or high water for all the world to see. And once one is one with one's ills one no longer needs outlets. Outlets such as yours—pusillanimous, not shameful—simply enshrine the disjunction between what you pretend and what you refuse to be. Know one thing, Grigorevitch, and know it well"—yet at this very moment if there was one being on the face of the earth least susceptible to exhortation, to the shame of insensibility, it was, in Xman's view, Grigorevitch—"we have never condemned our members for their shame—their slime—their symptoms. We thrive on slime. We have, on the contrary—ON THE CONTRARY—condemned them for a cowardly failure to make themselves one with their shame and possess it proudly. How many times have you heard us say, 'Chico, or Barrio, or Federipo, don't be ashamed of your symptoms but if you must be ashamed and I'm sure you must—you owe it to yourself—wear your shame proudly but not in such a way as to obliterate the burning intensity of the shame. Wear your shame as if it were anything but shame but not in such a manner as to cut the connection to its unique and incomparable capacity to revitalize and enrich. How many times, Grigo, tell me, how many times?"

"If you feel yourself to be one with your shame you will not dread judgement or torment yourself with disqualified-ness, invalidatedness, annihilation," said a voice definitively. Xman could not distinguish if it was Siegfried's or Fatima's. In the gloaming they perhaps had become one. "Yes, yes," he suddenly heard the doomed figure say. "You're right, I do feel this shame is mine after all. It is precisely shame that establishes my uniquity, spares me the biggest excruciation of all even though often it seems there is no excruciation bigger than shame after lapse." "But that is precisely our point"— the Fattie/S/M voice was still ambiguous—"you have taken the easy way out. Instead of the greatest—the most blessed— excruciation of all you have basely herniated to shame. Remember: One is always condemned not for the shame—not for the shameful acts—pitiful in their aspiration toward essential blasphemy—but for the disjunction—the iron wall— between self and acts. But with authentic excruciation—the excruciation beyond which there is no other—there is never said disjunction between self and act. Self becomes act, act self, in short, excruciation is a twenty-four hour a minute job and meshes perfectly with our . . . project." The condemned man began to weep. "Imagine my descent into the arena set aside for the satisfaction of compulsions such as mine. I don't have to draw pictures do I. A flight of stairs expires in a reddish half-light of peeling wallpaper punctured by writh-ing sconces out of Cocteau. But it is never the arena that terrifies—the arena in its nudity, its—abstraction—is after all home sweet home to the homeless one. Rather it is the alcoves, the niches, the outpouchings beyond, where men of my stamp can—can—" "Transact," Fatima declared. "Trans-

451

act, my friend." "And to their heart's content," S/M added, with a hopeless edge to his voice. Their voices were once again clearly distinguishable. Here the condemned man stopped weeping. "Stripped naked—do you understand or is it too difficult. After such frequentations how can I be expected to participate in a cause so noble—so exalted—as what has been so generously—so lovingly—mapped out for us here by the one—the only—"

Matter-of-factly, brushing all tribute aside, though not as quickly as she might have liked others to think, Fatima said, "Yes, yes, so it is an arena set aside for the purpose you describe—precisely that purpose and no other. You go and do what you have to do and then you leave. What could be simpler. I never resented your going—you know that. But you never came up with any deductions as a result of your going—fruits of abstraction from all that clatter, silence and slime. You never came back with clear-cut resemblances established between the deregulation rampant in those precincts—an only apparent deregulation, I might add—and our protocol. You never came back with descriptions that transcended the pettiness of your shame and making us gasp with awe pointed out how someone driven IN THAT DIRECTION could be equally though differently useful in the one—or ones—subtended by our own very special brand of social piety. It is your shortsightedness I resented and continue to resent. Never any attempt to analogize between that den of so-called unspeakability and the scrappy purlieus in which we are and will continue to be obliged to set foot if the world is to end with a lustral bang. Never any attempt to homologize between that outlet and this in a way that transcends both, leaves them far far behind in the name—and more far more than the name—to hell with mere names!—of a better world. In short, never any distinctions or connections made between slime A and slime B—for we are slime, I know it, but do you think I lose an hour's sleep over it—in a way that transcends both. Never any proof of acquisition—through such distinction—and connection-mongering—of a totally new element. A totally new element! Do you hear: a totally new element." Fatima appeared so distraughtly lacerating that even S/M was obliged to step in and urge her to contain herself. Fatima calmed herself. In a whisper she said: "Never a simple comparison between the way he was fondled there and the way we fondle our bombs, between the way a finger might have been inserted between his sagging buttocks and the way we painstakingly between the buttocks of the world, as it were, insert our little stick of dynamite. You go there, do what you have to do and then you leave, having seen nothing." Matter-of-factly, sadly, Siegfried said, "But this is precisely the problem, he refuses to accept the being of his symptom—the compulsion. He refuses the public places set aside specifically for the satisfaction—the relief—of compulsions such as his. It is almost more bearable to think he is at home nowhere than to realize there are indeed homelands for torments such as his and whose conformation might repay leisurely study." "Another reason for dismissing him!" cried a voice Xman could not identify. As if this was the cue Siegfried was waiting for he said: "And so we are discharging you not because of your ostensibly shameful practices—none are too shameful for our tastes—or rather our purposes—for we know how to assimilate everything, we know only too well how to shuck any manifestation to make the most of its usable kernel. But you have consistently given us nothing to shuck, poor boy. You haven't been willing to share your experiences. For too long you have hidden your symptoms—you hoarded them in the name—under the pretext of shame. It is not that we want you to confess pure and simple. In actual fact, we loathe confession here. It's as Fatima says: We wanted you to make comparisons, draw tentative conclusions, acquire abstractions of the too stench-ridden concrete and render concrete the fartlike consistency of the all too abstract. Your den of iniquity is an ideal exploratory site—an ideal field trip for the aspiring terrorist." In a sulkingly peasantlike tone of heartwarming sincerity that made Xman want to puke, Fatima added, "All we wanted was that you contribute your equipment, your apparatus, to the common cause—all we wanted was that you yield up your precious experiences in the den or rather render it reducible or better yet exaltable to our selfless aims." The condemned man looked around, especially hard at Xman. Then he said: "Before I go, at least let me speak of what I have endured. For I have endured enough to justify perhaps a staunch refusal to lay out my symptom for the good of the cause. Perhaps now—on my deathbed, as it were—I can rise to the distinctions and connections you heartily crave." After a deep breath with a sign from Fatima he was able to begin: "I came to this city—New York City, to be exact—to make myself unique. Maybe my hunger had—has—something to do with the fact that I was born an oversized orphan in Eunuque Falls, suburb of Old Balls, Iowa. Of course I was already saddled with certain symptoms—certain . . . problems before my arrival. New York didn't make me a sick man. At any rate, I thought the thirst to render myself unique, or rather the hunger, or rather the thirst, sometimes hunger sometimes thirst but never the twain shall meet, would do away with many of these problems and many of those haunting orphanage memories. And it did. The battle was fierce, as many of you well know." There was a generalized murmuring that Xman took to mean slightly embarrassed assent. "Of course I am not implying that the likes of this organization attracts only failures who have been unable to assert their uniqueness precisely because that uniquenes is too . . . unique. In any case—" he had, Xman noted, an odd disarming sometimes frightening frequently delightful habit of waving aside what he had just said as if it was not only of minimal significance but the sole obstacle on the way to authentic utterance, as if he was always able to demolish himself long before they—his worst enemies—could even begin to conceive of such a project much less boast of its triumphant consummation. "In any case I came here to make myself unique. Exhausting all legitimate channels I went on—or, as I put it to myself on more than one sodden occasion, progressed—to the illegitimate, thanks largely to a carnival barker named Rollins set up here as a uniqueness broker. Plenty of those running loose." When this condemned man on the way out mentioned Rollins Xman had a feeling of kinship never experienced before—maybe it was the man in the bushes behind the contagious hospital who had been severely reprimanded by Fa—at any rate, he, Xman was not throttled by this less kinship than hunger for same even if it called his uniqueness into question. Here was one who had encountered his own version of Rollins—he couldn't be the same man—who had suffered also: For a split second but no longer the delights of kinship overran its threat of diminished uniqueness.

"At first I tried to stay away from the lairs—back alleys—dens of iniquity recommended by this Rollins as 'eye-catching sources of potent raw material.' I tried to focus on uniqueness and uniqueness alone. On Sunday in winter to prove not only that I was doing nothing wrong but was incapable of so doing I would go to the Donnell Library on Fifty-third Street and read the newspapers. And when I had to piss I went across the street to the basement toilets in the Museum of Modern Art and relieved myself there. From my seat in the Donnell I made a point of noting—do you hear, Fatima, noting, noting, noting—the jarring scrolls of fluorescence launchingly reflected out into the pretzel-vendor-

455

laden dusk—slashing but without injuring—as a ballerina penetrating parts but never abuts on a thicket of corps members—the naked honey locust boughs subtilizing the pavement. Fifty-third Street. How far, alas, I have come from you, with your massive ocherous thighs propping me up against the onslaught of dusk. You represented and will go on representing, den of iniquity or no den, the exaltedness of occluded hopes. In any case—coming and going from Donnell to MOMA and back again and back again and back again— no matter how ravaged by a hunger to succumb—to deride and vilify my hunger for uniqueness through pursuit of other—even more unspeakable—hungers!—Fatima, I was not driven by desire, I was hunting for desire, I was not hungry, I was not driven by hunger, I was hunting for hunger, I was hunting to be driven by hunger—and maybe that is what you are doing, you and your merry men. How's that for a comparison. At any rate, no matter how ravaged by time and the hour I tried to model myself on the old Jewish men whom I saw sitting beside and behind me. No matter the horrible grief to which they might be wedded they always made it a point to dress neatly, formally, or better yet punctually, for presentation, as it were, hat in hand. I strove to be as they but with little success. The derelicts athwart the library's outlying chairs and benches were more the model my self-loathing was after. Whenever I tried to be as the old men the symptom gnawed away at inchoate impersonation, at me. And always after one of those flights of sublime fancy when seemingly most immune I succumbed.

"I would buy a ticket for the 2:30 film, ostensibly ready at a moment's notice to descend to second basement level with all the other wrecks. Yet what do I mean by wrecks. Then, just before the film was about to begin, I would take a walk, not a long walk, just a little stroll—but always in the direction of the den of iniquity, the lair, the foul pit of fecundating slime. I would stake out the site of my degradation—listen closely, Fatima, for the anagogic reverberations of the scene about to unfold as they impinge on this, your very own echo chamber—all the time descending upon it as if by chance, the merest chance, the merest caprice of the west wind or the north blowing me into its trash-infected precincts opposite a restaurant, or was it a bank. I would walk back and forth on the street, back and forth, back and forth, deciding whether or not to sell myself—for that is what it came to, shut your ears if you like—that is what it came to. I would walk back and forth on the same street—THE street—pretending to be waiting for someone, as if impatience could account for the throbbing in my vitals—there, Fatima, my ironic commentary on hunger trying to masquerade as casual impatience can surely be applied to some of our situations, how, for example, my colleagues and I should look waiting for our target of the day or week to arrive on the scene—of the crime—in short, I impersonated a waiter. Soon I knew the street by heart: shuttling a suffocating familiarity between bank at one corner and supermarket at the other. There were very few strollers, as a rule, and those who did stroll by always looked askance at this site of—of—either authentically taken by surprise or manufacturing a passing stance of shocked surprise—I came to know the street by heart and yet knew it not at all for I was all the time too busy converging on the moment—what about that, Fattie, eh, my colleagues and I converge not on victims but on the moment—THE MOMENT—when the den—the lair—the slime pit would be bypassed at last. All the time alert for specimens similar to my own I knew if I saw one resembling what I supposed I resembled yet succumbing without apparent shame then I would take the shamelessness as personal invitation aimed my way and follow, follow without hesitation—interesting, eh, Fa: Perhaps my colleagues and I can, while waiting for our targets, seize upon innocent bystanders as models and take their simpering hebetude for infectious audacity—and take it from me, absence of hesitation was nothing more than the sum of an infinity of excruciating hesitations instantaneously come to nought. How I hated myself—surely self-hate is an affliction of bomb throwers that must be overcome—at the same time free will, autonomy, or rather the masquerade of autonomy, free will, was enactable only in this sphere. On a crumbling street with bank at one end and supermarket at the other I played out its parody. And always just before I had every intention of running back to submit my ticket to the taker in the basement—apprentice grenade-throwers pay careful attention to my strategy or parody of same here. But as it turned out I was always after bigger basement game. In this arena of surrender vs. nonsurrender—perhaps this is one way, Fatima dear, to capture or at least entice our prey: Locate them each in his very own personal arena where surrender vs. nonsurrender to desire or the hunger to feel desire is played out to the crack of doom: Landlords, magnates, heads of state, must have their ration of unspeakables—far beyond the excruciated shame I pretended not to allow myself to see beyond, I experienced the thrill of strumming a little pocket of indeterminacy solely left me after centuries of thralldom. Don't you see, I never knew from minute to minute what I would finally do. Perhaps we should map out more conscientiously the itinerary of our victims based on their presumed love of a certain latitude of indeterminacy in every sphere of their existence—eating, fucking, shitting, voyeuring. Don't you see, I never knew, or thought I never knew, from minute to minute what I would finally do. And at the same time given up to the pacing I lost all connection with whatever real torments had driven me to this knight-aberrancy. So when on certain rare occasions the moment came for me to triumph over the urge—the hunger to hunger—it was with a stunned surprise I made my way back to the library—too late to see the film—to 'catch it' as good middle-class folk say— and my other—my real torments. For given up to the hunger, the urge, or rather the urge to hunger and the hunger to urge, incarnated blisslessly in skewedly sagittal pacing before the sacred den whose trajectory united hell, heaven and earth— within the radius of its hideous temptation—it was as if no other torments existed. This deviation—much like the deviation of bomb throwing or magnate assassination—this deviation from very real anguish—anguish over how barely to survive—put a little stale bread on the absent table and keep the landlords at bay—this overlay became the only real torment. Pacing back and forth loathing myself for wanting to succumb, all I could think of was getting rid of this torment in order to be free. Of myself most of all, I suppose, for in this torment, this rim of indeterminacy, I was most burningly myself. When I did, on occasion, triumph over the hunger to hunger, craving to crave, I would return to the life of men surprised I had any problems left to face. And surely we here have all felt that wondering sense of evisceration when our victim of the hour failed to show and we were thrown trudgingly back on the everyday world of supermarkets and subway kiosks." There was again, Xman noticed, a hum of assent though less vehement then previously. Though, Xman wondered, was it in fact "less vehement" or did it simply have to be less vehement to get him, Xman, through a painful interval. "Triumphing over the hunger for slime it had seemed all problems were momentarily vanished—vanquished by my repelling strength of purpose. Repelling strength of purpose, hahaha."

In a lower voice as if shamedly yet with an undercurrent of provoking sibilance Grigorevitch added, "There were times of course when I did not triumph over the hunger, no not by

459

a long shot. Then I entered. And what I saw! Oh, what I saw
and what I allowed others to see. How can I, having seen
what I have seen, dare come back here to you—to your purity of dedication. How come back to your likes after such
knowledge acquired among their likes. It is less what I did
than what I instinctively understood of what others did before my very eyes. I recoiled in horror from what I understood the minute I set foot in the slime. There could be no
pretense of failing to understand. There could be no possibility of impersonating someone who did not quite understand,
was at a loss, at sea. Instinctive understanding marked me
immediately as an untouchable. And my untouchability was
not mitigated, as was the others', by participation—by doing.
I abstained. Abstention merely raised the temperature of my
untouchability to the boiling point. Instinctive instantaneous perception of a corruption that is, I was and still am
sure, indecipherable to the mass of mankind—this was what
terrified and estranged me in advance from all those to
whom I had to return. Not so much acts—though there were
unspeakable acts in profusion—as instantaneous perception
of act, deliriously surefooted interpretation of signs inaccessible to the hausfrau cleanliness of others—this was what
bowled over and cast me into the deepest pit of hell stinking
of half-life as one long dissimulation. Acting—taking part—
would have purified. It was abstention in watching and instinctively understanding the acting of others that sullied
beyond repair. So how can we use all this, Fatima, since you
are so attuned to the usefulness of experience no matter how
brawny, brash and truculent. How can I apply the consequences of my perception-voracity to my situation here with
you and these merry maids. How can I make it work and get
ahead in the terrorism industry. How can I, Fatima Belle,
strike just the right balance between watching and acting,
calculating and doing, abstaining and leaping, that marks

the ever-ascending professional. How Fattie Belle, you tell me."

"Oh," he moaned, "how can you expect me to exist having witnessed what I witnessed under the red lights. If only they had been blue or green. But they were red, and worse, an etiolated red. How can I be expected to come back and participate when all being is necessarily a simulated being after contamination by what I have witnessed down there in the red hole. Only the incapacity to perceive is true innocence—understand, Fatima—blessedness, worthiness. As far as I am concerned consciousness is nothing but contaminatedness. And since Fatima—pay attention, I am making a connection, I am extrapolating to our wretched doings here in this greenish hole, not reddish but greenish—and since Fatima you wish us as contaminated as possible you should do your utmost to have us impregnated with consciousness, make sure our perception-voracity is functioning at highest speed. Then we will feel most contaminated by all the ugliness we see and most contaminated we will seek for release and what better release—what better vengeance on all we see—than to throw a grenade into the heart of a crowd fighting for the markdowns in a department store about to close for good."

Another recruit, as raw and as doomed as the first, cried out, "Only because we have been exposed to Fatima for so long do we associate perception with voracity—with evil—with contamination. How can we be expected not to curse apperception as you, Grigorevitch, have done among the reddish lights of the black hole given that whenever we look anything in the eye eventually we are sure to encounter her hideous gaze. We have never been able to witness—recognize—anything without her leaping into the stadium of our perception to broadcast an attack. She has always retaliated against our perception—perception, that is, independent of

461

her specifications. Never has she been able to endure this witnessing perception without a mammoth monstrous intercession ostensibly on our behalf. For she has never accepted her own ability to perceive, to identify objects and differentiate among details without undergoing each and every as a concerted attack directed against the hard won peace of mind consequent to suitable if makeshift arrangement of its predecessors. (And as Hegel never fails to inform us, the universal lifeblood is in every distinction.) She is a routine addict. So what does she do: She establishes herself as a destroyer of perception with branches all over the world. As a result of dealing with Fatima—this monster, this hideously deformed slime queen, guttersnipe *coya*, I don't care any more, I'm leaving, I'm getting out of the demolition circus—we have learned to pretend always to be seeing nothing lest we meet—en route to perception, en route to discovery—that hideous ubiquitous gaze preconizing perception gone beserk, missing nothing, misinterpreting everything, according to specifications permanently plastered to the world's lower left buttock, shit-smeared of course. Don't you see, Sabbatai, from incessant collisions not with the world but with Fatima's interventional thwarting of such collisions, you have come to view perception as evil in itself, as contaminating in itself. I am not saying this is necessarily untrue: It is simply your way of debouching on this truth— through the auspices of La Fatima—that I contest. Since she always seizes upon perception as the occasion for—for—she knows not what—the delirious reconstruction, let us say, of a sense of nonbeing, of nonrelation. For she loathes perception that is not focused on her as target. So we have come never to be surprised when she animadverts with equal vehemence on the temerity of a falling leaf, a conscienceless slumlord, and a belly dancer with a truly luscious behind— the kind we guys dream of penetrating going full speed ahead. And so, under the circumstances, or rather the non-circumstances, it is not surprising that you—that all of us—have assiduously cultivated an absolute incapacity to observe and interpret. When in doubt we simply throw grenades. Rather than scrutinize, rather than linger over figures in the landscape, we convert them immediately into targets and start tossing squibs. She—she—she"—he was pointing to Fatima's navel—"has taught us to hate our own capacity to perceive—to replace it with a capacity to destroy what we never even begin to perceive as target worthy of destruction. And so, Sabbatai Grigorevitch, they are letting you go, ostensibly because you haven't the courage to assume the full burden of terrorist consciousness. As if they have that courage! They are letting you go—seeing always what Fatima tells them to see or rather to avoid seeing—because you have been unable to put perception to rest, to reconcile your pristine perception-voracity with their contaminated conception of its contaminatedness. I know you don't believe what you just said about the reddish light district. Outrage was merely the schema for the possibility of presentation, of discourse, the only conceivable schema under these circumstances." Whisperingly, ever so sweetly, over the heads of her flock Fatima announced, "S/M, after our little meeting be so good as to take this young man into the New Jersey cornfields and when the sun is just about to set over our foul-smelling and indifferent planet you will—" S/M lowered his head as if to say, Her will be done. The young man turned to Fatima, now sewing upright and paying no heed, and said, "You see, Fatima, I have tried all these years to look back at you from different perspectives. When I was assigned to blow up a bridge I would long stand at one end before centering the explosives. And I would do the same just before assassinating some dignitary in an airport toilet. Yet from no perspective—even with Mendelssohn's "Variations sérieuses" strummed in the background—did you soften, were your war crimes mitigable. From no perspective was I inspired to LOOK BACK ON BEING and forgive and forget. Yes, you have made progress in the last few months—days—minutes. You are a bit more polite: Sewing seems to have a calming effect. But there comes a time and the time is now when you must be judged absolutely in a manner commensurate with the absoluteness of your viciousness—not toward so much the world as us your apostles—and not in terms of a very— an exclusively—relative progress. For that progress simply has been far too slow to substantively reverberate in our real world of flunkification woe." Sabbatai made a farting sound with his cheeks. "Oddly enough," he announced, "your com- ments do not comfort in the least. My only comfort is to believe that loathing Fatima—S/M—the entire cell—has no basis in reality, is a superfetatory fabrication of stark failure to survive in this privileged domain. At any rate all is over. But please let me finish my story, or rather, my glaring ab- sence of story, won't you. Circling round the den going up and down its street quickly became mesmerizingly gratui- tous, no longer a flight from torment outside my immediate circuit for the den usurped all other torments. I found myself in the darkness, the livid darkness, of the den of iniquity, giving way at long last to unspeakable cravings. Eventually I reemerged—my buttocks taut against further . . . violation— hoping not to be seen, never to be seen, and aware that the problem of the den—I mean, whether to succumb or re- frain—would never overcome all others. Gradually, coming back, after having succumbed or refrained—I always gradu- ally realized that I had all along been fleeing from real prob- lems, still unresolved, and that shame would never be sufficiently vastly reverberative to squelch those problems. And here, once again, Fatima, I have the generosity to exit from my shithole of a story and extrapolate to this—your—

state of affairs. Teach your men after I am gone to cultivate this sense that their only real problems concern throwing a bomb or stabbing a resistant sternum. Cultivate at the moment of attack this amnesia regarding the very real circumambient problems of everyday life. Here, I have once again very kindly extrapolated, made vital connections between this my shithole and this yours. At any rate, I skirted the Donnell and the Museum. Especially ashamed to show my ravaged face and figure to the old Jewish men sitting quietly in front of their printed matter. I tried to sit and concentrating on books I drew at random and unseeing from the shelves cultivate my thitherto shelved uniqueness. Inevitably I returned to the site of degradation. Until finally I stopped fighting the apparent opposition between those two poles: one of learning, culture, restraint, the other of slime, shamelessness. It was not as if one encroached on, got in the way of the other. They were both flights from, mirror images of, the same terror, and gradually I came to accept one as preliminary sketch of, way station to, the other. Both but only in concert sketched the true route of my being—its true career, that is, its careering. So one more extrapolation for the road, Fatima dear. Don't jump on your disciples—my comrades—when they seem to show an interest in other matters besides the church of the heavenly destruction. See their compulsions as feeding your own. See them as twin poles of the same syndrome. So much for a parting extrapolation, a valedictory connection- and distinction-making.

"There were times too equally differently painful. Equally differently painful, do you hear, when I simply could not manage to experience—to find—the hunger for what the den offered. Or rather, when I simply could not manage to induce a hunger for that hunger. At those times entering I panicked not so much at giving way—at the possibility of being seen—as at not being sufficiently mastered by compulsional desire to justify entry and render me momentarily indifferent—in the heat of my heat—to whether or not I was seen. In short, I had no localizable hunger to hunger only a hunger to hunger to hunger. It tormented me to think I might be found out, unmasked entering, when not overcome in fact by a superabundance—by even a whit—of uncontrollable craving. What then drove me at those moments when I had no real craving to give way to debasement, to spread my thighs and buttocks to the winds of slime, as it were, and—and—only a craving to crave to crave to give way at some remote point in the future. What drove me if not the simple craving to investigate craving—my craving—in the absence of obstructing manifestational details—to catch craving as it were unawares and the investigator unencumbered by obfuscating because overwhelming pulsations in the vitals. Yet simply too overwhelmed with fear that I might have been seen when I could very easily have abjured entry I learned, at those times, nothing. Here was the loathesome paradox: When inexorably driven by a flame in the buttocks I was too given up to the—symptom—to be able to study it and when not I was too given up to self-reprobation for giving way at all since, under these latter circumstances, I might have so easily abstained and thereby saved face. So let this be a lesson to you, Fattie—yes, you guessed it, a post-postscript of an extrapolation to your case at hand—when your men—our men—try to analyze their bomb-craving in the absence of authentic craving accept that such analysis is doomed I will not say to failure but incompletion. But you don't believe in analysis, you believe in action, so there is no problem. Getting back to the den—there were times too when I could only laughingly weep at my fatuous failure to accept the symptom without generating countersymptoms of shame and despair. In the dark I came to realize my symptom did not create a fissure in being too too wide for the world to caulk. Running to my den of iniquity—my lair—cast in a reddish light, remember—I did not 'incise the universe beyond repair' and placing myself thereby out of time and space induce a vertigo of jeremiad-tattered outrage others could never begin to hope to assimilate. No: I was always eminently labellable as one who ran from the cold into the heat and lurid light of the local den of iniquity with its unblinking marquee and superannuated ticket-taker propped a little to the right of the admission fee posted slap-dash. Simple as that—so remember, Fatima, when your pumpkin head begins to run away with you and you imagine—with fear and rapture—that through your men you have finally achieved a stance outside being, unassimilable to its outraged labels and lamentations—just remember you have achieved nothing of the kind and at that very moment being is snickering right up your flapping breeches in celebration of an ass—imilability too facile to be believed. But there is perhaps a positive aspect to your ass—imilability: It will keep you on your toes: Rage at being at last assimilable will make you fight harder against the powers that be—sole obstruction keeping you from the great white way of nonbeing. Just when I felt myself about to go mad because my compulsion—and its concomitant contacts and perceptions—was simply too gross for functioning in the world—Fatima's world of exalted notions—all of a sudden I realized what a slimy place this world in fact is. Suddenly there was nothing scandalously excessive about my unspeakable symptomed woe compared, that is, to the world's scandalous refusal of piacular symptoms in the face of its own atrocities. I realized the world—Fatima's world—could very easily come to terms with my unspeakable woe. There was, after all, nothing out of the ordinary in the symptom's brute content, even if the mediations to which it gave rise had a certain . . . frightfulness. It came to me—perhaps at the very moment when

467

some particularly slimy hand fingering my privates slipped a few coins, well-earned I might add, between my thighs that strength is not absence of compulsive symptomed infirmity but complete shamelessness in proud submission to the symptom's dictates, world's slithering and slimy huff-and-puffery be damned. World was suddenly unworthy even of my most loathesome transactions under a reddish bulb's sponsorship. No longer aghast and stunned at my spasm as colossal desecration of world's high contrast purity, I vowed never again to fear shooting my contaminating ray in its delicate void. For I suddenly understood—all the while my privates were being fingered, kneaded, molded—that my symptom's shame did not desecrate the world's porcelain but was simply one more labellable morsel for world's as-similating maw—one more labelled manifestation of its murk. So coming—coming—to this conclusion I was prompted to say out loud and out of the blue: Finger me here, there and everywhere, oh world. No, finger me there. And with that I remorselessly thrust my prick right down the world's bloody throat— Something in my tone told me I was now strong enough to put shameless iniquity on a par with all other facets of my being—stride, micturition, chomp of jowly jaws when devouring an apple—I loathe apples—con-sanguineous with each and every interplanetary manifesta-tion of protest, outrage and delight. Symptoms are not all outrage and protest. There is delight, for example, in having one's privates—Mr. Dick and Lord and Lady Balls—assessed at last by skilled pawnbroker hands. I vowed then and there I would never again allow anyone to manhandle my symptom. My privates were—and still are—another matter. But no one would ever fondly fondling or not put my symptoms in the service or the grinder of a grander design. There is nothing grander than a symptom (sung of course to that mock-anvil chorus, 'There is nothing like a dame')—than my symptom.

I had—I have—no reason to shamefacedly yield up that symptom to some putatively better purpose than my own enjoyment. Why rob it of its content in the name of some old battle-ax's striving to drown the world in her leers.

"Ah, alas this was the closest I ever came to tenderness. It was you, Fatima, you and your flunkey who incapacitated me for tenderness. I was made to believe my symptom or rather the network of relations to which it delivered me up but not deprived of its fleshly content was incompatible with tenderness within and without its sphere. And so I had to go all these centuries my way alone, excruciated by a fear of touch different from touch as it is perpetrated in the depths of the den with its reddish light casting greenish tints on brownish flesh. And of course there were moments when I could no longer yield myself up to the symptom's shamefulness and feared an abyss of boredom was about to engulf me. You must dread the onset of that boredom, Fatima. But I'm sure you arrange for another murder before you can be overcome. And without the well-intentioned terror and trepidation delivering me up to the symptom what did I have to look forward to. What was there to palpate on the face of the earth besides the intricacy of sidestreets leading all to that one and only impasse. So what if this symptom isolated me from all tenderness. Please turn: To this day I have never been able to decide what is worse: loss of credulity with respect to the symptom's heinousness (and consequent incompatibility with tenderness) or credulity still warm with the isolation stemming from everything witnessed under the symptom's unspeakable auspices of stark incompatibility with such recognizable human emotions as tenderness. But Fatima you have often told me how our operation here will purge the world of such dilemmas. At any rate, there came a moment when I did discover tenderness. You remember her: She worked for you but briefly and then disappeared.

No more was said of her. What was her name. I was drawn to
her deeply, to her innocence and quiet beauty, the line of her
cheek, her way of uttering my name. I was drawn to her at
the same time I was drawn to the symptom. Yes, I was drawn
to the symptom: never first to the dens of iniquity where I
could satisfy no questions asked an absolute and irrefutable
craving—never first to the dens, that came later. But to the
symptom. As a possibility, to desire as a possibility, as—a
way out. Being drawn to her did not I found obliterate convergence on the symptom, once more as a possibility. In fact
being drawn to her, call it A, reactivated convergence on the
symptom, called henceforth in this amphitheater of the absolute B, B and nothing but the B, convergence not in despair
but with a kind of joy now it was clear B would not hinder
preoccupation with, immersion in A.

"When we were together there were times when life was
unbearable—working for you was by no means easy. I gave
way on many occasions. To the symptom, I mean. B, I mean.
My life was unbearable—her life was unbearable—therefore
my flight to the den, to unspeakable acts, was justifiable or
at least conceivable but alas not to her. If our life is unbearable how can you allow yourself refuge in such a depth was
the response. You should be actively working, was the implication, for amelioration. Burdened in addition to life's everyday unbearability with the symptom I was delivered up to
(indemnified by?) all sorts of dialectical traps negotiable in
formulations such as these: —you see, Fatima, I am capable
of making distinctions and bringing them to you in the form
of pristine acquisitions that may—I say 'may'—be applicable
to the true work at hand— Running was never a running
toward satisfaction of cravings too unspeakable for naming
but rather toward restimulation of those cravings as antidote
against the excruciation of everyday. If I ran toward the den it
was not to escape from her but rather to celebrate—listen

carefully—to celebrate the unexpected compatibility among my tenderness for her and this panting penchant for an arena where tenderness played so minuscule a part—except during those moments few and far between when a few coins or bills were slipped into the crevice separating one buttock from the other. Running toward the symptom or toward hunger for the symptom's recrudescence was nothing less than a celebration of my tenderness—if not the sole schema for that celebration, as well as the best way of protecting her from the less neighborly other components of the amalgam in which tenderness was alas embedded. The great the overwhelming advantage of shameful descent after shameful descent was the subsequent unfailing sense (in retrospect as muddy veil of turbulence thrown in wake of the symptom's gratification over things terrestrial) that everyday excruciation could have been resolved easily enough if only I had stayed behind and steered clear of this far direr predicament. In the shadow of instantaneous retrospect cast over all things terrestrial by shame and satiety—the satiety of shame—and vicey-versey—everyday torments of everyday life with her—with my cellmates—with you, Fatima, and your witless unwitting gigolo—played out their own triumphant resolution organically." The speaker stopped and to Xman's surprise everyone applauded. S/M cried: "You have done it. What a demonstration. You must stay. We need you for the raw recruits—we need you to show them how to abstract from the brute content of their symptoms to a network of relations with center nowhere and contact points everywhere. Of course you might have gone even further. There was no need to become so utter a slave to shame and allow it to dictate so dreary an itinerary. Why did you confine your peregrinations to one street—we need people who like to ramify beyond the obscurest canyons of mamma tanta York—when there are so many beauties: East Twenty-second, for example, right near granny Gramercy; Tiemann Place, in the shadow of Ulysses S.; Gracie Mansion's Henderson; Sutton Place's Sutton Square; Pomander Walk—I could go on and on, like Leporello. But I know I speak for Fatima also when I say we are delighted, absolutely delighted, with how well you have come through utilizing the symptom as a springboard to abstraction, computations of resemblances and differences—ramifying beyond your own sticky tentacles and our petty little framework." Looking around for corroboration S/M grinned, Xman thought, like a hyena. "As a result, promoting you we want you to work simultaneously with Xman here, who needs to be able to vacate his symptoms of their overt content, as it were—oh he comprises more than he knows, a veritable plethora—and savor their succulent flesh as you have managed miraculously to do. Take him in hand—he cannot utilize his symptoms precisely because their content blinds him to their identity. THEIR CONTENT BLINDS HIM TO THEIR IDENTITY. Isn't that true, Fatima. At any rate your experience, might we say your triumph, proves how undogmatic in essence we are for all our excommunicatory proclamations. Properly handled surrender to a symptom with the subsequent pithing and gelding of inedible content need not be incompatible with the most mawkish tenderness, fulsome as a sweetmeat from the firm of Fanny FartMart." Fatima breathed deeply and said: "I don't want to delve too deeply into his personal history. Personal history, per say, is not my strong point. I prefer to think of him coming to us brand-new and newborn—without the slightest trace of a history—but I do believe that all his life has been spent escaping 'repressive middle-class origins' and the only conceivable happiness sadly indissociable from such origins. Having spent all his time running while standing still and in place finally his stance—of escape—has frozen. Having come to embody all he loathes he never thereby lets it take him unawares and finds himself revelling in its unsuspected charms so long rebuffed. Now he knows where bourgeois repressiveness is to be found and can go about denouncing it at leisure. He pays of course the supreme price for this luxury of incessant denunciation, I speak of self-obliteration in poisoning suppression of all he might have been. He has chosen, wisely to rage alone, without benefit of clergy—without wife and child like a thorn at his side obliged to drown in the overflowing spleen. Having had to liberate himself totally from the prospect of happiness alone he can indulge illimitably the denunciation that poisons along the way: Self-venomization renders denunciation more virulently powerful in addition to providing its only conceivable basis." Xman replied: "Everything you say is wrong. I have no symptoms. I live for the work tried and true." Though he spoke—though he knew he was speaking—a misrepresentation, the misrepresentation had an extenuating urgency beyond the vulgarity of trammelled plain truth. He spoke suddenly and uncharacteristically with the arrogance of the liar for whom the lie is trifling self-indemnification for plight outrageous and unmerited. And at the same time there was the exhilaration of inventing himself—cancelling truer stirrings by a simple proclamation. "And yet you are crucified by the true work's repletion—the repletion let us say of its raw materials," said Fatima. So she was playing along with his masking of an essential depletion. "The strength of the true work," he enunciated more for his own ears—so he wanted them suddenly to think—than for anybody else's, "is in its sum of parts. For a sum has interstices and in these interstices it is inaccessible." "In terrorism—in your work for us—you will be judged by single acts," said S/M, as if wormily casting doubt on his competence. Xman turned away. "But he is *au courant*," Fatima murmured. She was defending him! Out of the blue she was with quiet stress setting his gifts before them. S/M looked at him as if incapable of making a correlation between Xman and any kind of aptitude.

Then she surprised, horrified him saying: "This preoccupation with a true work that can never be is your symptom, Xman. The true work is your symptom! So far you have managed to keep it fairly well devoid of . . . overt content. But you must go further: It must first be stuffed full of content in order to be significantly purged of content. So far you have been able to keep yourself out of any group. For like Grigorevitch you dread discovery of a space—a den—set apart for your likes. As long as there is no such space the true work remains in its interstices, safely untested and safely uncontested. You will work with Gunhildo and perhaps in the course of our work you will stumble on a space common to true workers like yourself. And then you may have an epileptic fit of despair at being one among so many millraces. You will work with Gunhildo, né Grigorevitch. He will show you how the symptom can be emptied of its content in a space set apart for its subsequent insertion, successfully emptied, in a network of relations." Fatima and S/M turned toward the condemned man for one last look at his relation to his published shame. If on one level they blinked shocked fear of contamination, on another more basic scrupulosity overrode access as they proceeded to go about computing specific instances—in their line of work— of crying need for symptoms such as his.

Armed with a small map of the bridge to be blown up at the very moment a prominent slumlord was scheduled to traverse its sleek quarter-mile en route to eviction of several more of the elderly mad and poor with whom—which— whom—mamma York was becoming more and more infested Xman went out by subway to meet his assigned cohort. Alert and vigorous beneath the Jackson Heights El,

Gunhildo said: "You look like a limp dishrag." A rage greater
he suspected than any he might concoct for the likes of the
slumlord who, he suddenly remembered, was about to become ambassador to or president of a highly repressive Central American banana boat masquerading as yet another
people's republic suddenly threatened to undermine a desperately needed fusedness against that common target.
Though was it in fact desperately needed or were words, the
little devils, simply anastomosing again. Though enraged he
knew he mainly looked wounded. Hadn't Gunhildo detected
and on more than one occasion that his, Xman's, consecration to a total abstention from denigrating raillery stemmed
from the perceived inability to withstand retaliation. He was
even convinced Gunhildo had become trained to subscribe
to his program. Yet here he was—and in Jackson Heights, no
less—calling him in so many words a shit forgetting that
when he, Gunhildo, and on more than one occasion complained of unfair treatment at the hands of Fatima and S/M
he, Xman, had, and on every one of those occasions, made it
a point to more than magnanimously interject some perspi-
cacious compassionation aimed at shrinking the other's
mighty tumor of grievance. Yet here was Gunhildo—né Grigorevitch—so very much the blond beast simply refusing
more sharply than the serpent's tooth to render tit for tat, tat
for tit, and proving beyond the shadow of a doubt that he was
simply incapable of adhering on the requisite full-time and
unfissured basis to the unspoken terms of their latent vow of
mutual support through thick and thin compliments of both
abstention from raillery and simulated compassionation at a
moment's notice. These were Xman's tools. Here was Xman,
about to assist in annihilation of a bridge and its contents
focused exclusively on his loathing for his partner. At the
same time he felt he loathed Gunhildo not so much for a
comment he could hardly situate in the scheme of things as

for appropriating it long before he, Xman once again, could have any inkling he himself had been all along hungering after just such a comment to direct at somebody just like the likes of Gunhildo. Appropriation of that for which Xman had no recollection of a gnawing hunger was suddenly inducing infinite and unappeasable hunger. Gun's massively casual appropriation proved Xman's indoctrination had been a complete failure: The predilection for abstention from cruel raillery Xman had striven so hard to induce and instill through the sheer and passive insistence of inobtrusive demonstration at every twist and turn of the partnership—demonstration, one might add, of a spectacularly subdued clarity—had not been in the least induced. Gun was still outside his sway. He couldn't help feeling as he watched Gunhildo spread out the explosives on a narrow shelf of slope just below the bridge, which gleamed pitilessly in the winter sun, that his partner had leaped on the remark not from any particular desire to direct it at Xman for clearly he had no sense of what the remark meant directed at anybody but simply because being there for the taking he had determined to annex the space of its vacancy rather than see Xman get so blooming lucky in his old age. He had stepped into the foul-smelling lime pit of the remark not, Xman was sure, from the irrepressible vigor of natural conviction but in order to taunt the other, render him envious for what he had unwittingly relinquished unawares and for all time and all space. For two beings, however much welded to a common cause, could not occupy the same space of outlash at the same or different times. He had leaped into the pit of the remark not from throbbing affinity with its slurred import but to demonstrate how triumphantly refractory he had every intention of continuing to remain to that less than celebrated brand of tact Xman presumed pedagogically to peddle. For what was that tact, Gunhildo's sneer seemed to imply, but the stratagem of basest barest self-protection.

"Get ready," Gunhildo said, as if aware exactly at what point he was pushing his way into Xman's meditations. Something in Gunhildo's tone told him he would never get ready. He was too convulsed with hatred at the order, another window on death but not just any another, one affording, in this case, in fact too excruciatingly grandiose a perspective on self-debasement. Yet stronger—more encumbering—than his hatred for Gunhildo was the belief that, if he wished to be equal to himself, he would have to hate and hate hard. "Get ready," Gunhildo repeated. But Xman was incapacitated though he heard the car advancing over the bridge. The distant flues emitted ram's-thigh exhalations, hecatombs Homerically worthy of the most abject supplicant. "Get ready!" Gunhildo repeated. So convulsed with hatred Xman felt that he could not move. He found himself overrun with a craving to be conscientious. He began to take pleasure in his imminent conscientiousness until the pleasure inevitably triggered pain and he found himself wondering whether such conscientiousness, success as a bomber, would bring him closer to Rosalie or take him further away, bring him closer to a possible upsurge of the true work or further and further from any possibility in that potential space. What did success in this sphere—and he could only laugh heartily at spontaneous generation of the word "success" to describe pitifully accurate placement of some tiny utensil forwarded by Gunhildo in a tiny pillbox—bode for other spheres. He looked up at the sky, thought he could make out skywriting, perhaps it was only a scrawl of cirrus. At any rate the characters were unmistakable: Bodes nothing, schmuck. He proceeded to place his two sausage-shaped explosives exactly as Gunhildo had explained, even more perfectly, if that was possible. Once the car was blown up and its mass reduced to a supercharged nebula tottering over one of many gaps in the girded railing Gunhildo said, casually, even too casually, "Oh I never bother doing it as carefully as you," careful to invest his tone with a certain imitable world-weariness. The remark reminded Xman of something more than a mere homologous remark, but a little less than a cosmos of prophecy. They made their way slowly past the smokestacks to a maze of sidestreets that eventually deposited them in the heart of a local shopping district where, as it was Saturday afternoon, faces and figures overran the pavement and the odor of charred souvlaki made Xman want to puke. But he was far more nauseated by Gunhildo's having said, "Oh I never bother . . ." Had there been in the labyrinth of cubicles, eons ago, for the favors of O'Fish and McKay, the same petty competition among flunkeys masked as blithe disinterest in all such competition. On the subway back to Forty-second Street Xman could not resist asking: "Gunhildo." "Yes." "When I was placing my half of the bomb so carefully—even more carefully than you had taught me or so I seem to remember—were you a little jealous. And when you said: 'Oh I never bother—' " Gunhildo turned to him with a slowness of désinvolture too vast to be anything but the grossest dissimulation. "Did I say that?" said Gunhildo with a broad smile that proclaimed unabashedness in and over each and every nook and cranny of his acting soul. He looked cornered, his eyes grew bloodshot, he was more than ever the Gunhildo of the excruciated midnight confession in the hotel cellule. "So," he sneered, "you understand my mechanism." Xman surprised himself by saying: "Yet this is precisely what I do not wish to be saddled with—especially now since it cannot be deposited bones and all in the stewpot of the true work—your mechanism." "You mean you don't wish to be saddled with your understanding of that mechanism. You don't want to live with what you know you have acquired if it walls you off from the rest of humanity. What about the years I spent circling the den of iniquity and then entering—circling only to finally enter and note what cannot be divulged to any man. Yes, yes, it is terrible, you are absolutely right. It is terrible, terrible, to be caretaker of the world's lapsed anatomy. Yet here you are catching me in my nudity and at the same time obliged to endure my jaded sense of superiority toward what I loftily deem the wearisome machinations and delusional futilities of those I claim to have caught in theirs. Here you are obliged to bracket my deludedness right after it has been so busy bracketing the deludedness of others. Your conscientiousness revolted me. Especially when I was hoping you were going to turn out bereft of all dexterity. Yet suddenly there you were, setting the sausages exactly right and reminding me thereby of all my previous lapses. For I have truth be told never been one to pay attention to sausage placement—placing them the way you had the good sense to place them and on your first try no less—that is to say, at an angle of exactly forty-two degrees. Your clever move—the move of a mere raw recruit—becoming immediately an insufferable indelible strain on my legendary competence I had to erect all my past lapses—perhaps there has only been one in fact—too luridly cast in a sooty spotlight by this unwanted upsurge of true competence—had to erect them into the sign of a program, a calculated stratagem, the mark of intentional disregard unique to the prerogative of a true professional. But I didn't fool you, saddled instead with acquisition of this manifest disjunction between my inside and outside. No escape then from such disjunctions, not even in the world of terrorist enterprise." "But Fatima seemed to imply—" "Never mind that. I have elected you sole caretaker of an embodied contradiction. Suddenly you must accept the distance between Gunhildo and Xman as subtended by the distance between Gunhildo and Gunhildo. There is no escape from such distances, Xman, not even in terrorism. And why is it so painful to accept this distance. Is it because it proclaims the death of the wise, all-knowing parent with whom you may fuse when it suits the convenience of an intermittent flight from responsibility." Sulkingly Xman said, "Not only did you disguise—whitewash—your lapses as meteoric outpouchings of a carefully meditated program aimed at the firmament of the future but you lured me to a similar negligence. Ineptitude loves company, you could not bear my unblottedness." As they neared Pennsylvania Station Gunhildo cried out: "So you had to witness and metabolize this bald disjunction between what the aging flunkey said and what he really underwent. If you are lucky, Xman, this terror of disjunction will prolapse—herniate—to a more bearable because more stridently irascible form of discomfort—having to endure contamination by disjunction without some flauntable reward. Perhaps the only reward you seek is wounding me and all others to irreparable enlightenment in or out of the true work. But our kind does not seek enlightenment. Go back to the true work. Enlighten the true work as to my fatuous lapses on the field of battle. You can wound to irreparable enlightenment the creatures with which your true work intends to be populated and to your heart's content. But the search for a reward, in and out of the true work, that is nothing but a frantic search for escape from brute and definitive separation as the supreme datum concerning man and man. Virtue is, in short, its own reward. Your observation at the bombsite—what a lovely little bridge and I don't think it was in any way irreparably injured—puts the definitive seal on separatedness as a fact of life. At the very moment we should have been most united—when any two beings should be most united—blowing a scoundrel to bits—we were in fact most centrifugally at odds. Go and catch a falling true work and try to embed your perceived and acquired disjunction into that pulsating void for all posterity to applaud and acclaim." "And what enrages me even more," said Xman, tracing his own wound as a line of thought, "is knowing you have no intention of sustaining your allegiance to lapse. You have every intention once my back is turned of going back to conscientiously striving much harder now you have a competitor. But for the duration of your masquerade you stashed away that conscientiousness as *my* absurd antiquated derisory conscientiousness—graceless and excessive—yet strangely serviceable as a well-defined pinpoint of farce-laden reference crucial to the turbulent success of that masquerade. In short, the conscientiousness having to go somewhere you stashed away for further retrieval as much as you could in the coffers of my being less than beauteous." Gunhildo laughed as if among friends. "What can I do. I know when I'm licked. But you don't want the laughter of self-recognition. You want remorseful prostration before the intrepidity of a venture in behalf of my being wounded to quasi-irreparable enlightenment. Or maybe you simply begrudge the suppleness of my ability to accept exposure without feeling obliged in consequence to blow myself to bits. But we're wasting time and you're missing the whole point."

As they exited from the station, Xman said: "What is the point. We've killed a man sure as Times Square stinks to high hell of piss and dogshit. Is that the point." Yet Xman knew he, Xman, stank of mawkishness. Gunhildo smiled and said, "He deserved to die. In any case—the point is to keep our rage away from each other and expertly focused on the adversative billions out there. It's easy enough to release that rage on each other: I become the target of everything you mightily loathe in yourself. At the first sign of a resemblance to yourself I am loathed. And yet when I am clearly not at all like you in mien and bearing then I am purposefully playing at not being what indubitably I must be—you. I am making not being you—that is myself—a pathway to derisive commentary, a flaunting of immunity to your—my—humors. How do I win. I must maintain some context of resemblance within which significant difference may ultimately be undergone as difficult abstention from your—my—humors putting itself selflessly at the service, rather the mercy, of those most urgent of all humors—yours. I become the consolatory progenitor you crave not just another greasy orphanage stand-in for the real thing. But there is no place here for family life. But if we are to have a partnership—and we are, according to the higher-ups—then I must bloody well abstain from being you and at the same time I must not abstain, I mean, insofar as not being you—not being at all like you—is misinterpreted as a sneering challenge—a defiance—a ridicule—a contravention of all I must embody if you are, in turn, to stoop to connectedness with one standing in, on this bank and shoal of time, for being's all. But Xman, Xman, you must understand, we don't have time for these games. Yes, yes, you'd like me to play at not being you as proof of both my incapacity to sustain your pitch (but of what? of what, exactly?) and my eagerness to put starkly humbler—oh infinitely humbler—talents at the service of your condescendingly colossal if marginal participation in being. Your ad must run something like this: COMPENSATION SOUGHT FOR COLOSSAL FAVOR OF MARGINAL PARTICIPATION IN BEING. I refuse, Xman, I refuse to succumb to the exigencies of your proclaimed excruciation. I refuse to be you and I refuse not-to-be-you-so-as-to-avoid-distraction-from-those-most-pressing-of-all-contingencies-your-ill-defined-needs. I refused to have anything to do with you except insofar as we are partners consecrated to obliterating a sick civilization—sagittal figures of purgation. We have to consecrate ourselves to the targets out there, Xman. And we have to obliterate all sense of similarity to our targets." "But wasn't it the endless proliferation of analogies between ourselves and those we pretend to find inconceivable that sketched a connecting hatred in the first place. Wasn't it the very similarity between our targets and us that made us balk and recoil in the first place among ourselves and go on to seek targets elsewhere, outside the inner circle." Near Forty-second street there was no reason for the marquees to be blinking so luridly in the hallucinatory haze. "You have to stop hating me, Xman. Oh I don't mean you hate me because I am Gunhildo with this or that fixed character. No, you hate me simply through propinquity, through the fact that earning our bed and breakfast by the sweat of our balls, so to speak, we are forced to occupy the same workplace. You hate me because I remind you of who and what you are or rather you hate me because going about doing what I—what you—what we—have to do I remind you not so much of who and what you are but that you are—that you have to be and that being is not a gratuitous supererogatory gesture worthy of mammoth reparation. But you have to stop hating me—or rather you have to stop focusing on your hatred or you will destroy not only the texture of our comradeship but the very fabric of the operation—we are the hierodules, Xman, simple as that—we are weaving the fabric of—of—a destiny bigger than your measly forestalled specimen." "The only fabric that concerns me—" Xman began, but then he stopped short not so much from discretion as from fear that if Gunhildo was to learn of that astonishing horde of artisans for whom neither sleep nor refreshment mattered any longer once confronted with the imminence of so staggering a destiny as his he might very well— Instead he said, "Maybe all this hatred is simply a phase of apprentice-

483

ship, a symptom of the novitiate that disappears completely in time." As they entered the hotel, Gunhildo shoved a piece of paper into his hand. "Just a few of the key precepts from our manual." Going through the parlor door and smelling the familiar musty smell, a mixture of sweat and fried haddock, Xman read: "Focus on the Target Out There. Disregard—abolish!—all similarity with the Target Out There (even if with regard to target out there similarity was inspiriting basis of initial repugnancy)." Looking up he saw Fatima: "We must meet." Surprising himself by his temerity Xman gestured to the furniture as if to say, What's wrong with the here and now. "No, no, no. Not here, Paley Park, do you know it, not far from where Gunhildo operated his one-man shuttle between despairing iniquity and dreams sublime, but in the long run just as despairing." He did not answer nor did Fatima knowing he would probably be present require a forthright response. He went upstairs. "To dress for dinner," he murmured, laughing above the murmur. Finding a radio stashed away in the room's one closet he plugged it in and turned it on, it worked. The music transported him far far yet not far enough to blind him to the appalling disjunction between the brute round of days numbering encounter with the likes of Fatima B. among its farces and this sublime frolic of a Mendelssohn. Yet the further he got riding pillion the more appalling the vantage on his appalling rootedness in the quotidian. Transported to an overview of life in the midst of life, the sound from each plucked key at once needling the flesh and furnishing its own instantaneous suture, listening he became the music's less than tender but always tenderly expressed verdict on all of being adroitly bypassed. Yet blithely though not derisively obtrusive Fatima, S/M and Gun were still there, surviving beyond a verdict supremely and sublimely capable—and surely not according to only his famished ears—of putting them forever out of his misery. They survived beyond music beyond which if the music itself was to be believed nothing even if it wielded the scepter of invincible decay survived. He could not bear to listen any longer now that the music had proved definitively—or had been proven definitively—incapable of obliterating Fatima and company. Stashing the gadget back in its hole he went downstairs, past the kitchen where one of the recruits just back from an expedition similar surely to his own was chewing on an old pizza bone. Just before he reached the door he heard Gunhildo—the voice was unmistakable—say: "Have a real nice day." He was reminded of something. Though the inflection was well-modulated, well-intentioned, there was, there simply had to be, an undercurrent of mocking expectation of tormented apprehension. Or was he, Xman, merely displacing his own rage from Fatima and Siegfried (too vastly and overwhelmingly malevolent to serve as target of incising protest) to one well-intentioned and innocently stationed on the sidelines, a bystander as he had been among the Arabs. Yet as he advanced up Seventh Avenue he could not forget Gunhildo's wishing—in other words, assigning—him a nice day and incising thereby the anonymity that was his only weapon. For what did such a comment do—and for all to see and hear—but render him discernible, intelligible, one among the myriad subjected to the day's brute niceness. What did such a comment do but subject him to its echo's jurisdiction for as long as he cared to be annihilated by its preponderancy among all other urban clangors. Gunhildo had succeeded in assigning him a niche in being when all he really wanted at this moment and every other was to be on the fringe of being or at least impersonating someone on said fringe. Whoever assigned such a niche necessarily assigned himself one outside being. The radio should have blared forth this apothegm rather than oblige him to stumble on it quite by chance amid the wilds

of Seventh. Although it was close to five a strip of sun across
one of the tabletops in Paley Park embodied highest noon.
They—Fatima gaudily arrayed and Siegfried steely gray beside her—smiled, all the time looking as if trying to fire
themselves beyond sheepish pusillanimity to righteous indignation slow in coming. Watching them struggle Xman
noted with pleasure that he had no intention of throwing out
however neutral some remark that they, inflamed in impotence as they clearly already were, might easily deform into
one more piece of evidence in support of what not only the
milkman had been saying all along. "Fatima tells me you
have been encountering some problems," said S/M. "There is
much to be desired," Fatima interposed in lofty attenuation,
or was it exacerbation. He did not answer, noting that the
naked fronds of adjacent slender saplings abutted somewhere in the vicinity of the black wall of foam bereft of
identifiably discrete foamlets—this was enough of an answer
as far as he was concerned. He was surprised at his firm
control—this brazen display of disavowed culpability, where
did it come from. Wasn't he in fact a very sloppy apprentice
with every reason to cower at the prospect of this long over-
due assessment. Only—only—only—disgust and despair at
the fate meted out to the true work triturated their accusa-
tory glare in his own. They were here to judge. Good. As a
true worker so was he here to judge if need be all of mankind
falling short of its duty. He watched Siegfried, Lieutenant S/
M Mahatma Siegfried von Schtunk-Siegfriedovsky, his tou-
pee ajar, continue to try to claw toward some momentarily
inaccessible substratum of hysterical outrage applicable to
all contingencies including, as in this Xman's case a tyro's
indefatigable ineptitude and, be it known, chicanery. Xman
almost took pity on S/M rudely forced to remain in the
realm of normal feelings bereft of enough documentational

yeast to make those feelings paroxysmically, irrefutably, rise as the hefty loaf of evidence.

"It seems," Fatima said, taking a seat and motioning the men to follow suit, "you are . . . disoriented by the skill of your fellows who have it is true been in the business longer and consequently mastered the craft. The craft! the craft!" Taking a deep breath she went on more soberly, "They may have the craft but you are free to study them—for style." She looked at Siegfried for concurrence as she might have looked at the wall of water. "Not only the triumphs but the fiascos also—few and far between, I admit, when you are dealing with professionals of our caliber but edifying nonetheless, terrifyingly so, more so in fact than the triumphs, let me tell you." "He keeps himself too much in shadow," said Siegfried, his eye roving over some of the squatters in this picturesque little alcove of the urban attic. "And as a result of his recoil work—our work—looms inaccessible and grandiose whereas the fact remains—" communing with Fatima's constructed blankness and taking this as the goad he craved "—yes it is inaccessible to amateurs and even to some professionals and yes it is grandiose but at the same time and gently oozing out of the inaccessibility if one only knows how to lap up these oozings—" Then an extraordinary thing happened. Siegfried stopped speaking as long ago he had suddenly stopped speaking in the hotel room until all that was left to a certain young man, one fresh face in the big city, was the explosion of raster. Clearly Siegfried's physiologic need for the utterance—for utterance—had been satisfied faster than meaning could leak from that utterance and manifest itself. As if she had been eagerly following the conversation and was now disturbed at Xman's possible reaction Fatima hurriedly added: "If only you could loosen up and rub your nose in the mud of our calculations you would find the big event is after all in fact nothing more—" "—And nothing less, Fatima—" "—than a series of little decisions exquisitely calibrated against the gruesome inevitability of reprisal. In short, our edifice—like all edifices doomed to perdure—is an agglomeration of little chunks." He did not know what was coming over him, here among the honey locust fronds barely mating against the curdling marble of late winter but suddenly heard himself saying, "And if I get close enough to the much-touted mastaba concocted by incontrovertible masters in this subgenre I will no doubt find it swathed in nothing more substantial than the emperor's newest clothes—a sum of errors, miscalculations, stillborn skirmishes. Yes maybe you are right: Get close, as close as Gunhildo, and I will find the grandiose mechanism no longer looming and well on its way to becoming what it already is—if only I had the eyes to see—namely, over and done with." "But Siegfried, you must remember skill or no skill he always shows up. He is always present. This must count for something." Why was she defending him as if Siegfried's had been the last word. Had she finally discovered—and in Paley Park of all places—exploitable qualities of which she was loath to let go, negotiable subtalents to be gotten cheaper than she had ever dreamed, preeminently desirable if ultimately sabotaging to professed sabotaging aims.

"I can't stay here. Every time I am on the verge of learning the tricks of the trade I feel equally—no no no far more potently—that I am losing the true work—forever." Why was he speaking of the true work now—at this stage? But what stage was it. "So you feel tension, my dear Xman. Well that is all to the good. That means the symptom is sweating off its excess content fat. The basis of our work, in case you didn't know, is the capacity to sustain the most excruciating agony of tension. Our comrades—yours too—are nothing more than sets of gritted teeth." Fatima shrugged admiringly at Siegfried's bombast. "I fear the loss at every moment of what I hold most dear. As I was planting the sausages—I mean the bombs in the form of sausages—" "Exactly!" Siegfried shrieked so that the few remaining squatters impaled beneath the frond-flayed rays of twilight were obliged to look up dully from their cudless ruminations. "Sustaining the pedal point of excruciating tension requires fear of the loss at any moment of all you hold most dear. And you must reach the point where such fear—overriding and inexorable—never missing a beat—becomes utterly incompatible with a sense of actual possession of that all. If you can reach that point then—then then dear boy you will have no trouble surviving. What I mean is—and correct me if I'm wrong, Fattie Lu—as long as you continue to believe, oh so faithfully, oh so rackedly—like the sequacious little thurifer you undeniably are—in the hopeless and lurid interminability of your tension among the sausages—as long as you can sustain its pitch—terrorists adore tension, never forget that—unmitigated by the dimmest glimpse of what such submission may ultimate CONFER—if you can do all this, you may rest pretty damned assured you'll survive, my son, come hell or high water." Always the gadfly Fatima piped up with, "But he wants to do more than survive. Don't you—boy."

Choosing not to hear Siegfried said: "In short, the key is to undergo incessant panic over the loss of your prizest possessions so that you are never actually enjoying the fruits of possession, so that you can never point to yourself pointing and saying, 'Here he is having what he has.' And what is more a prized possession than your life. Among us you will never be sure of having it. And that is all to the good. Conscious at every moment of the loss of what you hold dearest you can be sure ultimately of holding on to what you hold though you will never of course be able to isolate this surety at any given moment. It will always elude you for if it didn't there would be a reduction of tension and what have we been saying all along about the dangers of tension-reduction in our line of work. Our line simply requires ever more complicated detours toward—toward—the final rest in the triumph of terrorism." Xman, for one, wondered why Siegfried, who loathed naming, had suddenly resorted to the labelling phrase, "triumph of terrorism." Did this hunger to name and thereby identify himself brand Siegfried and everyone connected with him as amateurs. It was as if he, Siegfried, had to be reminded of their conversation's ostensible subject lest unregenerated it vanish forever.

Softly Fatima added, "We cannot allow ourselves to acquire anything not even or rather most of all not our own tension. Acquiring—knowing we are acquiring—we are necessarily more indulgent toward our—clients. Those, that is, who come to us weighed down with commodities and begging for obliteration." Having spoken, having intoned the phrase that recreated the subject at hand, Siegfried looked prideful, ever so content, as if nothing less than epaulets had sprung up from the mossy dung of rhetoric—so prideful and content it suddenly became more than Xman's duty to refute all this balderdash about tension as exclusively the mainstay of terrorism—as if only this mode of endeavor had a patent on so fructive an entity—it became more than a duty, it became, in somebody's words, a pleasure. He cleared his throat, indispensable preliminary—so he had often observed and not only on the silver screen—to moving in for the kill. He tried for once to stand erect, head on a line with heels and hips—tried to leave behind centuries of inaction with their lusterless drooping near windowsills and mindless consumption of processed carbohydrate.

"It's absurd to talk about possession," said Xman, "not only of the tools of the trade of terrorism's terrible triumph but of my very being if at every moment consciousness of possession—of one's jagged contour in relation to the jagged contour of things—must be obliterated in the name of—" "Tension, yes, tension," Siegfried murmured. Fatima turned from the debate with a little shrug, mysterious, almost scent-laden, doubtless pinpointing the inconsequence of his own counterthrust. No, no, no, it wasn't that. He supplicated the honey locust frondlets. The shrug—she had seen—the shrug had been her seeing—that he, Xman, would refute her lover's glibness—yes, this much was clear, they were lovers to the death—and her shrug let him know she was nonetheless linked to that lover beyond, far beyond, questions of refutation or invincibility to same. The shrug said—yes, Xman knew it now—the shrug said, Xman's puny triumph was merely the sign—the glowing, nay molten, prefiguration—of far greater, perhaps irreversible, defeat in some other realm. "And what realm is that," Xman cried out. The squatters were gone. Their absence was palpable and echoed back, "What realm indeed."

Taking his cue from the frondlets, Siegfried was now intent on dispensing generous dollops of salty eloquence to the stew of Xman's widening wounds. "You're always looking to possess, Xman, dear boy. That won't do not only in the realm of terrorism but also in that of your so-called true work, dead and gone for ever hahahahohohohihih. Don't look to acquire—to possess. Don't look for results. Don't wait to be praised for placing the sausage bombs exactly right. Don't hunt for souvenirs among the debris of your latest victim. You want to believe in terrorism then believe. Don't expect any profit from understanding, belief, tension. Ah, but don't tell me. You've found a way to stretch it out to the point where it at last suffices for one of your ilk. You intend to use half of your belief—your understanding—your tension—to ACT, propelled of course by despair—and the other half to achieve a certain optimal distance from all this fussiness of despair whereby the insight that there is in fact no reason through tension to act—to throw the doughnut-shaped bombs into the ex-ambassador's motorcade facing north-west—and thereby dissipate the threat of possession—of doughnut—of bomb—of throw—may be acquired as acquisi-tion above all acquisitions. Bravo, little man." Fatima was noiselessly dozing, a frequent stratagem when she no longer felt herself the cynosure of all squints. "Hear that, Fattie Lu—he has a way of using half his energy to make like a terrorist consumed with purest despair of loathing for this foul fucking earth and the other half to stand calmly and quaintly BACK from all the pulling of triggers and unsheath-ing of swordpoints in order to acquire the ultimate verdict among verdicts—that triggers and swordpoints are com-pletely unnecessary, or rather that they are necessary but not their use. Listen, you little punk, you never become a good terrorist through approximation, through a calculation of probabilities which calculation always keeps three-quarters of its resources in reserve against the contingency of total collapse of all striving in the chosen realm. In short, stop looking for results. A man with a style never finishes, never has results to show for his efforts since more than anything he loathes giving satisfaction thereby to those vermin for whom results are *über alles*. He prefers to keep the wound of the negative—the 'without results'—wide open yet not from mere perversity cutting off its proverbial nose to spite its proverbial butt. When we blow up a bridge—as you did so successfully with dear Gunhildo—we do not think of it as a result, not even as bracketed nothingness." "Stop it!" Xman cried, so piercingly (though long after S/M had done) that Fatima stirred in her sleep. "Stop being so absolute. You know very well the blowing up of a bridge is a something about which the blowers can be bloody well damned proud.

I'm sick and tired of all this talk about the only worthwhile venture being that which is the absolute correlative of absolute and incorrigible uncertainty. Somebody expecting results so as to have something to show for his efforts—and not necessarily to vermin—is not lower than a turd. Sorry, Siggy, don't agree. What you are really saying—though refusing to say it—is that by acquiring a result, a fixed and contoured result, the acquirer himself or herself becomes fixedly contoured and therefore a suitable or at least a visible target of obliteration. A result proves the project is at a certain stage and for the being terrified of acquisition the visibility of a certain stage is indistinguishable from the reification of that stage. For our being terrified of acquisition is terrified precisely because he is so voracious of acquisition. At any rate, once the certain stage is reified it too becomes a target of the very obliteration our being terrified of acquisition is always incubating for THOSE OUT THERE. The possibility of the stage's obliteration becomes indistinguishable from the actuality of that obliteration given the omnipotence of our being's thought. So the stage drops dead and our acquirer is back to zero—at least in his own conception of the scheme of things. There is no going on only a going back to zero. That is why he dreads being reminded of his progress. But I do not dread being so reminded. I'm happy you have chosen to remind me of the successful obliteration of our ambassador. I know where I am situated on the grid of world destruction yet I do not feel on the verge of obliteration due to my high visibility." Xman felt he was impersonating somebody, impersonating madly. But whom? Top regional salesman at the semiannual marketing conference in Old Balls, Iowa.

Suddenly Fatima woke up from her doze to say, "We think it's best that UNDER THE CIRCUMSTANCES you go away for a while—a mission abroad, Nechayevian rouble equivalent of the grand tour." "Yeah, make yourself scarce, you little prick." Against the salmon-colored sky the frondlets made a "temper, temper" movement. Xman turned away from his embarrassment at this attempt to show she was completely aboveboard. Having just met at the rim of the park a couple kissed. The man obviously feeling awkward— this was so very much what he was supposed to be doing UNDER THE CIRCUMSTANCES (the same that oozed the rightness of Xman's business trip?)—made a kissing sound as he kissed. And Xman immediately understood how without the sound sign standing in for it the actual kissing would have been unbearable, because supremely bracketable and so very much of a piece with what was evoked by the caption: Young professional lovers meeting in the pocket park. Yes, yes, Xman understood so well. Somehow by making the kiss- ing sound, the male member crawled, so he felt, outside the demesne of the caption's dragnet. What sound did Xman need to make to allow him to crawl out of his caption's dragnet.

Yet at a little table right up against the wall of water, just below the horseplay of foamlets and fronds, serving almost as intentional corrective to this scene of crime, sat a young- ish man, fat but not repulsively so, with his arm around a young woman to whom taking a pleasure almost voluptuous in its lullabylike tenacity he persisted in offering what looked like consolation. At first Xman was afraid she was merely sullen and unattainable and hated her for that. But then as, although never looking his way, imbibing she began slowly to show herself comforted by the brute's mellifluity Xman began—began—to—to—like—neither her nor her lover but rather the situation ripe for a caption yet thanks to the brute's unusually delicate and indefatigable muttering of the usual banalities indifferent to its encroachment. Here was a man who was not afraid of captions, who did not permit himself to live within the time zone of their dreaded imminence. Come and get me, I dare you, his massaging of the loved one's elbow seemed to say. He was clearly indifferent to the overrated pitfalls of banality. Xman wanted somehow to pay homage to this indifference, to learn from it, to learn to be from it. The brute made the careful placement of the sausage bombs an embarrassing irrelevance. "Yes," said Fatima, as if guessing his thought, "you were always so afraid of THAT," (she pointed deftly so as not to disturb this idyll by which she too was mildly entranced, only Siegfried von Mahatma-Jones picking his nose and ears remained immune), "you ended up saying and doing nothing. Before you ever even opened your mouth you had already tabulated the trajectory of what you intended to say. You were always asking yourself, 'What is the point of saying this, saying that. Where will it take me.' " Looking at Siegfried who seemed to be daring her to order him to stop all this nosepicking she added, "Even then a preoccupation with acquisitions, packets to bring home to mamma, so to speak. And so deciding always that no everyday utterance had the capacity to take you where you needed to go—ostensibly closer to the true work but in fact—in actual fact—in point of fact— Your calculation, poor man, never took into account the modifying influence of another. That young man over there, the one you so much admire at this very moment, the one you love at this very moment—don't worry I wouldn't dream of suggesting an unnatural attachment—at any rate he not only takes into account the modifying influence of those robust little thighs, those rotund little forearms, he positively lives for it, positively stews in its juice, and to paraphrase my dear friend Preston S.—positively swills in its ale. But you have missed your chance to positively swill and swill, I might add, positively, poor boy. Let me remind you however that when you commit yourself to throwing a bomb, sausage-shaped or not, we expect you to go through with it—achieve the trajectory of the . . . tool. We don't want any of this pro-leptic undergoing of that trajectory for no amount of prolep-sis can account for the modifying influence of the medium through which the sausage or the doughnut deftly soars."

Remembering what Fatima had just said—about going away for a while—and not knowing how to feel, rather, how he felt about all this, Xman tried hard to feel. He did not know how he felt but he did know that if asked at that very moment he would be unable to contain the rage smoldering beneath the not knowing. Trying to understand how he now felt toward Fatima and S/M charting his destiny in this man-ner he could think of nothing but Gunhildo, his rival. He felt rage less at F and S/M than at Gunhildo's probable hilarity on the sidelines as it strove to lap up the consequences of this new disaster befalling his arch-rival. Gunhildo's doing nothing was somehow more excruciating, more of a flagrant riding roughshod over raw feelings, then the bravado mani-fest in the decision taken by the two little devils, Fattie Lu and S. Mahatma even if strictly speaking far more horrifying to imagine that in his absence he had been "brought under serious consideration" the way, earmarked for maximum ex-ploitation, any pawn in the game, any malleable entity, any inherent obstruction (but to what? to what?) is brought un-der serious consideration. Absence had not beautified him in their eyes, was simply a pretext for belittlement. Through this new decision reported sheepishly (proving there was a certain shame mixed up in it) he could not help catching a glimpse of himself as they must see him or rather as they must see the shred they had constructed from his leavings a little to the right or left of where he did not quite stand unsupported. He saw himself through—AS—the words minced in molding—moldering—his destiny—the words that ceaselessly flinging him aside ostensibly constructed his destiny. He saw himself the way their words surely saw him—as an obstruction to a final decision. Clearly he was always to be the one about whom others must feel a begrudging responsibility having remotely to do with some final decision about his well-being a little farther off. He had to be fair: Here in Paley Park where the very frondlets enjoined probity at all costs he had to admit their words no more bypassed him than he himself incessantly on the way to heat prostration before some more robust, wartier confrere, preferably a cyclist, or a truck, or collision with trucklike details whose contour seemed to prefigure that of the true work. Their words thinking of him in his absence—but never anastomosing far from his site of obloquy—had cancelled him incessantly in and out of absence. So here he was, ageless athwart a wicker chair in Manhattan's Paley Park, finding he had more than a little in common with those who unflinchingly sacrificed him to the hubbub on the front lines. The screen separating him from his tormentors was now impalpable, there was in fact no bloody screen. "In the meantime stick with Gunhildo," Fatima said. "He knows the ropes." Able to bear no more he cried out: "He's my rival, he knows nothing, he has usurped my terrain. Did he tell you how well I handled the explosives, eh. I have to find a whole other dimension in which to prove myself beyond usurpation. I must learn to abstain from transactions in that terrain effectuating his consecration and perpetuation of the myth of my obscure ineptitude." Fatima and Siggy Lu only stared unruffled, their silence making it painfully clear that in their view a true worker would be already well-advanced transmuting their brand of miscellaneous scoria into essential component while he found himself forever on the far fringe of exploitativeness, forever on the threshold of those ideal conditions apparently indispensable to commencement.

Walking quickly away without salutation he hurried up or was it down Fifth Avenue staring at what from the depths of shop windows vouchsafed a scattered glimpse of the correct approach to such phenomena as those to which he had been but a short time before superabundantly exposed—in short, these mannequins never mind the gender by gazing off to the side of his ineptitude's core at just the right angle of feigned indifference pinpointed better than any certified pedagogue the comportment crucial to transmutation of epiphenomenal shit into workerly lubricant—into significant core of potential workerly material. These mannequins, handbags and toy poodles knew how to contend with the likes of Fatima and Siegfried. In the beam cast by their skill he suddenly saw Fatima as authentic raw material and no longer as a mere obstruction requiring obliteration before the true work could begin. But did he feel this way only because he was at the corner of Fifty-sixth and Fifth at just the right breathing distance from the twig smoke of Central Park. On another street-corner all the old anguish would surely be refunded but this, for some reason, enjoined immediate jubilation over Fatima's utility. For split seconds—for as long as it took to traverse this or that square of pavement—pass this particular vitrine or that particular souvlaki vendor—he felt catapulted to a vantage whence commencement was no longer dependent on elimination of every living turd and wasps' nest of a fuming manhole strewn a little to the right of his primrose path. Here—at the corner of Fifty-sixth and Fifth— he was free at last of all that stood in the way of a beginning. And what stood in the way, he suddenly saw, were less the frothing fulsome fetid phenomena themselves—instantiated in turds and wasps' nests and frondlet-screened foamlets and

Siegfried's nosepicking and asspicking and Fatima's snoring awake—than the malevolent obstructions—ideas of obstruction—down into which he had whittled them—down into which abstention from the true work had whittled them. And what had all along stood in the way of the true work, he suddenly saw, for three minutes' time, that is, at the corner of Fifty-sixth and Fifth, a block and light years away from Fifty-sixth and Sixth, to say nothing of Fifty-seventh—for on Fifty-sixth and Fifth he was altogether different from what he might turn out to be on Fifty-sixth and Sixth or Fifty-seventh and Fifth—what had all along stood in its way were not these phenomena harmless after all in themselves but the insidious conceptions that had supervened to obnubilate their fertile contour. He thought he heard Fatima calling him back to phenomena, he did not want to see her, not now, he wanted to see Rosalie. Was it too late to exit from the sausage-bomb circus and take up the true work respectably, as a nine-to-five enterprise indistinguishable from every other nine-to-five enterprise.

Halfway through the park he remembered the little island traversable by tramway. Standing over its landscape he saddened at all he was losing, he could have been a true worker and family man, he was neither, would never be either. Going away for good he was not even going of his own initiative, he was being sent and, to recapitulate, for no discernible reason. Maybe it all had to do with the bursting of one of Siggy's hemorrhoids. He belched the phrase: We need you there, and laughed so uproariously the other passengers turned to him in a glorious diapason of contempt whence he looked away toward the coppery smudge deputizing as "sunset above the New Jersey shore." Merely to expose his credulity a smudge was standing in for sunset just as in Paley Park the fat young executive—had he been fat?—had made the sound of a kiss stand in for authentic affection toward—

Everything was a stand-in for the real on convalescent leave. You're taking THINGS TOO FAR, he told himself. You're busy concocting anthologizable observations that have no connection with your real feelings. But how can they not have a connection with those feelings.

High above Manhattan the new buildings starkly repudiated all notion of filigree as well as all leisurely and parodic exertions toward that end. Here and there a few townhouses squeezed between the newer monsters—as if they were the interlopers—still if closely examined oozed— and with a desperation only the likes of Xman could marshal—an exiguity of scrollwork on vasiform balusters. But he—somebody—had made that observation before. Noting a griffin vaguely resembling Rose B. when she spoke menacingly of the implications for reemployment of his suicide attempt(s) Xman felt once more—as he had at the corner of Fifty-sixth and Fifth but not, as it turned out, at the corner of Fifty-seventh and Fifth—completely outside the predicament that would surely haunt him for all eternity. He was now free—but for a split second only—to begin. For a split second turning on his heels though standing absolutely still he was deliriously—uncaptionably—outside—untraceable to—the inherent pathology of his predicament. But just as suddenly with the tramway docking invincibility died and he was once again the peer of turds, toads and flaming manholes and on the lookout for annihilating slights from these and related entities. And as far as he was concerned all entities were related in their effort to blow him to kingdom come. But hadn't he not so long ago—with the sausage-bombs—no regret—he was near obliteration himself—he would pay. As he walked toward the apartment complex invincibility reclaimed him but he did not know if he wanted to be reclaimed just yet. Better this way, he said, but with infinite delight anticipating how absence might purify him at last in their eyes, Rosalie's and the child's. He felt, entering the apartment building, totally impervious to pain, light-almost tenderhearted, the sum of torments and exhilarations that was he, Xman, miraculously cancelling themselves out. Passing through door connecting lobby with elevator the sum of torments and excruciations that was he simultaneously traversed a field in which their own pullulation inflamed and died: The most excruciating episodes of his past, with Rosalie, without—his past a substance of incompatible selves as dusk's Second Avenue was a substance of incompatible glare—managed like sun into black-eyed cloudpouch—to pass through the sieve of temporary oblivion. Yet why now. For no reason at all enjoying a few moments of peace and simultaneously finding it impossible to contend with this peace as offered pressing the correct floor button—five wasn't it—he was gripped with horror. Getting closer and closer to Rosalie and the child he wanted to cry out: What after all is peace and security here and now but anxiety momentarily gone beserk for want of a target. Trying to couple his momentary serenity to some target: A ripped half-full bag of potato chips on the floor, the emergency button, smell of underdone veal steak and finding none would do he decided serenity without target was as excruciating as—more excruciating than—anxiety.

Once out of the elevator he would be free of this excruciation stemming simply from a fleeting independence of stimuli and what stimuli normally ordered him to feel. Once out of the elevator he would be free of this excruciation stemming oh so simply from momentary independence of circumstance. He was too much in pain of eagerness to see Rosalie and the little one—to be able to master the intricacy of this dubious moment out of time. He did not like being, he was discovering, independent of what phenomena normally told him to feel. Though the elevator was slow, maddeningly slow, in opening he knew that if he could only detach himself from these immediate circumstances—this test tube and echo chamber—in which it was bred he would be able to cancel torment forever. As the elevator door suddenly opened it was no longer torment itself but those circumstances beneath which it festered that had to be eliminated. And if, for example, he succeeded in eliminating the circumstances—the stimuli—the epiphenomena—of terrorism then surely he would be able to see his way clear at last to—to—to—the true work and as a nine-to-five enterprise. At any rate, here in the elevator he was conspicuous, scandalously conspicuous, to torment but only under circumstances particular to such an elevator. It was this accursed trip in an elevator following hot on the heels of long walk up along the foul-smelling river from the tramway that was responsible for the torment of feeling free at last of the obligation to respond to contingency—stimulus—epiphenomenon—in the darkest way imaginable—the way, let us say, of Gunhildo né Grigorevitch under the reddish glare of the writhing sconces. He heard someone in the elevator adjacent cry: A bad true worker blames his tools: elevator, smell of steak, lowering river sky. Walking down the corridor he found himself next to a delivery boy from the pizzeria, which he suddenly remembered was a few doors down. Just before reaching her door Xman stopped to watch him stoop down and pick up the debris intentionally cast aside by a horde of brats that had just streamed past. Xman immediately leaped to frame this stooping to tidy up a corridor to which he, the delivery boy, was a mere visitor. And an ill-paid visitor, at that. Having framed he found himself wondering what would happen to an act so framed—packaged—against all eternity. Such an act was out of place in the world though the mistake might lie in—the incongruity might be the result of—his having framed it. Unperceived and unframed the act was perhaps very much of the world along with its perpetrator to whom Xman was generously lending his own desolated outrage. Trapped within the tragical and delicately futile intention loaned it by Xman— by a consciousness such as Xman's—no wonder the act was forcibly disintegrating before his—the world's—very eyes. No, no, no, framed or unframed such an act did not deserve such a world, a world of terrorizing hordes, tomorrow's apprentices to proper sausage placement. The Indian rose and turning to him said, "Once you might have salvaged my act from the heap rising steadily beside the waters of the Ganges. Now you can only, framing, destroy it." Did the Indian mean he, Xman, would one day try to blow him up. Did he mean without authentic commitment to a true work his quasi-hysterical framing was nothing more nor less than a form of annihilation. Did he mean Xman's fortuitous framing required a larger framework offered only by the true work he had renounced. "Your stooping to pick up the excretions of those brats deserves a better world particularly since the world is in so many ways a hideous female as depicted by a quasi-hysterical male—though grossly and grotesquely casual about exploiting already exhausted sites of tribulation—such as yours, my friend—in her infinite fragility she, the old bitch, has always to be protected against the greater grossness and grotesqueness of searing indictment. The world is slime, Indian boy—and that is why I refuse to deliver up at its reliquary the hecatomb of the truest work I know—the world is slime but innocent of anything as brute as stark perception of all it slimily perpetrates with such panache ends up forever suggesting nothing so much as unbruised purity rarissime. Members of the world community condemn my perception of world's slime but not the slime itself: Progenitor of the slime must at all cost be protected against the savage indelicacy of indictment. This is the true atrocity: to perceive and perceiving call slime's attention to the slime, thereby rendering oneself indistinguishable from—grosser than—that slime—as my good friend Gunhildo né Kirillov missing nothing of what was going on there rendered himself indistinguishable from—far grosser than—the lurid light of iniquity's den. Whereas in the active perpetration of whatever makes for the heaped perpetuation of slime—beside or beyond the Ganges—one is considered simply to be ploughing one's way past slime toward progress." "You might have salvaged my act from the slagheap. In a true work." "I cannot fight the slime," Xman replied. "You can only become a part of it," replied the Indian boy holding the wide flat white box very close to his flaring nostrils. There were grease stains at the corners, not at all eight, maybe three, five at most. Xman did not know if his nostrils were flaring but the words—the words!—forever anastomosing in his brain made it so faster than his perceptual apparatus could confirm or deny. "With your bombs and grenades you will become part of the slime." "Compassion drove me to rescue your stooping from the maw of unseeing," Xman shouted, for the boy was now far down the corridor. "Now it is framed—acquired—you want to flush it away, you don't know what to do with your acquisition especially as it begins to stink heartily of the stink of your contour. Framed my act needs—without the larger framework of a nurturing true work—to be flushed away out of sight out of mind. You'll blow it out your ass, maybe you'll get lucky and blow yourself away. And then you won't have to worry any more about being saddled with acts like mine." "That can only alert me to the disjunction between things as they alarmingly are and things as they should be. I hate you for stooping. Your stooping has caused me acute discomfort and me with my rheumatism. I hate myself for perceiving and becoming your stooping. Fatima may be the only way away from such useless acquisition. I'll confess my acquisition the way Gunhildo did." Thinking of him picking up after the little scoundrels made Xman too sick to ring the bell. He walked to the window at the end of the corridor open on the gusty twilight where distant clouds serving as backdrop for more distant boles, boughs, twigs and petioles strove to melt even the stoutest absence of heart entrenched in its own soot. The unbearably brilliant blue slowly descended to the most exquisitely lachrymal shades whose purity was best affirmed by adjacent rust of smokestacks and water towers. When Rosalie opened the door and he saw she was not in the least altered he couldn't stop talking, as if reunion was—had always only been—a matter of his once and for all making up his mind. And here it was made up at last, at least for the moment: He wanted to be back whatever that meant. He caught a glimpse of the child eating out of a narrow-rimmed dish in its high chair, lifting the tiny fork with aplomb, with the high seriousness of a being that will simply not tolerate any lapses at the dinner table. She stepped aside more, he noted with alarm, from a desire to avoid his eye than to encourage entry. "I have to go away soon." "That's why you always come," she said without rancor as if letting the words pursue their own anastomosing inevitability of intention. As his body followed the child's unmistakable scent into the kitchen the corner of his eye noted a third figure beneath the unsheathed bulb at war with the twilight. Its form cried out for the caption: Coping with a stranger's intrusion. Suddenly more than intrusive Xman began infinitely to pity this figure unmarred, from where he tentatively trembled, by ears, nose, throat, forearms, bulk. The features taking shape, "I might as well go," he said speaking from discomfort, no suffocation. He stood over the child, which challenged him with the same quizzically ironic look of the time before, or was it the time before that, had there been a time before that. "Finish up," said the gentle bass. "I might as well go even if the true work never makes itself known. At least I have had my collision—my intimate collision—with Milady Fate in her essence ... of repudiating hausfrau." Rosalie looked quizzical too but with the quizzicalness of wondering when the uninvited guest intended at last to have the decency to make himself forever scarce. "Yes, my intimate collision with fate," he continued, as if overruling an objection. "I have had a collision with fate to which few are privy and the privity somehow rises far above the infinite humiliation to which that demon goddess—her name is Rose—Rosalie—no, not Rosalie—never Rosalie—never had any scruple about exposing me. I have tasted fate in her essence: Fatima. In her adytum of adyta, there where she blithely withholds what she knows rightly mine fleetingly tangent to the ever-receding curb of my festive destiny—why isn't *Pace, pace, mio Dio* being played in the background—I share her mightiest secret. For her refusal to bequeath what is rightfully mine is ultimately infinitely revealing, about her more than about me. I'm nobody, what about you, are you nobody too. Who cares about me, after all. Do you: No, no, no, and rightly so. Can I take the child for a walk. Just one, Rosalie: It's a mild night. We share an earthshattering secret she and I—that is, if mother dearth still has the capacity to be forthrightly shattered given her—its—foul-smelling integument is of the thickest magma known to ichthyosaur—that of my shipwreck compliments of her perversity. But don't grieve or I'll have to depart. I am buoyed up if you must know by this privity of collusion in my own dilapidation. This secret knowledge of fate's active and invidious withholding of a destiny so heartily craved and—as you know better than anybody, Rosalie, my love—for so long may be enough to get me through the flagrant absence of a true work, even worse, sign of a true work's possibility imminent or otherwise. This privity of collusion is a vengeance—an active vengeance—so what if ultimately redounding—rebounding—to my very own discredit. Vengeance is vengeance, saith the Lord. Lord Balls, of course, I won't speak of his Lady-wife. Yes, privity of collusion in my own dilapidation may be enough to get me through—through. And through what, you are right to ask. Through. Through, simply.

Rosalie went toward her baby instinctively as if to protect it. A gesture that speaks volumes, Xman thought. Mesmerized by her gesture he repeated: "Enough to get me through." He did not mention that he was assigned to bomb one of Europe's great industrial headquarters (multinational) where many Nazis were reputed to be still actively engaged. The man of the house watched politely, if grimly. Looking at him Xman said, "You see New York has defeated me. I'm the first to admit it. Humility is one of my changes of garment. In New York—in case you haven't noticed—there is never a sense of the incompatibility of incompatibles. No matter what you annex to street, alley, parksite, it is never out of place. It is absurd therefore to speak of the outrage of incongruity. New York will never be done in by the incompatibility of its components. Blandly, facilely, I might summate intoning: New York is that incompatibility, no more, no less. Yet in my case—take me for example—every new act threatens an already fatuously fragile structural integrity with further insult, every new step threatens to threaten to outface the powers within quaking under a constant tentativeness. How call myself X if I do Y, how do B if already pledged to A. Having done B how resume doing A. My bosses have of course tried to assure me that for a terrorist there are no incompatibles. Or rather nothing is more incompatible with than anything else. But long ago I stopped listening to their conception of how to make others undergo doctrines crucially different from those others' own. As Rosalie will tell you, I don't traffic in doctrines." She was looking at the child and weeping. "Maybe I'd better leave," the other man said. "This is your home," Rosalie said staunchly as if defending her own version of doctrine, but it was clear from something deeper than mere tone of voice that she did want him to leave. Entering what he remembered to have been their bedroom Xman felt an unbearable upsurge of hope that Rosalie would take him back intensified by the proximity of this apparent good provider whose presence, present or absent, made such a change of tack highly improbable. Sitting across from him she gave free rein to her weeping. The child regarded respectfully. "Do you remember when you wept over me for being a fumbling little clerk on my way nowhere." He went to the window, a large photograph of the child on a tricyclette reflected in its depths. "My problem all along has been to think that through abstention from all recognizable acts I could be supremely inconspicuous. But you saw right through me." Stroking the child's scanty hair Rosalie said: "I think I saw you but I didn't always like myself for not liking what I saw." "I'm a terrorist now," he said. "I'm no longer doing the bare minimum necessary to survive in behalf of the true work." "A terrorist!" she cried. "A terrorist!" The child, infected by her laughter, began throwing morsels of lukewarm gruel in Xman's direction. Trying to maintain a certain seriousness, or at least equilibrium, as she stooped to pick up the morsels Rosalie intoned, "Yes, I was worried about what would happen to you once you were cast out into the street, blinded by the brilliance of your own cumulative ineptitude, your long unfamiliarity with the way of the world's insistence on competence and efficiency." Looking around Xman noticed the jacket from a blue suit hanging neatly over the chair far down the living room as well as an attaché case—the kind that proliferates madly on subway platforms during the rush hours—beside a worn-out cushion, color indecipherable in the growing gloam. "I had my true work!" he cried, in defiance less of her than of the attaché case and blue suit. But was it, in fact, less of her. "I was always banking on apotheosis via the true work." As she did not answer Xman bent over and kissed the child. "A farewell kiss," he said. Then, more brutally, "And now that I have finally abandoned a middling approach to success you are still discontented and you will never be content, at least with me. But you seem to have found what you were always looking for." "And you are able to give up your child to a stranger." In way of answer he said, "You know, when I am with you and look with you at what you see of me I feel utterly damned. Stop. And at the same time it is not so damning. Stop. For what does your seeing see—Stop—but my own blithe lack of awareness. All along I thought to perceive—to see what through their loathsome obtuseness others are not equipped to see was to trespass. And now I am suddenly told not seeing I trespass: quite refreshing. Stop. All along you were watching and damning when you seemed to have your eye on nothing—Stop—in particular. But watching and damning not my proverbial perception-voracity in high gear but on the contrary my failure to perceive, my blindness to being and my place therein. How could I not have sensed your verdict from the very beginning. This is what is so humiliating, so debasing. And at the same time— Stop—refreshing. If only I had all along been aware of your mounting exasperated despairing contempt for a flunkey's deplorable quiescence I wouldn't feel now so rawly exposed. I would never have allowed you to trick me into siring a—" But he did not say the words.

"And yet," she began, "it must as you say be something of a relief to see yourself as you claim I see you—a public man with grave vocational and therefore financial problems. Don't my solicitous tears—so what if evoked only retrospectively—purge you in a sense at least a little of all your private terrors. Doesn't my flat-footed concern for the public—the social—Xman allow said Xman prescinding from the torpid miscellany of private terror to metamorphose into any one of the myriad in blue suits/attaché cases. You know the type: caption: 'The boss has to pay me more if I'm going to put in THESE KIND OF hours.' My tears then—didn't they—don't they—paint you as archetypal everyman confronted with everyday excruciation and therefore purged of your personal purulence that under so many circumstances—even that of your aborted true work—was more a shackle than an asset. Isn't it something of a thrill—Stop—to be outside the cell of a private anguish promoted as it were to the prison courtyard among your congeners." "The novelty wears off fast," he said. "But please let me take the child out for a little walk." "We'll both go," she surprised him by saying, "wait, I'll get my coat and tell Jim we're going out." In the street they all three but not in unison sniffed the mild night, crossed the street and walked toward the river, suddenly he felt—from the way they turned to the river and this time all in unison, the way God meant it to be—this was something they did every night after dinner. For a split second he loved this membership in a family group. Then the walk began to feel imposed. He looked at the walk and felt suffocated in his chest. Then he wanted to puke less at the state of affairs than at the name for this state of affairs—family group member-ship. Will we ever look back on this cul-de-sac, he wanted to cry out, will we ever get beyond it. The child pointed at the water, which did not flow nor splash against the upraised rocks. "It's the river flowing," he remarked and was immedi-ately enthralled by the kindness in his tone, the imperson-ation of kindness. For the duration of the simple utterance he felt completely transformed and outside his destiny. De-ferring to—naming a phenomenon—paradoxically he felt further than he had ever been from what he had all along construed—constructed—as most suffocating of destinies, one amassed from such deferential naming. Calling a spade a spade deferring to the river by its right name he felt at last that he stood a chance of thwarting the loading of the deck— since as far back as the orphanage—that was his life. Naming with the right name, resigned to correctly naming he was suddenly calm enough to take the child, its odor irresistible still, in his arms, through the corner of his eye he saw Rosalie was moved, as he gave the child back to her she said, "But it's not a substitute for being there all the time, being there when he laughs, when he cries, watching him grow out of my nightmares and his own—" "I have to go now," he said. "I have so many last minute preparations to make." "It's just that for the last few years our life has been so difficult," she said.

He shook his head with disgust, suddenly feeling righteous yet disgusted with the possibility—the futility—of righteousness. "In the last few years. When you mean the last few months—weeks—days—minutes you say 'years' and when you mean the last few milliseconds you manage to say 'the last few years.' I can't keep up with your wearisome expansions and contractions of time." He would have liked her to ask, Why are you going, Why have you joined up with them, so he could reply this time without telegrammatic stop signs, Doing what they tell me to do I have a better idea of what the true work is, or rather, what it isn't. I would have liked my targets to undergo indirectly what I came close to choosing to depict. But that isn't possible. So I have no alternative BEFORE THE END but to blow up buildings, cars, bridges—anything that can be made to have the decency to stand still for the sketch of its own obliteration—and in this way I'm sure those involved undergo—but of course not indirectly. He wanted to burst out laughing "uncontrollably" but

511

was unable. During the ride back he did not look out on the city, he only thought: A week ago I first met Fatima, two weeks ago I had thrown myself in front of truck for the second time, three weeks ago . . . , fascinated by the supposedly stark contrast between two disparate events disjoined by a standard unit of measurement. A week before . . . two weeks before . . . here he was delivering up life-events or what he made pass for same to the economy of language so they might profit from that economy and attain among themselves and emphatically in relation to themselves a perduring distinctness as discretely delirious jumps—leaps—out of brute duration's continuous slime, at least from the vantage of one who ordinarily detested discontinuity, disorder, routine's violation. Violation of routine meant disintegration of Hopiesque cumulative impact presentable as indicated toward mammoth reparation for services rendered, excruciations endured, and all in the name of a destiny whose fabric was still patchy. Through language he was being allowed to undergo discontinuity, stark leaps though standing still. Had he striven to be meeting Fatima one week and leaping in front of a truck the next. By both establishing the distance of one week/two/three and dragging in their overload of connotation language imposed retrospective stark contrast within a limited interval, made a stew out of a clear soup. The leap of stark contrast retrospectively imposed did nothing, then, to disrupt the ever-cumulative behemothoid propulsion of routine. And he was even able to foresee yet another retrospect from whose heights he would surely be saying, One week ago I was with wife and son, bathing not far from a willow copse next to a cemetery overlooking the sea in a quiet lake among the mountains. As the tram docked, this time in Manhattan, he felt himself advancing—advancing—toward—toward— The plunge forward no matter what became his carefully guarded secret, bedrock of

his life's long dissimulation, sole trump card against his enemies should their derision suddenly become too mammoth.
I am advancing toward death, he said, where no one can hurt
me. To look at me who would think that I harbor this secret
being able to die. The secret made him feel infinitely strong,
even stronger knowing this was a secret nobody else harbored.

Returning from a last farewell to Rosalie and the child and
having identified his trump card he got off the tramway intending quickly to relish this being able to stand at a new
infinite distance from things, he looked around, purposely
cultivating an estrangement that his forefinger tapping
against his ear deemed nothing short of delicious. But then
obliged at the Fifty-ninth Street token booth to wait on line
at least twenty minutes for the downtown local he was immediately overcome with the old rage as sole vital figure in
the tapestry of his wretchedness. Stamping his foot and grit-
ting his teeth quickly demolished any recently cultivated
pretensions to a genteel, baffled, ethereal estrangement—to
a new life. Frustration, he knew, immediately identified
what he was and always would be, trump or no trump.
Scooping his four dollars' worth of coins he heard the token
vendor say, "You are not as delicately at a loss in the face of
phenomena as this brief abstention from phenomena managed to make you want to think. You simply hadn't yet come
across the right occasion for recrudescence of those gestures—renewed now, I see, without the slightest difficulty—
that tell you what you are, I mean, of course, a loathsome
failure. I know, I know, getting off the purificatory—the lustral—tramway you had for the briefest of intervals begun to
feel like everybody else, like everyman, as you had when . . ."
. . . Over his fate Rosalie had made it her business to weep
tears blindingly abject and precise. For the briefest of intervals he had been able to impersonate everyman as he, no-

body-man, imagined everyman to be. He had begun looking at phenomena—overpainted women in mink coats entering a fashionable department store, a pair of ugly lovers arguing next to a fire hydrant, a fire truck rising in the shadow of equestrian Bolívar to the challenge of a rut festooning the roadway—as he believed others—those without his trump card—must look—with both relish for a duration made to the measure of their essence and deference to distance from that busily populated duration. At last he had begun acquiring the communal jabbering delight in silent awe of the masses respecting duration of and distance from phenomena, or if not quite acquiring that plodding jabbering delight then shorn of the rage to collide with and plough through he was at least shedding the usual disgust that refusing to die, be done, have done, these phenomena were simply not yielding up their secrets fast enough for one with his garbled itinerary. But no, but no, things were as they had always been, once again more than ever he wanted to get through phenomena to extract their vital secret—their malevolent intention—for use by, in, the true work. The true work. He laughed out loud, for dear life hanging on to a strap though there were plenty of seats—laughed out loud at the unbridled preposterousness of such a pretension still refusing to say die—laughed so loud the few other passengers all looked up then away from yet another madman with whom it was injudicious to make even marginal eye contact. He laughed out loud for his raging impatience with regard to the things of the world was no different essentially than that triggering Fatima's truck with sausage-shaped bombs and doughnut-lustered grenades. One sitting contentedly with hands folded was clearly one of the blessed myriad who respected the duration of—"It takes, Mabel, as long as it has to take, my hemorrhoidectomy, I mean"—as well as distance from—"I liked my seat in the fourth ring: Some folks get fidgety and claim they can't see a single entrechat but I—" —phenomena, phenomena, the meat and potatoes of any self-respecting and phenomena-respecting true worker. About to relinquish strap and sit down to hands folded like a real man he suddenly remembered all that disqualified him for such a stance of rankest impersonation. At any rate, the train was pulling into foul familiar Forty-second.

Back at the hotel Fatima told him he would be leaving first-class the following night but that during the day they wanted him to attend the funeral of the fraud and scoundrel recently triturated by Gunhildo no longer né Grigorevitch and an Associate . . . Yes, yes, they had been a little hard on him in Paley Park, yes yes the frondlets had that effect on both of them, but this wasn't Paley and deep down they were conscious of "the kind of work he was trying to do." They sounded like some mustachioso who once long ago had been found—out—"chatting with boss and daughter." She absolutely insisted he attend—if the *Times* was to be believed and it was, always, this was the event of the year: At any rate he was being paid to put in more than an appearance at such functions, in fact there was a generous check waiting for him on the dresser upstairs, small recompense for a job damned well done. Something compelled him to say, "If only you could explain more clearly what is wanted, what is needed. I'm just a tiny bit adrift. Gunhildo has been here much longer than I but even he seems from time to time overwhelmed by a dark dank mass of preconceptions that simply, when you come right down to it, will not serve." Fatima sighed deeply. "Tomorrow at the funeral we will explain why we can't explain. In other words, why communication of the way to salvation is impossible. At the funeral, okay." Xman felt she spoke ominously or was trying to speak ominously.

He wanted to tell her he wasn't in the least afraid of funerals. But though sorely tempted he thought it best to say

515

nothing. Hadn't he been sorely tempted when Rose Baldachino asked about Rosalie's delicate condition to bypass the
garrulity of concerned husband and imminent father and
animadvert on the fates' perverse obstruction of a passage. to
Balanchiniana (minuet for four black duchesses, gigue, lord's
prayer, theme and variations).

Once they were on their way wearing a white turban and
pearl earrings, "It's not every day," she said, "that you get a
chance to go to the funeral of the visiting dignitary you
yourself have helped to blow to bits." S/M nodded sagely,
automatically. Xman said, "I thought he was a slumlord." At
first Fatima did not answer. "He is everything you think he is
and more. He is dead." Then death, Xman thought, must turn
out to be just the phenomenon I am looking for: captionless
and devoid of symptomal content. The main thoroughfare of
this outlying borough was deserted for better or worse: They
had it almost to themselves. In the funeral parlor the usual
little groups regarded each other with a contemptuous curiosity bordering on high sanctimony. The dead man, then,
was a hot property over which each strove to exert supreme
proprietary right based on the evident peerlessness of its
own inconsolable bereavement. Xman felt himself growing
more and more impatient to see not so much the dead man
as death as the epiphenomenal refutation of all captions and
all symptomlike content conducive to caption-making.
Once again as on the tramway he felt he was on the verge of
achieving an—the—optimal distance from phenomena vital
to the genesis of the true work's possibility. Near death he
felt closer than ever to the possibility of a true work's flowering. Before he even saw the coffin he wanted to be—to impersonate—the dead man. Then he wondered if he really did
have this feeling or was he trying to have it by impersonating
one who had it. He wanted to be born posthumously, like the
dead man. He heard someone say the pieces had been

patched together to create a plausible dead man. For a second he trembled. Surely, however, this remark did not mean the dead man was in any way captioned, reduced in stature, the stature of dimensionlessness, a looking back on life.

Xman squatted to look. The dead man looked back as if about to be born as everything he had in vain striven to be. Sitting down, overcome with excitement and envy, Xman observed Fatima commingling, commiserating. Didn't the others see make-up and turban set off authentic death's head. But merely because she was its embodiment did not mean she could understand his longing for . . . communion with death. Going back to the faint smile on the face of his victim he suddenly wanted to leave but saw it was now time to greet the diminutive and exquisitely well-dressed widow holding court more angry than grieving in a side parlor. Faces rose out of the crowd in that small room, each asserting its claim to primacy in grieving. The son, presumably of the deceased, stood proud and tall: With horror Xman realized he was being pushed toward the grieving dyad and with even greater horror that the son at the approach of each mourner was opening wide his arms like a true man of God or a vampire bat in order to bury them both in a global embrace, without the slightest trace of the ambivalence or sense of absurdity that was overwhelming Xman more and more in these moments of waiting. The embrace killed each mourner briefly then released him/her from death. Physical contact was death: If he was to do his true work he must steer clear of human flesh. With pure terror Xman realized once again and strangely without a tinge of regret that he was queuing up for his ration of communion. Could he say, Communion is not in my line. For the son, so decent you wanted to drag him out into the muted sunlight and strangle him on the spot, communion was clearly in everybody's line. Everybody stewing in the heterogeneity pot was capable and worthy of communion. As the bereaved took him under his wing, woolly and warm, Xman told himself: I am doing this not for the sake of Fatima and the boys—Rose B. was right, any display of enthusiasm for anything other than the true work had been, was, an impersonation, of which he, Xman, had hoped to become the biggest dupe—but for the true work. Under the wing of the bereaved he could see and hear nothing—could only imagine everybody else stopping dead in the tracks of their struggle for priority in bereavement to scrutinize his fatuity, no longer warm, no longer woolly. He could not respond to the embrace. He underwent the embrace announcing they were here to "share their pain." He was captioned, then, once again. Only a dead man eluded caption, he was sure of it. He intended to learn from the dead duck. What enraged was that he hadn't been allowed to choose this sharing of pain. It was assumed he wanted nothing more than to undergo an embrace saying, You too are my brother though I have never laid eyes on you in my life. If you are here then at some point, God damn it, or rather, God bless it, our paths must have crossed and we must have shared a moment that burned bright with mutual sympathy, similar to those shared every day of the work week by potbellied stockbrokers relieving themselves on adjacent johns. There was only one refuge from such suffocating presumptions: the true work. He had to get back to the true work, to somehow enclose this easily captionable chance encounter within the framework of that work. From his wing's inflection it was clear the bereaved believed he was not so much depriving Xman of a choice as sparing him its excruciation. How could he say, I would have preferred exclusion, he could not speak, for the event and its participants had long before been embroiled in and obliterated by a caption: We comfort each other in the moment of our pain. It was the caption that suffocated even more than the warm woolly wing of the bereaved's limp presumption. But was it in fact true that the caption suffocated more: Were words anastomosing again, even here, with supreme profaneness, in this house of the lord. He needed the true work. Only the true work would submerge these caption-events, events which became the bloodless epiphenomenon of the virulent vaunting captions they invoked. Never again did he want to be caught in a caption the way a tiger behind bars is caught by the leer of the proverbial fat boy (toy camera, peanut brittle, fly pried open by bulging belly). "Such a nice boy," he heard some nearby frump declare and at once he knew she must be very chic and in her bleached blond coiffure very much a part of the heterogeneity circus taking up temporary residence here. "Yes," said her companion with a whining piousness that invoked a landscape of doily-covered hibiscus. When he was released Fatima wandered over. He had his antennae out for the slightest sign of the dead man's captionization. "Don't you just loathe families," she murmured, taking his arm. "Do you remember the clan next to my hotel room that first night?" he dared. She did not respond. "Especially families 'pulling together in a crisis.' " Xman realized he too might have been captioned in just this way by some particularly acute onlooker. Reverting to the son still enfolding unwary mourners in his arms, he quickly turned away for the gesture, as oppressive as ever, only got in the way of its own reconstruction, attacked his far meatier vision of its true being. It was his gesture now. Turned away he played back the gesture over and over as Fatima babbled on. Yet playing it back he began barely to exorcise the demon—that is to say, the caption—not so latent in its steely genteelness. The hearty trust embodied was so straightforward as to be almost diabolical. Xman could not refrain from looking back one last time and catching a glimpse of a certain strain, even maniacal, in son's engagement with his latest conquest, was able perfectly to isolate the tyrannical rigidity generating the moments of the stance's unfolding. This stance stalwartly refused the evidence of the senses, abjuring the encroachment of any data other than that fostering an even more suffocating commitment to warmth, woolly woolly warmth, warmth as defiance, warmth with a vengeance, licensed to kill, warmth despotic despotically naive and shortsighted. Others were also looking around not like Xman as if lost but simply to manifest their ease, their sense of belonging to the grieving inner circle, their self-satisfied glances defying the riffraff to mar the occasion's solemn homogeneity of pious prostration before an authentic mentor. He felt Fatima pushing him forward. "Go to the son," she whispered, hadn't she seen him, he had to get used to orders, sure enough, the bereaved cradled him again, didn't seem to remember it was he, Xman. When he was able to extricate himself once again from the death-clasp of life-affirming hyperrigidity, moving off he tried to stay far from Fatima. He could see her in the distance giving helpful hints to widow and daughter-in-law. Even from a distance Xman perceived the daughter-in-law, plump and prim in the limelight, was beginning to loathe the likes of Fatima. When he began to feel uncomfortable for Fatima he remembered she was tone-deaf to—against—the amenities, the little graces, of everyday life, imprudently imposing herself and her points of view whenever and wherever they were least needed and solicited. Unlike Xman, Fatima did not dread outbursts, hostility and irritation—she relished them. Rebuff was eagerly solicited in order to be formulated—bracketed away for future reference—as outrageous ingratitude in the face of helpful hints perpetrated with master-class tact. As the widow intoned on the incomprehensibility of God's ways Xman was surprised to see that Fatima clasped her hands with evident passion. If she happened to be the local head of an international network she was also and just as passionately the vessel of a crude determined piety very much lost, during its accesses, to the world. Or was she merely playing at being lost. Was this simply another form of scrutiny. Wasn't it true that when seemingly most given up to her trances Fatima was at the height of vigilance.

As they all filed in for what the same blond frump of a short time before insisted was bound to be "a most beautiful service" one friend of the deceased—Xman was still on the lookout for demeaning captions—said to another, "I found him. I was the one. Lying there. The trees," (Gingkos? Xman tried hard to remember), "smelled like death. He smelled like death. But they smelled worse. I found him. First I thought he was one lousy drunk. Then I saw it was him. Our poker crony. The one who always made it his business to fart between rounds or during the game to distract his opponents. Lowest of the low." The old friend, newly elected star of the show, spoke sneeringly. But what was his target? Death? the gingkos? the friend discovered among the dead leaves? What was he denigrating or was death its own denigration, its own denigrating caption. Yes, death was its own denigration, denigrating caption, no longer a trump card elevating one enigmatically among the stars. This was the meaning of death. Xman spewed out the meaning: He was no friend to such meanings, fruit of the adroit anastomosis of words. Death was now as denigrating—no no no—as a walk down the corridor past cubicle after cubicle of Fish's or was it O'Kay's labyrinth of lucky devils. Death was now its own bad press. Death too was eminently captionable. No, no, no.

"Yes, yes, yes," Xman cried out as they descended the steps into the warmth of the chapel's early afternoon, "you were the goddamned star of the show, you little putz. You're not like the other mourners gathered here in the presumption of their insignificance. You're special! You're outside the grieving inner circle whose prestige comes down to nothing more than faster captionability. You see through the pretensions of the dead man. For what is more presumptuous—pretentious—than a dead man claiming as he lies there in state to have had the last word at last. And you are absolutely right to expose him for is there anything more scandalously bad-mannered than to drop down dead in gingko mush. A troublemaker, that's what he was, every corpse is. That's why we must shovel it away as soon as possible. And if it weren't for you—if you hadn't seen fit to rescue him from an improvised bier of smelly leafage where, to judge from the uncensored crooked smile even the mortician couldn't rectify, he seemed ever so content to lie—he'd still be decomposing there, a feast for dogs. You took one dirty dog out of the gutter and with the purest Old World tact, demanding no fee, procured for him some semblance of salvation." Several times Fatima made halfhearted efforts to silence him but her giving up quickly suggested she took a vicarious pleasure in his spewing forth. Once everyone was seated inside the chapel a lithe sallow young man who bore a marked resemblance to everybody's favorite undertaker's son—Xman was not ridiculing the man nor even the profession of undertaker, only a world that went to the trouble of sponsoring such possibilities, conceiving such captionabilities—advanced on the podium with what looked like a telegram ostentatiously dangling from one hand. "It bereaves and behooves me to announce," he remarked in the tone of one doing his utmost to suppress a giggle, "to announce that the reverend father—Father of the Marshalsea, to be exact—elected to deliver the farewell sermon has been blown up en route. We had no choice but to solicit the services of a surrogate. He will be arriving shortly." Before he finished speaking the undertaker's son (whose name was Bennett since a sibilant female or perhaps genderless voice was shrieking,

"Bennett! Bennett!" from the wings) was already looking above the heads of the congregation, past the double doors to the great outdoors of sky, leaf, turnpike, reminding Xman thereby of his Columbus Circle ploy—had it been his or some other's whose name escaped him—for foiling the lean guitarist striving at all costs to impose his bracketing soundtrack on the monochromatic motions of the nine-to-five crowd. Just when Xman thought the favorite son was about to descend he cleared his throat and added, "But please everybody, sit absolutely still. After all we all need spiritual guidance, a plan of life. We need to have this plan of life communicated to us by experts in the field, adepts, seers, soothsayers, and the like. We need to move forward. And so the very reverend surrogate seer will soon be here to move us all forward. Don't go 'way now folks." As Bennett moved up the aisle, Siegfried eyeing him obsequiously said, "Good, we have a few minutes. So—you'll be going off tonight. We have to get all your papers ready, you'll be meeting somebody by the name of Merdouille."

Emboldened by the chaos let loose on the world through the assassination of the man of God Xman cried: "You're giving me departure instructions when I need some form of spiritual guidance. Don't you see my one trump card—death—has been exploded. Death doesn't look back on all other states and is therefore not outside bracketing, labelling, straitjacketing, formulation, contempt. You heard that old geezer talking about our friend. Talking about him when I wanted to believe he—someone—was at last inconceivable to the forms of talk. His pals don't remember his leonine if piecemeal majesty set against the luminosity of fan-shaped gingko figments. No, they gripe at an old thug shamelessly allowing himself to be caught dead as a dog amid the suffocating stench of some grimy little leafheaps." Swallowing a sob Xman added: "I need somebody's advice because I'm leaving tonight—for a better world, hopefully—and I see that even in death—" Fatima snorted into the neighboring pew, he did not know quite why, the target was as unlocalizable as her shrug's centuries before in Paley Park. Siegfried said suddenly: "All direct communication defrauds the novice. What good is an experience you have not lived. And the defrauding is not only of the novice, namely you, but of the communicator, namely me. For if I tell you that when you arrive in such and such a port with such and such an ambience based on my experience you should do such and such, then I imply I am no longer an existing individual. I have become frozen, no longer subject to qualification, fixed and formulated beyond the intervention of all further, modifying, experience. I become your idealized dead man—the dead man your dead man refuses, and rightly, to become. And when I tell you to call on such and such an agent, to place your gun in such and such a position, then I am actively obliterating your relation to the great out-there. Your relationship to your vocation, to the blowing up of this or that structure, this or that dignitary, is no longer absolute and fruit of your absolute acumen and commitment. You are made to lose sight of the target in your submission to the rules of the game—my rules. I cannot do such a thing to my little Xman. You may fail—but fail on your own terms. Even if your failure has such unwelcome consequences for the project that we ultimately have no alternative but to plug you out in Jersey." Fatima giggled so volubly that a pew warmer had to turn around, almost but not quite reprovingly. "Tell him his memory will live on. Like the dead man's." "I want you to understand," said Siegfried, disregarding the giggles as if downright blasphemous to the purity of his intention, "that on my part it requires not a niggardliness of spirit but on the contrary special discipline to abstain from meddling with your relationship to the vocation—our vocation. At this very moment I'm sorely tempted to hold forth. But I refrain. Dear boy, I refrain. For true teacher that I am I know a direct relation between pupil and teacher does not exist. You'll never reach the truth I have reached through an apelike approximation process. In any case what I have reached has nothing to do with you even if we both seem to be after the same: right of peoples to life, liberty, pursuit of happiness, safe and decent workplace, holiday pay, insurance, pension fund, schooling opportunities for chips off the old block, etc.

"Communication—communication—I'm sick to death of it. Didn't we and only a short time ago undergo enough communication to last us a lifetime—I mean in the alcove with widow woman and her scrawney offspring taking everybody and his Dutch uncle under warm woolly wing. Communication—of results—is simply the most unnatural form of intercourse between man and man: Fondling of genitalia is far more truthful. All kidding aside, far more important than truth is the manner of its acquisition. The truth of sausage-bomb-throwing comes in the actual and particular throwing. My truth of bomb-throwing is, from your perspective, stark untruth. Truth is determined by its particular mode of acquisition but communication is not a viable mode of acquisition. If you live in the truth of bomb-throwing and I live in the truth of bomb-throwing then that living in the truth, of x, is by no means the cuddly communion of two sickeningly apoplectic Wall Street chumchums strutting arm-in-arm at midday across Hanover Square to the nearest chophouse, but rather the lordly separation within which each one of us persists in cuddling his individual truth of x.

"Do you think, Xman dear boy, you will be able to cuddle your truth in private without assistance from me. My words may have some resonance even for the true work since rumor has it you haven't completely relinquished your belief in that phantom—and I do not, for once, use the word 'phantom' denigratingly. In any case, Xman, it may take time to learn to cuddle that truth, to sing the song of yourself as our precursor Walt enjoined. And please Xman—" Siegfried said suddenly, bouncing forward from the back seat as if the conversation had long ago died, "Please don't write or wire us from abroad. Don't call us, we'll call you. Merdouille is a very competent fellow: he's bright, he knows what's going on, he'll take care of you!" Ogling Fatima conspiratorially he would have looked positively porcine if he hadn't been so haggard.

"He isn't always very subtle," Fatima said in a thick drugged voice as if with apparent inconspicuity prompting Siegfried. "Yes, yes, yes, he isn't very subtle. Exactly, he isn't very subtle. Exactly, he isn't very subtle. And that is why he may attempt to lasso you into some kind of misguided doctor/patient, apostle/disciple relationship. But don't be fooled. Don't become Merdouille's patient. Remember that every direct communication about how to place a bomb, how far away to stand from one's target, what kinds of food to consume to avoid, on the fateful day, preoccupations with farting and the like—every direct communication, remember, is a misunderstanding, can always only be a misunderstanding. Nothing will come of it—you'll be sadder, not wiser, never wiser, for the wisdom of another is equivalent to the emperor's newest clothes. Remember, Xman, at the present stage— and we can only speak of the present state of things—truth has become trivial. People's brains are crammed full of the inessential, the false, the meretricious. So that the art of communication becomes the art of subtraction, of abstention such as you claimed to practice when it came to collaborating on the celebrated fabric of your destiny. Yes, yes, yes, we know all about that fabric and the horde and the hierodules.

"Think of the benighted billions out there, their head full of the media's glaring imagery of folk wisdom: raster, cauli-flower, headlines, video game strategies. So that in such cases does rational communication consist in stuffing them full of even more junk or does it consist instead in taking some of it away or rather in abstaining from any form of mediation whatsoever—driving them crazy in other words with one's refusal to participate in the gourmandizing game. I'll answer for you. I'll tell you point blank. Communication consists in abstaining in order to drive them crazy—so crazy that the collective head is able at last to disgorge its fateful surfeit. I am tempted to say, so that they recant, but there is no question here of belief. They don't believe in what they embody, that with which they overflow. As you observed today, Fatima embodies death but refuses to believe in it. Xman—I'm going to give it to you straight from the shoul-der—when a man proclaims as loudly as you that he needs advice the key is either to abstain or furnish knowledge but in a form so strange it produces an utter and paroxysmal decentering of the assimilating organism: This form of knowledge-presentation is in fact the purest form of sub-tracting the inessential, the crude, crass, nasty, brutish and, alas, not short enough. The true teacher presents knowledge as strangeness with contours and facets that do nothing so much as disorient the jaded recipient although ultimately he may very well find he had more than enough equipment for assimilation of the quondam unassimilable. With such knowledge-presentation, the novice/pupil is suddenly re-quired to undergo data with all of his being. As Roland Barthes told me in Warsaw when we thought of blowing up the wheat commissariat, Landowska played Bach with far more than her fingertips. In any case, it is a paroxysmal undergoing that must take place. Once the pupil has somehow surmounted the blessed resistance of its matter—most beautiful word in the language: Resistance—he can—you can—be said to have assimilated knowledge. Nothing by the way, dearest Xman, comes to fruition without the most ungovernable resistance to the aim, professed or simply sniffed out with outrage."

"This is what I always sought to make of the true work," Xman said weakly, realizing with the deepest regret he had ever experienced that he was bereft of models. It was all a fiction—what had Siegfried called it a minute ago, phantom. He could no longer go wandering about the city as he had in the time of Rollins speaking only of the true work. No one was going to take him seriously without palpable proof of— of— "What," Fatima said dully.

"An occasion for undergoing—strenuous undergoing— whereby the initiand ultimately lives the phenomenon—in this case true work—with a force and vitality beyond whatever mere depiction may offer. The true work should— should have—both provoked and stymied—resisted—the initiand's undergoing of its depthless depth. But I see I will never live to play out my commitment to the true work. Don't you see, slobs that you are, the true work as a form of direct communication—yes, direct communication—would have circumvented the dilemma of direct communication by forcing recipient—pupil—spectator—to undergo even more strenuously than the producer. There is a message buried in the heart of the true work as there was an insidious intention buried not so very deep within the heart of every stimulus with which you had the audacity to afflict me on my way to this point. There was malevolence at the heart of the noise, Fatima, as there was malevolence in the fuming horseshit smearing the curb beneath the statue of Bolívar or is it San Martín, I can never remember. And need I in fact remember. Where was I, where was I. There is a message—a result—buried at the heart of the true work but the communication of this result does not cancel self-activity—undergoing—of personal appropriation on the part of spectator/consumer/consumer-pupil. And the result—the message—knows it will always be misunderstood and is able to assimilate all misunderstandings. In short, only with the true work is there a message—a direct communication—but the direct communication is precisely the receiver's sinuous undergoing of direct communication." "Keep trying," Siegfried murmured. "Keep trying, be your own man, glad to hear it. Only don't make the mistake of falling into that damned doctor/patient relation with Merdouille. There may be moments when Merdouille begins to see you as an interesting case. He may admire your technique, you may be tempted to undergo such admiration as a terrible waste of time. For haven't you come to Merdouille to be rehabilitated, admit it. No, you have not. You most certainly have not. And doesn't his admiration or at any rate his interest prove you are being insufficiently rehabilitated. There is no wounding here, you are thinking, wounding to irreparable enlightenment. You may start out prostrating yourself completely before the master 'from whom you have so so much to learn.' (It is not we responsible for such a delusion.) And little by little you discover there are striking similarities between you—master and pupil. After all, you both fart, piss, shit, eat strawberries and rancid cream. Little by little you affirm yourself and find he willingly lends his ear. And you are momentarily pleased, then disappointed. How dare he show any interest in you as an equal—even as an inferior with some similarities. You, in your smallness, should be inconceivable to him likewise inconceivable in his greatness to you. You feel therefore you are cancelling yourself away: Depicting yourself for his delectation becomes a form of cancellation. You wait for your true medicine: For you are a

529

patient, after all. Didn't Fatima first come upon you as a patient. Not that WE ever wished you to go there as a patient. But when you are being tortured you feel you are at last acquiring your rightful due—rehabilitation in substantive dosages. Tortured you are clearly in the presence of what will refund you to yourself and as more than yourself. Fighting against the other's diagnosis (in vain, since it is accepted from the start, earlier even than the start)—fighting against the inevitable—more real than its target—you—could ever turn out to be—turns out to be—exhilarating. But we don't want this to happen. We warn you in advance. Remember: Whatever is possible for Merdouille—as a master artisan, I mean—though he has been within the organization much longer—is possible for you. And any being who actively encourages your belief in his monopoly of that possibility by divine right or any other hocus-pocus is a charlatan. Do you hear—a charlatan."

When the spokesman surrogate finally arrived most of the congregation was fast asleep. Even the widow of the dead man looked as if she was about to succumb. Robustly fat he put both arms on the lectern and twitching from nave to chaps proceeded as follows: "We all know how the dear departed met his end. We all know how the Very Reverend met *his* end. Terrorism is being pawned off as a corrective for all ills. So before we all die—I have a premonition that we are all to die here and now—I believe it my duty—even if I am but a mere surrogate—to furnish a countercorrective. A countercorrective, yes, a countercorrective. There are enemies among us, yes, enemies. Don't look around. But these enemies consider themselves the good ones. The damned good, as it were. They don't seem to realize that we have a team of psychiatrists, psychologists, social workers, geneticists, and attorneys working day and night to pinpoint the childhood congeries responsible for the doings of such good ones. Don't they read the *New York Times, New York, Gotham Fartmobile.* At any rate since they refuse to be put in their place by the monumentality of these rags, to say nothing of the credentials of those who agree to publish there—I'm talking about a team of psychiatrists, psychologists, social workers, geneticists, and attorneys working day and night to pinpoint the childhood congeries responsible for the doings of such goods—I have no recourse but to turn them in. Not to the international mounted police nor to the diaper brigades of counterterrorism but to you, the people. They call themselves, the good. But they are not good. For good people ramify and evolve from a triumphant affirmation of what they are IN THEMSELVES. These slime in contrast affirm themselves in opposition to what is already there—outside. For our so-called good ones all action is reaction and by reaction they killed the dear departed. Out of the kindness of his heart he was determined to dedicate—no consecrate—the golden years to razing the wreckage of a city in decay to make way for a future of eye-healing hi-rises replete with burnished mullions, rooftop saunas, impeccably shod doormen. So what did these ingrates do—they made him a marked man, they did him in. If you look around—but don't look around, don't look around—you'll see them changing before your very eyes. For these good souls evolve from their target as an afterthought: Sucking its blood they feel themselves beginning to . . . be. But it is only an impersonation of being, a gross imposture. Yes, yes, yes, benighted ones, I know what you are going to say: Hasn't our friend and others like him been responsible for the eviction, deterioration and death of decent hardworking citizens—you know, DECENT HARDWORKING CITIZENS, phrase-prop of advertising and political campaigns. Yes, but we cannot expect blond beasts of prey like the dear departed to remain perpetually confined within the bounds of superconscientiousness, loyalty, and respect toward his own kind without once in a while craving a mere student prank or two. We must revere such lapses and not judge them as we judge the antics of the good ones. Who wouldn't prefer these blond beasts, inspiring through their hi-rises and rise-highers a happy mixture of triumphant fear and invigorating awe. How could we have expected our dearly beloved and dear departed not to have thirsted to overthrow, evict, triumph. The dear departed *was* his deed, his effort, his nisus. Never was there any behind—I mean being—BEHIND the deed free to come and go, free to choose the deed or reject the deed. It is only our good, seated secretly among us, who with their foul filthy propaganda are always making some unforgivably heavy-handed pitch for *this agent behind the deed* free to accept or repudiate its fulguration. But we know better, we know the dear departed could not be held accountable for his strength. And we also know that the goodies' cowering abstention from the deed is not—is never—an achievement, is never in itself a deed. It is what it is—weakness. But our dear departed embodied strength. I never knew the S.O.B. but I've heard tell. And the magnitude of his strength may be easily measured by the number of beings and institutions that had to be sacrificed to his impulse. Even he, crowned by gingko leaves, had to be so sacrificed. He ultimately stood—haha—in his own way. And here are our goodies—don't look around, don't look around—scouring the intestines of his, of all our pasts for ambiguities—clues—vindicating this orgy of suspiciousness and deceit. I guess what I'm basically saying folks and now I'll quit so you can go home and rustle up some grub and get some shut-eye is that our hero—our man of the hour—had no choice but to be a hero. His dreams were oceanic and they—the others—the goodies—interspersed among our butts could never venture beyond their pitiful little puddles of prudence. But they were not satisfied with the fringe bene-

fits of pusillanimity, no. They were not content to make do
with ventures determined on the basis of a calculation of
probabilities and performed to the siren song of the discretely quantitative, no. With the arrogance of the totally
talentless—for whom the absence of talent is the only authentic talent—proof of an unobstructed vantage on being—
and in a sense they are right but not in and for
themselves—they are right from the perspective of our beloved Creator for whom each man is an experiment and for
whom consequently they are most fascinating who lay
claim to the tiniest ration of resource. A taxi driver taught
me that, no not quite that, at any right I am inflecting his
observation for the better, best—where was I—oh yes, with
the arrogance of the totally talentless they demanded to be
considered our hero's peers and through their act—murder, I
say—murder most foul—murder will out—they came to believe they had achieved their dream of GETTING THEIR
RIGHTFUL DUE. They demand that the world underwrite
their 'youthful delusions of omnipotence,' and the world
complies since all it takes in fact is one worm, one madly
applauding worm—to confirm that their recoil from profit
and the greater glory of the profit motive and the reconstruction of Gotham from cellar to dome in the name of a breath-
taking skyline is a heroism infinitely nobler than that
evinced all through his career by ours truly, the dear departed, dearly beloved. All it takes is one little worm, one
failed worker, tried and true"—Was Xman imagining that he
was staring quite pointedly at his right cheek?—"to confirm
that their horror of free enterprise (glory of the capitalist
adventure) with its stocks and bonds, debentures and balance sheets, is not the scummy calculated prudence of the
boorishly weak but an imposing deed, a strong-willed
achievement reminiscent of the Borgias, Chet and Loocy.
But never forget, dearly gathered here to celebrate our man's

nuptials with the heavenly host, their so-called deed is never more than the shabbiest abstention—abstention in fact of the worst kind—too vile in fact to merit the name—festooned on occasion, surely you will agree, with riotous resonances that survive the moment. In fact, look around, no don't look around, this kind of abstention is no longer motivated even by prudence but rather by a kind of narcotized madness of monstrous accidie decking itself out in all the colors of monstrous exploit. All I am saying, then, is don't be ashamed of your profit-hungry impulses. Don't be ashamed when you feel yourself gliding like Balanchine's *sonnambula* toward the very heart of the marketplace garishly splashed with outcries of life's rapacity lived to the hilt come hell or high water. All I am saying is that the slime among us—" At this point the course of events went muddy and not only for Xman. As Fatima rose and shrieked, "Whoreson, bastard, bitch, lackey, liar, clerk, flunkey's clerk," evidently neck-deep in exception taken, Siegfried deploying like dagger from its sheath a broad and toothy smile threw Xman what resembled closely—even to Xman's toolilliterate eye—a sawed-off shotgun. Friends, relatives, bystanders and thrill-seekers making for the exits it was at this very moment, with Fatima still screaming at our man of the cloth refusing to abandon the pulpit on high and all it triggered of what he took to be eloquence and Siegfried still sporting his ear-to-ear grin—it was at this very moment that Xman began to fire, first at Fatima, until she was no longer Fatima Buckley but Bloodina Pulpina Buckley, then at the man of the cloth but more neatly, economically, even respectfully, so that his target was definitively downed after only three lean shots in the gowned groin. Turning to Siegfried Xman noted the smile was gone. And he hadn't seen it go. Once again he had been negligent, remiss, lapse-laden, with regard to the ebb and flow of phenomena that

just might have been useful—assimilable—to the true work
waxing ever brighter, ever more luminous. The smile was no
longer his to use. It had eluded the grasp of his perception-
voracity barely coming into its own. Rage, then, over the
surely eternal consequences of this momentary lapse in hy-
pervigilance prompted him to start firing again. Somehow S/
M managed all in a single spasm to leap, introduce and lose
himself among the horde some of whose members did not,
in contrast and due perhaps to his impish impetuosity self-
serving to the last, escape the lethal thrashing Xman seemed
most committed to inflicting on all of being. As he went on
and on firing Xman heard himself cry, "I simply cannot tell
the difference between good and bad, scoundrels and saints.
Impossible." Looking down he realized it was Fatima's pudgy
little bejewelled fingers responsible for this tearing and burning sensation deep within his kneecap. He had no recourse
but to bash her over the head with the stock of the weapon—
Xman was not quite clear what a stock was but he assumed
this segment proving so efficacious must be called a stock—
stock of the weapon transferred to his precincts and in colossal good faith by his erstwhile mentor and fellow fat-chewer
(causeways, causeways, and causeways) seconds before.
Xman himself then jumped into the crowd and became in
fact the most vociferous participant in its teamlike clamor-
ing for a way out, a way out. Behind the funeral parlor he
made for the slight declivity that wended its way ever so
gingerly into trash-infested underbrush stinking of corpse-
trimmings. All of a sudden he knew he was no longer in the
outskirts of the city, his mamma York, but IN THAT PLACE
TO WHICH FATIMA AND S/M HAD HAD EVERY INTEN-
TION OF SENDING HIM AND FROM WHOSE BOURN
NO TRAVELLER, HOWEVER WEARY, HOWEVER HOME-
SICK, EVER RETURNS. He looked around, all was fast fading, and tried to remember what Siegfried had shouted long

before: You cannot be condemned for your shamefulness.
You can only be condemned for your failure to appropriate
that shamefulness as your very own. He tried to remember
there in the hot sun all he had learned never mind from
whom. Were these soldiers with machine guns coming out
of the museum, had they been alerted to his true work, had
Merdouille betrayed him, he tried not to think of dying, told
himself, I am not afraid of death *per se* but of being done in—
bracketed—by the noisome and constricting particularity of
any number of describable—captionable—deaths orches-
trated each and every by the most humdrum of thugs, gov-
ernment-sponsored or otherwise. But what am I, I too am a
thug, thug without a symptom, true symptom, to his name.
Behind him were the ruins of the temple impressively riddled and fissured by the irreversible saunter of time. He remembered Fatima and the many careers of Fatima: ballerina,
lyric contralto, chamber actress. Had she in fact heroically
relinquished these careers or was all talk of relinquishment
the mere and frenzied fabrication of a misfit who had by the
sheerest chance stumbled on what managed to end up passing for a real vocation. Standing here he cursed what now
reverberated as her hollow pretension. Entrenched over and
over in her digressions he had had no choice but to revere all
they limned and dislimned of persistence in the face of obstacle, sometimes thunderboltish, sometimes glancing,
sometimes impalpable. Maybe he had only impersonated
one revering. He could not determine what was more excruciating to instantaneous retrospect: to have been authentically reverent in front of a sham or an equally shamming
impersonator of one authentically reverent. He, Xman,
could hear the insects buzzing their last before the fall of
winter and was grateful for their continuing patronage of his
precincts. Observing an ant making its way along what from
its perspective must loom as the loftiest of ramparts he was

suddenly terrified that continued persistence in his own being might very well depend on making such a creature understand a sunset—or worse, his conception of sunset, or a
stem's twinge against some untimely twilight gust, or a stro-
phe of Pindar. And there was always the danger that it might
leap out of its charmed circle and, no longer absorbed by or
reverent in front of the locus of all points equidistant from a
single point, rend him to pieces. Scrambling up out of the pit
he was at last shaken free of all the labels by which he had
come to be known always long long long after he had relinquished striving so hard to earn them one and all. He heard
himself say, "I want to escape," but there was no escaping
the landscape, a monologue always the same because always
infected with the slightest coefficient of difference. Oh the
lure of day already saturated with the scents normal men
usually associate not so much with night as with the onset
of night, with not so much night as onset of night.

Just before these toy soldiers shot at his gun he UNDER-
WENT a pain in the balls, might he say even an acute pain in
the balls, might he even say an acute pain in the balls-hip-
left eyelid axis so dear to psychopathologists. He could only
laugh hysterically at this completely supererogatory, gratuitous, excessively conscientious signalling of a decomposi-
tion long established beyond the shadow of even the wariest
plundering doubt. Suddenly besieged by too many symptoms
he could not even begin to begin to eviscerate for the ultimate purpose of their anastomosis amid the depthless pupil-
scorched depths of the truer-than-true work—too many
symptoms dutifully rushed in from Verisimilitude, Inc.,
brainchild of one Fatima Buckley, quondam wardrobe mistress and choreographer extraordinaire, he wanted just before falling to his knees—but not to genuflect before the
spinelessness of his demiurge—he wanted to tell them—
these hairy hierodules who had evidently and ignominiously

given up piecework on what should really have concerned—
obsessed—them long long before—he wanted to tell them to
stop working so hard on overdetermination of this blessed
state not worth determining in the first place. He had so
many symptoms he didn't know what to do. But none would
be, had ever been, a pathway to the dream time, balsam-
scented transmogrification against the fur, against the fur,
against the fur.

He cried out: "I have always prostrated myself before others," then threw the bomb, saw the soldiers go instantly up
in smoke. "I have always prostrated myself," he repeated, for
the salt of the word *prostrated* on his own tongue was new to
him. He looked: The soldiers continued to go up in smoke.
But better than their obliteration was hearing at last and
indubitably catalogued and shelved a plight on which he had
ever so thriftily spun out the shadow of a life. Using the word
prostrated, no longer appalled then by what it claimed to
evoke in the world of half-men, he at last acquired his impotence and consequently could no longer be identified with it.
Perhaps acquisition of its impotence was the obligatory first
stage in evolution of the true work. Now all he had to do was
find a way to insert this acquisition within the larger framework. Just before going completely prone he was overcome
not by the smell of sun; night; soldiers' boots; bomb shards;
sausage; funeral parlor shellac; but by dilemma, mother's
milk to impotents. Had he been ready just beforehand to
confront and acquire THE TRUTH OF HIS BEING—incessant prostration before the gaps in a succession of powers
that strove to be—and had therefore he stumbled lucidly on
the right—the only—the ebullition-quenching word. Or had
the word, as words are known in and out of anastomosis
notoriously to do, there being no question here of meritori-
ous evolution, simply stumbled on a usable site thereby enabling one more likely bystanding nondescript to seem to

consign the flammable putrefaction that was he to a state beyond shame, beyond shamelessness. At any rate, he murmured—to whatever chitinous exoskeleton was still willing to tolerate his wry falsetto—at any rate readiness for diagnosis means readiness for cure. Dead, he whispered, I am beyond my plight forever.